Pitkin County Library

120 North Mill Street
Aspen, Colorado 81611

DATE DUE		
JUN 8 2000	JUN 1 8 2001	
JUL 3	DEC 7 - 2001	
AUG 5 2000	NOV 2 9 2002	
AUG 2 5 2000	JAN 2 6 2008	
AUG 3 1 2000		
2000		
NOV 1 2000		
DEC 9 2000		

201-9500   PRINTED IN U.S.A.

WONDERFUL

TOWN

WONDERFUL

TOWN

NEW YORK STORIES FROM *THE NEW YORKER*

EDITED BY DAVID REMNICK

WITH SUSAN CHOI

RANDOM HOUSE | NEW YORK

Library of Congress Cataloging-in-Publication Data

Wonderful town : New York stories from The New Yorker / edited by David Remnick
with Susan Choi.
p.   cm.
ISBN 0-375-50356-0 (alk. paper)
1. New York (N.Y.)—Social life and customs—Fiction.   2. City and town life—
New York (State)—New York—Fiction.   3. Short stories, American—New York
(State)—New York.   4. American fiction—20th century.   I. Remnick, David.
II. Choi, Susan.
PS549.N5 W58   2000
813'.0108327471—dc21
99-048838

Random House website address: www.atrandom.com

Printed in the United States of America on acid-free paper

24689753

First Edition

Book design by Jo Anne Metsch

ACKNOWLEDGMENTS

The novelist and former *New Yorker* staff member Susan Choi worked tirelessly reading hundreds of short stories set in New York, from the sketches of the earliest days of *The New Yorker* onward. Her insight into the magazine's evolution over seventy-five years and her sensitivity as a reader were invaluable.

I am grateful, as well, to Roger Angell, who gave an order to the selections; to Bill Buford, Deborah Treisman, Cressida Leyshon, Alice Quinn, Meghan O'Rourke, and many others at the magazine (from John Updike, who is represented here, to some of the fact checkers, who will no doubt be in similar anthologies, sooner or later). Thanks are also due Pamela Maffei McCarthy and Eric Rayman at *The New Yorker* for making arrangements with Daniel Menaker and Ann Godoff of Random House; and thanks to Brenda Phipps, Beth Johnson, and Chris Shay and his library staff, all of whom were essential in making this book possible.

CONTENTS

INTRODUCTION

From the moment Harold Ross published the first issue of *The New Yorker,* seventy-five years ago (cover price: fifteen cents), the magazine has been a thing of its place, a magazine of the city. And yet the first issue is a curiosity, a thin slice of the city's life, considering all that came after. Dated February 21, 1925, it offers only a hint of the boldness and depth to come, just a whisper of the range of response to its place of origin. What was certainly there from the start, however, was a determinedly sophisticated lightness, a silvery urbane tone of the pre-Crash era that was true to its moment (in some neighborhoods) and which also became the magazine's signature. Of the issue's thirty-two pages, nearly all are taken up with jokes, light verse, anecdotes, squib-length reviews, abbreviated accounts of this or that incident, and harmless gossip about metropolitan life. With Rea Irvin's Eustace Tilley peering through his monocle at a butterfly on the cover, with its cartoons and drawings of uptown flappers, Fifth Avenue dowagers, and Wall Street men with their mistresses out on the town, with its very name, the magazine announced its identity—or at least the earliest version of it. There was a column called "In Our Midst" that delivered one-sentence news briefs on the city's forgotten and barely remembered ("Crosby Gaige, of here and Peekskill, is leaving for Miami next week to join the pleasure seekers in the sunny southland"); there was "Jottings About Town" by Busybody ("A newsstand where periodicals, books and candy may be procured is now to be found at Pennsylvania Station"); there were reports of overheard talk on "Fifth Avenue at 3 P.M.," musical notes by "Con

Brio," and theater notes by "Last Night." With an advisory board of editors
that included Irvin, George S. Kaufman, Dorothy Parker, and Alexander
Woolcott, Ross's first issue had the feel of an amusement put together by an
in-crowd of amused, and amusing, New York friends. One of the squibs,
called "From the Opinions of a New Yorker," is typical of the throwaway,
unearthshaking tone of that first issue:

> New York is noisy.
> New York is overcrowded.
> New York is ugly.
> New York is unhealthy.
> New York is outrageously expensive.
> New York is bitterly cold in winter.
> New York is steaming hot in summer.
> I wouldn't live outside New York for anything in the world.

It was essentially impossible to see what a various and ambitious publication *The New Yorker* would become. In his original prospectus for the
magazine, Ross said he intended to publish "prose and verse, short and
long, humorous, satirical and miscellaneous." No mention of fiction. The
literary side of things did not initially strike Ross as right for him or even
worth the struggle. For one thing, the competition for fiction seemed forbidding: *Collier's* and *The Saturday Evening Post*, fat with advertisements,
were publishing such authors as Fitzgerald and Hemingway, Lewis and Dos
Passos, and paying them handsomely. Often enough they wrote their novels for art, their stories to live. Ross would later admit that he didn't pursue
Hemingway "because we didn't pay anything." And as Thomas Kunkel,
Ross's wonderful biographer, points out, Ross's preferences ran to humorous sketches and commentary—"casuals." Any trace of seriousness made
him jumpy.

Fiction eventually became an essential part of the magazine for two reasons. When Ross hired Katharine White, in 1927, he was bringing into the
magazine someone of enormous literary sophistication, someone who
adored him but was willing to argue with him—and able to win. Her singular victory was the establishment of fiction as a regular component of
The New Yorker. The second reason for the rise of fiction in the magazine was
the American mood. With the Crash of the stock market, in 1929, the
magazine's chronically bemused tone suddenly seemed out of step and out
of tune. More and more, Katharine White succeeded in getting short stories—and short stories of a deeper sort—into the magazine.

But what *kinds* of stories? There have been many essays, some critical, some rather too defensive, describing a species of fiction known as "the *New Yorker* story"—a quiet, modest thing that tends to track the quiet despera- tion of a rather mild character and ends in some gentle aperçu of recogni- tion or dismay—or dismayed recognition. Or some such. The minor key, that was the essential matter. Somerset Maugham once described it as "those wonderful *New Yorker* stories which always end when the hero goes away, but he doesn't really go away, does he?" Even White herself despaired of the "slight, tiny, mood story." And while it is true that a certain kind of wan tone infects the lesser stories of the period, White, as well as her suc- cessor Gustave Lobrano, were remarkably successful in finding new young writers—often enough New York writers—who gave the magazine an orig- inal kind of vitality and its readers something mysterious and lasting to hold on to as the weekly issues came and went.

Among the first great New York writers that Katharine White began to publish was John Cheever, a shy young man then, in 1935, barely surviv- ing and writing stories in his three-dollar-a-week apartment in the Village. Rather than pant after the established writers that it could not yet afford, White's fiction department established a strong personal bond with Cheever, as it did with many other newcomers, and his name and voice be- came as much a part of the magazine's as E. B. White's and James Thurber's, A. J. Liebling's and Joseph Mitchell's. This was *The New Yorker* at its best, and the impact of new arrivals continues to energize the magazine.

It's not hard to imagine that these new voices will speak to different read- ers in different ways. When I was a student, Knopf published that great red volume, *The Stories of John Cheever.* Cheever was far from obscure—readers of *The New Yorker* had come to celebrate him as the most original of the fifties story writers—but my generation knew him far less well, not half as well as we knew Updike, Roth, and the emerging Raymond Carver, to say nothing of younger names like Richard Ford and Lorrie Moore. The reviews for the Cheever book were extraordinary and the word of mouth even bet- ter, and so it reached us. Read straight through, the earlier Cheever stories especially evoked an era as distant and as compelling to my generation as the loping steps of Joe DiMaggio or the tom-tom drums of Gene Krupa.

"These stories seem at times to be stories of a long-lost world when the city of New York was still filled with a river light, when you heard the Benny Goodman quartets from a radio in the corner stationery store, and when al- most everybody wore a hat," Cheever wrote in his preface. "Here is the last of that generation of chain-smokers who woke the world in the morning with their coughing, who used to get stoned at cocktail parties and perform obsolete dance steps like 'the Cleveland Chicken,' sail for Europe on ships, who were truly nostalgic for love and happiness, and whose gods were as ancient as yours and mine, whoever you are."

The secondary effect of that book was to drive me and many of my friends toward *The New Yorker*. And here we came upon writers as various as Ann Beattie and Donald Barthelme, Harold Brodkey and Max Frisch, Veronica Geng and Jamaica Kincaid.

CHEEVER'S evocation of "his" New York is resonant for everyone, but even when he was writing his earliest stories, he was evoking just one of a multitude of possible New Yorks. That diversity is a New York constant and a constant of *The New Yorker*. So it seemed a natural idea to gather some of the best examples of the magazine's city fiction and—as a celebration of the authors, the city, and the magazine—put them together in this book.

The stories here reflect the city's moods and crises over seventy-five years, from the highlife so artfully implied in Ludwig Bemelmans's "Mespoulets of the Splendide" to the AIDS catastrophe in Susan Sontag's "The Way We Live Now." It's true that the table of contents is less complete than one might wish. James Baldwin, Norman Mailer, Richard Wright, Zora Neale Hurston, William Burroughs, Oscar Hijuelos, Claude Brown, Richard Price—all these writers, and many more, have been underrepresented in, or absent from, the magazine. It's also true, by the way, that some of the grittiest stories we are publishing now are not set in New York. Junot Díaz, one of the magazine's most distinguished recent discoveries, writes of urban New Jersey, just across the Hudson. Still, what the magazine did publish, and the writers it did discover and nurture, are legion, and they have helped to create a powerful and complex portrait of New York—one that we hope will be well represented by this anthology.

The main criterion for inclusion in *Wonderful Town* was the quality of endurance. Which of our New York stories seemed to last? *The New Yorker* famously published Thomas Wolfe's "Only the Dead Know Brooklyn," but as much as one wants to include Wolfe, his dialect story doesn't seem to have it anymore. Similarly, as a great fan of "The Golden Spur" and other novels, I wish Dawn Powell's half-dozen efforts for *The New Yorker* in the late thirties were up to her standard; they aren't, really. Some chestnuts, such as Irwin Shaw's "The Girls in Their Summer Dresses," stood up just fine but perhaps not quite so well as the others that have been less often anthologized—in Shaw's case, "The Sailor off the *Bremen*." But where the chestnut also seemed supreme—Jean Stafford's "Children Are Bored on Sunday" is a prime example—there seemed no sense in exacting a perverse penalty of exclusion.

As with any anthology, this one will draw complaints. Where's Peter DeVries? (Well, his best stories are in the suburbs.) Where's Harold Brodkey? (In St. Louis, mainly.) And with such a wealth of writers to draw on, even a thousand pages would not have done the trick entirely. As there is barely enough room in this city to contain all of its busy, funny, angry, joyful, carping, and canny inhabitants, there was barely enough room to contain the wide range of stories we agreed upon. Argument is half the fun. After all, it was argument—the fierce and loving debate between Harold Ross and Katharine White way back when—that set *The New Yorker*'s fictional vessel on its course.

—*David Remnick*

WONDERFUL

TOWN

THE FIVE-FORTY-EIGHT

W HEN Blake stepped out of the elevator, he saw her. A few people, mostly men waiting for girls, stood in the lobby watching the elevator doors. She was among them. As he saw her, her face took on a look of such loathing and purpose that he realized she had been waiting for him. He did not approach her. She had no legitimate business with him. They had nothing to say. He turned and walked toward the glass doors at the end of the lobby, feeling that faint guilt and bewilderment we experience when we bypass some old friend or classmate who seems threadbare, or sick, or miserable in some other way. It was five-eighteen by the clock in the Western Union office. He could catch the express. As he waited his turn at the revolving doors, he saw that it was still raining. It had been raining all day, and he noticed now how much louder the rain made the noises of the street. Outside, he started walking briskly east toward Madison Avenue. Traffic was tied up, and horns were blowing urgently on a crosstown street in the distance. The sidewalk was crowded. He wondered what she had hoped to gain by a glimpse of him coming out of the office building at the end of the day. Then he wondered if she was following him.

Walking in the city, we seldom turn and look back. The habit restrained Blake. He listened for a minute—foolishly—as he walked, as if he could distinguish her footsteps from the worlds of sound in the city at the end of a rainy day. Then he noticed, ahead of him on the other side of the street, a break in the wall of buildings. Something had been torn down; something was being put up, but the steel structure had only just risen above the sidewalk fence and daylight poured through the gap. Blake stopped opposite here and looked into a store window. It was a decorator's or an auctioneer's. The window was arranged like a room in which people live and entertain their friends. There were cups on the coffee table, magazines to read, and flowers in the vases, but the flowers were dead and the cups were empty and the guests had not come. In the plate glass, Blake saw a clear reflection of himself and the crowds that were passing, like shadows, at his back. Then he saw her image—so close to him that it shocked him. She was standing only a foot or two behind him. He could have turned then and asked her what she wanted, but instead of recognizing her, he shied away abruptly from the reflection of her contorted face and went along the street. She might be meaning to do him harm—she might be meaning to kill him.

The suddenness with which he moved when he saw the reflection of her face tipped the water out of his hatbrim in such a way that some of it ran down his neck. It felt unpleasantly like the sweat of fear. Then the cold water falling into his face and onto his bare hands, the rancid smell of the wet gutters and pavings, the knowledge that his feet were beginning to get wet and that he might catch cold—all the common discomforts of walking in the rain—seemed to heighten the menace of his pursuer and to give him a morbid consciousness of his own physicalness and of the ease with which he could be hurt. He could see ahead of him the corner of Madison Avenue, where the lights were brighter. He felt that if he could get to Madison Avenue he would be all right. At the corner, there was a bakery shop with two entrances, and he went in by the door on the crosstown street, bought a coffee ring, like any other commuter, and went out the Madison Avenue door. As he started down Madison Avenue, he saw her waiting for him by a hut where newspapers were sold.

She was not clever. She would be easy to shake. He could get into a taxi by one door and leave by the other. He could speak to a policeman. He could run—although he was afraid that if he did run, it might precipitate the violence he now felt sure she had planned. He was approaching a part of the city that he knew well and where the maze of street-level and underground passages, elevator banks, and crowded lobbies made it easy for a man to lose a pursuer. The thought of this, and a whiff of sugary warmth from the coffee ring, cheered him. It was absurd to imagine being harmed on a crowded street. She was foolish, misled, lonely perhaps—that was all it could amount to. He was an insignificant man, and there was no point in anyone's following him from his office to the station. He knew no secrets of any consequence. The reports in his briefcase had no bearing on war, peace, the dope traffic, the hydrogen bomb, or any of the other international skulduggeries that he associated with pursuers, men in trench coats, and wet sidewalks. Then he saw ahead of him the door of a men's bar. Oh, it was so simple!

He ordered a Gibson and shouldered his way in between two other men at the bar, so that if she should be watching from the window she would lose sight of him. The place was crowded with commuters putting down a drink before the ride home. They had brought in on their clothes—on their shoes and umbrellas—the rancid smell of the wet dusk outside, but Blake began to relax as soon as he tasted his Gibson and looked around at the common, mostly not-young faces that surrounded him and that were worried, if they were worried at all, about tax rates and who would be put in charge of merchandising. He tried to remember her name—Miss Dent, Miss Bent, Miss Lent—and he was surprised to find that he could not remember it, although he was proud of the retentiveness and reach of his memory and it had only been six months ago.

Personnel had sent her up one afternoon—he was looking for a secretary. He saw a dark woman—in her twenties, perhaps—who was slender and shy. Her dress was simple, her figure was not much, one of her stockings was crooked, but her voice was soft and he had been willing to try her out. After she had been working for him a few days, she told him that she had been in the hospital for eight months and that it had been hard after this for her to find work, and she wanted to thank him for giving her a chance. Her hair was dark, her eyes were dark; she left with him a pleasant impression of darkness. As he got to know her better, he felt that she was oversensitive and, as a consequence, lonely. Once, when she was speaking to him of what she imagined his life to be—full of friendships, money, and a large and loving family—he had thought he recognized a peculiar feeling of deprivation. She seemed to imagine the lives of the rest of the world to be more brilliant than they were. Once, she had put a rose on his desk, and he had dropped it into the wastebasket. "I don't like roses," he told her.

She had been competent, punctual, and a good typist, and he had found only one thing in her that he could object to—her handwriting. He could not associate the crudeness of her handwriting with her appearance. He would have expected her to write a rounded backhand, and in her writing there were intermittent traces of this, mixed with clumsy printing. Her writing gave him the feeling that she had been the victim of some inner— some emotional—conflict that had in its violence broken the continuity of the lines she was able to make on paper. When she had been working for him three weeks—no longer—they stayed late one night and he offered, after work, to buy her a drink. "If you really want a drink," she said, "I have some whiskey at my place."

She lived in a room that seemed to him like a closet. There were suit boxes and hatboxes piled in a corner, and although the room seemed hardly big enough to hold the bed, the dresser, and the chair he sat in, there was an upright piano against one wall, with a book of Beethoven sonatas on the rack. She gave him a drink and said that she was going to put on something more comfortable. He urged her to; that was, after all, what he had come for. If he had had any qualms, they would have been practical. Her diffidence, the feeling of deprivation in her point of view, promised to protect him from any consequences. Most of the many women he had known had been picked for their lack of self-esteem.

When he put on his clothes again, an hour or so later, she was weeping. He felt too contented and warm and sleepy to worry much about her tears. As he was dressing, he noticed on the dresser a note she had written to a cleaning woman. The only light came from the bathroom—the door was ajar—and in this half light the hideously scrawled letters again seemed entirely wrong for her, and as if they must be the handwriting of some other and very gross woman. The next day, he did what he felt was the only sensible thing. When she was out for lunch, he called personnel and asked them to fire her. Then he took the afternoon off. A few days later, she came to the office, asking to see him. He told the switchboard girl not to let her in. He had not seen her again until this evening.

BLAKE drank a second Gibson and saw by the clock that he had missed the express. He would get the local—the five-forty-eight. When he left the bar the sky was still light; it was still raining. He looked carefully up and down the street and saw that the poor woman had gone. Once or twice, he looked over his shoulder, walking to the station, but he seemed to be safe. He was still not quite himself, he realized, because he had left his coffee ring at the bar, and he was not a man who forgot things. This lapse of memory pained him.

He bought a paper. The local was only half full when he boarded it, and he got a seat on the river side and took off his raincoat. He was a slender man with brown hair—undistinguished in every way, unless you could have divined in his pallor or his gray eyes his unpleasant tastes. He dressed—like the rest of us—as if he admitted the existence of sumptuary laws. His raincoat was the pale, buff color of a mushroom. His hat was dark brown; so was his suit. Except for the few bright threads in his necktie, there was a scrupulous lack of color in his clothing that seemed protective.

He looked around the car for neighbors. Mrs. Compton was several seats in front of him, to the right. She smiled, but her smile was fleeting. It died swiftly and horribly. Mr. Watkins was directly in front of Blake. Mr. Watkins needed a haircut, and he had broken the sumptuary laws; he was wearing a corduroy jacket. He and Blake had quarrelled, so they did not speak.

The swift death of Mrs. Compton's smile did not affect Blake at all. The Comptons lived in the house next to the Blakes, and Mrs. Compton had never understood the importance of minding her own business. Louise Blake took her troubles to Mrs. Compton, Blake knew, and instead of discouraging her crying jags, Mrs. Compton had come to imagine herself a sort of confessor and had developed a lively curiosity about the Blakes' intimate affairs. She had probably been given an account of their most recent quarrel. Blake had come home one night, overworked and tired, and had found that Louise had done nothing about getting supper. The gin bottle was half emptied, and the first three glasses he took from the bar were smeared with lipstick grease. He had gone into the kitchen, followed by Louise, and he had pointed out to her that the date was the fifth. He had drawn a circle around the date on the kitchen calendar. "One week is the twelfth," he had said. "Two weeks will be the nineteenth." He drew a circle around the nineteenth. "I'm not going to speak to you for two weeks," he had said. "That will be the nineteenth." She had wept, she had protested, but it had been eight or ten years since she had been able to touch him with her entreaties. Louise had got old. Now the lines in her face were ineradicable, and when she clapped her glasses onto her nose to read the evening paper she looked to him like an unpleasant stranger. The physical charms that had been her only attraction were gone. It had been nine years since Blake had built a bookshelf in the doorway that connected their rooms and had fitted into the bookshelf wooden doors that could be locked, since he did not want the children to see his books. But their prolonged estrangement didn't seem remarkable to Blake. He had quarrelled with his wife, but so did every other man born of woman. It was human nature. In any place where you can hear their voices—a hotel courtyard, an air shaft, a street on a summer evening—you will hear harsh words.

The hard feeling between Blake and Mr. Watkins also had to do with Blake's family, but it was not as serious or as troublesome as what lay behind Mrs. Compton's fleeting smile. The Watkinses rented. Mr. Watkins broke the sumptuary laws day after day—he once went to the eight-fourteen in a pair of sandals—and he made his living as a commercial artist. Blake's oldest son—Charlie was fourteen—had made friends with the Watkins boy. He had spent a lot of time in the sloppy rented house where the Watkinses lived. The friendship had affected his manners and his neatness. Then he had begun to take some meals with the Watkinses, and

to spend Saturday nights there. When he had moved most of his possessions over to the Watkinses' and had begun to spend more than half his
nights there, Blake had been forced to act. He had spoken not to Charlie but
to Mr. Watkins, and had, of necessity, said a number of things that must
have sounded critical. Mr. Watkins' long and dirty hair and his corduroy
jacket reassured Blake that he had been in the right.

But Mrs. Compton's dying smile and Mr. Watkins' dirty hair did not
lessen the pleasure Blake took in settling himself in an uncomfortable seat
on the five-forty-eight deep underground. The coach was old and smelled
oddly like a bomb shelter in which whole families had spent the night. The
light that spread from the ceiling down onto their heads and shoulders was
dim. The filth on the window glass was streaked with rain from some other
journey, and clouds of rank pipe and cigarette smoke had begun to rise
from behind each newspaper, but it was a scene that meant to Blake that he
was on a safe path, and after his brush with danger he even felt a little
warmth toward Mrs. Compton and Mr. Watkins.

The train travelled up from underground into the weak daylight, and the
slums and the city reminded Blake vaguely of the woman who had followed
him. To avoid speculation or remorse about her, he turned his attention to
the evening paper. Out of the corner of his eye he could see the landscape.
It was industrial and, at that hour, sad. There were machine sheds and
warehouses, and above these he saw a break in the clouds—a piece of yellow light. "Mr. Blake," someone said. He looked up. It was she. She was
standing there holding one hand on the back of the seat to steady herself in
the swaying coach. He remembered her name then—Miss Dent. "Hello,
Miss Dent," he said.

"Do you mind if I sit here?"

"I guess not."

"Thank you. It's very kind of you. I don't like to inconvenience you like
this. I don't want to . . ." He had been frightened when he looked up and
saw her, but her timid voice rapidly reassured him. He shifted his hams—
that futile and reflexive gesture of hospitality—and she sat down. She
sighed. He smelled her wet clothing. She wore a formless black hat with a
cheap crest stitched onto it. Her coat was thin cloth, he saw, and she wore
gloves and carried a large pocketbook.

"Are you living out in this direction now, Miss Dent?"

"No."

She opened her purse and reached for her handkerchief. She had begun
to cry. He turned his head to see if anyone in the car was looking, but no
one was. He had sat beside a thousand passengers on the evening train. He
had noticed their clothes, the holes in their gloves; and if they fell asleep

and mumbled he had wondered what their worries were. He had classified almost all of them briefly before he buried his nose in the paper. He had marked them as rich, poor, brilliant or dull, neighbors or strangers, but not one of the thousands had ever wept. When she opened her purse, he remembered her perfume. It had clung to his skin the night he went to her place for a drink.

"I've been very sick," she said. "This is the first time I've been out of bed in two weeks. I've been terribly sick."

"I'm sorry that you've been sick, Miss Dent," he said in a voice loud enough to be heard by Mr. Watkins and Mrs. Compton. "Where are you working now?"

"What?"

"Where are you working now?"

"Oh don't make me laugh," she said softly.

"I don't understand."

"You poisoned their minds."

He straightened his back and braced his shoulders. These wrenching movements expressed a brief—and hopeless—longing to be in some other place. She meant trouble. He took a breath. He looked with deep feeling at the half-filled, half-lighted coach to affirm his sense of actuality, of a world in which there was not very much bad trouble after all. He was conscious of her heavy breathing and the smell of her rain-soaked coat. The train stopped. A nun and a man in overalls got off. When it started again, Blake put on his hat and reached for his raincoat.

"Where are you going?" she said.

"I'm going up to the next car."

"Oh, no," she said. "No, no, no." She put her white face so close to his ear that he could feel her warm breath on his cheek. "Don't do that," she whispered. "Don't try and escape me. I have a pistol and I'll have to kill you and I don't want to. All I want to do is to talk with you. Don't move or I'll kill you. Don't, don't, don't!"

Blake sat back abruptly in his seat. If he had wanted to stand and shout for help, he would not have been able to. His tongue had swelled to twice its size, and when he tried to move it, it stuck horribly to the roof of his mouth. His legs were limp. All he could think of to do then was to wait for his heart to stop its hysterical beating, so that he could judge the extent of his danger. She was sitting a little sidewise, and in her pocketbook was the pistol, aimed at his belly.

"You understand me now, don't you?" she said. "You understand that I'm serious?" He tried to speak but he was still mute. He nodded his head. "Now we'll sit quietly for a little while," she said. "I got so excited that my thoughts are all confused. We'll sit quietly for a little while, until I can get my thoughts in order again."

Help would come, Blake thought. It was only a question of minutes. Someone, noticing the look on his face or her peculiar posture, would stop and interfere, and it would all be over. All he had to do was to wait until someone noticed his predicament. Out of the window he saw the river and the sky. The rain clouds were rolling down like a shutter, and while he watched, a streak of orange light on the horizon became brilliant. Its brilliance spread—he could see it move—across the waves until it raked the banks of the river with a dim firelight. Then it was put out. Help would come in a minute, he thought. Help would come before they stopped again; but the train stopped, there were some comings and goings, and Blake still lived on, at the mercy of the woman beside him. The possibility that help might not come was one that he could not face. The possibility that his predicament was not noticeable, that Mrs. Compton would guess that he was taking a poor relation out to dinner at Shady Hill, was something he would think about later. Then the saliva came back into his mouth and he was able to speak.

"Miss Dent?"

"Yes."

"What do you want?"

"I want to talk with you."

"You can come to my office."

"Oh, no. I went there every day for two weeks."

"You could make an appointment."

"No," she said. "I think we can talk here. I wrote you a letter but I've been too sick to go out and mail it. I've put down all my thoughts. I like to travel. I like trains. One of my troubles has always been that I could never afford to travel. I suppose you see this scenery every night and don't notice it anymore, but it's nice for someone who's been in bed a long time. They say that He's not in the river and the hills but I think He is. 'Where shall wisdom be found,' it says. 'Where is the place of understanding? The depth saith it is not in me; the sea saith it is not with me. Destruction and death say we have heard the force with our ears.'

"Oh, I know what you're thinking," she said. "You're thinking that I'm crazy, and I have been very sick again but I'm going to be better. It's going to make me better to talk with you. I was in the hospital all the time before I came to work for you but they never tried to cure me, they only wanted to take away my self-respect. I haven't had any work now for three months. Even if I did have to kill you, they wouldn't be able to do anything to me except put me back in the hospital, so you see I'm not afraid. But let's sit quietly for a little while longer. I have to be calm."

The train continued its halting progress up the bank of the river, and Blake tried to force himself to make some plans for escape, but the immediate threat to his life made this difficult, and instead of planning sensibly, he thought of the many ways in which he could have avoided her in the first place. As soon as he had felt these regrets, he realized their futility. It was like regretting his lack of suspicion when she first mentioned her months in the hospital. It was like regretting his failure to have been warned by her shyness, her diffidence, and the handwriting that looked like the marks of a claw. There was no way now of rectifying his mistakes, and he felt—for perhaps the first time in his mature life—the full force of regret. Out of the window, he saw some men fishing on the nearly dark river, and then a ramshackle boat club that seemed to have been nailed together out of scraps of wood that had been washed up on the shore.

Mr. Watkins had fallen asleep. He was snoring. Mrs. Compton read her paper. The train creaked, slowed, and halted infirmly at another station. Blake could see the southbound platform, where a few passengers were waiting to go into the city. There was a workman with a lunch pail, a dressed-up woman, and a man with a suitcase. They stood apart from one another. Some advertisements were posted on the wall behind them. There was a picture of a couple drinking a toast in wine, a picture of a Cat's Paw rubber heel, and a picture of a Hawaiian dancer. Their cheerful intent seemed to go no farther than the puddles of water on the platform and to expire there. The platform and the people on it looked lonely. The train drew away from the station into the scattered lights of a slum and then into the darkness of the country and the river.

"I want you to read my letter before we get to Shady Hill," she said. "It's on the seat. Pick it up. I would have mailed it to you, but I've been too sick to go out. I haven't gone out for two weeks. I haven't had any work for three months. I haven't spoken to anybody but the landlady. Please read my letter."

He picked up the letter from the seat where she had put it. The cheap paper felt abhorrent and filthy to his fingers. It was folded and refolded. "Dear Husband," she had written, in that crazy, wandering hand, "they say that human love leads us to divine love, but is this true? I dream about you every night. I have such terrible desires. I have always had a gift for dreams. I dreamed on Tuesday of a volcano erupting with blood. When I was in the hospital they said they wanted to cure me but they only wanted to take away my self-respect. They only wanted me to dream about sewing and basketwork but I protected my gift for dreams. I'm clairvoyant. I can tell when the telephone is going to ring. I've never had a true friend in my whole life. . . ."

The train stopped again. There was another platform, another picture of the couple drinking a toast, the rubber heel, and the Hawaiian dancer. Suddenly she pressed her face close to Blake's again and whispered in his ear. "I know what you're thinking. I can see it in your face. You're thinking you can get away from me in Shady Hill, aren't you? Oh, I've been planning this for weeks. It's all I've had to think about. I won't harm you if you'll let me talk. I've been thinking about devils. I mean if there are devils in the world, if there are people in the world who represent evil, is it our duty to exterminate them? I know that you always prey on weak people. I can tell. Oh, sometimes I think that I ought to kill you. Sometimes I think you're the only obstacle between me and my happiness. Sometimes . . ."

She touched Blake with the pistol. He felt the muzzle against his belly. The bullet, at that distance, would make a small hole where it entered, but it would rip out of his back a place as big as a soccer ball. He remembered the unburied dead he had seen in the war. The memory came in a rush: entrails, eyes, shattered bone, ordure, and other filth.

"All I've ever wanted in life is a little love," she said. She lightened the pressure of the gun. Mr. Watkins still slept. Mrs. Compton was sitting calmly with her hands folded in her lap. The coach rocked gently, and the coats and mushroom-colored raincoats that hung between the windows swayed a little as the car moved. Blake's elbow was on the window sill and his left shoe was on the guard above the steampipe. The car smelled like some dismal classroom. The passengers seemed asleep and apart, and Blake felt that he might never escape the smell of heat and wet clothing and the dimness of the light. He tried to summon the calculated self-deceptions with which he sometimes cheered himself, but he was left without any energy for hope or self-deception.

The conductor put his head in the door and said "Shady Hill, next, Shady Hill."

"Now," she said. "Now you get out ahead of me."

Mr. Watkins waked suddenly, put on his coat and hat, and smiled at Mrs. Compton, who was gathering her parcels to her in a series of maternal gestures. They went to the door. Blake joined them, but neither of them spoke to him or seemed to notice the woman at his back. The conductor threw open the door, and Blake saw on the platform of the next car a few other neighbors who had missed the express, waiting patiently and tiredly in the wan light for their trip to end. He raised his head to see through the open door the abandoned mansion outside of town, a no-trespassing sign nailed to a tree, and then the oil tanks. The concrete abutments of the bridge passed, so close to the open door that he could have touched them. Then he saw the first of the lampposts on the north-bound platform, the sign "SHADY HILL" in black and gold, and the little lawn and flower bed kept up by the Improvement Association, and then the cab stand and a corner of the old-fashioned depot. It was raining again; it was pouring. He could hear the splash of water and see the lights reflected in puddles and in the shining pavement, and the idle sound of splashing and dripping formed in his mind a conception of shelter, so light and strange that it seemed to belong to a time of his life that he could not remember.

He went down the steps with her at his back. A dozen or so cars were waiting by the station with their motors running. A few people got off from each of the other coaches; he recognized most of them, but none of them offered to give him a ride. They walked separately or in pairs—purposefully out of the rain to the shelter of the platform, where the car horns called to them. It was time to go home, time for a drink, time for love, time for supper, and he could see the lights on the hill—lights by which children were being bathed, meat cooked, dishes washed—shining in the rain. One by one, the cars picked up the heads of families, until there were only four left. Two of the stranded passengers drove off in the only taxi the village had. "I'm sorry, darling," a woman said tenderly to her husband when she drove up a few minutes later. "All our clocks are slow." The last man looked at his watch, looked at the rain, and then walked off into it, and Blake saw him go as if they had some reason to say goodbye—not as we say goodbye to friends after a party but as we say goodbye when we are faced with an inexorable and unwanted parting of the spirit and the heart. The man's footsteps sounded as he crossed the parking lot to the sidewalk, and then they were lost. In the station, a telephone began to ring. The ringing was loud, plaintive, evenly spaced, and unanswered. Someone wanted to know about the next train to Albany, but Mr. Flannagan, the stationmaster, had gone home an hour ago. He had turned on all his lights before he went away. They burned in the empty waiting room. They burned, tin-shaded, at intervals up and down the platform and with the peculiar sadness of dim and purposeless light. They lighted the Hawaiian dancer, the couple drinking a toast, the rubber heel.

"I've never been here before," she said. "I thought it would look different. I didn't think it would look so shabby. Let's get out of the light. Go over there."

His legs felt sore. All his strength was gone. "Go on," she said.

North of the station there was a freight house and a coalyard and an inlet where the butcher and the baker and the man who ran the service station moored the dinghies from which they fished on Sundays, sunk now to the gunwales with the rain. As he walked toward the freight house, he saw a movement on the ground and heard a scraping sound, and then he saw a rat take its head out of a paper bag and regard him. The rat seized the bag in its teeth and dragged it into a culvert.

"Stop," she said. "Turn around. Oh, I ought to feel sorry for you. Look at your poor face. But you don't know what I've been through. I'm afraid to go out in the daylight. I'm afraid the blue sky will fall down on me. I'm like poor Chicken-Licken. I only feel like myself when it begins to get dark. But still and all I'm better than you. I still have good dreams sometimes. I dream about picnics and Heaven and the brotherhood of man, and about castles in the moonlight and a river with willow trees all along the edge of it and foreign cities, and after all I know more about love than you."

He heard from off the dark river the drone of an outboard motor, a sound that drew slowly behind it across the dark water such a burden of clear, sweet memories of gone summers and gone pleasures that it made his flesh crawl, and he thought of dark in the mountains and the children singing. "They never wanted to cure me," she said. "They . . ." The noise of a train coming down from the north drowned out her voice, but she went on talking. The noise filled his ears, and the windows where people ate, drank, slept, and read flew past. When the train had passed beyond the bridge, the noise grew distant, and he heard her screaming at him, "*Kneel down!* Kneel down! Do what I say. *Kneel down!*"

He got to his knees. He bent his head. "There," she said. "You see, if you do what I say, I won't harm you, because I really don't want to harm you, I want to help you, but when I see your face it sometimes seems to me that I can't help you. Sometimes it seems to me that if I were good and loving and sane—oh, much better than I am—sometimes it seems to me that if I were all these things and young and beautiful, too, and if I called to show you the right way, you wouldn't heed me. Oh, I'm better than you, I'm better than you, and I shouldn't waste my time or spoil my life like this. Put your face in the dirt. *Put your face in the dirt!* Do what I say. Put your face in the dirt."

He fell forward in the filth. The coal skinned his face. He stretched out on the ground, weeping. "Now I feel better," she said. "Now I can wash my hands of you, I can wash my hands of all this, because you see there is some kindness, some saneness in me that I can find again and use. I can wash my hands." Then he heard her footsteps go away from him, over the rubble. He heard the clearer and more distant sound they made on the hard surface of the platform. He heard them diminish. He raised his head. He saw her climb the stairs of the wooden footbridge and cross it and go down to the other platform, where her figure in the dim light looked small, common, and harmless. He raised himself out of the dust—warily at first, until he saw by her attitude, her looks, that she had forgotten him; that she had completed what she had wanted to do, and that he was safe. He got to his feet and picked up his hat from the ground where it had fallen and walked home.

(1954)

ANN BEATTIE

DISTANT MUSIC

O N Friday she always sat in the park, waiting for him to come. At one-thirty, he came to this park bench (if someone was already sitting there, he loitered around it), and then they would sit side by side, talking quietly, like Ingrid Bergman and Cary Grant in "Notorious." Both believed in flying saucers and health food. They shared a hatred of laundromats, guilt about not sending presents to relatives on birthdays and at Christmas, and a dog—part weimaraner, part German shepherd—named Sam. She was twenty, and she worked in an office; she was pretty because she took a lot of time with makeup, the way a housewife who really cared might flute the edges of a piecrust with thumb and index finger. He was twenty-four, a graduate-school dropout (theatre), who collaborated on songs with his friend Gus Greeley, and he wanted, he fervently wanted, to make it big as a songwriter. His mother was Greek and French, his father American. This girl, Sharon, was not the first woman who had fallen in love with Jack because he was so handsome. She took the subway to get to the bench, which was in Washington Square Park; he walked from the basement apartment he lived in. Whichever of them had Sam that day (they kept the dog on alternating weeks) brought him. They could do this because her job only required her to work from eight to one, and he worked at home. They had gotten the dog because they feared for its life. A man had come up to them on West Tenth Street carrying a cardboard box, smiling, and saying, "Does the little lady want a kitty cat?" They peered inside. "Puppies," Jack said. "Well, who gives a damn?" the man had said, putting the box down, his face dark and contorted. Sharon and Jack had stared at the man; he had stared belligerently back. Neither of them was quite sure how things had suddenly turned ominous. She had wanted to get out of there right away, before the man took a swing at Jack, but to her surprise Jack smiled at the man and dipped into the box for a dog. He extracted the scrawny, wormy Sam. She took the dog first, because there was a veterinarian's office close to her apartment. Once the dog was cured of its worms, she gave it to Jack to begin its training. In his apartment, the puppy would fix its eyes on the parallelogram of sunlight that sometimes appeared on the wood floor in the late morning—sniffing it, backing up, edging up to it at the border. In her apartment, the puppy's object of fascination was a clarinet that a friend had left there when he moved. The puppy looked at it respectfully. She watched the dog for signs of maladjustment, wondering if it was too young to be shuttling back and forth, from home to home. (She herself had been raised by her mother, but she and her sister would fly to Seattle every summer to spend two months with their father.) The dog seemed happy enough.

At night, in Jack's one-room apartment, they would sometimes lie with their heads at the foot of the bed, staring at the ornately carved oak headboard and the old-fashioned light attached to it, with the little sticker still on the shade that said "From home of Lady Astor. $4.00." They had found the lamp in Ruckersville, Virginia, on the only long trip they ever took out of the city. On the bed with them there were usually sheets of music—songs that he was scoring. She would look at the pieces of paper with lyrics typed on them, and read them slowly to herself, appraisingly, as if they were poetry.

On weekends, they spent the days and nights together. There was a small but deep fireplace in his apartment, and when September came they would light a fire in the late afternoon, although it was not yet cold, and sometimes light a stick of sandalwood incense, and they would lean on each other or sit side by side, listening to Vivaldi. She knew very little about such music when she first met him, and much more about it by the time their first month had passed. There was no one thing she knew a great deal about—as he did about music—so there was really nothing that she could teach him.

"Where were you in 1974?" he asked her once.

"In school. In Ann Arbor."

"What about 1975?"

"In Boston. Working at a gallery."

"Where are you now?" he said.

She looked at him and frowned. "In New York," she said.

He turned toward her and kissed her arm. "I know," he said. "But why so serious?"

She knew that she was a serious person, and she liked it that he could make her smile. Sometimes, though, she did not quite understand him, so she was smiling now not out of appreciation but because she thought a smile would make things all right.

Carol, her closest friend, asked why she didn't move in with him. She did not want to tell Carol that it was because she had not been asked, so she said that the room he lived in was very small and that during the day he liked solitude, so he could work. She was also not sure if she would move in if he did ask her. He gave her the impression sometimes that he was the serious one, not she. Perhaps "serious" was the wrong word; it was more that he seemed despondent. He would get into moods and not snap out of them; he would drink red wine and play Billie Holiday records, and shake his head and say that if he had not made it as a songwriter by now chances were that he would never make it. She was not really familiar with Billie Holiday until he began playing the records for her. He would play a song that Billie had recorded early in her career, then play another record of the same song as she had sung it later. He said that he preferred her ruined voice. Two songs in particular stuck in her mind. One was "Solitude," and the first time she heard Billie Holiday sing the first three words, "In my solitude," she felt a physical sensation, as if someone were drawing something sharp over her heart, very lightly. The other record she kept thinking of was "Gloomy Sunday." He told her that it had been banned from the radio back then, because it was said that it had been responsible for suicides.

FOR Christmas that year, he gave her a small pearl ring that had been worn by his mother when she was a girl. The ring fitted perfectly; she only had to wiggle it slightly to get it to slide over the joint of her finger, and when it was in place it felt as if she were not wearing a ring at all. There were eight prongs holding the pearl in place. She often counted things: how many panes in a window, how many slats in a bench. Then, for her birthday, in January, he gave her a silver chain with a small sapphire stone, to be worn on the wrist. She was delighted; she wouldn't let him help her fasten the clasp.

"You like it?" he said. "That's all I've got."

She looked at him, a little startled. His mother had died the year before she met him; what he was saying was that he had given her the last of her things. There was a photograph of his mother on the bookcase—a black-and-white picture in a little silver frame of a smiling young woman, whose hair was barely darker than her skin. Because he kept the picture, she assumed that he worshipped his mother. One night he corrected that impression by saying that his mother had always tried to sing in her youth, when she had no voice, which had embarrassed everyone.

He said that she was a silent person; in the end, he said, you would have to say that she had done and said very little. He told Sharon that a few days after her death he and his father had gone through her possessions together, and in one of her drawers they had come upon a small wooden box shaped like a heart. Inside the box were two pieces of jewelry—the ring and the chain and sapphire. "So she kept some token, then," his father had said, staring down into the little box. "You gave them to her as presents?" he had asked his father. "No," his father had said apologetically. "They weren't from me." And then the two of them had stood there looking at each other, both understanding perfectly.

She said, "But what did you finally say to break the silence?"

"Something pointless, I'm sure," he said.

She thought to herself that that might explain why he had not backed down, on Tenth Street, when the man offering the puppies took a stance as though he wanted to fight. Jack was used to hearing bad things—things that took him by surprise. He had learned to react coolly. Later that winter, when she told him that she loved him, his face had stayed expressionless a split second too long, and then he had smiled his slow smile and given her a kiss.

The dog grew. It took to training quickly and walked at heel, and she was glad that they had saved it. She took it to the veterinarian to ask why it was so thin. She was told that the dog was growing fast, and that eventually it would start filling out. She did not tell Jack that she had taken the dog to the veterinarian, because he thought she doted on it too much. She wondered if he might not be a little jealous of the dog.

Slowly, things began to happen with his music. A band on the West Coast that played a song that he and Gus had written was getting a big name, and they had not dropped the song from their repertoire. In February he got a call from the band's agent, who said that they wanted more songs. He and Gus shut themselves in the basement apartment, and she went walking with Sam, the dog. She went to the park, until she ran into the crippled man too many times. He was a young man, rather handsome, who walked with two metal crutches and had a radio that hung from a strap around his neck and rested on his chest, playing loudly. The man always seemed to be walking in the direction she walked in, and she had to walk awkwardly to keep in line with him so they could talk. She really had nothing to talk to the man about, and he helped very little, and the dog was confused by the crutches and made little leaps toward the man, as though they were all three playing a game. She stayed away from the park for a while, and when she went back he was not there. One day in March, the park was more crowded than usual because it was an unusually warm, springlike afternoon, and, walking with Sam, half dreaming, she passed a heavily madeup woman on a bench, who was wearing a polka-dot turban, with a hand-lettered sign propped against her legs announcing that she was Miss Sydney, a fortune-teller. There was a young boy sitting next to Miss Sydney, and he called out to her, "Come on!" She smiled slightly and shook her head no. The boy was Italian, she thought, but the woman was hard to place. "Miss Sydney's going to tell you about fire and famine and early death," the boy said. He laughed, and she hurried on, thinking it was odd that the boy would know the word "famine."

She was still alone with Jack most of every weekend, but much of his talk now was about technical problems he was having with scoring, and she had trouble following him. Once, he became enraged and said that she had no interest in his career. He said that because he wanted to move to Los Angeles and she said she was staying in New York. She had said it assuming at once that he would go anyhow. When he made it clear that he would not leave without her, she started to cry, because she was so grateful that he was staying. He thought she was crying because he had yelled at her and said that she had no interest in his career. He took back what he had said; he told her that she was very tolerant, and that she often gave good advice. She had a good ear, even if she didn't express her opinions in complex technical terms. She cried again, and this time even she did not realize at first why. Later, she knew that it was because he had never said so many kind things to her at once. Actually, very few people in her life had ever gone out of their way to say something kind, and it had just been too much. She began to wonder if her nerves were getting bad. Once, she woke up in the night disoriented and sweating, having dreamed that she was out in the sun, with all her energy gone. It was stifling hot and she couldn't move. "The sun's a good thing," he said to her when she told him the dream. "Think about the bright beautiful sun in Los Angeles. Think about stretching out on a warm day with a warm breeze." Trembling, she left him and went into the kitchen for water. He did not know that if he had really set out for California she would have followed.

In June, when the air pollution got very bad and the air carried the smell that sidewalks get when they are baked through every day, he began to complain that it was her fault that they were in New York and not in California. "But I just don't like that way of life," she said. "If I went there I wouldn't be happy."

"What's so appealing about this uptight New York scene?" he said. "You wake up in the night in a sweat. You won't even walk through Washington Square Park anymore."

"It's because of that man with the crutches," she said. "People like that. I told you it was only because of him."

"So let's get away from all that. Let's go somewhere."

"You think there aren't people like that in California?" she said.

"It doesn't matter what I think about California, if I'm not going." He clamped earphones on his head.

THAT same month, while she and Jack and Gus were sharing a pot of cheese fondue, she found out that Jack had a wife. They were at Gus's apartment, when Gus casually said something about Myra. "Who's Myra?" she asked, and he said, "You know—Jack's wife, Myra." It seemed unreal to her—even more so because Gus's apartment was such an odd place; that night, Gus had plugged a defective lamp into an outlet and blown out a fuse. Then he had plugged in his only other lamp, which was a sunlamp. It glowed so brightly that he had to turn it, in its wire enclosure, to face the wall. As they sat on the floor eating, their three shadows were thrown up against the opposite wall. She had been looking at that—detached, the way you would stand back to appreciate a picture—when she tuned in on the conversation and heard them talking about someone named Myra.

"You didn't know?" Gus said to her. "O.K., I want you both out. I don't want any heavy scene in my place. I couldn't take it. Come on—I really mean it. I want you out. Please don't talk about it here."

On the street, walking beside Jack, it occurred to her that Gus's outburst was very strange, almost as strange as Jack not telling her about his wife.

"I didn't see what would be gained by telling you," Jack said.

They crossed the street. They passed the Riviera Café. She had once counted the number of panes of glass across the Riviera's front.

"Did you ever think about us getting married?" he said. "I thought about it. I thought that if you didn't want to follow me to California, of course you wouldn't want to marry me."

"You're already married," she said. She felt that she had just said something very sensible. "Do you think it was right to—"

He had started to walk ahead of her. She hurried to catch up. She wanted to call after him, "I would have gone!" She was panting.

"Listen," he said, "I'm like Gus. I don't want to hear it."

"You mean we can't even talk about this? You don't think that I'm entitled to hear about it?"

"I love you and I don't love Myra," he said.

"Where is she?" she said.

"In El Paso."

"If you don't love her, why aren't you divorced?"

"You think that everybody who doesn't love his wife gets divorced? I'm not the only one who doesn't do the logical thing, you know. You get nightmares from living in this sewer, and you won't get out of it."

"It's different," she said. What was he talking about?

"Until I met you, I didn't think about it. She was in El Paso, she was gone—period."

"Are you going to get a divorce?"

"Are you going to marry me?"

They were crossing Seventh Avenue. They both stopped still, halfway across the street, and were almost hit by a Checker cab. They hurried across, and on the other side of the street they stopped again. She looked at him, as surprised but as suddenly sure about something as he must have been the time he and his father had found the jewelry in the heart-shaped wooden box. She said no, she was not going to marry him.

IT dragged on for another month. During that time, unknown to her, he wrote the song that was going to launch his career. Months after he had left the city, she heard it on her AM radio one morning, and she knew that it was his song, even though he had never mentioned it to her. She leashed the dog and went out and walked to the record shop on Sixth Avenue— walking almost the same route they had walked the night she found out about his wife—and she went in, with the dog. Her face was so strange that the man behind the cash register allowed her to break the rule about dogs in the shop, because he did not want another hassle that day. She found the group's record album with the song on it, turned it over, and saw his name, in small type. She stared at the title, replaced the record, and went back outside, hunched as if it were winter.

During the month before he left, though, and before she ever heard the song, the two of them sat on the roof of his building one night, arguing. They were having a Tom Collins, because a musician who had been at his place the night before had brought his own mix and then left it behind. She had never had a Tom Collins. It tasted appropriately bitter, she thought. She held out the ring and the bracelet to him. He said that if she made him take them back, he would drop them over the railing. She believed him and put them back in her pocket. He said, and she agreed, that things had not been perfect between them even before she found out about his wife. Myra could play the guitar, and she could not; Myra loved to travel, and she was afraid to leave New York City. As she listened to what he said, she counted the posts—black iron and shaped like arrows—of the fence that wound around the roof. It was almost entirely dark, and she looked up to see if there were any stars. She yearned to be in the country, where she could always see them. She said she wanted him to borrow a car before he left, so that they could ride out into the woods in New Jersey. Two nights later, he picked her up at her apartment in a red Volvo, with Sam panting in the back, and they wound their way through the city and to the Lincoln Tunnel. Just as they were about to go under, another song began to play on the tape deck. It was Ringo Starr, singing "Octopus's Garden." Jack laughed. "That's a hell of a fine song to come on just before we enter the tunnel." Inside the tunnel, the dog flattened himself on the back seat. "You want to keep Sam, don't you?" he said. She was shocked, because she had never even thought of losing Sam. "Of course I do," she said, and unconsciously edged a little away from him. He had never said whose car it was. For no reason at all, she thought that the car must belong to a woman.

"I love that syrupy chorus of 'aaaaah' Lennon and McCartney sing," he said. "They really had a fine sense of humor."

"Is that a funny song?" she said. She had never thought about it.

They were on Boulevard East, in Weehawken, and she was staring out the window at the lights across the water. He saw that she was looking, and drove slower.

"This as good as stars for you?" he said.

"It's amazing."

"All yours," he said, taking his hand off the wheel to swoop it through the air in mock graciousness.

After he left, she would remember that as one of the little digs he had gotten in—one of the less than nice things he had said. That night, though, impressed by the beauty of the city, she let it go by; in fact, she would have to work on herself later to reinterpret many of the things he had said as being nasty. That made it easier to deal with his absence. She would block out the memory of his pulling over and kissing her, of the two of them getting out of the car and, with Sam between them, walking.

One of the last times she saw him, she went to his apartment on a night when five other people were there—people she had never met. His father had shipped him some eight-millimetre home movies and a projector, and the people all sat on the floor, smoking grass and talking, laughing at the movies of children (Jack at his fourth birthday party; Jack in the Halloween parade at school; Jack on Easter, collecting eggs). One of the people on the floor said, "Hey, get that big dog out of the way," and she glared at him, hating him for not liking the dog. What if his shadow had briefly darkened the screen? She felt angry enough to scream, angry enough to say that the dog had grown up in the apartment and had the right to walk around. Looking at the home movies, she tried to concentrate on Jack's blunders: dropping an Easter egg, running down the hill after the egg, going so fast he stumbled into some blur, perhaps his mother's arms. But what she mostly thought about was what a beautiful child he was, what a happy-looking little boy. There was no sense in her staying there and getting sentimental, so she made her excuses and left early. Outside, she saw the red Volvo, gleaming as though it had been newly painted. She was sure that it belonged to an Indian woman in a blue sari who had been there, sitting close to Jack. Sharon was glad that as she had been leaving, Sam raised his hackles and growled at one of the people there. She had scolded him, but out on the street she had patted him, secretly glad. Jack had not asked her again to come to California with him, and she told herself that she probably would not have changed her mind if he had. The tears that began to well up in her eyes were because a cab wouldn't stop for her when the driver saw that she had a dog, she told herself. She ended up walking blocks and blocks back to her apartment that night; it made her more certain than ever that she loved the dog and that she did not love Jack.

ABOUT the time she got the first postcard from Jack, things started to get a little bad with Sam. She was afraid that he might have distemper, so she took him to the veterinarian, waited her turn, and told the doctor that the dog was growling at some people and she had no idea why. He assured her that there was nothing physically wrong with the dog, and blamed it on the heat. When another month passed and it was less hot, she visited the veterinarian again. "It's the breeding," he said, and sighed. "It's a bad mix. A weimaraner is a mean dog, and that cross isn't a good one. He's part German shepherd, isn't he?"

"Yes," she said.

"Well—that's it, I'm afraid."

"There isn't any medication?"

"It's the breeding," he said. "Believe me. I've seen it before."

"What happens?" she said.

"What happens to the dog?"

"Yes."

"Well—watch him. See how things go. He hasn't bitten anybody, has he?"

"No," she said. "Of course not."

"Well—don't say of course not. Be careful with him."

"I'm careful with him," she said. She said it indignantly. But she wanted to hear something else. She didn't want to leave.

Walking home, she thought about what she could do. Maybe she could take Sam to her sister's house in Morristown for a while. Maybe if he could run more, and keep cool, he would calm down. She put aside her knowledge that it was late September and already much cooler, and that the dog growled more, not less. He had growled at the teen-age boy she had given money to to help her carry her groceries upstairs. It was the boy's extreme reaction to Sam that had made it worse, though. You had to act calm around Sam when he got like that, and the boy had panicked.

She persuaded her sister to take Sam, and her brother-in-law drove into New York on Sunday and drove them out to New Jersey. Sam was put on a chain attached to a rope her brother-in-law had strung up in the back yard, between two huge trees. To her surprise, Sam did not seem to mind it. He did not bark and strain at the chain until he saw her drive away, late that afternoon; her sister was driving, and she was in the back seat with her niece, and she looked back and saw him lunging at the chain.

The rest of it was predictable, even to her. Even as they drove away, she almost knew it all. The dog would bite the child. Of course, the child should not have annoyed the dog, but she did, and the dog bit her, and then there was a hysterical call from her sister and another call from her brother-in-law, saying that she must come get the dog immediately—that he would come for her so she could get him—and blaming her for bringing it to them in the first place. Her sister had never really liked her, and the incident with the dog was probably just what she had been waiting for to sever contact.

When Sam came back to the city, things got no better. He turned against everyone and it was difficult even to walk him, because he had become so aggressive. Sometimes a day would pass without any of that, and she would tell herself that it was over now—an awful period but over—and then the next morning the dog would bare its teeth at some person they passed. There began to be little signs that the dog had it in for her, too, and when that happened she turned her bedroom over to him. She hauled her mattress to the living room, and let him have his own room. She left the door cracked, so he would not think he was being punished. But she knew, and Sam knew, that it was best he stay in the room. If nothing else, he was an exceptionally smart dog.

SHE heard from Jack for over a year—sporadically, but then sometimes two postcards in a single week. He was doing well, playing in a band as well as writing music. When she stopped hearing from him—and when it became clear that something had to be done about the dog, and something had been done—she was twenty-two. On a date with a man she liked as a friend, she suggested that they go over to Jersey and drive down Boulevard East. The man was new to New York, and when they got there he said that he was more impressed with that view of the city than with the view from the top of the RCA Building. "All ours," she said, gesturing with her arm, and he, smiling and excited by what she said, had taken her hand when it had finished its sweep and kissed it, and continued to stare with awe at the lights across the water. That summer, she heard another song of Jack's on the radio, which alluded, as so many of his songs did, to times in New York she remembered well. In this particular song there was a couplet about a man on the street offering kittens in a box that actually contained a dog named Sam. In the context of the song, it was an amusing episode—another "you can't always get what you want" sort of thing—and she could imagine Jack in California, not knowing what had happened to Sam, and, always the one to appreciate little jokes in songs, smiling.

(1977)

SAILOR OFF THE BREMEN

THEY sat in the small white kitchen, Ernest and his brother Charlie and Preminger and Dr. Slater, all bunched around the porcelain-topped table, so that the kitchen seemed to be overflowing with men. Sally stood at the stove turning griddlecakes over thoughtfully, listening to what Preminger was saying.

"So everything was excellent. The Comrades arrived, dressed in evening gowns and—what do you call them?"

"Tuxedos," Charlie said.

"Tuxedos." Preminger nodded. "Very handsome people," he said, his English precise and educated, but with a definite German accent. "Mixing with all the other handsome people who came to say goodbye to their friends on the boat, everybody very gay, everybody with a little whiskey on the breath, nobody would suspect they were Party members, they were so clean and upper-class." He laughed at his own joke. With his crew-cut hair and his straight nose and blue eyes, he looked like a young boy from a Middle-Western college. His laugh was a little high and short and he talked fast, as though he wanted to get a great many words out to beat a certain deadline, but otherwise being a Communist in Germany and a deck officer on the *Bremen* had not left any mark on him. "It is a wonderful thing," he said, "how many pretty girls there are in the Party in the United States."

They all laughed, even Ernest, who put his hand up to cover the empty spaces in his front teeth. His hand covered his mouth and the fingers cupped around the neat black patch over his eye, and he smiled at his wife behind that concealment, getting his merriment over with swiftly so he could take his hand down and compose his face. Sally watched him from the stove. "Here," she said, dumping three griddlecakes onto a plate and putting them before Preminger. "Better than Childs restaurant."

"Wonderful," Preminger said, dousing the cakes with syrup. "Each time I come to America, I feast on these. There is nothing like it in the whole continent of Europe."

"All right," Charlie said. He leaned across the kitchen table, practically covering it because he was so big. "Finish the story."

"So I gave the signal," Preminger said, waving his fork, "when everything was nice and ready, everybody having a good time, stewards running this way, that way, with champagne, and we had a very nice little demonstration. Nice signs, good, loud yelling, the Nazi flag cut down one, two, three from the pole, the girls standing together singing like angels, everybody running there from all parts of the ship." He smeared butter methodically on the top cake. "So then the rough business. Expected. Naturally. After all, we all know it is no cocktail party for Lady Astor." He squinted at his plate. "A little pushing, expected. Maybe a little crack over the head here and there, expected. Justice comes with a headache these days, we all know that. But my people, the Germans, you must always expect the worst from them. They organize like lightning. Method. How to treat a riot on a ship. Every steward, every oiler, every sailor was there in a minute and a half. Two men would hold a Comrade, another would beat him. Nothing left to accident."

"What's the sense in going over the whole thing again?" Ernest said. "It's all over."

"Shut up," Charlie said.

"Two stewards got hold of Ernest," Preminger said softly, "and another one did the beating. Stewards are worse than sailors. All day long they take orders, they hate the world. Ernest was unlucky. The steward who beat him up is a member of the Nazi party. He is an Austrian. He is not a normal man."

"Sally," Ernest said, "give Mr. Preminger some more milk."

"He kept hitting Ernest," Preminger said, tapping on the porcelain top with his fork. "And he kept laughing and laughing."

"You're sure you know who he is?" Charlie asked.

"I know who he is. He is twenty-five years old, very dark and good-looking, and he sleeps with at least two ladies a voyage." Preminger slopped his milk around in the bottom of his glass. "His name is Lueger. He spies on the crew for the Nazis. He has sent two men already to concentration camps. He knew what he was doing when he kept hitting Ernest in the eye. I tried to get to him, but I was in the middle of a thousand people screaming and running. If something happens to that Lueger, it will be a very good thing."

"Have a cigar," Ernest said, pulling two out of his pocket.

"Something'll happen to him," Charlie said. He took a deep breath and leaned back from the table.

"What do you prove if you beat up one stupid sailor?" Ernest said.

"I don't prove anything," Charlie said. "I'm just going to have a good time with the boy that knocked my brother's eye out. That's all."

"It's not a personal thing," Ernest said in a tired voice. "It's the movement of Fascism. You don't stop Fascism with a personal crusade against one German. If I thought it would do some good, I'd say sure, go ahead."

"My brother, the Communist," Charlie said bitterly. "He goes out and gets ruined and still he talks dialectics. The Red saint with the long view. The long view gives me a pain. I'm taking a very short view of Mr. Lueger."

"Speaking as a Party member," Preminger said, "I approve of your brother's attitude, Charlie. Speaking as a man, please put Lueger on his back for at least six months. Where is that cigar, Ernest?"

Dr. Slater spoke up in his polite, dentist's voice. "As you know," he said, "I'm not the type for violence." Dr. Slater weighed a hundred and thirty-three pounds and it was almost possible to see through his wrists, he was so frail. "But as Ernest's friend, I think there'd be a definite satisfaction for all of us, including Ernest, if this Lueger was taken care of. You may count on me for anything within my powers." His voice was even drier than usual, and he spoke as if he had reasoned the whole thing out slowly and carefully and had decided to disregard the fear, the worry, the possible great damage. "That's my opinion," he said.

"Sally," Ernest said, "talk to these damn fools."

"I think," Sally said, looking at her husband's face, which was stiffly composed now, like a corpse's face, "I think they know what they're talking about."

Ernest shrugged. "Emotionalism. A large, useless gesture. You're all tainted by Charlie's philosophy. He's a football player, he has a football player's philosophy. Somebody knocks you down, you knock him down, everything is fine."

"Please shut up, Ernest." Charlie stood up and banged on the table. "I've got my stomach full of Communist tactics. I'm acting strictly in the capacity of your brother. If you'd had any brains, you'd have stayed away from that lousy boat. You're a painter, an artist, you make water colors. What the hell is it your business if lunatics're running Germany? But you go and get your eye beat out. O.K. Now I step in. Purely personal. None of your business. Please go and lie down in the bedroom. We have arrangements to make here."

Ernest stood up, hiding his mouth, which was twitching, and walked into the bedroom, closed the door, and lay down on the bed in the dark, with his eye open.

THE next day, Charlie and Dr. Slater and Sally went down to the *Bremen* an hour before sailing time and boarded the ship on different gangplanks. They stood separately on the A deck, up forward, waiting for Preminger. Eventually he appeared, very boyish and crisp in his blue uniform. He walked past them, touched a steward on the arm—a dark, good-looking young steward—said something to him, and went aft. Charlie and Dr. Slater examined the steward closely, so that when the time came, on a dark street, there would be no mistake. Then they went home, leaving Sally there, smiling at Lueger.

"YES," Sally said two weeks later, "it is very clear. I'll have dinner with him, and I'll go to a movie with him and get him to take at least two drinks, and I'll tell him I live on West Twelfth Street, near West Street. There's a whole block of apartment houses there. I'll get him down to West Twelfth Street between a quarter to one and one in the morning, and you'll be waiting—you and Slater—on Greenwich Street, at the corner, under the Ninth Avenue 'L.' And you'll say, 'Pardon me, can you direct me to Sheridan Square?' and I'll start running."

"That's right," Charlie said. "That's fine." He blew reflectively on his huge hands. "That's the whole story for Mr. Lueger. You'll go through with it now, Sally? You're sure you can manage it?"

"I'll go through with it," Sally said. "I had a long talk with him today when the boat came in. He's very—anxious. He likes small girls like me, he says, with black hair."

"What's Ernest going to do tonight?" Dr. Slater asked. In the two weeks of waiting his throat had become so dry he had to swallow desperately every five or six words. "Somebody ought to take care of Ernest tonight."

"He's going to Carnegie Hall," Sally said. "They're playing Brahms and Debussy."

SAILOR OFF THE BREMEN

"That's a good way to spend an evening," Charlie said. He opened his collar and pulled down his tie. "The only place I can go with Ernest these days is the movies. It's dark, so I don't have to look at him."

"He'll pull through," Dr. Slater said professionally. "I'm making him new teeth. He won't be so self-conscious. He'll adjust himself."

"He hardly paints anymore," Sally said. "He just sits around the house and looks at his old pictures."

"He used to be a very merry man," Slater said. "Always laughing. Always sure of what he was saying. Before he was married we used to go out together all the time and all the time the girls—my girl and his girl, no matter who they were—would give all their attention to him. All the time. I didn't mind. I love your brother Ernest as if he was my younger brother. I could cry when I see him sitting now, covering his eye and his teeth, not saying anything, just listening to what other people have to say."

"Mr. Lueger," Charlie said. "Our pal, Mr. Lueger."

"He carries a picture of Hitler," Sally said. "In his watch. He showed me. He says he's lonely."

"I have a theory," Slater said. "My theory is that when Ernest finds out what happens to this Lueger, he'll pick up. It'll be a kind of springboard to him. It's my private notion of the psychology of the situation." He swallowed nervously. "How big is this Lueger?"

"He's a large, strong man," Sally said.

"I think you ought to have an instrument of some kind, Charlie," Slater said. "Really I do."

Charlie laughed. He extended his two hands, palms up, the fingers curved a little, broad and muscular. "I want to take care of Mr. Lueger with my bare fists."

"There is no telling what—"

"Don't worry, Slater," Charlie said. "Don't worry one bit."

AT twelve that night, Sally and Lueger walked down Eighth Avenue from the Fourteenth Street subway station. Lueger held Sally's arm as they walked, his fingers moving up and down, occasionally grasping the loose cloth of her coat.

"I like you," he said, walking very close to her. "You are a good girl. You are made excellent. I am happy to accompany you home. You are sure you live alone?"

"Don't worry," Sally said. "I'd like a drink."

"Aaah," Lueger said. "Waste time."

"I'll pay for it," Sally said. She had learned a lot about him in the evening. "My own money. Drinks for you and me."

"If you say so," Lueger said, steering her into a bar. "One drink, because we have something to do tonight." He pinched her playfully and laughed, looking obliquely into her eyes with a kind of technical suggestiveness.

UNDER the Ninth Avenue "L" at Twelfth Street, Charlie and Dr. Slater leaned against an Elevated pillar, in deep shadow.

"I wonder if they're coming," Slater said finally, in a flat, high whisper.

"They'll come," Charlie said, keeping his eyes on the little triangular park up Twelfth Street where it joins Eighth Avenue. "That Sally has guts. That Sally loves my dumb brother like he was the President of the United States. As if he was a combination of Lenin and Michelangelo. And he had to go and get his eye batted out."

"He's a very fine man," Slater said, "your brother Ernest. A man with true ideals. I am very sorry to see what has happened to his character since—is that them?"

"No," Charlie said. "It's two girls from the Y.W.C.A. on the corner."

"He used to be a very happy man," Slater said. "Always laughing."

"Yeah," Charlie said. "Yeah. Why don't you keep quiet, Slater?"

"Excuse me," Slater said. "I don't like to bother you. But I must talk. Otherwise, if I just stand here keeping still, I will suddenly start running and I'll run right up to Forty-second Street. I can't keep quiet at the moment, excuse me."

"Go ahead and talk then," Charlie said, patting him on the shoulder. "Shoot your mouth right off, all you want."

"I am only doing this because I think it will help Ernest," Slater said, leaning hard against the pillar, in the shadow, to keep his knees straight. The Elevated was like a dark roof stretching all the way across from building line to building line. "We should have brought an instrument with us, though. A club, a knife, brass knuckles." Slater put his hands in his pockets, holding them tight against the cloth to keep them from trembling. "It will be very bad if we mess this up. Won't it be very bad, Charlie?"

"Sh-h-h," Charlie said.

Slater looked up the street. "That's them. That's Sally, that's her coat."

"Sh-h-h, Slater. Sh-h-h."

"I feel very cold, Charlie. Do you feel cold? It's a warm night but I—"

"For Christ's sake, shut up!"

"We'll fix him," Slater whispered. "Yes, Charlie, I'll shut up. Sure, I'll shut up, depend on me, Charlie."

SALLY and Lueger walked slowly down Twelfth Street. Lueger had his arm around Sally's waist. "That was a very fine film tonight," he was saying. "I enjoy Deanna Durbin. Very young, fresh, sweet. Like you." He grinned at Sally in the dark and held tighter to her waist. "A small young maid. You are just the kind I like." When he tried to kiss her, Sally turned her head away.

"Let's walk fast," she said, watching Charlie and Slater move out from the "L" shadow. "Let's not waste time."

Lueger laughed happily. "That's it. That's the way a girl should talk."

They walked swiftly toward the Elevated, Lueger laughing, his hand on her hip in certainty and possession.

"Pardon me," Slater said. "Could you direct me to Sheridan Square?"

"Well," said Sally, stopping, "it's—"

Charlie swung, and Sally started running as soon as she heard the wooden little noise a fist makes on a man's face. Charlie held Lueger up with one hand and chopped the lolling head with the other. Then he carried Lueger back into the shadows against a high iron fence. He hung Lueger by his overcoat against one of the iron points, so he could use both hands on him. Slater watched for a moment, then turned and looked up at Eighth Avenue.

Charlie worked very methodically, getting his two hundred pounds behind short, accurate, smashing blows that made Lueger's head jump and loll and roll against the iron pikes. Charlie hit him in the nose three times, squarely, using his fist the way a carpenter uses a hammer. Each time Slater heard the sound of bone breaking, cartilage tearing. When Charlie got through with the nose, he went after the mouth, hooking along the side of the jaws with both hands until teeth fell out and the jaw hung open, smashed, loose with the queer looseness of flesh that is no longer moored to solid bone. Charlie started crying, the tears running down into his mouth, the sobs shaking him as he swung his fists. Even then Slater didn't turn around. He just put his hands to his ears and looked steadfastly at Eighth Avenue.

Charlie was talking. "You bastard!" he was saying. "Oh you dumb, mean, skirt-chasing, sonofabitch bastard!" And he kept hitting with fury and deliberation at the shattered face.

A car came up Twelfth Street from the waterfront and slowed down at the corner. Slater jumped on the running board. "Keep moving," he said, very tough, "if you know what's good for you." Then he jumped off the running board and watched the car speed away.

Charlie, still sobbing, pounded Lueger in the chest and belly. With each blow, Lueger slammed against the iron fence with a noise like a carpet being beaten until his coat ripped off the pike and he slid to the sidewalk. Charlie stood back then, his fists swaying, the sweat running down his face inside his collar, his clothes stained with blood. "O.K.," he said. "O.K., you bastard." He walked swiftly uptown under the "L" in the shadows, and Slater hurried after him.

MUCH later, in the hospital, Preminger stood over the bed in which Lueger lay unconscious, in splints and bandages.

"Yes," he said to the detective and the doctor, "that's our man. Lueger. A steward. The papers on him are correct."

"Who do you think done it?" the detective asked in a routine voice. "Did he have any enemies?"

"Not that I know of," Preminger said. "He was a very popular boy. Especially with the ladies."

The detective started out of the ward. "Well," he said, "he won't be a very popular boy when he gets out of here."

Preminger shook his head. "You must be very careful in a strange city," he said to the interne, and went back to his ship.

(1939)

PHYSICS

A FTER I got my hair cut at High Style 2000 on Lexington Avenue, I was hit by a car. It wasn't even a very nice vehicle, just a blue-and-white Pinto. I was trying to cross the street in the middle of the block, and the car backed up and hit me in the legs at knee level. I didn't realize that I'd been struck by a car; it felt more as if someone came along and punched me in the legs. Then it pulled forward. I was stunned. I kept staring at the license plate: it said 867-UHH. I tried to memorize it. The car wasn't going anywhere—I guess the driver was waiting to see if I was seriously damaged. I was angry, even if it *was* my fault. I glared at the car and tried to give the driver the evil eye. He leaned out the window and yelled at me, "You stupid, or what? Didn't you see how far away from you I was?"

Now, I am a word person and have never been good with mathematical problems—how many miles a train can travel in five hours if its speed is forty miles per hour, and so forth. I always think, What if a cow gets in the way? Probably because of this, I almost flunked high-school physics. Every night my mother made me memorize phrases from the textbook, but it didn't do any good. The teacher tried to help me after school, but I still got a D. Faced with the driver's hard question on Lexington Avenue, I wanted to do something—go scream at him, for instance—but I was afraid. I remembered my mother telling me how, at age two, she was taken on a trip from Atlanta to Manhattan and when her mother took her outside to play in the courtyard of the building they were staying in someone opened a window and poured a pail of water onto my mother's head. Whoever it was didn't like the fact that my mother was singing under that window at nine o'clock on a Sunday morning. Of course, my grandmother dried her off (or the water evaporated quickly or slowly, depending on the coefficient of diffusion) and called the police and the newspapers. My mother still had the clipping with the photo from the *Herald Tribune*, captioned "A MINUTE MYSTERY." It showed her in Shirley Temple ringlets, with chubby legs, and the article described how little Sonia Silverman, up from Georgia on a visit, had been the victim of a nasty prank.

I stood in the gutter. I was trembling. Either I was extremely happy or I had just received a shot of adrenaline from being hit. It was hard to tell the difference. I wasn't dead. It was like finding twenty dollars in the gutter. What a thing I was! I went across the street and into a pizzeria, and I ordered a piece of pizza—pepperoni, mushrooms, onions, and peppers. I had to wait on line while it was heating in the oven.

There was another girl waiting ahead of me, and when the cook finally took out her slice I tried to reach for it, but she reached first and the cook handed it to her. "Is this the type that you ordered?" I said. I rarely speak to strangers, but I had to say something. I didn't believe the girl had gotten the same type of pizza as mine, because (a) it was an unusual choice to make, and (b) almost everyone else seemed to be ordering the plain slices.

The girl gave me a dirty look. "Yes, it is," she said snippily.

The cook said to me, "Don't get impatient, honey. Just relax." This only made me feel more foolish. The slice that he gave me, however, was really sparse. Most of the ingredients had slid off into the oven. I was embarrassed and would have said something along the lines of "I can assure you I'm not impatient," but nothing came out of my mouth. The cook, I was certain, had gone out of his way to make me look pushy, when obviously it was unintentional on my part.

The pizza was like a metaphor for my entropic life. The girl whose slice I tried to steal was carrying one of these trashy novels about Hollywood. I was incensed. This was her reading material, yet she felt superior to me. At first I thought she was about to take the only table left and I would be forced to sit with her. My hot pizza was leaking through the paper plate. But finally I found another empty table. I felt so grateful I almost threw myself into my seat. At the next table was a woman with a crew cut, a kid about six years old, and a guy with pale-blue hair who looked like the woman's brother. He kept taking food from the little kid's plate, and the kid said, in a fury, practically heartbroken, "Leave my food alone." He was eating spaghetti. I wondered if it tasted as good as my pizza, which, though skimpy, was absolutely delicious—chunks of chewy mushrooms, dense and meaty, cheese like stringy bubble gum, and salty, sparky bits of pepperoni.

On the ceiling, over the steam trays, giant papier-mâché haunches of meat were hanging from ropes. I kept thinking, "I was just hit by a car."

ON the bus home, I reminded myself not to tell Stash, my boyfriend, about what had happened, or he would kill me. How would it be if he picked up the *Post* and saw "JEWELRY DESIGNER, 28, KILLED BY HIT-AND-RUN"? First of all, everyone would know that I got my hair cut in an outré joint on Lexington Avenue and not at some SoHo or East Village spot. Plus, who would come to my funeral? I had no friends. All the other jewelry designers I knew had plenty of friends. They threw big parties for themselves at various clubs, and their pictures were published in the most fashionable magazines. Maybe they were receiving outside financial assistance. I had no money to throw parties, although I had a hunger for things I knew I didn't actually care for.

When I got in the door, Stash was lying on the bed next to Andrew, our Dalmatian. Stash's thick blond hair, loose from its ponytail, was practically covering his face. He had an ominous, unshaven look. He wasn't wearing a shirt; his hairy chest had an animal ferocity. Andrew's legs were sticking up in the air, and his neck was resting on Stash's arm. Andrew had a snoring problem; he snored so loudly that he used to wake Stash and me several times a night, until Stash devised a solution: he attached a rope to Andrew's bed, and during the night whenever Andrew began to snore Stash would yank the rope and the abrupt movement would wake Andrew and he would stop snoring for a while. I used to tease Stash, telling him this was cruelty to animals—after all, would he have liked it if someone tied a rope to our bed and gave it a jerk every time we drifted off to sleep? But Andrew was so good-natured—or dumb—he didn't seem to mind.

Stash and Andrew didn't even look at me. I felt left out. "Hi," I said. "I got my hair cut." I had red corkscrew curls, almost to my waist; my hair didn't have a real style, it was just a mess. Stash had begged me never to change it. "It doesn't look one iota different, does it? I spent ten dollars and told them to snip the ends. What do you think? Will I look nice tonight?"

Stash didn't answer.

"Is something wrong?" I said.

"No."

"Are you sick? You have an earache?"

"No."

"Did you eat today?"

"Yes."

"What did I do?" I said. "I forgot to defrost the refrigerator? Is that it? *You* defrost the goddam refrigerator."

"Eleanor, I would have defrosted the refrigerator, but you've got too much stuff in there. You made me help you pick eight quarts of cherries last summer and you never made pies. Why don't you throw them out?"

"I didn't make pies because you said we were on a diet. I come home and you're mad at me about the refrigerator?"

"I wasn't even thinking about the refrigerator until you reminded me. I'm mad about that article on the table. Go look at it."

Sometimes I felt as if I were the sole member of the Bomb Squad: I had to defuse Stash. I picked up the magazine lying on the table. It was a nice table, like something that might be found in a campers' dining hall. Stash had bought it for me a few months back, saying that since I complained so much about not being able to have anyone over to dinner he would get me a table. So far, though, every time I suggested we invite someone over he said the house was too messy and gave examples. No. 1, I had stuck black and white adhesive tiles in the space between the kitchen counter and the cabinets, and when they peeled off, a short time later, all the paint on the wall peeled off with them, leaving brown spots.

In the magazine was a reproduction of one of Stash's paintings, "The Wisdom of Solomon," in which Quick Draw McGraw and Baba Looey are sawing an Eskimo baby in half. Underneath the picture was a long article. In the first paragraph the author said that while he couldn't dismiss Stash's work entirely, it was nevertheless the mindless scrawling of a Neanderthal.

"Well, that doesn't sound so bad," I said when I put it down.

"Doesn't sound so bad?" Stash said. He shook his head disbelievingly. "Sometimes you amaze me."

"Well, things could always be worse," I said. "This could be Russia, where they come and knock on your door and take you away and shoot you if they don't like what you do."

"Russian Constructivist art is my favorite," Stash said.

"At least you're getting attention!" I said. "I'd be thrilled if anyone wrote an article about me, even a negative one."

"I don't know if I feel like going to the dinner tonight," Stash said.

A fancy dinner for thirty of the country's most famous artists was going to be held at a swank Italian restaurant, to honor the fact that they had agreed to decorate a night club. Stash was one of them; they would all be there this evening. My girlfriend had told me that at this restaurant dinner for two, with one bottle of champagne, could cost more than two hundred dollars. Luckily, we wouldn't be paying.

"You do too feel like going out tonight," I said. "All the other artists will envy your appearance in that magazine."

"Do you think?" Stash said. "I don't know."

"First of all, everyone wants publicity," I said. "Secondly, as long as you're an underdog you can have respect—like Vincent van Gogh. If you get too popular it makes you seem phony and commercial." I probably would have said anything—I really wanted to go to the dinner. It was going to be an event: never had so many diverse and famous artists been collected under one roof. They ranged from people famous for sports illustration to the latest East Village star.

"I was in a good mood until I saw this article," Stash said. "Then when I got home I found you still hadn't defrosted the refrigerator. Not only will I never be able to get the money to buy a loft now, I don't see the point anyway. If we did have a decent place to live, it would always be a complete mess."

"Didn't you ever hear of a self-defrosting refrigerator?" I said. "You were just looking for an excuse. Don't you try and punish me, Stash."

"How am I punishing you?"

"Because you promised me we'd start looking for a bigger space to live in, and now you're going to try and weasel out." One half of me had known all along we would never move: we were too uncomfortable here. Low rent (subsidized housing for artists) and a nice river view—we were used to it. On the other hand, a friend of Stash's was trying to buy a building nearby, and Stash liked the way the deal sounded. He could buy a whole floor and rent out half, thus making his mortgage payments.

I started to get the things out of the refrigerator and put them into the sink. I'd defrost overnight. I felt like clobbering Stash over the head. I was practically thirty years old, unmarried, and my marketability was going downhill fast. My career hadn't taken off the way I'd hoped. I had had to quit working on my jewelry full time in order to take on a job two days a week as copy editor for an East Village newspaper. I also had to be burdened with my lousy personality. If I had been more outgoing maybe I could have been more successful with my jewelry. That was the way things worked in Manhattan.

Where I grew up, in South Carolina, social graces didn't count. Max, my father, had a mail-order gardening business. We raised peonies, daffodils, daylilies, hyacinths, irises, all kinds of bulbs and perennials. For my fourteenth birthday, Max named a new variety of pink camellia after me. I wasn't thrilled—I really wanted a subscription to *Seventeen*—but I kept my mouth shut. Max also taught horticulture at the local university part time. When we children came home from school, everyone had a job to do. The stove was full of baked potatoes, and that's what we'd have—baked potatoes with yogurt and goat cheese. My mother raised angora goats and sold the wool to weavers across the country. My parents had made a choice: they would remain poor but live off the land, in a style unaffected by the progressively commercial and false world around them. It was taken for granted that we would all work hard. In other words, we didn't have a TV set.

Well, I had also made a choice: I would rebel against my parents and join the rat race. I wanted things, and the things I wanted weren't inexpensive. Unfortunately, somewhere along the line I got sidetracked. For one thing, I had never, in my wackiest dreams, imagined that I would grow up to be a poor person. My mother had warned me about New York, but I was prepared to work hard, and I figured eventually I'd make it. I wasn't the only one in my situation. Most of the people I knew were doing one thing but considered themselves to be something else: all the waitresses I knew were really actresses, all the Xeroxers in the Xerox place were really novelists, all the receptionists were artists. There were enough examples of people who had been receptionists and went on to become famous artists that the receptionists felt it was O.K. to call themselves artists. But if I was going to have to do something like copy-edit two or three days a week, I didn't want to lie to myself and say I was a jewelry designer. I figured I should just accept reality and say I was a copy editor.

I was embittered. It was hard to live in New York and not be full of rage. I was thinking of all this while I fixed some instant flan, using up all the rest of the milk so it wouldn't go bad being outside the refrigerator overnight. On the side of the box the only ingredient listed was sugar. I felt I should have made Stash flan from scratch.

At that moment he came into the kitchen. "What are you doing?" he said. "You can't even focus on one activity! You're trying to defrost the refrigerator and cook at the same time!"

It was strange how most of the time we got along so well, but then there were these periods when it was a good thing the knives were in the drawer and not out on display. "You're picking on me!" I said. "I do things as I please! Look around you—the junk that's here is yours, not mine. I had to clear off four of my bookshelves and mail my books back to my mother so you could have someplace to put all that junk from the table—and now the table has new junk on it."

While I yelled, Stash hacked at some of the loose ice on the freezer. When he had filled a bowl, he carried it over to the sink. "Where should I put it?" he said. "The sink is full of food—plus the dirty spaghetti pot."

"In the tub."

"I can't throw it in the tub," he said. "I'm going to take a shower."

"Well, run some hot water on it," I said. "The melting point of ice is zero degrees Celsius or thirty-two degrees Fahrenheit."

It was obvious that he had to restrain himself from throwing the ice at me. "How can I buy a loft when you put too much food in the refrigerator? Why should I go into debt when you're going to turn a new place into the same kind of disaster as here?" he said.

"You lash out at me because you're angry about the article!" I said as he went into the bathroom.

I imagined grabbing my clothing, throwing it into a suitcase, and storming out. This seemed so real to me that when Stash came out of the shower, wrapped in a towel, arms extended toward me, I was surprised.

He clutched me like an orangutan. "Let's be friends," he said.

"Don't pick on me every second of my existence," I said into his ear. "It makes me feel like I'm a fly and you're pulling off my wings."

"Yeah?" Stash said. "Don't give me that wings-being-picked-off business."

I knew he was afraid of letting me get too sure of myself; this was as much of an apology as I was going to get. He said we could go to the party.

Quickly I slurped down a yogurt before we went out. It tasted exactly like cold cream. I was only interested in helping the stomach not to complain, with its little lump of cold cream balanced neatly in the center. At these dinners, food wasn't served until eleven o'clock, or even eleven-thirty.

EVEN though the dinner was scheduled for ten, we didn't get there until ten-thirty, and most of the other people were just arriving. At the door, we had to sign a release stating that if our pictures were taken they could be used in publicity.

The restaurant was quite a pretty place. Every table had a mammoth floral display, as big as a tree, in the center, and there were little place cards and gifts at each place. My card said "Guest of Mr. Stosz"—I was seated next to the place card of "Stash Stosz"—and my gift was selected by someone who must have known my situation as well as my vocation: it was a large fake diamond engagement-and-wedding-ring set. Stash got a set of tattoos, water-soluble, and a toy motorcycle—Stash owned a motorcycle—which, when he wound it up, zipped across the table and fell over. Other artists received Etch A Sketch kits, voodoo dolls, exploding cigars, windup jack-in-the-boxes in the shape of clamshells which contained Botticelli's Venus leaping out to music, and their signatures made into rubber stamps.

The food was really delicious: slices of raw meat, thin as paper; angel-hair pasta speckled with shreds of crabmeat and roasted peppers; little fried fish, hot and curling on platters, with their astonished eyes still intact. In one corner of the room a man played the accordion—various haunting tunes—possibly as a special treat in honor of the occasion. Or maybe he was there all the time. For an appetizer I had a plate of slightly sandy mussels in a sauce of vermouth and garlic. Stash had smoked mozzarella with basil and tomatoes. We had agreed to share. But, frankly, I couldn't enjoy it as much as I would have liked. For one thing, by eleven-thirty my appetite was gone and I was ready to go to sleep, and, for another, I only liked to eat alone with Stash. I wanted to relish my food without having to worry about why I wasn't being included in the conversation or whether I was getting food on my chin. This was my small but sad handicap, not something that revealed a character trait: sometimes food or grease would get on my chin and I couldn't feel it. I had had a minor operation when I was fifteen and sensation on my chin never returned. It wasn't the most glamorous of handicaps to have, but it was mine. The one handicap that really appealed to me as tragic and romantic was the one that Laura had, Laura of "The Glass Menagerie." She was lame. There aren't too many lame people around anymore. Nowadays they just limp.

I was seated next to a girl wearing a rubber dress; it looked like a coat of latex paint. The card in front of her plate said "Samantha Binghamton," and every two seconds one of the photographers would come and snap her picture. She had wild black hair (maybe a wig) and a long, skinny neck, which was either very elegant or goosey—I couldn't decide. So much for my one fancy evening outfit of sequinned top and black velvet skirt—it was nothing compared to what Rubbermaid had on. I could have strangled her. The people across from me pretended I didn't exist. While twirling pasta with my fork, I quizzed Samantha on her life story. She had known her husband—he was seated on her other side—since second grade. He came from a fabulously wealthy family and now had one of the hottest galleries in New York. She used to be a top-notch agent—she was best friends with Dustin Hoffman and John Huston, and one of her clients was in the movie that swept the Academy Awards the year before. But even though she was only twenty-eight years old and close to the top of her profession, she decided she wasn't happy. Since her husband could support her and she didn't really need to work, she quit two weeks ago to become a rock star. This was what she really wanted to do. So far she hadn't landed a manager, but it seemed likely that this would happen soon.

Maybe I had had a little too much champagne; it certainly was delicious, with large, real raspberries stuck in the bottom of every glass. "Isn't it strange," I said, "to be trying to land an agent and a record contract when this is what you used to do for other people?"

"No."

Her best friend, in a feathered tutu, was seated across from us, and when the tutu girl got up to go buy cigarettes I asked Samantha what her friend did. "She goes out with Fritz," Samantha said. Fritz was a sculptor, famous for his work in lemons and mirrors. "She's only eighteen and a real witch." So much for best friends, I thought.

In the rest room we applied various kinds of makeup from Samantha's handbag. "That guy next to you," she said as she powdered her nose, "you're with him, right?"

"We live together," I said. "That's Stash."

"That's what I was going to ask you," she said. "He's Stash Stosz, right? Who just got a terrible review?"

"Yeah," I said.

She took a joint out of her bag. "Is he rich?" she said, lighting the joint and handing it to me.

"No," I said.

"Are you?"

"No."

"Well, why would you go out with him?" she said.

"I—" I said. I was stunned.

"Come out with us after the dinner," she said. "My husband has a brother who'd love to meet you. We'll all go to the club."

I smoked some of the joint with her. Maybe she had had too much to drink, too.

Back at the table Stash was having an active argument with a racehorse painter, a man with a goatee and rabbit teeth. "What you're doing, that's not art," the horse painter was saying. He was wearing a cowboy hat of soft and furry felt.

"I've seen your work," I said to him. "My mother bought some paper plates one time, for a cookout, and your paintings were on them."

Everyone had changed places. A photographer was walking around taking candid pictures. One artist, with his long white arms curled around the back of the chair next to him, and his round, bloblike head, resembled an octopus. Another made strange movements with his mouth like a kissing gourami. One artist was so famous he refused to sit with the rest of us: he had his own private table on the balcony, where he was seated with a famous French movie actress. The one sitting across from me was quite drunk; he had a red face and a superior attitude. While he was talking to someone he picked up a full ashtray in front of him and emptied it under the table.

When the dinner was over, one of the artists took a plate of cake (a special kind of Venetian cake known as a pick-me-up) and dumped it on the head of a less famous artist. The less famous artist didn't even blink; he just called for the photographer to come over.

Stash got stuck talking to someone at the coatroom, and I went outside. Samantha rolled down the window of a limousine and leaned out. "Eleanor, come here," she said. "I want you to meet my brother-in-law, Mitch."

I squinted in the window. Some guy with red hair and a beard was sitting next to Samantha. He had the wild eyes of a trotter at a fifth-rate racetrack, hopped up on who knew what. "Nice to meet you, Mitch," I said. He handed me a glass of champagne.

"Where are you going now, Eleanor?" Samantha said.

"Downtown."

"Come on, get in with us," she said. "We'll take you."

I thought for a second. I should wait for Stash, go home with him, walk the dog, and watch TV. I'd try to tell him about why all these people drove me crazy. How I was tired of their all being so wrapped up in themselves. But I knew he would just say that I'd had too much to drink. Or I could open the car door, jump in, and whiz off someplace. If I did, Stash would probably forgive me, eventually.

"Stash is still inside," I said. "I'm waiting for him. I don't want to keep you. I'll call you next week. Bye, Mitch."

Samantha shrugged and the window rolled back up. I was left standing on the curb with a glass of champagne in my hand.

BY the time we got home I was pretty depressed. While I brushed my teeth and cleaned my contact lenses, I thought about Samantha, in her rubber dress. Let's face it, she wasn't prettier than I, or more intelligent, and what did she do? Just one out of the millions who want to be rock stars. So how come she kept getting her picture taken, and how come all the men were making a fuss over her and asking if they could snap her latexwear? Because (a) she had an important husband, who ran a big gallery, and (b) she probably hung out with these people every night, taking drugs—cocaine or whatever—whereas it was a rare thing for me just to smoke marijuana. On the other hand, maybe she really had a better personality than I, and really was more attractive physically and psychically, and I was just deluding myself.

I realized that I really did want to be where I was—with Stash, in this hovel. I ran through all the parts of my life, trying to figure out which thing in particular wasn't working for me. I supposed I could get a nose job and take one of those courses that teach chutzpah. (I had read the leaflet on it in the supermarket.) But would this make me a more spiritual person? I doubted it. It was hard for me to keep up with all the various aspects of reality. Finally I figured it out: I wanted a baby. Obviously, based on this evening and others like it, I wasn't meant for any glamorous night life or fast lane, but I would be a good mother.

I pictured myself with a giant Buddha baby with a fat belly, a shock of blond hair, and a surprised expression. I would give it baths in a basin and wheel it around the block in a little go-cart, speaking to the other mothers. Stash could take it to openings strapped on his back. I had often seen men doing this in art galleries or at night clubs. Finally, when it grew up, it could tell me how wonderful I was. Stash and I would at last be bonded and we could have a joint checking account and I wouldn't have to be so worried about finances. These weren't such great reasons, but what counted was the unconscious level—the feeling that something was missing from my life and I had finally guessed what it was.

I went out into the bedroom—anyway, the end of our apartment where the bed was. "Listen, Stash," I said. "I've been thinking. You're middle-aged, and I'm not so young, either. It would be a good time to have a baby. We've been kidding about it for a while, but let's be serious." Looking at him, I knew that our baby would be cute, though if it inherited Stash's chest hair and my head hair it would practically be a gorilla. There wouldn't be one hairless inch.

"What are you—drunk?" Stash said. He was lying on the bed, watching a Frankenstein movie on TV, Andrew alongside him. "You can't bring a baby into this world. At least not in the city. Didn't you hear the news before?"

"I was brushing my teeth."

"This forty-nine-year-old widow was walking down the street and all of a sudden a thirty-five-ton crane toppled over and hit her. She was pinned under it for nearly six hours, partially crushed, just like that. That's why you can't have children in New York." Stash looked as if he was ready to kill me. It was hard for him to believe that a person could be so stupid. I knew I irritated Stash in the same way that my younger brother used to irritate me when I was a kid. Roland's foot-tapping used to send me into a rage; I would start to scream at him when he wasn't even aware of what he was doing. Now I knew what it was like to be the source of irritation without being irritated in return. I looked at Stash with the same puzzled, hurt expression that my brother had when I lashed out at him for no good reason.

"I'm taking the dog out," I said. "Come on, Andrew."

Andrew shot up and plunged up and down at my feet. Every time he went out he acted as if he had been locked up in a kennel for a year. His whip tail slashed my legs. Unfortunately, this was the only time he ever paid any attention to me, even though I had been with him since he was a year and a half old. He was Stash's dog. I had worked hard to make him love me. He was wearing a collar I had designed for him—plastic dinosaurs, turtles, and square, varicolored rhinestones, which I had attached to the leather with little grommets. I had done all kinds of things for Andrew. I decorated him, sometimes with baseball caps, sometimes with slogan sweatshirts I cut down from Woolworth's boys' department, and once I had painted additional spots on him with food coloring. Well, Andrew wasn't the brightest of dogs, but he did have a sense of humor and a certain dappled elegance.

It was late at night, and I didn't bother to put him on the leash. He sniffed the stunted trees and the metal signposts with the utmost delicacy, as if he were rooting for truffles. A fishy wind blew off the Hudson. Stash was probably feeling guilty and would be nice to me. Probably I had made the right choice. If I had gone off with Samantha and taken drugs I would have shifted into higher gear, but how long could I keep that up?

"Get over here, Andrew," I said. I wanted to go upstairs. "Hurry up." Of course he wouldn't move. He was deaf when he wanted to be. I gritted my teeth, annoyed. He went on calmly rooting as if I weren't even there. The rotten animal obeyed Stash, but not me.

Finally, he followed. The elevator was broken and we had to walk up seven flights. I'm not in such great shape. Believe me, I'd like to be one of those women with all the muscles, but, frankly, I don't like the idea of doing all that work. Once I took an aerobics class—I thought it would give me more energy—but every day I had to come home after class and sleep for a couple of hours.

When we made it back to the apartment Stash was standing near the window with a funny look on his face. "You wouldn't believe what just happened," he said.

"What?" I said.

"A transvestite and a john came over to the bushes under the window. Well, I don't want transvestites and tricks in our courtyard. So I went to the sink and took the spaghetti pot and dumped the water in it onto them. A direct hit!"

I started to laugh, involuntarily, but I stopped. "Stash," I said.

"Well, I didn't know that there were things in the pot," Stash said. "I really was mad, and I just dumped the whole soapy contents out, and I didn't realize there were some spoons and a bowl in it."

"My Russel Wright dish!" I said. "Stash, how could you do such a thing?"

"What do you mean?" he said. "You were out there with Andrew. Something could have happened to you. I wanted them to get the idea they can't come around here."

"What happened when the water hit them?" I said.

"They just walked away, shaking their heads."

"You could have killed someone," I said. I felt very bad about the transvestite: she was just trying to get along in the world and had ended up covered with soapy, greasy water—spaghetti water—and would probably be freezing cold for the rest of the night.

"The bowl hit the trees, it didn't hit her," Stash said.

"It's not your job to throw water on people," I said. "You should either have yelled something to chase them away or called the guard."

"I did feel sort of demonically possessed when I did it," Stash admitted. "What do you want? I'm only a mindless Neanderthal." I could tell he would have liked to undo it as soon as the water was halfway down, but it was too late—as had been demonstrated in another age by Galileo, who threw some stuff off the Leaning Tower of Pisa.

I suddenly wished I could go back to school and take physics again; I knew that this time I would understand it. The notion of random particles, random events, didn't seem at all difficult to comprehend. The whole business was like understanding traffic patterns, with unplanned crackups and hit-and-run accidents. Somewhere I had read that increasing the rate of collisions between positrons and electrons will result in interesting "events" that physicists can study. Quarks, quirks, leptons, protons, valence electrons, tracers, kryptons, isotopes—who knew what powerful forces were at work? I saw how emotions caused objects to go whizzing about. If I had gotten into the limousine earlier that night I'd be in the same mess only in a different neighborhood; at least in this place I had love, a feeling that came at a person like a Dodg'em car in an amusement park, where the sign says "Proceed at Own Risk."

(1985)

THE WHORE OF MENSA

O NE thing about being a private investigator, you've got to learn to go with your hunches. That's why when a quivering pat of butter named Word Babcock walked into my office and laid his cards on the table, I should have trusted the cold chill that shot up my spine.

"Kaiser?" he said. "Kaiser Lupowitz?"

"That's what it says on my license," I owned up.

"You've got to help me. I'm being blackmailed. Please!"

He was shaking like the lead singer in a rumba band. I pushed a glass across the desk top and a bottle of rye I keep handy for nonmedicinal purposes. "Suppose you relax and tell me all about it."

"You . . . you won't tell my wife?"

"Level with me, Word. I can't make any promises."

He tried pouring a drink, but you could hear the clicking sound across the street, and most of the stuff wound up in his shoes.

"I'm a working guy," he said. "Mechanical maintenance. I build and service joy buzzers. You know—those little fun gimmicks that give people a shock when they shake hands?"

"So?"

"A lot of your executives like 'em. Particularly down on Wall Street."

"Get to the point."

"I'm on the road a lot. You know how it is—lonely. Oh, not what you're thinking. See, Kaiser, I'm basically an intellectual. Sure, a guy can meet all the bimbos he wants. But the really brainy women—they're not so easy to find on short notice."

"Keep talking."

"Well, I heard of this young girl. Eighteen years old. A Vassar student. For a price, she'll come over and discuss any subject—Proust, Yeats, anthropology. Exchange of ideas. You see what I'm driving at?"

"Not exactly."

"I mean, my wife is great, don't get me wrong. But she won't discuss Pound with me. Or Eliot. I didn't know that when I married her. See, I need a woman who's mentally stimulating, Kaiser. And I'm willing to pay for it. I don't want an involvement—I want a quick intellectual experience, then I want the girl to leave. Christ, Kaiser, I'm a happily married man."

"How long has this been going on?"

"Six months. Whenever I have that craving, I call Flossie. She's a madam, with a master's in Comparative Lit. She sends me over an intellectual, see?"

So he was one of those guys whose weakness was really bright women. I felt sorry for the poor sap. I figured there must be a lot of jokers in his position, who were starved for a little intellectual communication with the opposite sex and would pay through the nose for it.

"Now she's threatening to tell my wife," he said.

"Who is?"

"Flossie. They bugged the motel room. They got tapes of me discussing 'The Waste Land' and 'Styles of Radical Will,' and, well, really getting into some issues. They want ten grand or they go to Carla. Kaiser, you've got to help me! Carla would die if she knew she didn't turn me on up here."

The old call-girl racket. I had heard rumors that the boys at headquarters were on to something involving a group of educated women, but so far they were stymied.

"Get Flossie on the phone for me."

"What?"

"I'll take your case, Word. But I get fifty dollars a day, plus expenses. You'll have to repair a lot of joy buzzers."

"It won't be ten Gs' worth, I'm sure of that," he said with a grin, and picked up the phone and dialled a number. I took it from him and winked. I was beginning to like him.

Seconds later, a silky voice answered, and I told her what was on my mind. "I understand you can help me set up an hour of good chat," I said.

"Sure, honey. What do you have in mind?"

"I'd like to discuss Melville."

" 'Moby Dick' or the shorter novels?"

"What's the difference?"

"The price. That's all. Symbolism's extra."

"What'll it run me?"

"Fifty, maybe a hundred for 'Moby Dick.' You want a comparative discussion—Melville and Hawthorne? That could be arranged for a hundred."

"The dough's fine," I told her and gave her the number of a room at the Plaza.

"You want a blonde or a brunette?"

"Surprise me," I said, and hung up.

I shaved and grabbed some black coffee while I checked over the Monarch College Outline series. Hardly an hour had passed before there was a knock on my door. I opened it, and standing there was a young redhead who was packed into her slacks like two big scoops of vanilla ice cream.

"Hi, I'm Sherry."

They really knew how to appeal to your fantasies. Long straight hair, leather bag, silver earrings, no makeup.

"I'm surprised you weren't stopped, walking into the hotel dressed like that," I said. "The house dick can usually spot an intellectual."

"A five-spot cools him."

"Shall we begin?" I said, motioning her to the couch.

She lit a cigarette and got right to it. "I think we could start by approaching 'Billy Budd' as Melville's justification of the ways of God to man, n'est-ce pas?"

"Interestingly, though, not in a Miltonian sense." I was bluffing. I wanted to see if she'd go for it.

"No. 'Paradise Lost' lacked the substructure of pessimism." She did.

"Right, right. God, you're right," I murmured.

"I think Melville reaffirmed the virtues of innocence in a naïve yet sophisticated sense—don't you agree?"

I let her go on. She was barely nineteen years old, but already she had developed the hardened facility of the pseudo-intellectual. She rattled off her ideas glibly, but it was all mechanical. Whenever I offered an insight, she faked a response: "Oh, yes, Kaiser. Yes, baby, that's deep. A platonic comprehension of Christianity—why didn't I see it before?"

We talked for about an hour and then she said she had to go. She stood up and I laid a C-note on her.

"Thanks, honey."

"There's plenty more where that came from."

"What are you trying to say?"

I had piqued her curiosity. She sat down again.

"Suppose I wanted to—have a party?" I said.

"Like, what kind of party?"

"Suppose I wanted Noam Chomsky explained to me by two girls?"

"Oh, wow."

"If you'd rather forget it . . ."

"You'd have to speak with Flossie," she said. "It'd cost you."

Now was the time to tighten the screws. I flashed my private-investigator's badge and informed her it was a bust.

"What!"

"I'm fuzz, sugar, and discussing Melville for money is an 802. You can do time."

"You louse!"

"Better come clean, baby. Unless you want to tell your story down at Alfred Kazin's office, and I don't think he'd be too happy to hear it."

She began to cry. "Don't turn me in, Kaiser," she said. "I needed the money to complete my master's. I've been turned down for a grant. *Twice.* Oh, Christ . . ."

It all poured out—the whole story. Central Park West upbringing, Socialist summer camps, Brandeis. She was every dame you saw waiting in line at the Elgin or the Thalia, or pencilling the words "Yes, very true" into the margin of some book on Kant. Only somewhere along the line she had made a wrong turn.

"I needed cash. A girl friend said she knew a married guy whose wife wasn't very profound. He was into Blake. She couldn't hack it. I said sure, for a price I'd talk Blake with him. I was nervous at first. I faked a lot of it. He didn't care. My friend said there were others. Oh, I've been busted before. I got caught reading *Commentary* in a parked car, and I was once stopped and frisked at Tanglewood. Once more and I'm a three-time loser."

"Then take me to Flossie."

She bit her lip and said, "The Hunter College Book Store is a front."

"Yes?"

"Like those bookie joints that have barbershops outside for show. You'll see."

I made a quick call to headquarters and then said to her, "O.K., sugar. You're off the hook. But don't leave town."

She tilted her face up toward mine gratefully. "I can get you photographs of Dwight Macdonald reading," she said.

"Some other time."

I walked into the Hunter College Book Store. The salesman, a young man with sensitive eyes, came up to me. "Can I help you?" he said.

"I'm looking for a special edition of 'Advertisements for Myself.' I understand the author had several thousand gold-leaf copies printed up for friends."

"I'll have to check," he said. "We have a WATS line to Mailer's house."

I fixed him with a look. "Sherry sent me," I said.

"Oh, in that case, go on back," he said. He pressed a button. A wall of books opened, and I walked like a lamb into that bustling pleasure palace known as Flossie's.

Red flocked wallpaper and a Victorian décor set the tone. Pale, nervous girls with black-rimmed glasses and blunt-cut hair lolled around on sofas, riffling Penguin Classics provocatively. A blonde with a big smile winked at me, nodded toward a room upstairs, and said, "Wallace Stevens, eh?" But it wasn't just intellectual experiences—they were peddling emotional ones, too. For fifty bucks, I learned, you could "relate without getting close." For a hundred, a girl would lend you her Bartók records, have dinner, and then let you watch while she had an anxiety attack. For one-fifty, you could listen to FM radio with twins. For three bills, you got the works: A thin Jewish brunette would pretend to pick you up at the Museum of Modern Art, let you read her master's, get you involved in a screaming quarrel at Elaine's over Freud's conception of women, and then fake a suicide of your choosing—the perfect evening, for some guys. Nice racket. Great town, New York.

"Like what you see?" a voice said behind me. I turned and suddenly found myself standing face to face with the business end of a .38. I'm a guy with a strong stomach, but this time it did a back flip. It was Flossie, all right. The voice was the same, but Flossie was a man. His face was hidden by a mask.

"You'll never believe this," he said, "but I don't even have a college degree. I was thrown out for low grades."

"Is that why you wear that mask?"

"I devised a complicated scheme to take over *The New York Review of Books*, but it meant I had to pass for Lionel Trilling. I went to Mexico for an operation. There's a doctor in Juarez who gives people Trilling's features— for a price. Something went wrong. I came out looking like Auden, with

Mary McCarthy's voice. That's when I started working the other side of the law."

Quickly, before he could tighten his finger on the trigger, I went into action. Heaving forward, I snapped my elbow across his jaw and grabbed the gun as he fell back. He hit the ground like a ton of bricks. He was still whimpering when the police showed up.

"Nice work, Kaiser," Sergeant Holmes said. "When we're through with this guy, the F.B.I. wants to have a talk with him. A little matter involving some gamblers and an annotated copy of Dante's 'Inferno.' Take him away, boys."

Later that night, I looked up an old account of mine named Gloria. She was blond. She had graduated *cum laude*. The difference was she majored in physical education. It felt good.

(1974)

WHAT IT WAS LIKE, SEEING CHRIS

WHILE I sit with all the other patients in the waiting room, I always think that I will ask Dr. Wald what exactly is happening to my eyes, but when I go into his examining room alone it is dark, with a circle of light on the wall, and the doctor is standing with his back to me arranging silver instruments on a cloth. The big chair is empty for me to go sit in, and each time then I feel as if I have gone into a dream straight from being awake, the way you do sometimes at night, and I go to the chair without saying anything.

The doctor prepares to look at my eyes through a machine. I put my forehead and chin against the metal bands and look into the tiny ring of blue light while the doctor dabs quickly at my eye with something, but my head starts to feel numb, and I have to lift it back. "Sorry," I say. I shake my head and put it back against the metal. Then I stare into the blue light and try to hold my head still, and to convince myself that there is no needle coming toward my eye, that my eye is not anesthetized.

"Breathe," Dr. Wald says. "Breathe." But my head always goes numb again, and I pull away, and Dr. Wald has to wait for me to resettle myself against the machine. "Nervous today, Laurel?" he asks, not interested.

ONE Saturday after I had started going to Dr. Wald, Maureen and I walked around outside our old school. We dangled on the little swings with our knees bunched while the dry leaves blew around us, and Maureen told me she was sleeping with Kevin. Kevin is a sophomore, and to me he had seemed much older than we were when we'd begun high school in September. "What is it like?" I asked.

"Fine." Maureen shrugged. "Who do you like these days, anyhow? I notice you haven't been talking much about Dougie."

"No one," I said. Maureen stopped her swing and looked at me with one eyebrow raised, so I told her—although I was sorry as soon as I opened my mouth—that I'd met someone in the city.

"In the city?" she said. Naturally, she was annoyed. "How did you get to meet someone in the city?"

It was just by accident, I told her, because of going to the eye doctor, and anyway it was not some big thing. That was what I told Maureen, but I remembered the first time I had seen Chris as surely as if it were a stone I could hold in my hand.

IT was right after my first appointment with Dr. Wald. I had taken the train into the city after school, and when the doctor was finished with me I was supposed to take a taxi to my sister Penelope's dancing school, which was on the east side of the Park, and do homework there until Penelope's class was over and Mother picked us up. Friends of my parents ask me if I want to be a dancer, too, but they are being polite. There is Penelope, and there is me.

Across the street from the doctor's office, I saw a place called Jake's. I stared through the window at the long shining bar and mirrors and round tables, and it seemed to me I would never be inside a place like that, but then I thought how much I hated sitting outside Penelope's class and how much I hated the doctor's office, and I opened the door and walked right in.

I sat down at a table near the wall, and I ordered a Coke. I looked around at all the people with their glasses of colored liquids, and I thought how happy they were—vivid and free and sort of the same, as if they were playing.

I watched the bartender as he gestured and talked. He was really putting on a show telling a story to some people I could only see from the back. There was a man with shiny, straight hair that shifted like a curtain when he laughed, and a man with curly blond hair, and between them a girl in a fluffy sweater. The men—or boys (I couldn't tell, and I still don't know)— wore shirts with seams on the back that curved up from their belts to their shoulders. I watched their shirts, and I watched in the mirror behind the bar as their beautiful goldish faces settled from laughing. I looked at them in the mirror, and I particularly noticed the one with the shiny hair, and I watched his eyes get like crescents, as if he were listening to another story, but then I saw he was smiling. He was smiling into the mirror in front of him, and in the mirror I was just staring, staring at him, and he was smiling back into the mirror at me.

The next week I went back to Dr. Wald for some tests, and when I was finished, although I'd planned to go do homework at Penelope's dancing school, I went straight to Jake's instead. The same two men were at the bar, but a different girl was with them. I pretended not to notice them as I went to the table I had sat at before.

I had a Coke, and when I went up to the bar to pay, the one with the shiny hair turned right around in front of me. "Clothes-abuse squad," he said, prizing my wadded-up coat out of my arms. He shook it out and smiled at me. "I'm Chris," he said, "and this is Mark." His friend turned to me like a soldier who has been waiting, but the girl with them only glanced at me and turned to talk to someone else.

Chris helped me into my coat, and then he buttoned it up, as if I were a little child. "Who are you?" he said.

"Laurel," I said.

Chris nodded slowly. "Laurel," he said. And when he said that, I felt a shock on my face and hands and front as if I had pitched against flat water.

"SO are you going out with this guy, or what?" Maureen asked me.

"Maureen," I said. "He's just a person I met." Maureen looked at me again, but I just looked back at her. We twisted our swings up and let ourselves twirl out.

"So what's the matter with your eyes?" Maureen said. "Can't you just wear glasses?"

"Well, the doctor said he couldn't tell exactly what was wrong yet," I said. "He says he wants to keep me under observation, because there might be something happening to my retina." But I realized then that I didn't understand what that meant at all, and I also realized that I was really, but really, scared.

Maureen and I wandered over to the school building and looked in the window of the fourth-grade room, and I thought how strange it was that I used to fit in those miniature chairs, and that a few years later Penelope did, and that my little brother Paul fit in them now. There was a sickly old turtle in an aquarium on the sill just like the one we'd had. I wondered if it was the same one. I think they're sort of prehistoric, and some of them live to be a hundred or two hundred years old.

"I bet your mother is completely hysterical," Maureen said.

I smiled. Maureen thinks it's hilarious the way my mother expects everything in her life (*her* life!) to be perfect. "I had to bring her with me last week," I said.

"Ick," Maureen said sympathetically, and I remembered how awful it had been, sitting and waiting next to Mother. Whenever Mother moved— to cross her legs or smooth out her skirt or pick up a magazine—the clean smell of her perfume came over to me. Mother's perfume made a nice little space for her there in the stale office. We didn't talk at all, and it seemed like a long time before an Asian woman took me into a small white room and turned off the light. The woman had a serious face, like an angel, and she wore a white hospital coat over her clothes. She didn't seem to speak much English. She sat me down in front of something hanging on the wall which looked like a map of planets drawn in white on black.

The woman moved a wand across the map, and the end of the wand glimmered. "You say when you see light," she told me. In the silence I made myself say "Now" over and over as I saw the light blinking here and there upon the planet map. Finally the woman turned on the light in the room and smiled at me. She rolled up the map and put it with the wand into a cupboard.

"Where are you from?" I asked her, to shake off the sound of my voice saying "Now."

She hesitated, and I felt sick, because I thought I had said something rude, but finally the meaning of the question seemed to reach her. "Japanese," she said. She put the back of her hand against my hair. "Very pretty," she said. "Very pretty."

Then Dr. Wald looked at my eyes, and after that Mother and I were brought into his consulting room. We waited, facing the huge desk, and eventually the doctor walked in. There was just a tiny moment when he saw Mother, but then he sat right down and explained, in a sincere, televisionish voice I had never heard him use before, that he wanted to see me once a month. He told my mother there might or might not be "cause for concern," and he spoke right to her, with a little frown as she looked down at her clasped hands. Men always get important like that when they're talking to her, and she and the doctor both looked extra serious, as if they were re- minding themselves that it was me they were talking about, not each other. While Mother scheduled me for the last week of each month (on Thursday, because of Penelope's class) the cross-looking receptionist seemed to be fig- uring out how much Mother's clothes cost.

When Mother and I parked in front of Penelope's dancing school, Penelope was just coming out with some of the other girls. They were in jeans, but they all had their hair still pulled up tightly on top of their heads, and Penelope had the floaty, peaceful look she gets after class. Mother smiled at her and waved, but then she looked suddenly at me. "Poor Laurel," she said. Tears had come into her eyes, and answering tears sprang into my own, but mine were tears of unexpected rage. I saw how pleased Mother was, thinking that we were having that moment together, but what I was thinking, as we looked at each other, was that even though I hadn't been able to go to Jake's that afternoon because of her, at least now I would be able to go back once a month and see Chris.

"And all week," I told Maureen, "Mother has been saying I got it from my father's family, and my father says it's glaucoma in his family and his genes have nothing to do with retinas."

"Really?" Maureen asked. "Is something wrong with your dad?"

Maureen is always talking about my father and saying how "attractive" he is. If she only knew the way he talks about her! When she comes over, he sits down and tells her jokes. A few weeks ago when she came by for me, he took her outside in back to show her something and I had to wait a long time. But when she isn't at our house, he acts as if she's just some stranger. Once he said to me that she was cheap.

OF course, there was no reason for me to think that Chris would be at Jake's the next time I went to the doctor's, but he was. He and Mark were at the bar as if they'd never moved. I went to my little table, and while I drank my Coke I wondered whether Chris could have noticed that I was there. Then I realized that he might not remember me at all.

I was stalling with the ice in the bottom of my glass when Chris sat down next to me. I hadn't even seen him leave the bar. He asked me a lot of things—all about my family and where I lived, and how I came to be at Jake's.

"I go to a doctor right near here," I told him.

"Psychiatrist?" he asked.

All I said was no, but I felt my face stain red.

"I'm twenty-seven," he said. "Doesn't that seem strange to you?"

"Well, some people are," I said.

I was hoping Chris would assume I was much older than I was. People usually did, because I was tall. And it was usually a problem, because they were disappointed in me for not acting older (even if they knew exactly how old I was, like my teachers). But what Chris said was "I'm much, much older than you. Probably almost twice as old." And I understood that he wanted me to see that he knew perfectly well how old I was. He wanted me to see it, and he wanted me to think it was strange.

When I had to leave, Chris walked me to the bar to say hello to Mark, who was talking to a girl.

"Look," the girl said. She held a lock of my hair up to Mark's, and you couldn't tell whose pale curl was whose. Mark's eyes, so close, also looked just like mine, I saw.

"We could be brother and sister," Mark said, but his voice sounded like a recording of a voice, and for a moment I forgot how things are divided up, and I thought Mark must be having trouble with his eyes, too.

From then on, I always went straight to Jake's after leaving the doctor, and when I passed by the bar I could never help glancing into the mirror to see Chris's face. I would just sit at my table and drink my Coke and listen for his laugh, and when I heard it I felt completely still, the way you do when you have a fever and someone puts his hand on your forehead. And sometimes Chris would come sit with me and talk.

At home and at school, I thought about all the different girls who hung around with Chris and Mark. I thought about them one by one, as if they were little figurines I could take down from a glass case to inspect. I thought about how they looked, and I thought about the girls at school and about Penelope, and I looked in the mirror.

I looked in the mirror over at Maureen's house while Maureen put on nail polish, and I tried to make myself see my sister. We are both pale and long, but Penelope is beautiful, as everyone has always pointed out, and I, I saw, just looked unsettled.

"You could use some makeup," Maureen said, shaking her hands dry, "but you look fine. You're lucky that you're tall. It means you'll be able to wear clothes."

I love to go over to Maureen's house. Maureen is an only child, and her father lives in California. Her mother is away a lot, too, and when she is, Carolina, the maid, stays over. Carolina was there that night, and she let us order in pizza for dinner.

"Maureen is my girl. She is my girl," Carolina said after dinner, putting her arms around Maureen. Maureen almost always has some big expression on her face, but when Carolina does that she just goes blank.

Later I asked Maureen about Chris. I was afraid of talking about him, because it seemed as if he might dissolve if I did, but I needed Maureen's advice badly. I told her it was just like French class, where there were two words for "you." Sometimes when Chris said "you" to me I would turn red, as if he had used some special word. And I could hardly say "you" to him. It seemed amazing to me sometimes when I was talking to Chris that a person could just walk up to another person and say "you."

"Does that mean something about him?" I asked. "Or is it just about me?"

"It's just you," Maureen said. "It doesn't count. It's just like when you sit down on a bus next to a stranger and you know that your knee is touching his but you pretend it isn't."

OF course Maureen was almost sure to be right. Why wouldn't she be? Still, I kept thinking that it was just possible that she might be wrong, and the next time I saw Chris something happened to make me think she was.

My vision had fuzzed up a lot during that week, and when Dr. Wald looked at my eyes he didn't get up. "Any trouble lately with that sensation of haziness?" he asked.

I got scorching hot when he said that, and I felt like lying. "Not really," I said. "Yes, a bit."

He put some drops in my eyes and sent me to the waiting room, where I looked at bust exercises in *Redbook* till the drops started to work and the print melted on the page. I had never noticed before how practically no one in the waiting room was even pretending to read. One woman had bandages over her eyes, and most people were just staring and blinking. A little boy was halfheartedly moving a stiff plastic horse on the floor in front of him, but he wasn't even looking at it.

The doctor examined my eyes with the light so bright it made the back of my head sting. "Good," he said. "I'll see you in—what is it?—a month."

I was out on the street before I realized that I still couldn't see. My vision was like a piece of loosely woven cloth that was pulling apart. In the street everything seemed to be moving off, and all the lights looked like huge haloed globes, bobbing and then dipping suddenly into the pocketed air. The noises were one big pool of sound—horns and brakes and people yelling—and to cross the street I had to plunge into a mob of people and rush along wherever it was they were going.

When I finally got through to Jake's my legs were trembling badly, and I just went right up to Chris at the bar, where he was listening to his friend Sherman tell a story. Without even glancing at me, Chris put his hand around my wrist, and I just stood there next to him, with my wrist in his hand, and I listened, too.

Sherman was telling how he and his band had been playing at some club the night before and during a break, when he'd been sitting with his girl-friend, Candy, a man had come up to their table. "He's completely destroyed," Sherman said, "and Candy and I are not exactly on top of things ourselves. But the guy keeps waving this ring, and the basic idea seems to be that it's his wife's wedding ring. He's come home earlier and his wife isn't there, but the ring is, and he's sure his wife's out playing around. So the guy keeps telling me about it over and over, and I can't get him to shut up, but finally he notices Candy and he says, 'That your old lady?' 'Yeah,' I tell him. 'Good-looking broad,' the guy says, and he hands me the ring. 'Keep it,' the guy says. 'It's for you—not for this bitch with you.' "

One of the girls at the bar reached over and touched the flashing ring that was on a chain around Sherman's neck. "Pretty," she said. "Don't you want it, Candy?" But the girl she had spoken to remained perched on her barstool, with her legs crossed, smiling down at her drink.

"So what did you think of that?" Chris said as he walked me over to my table and sat down with me. I didn't say anything. "Sherman can be sort of disgusting. But it's not an important thing," Chris said.

The story had made me think about the kids at school—that we don't know yet what our lives are really going to be like. It made me feel that anything might be a thing that's important, and I started to cry, because I had never noticed that I was always lonely in my life until just then, when Chris had understood how much the story had upset me, and had said something to make me feel better.

Chris dipped a napkin into a glass of water and mopped off my face, but I was clutching a pencil in my pocket so hard I broke it, and that started me crying again.

"Hey," Chris said. "Look. It's not dead." He grabbed another napkin and scribbled on it with each half of the pencil. "It's fine, see? Look. That's just how they reproduce. Don't they teach you anything at school? Here," he said. "We'll just tuck them under this and we'll have two very happy little pencils."

And then, after a while, when I was laughing and talking, all at once he stood up. "I'm sorry to have to leave you like this," he said, "but I promised Mark I'd help him with something." And I saw that Mark and a girl were standing at the bar, looking at us. "Ready," Chris called over to them. "Honey," he said, and a waitress materialized next to him. "Get this lady something to drink and put it on my tab. Thanks," he said. And then he walked out, with Mark and the girl.

But the strange thing was that I don't think Mark had actually been waiting for Chris. I don't think Chris had promised Mark anything. I think Mark and the girl had only been looking at us to look, because I could see that they were surprised when Chris called over to them, and also the three of them stood talking on the sidewalk before they went on together. And right then was when I thought for a minute that Maureen had been wrong about me and Chris. It was not when Chris held my wrist, and not when Chris understood how upset I was, and not when Chris dried off my tears, but it was when Chris left, that I thought Maureen was wrong.

MY grades were getting a lot worse, and my father decided to help me with my homework every night after dinner. "All right," he would say, standing behind my chair and leaning over me. "Think. If you want to make an equation out of this question, how do you have to start? We've talked about how to do this, Laurel." But I hated his standing behind me like that so much all I could do was try to send out rays from my back that would make him stand farther away. Too bad I wasn't Maureen. She would have loved it.

FOR me, every day pointed forward or backward to the last Thursday of each month, but those Thursdays came and went without anything really changing, either at the doctor's or at Jake's, until finally in the spring. Everyone else in my class had spent most of a whole year getting excited or upset about classes and parties and exams and sports, but all those things were one thing to me—a nasty fog that was all around me while I waited.

And then came a Thursday when Chris put his arm around me as soon as I walked into Jake's. "I have to do an errand," he said. "Want a Coke first?"

"I'm supposed to be at my sister's class by six," I said. In case he hadn't been asking me to go with him, I would just seem to be saying something factual.

"I'll get you there," Chris said. He stood in back of me and put both arms around my shoulders, and I could feel exactly where he was touching me. Chris's friends had neutral expressions on their faces as if nothing was happening, and I tried to look as if nothing was happening, too.

As we were going out the door, a girl coming in grabbed Chris. "Are you leaving?" she said.

"Yeh," Chris told her.

"Well, when can I talk to you?" she asked.

"I'll be around later, honey," Chris said, but he just kept walking. "Christ, what a bimbo," he said to me, shaking his head, and I felt ashamed for no reason.

When Chris drove his fast little bright car it seemed like part of him, and there I was, inside it, too. I felt that we were inside a shell together, and we could see everything that was outside it, and we drove and drove and Chris turned the music loud. And suddenly Chris said, "I'd really like to see you a lot more. It's too bad you can't come into the city more often." I didn't know what to say, but I gathered that he didn't expect me to say anything.

We parked in a part of the city where the buildings were huge and squat. Chris rang a bell and we ran up flights of wooden stairs to where a man in white slacks and an unbuttoned shirt was waiting.

"Joel, this is Laurel," Chris said.

"Hello, Laurel," Joel said. He seemed to think there was something funny about my name, and he looked at me the way I've noticed grown men often do, as if I couldn't see them back perfectly well.

Inside, Chris and Joel went through a door, leaving me in an enormous room with white sofas and floating mobiles. The room was immaculate except for a silky purple-and-gold kimono lying on the floor. I picked up the kimono and rubbed it against my cheek and put it on over my clothes. Then I went and looked out the window at the city stretching on and on. In a building across the street, figures moved slowly behind dirty glass. They were making things, I suppose.

After a while Chris and Joel burst back into the room. Chris's eyes were shiny, and he was grinning like crazy.

"Hey," Joel said, grabbing the edges of the kimono I was wearing. "That thing looks better on her than on me."

"What wouldn't?" Chris said. Joel stepped back as Chris put his arms around me from behind again.

"I resent that, I resent that! But I don't deny it!" Joel said. Chris was kissing my neck and my ears, and both he and Joel were giggling.

I wondered what would happen if Chris and I were late and Mother saw me drive up in Chris's car, but we darted around in the traffic and shot along the avenues and pulled up near Penelope's dancing school with ten minutes to spare. Then, instead of saying anything, Chris just sat there with one hand still on the wheel and the other on the shift, and he didn't even look at me. When I just experimentally touched his sleeve and he still didn't move, I more or less flung myself on top of him and started crying into his shirt. I was in his lap, all tangled up, and I was kissing him and kissing him, and my hands were moving by themselves.

Suddenly I thought of all the people outside the car walking their bouncy little dogs, and I thought how my mother might pull up at any second, and I sat up fast and opened my eyes. Everything looked slightly different from the way it had been looking inside my head—a bit smaller and farther away—and I realized that Chris had been sitting absolutely still, and he was staring straight ahead.

"Goodbye," I said, but Chris still didn't move or even look at me. I couldn't understand what had happened to Chris.

"Wait," Chris said, still without looking at me. "Here's my phone number." He shook himself and wrote it out slowly.

At the corner I looked back and saw that Chris was still there, leaning back and staring out the windshield.

"WHY did he give me his phone number, do you think?" I asked Maureen. We were at a party in Peter Klingeman's basement.

"I guess he wants you to call him," Maureen said. I knew she didn't really feel like talking. Kevin was standing there, with his hand under her shirt, and she was sort of jumpy. "Frankly, Laurel, he sounds a bit weird to me, if you don't mind my saying," Maureen said. I felt ashamed again. I wanted to talk to Maureen more, but Kevin was pulling her off to the Klingemans' TV room.

Then Dougie Pfeiffer sat down next to me. "I think Maureen and Kevin have a really good relationship," he said.

I was wondering how I ever could have had a crush on him in eighth grade when I realized it was my turn to say something. "Did you ever notice," I said, "how some people say 'in eighth grade' and other people say 'in *the* eighth grade'?"

"Laurel," Dougie said, and he grabbed me, shoving his tongue into my mouth. Then he took his tongue back out and let me go. "God, I'm sorry, Laurel," he said.

I didn't really care what he did with his tongue. I thought how his body, under his clothes, was just sort of an outline, like a kid's drawing, and I thought of the long zipper on Chris's leather jacket, and a little rip I noticed once in his jeans, and the weave of the shirt that I'd cried on.

I carried Chris's phone number around with me everywhere, and finally I asked my mother if I could go into the city after school on Thursday and then meet her at Penelope's class.

"No," Mother said.

"Why not?" I said.

"We needn't discuss this, Laurel," my mother said.

"You let me go in to see Dr. Wald," I said.

"Don't," Mother said. "Anyhow, you can't just . . . wander around in New York."

"I have to do some shopping," I said idiotically.

Mother started to say something, but then she stopped, and she looked at me as if she couldn't quite remember who I was. "Oh, who cares?" she said, not especially to me.

There was a permanent little line between Mother's eyebrows, I noticed, and suddenly I felt I was seeing her through a window. I went up to my room and cried and cried, but later I couldn't get to sleep, thinking about Chris.

I called him Thursday.

"What time is it?" he said with his blistery laugh. "I just woke up." He told me he went to a party the night before and when he came out his car had been stolen. He was stoned, and he thought the sensible thing was to walk over to Mark's place, which is miles from his, but on the way he found his car parked out on the street. "I should've reported it, but I figured, hey, what a great opportunity, so I just stole it back."

Chris didn't mention anything about our seeing each other.

"I've got to come into the city today to do some stuff," I said.

"Yeh," Chris said. "I've got a lot to do today myself."

Well, that was that, obviously, unless I did something drastic. "I thought I'd stop in and say hi, if you're going to be around," I said. My heart was jumping so much it almost knocked me down.

"Great," Chris said. "That's really sweet." But his voice sounded muted, and I wasn't at all surprised when I got to Jake's and he wasn't there. I was on my third Coke when Chris walked in, but a girl wearing lots of bracelets waylaid him at the bar, and he sat down with her.

I didn't dare finish my Coke or ask for my check. All I could do was stay put and do whatever Chris made me do. Finally the girl at the bar left, giving Chris a big, meaty kiss, and he wandered over and sat down with me.

"God. Did you see that girl who was sitting with me?" he said. "That girl is so crazy. There's nothing she won't put in her mouth. I was at some party a few weeks ago, and I walk in through this door, 'cause I'm looking for the john, and there's Beverly, lying on the floor stark naked. So you know what she does?"

"No," I said.

"She says, 'Excuse me,' and instead of putting something on she reaches up and turns out the light. Now, that's thinkin', huh?" He laughed. "Have you finished all those things you had to do?" he asked me.

"Yes," I said.

"That's great," Chris said. "I'm really running around like a chicken today. Honey," he said to a waitress, "put that on my tab, will you?" He pointed at my watery Coke.

"Sandra was looking for you," the waitress said. "Did she find you?"

"Yeah, thanks," Chris said. He gave me a kiss on the cheek, which was the first time he had kissed me at all, except at Joel's, and he left.

I knew I had made some kind of mistake, but I couldn't figure out what it was. I would only be able to figure it out from Chris, but it would be two weeks until I saw him again. Every night, I looked out the window at the red glow of the city beyond all the quiet little houses and yards, and every night after I got into bed I felt it draw nearer and nearer, hovering just beyond my closed eyes, with Chris inside it. While I slept, it receded again; but by morning, when I woke up and put on my school clothes, I had come one day closer.

After my next appointment with Dr. Wald, Chris wasn't at Jake's. For the first time since I had gone to Jake's, Chris didn't come at all.

On the way home it was all I could do not to cry in front of Mother and Penelope. And I wondered what I was going to do from that afternoon on.

"And how was Dr. Wald today?" my father said when we sat down for dinner.

"I didn't ask," I said.

My father paused to acknowledge my little joke.

"What I meant," he said, "was how is my lovely daughter?"

I knew he was trying to say something nice, but he could have picked something sincere for once. I hated the way he had taken off his jacket and opened up his collar and rolled up his sleeves, and I thought I would be sick if he stood behind my chair later. "Penelope is your lovely daughter," I said, and threw my silverware onto the table.

From upstairs I listened. I knew that Penelope would have frozen, the way she does when someone says in front of me how pretty she is, but no one said anything about me that I could hear.

Later, Penelope and Paul and I made up a story together, the way we had when we were younger. Paul fell asleep suddenly in the middle with little tears in the corners of his eyes, and I tucked Penelope into bed. When I smoothed out the covers, a shadow of relief crossed her face.

THAT Saturday, Mother took me shopping in the city without Penelope or Paul. "I thought we should get you a present," Mother said. "Something pretty." She smiled at me in a strange, stiff way.

"Thank you," I said. I felt good that we were driving together, but I was sad, too, that Mother was trying to bring me into the clean, bright, fancy, daytime part of New York that Penelope's dancing school was in, because when would she accept that there was no place there for me? I wondered if Mother wanted to say something to me, but we just drove silently, except for once, when Mother pointed out a lady in a big white, flossy fur coat.

At Bonwit's, Mother picked out an expensive dress for me. "What do you think?" she said when I tried it on.

I was glad that Mother had chosen it, because it was very pretty, and it was white, and it was expensive, but in the mirror I just looked skinny and dazed. "I like it," I said. "But don't you think it looks wrong on me?"

"Well, it seems fine to me, but it's up to you," Mother said. "You can have it if you want."

"But look, Mother," I said. "Look. Do you think it's all right?"

"If you don't like it, don't get it," she said. "It's your present."

At home after dinner I tried the white dress on again and stared at myself in the mirror, and I thought maybe it looked a little better.

I went down to the living room, where Mother was stretched out on the sofa with her feet on my father's lap. When I walked in he started to get up, but Mother didn't move. "My God," my father said. "It's Lucia."

My mother giggled. "Wedding scene or mad scene?" she said.

Upstairs I folded the dress back into the box for Bonwit's to pick up. At night I watched bright dancing patterns in the dark and I dreaded going back to Dr. Wald.

THE doctor didn't seem to notice anything unusual at my next appointment. I still had to face walking the short distance to Jake's, though. I practically fell over from relief when I saw Chris at the bar, and he reached out as I went by and reeled me in, smiling. He was talking to Mark and some other friends, and he stood me with my back to him and rubbed my shoulders and temples. I tried to smile hello to Mark, who was staring at me with his pale eyes, but he just kept staring, listening to Chris. I closed my eyes and leaned back against Chris, who folded his arms around me. When Chris finished his story, everyone laughed except me. Chris blew a little stream of air into my hair, ruffling it up. "Want to take a ride?" he said.

We drove for a while, fast, circling the city, and Chris slammed tapes into the tape deck. Then we parked and Chris turned and looked at me.

"What do you want to do?" Chris asked me.

"Now?" I said, but he just looked at me, and I didn't know what he meant. "Nothing," I said.

"Have I seemed preoccupied to you lately, honey?" he asked.

"I guess maybe a little," I said, even though I hadn't really ever thought about how he seemed. He just seemed like himself. But he told me that yes, he had been preoccupied. He had borrowed some money to start an audio business, but he had to help out a cousin, too. I couldn't make any sense of what he was talking about, and I didn't really care, either. I was thinking that now he had finally called me "honey." It made me so happy, so happy, even though "honey" was what he called everyone, and I had been the only Laurel.

Chris kept talking, and I watched his mouth as the words came out. "I know you wonder what's going on with me," he said. "What it is is I worry that you're so young. I'm a difficult person. There are a lot of strange things about me. I'm really crazy about you, you know. I'm really crazy about you, but I can't ask you to see me."

"Why don't I come in and stay over with you a week from Friday," I said. "Can I?"

Chris blinked. "Terrific, honey," he said cautiously. "That's a date."

I arranged it with Maureen that I would say I was staying at her house. "Don't wear underwear," Maureen told me. "That really turns guys on."

Chris and I met at Jake's, but we didn't stay there long. We drove all over the city, stopping at different places. Chris knew people everywhere, and we would sit down at the bar and talk to them. We went to an apartment with some of the people we ran into, where everyone lay around listening to tapes. And once we went to a club and watched crowds of people change like waves with the music, under flashing lights.

Chris didn't touch me, not once, not even accidentally, all during that time.

Sometime between things, we stopped for food. I couldn't eat, but Chris seemed starving. He ate his cheeseburger and French fries, and then he ate mine. And then he had a big piece of pecan pie.

Late, very late, we climbed into the car again, but there was nothing left to do. "Home?" Chris said without turning to me.

Chris's apartment seemed so strange, and maybe that was just because it was real. But I had surely never been inside such a small, plain place to live before, and Chris hardly seemed to own anything. There were a few books on a shelf, and a little kitchen off in the corner, with a pot on the stove. It was up several flights of dark stairs, in a brick building, and it must have been on the edge of the city, because I could see water out of the window, and ribbons of highway elevated on huge concrete pillars, and dark piers.

Chris's bed, which was tightly made with the sheet turned back over the blanket, looked very narrow. All the music we had been hearing all night was rocketing around in my brain, and I felt jittery and a bit sick. Chris passed a joint to me, and he lay down with his hands over his eyes. I sat down on the edge of the bed next to him and waited, but he didn't move. "Remember when I asked you a while ago what you wanted to do and you said 'Nothing'?" Chris asked me.

"But that was—" I started to say, and then the funny sound of Chris's voice caught up with me, and all the noise in my head shut off.

"I remember," Chris said. Then a long time went by.

"Why did you come here, Laurel?" Chris said.

When I didn't answer, he said, "Why? Why did you come here? You're old enough now to think about what you're doing." And I remembered I had never been alone with him before, except in his car.

"Yes," I said into the dead air. Whatever I'd been waiting for all that time had vanished. "It's all right."

"It's all right?" Chris said furiously. "Well, good. It's all right, then." He was still lying on his back with his hands over his eyes, and neither of us moved. I thought I might shatter.

Sometime in the night Chris spoke again. "Why are you angry?" he said. His voice was blurred, as if he'd been asleep. I wanted to tell him I wasn't angry, but it seemed wrong, and I was afraid of what would happen if I did. I put my arms around him and started kissing him. He didn't move a muscle, but I kept right on. I knew it was my only chance, and I thought that if I stopped I would have to leave. "Don't be angry," he said.

Sometime in the night I sprang awake. Chris was holding my wrists behind my back with one hand and unbuttoning my shirt with the other, and his body felt very tense. "Don't!" I said, before I understood.

" 'Don't!' " echoed Chris, letting go of me. He said it just the way I had, sounding just as frightened. He fell asleep immediately then, sprawled out, but I couldn't sleep anymore, and later, when Chris spoke suddenly into the dark, I felt I'd been expecting him to. "Your parents are going to worry," he said deliberately, as if he were reading.

"No," I said. I wondered how long he had been awake. "They think I'm at Maureen's." And then I realized how foolish it was for me to have said that.

"They'll worry," he said. "They will worry. They'll be very frightened."

And then I was so frightened myself that the room bulged and there was a sound in my ears like ball bearings rolling around wildly. I put my hands against my hot face, and my skin felt to me as if it belonged to a stranger. It felt like a marvel—brand-new and slightly moist—and I wondered if anyone else would ever touch it and feel what I had felt.

"Look—" Chris said. He sounded blurry again, and helpless and sad. "Look—see how bad I am for you, Laurel? See how I make you cry?" Then he put his arms around me, and we lay there on top of the bed for a long, long time, and sometimes we kissed each other. My shirtsleeve was twisted and it hurt against my arm, but I didn't move.

When the night red began finally to bleach out of the sky, I touched

Chris's wrist. "I have to go now," I said. That wasn't true, of course. My parents would expect me to stay at Maureen's till at least noon. "I have to be home when it gets light."

"Do you?" Chris said, but his eyes were closed.

I stood up and buttoned my shirt.

"I'll take you to the train," Chris said.

At first he didn't move, but finally he stood up, too. "I need some coffee," he said. And when he looked at me my heart sank. He was smiling. He looked as if he wanted to start it up—start it all again.

I went into the bathroom, so I wouldn't be looking at Chris. There was a tub and a sink and a toilet. Chris uses them, I thought, as if that would explain something to me, but the thought was like a sealed package. Stuck in the corner of the mirror over the sink was a picture of a man's face torn from a magazine. It was a handsome face, but I didn't like it.

"That's a guy I went to high school with," Chris said from behind me. "He's a very successful actor now."

"That's nice," I said, and waited as long as I could. "Look—it's almost light."

And in the instant that Chris glanced at the window, where in fact the faintest dawn was showing, I stepped over to the door and opened it.

In the car, Chris seemed the way he usually did. "I'm sorry I'm so tired, honey," he said. "I've been having a rough time lately. We'll get together another time, when I'm not so hassled."

"Yes," I said. "Good." I don't think he really remembered the things we had said in the dark.

When we stopped at the station, Chris put his arm across me, but instead of opening the door he just held the handle. "You think I'm really weird, don't you?" he said, and smiled at me.

"I think you're tired," I said, making myself smile back. And Chris released the handle and let me out.

I took the train through the dawn and walked from the station, pausing carefully if it looked as though someone was awake inside a house I was passing. Once a dog barked, and I stood absolutely still for minutes.

I threw chunks from the lawn at Maureen's window, so Carolina wouldn't wake up, but I was afraid the whole town would be out by the time Maureen heard.

Maureen came down the back way and got me. We each put on one of her bathrobes, and we made a pot of coffee, which is something I'm not allowed to drink.

"What happened?" Maureen asked.

"I don't know," I said.

"What do you mean, you don't know?" Maureen said. "You were there."
Even though my face was in my hands, I could tell Maureen was staring
at me. "Well," she said after a while. "Hey. Want to play some Clue?" She
got the Clue board down from her room, and we played about ten games.

THE next week I really did stay over at Maureen's.

"Again?" my mother said. "We must do something for Mrs. MacIntyre.
She's been so nice to you."

Dougie and Kevin showed up together after Maureen and Carolina and I
had eaten a barbecued chicken from the deli and Carolina had gone to her
room to watch the little TV that Mrs. MacIntyre had put there. I figured it
was no accident that Dougie had shown up with Kevin. It had to be a brain-
storm of Maureen's, and I thought, Well, so what. So after Maureen and
Kevin went up to Maureen's room I went into the den with Dougie. We
pretty much knew from classes and books and stuff what to do, so we did it.
The thing that surprised me most was that you always read in books about
"stained sheets," "stained sheets," and I never knew what that meant, but
I guess I thought it would be pretty interesting, and that it would be some
kind of sign that things had changed—that everything would be a new
color. But I still don't know what it means, because everything seemed exactly the same, except that I wished Dougie would completely disappear.

We went back into the living room to wait, and I sat while Dougie walked
around poking at things on the shelves. "Look," Dougie said, "Clue." But I
just shrugged, and after a while Maureen and Kevin came downstairs looking pretty pleased with themselves.

I sat while Dr. Wald finished at the machine, and I waited for him to say
something, but he didn't.

"Am I going to go blind?" I asked him finally, after all those months.

"What?" he said. Then he remembered to look at me and smile. "Oh, no,
no. We won't let it come to that."

I knew what I would find at Jake's, but I had to go anyway, just to finish.
"Have you seen Chris?" I asked one of the waitresses. "Or Mark?"

"They haven't been around for a while," she said. "Sheila," she called
over to another waitress, "where's Chris these days?"

"Don't ask me," Sheila said sourly, and both of them stared at me.

I could feel my blood travelling in its slow loop, carrying a heavy proudness through every part of my body. I had known Chris could injure me, and I had never cared how much he could injure me, and it had never occurred to me until this moment that I could do anything to him.

OUTSIDE, it was hot. There were big bins of things for sale on the sidewalk, and horns were honking, and the sun was yellow and syrupy. I noticed two people who must have been mother and daughter, even though you couldn't really tell how old either of them was. One of them was sort of crippled, and the other was very peculiar-looking, and they were all dressed up in stiff, cheap party dresses. They looked so pathetic with their sweaty, eager faces and ugly dresses that I felt like crying. But then I thought that they might be happy, much happier than I was, and that I just felt sorry for them because I thought I was better than they were. And I realized that I wasn't really different from them anyhow—that every person just had one body or another, and some of them looked right and worked right and some of them didn't—and I thought maybe it was myself I was feeling sorry for, because of Chris, or maybe because it was obvious even to me, a total stranger, how much that mother loved her homely daughter in that awful dress.

When Mother and Penelope and I got back home, I walked over to Maureen's house, but I decided not to stop. I walked by the playground and looked in at the fourth-grade room and the turtle that was still lumbering around its dingy aquarium, and it came into my mind how even Paul was older now than the kids who would be sitting in those tiny chairs in the fall, and I thought about all the millions and billions of people in the world, all getting older, all trapped in things that had already happened to them.

When I was a kid, I used to wonder (I bet everyone did) whether there was somebody somewhere on the earth, or even in the universe, or ever had been in all of time, who had had exactly the same experience that I was having at that moment, and I hoped so badly that there was. But I realized then that that could never occur, because every moment is all the things that have happened before and all the things that are going to happen, and every moment is just the way all those things look at one point on their way along a line. And I thought how maybe once there was, say, a princess who lost her mother's ring in a forest, and how in some other galaxy a strange creature might fall, screaming, on the shore of a red lake, and how right that second there could be a man standing at a window overlooking a busy street, aiming a loaded revolver, but how it was just me, there, after Chris, staring at that turtle in the fourth-grade room and wondering if it would die before I stopped being able to see it.

(1985)

DRAWING ROOM B

NOBODY big had taken Leda Pentleigh to the train, and the young man from the publicity department who had taken her was not authorized to hire the Rolls or Packard that used to be provided for her New York visits. Nor had they taken their brief ride from the Waldorf to Grand Central. This time, she was riding West on the Broadway and not the Century, and she had come to the station in an ordinary taxicab, from a good but unspectacular hotel north of Sixtieth Street. Mr. Egan, it is true, was dead, but his successor at Penn Station, if any, did not personally escort Leda to the train. She just went along with the pleasant young hundred-and-fifty-a-week man from the publicity department, her eyes cast down in the manner which, after eighteen years, was second nature to her in railroad stations and hotel lobbies, at tennis matches and football games. Nobody stopped her for her autograph, or to swipe the corsage that the publicity young man's boss had sent instead of attending her himself. Pounding her Delman heels on the Penn Station floor, she recalled a remark which she was almost sure she had originated, something about the autograph hounds not bothering her: it was when they didn't bother you that they bothered you. Of course, it was Will Rogers or John Boles or Bill Powell or somebody who first uttered the thought, but Leda preferred her way of putting it. The thought, after all, had been thought by thousands of people, but she noticed it was the way *she* expressed it that was popular among the recent Johnny-come-latelies when they were interviewed by the fan magazines. Well, whoever had said it first could have it; she wouldn't quarrel over it. At the moment of marching across Penn Station, there seemed to be mighty few travellers who would take sides for or against her in a controversy over the origin of one of her routine wisecracks. Far from saying, "There goes Leda Pentleigh, who first said . . ." the travellers were not even saying, "There goes Leda Pentleigh—period." The few times she permitted her gaze to rise to the height of her fellowmen were unsatisfactory: one of the older porters raised his hat and smiled and bowed; two or three nice-appearing men recognized her—but they probably were Philadelphians in their thirties or forties, who would go home and tell their wives that they had seen Leda Pentleigh in Penn Station, and their wives would say, "Oh, yes. I remember her," or "Oh, yes. She was in Katie Hepburn's picture. She played the society bitch, and I'll bet she's qualified." Katie Hepburn, indeed! It wasn't as if Katie Hepburn hadn't been in pictures fifteen years. But no use getting sore at Katie Hepburn because Katie was a few years younger and still a star. At this thought, Leda permitted herself a glance at a Philadelphia-type man, a man who had that look of being just about to get into or out of riding togs, as Leda called them. He frowned a little, then raised his hat, and because he was so obviously baffled, she gave him almost the complete Pentleigh smile. Even then he was baffled, had not the faintest idea who she was. A real huntin'-shootin' dope, and she knew what he was thinking—that here was a woman either from Philadelphia or going to Philadelphia and therefore someone he must know. The gate was opened, and Leda and Publicity went down to her car. Publicity saw that she was, as he said, all squared away, and she thanked him and he left, assuring her that "somebody" from the Chicago office would meet her at Chicago, in case she needed anything. Her car was one of the through cars, which meant she did not have to change trains at Chicago, but just in case she needed anything. (Like what, she said to herself. Like getting up at seven-thirty in the morning to be ready to pose for photographs in the station? Oh, yes? And let every son of a bitch in the Pump Room know that Leda Pentleigh no longer rated the star treatment?)

IN her drawing room, Leda decided to leave the door open. There might, after all, be a Coast friend on the train. If she wanted to play gin with him—or her—she could do it, or if she wanted to give her—or him—the brush, she knew how to do that, too. Her window was on the wrong side of the car to watch people on the platform, and she sat in a corner where she could get a good look at the passengers going by her door. She opened a high-class book and watched the public (no longer so completely hers) going by. They

all had that beaten look of people trying to find their space, bent over—
surely not from the weight of their jewelry boxes and briefcases—and then
peering up at the initial on her drawing room, although they could plainly
see that the room was occupied by a striking, stunning, chic, glamorous,
sophisticated woman, who had spent most of the past week in New York
City, wishing she were dead.

She drove that little thought out of her mind. It would do no good to
dwell on that visit, ending now as the train began to pull out—her first visit
to New York in four years, and the unhappiest in all her life. What the hell
was the use of thinking back to the young punk from one of the dailies who
had got her confused with Renée Adorée? What difference the wrong tables
in restaurants and the inconveniently timed appointments at hairdressers'
and the night of sitting alone in her hotel room while a forty-dollar pair of
theatre tickets went to waste? The benefit in Union City, New Jersey? The
standup by Ken Englander, the aging architect, who had been glad enough
in other days to get once around the floor with her at the Mayfair dances?
The being made to wait on the telephone by the New York office of her
agent, her own agent? The ruined Sophie dress and the lost earring at that
South American's apartment? Why think of those things? Why not think of
the pleasanter details of her visit?

Think, for instance, of the nice things that had been said about her on
that morning radio program. Her appearance had been for free, but the
publicity was said to be valuable, covering the entire metropolitan area and
sometimes heard in Pennsylvania. Then there was the swell chat with Ike
Bord, publicity man for a company she had once been under contract to.
"Whenner you coming back to us, Leda? . . . Anything I can do for you
while you're in town, only too glad, you know. I didn't even know you were
here. Those bums where you are now, they never get anything in the papers." And it was comforting to know she could still charge things at
Hattie's, where she had not bought anything in four years. And the amusing taxidriver: "Lady, I made you right away. I siss, 'Lydia Penley. Gay me an
autograft fa Harry.' Harry's my kid was killed in the U.S. Marines.
Guadalcanal. Sure, I remembered you." And, of course, her brother, who
had come down all the way from Bridgeport with his wife, bringing Leda a
pair of nylons and a bona-fide cash offer, in case she had a clean car she
wasn't using. The telephone service at her hotel had been something extra
special because one of the operators formerly had been president of Leda's
Brooklyn fan club. Through it all was the knowledge that her train fare and
hotel bill were paid for by the company because she obligingly posed for
fashion stills for the young-matron departments of the women's magazines, so the whole trip was not costing her more than eight or nine hun-

dred dollars, including the visit to Hattie's. There were some nice things to remember, and she remembered them.

THE train rolled through Chester County, and it was new country to Leda. It reminded her of the English countryside and of American primitives.

She got up and closed her door once, before washing her hands, but reopened it when she was comfortable. Traffic in the passageway had become light. The train conductor and the Pullman conductor came to collect her tickets and asked for her last name. "Leda Pentleigh," she said. This signified nothing to the representative of the Pennsylvania Railroad, but the Pullman conductor said, "Oh, yes, Miss Pentleigh. Hope you have an enjoyable trip," and Leda thanked him and said she was sure she would, lying in her beautiful teeth. She was thinking about sending the porter for a menu when the huntin'-shootin' type stood himself in her doorway and knocked.

"Yes?" she said.

"Could a member of Actors' Equity speak to you for a moment, Miss Pentleigh?" he said. He didn't so much say the line as read it. She knew that much—that rehearsal was behind the words and the way he spoke them.

"To be sure," she said. "Sit down, won't you?"

"Let me introduce myself. My name is Kenyon Littlejohn, which of course doesn't mean anything to you, unless you've *seen* me?"

"I confess I did see you in the station, Mr. Littlejohn. In fact, I almost spoke to you. I thought I recognized you."

He smiled, showing teeth that were a challenge to her own. He took a long gold case out of his inside coat pocket and she took a cigarette. "That can mean two things," he said. "Either you've seen me—I've been around a rather long time, never any terribly good parts. I've usually got the sort of part where I come on and say, 'Hullo, thuh, what's for tea? Oh, crom-pits! How jolly!' " She laughed and he laughed. "Or else you know my almost-double. Man called Crosby? Very Back Bay-Louisburg Square chap from Boston. Whenever I've played Boston, people are always coming up to me and saying, 'Hello, Francis.' "

"Oh, I've met Francis Crosby. He used to come to Santa Barbara and Midwick for the polo."

"That's the chap," said Kenyon Littlejohn, in his gray flannel Brooks suit, Brooks shirt, Peal shoes, Players Club tie, and signet ring. "No wonder you thought you knew me, although I'm a bit disappointed it was Crosby you knew and not me."

"Perhaps I did know you, though. Let me see—"

"No. Please don't. On second thought, the things I've been in—well, the things I've been in have been all right, mostly, but as I said before, the parts I've had weren't anything I particularly care to remember. Please let me start our acquaintance from scratch."

"All right," she said.

He took a long drag on his cigarette before going on. "I hope you don't think I'm pushy or anything of that sort, Miss Pentleigh, but the fact is I came to ask your advice."

"You mean about acting?" She spoke coldly, so that this insipid hambo wouldn't think he was pulling any age stuff on her.

"Well, hardly that," he said. He spoke as coldly as he dared. "I've very seldom been without work and I've lived quite nicely. My simple needs and wants. No, you see, I've just signed my first picture contract—or, rather, it's almost signed. I'm going out to California to make tests for the older-brother part in 'Strange Virgin.' "

"Oh, yes. David's doing that, isn't he?"

"Uh—yes. They're paying my expenses and a flat sum to make the test, and, if they like me, a contract. I was wondering, do you think I ought to have an agent out there? I've never had one, you know. Gilbert and Vinton and Brock and the other managers, they usually engage me themselves, a season ahead of time, and I've never *needed* an agent, but everybody tells me I ought to have one out there. Do you agree that that's true?"

"Well, of course, to some extent that depends on how good you are at reading contracts."

"I had a year at law school, Miss Pentleigh. That part doesn't bother me. It's the haggling over money that goes on out there, and I understand none of the important people deal directly with the producers."

"Oh, you're planning on staying?"

"Well . . ."

"New York actors come out just for one picture, or, at least, that's what they say. Of course, they have to protect themselves in case they're floperoos in Hollywood. Then they can always say they never planned to stay out there, and come back to New York and pan pictures till the next offer comes along, if it ever does."

"Yes, that's true," said Mr. Littlejohn.

" 'That place,' they say. 'They put caps on your teeth and some fat Czechoslovakian that can't speak English tries to tell you how to act in a horse opera,' forgetting that the fat Czechoslovakian knows more about acting in his little finger than half the hambos in New York. Nothing *personal*, of course, Mr. Little."

"Thank you," said Mr. Littlejohn.

"But I've got a bellyful of two-hundred-dollar-a-week Warfields coming out and trying to high-hat us, trying to steal scenes and finding themselves on the cutting-room floor because they don't know the first thing about picture technique, and it serves them right when they find themselves out on their duffs and on the way back to their Algonquins and their truck-garden patches in Jackson Heights, or wherever they live. God damn it to hell, making pictures is work!"

"I realize—"

"Don't give me any of that I-realize. Wait'll you've got up at five and sweated out a scene all day and gone to the desert on location and had to chase rattlesnakes before you could go to bed. Find out what it's like and then go back and tell the boys at the Lambs Club. Do that for twenty or fifteen years." She stopped, partly for breath and partly because she didn't know what was making her go on like this.

"But we're not all like that, Miss Pentleigh," said Littlejohn when she did not go on.

His speaking reminded her that she had been talking to an unoffending human being and not merely voicing her hatred of New York. But his being there to hear it all (and to repeat it later, first chance he got) made her angry at him in particular. "I happen to think you are, eef you don't mind," she said. "I don't care if you're Lunt and Fontanne or Helen Hayes or Joe Blow from Kokomo—if you don't click in Hollywood, it's because you're not good enough. And, oh, boy, don't those managers come out begging for us people that can't act to do a part in their new show. When they want a name, they want a movie name. Why, in less than a week, I had chances to do a half a dozen plays, including a piece of the shows. What good can New York do me, I ask you?"

"The satisfaction of a live audience," he said, answering what was not a question. "Playing before a—"

"A live audience! On a big set you play to as many people as some of the turkeys on Broadway. Live audience! Go to a première at Grauman's Chinese or the Carthay Circle and you have people, thousands, waiting there since two o'clock in the afternoon just to get a look at you and hear you say a few words into the microphone. In New York, they think if they have three hundred people and two cops on horses, they have a crowd. On the Coast, we have better than that at a preview. A *sneak* preview! But of course you wouldn't know what that is."

"Really, Miss Pentleigh, I'm very glad to be going to Hollywood, but I didn't have to go if I didn't want to."

"That wasn't your attitude. You sat down here as if you were patronizing me, *me*! And started in talking about agents and producers as if Hollywood people were pinheads from Mars. Take a good gander at some of the swishes and chisellers on Broadway."

"Oh, I know a lot about them."

"Well, then, what are you asking me for advice for?"

"I'm terribly sorry," he said, and got up and left.

"Yes, and I think you're a bit of a swish yourself," said Leda to the closed door. She got a bottle of bourbon out of her bag and poured herself a few drinks into doubled paper cups and rang for the porter.

PRESENTLY, a waiter brought a menu, and by that time Leda was feeling fine, with New York a couple of hundred miles and a week and a lifetime behind her. Dinner was served, and she ate everything put before her. She had a few more shots and agreed with her conscience that perhaps she had been a little rough on the actor, but she had to take it out on somebody. He wasn't really too bad, and she forgave him and decided to go out of her way to be nice to him the next time she saw him. She thereupon rang for the porter.

"Yes, Ma'am?" said the porter.

"There's a Mr. Applegate—no, that's not his name. Littlefield. That's it. Littlefield. Mr. Littlefield is on the train. He's going to California. Do you think you could find 'im and ask 'im that I'd tell 'im I'd like to speak to 'im, please?"

"The gentleman just in here before you had your dinner, Ma'am?"

"Yes, that's the one."

"Mr. Littlejohn. He's in this same car, PA29. I'll give him your message, Ma'am."

"Do that," she said, handing the porter a ten-dollar bill.

She straightened her hair, which needed just a little straightening, and assumed her position—languor with dignity—on the Pullman seat, gazed with something between approval and enchantment at the dark Pennsylvania countryside, and looked forward to home, California, and the friends she loved. She could be a help to Mr. Littlejohn (*that* name would have to be changed). She *would* be a help to Mr. Littlejohn. "That I will, that I will," she said.

(1947)

PETER TAYLOR

A SENTIMENTAL JOURNEY

FIFTEEN years ago, in 1939, Jim Prewitt and I drove to New York City to spend our Thanksgiving holiday. Jim and I were then in our senior year at Kenyon College. There at Kenyon, which is located in the little village of Gambier, Ohio, he and I had for two years shared a room on the second floor of old Douglass House. I say "old" because at Kenyon in those days there was still a tendency to prefix that adjective to the name of everything of any worth on the campus or in the village. Oldness had for so many years been the most respected attribute of the college that it was natural for its prestige to linger on a few years after what we considered the new dispensation and the intellectual awakening. Old Douglass House *was* an oldish house, but it had only been given over for use as a dormitory the year that Jim and I—and most of our friends—came to Kenyon. The nine of us moved into it just a few weeks after its former occupants—a retired professor and his wife, I believe—had moved out. And we lived there during our three years at Kenyon (all of us having transferred from other colleges as sophomores)—lived there without ever caring to inquire into the age or history of the house. We were not the kind of students who cared about such things. We were hardly aware, even, of just how quaint the appearance of the house was, with its steep white gables laced with gingerbread-work, and its Gothic windows and their arched window blinds. Our unawareness—Jim's and mine—was probably never more profound than on the late afternoon in November, in our third year at

Kenyon, when we set out from Douglass House for New York City. Our plan was to spend two days in Manhattan and then go on to Boston for a day with Jim's family.

During the previous summer, Jim Prewitt had become engaged to a glorious, talented girl with long flaxen hair, whom he had met at a student writers' conference somewhere out West. And I, more attached to things at home in St. Louis than Jim was to things in Boston—*I* had been "accepted" by an equally glorious dark-eyed girl in whose veins ran the Creole blood of old-time St. Louis. By a happy coincidence both of these glorious girls were now in New York. Carol Crawford, with her flaxen hair fixed in a bun on the back of her neck and a four-hundred-page manuscript in her suitcase, had headed East from the fateful writers' conference in search of a publisher for her novel. Nancy Gibault had left St. Louis in September to study painting at the National Academy. The two girls were as yet unacquainted, and it was partly to the correcting of this that Jim and I meant to dedicate our Thanksgiving holiday.

It was four o'clock in the afternoon when we left the village of Gambier. We had had to wait till the afternoon mail was put up because each of us was expecting a check from home. Mine came. Jim's did not. But mine was enough to get us there, and Jim's would be enough to get us back. "Enough to get back, *if* we come back!" That became our motto for the trip. We had both expressed the thought in precisely the same words and at precisely the same moment as we came out of the post office. And during the short time it took us to dash back across the village street, with its wide green in the center, and climb the steps up to Douglass House and then dash down again with our suitcases to the car, we found half a dozen excuses for repeating our motto.

The day was freakishly warm, and all of our housemates were gathered on the front stoop when we made our departure. In their presence, we took new pleasure in proclaiming our motto and repeating it over and over as we threw our things into the car. The other boys didn't respond, however, as we hoped they would. They leaned against the iron railing of the stoop, or sat on the stone steps leaning against one another, and refused to admit any interest in our "childish" insinuation: *if* we came back. All seven of them were there and all seven were in agreement on the "utter stupidity" of our long Thanksgiving trip as well as that of our present behavior. But they didn't know about the two glorious girls. Or at least I don't think they did.

Altogether, the boys who lived in Douglass House were a sad, shabby, shaggy-looking lot. Yet they were not studiedly so, I think. You have probably seen students who look the way we did—especially if you have ever vis-

ited Bard College or Black Mountain or Rollins. Such students seem to affect a kind of hungry, unkempt look. And yet they don't really know what
kind of impression they want to make; they only know that there are certain kinds they *don't* want to make.

Generally speaking, we at Douglass House were reviled by the rest of the
student body, all of whom lived in the vine-covered dormitories facing the
campus, and by a certain proportion of the faculty. I am sure we were
thought of as a group as closely knit as any other in the college. We were
even considered a sort of fraternity. But we didn't see ourselves that way.
We would have none of that. Under that high gabled roof, we were all independents and meant to remain so. Housing us "transfers" together this way
had been the inspiration of the Dean or the President under the necessity of
solving a problem of overflow in the dormitories. Yet we did not object to his
solution, and of our own accord we ate together in the Commons, we hiked
together about the countryside, we went together to see girls in nearby
Mount Vernon, we enrolled in the same classes, flocked more or less after
the same professors, and met every Thursday night at the Creative Writing
class, which we all acknowledged as our reason for being at Kenyon. But
think of ourselves as a club, or as dependent upon each other for compan-
ionship or for anything else, we would not. There were times when each of
us talked of leaving Kenyon and going back to the college or university
from which he had come—back to Ann Arbor or Olivet, back to Chapel Hill,
to Vanderbilt, to Southwestern, or back to Harvard or Yale. It was a moder-
ately polite way each of us had of telling the others that *they* were a bunch
of Kenyon boys but that *he* knew something of a less cloistered existence
and was not to be confused with their kind. We were so jealous of every aspect of our independence and individuality that one time, I remember,
Bruce Gordon nearly fought with Bill Anderson because Bill, for some
strange reason, had managed to tune in, with his radio, on a Hindemith
sonata that Bruce was playing on the electric phonograph in his own room.

Most of us had separate rooms. Only Jim Prewitt and I shared a room,
and ours was three or four times as big as most dormitory cubicles. It
opened off the hall on the second floor, but it was on a somewhat lower
level than the hall. And so when you entered the door, you found yourself
at the head of a little flight of steps, with the top of your head almost
against the ceiling. This made the room seem even larger than it was, as did
the scarcity and peculiar arrangement of the furniture. Our beds, with our
desks beside them, were placed in diagonally opposite corners, and we each
had a wobbly five-foot bookshelf set up at the foot of his bed, like a hospital
screen. The only thing we shared was a little three-legged oak table in the
very center of the room, on which were a hot plate and an electric cof-

feepot, and from which two long black extension cords reached up to the light fixture overhead.

THE car that Jim and I were driving to New York did not belong to either of us. It didn't at that time belong to anybody, really, and I don't know what ever became of it. At the end of our holiday, we left it parked on Marlborough Street in Boston, with the ignition key lost somewhere in the gutter. I suppose Jim's parents finally disposed of the car in some way or other. It had come into our hands the spring before, when its last owner had abandoned it behind the college library and left the keys on Jim's desk up in our room. He, the last owner, had been one of us in Douglass House for a while—though it was, indeed, for a very short while. He was a poor boy who had been at Harvard the year that Jim was there, before Jim transferred to Kenyon, and he was enormously ambitious and possessed enough creative energy to produce in a month the quantity of writing that most of us were hoping to produce in a lifetime. He was a very handsome fellow, with a shock of yellow hair and the physique of a good track man. On him the cheapest department-store clothes looked as though they were tailor-made, and he could never have looked like the rest of us, no matter how hard he might have tried. I am not sure that he ever actually matriculated at Kenyon, but he was there in Douglass House for about two months, clicking away on first one typewriter and then another (since he had none of his own); I shall never forget the bulk of manuscript that he turned out during his stay, most of which he left behind in the house or in the trunk of the car. The sight of it depressed me then, and it depresses me now to think of it. His neatly typed manuscripts were in every room in the house—novels, poetic dramas, drawing-room comedies, lyrics, epic poems, short stories, scenarios. He wasn't at all like the rest of us. And except for his car he has no place in this account of our trip to New York. Yet since I have digressed this far, there is something more that I somehow feel I ought to say about him.

Kenyon was to him only a convenient place to rest awhile (for writing was not work to him) on his long but certain journey from Harvard College to Hollywood. He used to say to us that he wished he could do the way we were doing and really dig in at Kenyon for a year or so and get his degree. The place appealed to him, he said, with its luxuriant countryside, and its old stone buildings sending up turrets and steeples and spires above the treetops. If he stayed, he would join a fraternity, so he said, and walk the Middle Path with the other fraternity boys on Tuesday nights, singing fraternity songs and songs of old Kenyon. He said he envied us—and yet he hadn't himself time to stay at Kenyon. He was there for two months, and while he was there he was universally admired by the boys in Douglass House. But when he had gone, we all hated him. Perhaps we were jealous. For in no time at all stories and poems of his began appearing in the quarterlies as well as in the popular magazines. Pretty soon one of his plays had a good run on Broadway, and I believe he had a novel out even before that. He didn't actually get to Hollywood till after the war, but get there at last he did, and now, I am told, he has a house in the San Fernando Valley and has the two requisite swimming pools, too.

To us at Kenyon he left his car. It was a car given to him by an elderly benefactor in Cambridge, but a car that had been finally and quite suddenly rendered worthless in his eyes by a publisher's advance, which sent him flying out of our world by the first plane he could get passage on. He left us the car without any regret, left it in the same spirit that American tourists left their cars on the docks at European ports when war broke out that same year. In effect, he tossed us his keys from the first-class deck of the giant ship he had boarded at the end of his plane trip, glad to know that he would never need the old rattletrap again and glad to be out of the mess that all of us were in for life.

I have said that I somehow felt obliged to include everything I have about our car's last real owner. And now I know why I felt so. Without that digression it would have been impossible to explain what the other boys were thinking—or what we thought they were thinking—when we left them hanging about the front stoop that afternoon. They were thinking that there was a chance Jim and I had had an "offer" of some kind, that we had "sold out" and were headed in the same direction that our repudiated brother had taken last spring. Perhaps they did not actually think that, but that was how we interpreted the sullen and brooding expressions on their faces when we were preparing to leave that afternoon.

Of course, what their brooding expressions meant made no difference to Jim or to me. And we said so to each other as, with Jim at the wheel, we backed out of the little alleyway beside the House and turned in to the village street. We cared not a hoot in hell for what they thought of us or of our trip to New York. Further, we cared no more—Jim and I—for each other's approval or disapproval, and we reminded each other of this then and there.

We were all independents in Douglass House. There was no spirit of camaraderie among us. We were not the kind of students who cared about such things as camaraderie. Besides, we felt that there was more than enough of that spirit abroad at Kenyon, among the students who lived in the regular dormitories and whose fraternity lodges were scattered about the wooded hillside beyond the village. In those days, the student body at Kenyon was almost as picturesque as the old vine-clad buildings and the rolling countryside itself. So it seemed to us, at least. We used to sit on the front stoop or in the upstairs windows of Douglass House and watch the fops and dandies of the campus go strolling and strutting by on their way to the post office or the bank, or to Jean Val Dean's short-order joint. Those three establishments, along with two small grocery stores, the barbershop, the filling station, and the bakery, constituted the business district of Gambier. And it was in their midst that Douglass House was situated. Actually, those places of business were strung along just one block of the village's main thoroughfare. Each was housed in its separate little store building or in a converted dwelling house, and in the spring and in the fall, while the leaves were still on the low-hanging branches of the trees, a stranger in town would hardly notice that they were places of business at all.

From the windows of Douglass House, between the bakery and the barbershop, we could look down on the dormitory students who passed along the sidewalk, and could make our comment on what we considered their silly affectations—on their provincial manners and their foppish, collegiate clothing. In midwinter, when all the leaves were off the trees, we could see out into the parkway that divided the street into two lanes—and in the center of the parkway was the Middle Path. For us, the Middle Path was the epitome of everything about Kenyon that we wanted no part of. It was a broad gravel walkway extending not merely the length of the village green; it had its beginning, rather, at the far end of the campus, at the worn doorstep of the dormitory known as Old Kenyon, and ran the length of the campus, on through the village, then through the wooded area where most of the faculty houses were, and ended at the door of Bexley Hall, Kenyon's Episcopal seminary. In the late afternoon, boys on horseback rode along it as they returned from the Polo Field. At noon, sometimes, boys who had just come up from Kenyon's private airfield appeared on the Middle Path still wearing their helmets and goggles. And after dinner every Tuesday night the fraternity boys marched up and down the Path singing their fraternity songs and singing fine old songs about early days at Kenyon and about its founder, Bishop Philander Chase:

> The first of Kenyon's goodly race
> Was that great man Philander Chase.
> He climbed the hill and said a prayer
> And founded Kenyon College there.
>
> He dug up stones, he chopped down trees,
> He sailed across the stormy seas,
> And begged at ev'ry noble's door,
> And also that of Hannah Moore.

He built the college, built the dam,
He milked the cow, he smoked the ham;
He taught the classes, rang the bell,
And spanked the naughty freshmen well.

At Douglass House we wanted none of that. We had all come to Kenyon because we were bent upon becoming writers of some kind or other and the new President of the college had just appointed a famous and distinguished poet to the staff of the English Department. Kenyon was, in our opinion, an obscure little college that had for more than a hundred years slept the sweet, sound sleep that only a small Episcopal college can ever afford to sleep. It was a quaint and pretty spot. We recognized that, but we held that against it. That was not what we were looking for. We even collected stories about other people who had resisted the beauties of the campus and the surrounding countryside. A famous English critic had stopped here on his way home from a long stay in the Orient, and when asked if he did not admire our landscape he replied, "No. It's too rich for my blood." We all felt it was too rich for ours, too. Another English visitor was asked if the college buildings did not remind him of Oxford, and by way of reply he permitted his mouth to fall open while he stared in blank amazement at his questioner.

Despite our feeling that the countryside was too rich for our blood, we came to know it a great deal better—or at least in more detail—than did the polo players or the fliers or the members of the champion tennis team. For we were nearly all of us walkers. We walked the country roads for miles in every direction, talking every step of the way about ourselves or about our writing, or if we exhausted those two dearer subjects, we talked about whatever we were reading at the time. We read W. H. Auden and Yvor Winters and Wyndham Lewis and Joyce and Christopher Dawson. We read "The Wings of the Dove" (aloud!) and "The Cosmological Eye" and "The Last Puritan" and "In Dreams Begin Responsibilities." (Of course, I am speaking only of books that didn't come within the range of the formal courses we were taking in the college.) On our walks through the country—never more than two or three of us together—we talked and talked, but I think none of us ever listened to anyone's talk but his own. Our talk seemed always to come to nothing. But our walking took us past the sheep farms and orchards and past some of the old stone farmhouses that are scattered throughout that township. It brought us to the old quarry from which most of the stone for the college buildings and for the farmhouses had been taken, and brought us to Quarry Chapel, a long since deserted and "deconsecrated" chapel, standing on a hill two miles from the college and symbolizing there the failure of Episcopalianism to take root among the Ohio countrypeople. Sometimes we walked along the railroad track through the valley at the foot of the college hill, and I remember more than once coming upon two or three tramps warming themselves by a little fire they had built or even cooking a meal over it. We would see them maybe a hundred yards ahead, and we would get close enough to hear them laughing and talking together. But as soon as they noticed us we would turn back and walk in the other direction, for we pitied them and felt that our presence was an intrusion. And yet, looking back on it, I remember how happy those tramps always seemed. And how sad and serious we were.

JIM and I headed due east from Gambier on the road to Coshocton and Pittsburgh. Darkness overtook us long before we ever reached the Pennsylvania state line. We were in Pittsburgh by about 9 P.M., and then there lay ahead of us the whole long night of driving. Nothing could have better suited our mood than the prospect of this ride through the dark, wooded countryside of Pennsylvania on that autumn night. This being before the days of the turnpike—or at least before its completion—the roads wound about the great, domelike hills of that region and through the deep valleys in a way that answered some need we both felt. We spoke of it many times during the night, and Jim said he felt he knew for the first time the meaning of "verdurous glooms and winding mossy ways." The two of us were setting out on this trip not in search of the kind of quick success in the world that had so degraded our former friend in our eyes; we sought, rather, a taste—or foretaste—of "life's deeper and more real experience," the kind that dormitory life seemed to deprive us of. We expressed these yearnings in just those words that I have put in quotation marks, not feeling the need for any show of delicate restraint. We, at twenty, had no abhorrence of raw ideas or explicit statement. We didn't hesitate to say what we wanted to be and what we felt we must have in order to become that. We wanted to be writers, and we knew well enough that before we could write we had to have "mature and adult experience." And, by God, we *said* so to each other, there in the car as we sped through towns like Turtle Creek and Greensburg and Acme.

I have observed in recent years that boys the age we were then and with our inclinations tend to value ideas of this sort above all else. They are apt to find their own crude obsession with mere ideas the greatest barrier to producing the works of art they are after. I have observed this from the vantage ground of the college professor's desk, behind which the irony of fate has placed me from time to time. From there, I have also had the chance to observe something about *girls* of an artistic bent or temperament, and for that reason I am able to tell you more about the two girls we were going to see in New York than I could possibly have known then.

At the time—that is, during the dark hours of the drive East—each of us carried in his mind an image of the girl who had inspired him to make this journey. In each case, the image of the girl's face and form was more or less accurate. In my mind was the image of a brunette with dark eyes and a heart-shaped face. In Jim's was that of a blonde, somewhat above average height, with green eyes and perhaps a few freckles on her nose. That, in general, was how we pictured them, but neither of us would have been dogmatic about the accuracy of his picture. Perhaps Carol Crawford didn't have any freckles. Jim wasn't sure. And maybe her eyes were more blue than green. As for me, I wouldn't have contradicted anyone who said Nancy Gibault's face was actually slightly elongated, rather than heart-shaped, or that her hair had a decided reddish cast to it. Our impressions of this kind were only more or less accurate, and we would have been the first to admit it.

But as to the talent and the character and the original mind of the two glorious girls, we would have brooked no questioning of our concepts. Just after we passed through Acme, Pennsylvania, our talk turned from ourselves to these girls—from our inner yearnings for mature and adult experience to the particular objects toward which we were being led by these yearnings. We agreed that the quality we most valued in Nancy and Carol was their "critical" and "objective" view of life, their unwillingness to accept the standards of "the world." I remember telling Jim that Nancy Gibault could always take a genuinely "disinterested" view of any matter— "disinterested in the best sense of the word." And Jim assured me that, whatever else I might perceive about Carol, I would sense at once the originality of her mind and "the absence of anything commonplace or banal in her intellectual makeup."

It seems hard to believe now, but that was how we spoke to each other about our girls. That was what we thought we believed and felt about them then. And despite our change of opinions by the time we headed back to Kenyon, despite our complete and permanent disenchantment, despite their unkind treatment of us—as worldly and as commonplace as could be—I know now that those two girls were as near the concepts we had of them to begin with as any two girls their age might be, or should be. And I believe now that the decisions *they* made about *us* were the right decisions for *them* to make. I have only the vaguest notion of how Nancy Gibault has fared in later life. I know only that she went back to St. Louis the following spring and was married that summer to Lon Havemeyer. But as for Carol Crawford, everybody with any interest in literary matters knows what became of her. Her novels are read everywhere. They have even been translated into Javanese. She is, in her way, even more successful than the boy who made the long pull from Harvard College to Hollywood.

Probably I seem to be saying too much about things that I understood only long after the events of my story. But the need for the above digression seemed no less urgent to me than did that concerning the former owner of our car. In his case, the digression dealt mostly with events of a slightly earlier time. Here it has dealt with a wisdom acquired at a much later time. And now I find that I am still not quite finished with speaking of that later time and wisdom. Before seeing me again in the car that November night in 1939, picture me for just a moment—much changed in appearance and looking at you through gold-rimmed spectacles—behind the lectern in a classroom. I stand before the class as a kind of journeyman writer, a type of whom Trollope might have approved, but one who has known neither the financial success of the facile Harvard boy nor the reputation of Carol Crawford. Yet this man behind the lectern is a man who seems happy in the knowledge that he knows—or thinks he knows—what he is about. And from behind his lectern he is saying that any story that is written in the form of a memoir should give offense to no one, because before a writer can make a person he has known fit into such a story—or any story, for that matter—he must do more than change the real name of that person. He must inevitably do such violence to that person's character that the so-called original is forever lost to the story.

THE last lap of Jim's and my all-night drive was the toughest. The night had begun as an unseasonably warm one. I recall that there were even a good many insects splattered on our windshield in the hours just after dark. But by the time we had got through Pittsburgh the sky was overcast and the temperature had begun to drop. Soon after 1 A.M. we noticed the first big, soft flakes of snow. I was driving at the time, and Jim was doing most of the talking. I raised one finger from the steering wheel to point out the snow to Jim, and he shook his head unhappily. But he went on talking. We had maintained our steady stream of talk during the first hours of the night partly to keep whoever was at the wheel from going to sleep, but from this point on it was more for the purpose of making us forget the threatening weather. We knew that a really heavy snowstorm could throw our holiday schedule completely out of gear. All night long we talked. Sometimes the snow fell thick and fast, but there were times, too, when it stopped altogether. There was a short period just before dawn when the snow turned to rain—a cold rain, worse than the snow, since it began to freeze on our windshield. By this time, however, we had passed through Philadelphia and we knew that somehow or other we would make it on to New York.

We had left Kenyon at four o'clock in the afternoon, and at eight the next morning we came to the first traffic rotary outside New York, in New Jersey. Half an hour later we saw the skyline of the city, and at the sight of it we both fell silent. I think we were both conscious at that moment not so much of having arrived at our destination as of having only then put Kenyon College behind us. I remember feeling that if I glanced over my shoulder I might still see on the horizon the tower of Peirce Hall and the spires of Old Kenyon Dormitory. And in my mind's eye I saw the other Douglass House boys—all seven of them—still lingering on the stone steps of the front stoop, leaning against the iron railing and against one another, staring after us. But more than that, after the image had gone I realized suddenly that I had pictured not seven but *nine* figures there before the house, and that among the other faces I had glimpsed my own face and that of Jim Prewitt. It seemed to me that we had been staring after ourselves with the same fixed, brooding expression in our eyes that I saw in the eyes of the other boys.

NANCY Gibault was staying in a sort of girls' hotel, or rooming house, on 114th Street. Before she came down from her room that Thanksgiving morning, she kept me waiting in the lobby for nearly forty-five minutes. No doubt she had planned this as a way of preparing me for worse things to come. As I sat there, I had ample time to reflect upon various dire possibilities. I wondered if she had been out terribly late the night before and, if so, with whom. I thought of the possibility that she was angry with me for not letting her know what day I would get there. (I had had to wait on my check from home, and there had not been time to let her know exactly when we would arrive.) I reflected, even, that there was a remote chance she had not wanted me to come at all. What didn't occur to me was the possibility that *all* of these things were true. I sat in that dreary, overheated waiting room, still wearing my overcoat and holding my hat in my lap. When Nancy finally came down, she burst into laughter at the sight of me. I rose slowly from my chair and said angrily, "What are you laughing at? At how long I've waited?"

"No, my dear," she said, crossing the room to where I stood. "I was laughing at the way you were sitting there in your overcoat with your hat in your lap like a little boy."

"I'm sweating like a horse," I said, and began unbuttoning my coat. By this time Nancy was standing directly in front of me, and I leaned forward to kiss her. She drew back with an expression of revulsion on her face.

"Keep your coat on!" she commanded. Then she began giggling and backing away from me. "If you expect me to be seen with you," she said, "you'll go back to wherever you're staying and shave that fuzz off your lip." For three weeks I had been growing a mustache.

I had not yet been to the hotel where Jim and I planned to stay. It was a place that Jim knew about, only three or four blocks from where Nancy was living, and I now set out for it on foot, carrying my suitcase. Our car had broken down just after we came up out of the Holland Tunnel. It had been knocking fiercely for the last hour of the trip, and we learned from the garageman with whom we left it that the crankcase was broken. It seems we had burned out a bearing, because we had forgotten to put any oil in the crankcase. I don't think we realized at the time how lucky we were to find a garage open on Thanksgiving morning and, more than that, one that would have the car ready to run again by the following night.

After I had shaved, I went back to Nancy's place. She had gone upstairs again, but this time she did not keep me waiting so long. She came down wearing a small black hat and carrying a chesterfield coat. Back in St. Louis, she had seldom worn a hat when we went out together, and the sight of her in one now made me feel uncomfortable. We sat down together near the front bay window of that depressing room where I had waited so long, and we talked there for an hour, until it was time to meet Jim and Carol for lunch.

While we talked that morning, Nancy did not tell me that Lon Havemeyer was in town from St. Louis, much less that she had spent all her waking hours with him during the past week. I could not have expected her to tell me at once that she was now engaged to marry him, instead of me, but I did feel afterward that she could have begun at once by telling me that she had been seeing Lon and that he was still in town. It would have kept me from feeling quite so much at sea during the first hours I was with her. Lon was at least seven or eight years older than Nancy, and for five or six years he had been escorting débutantes to parties in St. Louis. His family were of German origin and were as new to society there as members of Nancy's family were old to it. The Havemeyers were also as rich nowadays as the Gibaults were poor. Just after Nancy graduated from Mary Institute, Lon had begun paying her attentions. They went about together a good deal while I was away at college, but between Nancy and me it had always been a great joke. To us, Lon was the essence of all that we were determined to get away from there at home. I don't know what he was really like. I had heard an older cousin of mine say that Lon Havemeyer managed to give the impression of not being dry behind the ears but that the truth was he was "as slick as a newborn babe." But I never exchanged two sentences with him in my life—not even during the miserable day and a half that I was to tag along with him and Nancy in New York.

It may be that Nancy had not known that she was in love with Lon or that she was going to marry him until she saw me there, with the fuzz on my upper lip, that morning. Certainly I must have been an awful sight. Even after I had shaved my mustache, I was still the seedy-looking undergraduate in search of "mature experience." It must have been a frightful embarrassment to her to have to go traipsing about the city with me on Thanksgiving Day. My hair was long, my clothes, though quite genteel, were unpressed, and even rather dirty, and for some reason I was wearing a pair of heavy brogans. Nancy had never seen me out of St. Louis before, and since she had seen me last, she had seen Manhattan. To be fair to her, though, she had seen something more important than that. She had, for better or for worse, seen herself.

We had lunch with Jim and Carol at a little joint over near Columbia, and it was only after we had left them that Nancy told me Lon Havemeyer was in town and waiting that very moment to go with us to the Metropolitan Museum. I burst out laughing when she told me, and she laughed a little, too. I don't remember when I fully realized the significance of Lon's presence in New York. It wasn't that afternoon, or that night, even. It was some time during the next day, which was Friday. I suppose that I should have realized it earlier and that I just wouldn't. From the time we met Lon on the museum steps, he was with us almost continuously until the last half hour before I took my leave of Nancy the following night. Sometimes I would laugh to myself at the thought of this big German oaf's trailing along with us through the galleries in the afternoon and then to the ballet that night. But I was also angry at Nancy from the start for having let him horn in on our holiday together, and at various moments I pulled her aside and expressed my anger. She would only look at me helplessly, shrug, and say, "I couldn't help it. You really have got to try to see that I couldn't help it."

AFTER the ballet, we joined a group of people who seemed to be business acquaintances of Lon's and went to a Russian night club—on Fourteenth Street, I think. (I don't know exactly where it was, for I was lost in New York and kept asking Nancy what part of town we were in.) The next morning, about ten, Nancy and I took the subway down to the neighborhood of Fifty-seventh Street, where we met Lon for breakfast. Later we looked at pictures in some of the galleries. I don't know what became of the afternoon. We saw an awful play that night. I know it was awful, but I don't remember what it was. The events of that second day are almost entirely blotted from my memory. I only know that the mixture of anger and humiliation I felt kept me from ducking out long before the evening was over—a mixture of anger and humiliation and something else, something that I had begun to feel the day before when Nancy and I were having lunch with Jim and Carol Crawford.

Friday night, I was somehow or other permitted to take Nancy home alone from the theatre. We went in a taxi, and neither of us spoke until a few blocks before we reached 114th Street. Finally I said, "Nancy." And Nancy burst into tears.

"You won't understand, and you will never forgive me," she said through her tears, "but I am so terribly in love with him."

I didn't say anything till we had gone another block. Then I said, "How have things gone at the art school?"

Nancy blew her nose and turned her face to me, as she had not done when she spoke before. "Well, I've learned that I'm not an artist. They've made me see that."

"Oh," I said. Then, "Does that make it necessary to—"

"It makes everything in the world look different. If I could only have known in time to write you."

"When did you know?"

"I don't know. I don't know when I knew."

"Well, it's a good thing you came to New York," I said. "You almost made a bad mistake."

"No," she said. "You mustn't think I feel that about you."

"Oh, not about me," I said quickly. "About being an artist. When we were at lunch yesterday, you know, with Jim and his girl, it came over me suddenly that you weren't an artist. Just by looking at you I could tell."

"What a cruel thing to say," she said quietly. All the emotion had gone out of her voice. "Only a child could be so cruel," she said.

When the taxi stopped in front of her place, I opened the door for her but didn't get out, and neither of us said goodbye. I told the driver to wait until she was inside and then gave him the address of my hotel. When, five minutes later, I was getting out and paying the driver, I didn't know how much to tip him. I gave him fifteen cents. He sat with his motor running for a moment, and then, just before he pulled away, he threw the dime and the nickel out on the sidewalk and called out to me at the top of his voice, "You brat!"

THE meeting between Nancy and Carol was supposed to be one of the high points of our trip. The four of us ate lunch together that first day sitting in the front booth of a little place that was crowded with Columbia University students. Because this was at noon on Thanksgiving Day, probably not too many restaurants in that neighborhood were open. But I felt that every student in the dark little lunchroom was exulting in his freedom from a certain turkey dinner somewhere, and from some particular family gathering. We four had to sit in the very front booth, which was actually no booth at all but a table and two benches set right in the window. Some people happened to be getting up from that table just as we came in, and Carol, who had brought us here, said, "Quick! We must take this one." Nancy had raised up on her tiptoes and craned her neck, looking for a booth not quite so exposed.

"I think there may be some people leaving back there," she said.

"No," said Carol in a whisper. "Quick! In here." And when we had sat down, she said, "There are some dreadful people I know back there. I'd rather die than have to talk to them."

Nancy and I sat with our backs almost against the plate-glass window. There was scarcely room for the two of us on the bench we shared. I am sure the same was true for Jim and Carol, and they faced us across a table so narrow that when our sandwiches were brought, the four plates could only be arranged in one straight row. There wasn't much conversation while we ate, though Jim and I tried to make a few jokes about our drive through the snow and about how the car broke down. Once, in the middle of something Jim was saying, Carol suddenly ducked her head almost under the table. "Oh, God!" she gasped. "Just my luck!" Jim sat up straighter and started peering out into the street. Nancy and I looked over our shoulders. There was a man walking along the sidewalk on the other side of the broad street.

"You mean that man way over there?" Nancy asked.

"Holy God, yes," hissed Carol. "Do please stop looking around at him."

Nancy giggled. "Is he dreadful, too?" she asked.

Carol straightened and took a sip of her coffee. "No, he's not exactly dreadful. He's the critic Melville Bland." And after a moment: "He's a full professor at Columbia. I was supposed to have dinner today with him and his stupid wife—she's the playwright Dorothy Lewis and simply *stupid*—at some chichi place in the East Sixties, and I told them an awful lie about my going out to Connecticut for the day. I'd rather be shot than talk to either of them for five minutes."

I was sitting directly across the table from Carol. While we were there, I had ample opportunity to observe her, without her seeming to notice that I was doing so. My opportunity came each time anyone entered the restaurant or left it. For nobody could approach the glass front door, either from the street or from inside, without Carol's fastening her eyes upon that person and seeming to take in every detail of his or her appearance. Here, I said to myself, is a real novelist observing people—*objectively* and *critically*. And I was favorably impressed by her obvious concern with literary personages; it showed how committed she was to a life of writing. Carol seemed to me just the girl that Jim had described. Her blond hair was not really flaxen. (It was golden, which is prettier but which doesn't sound as interesting as flaxen.) It was long and carelessly arranged. I believe Jim was right about its being fixed in a knot on the back of her neck. Her whole appearance showed that she cared as little about it as either Jim or I did about ours. . . . Perhaps *this* was what one's girl really ought to look like.

When we got up to leave, Nancy lingered at the table to put on fresh lipstick. Carol wandered to the newspaper stand beside the front door. Jim and I went together to pay our bills at the counter. As we waited for our change, I said an amiable, pointless "Well?"

"Well what?" Jim said petulantly.

"Well, they've met," I said.

"Yeah," he said. "They've met." He grinned and gave his head a little shake. "But Nancy's just another society girl, old man," he said. "I had expected something more than that." He suddenly looked very unhappy, and rather angry, too. I felt the blood rising in my cheeks and knew in a moment that I had turned quite red. Jim was much heavier than I was, and I would have been no match for him in any real fight, but my impulse was to hit him squarely in the face with my open hand. He must have guessed what I had in mind, for with one movement he jerked off his horn-rimmed glasses and jammed them into the pocket of his jacket.

At that moment, the man behind the counter said, "Do you want this change or not, fellows?"

We took our change and then glared at one another again. I had now had time to wonder what had come over Jim. Out of the corner of my eye I caught a glimpse of Carol at the newsstand and took in for the first time, in that quick glance, that she was wearing huaraches and a peasant skirt and blouse, and that what she now had thrown around her shoulders was not a topcoat but a long green cape. "At least," I said aloud to Jim, "Nancy's not the usual bohemian. She's not the run-of-the-mill arty type."

I fully expected Jim to take a swing at me after that. But, instead, a peculiar expression came over his face and he stood for a moment staring at Carol over there by the newsstand. I recognized the expression as the same one I had seen on his face sometimes in the classroom when his interpretation of a line of poetry had been questioned. He was reconsidering.

When Nancy joined us, Jim spoke to her very politely. But once we were out in the street there was no more conversation between the two couples. We parted at the first street corner, and in parting there was no mention of our joining forces again. That was the last time I ever saw Carol Crawford, and I am sure that Jim and Nancy never met again. At the corner, Nancy and I turned in the direction of her place on 114th Street. We walked for nearly a block without either of us speaking. Then I said, "Since when did you take to wearing a hat everywhere?"

Nancy didn't answer. When we got to her place, she went upstairs for a few minutes, and it was when she came down again that she told me Lon Havemeyer was going to join us at the Metropolitan. Looking back on it, I feel that it may have been only when I asked that question about her hat that Nancy decided definitely about how much Lon and I were going to be seeing of each other during the next thirty-six hours. It is possible, at least, that she called him on the telephone while she was upstairs.

I didn't know about it then, of course, but the reception that Jim Prewitt found awaiting him that morning had, in a sense, been worse even than mine. I didn't know about it and Jim didn't tell me until the following spring, just a few weeks before our graduation from Kenyon. By that time, it all seemed to us like something in the remote past, and Jim made no effort to give me a complete picture of his two days with Carol. The thing he said most about was his reception upon arriving.

He must have arrived at Carol's apartment, somewhere on Morningside Heights, at almost the same moment that I arrived at Nancy's place. He was not, however, kept waiting for forty-five minutes. He was met at the door by a man whom he described as a flabby middle-aged man wearing a patch over one eye, a T-shirt, and denim trousers. The man did not introduce himself or ask for Jim's name. He only jerked his head to one side, to indicate that Jim should come in. Even before the door opened, Jim had heard strains of the Brandenburg Concerto from within. Now, as he stepped into the little entryway, the music seemed almost deafening, and when he was led into the room where the phonograph was playing, he could not resist the impulse to make a wry face and clap his hands over his ears.

But although there were half a dozen people in the room, nobody saw the gesture or the face he made. The man with the patch over his eye had preceded him into the room, and everyone else was sitting with eyes cast down or actually closed. Carol sat on the floor tailor-fashion, with an elbow on each knee and her face in her hands. The man with the patch went to her and touched the sole of one of her huaraches with his foot. When she looked up and saw Jim, she gave him no immediate sign of recognition. First she eyed him from head to foot with an air of disapproval. Jim's attire that day, unlike my own, was extremely conventional (though I won't say he ever really looked conventional for a moment). At Kenyon, he was usually the most slovenly and ragged-looking of us all. He really went about in tatters, sometimes even with the soles hanging loose from his shoes. But in his closet, off our room, there were always to be found his "good" shoes, his "good" suit, his "good" coat, his "good" hat, all of which had been purchased for him at Brooks Brothers by his mother. Today he had on his "good" things. Probably it was that that made Carol stare at him as she did. At last she gave him a friendly but slightly casual smile, placed a silencing forefinger over her lips, and motioned for him to come sit down beside her and listen to the deafening tones of the concerto.

While the automatic phonograph was changing records, Carol introduced Jim to the other people in the room. She introduced him and everyone else—men and women alike—by their surnames only: "Prewitt, this is Carlson. Meyer, this is Prewitt." Everyone nodded, and the music began again at the same volume. After the Bach there was a Mozart symphony. Finally Jim, without warning, seized Carol by the wrist, forcibly led her from the room, and closed the door after them. He was prepared to tell her precisely what he thought of his reception, but he had no chance to. "Listen to me," Carol began at once—belligerently, threateningly, all but shaking her finger in his face. "I have sold my novel. It was definitely accepted three days ago and is going to be published in the spring. And two sections from it are going to be printed as stories in the *Partisan Review.*"

From that moment, Jim and Carol were no more alone than Nancy and I were. Nearly everywhere they went, they went with the group that had been in Carol's apartment that morning. After lunch with us that first noon, they rejoined the same party at someone else's apartment, down in Greenwich Village. When Jim told me about it, he said he could never be sure whose apartment he was in, for they always behaved just as they did at Carol's. He said that once or twice he even found himself answering a knock at the door in some strange apartment and jerking his head at whoever stood outside. The man with the patch over his eye turned out to be a musicologist and composer. Two others in the party were writers whose work Jim had read in New Directions anthologies and in various little magazines, but they seemed to have no interest in anything he had to say about what they had written, and he noticed that their favorite way of disparaging any piece of writing was to say it was "*so* naïve, *so* undergraduate." After Jim got our car from the garage late Friday afternoon, they all decided to drive to New Jersey to see some "established writer" over there, but when they arrived at his house the "established writer" would not receive them.

Jim said there were actually a few times when he managed to get Carol away from her friends. But her book—the book that had been accepted by a publisher—was Carol's Lon Havemeyer, and her book was always with them.

Poor Carol Crawford! How unfair it is to describe her as she was that Thanksgiving weekend in 1939. Ever since she was a little girl on a dairy farm in Wisconsin she had dreamed of becoming a writer and going to live in New York City. She had not merely dreamed of it. She had worked toward it every waking hour of her life, taking jobs after school in the wintertime, and full-time jobs in the summer, always saving the money to put herself through the state university. She had made herself the best student—the prize pupil—in every grade of grammar school and high school. At the university she had managed to win every scholarship in sight. Through all those years she had had but one ambition, and yet I could not have met her at a worse moment in her life. Poor girl, she had just learned that she *was* a writer.

DRIVING to Boston on Saturday, Jim and I took turns at the wheel again. But now there was no talk about ourselves or about much of anything else. One of us drove while the other slept. Before we reached Boston, in midafternoon, it was snowing again. By night, there was a terrible blizzard in Boston.

As soon as we arrived, Jim's father announced that he would not hear of our trying to drive back to Kenyon in such weather and in such a car. Mrs. Prewitt got on the telephone and obtained a train schedule that would start us on our way early the next morning and put us in Cleveland sometime the next night. (From Cleveland we would take a bus to Gambier.) After dinner at the Prewitts' house, I went with Jim over to Cambridge to see some of his prep-school friends who were still at Harvard. The dinner with his parents had been painful enough, since he and I were hardly speaking to each other, but the evening with him and his friends was even worse for me. In the room of one of these friends, they spent the time drinking beer and talking about undergraduate politics at Harvard and about the Shelley Poetry Prize. One of the friends was editor of the *Crimson*, I believe, and another was editor of the *Advocate*—or perhaps he was just on the staff. I sat in the corner pretending to read old copies of the *Advocate*. It was the first time I had been to Boston or to Cambridge, and ordinarily I would have been interested in forming my own impressions of how people like the Prewitts lived and of what Harvard students were like. But, as things were, I only sat cursing the fate that had made it necessary for me to come on to Boston instead of returning directly to Kenyon. That is, my own money having been exhausted, I was dependent upon the money Jim would get from his parents to pay for the return trip.

Shortly before seven o'clock Sunday morning, I followed Jim down two flights of stairs from his room on the third floor of his family's house. A taxi was waiting for us in the street outside. We were just barely going to make the train. In the hall I shook hands with each of his parents, and he kissed them goodbye. We dashed out the front door and down the steps to the street. Just as we were about to climb into the taxi, Mrs. Prewitt came rushing out, bareheaded and without a wrap, calling to us that we had forgotten to leave the key to the car, which was parked there in front of the house. I dug down into my pocket and pulled out the key along with a pocketful of change. But as I turned back toward Mrs. Prewitt I stumbled on the curb, and the key and the change went flying in every direction and were lost from sight in the deep snow that lay on the ground that morning. Jim and Mrs. Prewitt and I began to search for the key, but Mr. Prewitt called from the doorway that we should go ahead, that we would miss our train. We hopped in the taxi, and it pulled away. When I looked back through the rear window I saw Mrs. Prewitt still searching in the snow and Mr. Prewitt moving slowly down the steps from the house, shaking his head.

ON the train that morning Jim and I didn't exchange a word or a glance. We sat in the same coach but in different seats, and we did not go into the diner together for lunch. It wasn't until almost dinnertime that the coach became so crowded that I had either to share my seat with a stranger or to go and sit beside Jim. The day had been long, I had done all the thinking I wanted to do about the way things had turned out in New York. Further, toward the middle of the afternoon I had begun writing in my notebook, and I now had several pages of uncommonly fine prose fiction, which I did not feel averse to reading aloud to someone.

I sat down beside Jim and noticed at once that *his* notebook was open, too. On the white, unlined page that lay open in his lap I saw the twenty or thirty lines of verse he had been working on. It was in pencil, quite smudged from many erasures, and was set down in Jim's own vigorous brand of progressive-school printing.

"What do you have there?" I said indifferently.

"You want to hear it?" he said with equal indifference.

"I guess so," I said. I glanced over at the poem's title, which was "For the Schoolboys of Douglass House," and immediately wished I had not got myself into this. The one thing I didn't want to hear was a preachment from him on his "mature experience" over the holiday. He began reading, and what he read was very nearly this (I have copied this part of the poem down as it later appeared in *Hika*, our undergraduate magazine at Kenyon):

> Today while we are admissibly ungrown,
> Now when we are each half boy, half man,
> Let us each contrast himself with himself,
> And weighing the halves well, let us each regard
> In what manner he has not become a man.

> Today let us expose, and count as good,
> What is mature. And childish peccadillos
> Let us laugh out of our didactic house—
> The rident punishment one with reward
> For him bringing lack of manliness to light.

But I could take no more than the first two stanzas. And I knew how to stop him. I touched my hand to his sleeve and whispered, "Shades of W. B. Yeats." And I commenced reciting,

> "Now that we're almost settled in our house
> I'll name the friends that cannot sup with us
> Beside a fire of turf in th'ancient tower . . ."

Before I knew it, Jim had snatched my notebook from my hands, and began reading aloud from it:

"She had told him—Janet Monet had, for some inscrutable reason which she herself could not fathom, and which, had he known—as she so positively and with such likely assurance thought he knew—that if he came on to New York in the weeks ensuing her so unbenign father's funeral, she could not entertain him alone."

Then he closed my notebook and returned it to me. "I can put it into rhyme for you, Mr. Henry James," he said. "It goes like this:

> She knew that he knew that her father was dead,
> And she knew that he knew what a life he had led—"

While he was reciting, with a broad grin on his face and his eyes closed, I left him and went up into the diner to eat dinner. The next time we met was in the smoking compartment, at eight o'clock, an hour before we got into Cleveland.

IT was I who wandered into the smoking compartment first. I went there not to smoke, for neither Jim nor I started smoking till after we left college, but in the hope that it might be empty, which, oddly enough, it was at that moment. I sat down by the window, at the end of the long leather seat. But I had scarcely settled myself there and begun staring out into the dark when the green curtain in the doorway was drawn back. I saw the light it let in reflected in the windowpane, and I turned around. Jim was standing in the doorway with the green curtain draped back over his head and shoulders. I don't know why, but it was only then that I realized that Jim, too, had been jilted. Perhaps it was the expression on his face—an expression of disappointment at not finding the smoking compartment empty, at being deprived of his one last chance for solitude before returning to Douglass House. And now—more than I had all day—I hated the sight of him. My lips parted to speak, but he literally took the sarcastic words out of my mouth.

"Ah, you'll get over it, little friend," he said.

Suddenly I was off the leather seat and lunging toward him. And he had snatched off his glasses, with the same swift gesture he had used in the restaurant, and tossed them onto the seat. The train was moving at great speed and must have taken a sharp turn just then. I felt myself thrown forward with more force than I could possibly have mustered in the three or four steps I took. When I hit him, it was not with my fists, or even my open hands, but with my shoulder, as though I were blocking in a game of football. He staggered back through the doorway and into the narrow passage, and for a moment the green curtain separated us. Then he came back. He came at me just as I had come at him, with his arms half folded over his chest. The blow he struck me with his shoulders sent me into the corner of the leather seat again. But I, too, came back.

Apparently neither of us felt any impulse to strike the other with his fist or to take hold and wrestle. On the contrary, I think we felt a mutual abhorrence and revulsion toward any kind of physical contact between us, and if our fight had taken any other form than the one it did, I think that murder would almost certainly have been committed in the smoking compartment that night. We shoved each other about the little room for nearly half an hour, with ever increasing violence, our purpose always seeming to be to get the other through the narrow doorway and into the passage—out of sight behind the green curtain.

From time to time, after our first exchange of shoves, various would-be smokers appeared in the doorway. But they invariably beat a quick retreat. At last one of them found the conductor and sent him in to stop us. By then it was all over, however. The conductor stood in the doorway a moment before he spoke, and we stared at him from opposite corners of the room. He was an old man with an inquiring and rather friendly expression on his face. He looked like a man who might have fought gamecocks in his day, and I think he must have waited that moment in the doorway in the hope of seeing something of the spectacle that had been described to him. But by then each of us was drenched in sweat, and I know from a later examination of my arms and chest and back that I was covered with bruises.

When the old conductor was satisfied that there was not going to be another rush from either of us, he glanced about the room to see if we had done any damage. We had not even upset the spittoon. Even Jim's glasses were safe on the leather seat. "If you boys want to stay on this train," the conductor said finally, "you'll hightail it back to your places before I pull that emergency cord."

We were only thirty minutes out of Cleveland then, but when I got back to my seat in the coach I fell asleep at once. It was a blissful kind of sleep, despite the fact that I woke up every five minutes or so and peered out into the night to see if I could see the lights of Cleveland yet. Each time, as I dropped off to sleep again, I would say to myself what a fine sort of sleep it was, and each time it seemed that the wheels of the train were saying *Not yet, not yet, not yet.*

After Cleveland there was a four-hour ride by bus to Gambier. Sitting side by side in the bus, Jim and I kept up a continuous flow of uninhibited and even confidential talk about ourselves, about our writing, and even about the possibility of going to graduate school next year if the Army didn't take us. I don't think we were silent a moment until we were off the bus and, as we paced along the Middle Path, came in sight of Douglass House. It was 1 A.M., but through the bare branches of the trees we saw a light burning in the front dormer of our room. Immediately our talk was hushed, and we stopped dead still. Then, though we were as yet two hundred feet from the house and there was a blanket of snow on the ground, we began running on tiptoe and whispering our conjectures about what was going on in our room. We took the steps of the front stoop two at a time, and when we opened the front door, we were met by the odor of something cooking—bacon, or perhaps ham. We went up the long flight to the second floor on tiptoe, being careful not to bump our suitcases against the wall or the banisters. The door to our room was the first one at the top of the stairs. Jim seized the knob and threw the door open. The seven whom we had left lolling around the stoop on Wednesday were sprawled about our big room in various stages of undress, and all of them were eating. Bruce Gordon and Bill Anderson were in the center of the room, leaning over my hot plate.

Jim and I pushed through the doorway and stood on the doorstep looking down at them. I have never before or since seen seven such sober—no, such frightened-looking—people. Most eyes were directed at me, because it was my hot plate. But when Jim stepped down into the room, the two boys lounging back on his bed quickly stood up.

I remember my first feeling of outrage. The sacred privacy of that room under the eaves of Douglass House had been violated; this on top of what had happened in New York seemed for a moment more than flesh and blood could bear. Then, all of a sudden, Jim Prewitt and I began to laugh. Jim dropped his suitcase and went over to where the cooking was going on and said, "Give me something to eat. I haven't eaten all day."

I stood for a while leaning against the wall just inside the door. I was thinking of the tramps we had seen cooking down along the railroad track in the valley. Finally I said, "What a bunch of hoboes!" Everyone laughed—a little nervously, perhaps, but with a certain heartiness, too.

I continued to stand just inside the door, and presently I leaned my head against the wall and shut my eyes. My head swam for a moment. I had the sensation of being on the train again, swaying from side to side. It was hard to believe that I was really back in Douglass House and that the trip was over. I don't know how long I stood there that way. I was dead for sleep, and as I stood there with my eyes closed I could still hear the train wheels saying *Not yet, not yet, not yet.*

(1955)

DONALD BARTHELME

THE BALLOON

THE balloon, beginning at a point on Fourteenth Street, the exact location of which I cannot reveal, expanded northward all one night,
while people were sleeping, until it reached the Park. There I stopped it. At
dawn the northernmost edges lay over the Plaza; the free-hanging motion
was frivolous and gentle. But experiencing a faint irritation at stopping,
even to protect the trees, and seeing no reason the balloon should not be
allowed to expand upward, over the parts of the city it was already covering into the "air space" to be found there, I asked the engineers to see to it.
This expansion took place throughout the morning, a soft imperceptible
sighing of gas through the valves. The balloon then covered forty-five
blocks north-south and an irregular area east-west, as many as six crosstown blocks on either side of the Avenue in some places. That was the situation, then.

But it is wrong to speak of "situations," implying sets of circumstances
leading to some resolution, some escape of tension; there were no situations, simply the balloon hanging there—muted heavy grays and browns
for the most part, contrasting with walnut and soft yellows. A deliberate
lack of finish, enhanced by skillful installation, gave the surface a rough,
forgotten quality; sliding weights on the inside, carefully adjusted, anchored the great, vari-shaped mass at a number of points. Now, we have
had a flood of original ideas in all media, works of singular beauty as well
as significant milestones in the history of inflation, but at that moment
there was only *this balloon,* concrete particular, hanging there.

There were reactions. Some people found the balloon "interesting." As a response this seemed inadequate to the immensity of the balloon, the suddenness of its appearance over the city; on the other hand, in the absence of hysteria or other societally induced anxiety, it must be judged a calm, "mature" one. There was a certain amount of initial argumentation about the "meaning" of the balloon; this subsided, because we have learned not to insist on meanings, and they are rarely even looked for now, except in cases involving the simplest, safest phenomena. It was agreed that since the meaning of the balloon could never be known absolutely, extended discussion was pointless, or at least less meaningful than the activities of those who, for example, hung green and blue paper lanterns from the warm gray underside, in certain streets, or seized the occasion to write messages on the surface, announcing their availability for the performance of unnatural acts, or the availability of acquaintances.

Daring children jumped, especially at those points where the balloon hovered close to a building, so that the gap between balloon and building was a matter of a few inches, or points where the balloon actually made contact, exerting an ever-so-slight pressure against the side of a building, so that balloon and building seemed a unity. The upper surface was so structured that a "landscape" was presented, small valleys as well as slight knolls, or mounds; once atop the balloon, a stroll was possible, or even a trip, from one place to another. There was pleasure in being able to run down an incline, then up the opposing slope, both gently graded, or in making a leap from one side to the other. Bouncing was possible, because of the pneumaticity of the surface, and even falling, if that was your wish. That all these varied motions, as well as others, were within one's possibilities, in experiencing the "up" side of the balloon, was extremely exciting for children, accustomed to the city's flat, hard skin. But the purpose of the balloon was not to amuse children.

Too, the number of people, children and adults, who took advantage of the opportunities described was not so large as it might have been: a certain timidity, lack of trust in the balloon, was seen. There was, furthermore, some hostility. Because we had hidden the pumps, which fed helium to the interior, and because the surface was so vast that the authorities could not determine the point of entry—that is, the point at which the gas was injected—a degree of frustration was evidenced by those city officers into whose province such manifestations normally fell. The apparent purposelessness of the balloon was vexing (as was the fact that it was "there" at all). Had we painted, in great letters, "LABORATORY TESTS PROVE" or "18% MORE EFFECTIVE" on the sides of the balloon, this difficulty would have been circumvented, but I could not bear to do so. On the whole, these officers were remarkably tolerant, considering the dimensions of the anomaly, this toler-ance being the result of, first, secret tests conducted by night that con-vinced them that little or nothing could be done in the way of removing or destroying the balloon, and, secondly, a public warmth that arose (not un-colored by touches of the aforementioned hostility) toward the balloon, from ordinary citizens.

As a single balloon must stand for a lifetime of thinking about balloons, so each citizen expressed, in the attitude he chose, a complex of attitudes. One man might consider that the balloon had to do with the notion *sullied,* as in the sentence *The big balloon sullied the otherwise clear and radiant Manhattan sky.* That is, the balloon was, in this man's view, an imposture, something inferior to the sky that had formerly been there, something in-terposed between the people and their "sky." But in fact it was January, the sky was dark and ugly; it was not a sky you could look up into, lying on your back in the street, with pleasure, unless pleasure, for you, proceeded from having been threatened, from having been misused. And the underside of the balloon, by contrast, was a pleasure to look up into—we had seen to that. Muted grays and browns for the most part, contrasted with walnut and soft, forgotten yellows. And so, while this man was thinking *sullied,* still there was an admixture of pleasurable cognition in his thinking, struggling with the original perception.

Another man, on the other hand, might view the balloon as if it were part of a system of unanticipated rewards, as when one's employer walks in and says, "Here, Henry, take this package of money I have wrapped for you, because we have been doing so well in the business here, and I admire the way you bruise the tulips, without which bruising your department would not be a success, or at least not the success that it is." For this man the balloon might be a brilliantly heroic "muscle and pluck" experience, even if an experience poorly understood.

Another man might say, "Without the example of ———, it is doubtful that ——— would exist today in its present form," and find many to agree with him, or to argue with him. Ideas of "bloat" and "float" were intro-duced, as well as concepts of dream and responsibility. Others engaged in remarkably detailed fantasies having to do with a wish either to lose them-selves in the balloon, or to engorge it. The private character of these wishes, of their origins, deeply buried and unknown, was such that they were not much spoken of; yet there is evidence that they were widespread. It was also argued that what was important was what you felt when you stood under the balloon; some people claimed that they felt sheltered, warmed, as never before, while enemies of the balloon felt, or reported feeling, constrained, a "heavy" feeling.

Critical opinion was divided:

"monstrous pourings"

"harp"

XXXXXXX "certain contrasts
with darker portions"

"inner joy"

"large, square corners"

"conservative eclecticism that has so far
governed modern balloon design"

: : : : : : : "abnormal vigor"

"warm, soft, lazy passages"

"Has unity been sacrificed for a
sprawling quality?"

"Quelle catastrophe!"

"munching"

People began, in a curious way, to locate themselves in relation to aspects of the balloon: "I'll be at that place where it dips down into Forty-seventh Street almost to the sidewalk, near the Alamo Chile House," or "Why don't we go stand on top, and take the air, and maybe walk about a bit, where it forms a tight, curving line with the façade of the Gallery of Modern Art—" Marginal intersections offered entrances within a given time duration, as well as "warm, soft, lazy passages" in which . . . But it is wrong to speak of "marginal intersections." Each intersection was crucial, none could be ignored (as if, walking there, you might not find someone capable of turning your attention, in a flash, from old exercises to new exercises). Each intersection was crucial, meeting of balloon and building, meeting of balloon and man, meeting of balloon and balloon.

IT was suggested that what was admired about the balloon was finally this: that it was not limited, or defined. Sometimes a bulge, blister, or sub-section would carry all the way east to the river on its own initiative, in the manner of an army's movements on a map, as seen in a headquarters remote from the fighting. Then that part would be, as it were, thrown back again, or would withdraw into new dispositions; the next morning, that part would have made another sortie, or disappeared altogether. This ability on the part of the balloon to shift its shape, to change, was very pleasing, especially to people whose lives were rather rigidly patterned, persons to whom change, although desired, was not available. The balloon, for the twenty-two days of its existence, offered the possibility, in its randomness, of getting lost, of losing oneself, in contradistinction to the grid of precise, rectangular pathways under our feet. The amount of specialized training currently needed, and the consequent desirability of long-term commitments, has been occasioned by the steadily growing importance of complex machinery, in virtually all kinds of operations; as this tendency increases, more and more people will turn, in bewildered inadequacy, to solutions for which the balloon may stand as a prototype, or "rough draft."

I met you under the balloon, on the occasion of your return from Norway. You asked if it was mine; I said it was. The balloon, I said, is a spontaneous autobiographical disclosure, having to do with the unease I felt at your absence, and with sexual deprivation, but now that your visit to Bergen has been terminated, it is no longer necessary or appropriate. Removal of the balloon was easy; trailer trucks carried away the depleted fabric, which is now stored in West Virginia, awaiting some other time of unhappiness, sometime, perhaps, when we are angry with one another.

(1966)

SMART MONEY

W HAT the hell are you doing on a bus, with your dough?"
It was a small, husky young fellow with a short haircut and a
new business suit who wanted to know; he had been daydreaming over an
automotive magazine until he saw who was sitting next to him. That was
all it took to charge him up.

Undaunted by Zuckerman's unobliging reply—on a bus to be trans-
ported through space—he happily offered his advice. These days everybody
did, if they could find him. "You should buy a helicopter. That's how I'd do
it. Rent the landing rights up on apartment buildings and fly straight over
the dog-poop. Hey, see this guy?" This second question was to a man standing in the aisle reading his *Times*.

The bus was travelling south on Fifth Avenue, downtown from Zuckerman's new upper–East Side address. He was off to see an investment specialist on Fifty-second Street, a meeting arranged by his agent, André
Schevitz, to get him to diversify his capital. Gone were the days when
Zuckerman had only to worry about Zuckerman making money: hence-
forth he would have to worry about his money making money. "Where do
you have it right now?" the investment specialist had asked when
Zuckerman finally phoned. "In my shoe," Zuckerman told him. The investment specialist laughed. "You intend to keep it there?" Though the answer
was yes, it was easier for the moment to say no. Zuckerman had privately
declared a one-year moratorium on all serious decisions arising out of his
smashing success. When he could think straight again, he would act again.

All this, this luck—what did it mean? Coming so suddenly, and on such a scale, it was as baffling as a misfortune.

Because Zuckerman was not ordinarily going anywhere at the morning rush hour—except into his study with his coffee cup to reread the paragraphs from the day before—he hadn't realized until too late that it was a bad time to be taking a bus. But then he still refused to believe that he was any less free than he'd been six weeks before to come and go as he liked, when he liked, without having to remember beforehand who he was. Ordinary everyday thoughts on the subject of who one was were lavish enough without an extra hump of narcissism to carry around.

"Hey. *Hey.*" Zuckerman's excited neighbor was trying again to distract the man in the aisle from his *Times.* "See this guy next to me?"

"I do now," came the stern, affronted reply.

"He's the guy who wrote 'Carnovsky.' Didn't you read about it in the papers? He just made a million bucks and he's taking a bus."

Upon hearing that a millionaire was on board, two girls in identical gray uniforms—two frail, sweet-looking children, undoubtedly well-bred little sisters on their way to convent school—turned to look at him.

"Veronica," said the smaller of the two, "it's the man who wrote the book that Mummy's reading. It's Carnovsky."

The children kneeled on their seats so as to face him. A middle-aged couple in the row across from the children also turned to get a look.

"Go on, girls," said Zuckerman lightly. "Back to your homework."

"Our mother," said the older child, taking charge, "is reading your book, Mr. Carnovsky."

"Fine. But Mummy wouldn't want you to stare on the bus."

No luck. Must be phrenology they were studying at St. Mary's.

Zuckerman's companion had meanwhile turned to the seat directly behind to explain to the woman there the big goings on. Make her a part of it. The family of man. "I'm sitting next to a guy who just made a million bucks. Probably two."

"Well," said a gentle, ladylike voice, "I hope all that money doesn't change him."

Fifteen blocks north of the investment specialist's office, Zuckerman pulled the cord and got off. Surely here, in the garden spot of anomie, it was still possible to be nobody on the rush-hour streets. If not, try a mustache. This may be far from life as you feel, see, know, and wish to know it, but if all it takes is a mustache, then for Christ's sake grow one. You are not Paul Newman, but you're no longer who you used to be, either. A mustache. Contact lenses. Maybe a colorful costume would help. Try looking the way everybody does today instead of the way everybody looked twenty years ago in Humanities 2. Less like Albert Einstein, more like Jimi Hendrix, and you won't stick out so much. And what about your gait while you're at it? He was always meaning to work on that anyway. Zuckerman moved with his knees too close together and at a much too hurried pace. A man six feet tall should *amble* more. But he could never remember about ambling after the first dozen steps—twenty, thirty paces and he was lost in his thoughts instead of thinking about his stride. Well, now was the time to get on with it, especially with his sex credentials coming under scrutiny in the press. As aggressive in the walk as in the work. You're a millionaire, walk like one. People are watching.

The joke was on him. Someone was—the woman who'd had to be told on the bus why everyone else was agog. A tall, thin, elderly woman, her face heavily powdered . . . only why was she running after him? And undoing the latch on her purse? Suddenly his adrenaline advised Zuckerman to run too.

You see, not everybody was delighted by this book that was making Zuckerman a fortune. Plenty of people had already written to tell him off. "For depicting Jews in a peep-show atmosphere of total perversion, for depicting Jews in acts of adultery, exhibitionism, masturbation, sodomy, fetishism, and whoremongery," somebody with letterhead stationery as impressive as the President's had even suggested that he "ought to be shot." And in the spring of 1969 this was no longer just an expression. Vietnam was a slaughterhouse, and, off the battlefield as well as on, many Americans had gone berserk. Just about a year before, Martin Luther King and Robert Kennedy had been gunned down by assassins. Closer to home, a former teacher of Zuckerman's was still hiding out because a rifle had been fired at him through his kitchen window as he was sitting at his table one night with a glass of warm milk and a Wodehouse novel. The retired bachelor had taught Middle English at the University of Chicago for thirty-five years. The course had been hard, though not that hard. But a bloody nose wasn't enough anymore. Blowing people apart seemed to have replaced the roundhouse punch in the daydreams of the aggrieved: only annihilation gave satisfaction that lasted. At the Democratic Convention the year before, hundreds had been beaten with clubs and trampled by horses and thrown through plate-glass windows for offenses against order and decency less grave than Zuckerman's were thought to be by any number of his correspondents. It didn't strike Zuckerman as at all unlikely that in a seedy room somewhere the *Life* cover featuring his face (unmustached) had been tacked up within dart-throwing distance of the bed of some "loner." Those cover stories were enough of a trial for a writer's writer friends, let alone for a semi-literate psychopath who might not know about all the good deeds he did at the PEN Club. Oh, Madam, if only you knew the real me! Don't shoot! I am a serious writer as well as one of the boys!

But it was too late to plead his cause. Behind her rimless spectacles, the powdered zealot's pale-green eyes were glazed with conviction; at point-blank range she had hold of his arm. "Don't"—she was not young, and it was a struggle for her to catch her breath—"don't let all that money change you, whoever you may be. Money never made anybody happy. Only He can do that." And from her Luger-sized purse she removed a picture postcard of Jesus and pressed it into his hand. " 'There is not a just man upon earth,' " she reminded him, " 'that doeth good and sinneth not. If we say that we have no sin, we deceive ourselves, and the truth is not in us.' "

HE was sipping coffee later that morning at a counter around the corner from the office of the investment specialist—studying, for the first time in his life, the business page of the morning paper—when a smiling middle-aged woman came up to tell him that from reading about his sexual liberation in "Carnovsky" she was less "uptight" now herself. In the bank at Rockefeller Plaza where he went to cash a check, the long-haired guard asked in a whisper if he could touch Mr. Zuckerman's coat: he wanted to tell his wife about it when he got home that night. While he was walking through the Park, a nicely dressed young East Side mother out with her baby and her dog stepped into his path and said, "You need love, and you need it all the time. I feel sorry for you." In the periodical room of the Public Library an elderly gentleman tapped him on the shoulder and in heavily accented English— Zuckerman's grandfather's English—told him how sorry he felt for his parents. "You didn't put in your whole life," he said sadly. "There's much more to your life than that. But you just leave it out. To get even." And then, at last, at home, a large jovial black man from Con Ed who was waiting in the hall to read his meter. "Hey, you do all that stuff in that book? With all those chicks? You are something else, man." The meter reader. But people didn't just read meters anymore, they also read that book.

Zuckerman was tall, but not as tall as Wilt Chamberlain. He was thin, but not as thin as Mahatma Gandhi. In his customary getup of tan corduroy coat, gray turtleneck sweater, and cotton khaki trousers he was neatly attired, but hardly Rubirosa. Nor was dark hair and a prominent nose the distinguishing mark in New York that it would have been in Reykjavik or Helsinki. But two, three, four times a week they spotted him anyway. "It's Carnovsky!" "Hey, careful, Carnovsky, they arrest people for that!" "Hey, want to see my underwear, Gil?" In the beginning, when he heard someone call after him out on the street, he would wave hello to show what a good sport he was. It was the easiest thing to do, so he did it. Then the easiest thing was to pretend not to hear and keep going. Then the easiest thing was to pretend that he was hearing things, to realize that it was happening in a world that didn't exist. They had mistaken impersonation for confession and were calling out to a character who lived in a book. Zuckerman tried taking it as praise—he had made real people believe Carnovsky was real too—but in the end he pretended he was only himself, and with his quick, small steps hurried on.

AT the end of the day he walked out of his new neighborhood and over to Yorkville, and on Second Avenue found the haven he was looking for. Just the place to be left to himself with the evening paper, or so he thought when he peered between the salamis strung up in the window: a sixty-year-old waitress in runny eye-shadow and crumbling house slippers, and behind the sandwich counter, wearing an apron about as fresh as a Manhattan snowdrift, a colossus with a carving knife. It was a few minutes after six. He could grab a sandwich and be off the streets by seven.

"Pardon me."

Zuckerman looked up from the fraying menu at a man in a dark raincoat who was standing beside his table. The dozen or so other tables were empty. The stranger was carrying a hat in his hands in a way that restored to that expression its original metaphorical lustre.

"Pardon me. I only want to say thank you."

He was a large man, chesty, with big sloping shoulders and a heavy neck. A single strand of hair looped over his bald head, but otherwise his face was a boy's: shining smooth cheeks, emotional brown eyes, an impudent, owlish little beak.

"Thank me? For what?" The first time in the six weeks that it had occurred to Zuckerman to pretend that he was another person entirely. He was learning.

His admirer took it for humility. The lively, lachrymose eyes deepened with feeling. "God! For everything. The humor. The compassion. The understanding of our deepest drives. For all you have reminded us about the human comedy."

Compassion? Understanding? Only hours earlier the old man in the library had told him how sorry he felt for his family. They had him coming and going today.

"Well," said Zuckerman, "that's very kind."

The stranger pointed to the menu in Zuckerman's hand. "Please, order. I didn't mean to obtrude. I was in the washroom, and when I came out I couldn't believe my eyes. To see you in a place like this. I just had to come up and say thanks before I left."

"Quite all right."

"What makes it unbelievable is that I'm a Newarker myself."

"Are you?"

"Born and bred. You got out in '49, right? Well, it's a different city today. You wouldn't recognize it. You wouldn't want to."

"So I hear."

"Me, I'm still over there, pounding away."

Zuckerman nodded, and signalled for the waitress.

"I don't think people can appreciate what you're doing for the old Newark unless they're from there themselves."

Zuckerman ordered his sandwich and some tea. How does he know I left in '49? I suppose from *Life*.

He smiled and waited for the fellow to be on his way back across the river.

"You're our Marcel Proust, Mr. Zuckerman."

Zuckerman laughed. It wasn't exactly how he saw it.

"I mean it. It's not a put-on. God forbid. In my estimation you are up there with Stephen Crane. You are the two great Newark writers."

"Well, that's kind of you."

"There's Mary Mapes Dodge, but however much you may admire 'Hans Brinker,' it's still only a book for children. I would have to place her third. Then there is LeRoi Jones, but him I have no trouble placing fourth. I say this without racial prejudice, and not as a result of the tragedy that has happened to the city in recent years, but what he writes is not literature. In my estimation it is black propaganda. No, in literature we have got you and Stephen Crane, in acting we have got Rod Steiger and Vivian Blaine, in playwrighting we have got Dore Schary, in singing we have got Sarah Vaughan, and in sports we have got Gene Hermanski and Herb Krautblatt. Not that you can mention sports and what you have accomplished in the same breath. In years to come I honestly see schoolchildren visiting the city of Newark—"

"Oh," said Zuckerman, amused again, but uncertain as to what might be feeding such effusiveness, "oh, I think it's going to take more than me to bring the schoolchildren in. Especially with the Empire shut down." The Empire was the Washington Street burlesque house, long defunct, where many a New Jersey boy had in the half-light seen his first G-string. Zuckerman was one, Gilbert Carnovsky another.

The fellow raised his arms—and his hat: gesture of helpless surrender. "Well, you have got the great sense of humor in life too. No comeback from me could equal that. But you'll see. It'll be you they turn to in the future when they want to remember what it was like in the old days. In 'Carnovsky' you have pinned down for all time growing up in that town as a Jew."

"Well, thanks again. Thank you, really, for all the kind remarks."

The waitress appeared with his sandwich. That should end it. On a pleasant note, actually. Behind the effusiveness lay nothing but somebody who had enjoyed a book. Fine. "Thank you," said Zuckerman—the fourth time—and ceremoniously lifted half of his sandwich.

"I went to South Side. Class of '43."

South Side High, at the decaying heart of the old industrial city, had been almost half black even in Zuckerman's day, when Newark was still mostly white. His own school district, at the far edge of a newer residential Newark, had been populated in the twenties and thirties by Jews leaving the run-down immigrant enclaves in the central wards to rear children bound for college and the professions and, in time, for the Orange suburbs, where Zuckerman's own brother, Henry, now owned a big house.

"You're Weequahic '49."

"Look," said Zuckerman apologetically, "I have to eat and run. I'm sorry."

"Forgive me, please. I only wanted to say—well, I said it, didn't I?" He smiled regretfully at his own insistence. "Thank you, thank you again. For everything. It's been a pleasure. It's been a thrill. I didn't mean to bug you, God knows."

Zuckerman watched him move off to the register to pay for his meal. Younger than he seemed from the dark clothes and the beefy build and the vanquished air, but more ungainly and, with his heavy splayfooted walk, more pathetic than Zuckerman had realized.

"Excuse me. I'm sorry."

Hat in hand again. Zuckerman was sure he had seen him go out the door with it on his head.

"Yes?"

"This is probably going to make you laugh. But I'm trying to write myself. You don't have to worry about the competition, I assure you. When you try your hand at it, then you really admire the stupendous accomplishment of somebody like yourself. The patience alone is phenomenal. Day in and day out facing that white piece of paper."

Zuckerman had been thinking that he should have had the good grace to ask him to sit and chat, if only for a moment. He had even begun to feel a sentimental connection, remembering him standing beside the table announcing, "I'm a Newarker myself." He was feeling less sentimental with the Newarker standing back beside the table announcing that he was a writer too.

"I was wondering if you could recommend an editor or an agent who might be able to help someone like me."

"No."

"O.K. Fine. No problem. Just asking. I already have a producer, you see, who wants to make a musical out of my life. My own feeling is that it should come out first in public as a serious book. With all the facts."

Silence.

"That sounds preposterous to you, I know, even if you're too polite to say so. But it's true. It has nothing to do with me being anybody who matters. I ain't and I don't. One look and you know that. It's what happened to me that'll make the musical."

Silence.

"I'm Alvin Pepler."

Well, he wasn't Houdini. For a moment, that had seemed in the cards.

Alvin Pepler waited to hear what Nathan Zuckerman made of meeting Alvin Pepler. When he heard nothing, he quickly came to Zuckerman's aid. And his own. "Of course to people like you the name can't mean a thing. You have better things to do with your time than waste it on TV. But I thought, as we're *landsmen,* that maybe your family might have mentioned me to you. I didn't say this earlier, I didn't think it was in order, but your father's cousin, Essie Slifer, happened to go to Central with my mother's sister Lottie way back when. They were one year apart. I don't know if this helps, but I'm the one they called in the papers 'Pepler the Man of the People.' I'm 'Alvin the Jewish Marine.' "

"Why, then," said Zuckerman, relieved at last to have something to say, "you're the quiz contestant, no? You were on one of those shows."

Oh, there was more to it than that. The syrupy brown eyes went mournful and angry, filling up not with tears but what was worse, with *truth.* "Mr. Zuckerman, for three consecutive weeks I was the winner on the biggest of them all. Bigger than 'Twenty-One.' In terms of dollars given away, bigger than 'The $64,000 Question.' I was the winner on 'Smart Money.' "

Zuckerman couldn't remember ever seeing any of those quiz shows back in the late fifties, and didn't know one from another; he and his first wife, Betsy, hadn't even owned a television set. Still, he thought he could remember somebody in his family—more than likely Cousin Essie—once mentioning a Pepler family from Newark and their oddball son, the quiz contestant and ex-Marine.

"It was Alvin Pepler they cut down to make way for the great Hewlett Lincoln. That is the subject of my book. The fraud perpetrated on the American public. The manipulation of the trust of tens of millions of innocent people. And how for admitting it I have been turned into a pariah until this day. They made me and then they destroyed me, and, Mr. Zuckerman, they haven't finished with me yet. The others involved have all gone on, onward and upward in corporate America, and nobody cares a good God damn what thieves and liars they were. But because I wouldn't lie for those miserable crooks, I have spent ten years as a marked man. A McCarthy victim is better off than I am. The whole country rose up against that bastard, and vindicated the innocent and so on, till at least some justice was restored. But Alvin Pepler, to this day, is a dirty name throughout the American broadcasting industry."

Zuckerman was remembering more clearly now the stir those quiz shows had made, remembering not so much Pepler but Hewlett Lincoln, the philosophical young country newspaperman and son of the Republican governor of Maine, and, while he was a contestant, the most famous television celebrity in America, admired by schoolchildren, their teachers, their parents, their grandparents—until the scandal broke, and the schoolchildren learned that the answers that came trippingly off the tongue of Hewlett Lincoln in the contestants' isolation booth had been slipped to him days earlier by the show's producers. There were front-page stories in the papers, and as Zuckerman recalled, the ludicrous finale had been a congressional investigation.

"I wouldn't dream," Pepler was saying, "of comparing the two of us. An educated artist like yourself and a person who happens to be born with a photographic memory are two different things entirely. But while I was on 'Smart Money,' deservedly or not I had the respect of the entire nation. If I have to say so myself, I don't think it did the Jewish people any harm having a Marine veteran of two wars representing them on prime-time national television for three consecutive weeks. You may have contempt for quiz programs, even the honest ones. You have a right to—you more than anybody. But the average person didn't see it that way in those days. That's why when I was on top for those three great weeks, I made no bones about my religion. I said it right out. I wanted the country to know that a Jew in the Marine Corps could be as tough on the battlefield as anyone. I never claimed I was a war hero. Far from it. I shook like the next guy in a foxhole, but I never ran, even under fire. Of course there were a lot of Jews in combat, and braver men than me. But I was the one who got that point across to the great mass of the American people, and if I did it by way of a quiz show—well, that was the way that was given to me. Then, of course, *Variety* started calling me names, calling me 'quizling' and so on, and that was the beginning of the end. Quizling, with a 'z.' When I was the only one who didn't want their answers to begin with! When all I wanted was for them to give me the subject, to let me study and memorize, and then to fight it out fair and square! I could fill volumes about those people and what they did to me. That's why running into you, coming upon Newark's great writer out of the blue—well, it strikes me as practically a miracle at this point in my life. Because if I could write a publishable book, I honestly think that people would read it and that they would believe it. My name would be restored to what it was. That little bit of good I did would not be wiped away forever, as it is now. Whoever innocent I harmed and left besmirched, all the millions I let down, Jews particularly—well, they would finally understand the truth of what happened. They would forgive me."

His own aria had not left him unmoved. The deep-brown irises were cups of ore fresh from the furnace—as though a drop of Pepler's eyes could burn a hole right through you.

"Well, if that's the case," said Zuckerman, "you should work at it."

"I have." Pepler smiled the best he could. "Ten years of my life. May I?" He pointed to the empty chair across the table.

"Why not?" said Zuckerman, and tried not to think of all the reasons.

"I've worked at nothing else," said Pepler, plunging excitedly onto the seat. "I've worked at nothing else every night *for ten years*. But I don't have the gift. That's what they tell me anyway. I have sent my book to twenty-two publishers. I have rewritten it five times. I pay a young teacher from Columbia High in South Orange, which is still an A-rated school—I pay her by the hour to correct my grammar and punctuation wherever it's wrong. I wouldn't dream of submitting a single page of this book without her going over it beforehand for my errors. It's all too important for that. But if in their estimation you don't have the great gift—well, that's it. You may chalk this up to bitterness. I would too in your shoes. But Miss Diamond, this teacher working with me, she agrees: by now all they have to see is that Alvin Pepler is the author and they throw it in the pile marked trash. I don't think they read past my name. By now I'm one big laugh, even to the lowliest editor on Publishers' Row." The speech was fervent, yet the gaze, now that he was at the level of the table, seemed drawn to what was uneaten on Zuckerman's plate. "That's why I asked you about an agent, an editor—somebody fresh who wouldn't be prejudiced right off. Who would understand that this is *serious*."

Zuckerman, sucker though he was for seriousness, was still not going to be drawn into a discussion about agents and editors. If ever there was a reason for an American writer to seek asylum in Red China, it would be to put ten thousand miles between himself and those discussions.

"There's still the musical," Zuckerman reminded him.

"A serious book is one thing, and a Broadway musical is something else."

Another discussion Zuckerman would as soon avoid. Sounded like the premise for a course at the New School.

"If," said Pepler weakly, "it even gets made."

Optimistic Zuckerman: "Well, if you've got a producer . . ."

"Yes, but so far it's only a gentlemen's agreement. No money has changed hands, nobody's signed anything. The work is supposed to start when he gets back. That's when we make the real deal."

"Well, *that's* something."

"It's why I'm in New York. I'm living over at his place, talking into a tape machine. That's all I'm supposed to do. He doesn't want to read what I wrote any more than the moguls on Publishers' Row. Just talk into the machine till he gets back. And leave out the thoughts. Just the stories. Well, beggars can't be choosers."

As good a note as any to leave on.

"But," said Pepler, when he saw Zuckerman get to his feet, "but you've eaten only half a sandwich!"

"Can't." He indicated the hour on his watch. "Someone waiting. Meeting."

"Oh, forgive me, Mr. Zuckerman, I'm sorry."

"Good luck with the musical." He reached down and shook Pepler's hand. "Good luck all around." Pepler was unable to hide the disappointment. Pepler was unable to hide *anything*. Or was that hiding everything? Impossible to tell, and another reason to go.

"Thanks a million." Then, with resignation, "Look, to switch from the sublime . . ."

What now?

"You don't mind, do you, if I eat your pickle?"

Was this a joke? Was this satire?

"I can't stay away from this stuff," he explained. "Childhood hangup."

"Please," said Zuckerman, "go right ahead."

"Sure you don't—"

"No, no."

He was also eying the uneaten half of Zuckerman's sandwich. And it was no joke. Too driven for that. "While I'm at it . . ." he said, with a self-deprecating smile.

"Sure, why not."

"See, there's no food in their refrigerator. I talk into that tape machine with all those stories and I get starved. I wake up in the night with something I forgot for the machine, and there's nothing to eat." He began wrapping the half sandwich in a napkin from the dispenser on the table. "Everything is send-out."

But Zuckerman was well on his way. At the register he put down a five and kept going.

Pepler popped up two blocks to the west, while Zuckerman waited for a light on Lexington. "One last thing—"

"Look—"

"Don't worry," said Pepler, "I'm not going to ask you to read my book. Nuts I am"—the admission registered in Zuckerman's chest with a light thud—"but not that nuts. You don't ask Einstein to check your bank statements."

The novelist's apprehension was hardly mitigated by the flattery. "Mr. Pepler, what do you want from me?"

"I just wonder if you think this project is right for a producer like Marty Paté. Because that's who's after it. I didn't want to bandy names around, but, O.K., that's who it is. My worry isn't even the money. I don't intend to get screwed—not again—but the hell with the money for now. What I'm wondering to myself is if I can trust him to do justice to my life, to what I have been put through in this country *all my life.*"

Scorn, betrayal, humiliation—the eyes disclosed for Zuckerman everything Pepler had been put through, and without "thoughts."

Zuckerman looked for a taxi. "Couldn't say."

"But you know Paté."

"Never heard of him."

"Marty Paté. The Broadway producer."

"Nope."

"But—" He looked like some large animal just batted on the head at the abattoir, badly stunned but not quite out. He looked in agony. "But—he knows *you.* He met you—through Miss O'Shea. When you were all in Ireland. For her birthday."

According to the columnists, the movie star Caesara O'Shea and the novelist Nathan Zuckerman were an "item." Actually, off the screen, Zuckerman had met with her but once in his life, as her dinner partner at the Schevitzes' some ten days before.

"Hey, how is Miss O'Shea, by the way? I wish," said Pepler, now suddenly wistful, "I could tell her—I wish you could tell her *for* me—what a great lady she is. To the public. To my mind she is the only real lady left in the movies today. Nothing they say could besmirch Miss O'Shea. I mean that."

"I'll tell her." The easiest way. Short of running for it.

"I stayed up Tuesday to watch her—she was on the Late Show. 'Divine Mission.' Another incredible coincidence. Watching that and then meeting you. I watched with Paté's father. You remember Marty's old man? From Ireland? Mr. Perlmutter?"

"Vaguely." Why not, if it brought this fellow's fever down?

By now the light had changed several times. When Zuckerman crossed, Pepler did too.

"He lives with Paté. In the town house. You ought to get a load of the layout over there," Pepler said. "Offices downstairs on the main floor. Autographed photos all along the hallway coming in. You should see of who. Victor Hugo, Sarah Bernhardt, Enrico Caruso. Marty has a dealer who gets them for him. Names like that, and by the yard. There's a fourteen-carat chandelier, there's an oil painting of Napoleon, there's velvet drapes right to the floor. And this is only the office. There's a harp in the hallway, just sitting there. Mr. Perlmutter says Marty directed all the decoration himself. From pictures of Versailles. He has a valuable collection from the Napoleonic era. The drinking glasses even have gold rims, like Napoleon had. Then upstairs, where Marty actually lives, resides, completely done up in modern design. Red leather, recessed lights, pitch-black walls. Plants like in an oasis. You should see the bathroom. Cut flowers *in the bathroom*. The floral bill is a thousand a month. Toilets like dolphins and the handles on everything gold plate. And the food is all send-out, down to salt and pepper. Nobody prepares anything. Nobody washes a dish. He's got a million-dollar kitchen in there and I don't think anybody's ever used it except to get water for an aspirin. A line on the phone direct to the restaurant next door. The old man calls down, and the next thing—shish kebab. In flames. You know who else is living there right now? Of course she comes and she goes, but she was the one who let me in with my suitcase when I got here Monday. She showed me to my room. She found me my towels. Gayle Gibraltar."

The name meant nothing to Zuckerman. All he could think was that if he kept walking, he was going to have Pepler with him all the way home, and if he hailed a cab, Pepler would hop in.

"I wouldn't want to take you out of your way," Zuckerman said.

"No problem. Paté's on Sixty-second and Madison. We're almost neighbors."

How did he know that?

"You're a very approachable guy, really, aren't you? I was terrified even to come up to you. My heart was pounding. I didn't think I had the nerve. I read in the *Star-Ledger* where fans bugged you so much you went around in a limousine with drawn shutters and two gorillas for bodyguards." The *Star-Ledger* was Newark's morning paper.

"That's Sinatra."

Pepler enjoyed that one. "Well, it's like the critics say, nobody can top you with the one-liner. Of course, Sinatra's from Jersey too. Hoboken's own. He still comes back to see his mother. People don't realize how many of us there are."

"Us?"

"Boys from Jersey who became household words. You wouldn't be offended, would you, if I eat the sandwich now? It can get pretty greasy carrying around."

"Suit yourself."

"I don't want to embarrass you. The hick from home. This is your town, and you being you—"

"Mr. Pepler, it means nothing to me either way."

Gently undoing the paper napkin like a surgical dressing, leaning forward so as not to soil himself, Pepler prepared for the first bite. "I shouldn't eat this stuff," he told Zuckerman. "Not anymore. In the service I was the guy who could eat anything. I was a joke. Pepler the human garbage can. I was famous for it. Under fire in Korea I survived on stuff you wouldn't feed a dog. Washed down with snow. You wouldn't believe what I had to eat. But then those bastards made me lose to Lincoln on only my third week—a three-part question on Americana I could have answered in my sleep—and my stomach trouble dates from that night. *All* my trouble dates from that night. That's a fact. That was the night that did me in. I can document it with doctors' reports. It's all in the book." That said, he bit into the sandwich. A quick second bite. A third. Gone. No sense prolonging the agony.

Zuckerman offered his handkerchief.

"Thanks," said Pepler. "My God, look at me, wiping my mouth with Nathan Zuckerman's hankie."

Zuckerman raised a hand to indicate that he should take it in stride. Pepler laughed uproariously.

"But," he said, carefully cleaning his fingers, "getting back to Paté, what you're saying, Nathan—"

Nathan.

"—is that by and large I shouldn't have much worry with a producer of his calibre, and the kind of outfit he runs."

"I didn't say anything of the sort."

"But"—alarmed! again the abattoir!—"you know him, you met him in Ireland. You said so!"

"Briefly."

"Ah, but that's how Marty meets everybody. He wouldn't get everything in otherwise. The phone rings and you hear the secretary over the intercom telling the old man to pick up, and you can't believe your ears."

"Victor Hugo on the line."

Pepler's laughter was uncontrollable. "Not far from it, Nathan." He was having an awfully good time now. And, Zuckerman had to admit it, so was he. Once you relaxed with this guy, he wasn't unentertaining. You could pick up worse on the way home from the delicatessen.

Except how does he know we're almost neighbors? And how do you shake him off?

"It's a Who's Who of International Entertainment, the calls coming into that place. I tell you what gives me the greatest faith in this project getting off the ground, and that's where Marty happens to be right now. On business. Take a guess."

"No idea."

"Take a guess. You especially will be impressed."

"I especially."

"Absolutely."

"You've got me, Alvin." Alvin.

"Israel," announced Pepler. "With Moshe Dayan."

"Well, well."

"He's got an option on the Six-Day War, for a musical. Yul Brynner is already as good as signed to star as Dayan. With Brynner it could be something for the Jews."

"And for Paté too, no?"

"Christ, how can he miss? He'll rake it in. They're all but sold out the first year on theatre parties alone. This is without even a script. Mr. Perlmutter has sounded them out. They're ecstatic from just the idea. I tell you something else. Highly classified. When he gets back next week from Israel, I wouldn't be surprised if he approaches Nathan Zuckerman to do the adaptation of the war for the stage."

"They're thinking of me."

"You, Herman Wouk, and Harold Pinter. Those are the three names they're kicking around."

"Mr. Pepler."

" 'Alvin' is fine."

"Alvin, who told you all this?"

"Gayle. Gibraltar."

"How does she come by such classified information?"

"Oh, well, God. For one thing, she's a terrific business brain. People don't realize, because the beauty is all they see. But before she became a Playmate, she used to work as a guide at the United Nations. She speaks four languages. It was Playmate of the Month that launched her, of course."

"Into?"

"You name it. She and Paté literally don't stop. Those two are the secret of perpetual motion. Marty found out before he left that it was Dayan's son's birthday and so Gayle went out and got him a present: a solid-chocolate chess set. And the boy loved it. Last night she went up to Massachusetts to jump from an airplane today for UNESCO. It was a benefit. And in the Sardinian film they just finished, she did her own stunts on the horse."

"So she's an actress too. In Sardinian films."

"Well, it was a Sardinian corporation. The film was international. Look"—suddenly shyness overcame him—"she's not Miss O'Shea, not by a long shot. Miss O'Shea has style. Miss O'Shea has class. Gayle is some-body . . . without hangups. That's what she projects, you see. When you're with her."

Pepler turned a bright red speaking about what was projected by Gayle Gibraltar when you were with her.

"Which are her four languages?" asked Zuckerman.

"I'm not sure. English, of course, is one. I haven't had a chance to check out the others."

"I would, in your shoes."

"Well, O.K., I will. Good idea. Latvian must be another. That's where she was born."

"And Paté's father. Which four languages does he speak?"

Pepler saw he was being needled. But then, not by just anybody; he took it, after a moment, with another hearty, appreciative laugh. "Oh, don't worry. It's all straight from the shoulder with that guy. You couldn't meet a finer old-timer. Shakes your hand whenever you come in. Beautifully turned out, but in a sedate manner, always. Always with this nice, respect-ful, soft-spoken air. No, the one who gives me the confidence, frankly, is this lovely, dignified old gentleman. He keeps the books, he signs the checks, and when the decisions are made, I tell you, in his own quiet, respectful way, he makes them. He hasn't got Marty's go-go razzle-dazzle, but this is the rock, the foundation."

"I hope so."

"Please, don't worry about me. I learned my lesson. They wiped me out worse than you can begin to imagine back when they wiped me out. I haven't been the same person since. I start back after the war, and then there's Korea. I start back again after that, fight my way to the absolute top, and whammo. This actually is the best week I have had in ten years, being here in New York City with finally, *finally*, some kind of door to the future opening up. My good name, my robust health, my Marine record, and then my lovely, loyal fiancée, who took to the hills. I never saw her again. I became a walking disgrace because of those crooked bastards, and I'm not about to lay myself open like that ever again. I understand what you're trying to warn me about in your own humorous way. Well, don't worry, the one-liners aren't wasted on me. I'm warned. I'm not the wide-eyed little yokel I was back in '59. I don't think I'm with a great man anymore just because a guy has got a hundred pairs of shoes in the closet and a Jacuzzi bathtub ten feet long. They were going to make me a sportscaster on the Sunday-night news, did you know that? I was supposed to be Stan Lomax by now. I was supposed to be Bill Stern."

"But they didn't do it," said Zuckerman.

"May I speak frankly, Nathan? I would give anything to sit down with you for one evening, any night you wanted, and tell you what was going on in this country in the reign of Ike the Great. In my opinion the beginning of the end of what's good in this country were those quiz shows and the crooks that ran them and the public that swallowed it like so many dopes. There is where it began, and where it has ended is with another war again, and one this time that makes you want to scream. And a liar like Nixon as President of the United States. Eisenhower's gift to America. That schmegeggy in his golf shoes—this is what he leaves for posterity. But this is all in my book, spelled out in detail, step by step, the decline of every decent American thing into liars and lies. You can well understand why I have my own reasons for being nervous about throwing my lot in with anybody, Marty Paté included. After all, mine is not the kind of criticism of a country that you are used to finding in a Broadway musical. Do you agree? Can such a thing even be made into a musical without watering down the condemnation I make of the system?"

"I don't know."

"They promised me a job as a sportscaster if I didn't admit to the D.A. about how the thing was rigged from the day it started, how even that little girl they had on, age eleven and in pigtails, they gave her the answers and didn't even tell her mother. They were going to put me on TV every Sunday night with the sports results. It was all arranged. So they told me. 'Al Pepler and the Weekend Roundup.' And from there to broadcasting the Yankee home games. What it came down to was that they couldn't afford to let a Jew be a big winner too long on 'Smart Money.' Especially a Jew who made no bones about it. They were afraid about the ratings. They were terrified they would rub the country the wrong way. Bateman and Schachtman, the producers, would have meetings about things like this and talk about it together till all hours. They would talk about whether to have an armed guard come on the stage with the questions, or the president of a bank.

They would talk about whether the isolation booth should be waiting on the stage at the beginning or whether it should be rolled out by a squad of Eagle Scouts. They would talk all night long, two grown men, about what kind of tie I should wear. This is all true, Nathan. But my point is that if you study the programs the way I have, you'll see that my theory about the Jews is borne out. There were twenty quiz shows on three networks, seven of them in action five days a week. On an average week they gave away half a million bucks. I'm talking about true quiz shows, exclusive of panel shows and stunt shows and those do-good shows, where you could only get on if you had palsy or no feet. Half a million bucks a week, and yet over the bonanza period, from '55 till '58, you won't find a single Jew who won over a hundred thousand. That was the limit for a Jew to win, and this is on programs where the producers, nearly every single one, were Jews themselves. To break the bank you had to be a goy like Hewlett. The bigger the goy, the bigger the haul. This is on programs *run* by Jews. This is what still drives me crazy. 'I will study and get ready, and maybe the chance will come.' You know who said that? Abraham Lincoln. The real Lincoln. That was who I quoted from on nationwide TV my first night on the show, before I got into the booth. Little did I know that because my father wasn't governor of Maine and I didn't go to Dartmouth College, my chance wasn't going to be the same as the next guy's, that three weeks later I'd be as good as dead. Because I didn't commune with nature, you see, up there in the Maine woods. Because while Hewlett was sitting on his ass studying to lie at Dartmouth College, I was serving this country in *two* wars. Two years in World War II and then I get called back for Korea! But this is all in my book. Whether it's all going to get in the musical—well, how could it? Face facts. You know this country better than anybody. There are people that, as soon as word gets out that I'm working on what I'm working on with Marty Paté, who are going to put the pressure on him to drop me like a hot potato. I wouldn't even rule out payoffs from the networks. I wouldn't rule out the F.C.C. taking him aside. I can see Nixon himself getting involved to quash it. I'm supposed to be a disturbed and unstable person, you see. That's what they'll tell Marty to scare him off. That's what they told everybody, including me, including the parents of my stupid fiancée, including finally a special subcommittee from the United States House of Representatives. That was the story when I refused to go along with being dethroned for no reason after only three weeks. Bateman was practically in tears from worrying about my mental stability. 'If you knew the discussions we have had about your character, Alvin. If you knew the surprise it has been to us, that you have not turned out to be the trustworthy fellow we all so believed in. We're so worried about you,' he tells me, 'we've decided to pay for a psychiatrist for you. We want you to see him until you have gotten over your neurosis and are yourself again.' 'Absolutely,' Schachtman says. 'I want Alvin to see Dr. Eisenberg. I see Dr. Eisenberg, why shouldn't Alvin see Dr. Eisenberg? This organization is not going to save a few lousy dollars at the expense of Alvin's mental stability.' This is how they were going to discredit me, by setting me up as a nut. Well, that tune changed fast. Because one, I wasn't going in for any psychiatric treatment, and two, what I wanted was a written agreement from them guaranteeing that first Hewlett and I fight to a draw for three consecutive weeks and *then* I leave. And one month later, by popular request, a rematch, which he would win by a hair in the last second. But not on the subject of Americana. I was not going to let a goy beat a Jew again on that, not while the entire country was watching. Let him beat me on a subject like Trees, I said, which is their specialty and doesn't mean anything to anybody anyway. But I refuse to let the Jewish people go down on prime-time TV as not knowing their Americana. Either I had all that in writing, I said, or I would go to the press with the truth, including the stuff about the little girl with the braids and how they set her up too, first with the answers and then to take a dive. You should have heard Bateman then, and how much he was worried about my mental condition. 'Do you want to destroy my career, Alvin? Why? Why me? Why Schachtman and Bateman, after all we've done for you? Didn't we get your teeth cleaned? Sharp new suits? A dermatologist? Is this the way you plan to pay us back, by going up to people in the street and telling them Hewlett is a fake? Alvin, all these threats, all this blackmail. Alvin, we are not hardened criminals—we are in show business. You cannot ask random questions of people and have a show. We want "Smart Money" to be something the people of America can look forward to every week with excitement. But if you just ask random questions, you know you would have nobody knowing the answer two times in a row. You would have just failure, and failure does not make entertainment. You have to have a plot, like in "Hamlet" or anything else first-class. To the audience, Alvin, maybe you are only contestants. But to us you are far more. You are performers. You are artists. Artists making art for America, just the way Shakespeare made it in his day for England. And that is with a plot, and conflict, and suspense, and a resolution. And the resolution is that you should lose to Hewlett, and we have a new face on the show. Does Hamlet get up from the stage and say I don't want to die at the end of the play? No, his part is over and he lies there. That is the difference, in point of fact, between schlock and art. Schlock goes every which way and couldn't care less about anything but the buck, and art is *controlled,* art is *managed,* art is *always* rigged. That is how it takes hold of the human heart.' And this is where Schachtman pipes up and tells me that they are going to make a sportscaster out of me, as a reward, if I keep my mouth shut and go down for the count. So I did. But did they, *did they*, after telling me that *I* wasn't the one to be trusted?"

"No," said Zuckerman.

"You can say that again. Three weeks, and that was it. They cleaned my teeth and they kissed my ass, and for three weeks I was their hero. The mayor had me into his office. Did I tell you that? 'You have placed the name of the city of Newark before the whole country.' He said this to me in front of the City Council, who clapped. I went to Lindy's and signed a picture of myself for their wall. Milton Berle came up to my table and asked me some questions, as a gag. One week they're taking me for cheesecake to Lindy's and the next week they tell me I'm washed up. And call me names into the bargain. 'Alvin,' Schachtman says to me, 'is this what you're going to turn out to be, you who have done so much good for Newark and your family and the Marines and the Jews? Just another exhibitionist who has no motive but greed?' I was furious. 'What is your motive, Schachtman? What is Bateman's motive? What is the sponsor's motive? What is the network's motive?' And the truth is that greed had nothing to do with it. It was by this time my self-respect. As a man! As a war veteran! As a war veteran twice over! As a Newarker! As a Jew! What they were saying, you understand, was that all these things that made up Alvin Pepler and his pride in himself were unadulterated crap next to a Hewlett Lincoln. One hundred and seventy-three thousand dollars, that's what he wound up with, that fake. Thirty thousand fan letters. Interviewed by more than five hundred newsmen from around the world. Another face? Another *religion*, that's the ugly truth of it! This hurt me, Nathan. I am hurt still, and it isn't just egotistically either, I swear to you. This is why I'm fighting them, why I'll fight them right to the end, until my true story is before the American public. If Paté is my chance, then don't you see, I *have* to jump for it. If it has to be a musical first and *then* the book, then that's the way it has to be until my name is cleared!"

Perspiration streamed from beneath his dark rain hat, and with the handkerchief Zuckerman had given him earlier he reached up to wipe it off—enabling Zuckerman to step away from the street-corner mailbox where Pepler had him pinned. In fifteen minutes, the two Newarkers had travelled one block.

Across the street from where they stood was a Baskin-Robbins ice-cream parlor. The evening was cool, yet customers walked in and out as though it were already summertime. Inside the lighted store there was a small crowd waiting at the counter to be served.

Because he didn't know how to begin to reply, and probably because Pepler was perspiring so, Zuckerman heard himself ask, "What about an ice cream?" Of course, what Pepler would have preferred from Zuckerman was this: *You were robbed, ruined, brutally betrayed—"Carnovsky"'s author commits his strength to the redress of Pepler's grievance.* But the best Zuckerman could do was to offer an ice-cream snack. He doubted if anyone could do better.

"Oh, forgive me," said Pepler. "I'm sorry for this. Of course you've got to be starving, with me talking your ear off and then eating half your dinner in the bargain. Forgive me, please, if I got carried away on this subject. Meeting you has just thrown me for a loop. I don't usually go off half cocked like this, telling everybody my troubles out on the street. I'm so quiet with people, their first impression is I'm death warmed over. Someone like Miss Gibraltar," he said, reddening, "thinks I'm practically a deaf-mute. Hey, let *me* buy *you.*"

"No, no, not necessary."

But as they crossed the street, Pepler insisted. "After the pleasure you've given to me as a reader? After the earful I just gave you?" Refusing even to let Zuckerman enter the store with his money, Pepler cried, "Yes, yes, my treat, absolutely. For our great Newark writer who has cast his spell over the entire country! For that great magician who has pulled a living, breathing Carnovsky out of his artistic hat! Who has hypnotized the U.S.A.! Here's to the author of that wonderful best-selling book!" And then, suddenly, he was looking at Zuckerman as tenderly as a father on an outing with his darling baby boy. "Do you want jimmies on top, Nathan?"

"Sure."

"And flavor?"

"Chocolate is fine."

"Both dips?"

"Fine."

Comically tapping at his skull to indicate that the order was tucked safely away in the photographic memory that was once the pride of Newark, the nation, and the Jews, Pepler hurried into the store. Zuckerman waited out on the pavement alone.

But for what?

Would Mary Mapes Dodge wait like this for an ice-cream cone?

Would Frank Sinatra?

Would a ten-year-old child with any brains?

As though passing the time on a pleasant evening, he practiced ambling toward the corner. Then he ran. Down the side street, unpursued.

(1981)

ANOTHER MARVELLOUS THING

O N a cold, rainy morning in February, Freddie Delielle stood by the window of her hospital room looking out over Central Park. She was a week and a half from the time her baby was due to be born, and she had been put into the hospital because her blood pressure had suddenly gone up and her doctor wanted her constantly monitored and on bed rest.

A solitary jogger in bright-red foul-weather gear ran slowly down the glistening path. The trees were black and the branches were bare. There was not another soul out. Freddie had been in the hospital for five days. The first morning she had woken to the sound of squawking. Since her room was next door to the nursery, she assumed this was a sound some newborns made. The next day she got out of bed at dawn and saw that the meadow was full of seagulls who congregated each morning before the sun came up.

The nursery was an enormous room painted soft yellow. When Freddie went to take the one short walk a day allowed her, she would avert her eyes from the neat rows of babies in their little plastic bins, but once in a while she found herself hungry for the sight of them. Taped to each crib was a blue (I'M A BOY) or pink (I'M A GIRL) card telling mother's name, the time of birth, and birth weight. Freddie was impressed by the surprising range of noises the babies made: mewing, squawking, bleating, piping, and squealing. The fact that she was about to have one of these creatures herself filled her with a combination of bafflement, dread, and longing.

For the past two months her chief entertainment had been to lie in bed and observe her unborn child moving under her skin. It had knocked a paperback book off her stomach and caused the saucer of her coffee cup to jiggle and dance.

Freddie's husband, Grey, was by profession a lawyer, but by temperament and inclination he was a naturalist. Having a baby was right up his street. Books on neonatology and infant psychology replaced the astronomy and bird books on his night table. He gave up reading mysteries for texts on childbirth. One of these books had informed him that babies can hear in the womb, so each night he sang "I'm an Old Cowhand" directly into Freddie's stomach. Another suggested that the educational process could begin before birth. Grey thought he might try to teach the unborn to count.

"Why stop there?" Freddie said. "Teach it fractions."

Freddie was an economic historian. She had a horror of the sentimental. In secret—for she would rather have died than show it—the thought of her own baby brought her to tears. Her dreams were full of infants. Babies appeared everywhere. The buses abounded with pregnant women. The whole process seemed to her one half miraculous and the other half preposterous. She looked around her on a crowded street and said to herself, "Every single one of these people was *born*."

Her oldest friend, Penny Stern, said to her, "We all hope that this pregnancy will force you to wear maternity clothes, because they will be so much nicer than what you usually wear." Freddie usually wore her younger brother's castoff shirts, Grey's worn-out sweaters, and a couple of very old skirts. She went shopping for maternity clothes and came home empty-handed. She said, "I don't wear puffed sleeves and frilly bibs and ribbons around my neck when I'm not pregnant, so I don't see why I should have to just because I am pregnant." In the end, she wore Grey's sweaters, and two shapeless skirts with elastic waistbands. Penny forced her to buy one nice black dress, which she wore to teach her weekly class in economic history at the business school.

Grey set about renovating a small spare room that had been used for storage. He scraped and polished the floor, built shelves, and painted the walls pale pink, with the ceiling and moldings glossy white. They had once called this room the lumber room. Now they referred to it as the nursery. On one of the top shelves Grey put his collection of glass-encased bird's nests. He already had in mind a child who would go on nature hikes with him.

As for Freddie, she grimly and without expression submitted herself to the number of advances science had come up with in the field of obstetrics. It was possible to have amniotic fluid withdrawn and analyzed to find out the genetic health of the unborn and, if you wanted to know, its sex. It was possible to lie on a table and with the aid of an ultrasonic scanner see your unborn child in the womb, and to have a photograph of this view. As for

Grey, he wished Freddie could have had a sonogram every week, and he watched avidly while Freddie's doctor, a handsome, rather melancholy South African named Jordan Bell, identified a series of blobs and clouds as head, shoulders, and back. Every month in Jordan Bell's office, Freddie heard the amplified sound of her child's heart, and what she heard sounded like galloping horses in the distance.

Freddie went about her business outwardly unflapped. She continued to teach, and she worked on her dissertation. In between, when she was not napping, she made lists of baby things: crib sheets, a stroller, T-shirts, diapers, blankets. Two months before the baby was due, she and Penny went out and bought what was needed. She was glad she had not saved this until the last minute, because after an uneventful pregnancy she was put in the hospital at the beginning of her ninth month. She was monitored constantly. The sense of isolation she had cherished—just herself, Grey, and the unborn baby—was gone. She was in the hands of nurses she had never seen before and she found herself having long conversations with them. She was exhausted, uncertain, and lonely in her hospital room.

FREDDIE was admitted wearing the nice black dress Penny had made her buy, and taken to a private room that overlooked the Park. At the bottom of her bed were two towels and a hospital gown that tied up the back. Getting undressed to go to bed in the afternoon made her feel like a child banished for a nap. She did not put on the hospital gown. Instead, she put on the plaid flannel nightshirt of Grey's that she had packed in her bag weeks before in case she went into labor in the middle of the night.

"I hate it here already," Freddie said.

"It's an awfully nice view," Grey said. "If it were a little further along in the season, I could bring my field glasses and see what's nesting."

"I'll never get out of here," Freddie said.

"Not only will you get out of here," said Grey, "you will be released a totally transformed woman. You have heard Jordan say many times, 'All babies get born, one way or another.' "

Grey and Freddie had met as children at school in London, where they, along with Penny Stern, were members of a small band of Americans. They knew each other practically by heart. When Freddie was exasperated, she pushed her lank, brown hair out of her eyes. When tired, she rubbed her face. When upset, she tightened her jaw. But Grey had never seen her so upset before. He held her hand. "Don't worry," he said. "Jordan said this isn't serious. It's just a complication. The baby will be fine and you'll be fine. Besides, it won't know how to be a baby and we won't know how to be parents."

Grey had taken off his jacket and he felt a wet place where Freddie had laid her cheek. He did not know how to comfort her.

"I thought nature was supposed to take over and do all this for us," Freddie said into his arm.

"It will," Grey said.

Visiting hours began at seven o'clock. Even with the door closed Freddie could hear shrieks and coos and laughter. With her door open she could hear champagne corks being popped.

Grey closed the door. "You didn't eat much dinner," he said. "Why don't I go around the corner to the delicatessen and get you something?"

"I'm not hungry," Freddie said. She did not know what was in front of her, or how long she would be in this room, or how and when the baby would be born.

"I'll call Penny and have her bring something," Grey said.

"I already talked to her," Freddie said. "She and David are taking you out to dinner." David was Penny's husband, David Hooks.

"You're trying to get rid of me," Grey said.

"I'm not," Freddie said. "You've been here all day, practically. I just want the comfort of knowing that you're being fed and looked after. I think you should go soon."

"It's too early," said Grey. "Fathers don't have to leave when visiting hours are over."

"You're not a father yet," Freddie said. "Go."

After he left, she stood by the window to watch him cross the street and wait for the bus. It was dark and cold and it had begun to sleet. When she saw him, she felt pierced with desolation. He was wearing his old camel's-hair coat, and the wind blew through his wavy hair. He stood back on his heels as he had as a boy. He turned around and scanned the building for her window. When he saw her, he waved and smiled. Freddie waved back. A taxi, thinking it was being hailed, stopped. Grey got in, and was driven off.

EVERY three hours a nurse appeared to take Freddie's temperature, blood pressure, and pulse. After Grey had gone, the night nurse appeared. She was a tall, middle-aged black woman named Mrs. Perch. In her hand she carried what looked like a suitcase full of dials and wires.

"Don't be alarmed," Mrs. Perch said. She had a soft West Indian accent. "It is only a portable fetal-heart monitor. You get to say good morning and good evening to your child." She squirted a blob of cold blue jelly on Freddie's stomach and pushed a transducer around in it, listening for the beat. At once Freddie heard the sound of galloping hooves. Mrs. Perch timed the beats against her watch.

"Nice and healthy," Mrs. Perch said.

"Which part of this baby is where?" Freddie said.

"Well, his head is back here, and his back is there, and here is the rump, and the feet are near your ribs. Or hers, of course."

"I wondered if that was a foot kicking me," Freddie said.

"My second boy got his foot under my ribs and kicked with all his might," Mrs. Perch said.

Freddie sat up in bed. She grabbed Mrs. Perch's hand. "Is this baby going to be all right?" she said.

"Oh my, yes," Mrs. Perch said. "You're not a very interesting case. Many others much more complicated than you have come out fine, and you'll be fine, too."

At four in the morning, another nurse appeared—a florid Englishwoman. Freddie had spent a restless night, her heart pounding, her throat dry.

"Your pressure's up, dear," said the nurse, whose tag read "M. Whitely." "Dr. Bell has written orders that if your pressure goes up you're to have a shot of hydrolozine. It doesn't hurt baby—did he explain that to you?"

"Yes," said Freddie groggily.

"It may give you a little headache."

"What else?"

"That's all," Miss Whitely said.

The shot put Freddie to sleep, and she woke with a pounding headache. When she rang the bell, the nurse who had admitted her appeared. Her name was Bonnie Near, and she was Freddie's day nurse. She gave Freddie a pill and then taped a tongue depressor wrapped in gauze over her bed.

"What's that for?" Freddie said.

"Don't ask."

"I want to know."

Bonnie Near sat down on the end of the bed. She was a few years older than Freddie, trim and wiry, with short hair and tiny diamond earrings.

"It's hospital policy," she said. "The hydrolozine gives you a headache, right? You ring to get something to make it go away, and because you have high blood pressure everyone assumes that the blood pressure caused it, not the drug. So this thing gets taped above your bed in case of the one chance in about fifty-five million you have a convulsion."

Freddie turned her face away and stared out the window.

"Hey, hey," said Bonnie Near. "None of this. I noticed yesterday that you're quite a worrier. Are you like this when you're not in the hospital? I would tell you if I was worried about you. I'm not. You're just the common garden variety."

EVERY morning Grey appeared with two cups of coffee and the morning paper. He sat in a chair and he and Freddie read the paper together as they did at home.

"Is the house still standing?" Freddie asked after several days. "Are the banks open? Did you bring the mail? I feel I've been here ten months, instead of a week."

"The mail was very boring," Grey said. "Except for this booklet from the Minnesota Loon Society. You'll be happy to know that you can order a record called 'Loon Music.' Would you like a copy?"

"If I moved over," Freddie said, "would you take off your jacket and come next to me?"

Grey took off his jacket and shoes and curled up next to Freddie. He pressed his nose into her hair and looked as if he could drift off to sleep in a second. "Child World called about the crib," he said sleepily. "They want to know if we want white paint or natural pine. I said natural."

"That's what I think I ordered," Freddie said. "They let the husbands stay over in this place. They call them 'dads.' "

"I'm not a dad yet, as you pointed out," Grey said. "Maybe they'll just let me take naps here."

There was a knock on the door. Grey sprang to his feet, and Jordan Bell appeared. "Don't look so nervous, Freddie," he said. "I have good news. I think we want to get this baby born if your pressure isn't going to go down. I think we ought to induce you."

Freddie and Grey were silent.

"The way it works is that we put you on a drip of pitocin, which is a synthetic of the chemical your brain produces when you go into labor."

"We know," said Freddie. "Katherine went over it in childbirth class." Katherine Walden was Jordan Bell's nurse. "When do you want to do this?"

"Tomorrow," Jordan Bell said.

"And if it doesn't work?"

"It usually does," said Jordan Bell. "If it doesn't, we do a second-day induction."

"And if that doesn't work?"

"It generally does. If it doesn't, we do a cesarean section, but you'll be awake and Grey can hold your hand."

"Oh, what fun," said Freddie.

When Jordan Bell left, Freddie burst into tears. "Why isn't anything normal?" she said. "Why do I have to lie here day after day listening to other people's babies crying? Why is my body betraying me like this?"

Grey kissed her and then took her hands. "There is no such thing as normal," he said. "Everyone we've talked to has some story or other—heads that are too big, babies that won't budge, thirty-hour labors. A cesarean is a perfectly respectable way of getting born."

"What about me? What about me getting all stuck up with tubes and cut up into little pieces?" Freddie said, and she was instantly ashamed. "I hate being like this. I feel I've lost myself and some horrible, whimpering, whining person has taken me over."

"Think about how in two months we'll have a two-month-old baby to take to the Park."

"Do you really think everything is going to be all right?" Freddie said.

"Yes," said Grey. "I do. In six months we'll all be in Maine."

FREDDIE lay in bed with her door closed reading her brochure from the Loon Society. She thought about the cottage she and Grey rented every August in Jewell Neck, Maine, on a lagoon. There at night, with blackness all around them and not a light to be seen, they heard great horned owls and loons calling their night cries to one another. Loon mothers carried their chicks on their backs, Freddie knew. The last time she had heard those cries she had been just three months pregnant. The next time she heard them, she would have a child.

She thought about the baby shower Penny had given her—a lunch party for ten women. At the end of it, Freddie and Grey's unborn child had received cotton and wool blankets, little sweaters, tiny garments with feet, and two splendid Teddy bears. The Teddy bears had sat on the coffee table. Freddie remembered the strange, light feeling in her chest as she looked at them. She had picked them both up and laughed with astonishment.

At a red light on the way home in a taxi, surrounded by boxes and bags of baby presents, she saw something that made her heart stop: a man in a familiar tweed coat and a long paisley scarf walking down the street. It was James Clemens, who for two years had been her illicit lover.

With the exception of her family, Freddie was close only to Grey and Penny Stern. She had never been the subject of anyone's romantic passion. She and Grey, after all, had been fated to marry. She had loved him all her life. But James had pursued her; no one had ever pursued her before. He had two grown sons and had prematurely retired from his investment-banking firm to write a book on economics and architecture. He behaved as if he had little else to do in life than be amused by Freddie.

The usual signs of romance were as unknown to Freddie as the workings of a cyclotron. Crushes, she felt, were for children. She did not really believe that adults had them. One day when James came to visit wearing his tweed coat and the ridiculously long paisley scarf he affected, after many visits, lunches, and meetings Freddie had believed to be accidental, she realized with despair that she loved him.

The fact of James was the most exotic thing that had ever happened in Freddie's fairly stolid, uneventful life. He was as brilliant as a painted bunting. He was also, in marked contrast to Freddie, beautifully dressed. He did not know one tree from another. To him all birds were either robins or crows. He was avowedly urban and his pleasures were urban. He loved opera, cocktail parties, and lunches. They did not agree about economic theory, either. Nevertheless, they began to spend what now seemed to Freddie an amazing amount of time together. She learned that a pair of lovers constitute an entity not unlike a primitive society, with rules, songs and chants, taboos, and rituals. When she fell in love, she fell as if backward into a swimming pool. In the end she felt her life was being ruined.

She had not seen James for a long time. In that brief glance at the red light she saw his paisley scarf. She could see its long fringes flapping in the breeze. It was amazing that someone who had been so close to her did not know that she was having a baby. As the cab pulled away, she did not look back. She stared rigidly forward, flanked on either side by presents for her unborn child.

The baby kicked. Mothers-to-be should not be lying in hospital beds thinking about illicit love affairs. Of course, if you were like the other mothers on the maternity floor and had never had an illicit love affair, you would not be punished by lying in the hospital in the first place. You would go into labor like everyone else, and come rushing into Maternity Admitting with your husband and your suitcase. By this time tomorrow she would have her baby in her arms, just like everyone else.

AT six in the morning, Bonnie Near woke her. "You can brush your teeth," she said. "But don't drink any water. And your therapist is here to see you, but don't be long."

The door opened and Penny walked in. "And how are we today?" she said. "Any strange dreams or odd thoughts?"

"How did you get in here?" Freddie said.

"I said I was your psychiatrist and that you were being induced today and so forth," Penny said. "I just came to say good luck. Here's all the change we had in the house. Tell Grey to call constantly. I'll see you all tonight."

Freddie was taken to the labor floor and hooked up to a fetal-heart monitor, whose transducers were kept on her abdomen by a large elastic cummerbund. A stylish-looking nurse wearing hospital greens, a string of pearls, and perfectly applied pink lipstick poked her head through the door.

"Hi!" she said in a bright voice. "I'm Joanne Kelly. You're my patient today." She had the kind of voice and smile Freddie could not imagine anyone's using in private. "Now, how are we? Fine? All right. Here's what we're going to do. First of all, we're going to put this I.V. into your arm. It will only hurt a little, and then we're going to hook you up to something called pitocin. Has Dr. Bell explained any of this to you?"

"All," said Freddie.

"Neat," Joanne Kelly said. "We *like* an informed patient. Put your arm out, please." Freddie stuck out her arm. Joanne Kelly wrapped a rubber thong under her elbow. "Nice veins," she said. "You would have made a lovely junkie.

"Now we're going to start the pitocin," Joanne Kelly said. "We start off slow to see how you do. Then we escalate." She looked Freddie up and down. "O.K.," she said. "We're off and running. Now, I've got a lady moaning and groaning in the next room, so I have to go and coach her. I'll be back real soon."

Freddie lay looking at the clock, or watching the pitocin and glucose drip into her arm. She could not get a comfortable position, and the noise of the fetal-heart monitor was loud and harsh. The machine itself spat out a continual line of data.

Jordan Bell appeared at the foot of her bed. "An exciting day—yes, Freddie?" he said. "What time is Grey coming?"

"I told him to sleep late," Freddie said. "All the nurses told me that this can take a long time. How am I supposed to feel when it starts working?"

"If all goes well, you'll start to have contractions, and then they'll get stronger, and then you'll have your baby."

"Just like that?" said Freddie.

"Pretty much just like that."

But by five o'clock nothing much had happened. Grey sat in a chair next to the bed. From time to time, he checked the data. He had been checking them all day. "That contraction went right off the paper," he said. "What did it feel like?"

"Intense," Freddie said. "It just doesn't hurt."

"You're still in the early stages," said Jordan Bell when he came to check her. "I'm willing to stay on if you want to continue, but the baby might not be born till tomorrow."

"I'm beat," said Freddie.

"Here's what we can do," Jordan Bell said. "We can keep going or we can start again tomorrow."

"Tomorrow," said Freddie.

SHE woke up exhausted, with her head pounding. The sky was cloudy and the glare hurt her eyes. In the night, her blood pressure had gone up. She had begged not to have a shot—she did not see how she could go into labor feeling so terrible—but the shot was given. It had been a long, sleepless night.

She had been taken to a different labor room, where she lay alone with a towel covering one eye, trying to nap, when a new nurse appeared by her side. This one looked very young, had curly hair, and thick, slightly rose-tinted glasses. Her tag read "EVA GOTTLIEB." Underneath she wore a button that said "EVA: WE DELIVER."

"Hi," said Eva Gottlieb. "I'm sorry I woke you, but I'm your nurse for the day and I have to get you started."

"I'm here for a lobotomy," Freddie said. "What are you going to do to me?"

"I'm going to run a line in you," Eva Gottlieb said. "And then I don't know what. Because your blood pressure is high, I'm supposed to wait until Jordan gets here." She looked at Freddie carefully. "I know it's scary," she said. "But the worst that can happen is that you have to be sectioned and that's not so bad."

Freddie's head throbbed. "That's easy for you to say," she said. "I'm the section."

Eva Gottlieb smiled. "I'm a terrific nurse," she said. "I'll stay with you."

Tears sprang into Freddie's eyes. "Why will you?"

"Well, first of all, it's my job," said Eva. "And second of all, you look like a reasonable person."

Freddie looked at Eva carefully. She felt instant, total trust. Perhaps that was part of being in hospitals and having babies. Everyone you came into contact with came very close very fast.

Freddie's head throbbed. Eva was hooking her up to the fetal-heart monitor. Her touch was strong and sure, and she seemed to know Freddie did not want to be talked to. She flicked the machine on, and Freddie heard the familiar sound of galloping hooves.

"Is there any way to turn it down?" Freddie said.

"Sure," said Eva. "But some people find it consoling."

As the morning wore on, Freddie's blood pressure continued to rise. Eva was with her constantly.

"What are they going to do to me?" Freddie asked.

"I think they're probably going to give you magnesium sulfate to get your blood pressure down and then they're going to section you. Jordan does a gorgeous job, believe me. I won't let them do anything to you without explaining it first, and if you get out of bed first thing tomorrow and start moving around you'll be fine."

Twenty minutes later, a doctor Freddie had never seen before administered a dose of magnesium sulfate.

"Can't you do this?" Freddie asked Eva.

"It's heavy-duty stuff," Eva said. "It has to be done by a doctor."

"Can they wait until my husband gets here?"

"It's too dangerous," said Eva. "It has to be done. I'll stay with you."

The drug made her hot and flushed, and brought her blood pressure straight down. For the next hour, Freddie tried to sleep. She had never been so tired. Eva brought her cracked ice to suck on and a cool cloth for her head. The baby wiggled and writhed, and the fetal-heart monitor recorded its every move. Finally, Grey and Jordan Bell were standing at the foot of her bed.

"O.K., Freddie," said Jordan Bell. "Today's the day. We must get that baby out. I've explained to Grey about the mag sulfate. We both agree that you must have a cesarean."

"When?" Freddie said.

"In the next hour I have to check two patients and then we're off to the races."

"What do you think?" Freddie asked Grey.

"It's right," Grey said.

"And what about you?" Freddie said to Eva.

"It has to be done," Eva said.

Jordan Bell was smiling a genuine smile and he looked dashing and happy.

"Why is he so uplifted?" Freddie asked Eva after he had rushed down the hall.

"He loves the O.R.," she said. "He loves deliveries. Think of it this way: you're going to get your baby at last."

FREDDIE lay on a gurney, waiting to be rolled down the hall. Grey, wearing hospital scrubs, stood beside her, holding her hand. She had been prepped and given an epidural anesthesia, and she could no longer feel her legs. "Look at me," she said to Grey. "I'm a mass of tubes. I'm a miracle of modern science." She put his hand over her eyes.

Grey squatted down to put his head near hers. He looked expectant, exhausted, and worried, but when he saw her scanning his face he smiled. "It's going to be swell," Grey said. "We'll find out if it's little William or little Ella."

Freddie paced her breathing to try to breathe away her fear, but she thought she ought to say something to keep up the side. She said, "I knew we never should have had sexual intercourse." Grey gripped her hand tight and smiled. Eva laughed. "Don't you guys leave me," Freddie said.

Freddie was wheeled down the hall by an orderly. Grey held one hand, Eva held the other. Then they left her to scrub.

She was taken to a large, pale-green room. Paint was peeling on the ceiling in the corner. An enormous lamp hung over her head. The anesthesiologist appeared and tapped her foot. "Can you feel this?" he said.

"It doesn't feel like feeling," Freddie said. She was trying to keep her breathing steady.

"Excellent," he said.

Then Jordan Bell appeared at her feet, and Grey stood by her head.

Eva bent down. "I know you'll hate this, but I have to tape your hands down, and I have to put this oxygen mask over your face. It comes off as soon as the baby's born, and it's good for you and the baby."

Freddie took a deep breath. The room was very hot. A screen was placed over her chest.

"It's so you can't see," said Eva. "Here's the mask. I know it'll freak you out, but just breathe nice and easy. Believe me, this is going to be fast."

Freddie's arms were taped, her legs were numb, and a clear plastic mask was placed over her nose and mouth. She was so frightened she wanted to cry out, but it was impossible. Instead, she breathed as Katherine Walden had taught her to. Every time a wave of panic rose, she breathed it down. Grey held her hand. His face was blank and his glasses were fogged. His hair was covered by a green cap and his brow was wet. There was nothing she could do for him, except squeeze his hand.

"Now, Freddie," said Jordan Bell, "you'll feel something cold on your stomach. I'm painting you with Betadine. All right, here we go."

Freddie felt something like dull tugging. She heard the sound of foamy water. Then she felt the baby being slipped from her. She turned to Grey. His glasses had unfogged and his eyes were round as quarters. She heard a high, angry scream.

"Here's your boy," said Jordan Bell. "It's a beautiful, healthy boy."

Eva lifted the mask off Freddie's face.

"He's perfectly healthy," Eva said. "Listen to those lungs!" She took the baby to be weighed and tested. Then she came back to Freddie. "He's perfect, but he's little—just under five pounds. We have to take him upstairs to the preemie nursery. It's policy when they're not five pounds."

"Give him to me," Freddie said. She tried to free her hands, but they were securely taped.

"I'll bring him to you," Eva said. "But he can't stay down here. He's too small. It's for the baby's safety, I promise you. . . . Look, here he is."

The baby was held against her forehead. The moment he came near her he stopped shrieking. He was mottled and wet.

"Please let me have him," Freddie said.

"He'll be fine," Eva said. Then she took him away.

THE next morning Freddie rang for the nurse and demanded that her I.V. be disconnected. Twenty minutes later she was out of bed and slowly walking.

"I feel as if someone had crushed my pelvic bones," Freddie said.

"Someone did," said the nurse.

Two hours later, she was put into a wheelchair and pushed by a nurse into the elevator and taken to the Infant Intensive Care Unit. At the door, the nurse said, "I'll wheel you in."

"I can walk," Freddie said. "But thank you very much."

Inside, she was instructed to scrub with surgical soap and to put on a sterile gown. Then she walked very slowly and very stiffly down the hall. A Chinese nurse stopped her.

"I'm William Delielle's mother," she said. "Where is he?"

The nurse consulted a clipboard, and pointed Freddie down a hallway. Another nurse in a side room pointed to an isolette—a large plastic case with porthole windows. There, on a white cloth, lay her child.

He was fast asleep on his stomach, his little arm stretched in front of him—an exact replica of Grey's sleeping posture. On his back were two discs the size of nickels, hooked up to wires that measured his temperature and his heart and respiration rates on a console above his isolette. He was long and skinny and beautiful.

"He looks like a little chicken," said Freddie. "May I hold him?"

"Oh, no," said the nurse. "Not for a while. He mustn't be stressed." She gave Freddie a long look and said, "But you can open the windows and touch him."

Freddie opened a porthole window and touched his leg. He shivered slightly. She wanted to disconnect his probes, scoop him up, and hold him next to her. She stood quietly, her hand resting lightly on his calf.

The room was bright, hot, and busy. Nurses came and went, washing their hands, checking charts, making notes, diapering, changing bottles of glucose solution. There were three other children in the room. One was very tiny and had a miniature I.V. attached to a vein in her head. A pink card was taped on her isolette. Freddie looked on the side of William's isolette. There was a blue card, and in Grey's tiny printing was written "WILLIAM DELIELLE."

LATER in the morning, when Grey appeared in her room, he found Freddie sitting next to a glass-encased pump.

"This is the well-known breast pump. Electric. Made in Switzerland," Freddie said.

"It's like the medieval clock at Salisbury Cathedral," Grey said, peering into the glass case. "I just came from seeing William. He's much *longer* than I thought. I called all the grandparents. In fact, I was on the telephone all night after I left you." He gave her a list of messages. "They're feeding him in half an hour."

Freddie looked at her watch. To begin with, she had been instructed to use the pump for three minutes on each breast. Her milk, however, would not be given to William, who, the doctors said, was too little to nurse. He would be given carefully measured formula, and Freddie would eventually have to wean him from the bottle and to herself. The prospect of this seemed very remote.

As the days went by, Freddie's room filled with books and flowers, but she spent most of her time in the Infant I.C.U. She could touch William but not hold him. The morning before she was to be discharged, Freddie went to William's eight-o'clock feeding. She thought how lovely it would be to feed him at home, how they might sit in the rocking chair and watch the birds in the garden below. In William's present home, there was no morning and no night. He had never been in a dark room, or heard bird sounds or traffic noise or felt a cool draft.

William was asleep wearing a diaper and a little T-shirt. The sight of him seized Freddie with emotion.

"You can hold him today," the nurse said.

"Yes?"

"Yes, and you can feed him today, too."

Freddie bowed her head. She took a steadying breath. "How can I hold him with all this hardware on him?" she said.

"I'll show you," said the nurse. She switched off the console, reached into the isolette, and gently untaped William's probes. Then she showed Freddie how to change him, put on his T-shirt, and swaddle him in a cotton blanket. In an instant, he was in Freddie's arms.

He was still asleep, but he made little screeching noises and wrinkled his nose. He moved against her and nudged his head into her neck. The nurse led her to a rocking chair, and for the first time she sat down with her baby. All around her, lights blazed. The radio was on and a sweet male voice sang, "I want you to be mine, I want you to be mine, I want to take you home, I want you to be mine."

William opened his eyes and blinked. Then he yawned and began to cry.

"He's hungry," the nurse said, putting a small bottle into Freddie's hand.

She fed him and burped him, and then she held him in her arms and rocked him to sleep. In the process, she fell asleep, too, and was woken by the nurse and Grey, who had come from work.

"You must put him back now," said the nurse. "He's been out a long time, and we don't want to stress him."

"It's awful to think that being with his mother creates stress," Freddie said.

"Oh, no!" the nurse said. "That's not what I mean. I mean his isolette is temperature-controlled."

ONCE Freddie was discharged from the hospital she had to commute to see William. She went to the two morning feedings, came home for a nap, and met Grey for the five-o'clock. They raced out for dinner and came back for the eight. Grey would not let Freddie stay for the eleven.

Each morning, she saw Dr. Edmunds, the head of neonatology. He was a tall, slow-talking, sandy-haired man with horn-rimmed glasses.

"I know you will never want to hear this under any other circumstances," he said to Freddie, "but your baby is very boring."

"How boring?"

"Very boring. He's doing just what he ought to do." William had gone to the bottom of his growth curve and was beginning to gain a little. "As soon as he's a bit fatter, he's all yours."

Freddie stood in front of William's isolette watching him sleep. "This is like having an affair with a married man," Freddie said to the nurse who was folding diapers next to her.

The nurse looked at her uncomprehendingly.

"I mean you love the person but can only see him at certain times," said Freddie.

The nurse was young and plump. "I guess I see what you mean," she said.

At home, William's room was waiting. The crib had been delivered and put together by Grey. While Freddie was in the hospital, Grey had finished William's room. The Teddy bears sat on the shelves. A mobile of ducks and geese hung over the crib. Grey had bought a secondhand rocking chair and had painted it red. Freddie had thought that she would be unable to face William's empty room. Instead, she found that she could scarcely stay out of it. She folded and refolded his clothes, reorganized his drawers, arranged his crib blankets. She decided what should be his homecoming clothes and set them out on the changing table along with a cotton receiving blanket and a wool shawl. But even though he did not look at all fragile—he looked spidery and tough—the days were very long and it often felt to Freddie that she would never have him. She and Grey had been told that William's entire hospital stay, from day of birth, would be ten days to two weeks.

One day when she felt she could not stand much more, Freddie was told that she might try nursing him.

She was put behind a screen in William's room, near an isolette containing an enormous baby who was having breathing difficulties. She was told to keep on her sterile gown, and was given sterile water to wash her breasts with. At the sight of his mother's naked bosom, William began to howl. The sterile gown dropped onto his face. Freddie began to sweat. All around her the nurses chatted, clattered, and dropped diapers into metal bins and slammed the tops down.

"Come on, William," Freddie said. "The books say that this is the blissful union of mother and child."

But William began to scream. The nurse appeared with the formula bottle, and William instantly stopped screaming and began to drink happily.

"Don't worry," the nurse said. "He'll catch on."

At home at night she sat by the window. She could not sleep. She had never felt so separated from anything in her life. Grey, to distract himself, was stencilling the wall under the molding in William's room. He had found an Early American design of wheat and cornflowers. He stood on a ladder in his bluejeans carefully applying the stencil in pale-blue paint.

One night Freddie went to the door of the baby's room to watch him, but Grey was not on the ladder. He was sitting in the rocking chair with his head in his hands. His shoulders were shaking slightly. He had the radio on, and he did not hear her.

He had been so brave and cheerful. He had held her hand while William was born. He had told her it was like watching a magician sawing his wife in half. He had taken photos of William in his isolette and sent them to their parents and all their friends. He had read up on growth curves and had found Freddie a book on breast-feeding. He had also purloined his hospital greens to wear each year on William's birthday. Now *he* had broken down.

She made a noise coming into the room, and then bent down and stroked his hair. He smelled of soap and paint thinner. She put her arms around him and she did not let go for a long time.

THREE times a day, Freddie tried to nurse William behind a screen and each time she ended up giving him his formula. Finally, she asked a nurse, "Is there some room I could sit in alone with this child?"

"We're not set up for it," the nurse said. "But I could put you in the utility closet."

There, amidst unused isolettes and cardboard boxes of sterile water, on the second try, William nursed for the first time. She touched his cheek. He turned to her, just as it said in the book. Then her eyes crossed. "Oh, my God!" she said.

A nurse walked in. "Hurts, right?" she said. "Good for him. That means he's got it. It won't hurt for long."

At his evening feeding he howled again.

"The course of true love never did run smooth," said Grey. He and Freddie walked slowly past the Park on their way home. It was a cold, wet night.

"I am a childless mother," Freddie said.

Two days later William was taken out of his isolette and put into a plastic bin. He had no temperature or respiration or heart-rate probes, and Freddie could pick him up without having to disconnect anything. At his evening feeding when the unit was quiet, she took him out in the hallway and walked up and down with him.

The next day she was greeted by Dr. Edmunds. "I've just had a chat with your pediatrician," he said. "How would you like to take your boring baby home with you?"

"When?" said Freddie.

"Right now, if you have his clothes," Dr. Edmunds said. "Dr. Jacobson will be up in a few minutes and can officially release him."

She ran down the hall and called Grey at work. "They're springing him. Come and get us."

"You mean we can just walk out of there with him?" Grey said. "I mean just walk out with him under our arm? He barely knows us."

"Just get here. And don't forget the blankets."

A nurse helped Freddie dress William. He was wrapped in a green-and-white receiving blanket and covered with a white wool shawl. On his head was a blue-and-green knitted cap that had been Grey's. It slipped slightly sideways, giving him a rather raffish look.

They were accompanied in the elevator by a nurse. It was hospital policy that a nurse hold the baby, and hand it over at the door.

It made Freddie feel light-headed to be standing out-of-doors with her child. She felt she had just robbed a bank and gotten away with it.

In the taxi, Grey gave the driver their address.

"Not door to door," Freddie said. "Can we get out at the avenue and walk down the street just like everyone else?"

When the taxi stopped, they got out carefully. The sky was full of silver clouds and the air was blustery and chill. William squinted at the light and wrinkled his nose.

Then, with William tight in Freddie's arm, the three of them walked down the street just like everyone else.

(1985)

THE FAILURE

D OWN the long concourse they came unsteadily, Enid favoring her damaged hip, Alfred paddling at the air with loose-hinged hands and slapping the airport carpeting with poorly controlled feet, both of them carrying Nordic Pleasurelines shoulder bags and concentrating on the floor in front of them, measuring out the hazardous distance three paces at a time. To anyone who saw them averting their eyes from the dark-haired New Yorkers careering past them, to anyone who caught a glimpse of Alfred's straw fedora looming at the height of Iowa corn on Labor Day, or the yellow wool of the slacks stretching over Enid's outslung hip, it was obvious that they were Midwestern and intimidated. But to Chip Lambert, who was waiting for them just beyond the security checkpoint, they were killers.

Chip had crossed his arms defensively and raised one hand to pull on the wrought-iron rivet in his ear. He worried that he might tear the rivet right out of his earlobe—that the maximum pain his ear's nerves could generate was less pain than he needed now to steady himself. From his station by the metal detectors he watched an azure-haired girl overtake his parents, an azure-haired girl of college age, a very wantable stranger with pierced lips and eyebrows. It struck him that if he could have sex with this girl for one second he could face his parents confidently, and that if he could keep on having sex with this girl once every minute for as long as his parents were in town he could survive their entire visit. Chip was a tall, gym-built man with crow's-feet and sparse butter-yellow hair; if the girl had noticed him, she might have thought he was a little too old for the leather he was wearing. As she hurried past him, he pulled harder on his rivet to offset the pain of her departure from his life forever and to focus his attention on his father, whose face was brightening at the discovery of a son among so many strangers. In the lunging manner of a man floundering in water, Alfred fell upon Chip and grabbed Chip's hand and wrist as if they were a rope he'd been thrown. "Well!" he said. "Well!"

Enid came limping up behind him. "Chip," she cried, "what have you done to your *ears?*"

"Dad, Mom," Chip murmured through his teeth, hoping the azure-haired girl was out of earshot. "Good to see you."

He had time for one subversive thought about his parents' Nordic Pleasurelines shoulder bags—either Nordic Pleasurelines sent bags like these to every booker of its cruises as a cynical means of getting inexpensive walk-about publicity or as a practical means of tagging the cruise participants for greater ease of handling at embarkation points or as a benign means of building esprit de corps; or else Enid and Alfred had deliberately saved the bags from some previous Nordic Pleasurelines cruise and, out of a misguided sense of loyalty, had chosen to carry them on their upcoming cruise as well; and in either case Chip was appalled by his parents' willingness to make themselves vectors of corporate advertising—before he shouldered the bags himself and assumed the burden of seeing LaGuardia Airport and New York City and his life and clothes and body through the disappointed eyes of his parents.

He noticed, as if for the first time, the dirty linoleum, the assassinlike chauffeurs holding up signs with other people's names on them, the snarl of wires dangling from a hole in the ceiling. He distinctly heard the word "motherfucker." Outside the big windows on the baggage level, two Bangladeshi men were pushing a disabled cab through rain and angry honking.

"We have to be at the pier by four," Enid said to Chip. "And I think Dad was hoping to see your desk at the *Wall Street Journal.*" She raised her voice. "Al? Al?"

Though stooped in the neck now, Alfred was still an imposing figure. His hair was white and thick and sleek, like a polar bear's, and the powerful long muscles of his shoulders, which Chip remembered laboring in the spanking of a child, usually Chip himself, still filled the gray tweed shoulders of his sports coat.

"Al, didn't you say you wanted to see where Chip worked?" Enid shouted. Alfred shook his head. "There's no time."

The baggage carrousel circulated nothing.

"Did you take your pill?" Enid said.

"Yes," Alfred said. He closed his eyes and repeated slowly, "I took my pill. I took my pill. I took my pill."

"Dr. Hedgpeth has him on a new medication," Enid explained to Chip, who was quite certain that his father had not, in fact, expressed interest in seeing his office. And since Chip had no association with the *Wall Street Journal*—the publication to which he made unpaid contributions was the *Warren Street Journal: A Monthly of the Transgressive Arts;* he'd also very recently completed a screenplay, and he'd been working part-time as a legal proofreader at Bragg Knuter & Speigh for the nearly two years since he'd lost his assistant professorship in Renaissance Studies and Critical Theory at C—— College, in Connecticut, as a result of an offense involving a female undergraduate which had fallen just short of the legally actionable, and which, though his parents never learned of it, had interrupted the parade of accomplishments that his mother could brag about, back home in St. Jude; he'd told his parents that he'd quit teaching in order to pursue a career in writing, and when, more recently, his mother had pressed him for details, he'd mentioned the *Warren Street Journal,* the name of which his mother had misheard and instantly begun to trumpet to her friends Esther Root and Bea Meisner and Mary Beth Schumpert, and though Chip in his monthly phone calls home had had many opportunities to disabuse her he'd instead actively fostered the misunderstanding; and here things became rather complex, not only because the *Wall Street Journal* was available in St. Jude and his mother had never mentioned looking for his work and failing to find it (meaning that some part of her knew perfectly well that he didn't write for the paper) but also because the author of articles like "Consensual Incest" and "Self/Abuse" was conspiring to preserve, in his mother, precisely the kind of illusion that the *Warren Street Journal* was dedicated to exploding, and he was thirty-nine years old, and he blamed his parents for the person he had become—he was happy when his mother let the subject drop.

"His tremor's much better," Enid added in a voice inaudible to Alfred. "The only side effect is that he *may* hallucinate."

"That's quite a side effect," Chip said.

"Dr. Hedgpeth says that what he has is very mild and almost completely controllable with medication."

Alfred was surveying the baggage-claim cavern while pale travellers angled for position at the carrousel. There was a confusion of tread patterns on the linoleum, gray with the pollutants that the rain had brought down. The light was the color of car sickness. "New York City!" Alfred said.

Enid frowned at Chip's pants. "Those aren't *leather*, are they?"

"Yes."

"How do you wash them?"

"They're leather. They're like a second skin."

"We have to be at the pier no later than four o'clock," Enid said.

The carrousel coughed up some suitcases.

"Chip, help me," his father said.

Soon Chip was staggering out into the wind-blown rain with all four of his parents' bags. Alfred shuffled after him with the jerking momentum of a man who knew there would be trouble if he had to stop and start again. Enid lagged behind, intent on the pain in her hip. She'd put on weight and maybe lost a little height since Chip had last seen her. She'd always been a pretty woman, but to Chip she was so much a personality and so little anything else that even staring straight at her he had no idea what she really looked like.

"What's that—wrought iron?" Alfred asked him as the taxi line crept forward.

"Yes," Chip said, touching his ear.

"Looks like an old quarter-inch rivet."

"Yes."

"What do you do—crimp that? Hammer it?"

"It's hammered," Chip said.

Alfred winced and gave a low, inhaling whistle.

"We're doing a Luxury Fall Color Cruise," Enid said when the three of them were in a yellow cab, speeding through Queens. "We sail up to Quebec, and then we enjoy the changing leaves all the way back down to Newport. Dad so enjoyed the last cruise we were on. Didn't you, Al? Didn't you have a good time on that cruise?"

The brick palisades of the East River waterfront were taking an angry beating from the rain. Chip could have wished for a sunny day, a clear view of landmarks and blue water, with nothing to hide. The only colors on the road this morning were the smeared reds of brake lights.

"This is one of the great cities of the world," Alfred said with emotion.

"How are you feeling these days, Dad," Chip managed to ask.

"Any better I'd be in Heaven, any worse I'd be in Hell."

"We're excited about your new job," Enid said.

"One of the great papers in the country," Alfred said. "The *Wall Street Journal*."

"Does anybody smell fish, though?"

"We're near the ocean," Chip said.

"No, it's you." Enid leaned and buried her face in Chip's leather jacket. "Your jacket smells *strongly* of fish."

He wrenched free of her. "Mother. Please."

CHIP'S problem was a loss of confidence. Gone were the days when he could afford to *épater les bourgeois*. Except for his Manhattan apartment and his handsome girlfriend, Julia Vrais, he now had almost nothing to persuade himself that he was a functioning male adult, no accomplishments to compare with those of his sister, Denise, who at the age of thirty-two was the executive chef and co-owner of a large new high-end restaurant in Philadelphia. Chip had hoped he might have sold his screenplay by now, but he hadn't finished a draft until after midnight on Tuesday, and then he'd had to work three fourteen-hour shifts at Bragg Knuter & Speigh to raise cash to pay his August rent and reassure his landlord about his September and October rent, and then there was a lunch to be shopped for and an apartment to be cleaned and, finally, sometime before dawn this morning, a long-hoarded Xanax to be swallowed. Meanwhile, nearly a week had gone by without his seeing Julia or speaking to her directly. In response to the many nervous messages he'd left on her voice mail in the last forty-eight hours, asking her to meet him and his parents and Denise at his apartment at noon on Saturday and also, please, if possible, not to mention to his parents that she was married to someone else, Julia had maintained a total phone and E-mail silence from which even a more stable man than Chip might have drawn disturbing conclusions.

It was raining so hard in Manhattan that water was streaming down façades and frothing at the mouths of sewers. Outside his building, on East Ninth Street, Chip took money from Enid and handed it through the cab's partition, and even as the turbaned driver thanked him he realized the tip was too small. From his own wallet he took two singles and dangled them near the driver's shoulder.

"That's enough, that's enough," Enid squeaked, reaching for Chip's wrist. "He already said thank you."

But the money was gone. Alfred was trying to open the door by pulling on the window crank. "Here, Dad, it's this one," Chip said and leaned across him to pop the door.

"How big a tip was that?" Enid asked Chip on the sidewalk, under his building's marquee, as the driver heaved luggage from the trunk.

"About fifteen per cent," Chip said.

"More like twenty, I'd say," Enid said.

"Let's have a fight about this, why don't we."

"Twenty per cent's too much, Chip," Alfred pronounced in a booming voice. "It's not reasonable."

"You all have a good day now," the taxi-driver said with no apparent irony.

"A tip is for service and comportment," Enid said. "If the service and comportment are especially good I might give fifteen per cent. But if you *automatically* tip—"

"I've suffered from depression all my life," Alfred said, or seemed to say.

"Excuse me?" Chip said.

"Depression years changed me. They changed the meaning of a dollar."

"An economic depression, we're talking about."

"Then when the service really *is* especially good or especially bad," Enid pursued, "there's no way to express it monetarily."

"A dollar is still a lot of money," Alfred said.

"Fifteen per cent if the service is exceptional, really exceptional."

"I'm wondering why we're having this particular conversation," Chip said to his mother. "Why this conversation and not some other conversation."

"We're both terribly anxious," Enid replied, "to see where you work."

Chip's doorman, Zoroaster, hurried out to help with the luggage and installed the Lamberts in the building's balky elevator. Enid said, "I ran into your old friend Dean Driblett at the bank the other day. I never run into Dean but where he doesn't ask about you. He was impressed with your new writing job."

"Dean Driblett was a classmate, not a friend," Chip said.

"He and his wife just had their fourth child. I told you, didn't I, they built that *enormous* house out in Paradise Valley—Al, didn't you count eight bedrooms?"

Alfred gave her a steady, unblinking look. Chip leaned on the Door Close button.

"Dean's mother Honey and I are good friends, you know," Enid said, "and Dad and I were at the housewarming in June. It was spectacular. They'd had it catered, and they had *pyramids* of shrimp. It was solid shrimp, in pyramids. I've never seen anything like it."

"Pyramids of shrimp," Chip said. The elevator door finally closed.

"Anyway, it's a beautiful house," Enid said. "There are at least six bedrooms, and, you know, it looks like they're going to fill them. Dean's tremendously successful. He started that lawn-care business when he decided the mortuary business wasn't for him, well, you know, Dale Driblett's his stepdad, *you* know, the Driblett Chapel, and now his billboards are everywhere and he's started an H.M.O. I saw in the paper where it's the fastest-growing H.M.O. in St. Jude, it's called DeeDeeCare, same as the lawn-care business, and there are billboards for the H.M.O. now, too. He's quite the entrepreneur, *I'd* say."

"Slo-o-o-o-w elevator," Alfred said.

"This is a prewar building," Chip explained in a tight voice. "An extremely desirable building."

"But you know what he told me he's doing for his mother's birthday? It's still a surprise for her, but I can tell you. He's taking her to Paris for eight days. Two first-class tickets, eight nights at the Ritz! That's the kind of person Dean is, very family-oriented. But can you believe that kind of birthday present? Al, didn't you say the house alone probably cost a million dollars? Al?"

"It's a large house but cheaply done," Alfred said with sudden vigor. "The walls are like paper."

"All the new houses are like that," Enid said.

"You asked me if I was impressed with the house. I thought it was ostentatious. I thought the shrimp was ostentatious. It was poor."

"It may have been frozen," Enid said.

"People are easily impressed with things like that," Alfred said. "They'll talk for months about the pyramids of shrimp. Well, see for yourself," he said to Chip, as to a neutral bystander. "Your mother's still talking about it."

For a moment Chip was tempted to believe that his father had become a likable old stranger; but he knew Alfred, underneath, to be a shouter and a punisher. The last time Chip had visited his parents in St. Jude, four years earlier, he'd taken along his then-girlfriend Ruthie, a peroxided young Marxist from the North of England, who, after committing numberless offenses against Enid's sensibilities (she lit a cigarette indoors, laughed out loud at Enid's favorite watercolors of Buckingham Palace, came to dinner without a bra, and failed to take even one bite of the "salad" of water chestnuts and green peas and cheddar-cheese cubes in a thick mayonnaise sauce which Enid made for festive occasions), had needled and baited Alfred until he pronounced that "the blacks" would be the ruination of this country, "the blacks" were incapable of coexisting with whites, they expected the government to take care of them, they didn't know the meaning of hard work, what they lacked above all was *discipline*, it was going to end with slaughter in the streets, *with slaughter in the streets,* and he didn't give a damn what Ruthie thought of him, she was a visitor in *his* house and *his* country, and she had no right to criticize things she didn't understand; whereupon Chip, who'd already warned Ruthie that his parents were the squarest people in America, had smiled at her as if to say, *You see? Exactly as advertised.* Coincidentally or not, Ruthie had dumped him two weeks later.

"Al," Enid said as the elevator lurched to a halt, "you have to admit that it was a very, very nice party, and that it was *very* nice of Dean to invite us." Alfred seemed not to have heard her.

Propped outside Chip's apartment was a clear-plastic umbrella that Chip recognized, with relief, as Julia Vrais's. He was herding the parental luggage from the elevator when his apartment door swung open and Julia herself stepped out. "Oh. Oh!" she said, as though flustered. "You're early!"

By Chip's watch it was eleven-thirty-five. Julia was wearing a shapeless lavender raincoat and holding a DreamWorks tote bag. Her hair, which was long and the color of dark chocolate, was big with humidity and rain. In the tone of a person being friendly to large animals she said "Hi" to Alfred and "Hi," separately, to Enid. Alfred and Enid bayed their names at her and extended hands to shake, driving her back into the apartment, where Enid began to pepper her with questions in which Chip, as he followed with the luggage, could hear subtexts and agendas.

"Do you live in the city?" Enid said. *(You're not cohabiting with our son, are you?)* "And you work in the city, too?" *(You are gainfully employed? You're not from an alien, snobbish, moneyed Eastern family?)* "Did you grow up here?" *(Or do you come from a trans-Appalachian state where people are warmhearted and down-to-earth and unlikely to be Jewish?)* "Oh, and do you still have family in Ohio?" *(Have your parents perhaps taken the morally dubious modern step of getting divorced?)* "Do you have brothers or sisters?" *(Are you a spoiled only child or a Catholic with a zillion siblings?)*

Julia having passed this initial examination, Enid turned her attention to the apartment. Chip, in a late crisis of confidence, had bought a stain-removal kit and lifted the big semen stain off the red chaise lounge, dismantled the wall of wine-bottle corks with which he'd been bricking in the niche above his fireplace at a rate of half a dozen Merlots and Pinot Grigios a week, taken down from his bathroom wall the photographs of semierect penises which were the flower of his art collection, and replaced them with the three diplomas that Enid had long ago insisted on having framed for him.

"This is about the size of Dean Driblett's bathroom," Enid said. "Wouldn't you say, Al?"

Alfred rotated his bobbing hands and examined their dorsal sides.

"I'd never seen such an enormous bathroom."

"Enid, you have no tact," Alfred said.

It might have occurred to Chip that this, too, was a tactless remark, since it implied that his father concurred in his mother's criticism of the apartment and objected only to her airing of it. But Chip was unable to focus on anything but the hair dryer protruding from Julia's DreamWorks tote bag.

It was the hair dryer that she kept in his bathroom. She seemed, actually, to be heading out the door.

"Dean and Trish have a whirlpool *and* a shower stall *and* a tub, all separate," Enid went on. "The sinks are his 'n' hers."

"Chip, I'm sorry," Julia said.

He raised a hand to put her on hold. "We're going to have lunch here as soon as Denise comes," he announced to his parents. "It's a very simple lunch. Just make yourselves at home."

"It was nice to meet you both," Julia called to Enid and Alfred. To Chip in a lower voice she said, "Denise will be here. You'll be fine."

She opened the door.

"Mom, Dad," Chip said, "just one second."

He followed Julia out of the apartment and let the door fall shut behind him.

"This is really unfortunate timing," he said. "Just really, really unfortunate."

Julia shook her hair back off her temples. "I'm feeling good about the fact that it's the first time in my life I've ever acted self-interestedly in a relationship."

"That's nice. That's a big step." Chip made an effort to smile. "But what about the script? Is Eden reading it?"

"I think maybe this weekend sometime."

"What about you?"

"I read, um," Julia looked away, "most of it."

"My idea," Chip said, "was to have this 'hump' that the moviegoer has to get over. Putting something off-putting at the beginning, it's a classic modernist strategy. There's a lot of rich suspense toward the end."

Julia turned toward the elevator and didn't reply.

"*Did* you get to the end yet?" Chip asked.

"Oh, Chip," she burst out miserably, "your script starts off with a six-page lecture about anxieties of the phallus in Tudor drama!"

He was aware of this. Indeed, for weeks now, he'd been awakening most nights before dawn, his stomach churning and his teeth clenched, and had wrestled with the nightmarish certainty that a long academic monologue on Tudor drama had no place in Act I of a commercial script. Often it took him hours—took getting out of bed, pacing around, drinking vodka—to regain his conviction that a theory-driven opening monologue was not only not a mistake but the script's most powerful selling point; and now, with a single glance at Julia, he could see that he was wrong.

Nodding in heartfelt agreement with her criticism, he opened the door of his apartment and called to his parents, "One second, Mom, Dad. Just one second." As he shut the door again, however, the old arguments came back to him. "You see, though," he said, "the entire story is prefigured in that monologue. Every single theme is there in capsule form—gender, power, identity, authenticity—and the thing is . . . wait. Wait. Julia?"

Bowing her head sheepishly, as though she'd somehow hoped he wouldn't notice she was leaving, Julia turned away from the elevator and back toward him.

"The thing is," he said, "the girl is sitting in the front row of the classroom *listening* to the lecture. The fact that *he* is controlling the discourse—"

"And it's a little creepy, though," Julia said, "the way you keep talking about her breasts."

This, too, was true. That it was true, however, seemed unfair and cruel to Chip, who would never have had the heart to write the script at all without the lure of imagining the breasts of his young female lead. "You're probably right," he said. "Although some of the physicality there is intentional. Because that's the irony, see, that she's attracted to his mind while he's attracted to her—"

"But for a woman reading it," Julia said obstinately, "it's sort of like the poultry department. Breast, breast, breast, thigh, leg."

"I can remove some of those references," Chip said in a low voice. "I can also shorten the opening lecture. The thing is, though, I want there to be a 'hump'—"

"Right, for the moviegoer to get over. That's a neat idea."

"Please come and have lunch. Please. Julia?"

The elevator door had opened at her touch.

"I'm saying it's a tiny bit insulting to a person somehow."

"But that's not you. It's not even based on you."

"Oh, great. It's somebody else's breasts."

"Jesus. Please. One second." Chip turned back to his apartment door and opened it, and this time he was startled to find himself face to face with his father. Alfred's big hands were shaking violently.

"Dad, hi, just another minute here."

"Chip," Alfred said, "ask her to stay! Tell her we want her to stay!"

Chip nodded and closed the door in the old man's face; but in the few seconds that his back had been turned the elevator swallowed Julia. He punched the call button, to no avail, and then opened the fire door and ran down the spiral of the service stairwell. *After a series of effulgent lectures celebrating the unfettered pursuit of pleasure as a strategy of subverting the bureaucracy of rationalism, BILL QUAINTENCE, an attractive young professor of Renaissance Studies and Critical Theory, is seduced by his beautiful and adoring student MONA. Their wildly erotic affair has hardly begun, however, when they*

are discovered by BILL'*s estranged wife,* HILLAIRE. *In a tense confrontation representing the clash of Therapeutic and Transgressive world views,* BILL *and*
HILLAIRE *struggle for the soul of young* MONA, *who lies naked between them on
tangled sheets.* HILLAIRE *succeeds in seducing* MONA *with her crypto-repressive
rhetoric, and* MONA *publicly denounces* BILL. BILL *loses his job but soon discovers
E-mail records proving that* HILLAIRE *has given* MONA *money to ruin his career.
As* BILL *is driving to see his lawyer with a diskette containing the incriminating
evidence, his car is run off the road into the raging C—— River, and the diskette
floats free of the sunken car and is borne by ceaseless, indomitable currents into
the raging, erotic/chaotic open sea, and the crash is ruled vehicular suicide, and in
the film's final scenes* HILLAIRE *is hired to replace* BILL *on the faculty and is seen
lecturing on the evils of unfettered pleasure to a classroom in which is seated
her diabolical lesbian lover,* MONA. This was the one-page précis that Chip had
assembled with the aid of store-bought screenwriting manuals and had
faxed, one winter morning, to a Manhattan-based film producer named
Eden Procuro. Five minutes later he'd answered his phone to the cool,
blank voice of a young woman saying, "Please hold for Eden Procuro," followed by Eden Procuro herself crying, "I love it, love it, love it, love it, *love
it!*" But now a year and a half had passed. Now the one-page précis had
become a hundred-and-twenty-four-page script called "The Academy
Purple," and now Julia Vrais, the chocolate-haired owner of that cool,
blank personal assistant's voice, was running away from him, and as he
raced downstairs to intercept her, planting his feet sidewise to take the steps
three and four at a time, grabbing the newel at each landing and reversing
his trajectory with a jerk, all he could see or think of was a damning entry
in his nearly photographic mental concordance of those hundred and
twenty-four pages:

3: bee-stung lips, high round **breasts,** narrow hips and
3: over the cashmere sweater that snugly hugs her **breasts**
4: forward raptly, her perfect adolescent **breasts** eagerly
8: (eying her **breasts**)
9: (eying her **breasts**)
9: (his eyes drawn helplessly to her perfect **breasts**)
11: (eying her **breasts**)
12: (mentally fondling her perfect **breasts**)
15: (eying and eying her perfect adolescent **breasts**)
23: (clinch, her perfect **breasts** surging against his
24: the repressive bra to unfetter her subversive **breasts.**)
28: to pinkly tongue one sweat-sheened **breast.**)
29: phallically jutting nipple of her sweat-drenched **breast**
29: I like your **breasts.**

30: absolutely adore your honeyed, heavy **breasts.**
33: (H<small>ILLAIRE</small>'S **breasts,** like twin Gestapo bullets, can be
36: barbed glare as if to puncture and deflate her **breasts**
44: Arcadian **breasts** with stern puritanical terry cloth and
45: cowering, ashamed, the towel clutched to her **breasts.**)
76: her guileless **breasts** shrouded now in militaristic
83: I miss your mouth, I miss your perfect **breasts,** I
117: drowned headlights fading like two milk-white **breasts.**

And there were probably even more! More than he could remember! And the only two readers who mattered now were women! It seemed to Chip that Julia was leaving him because "The Academy Purple" had too many breast references and a draggy opening, and that if he could correct these few obvious problems, both on Julia's copy of the script and, more important, on the copy he'd specially laser-printed on twenty-four-pound ivory bond paper for Eden Procuro, there might be hope not only for his finances but also for his chances of ever again unfettering and fondling Julia's own guileless, milk-white breasts. Which by this point in the day, as by late morning of almost every day in recent months, was one of the last activities on earth in which he could still reasonably expect to take solace for his failures.

Exiting the stairwell into the lobby, he found the elevator waiting to torment its next rider. Through the open street door he saw a taxi extinguish its roof light and pull away. Zoroaster was mopping up inblown water from the lobby's checkerboard marble. "Goodbye, Mister Chip!" he quipped, by no means for the first time, as Chip ran outside.

Through the bead curtain of water coming off the marquee, he saw Julia's cab brake for a yellow light. Directly across the street, another cab had stopped to discharge a passenger, and it occurred to Chip that he could take this other cab and ask the driver to follow Julia. The idea was tempting; but there were difficulties.

One difficulty was that by chasing Julia he would arguably be committing the worst of the offenses for which the general counsel of C—— College, in a shrill, moralistic lawyer's letter, had once upon a time threatened to countersue him or have him prosecuted. The alleged offenses had included fraud, breach of contract, kidnap, Title IX sexual harassment, serving liquor to a student under the legal drinking age, and possession and sale of a controlled substance; but it was the accusation of stalking—of making "obscene" and "threatening" and "abusive" telephone calls and trespassing with intent to violate a young woman's privacy—that had really scared Chip and scared him still.

A more immediate difficulty was that he had four dollars in his wallet,
less than ten dollars in his checking account, no credit to speak of on any of
his major credit cards, and no prospect of further proofreading work until
Monday afternoon. Considering that the last time he'd seen Julia, six days
ago, she'd specifically complained that he "always" wanted to stay home
and eat pasta and "always" be kissing her and having sex (she'd said that
sometimes she almost felt like he used sex as a kind of medication, and that
maybe the reason he didn't just go ahead and self-medicate with crack or
heroin instead was that sex was free and he was turning into such a cheap-
skate; she'd said that now that she was taking an actual prescription medication herself she sometimes felt like she was taking it for both of them and
that this seemed doubly unfair, because she was the one who paid for the
medication and because the medication made her slightly less interested in
sex than she used to be; she'd said that if it were up to Chip, like, they probably wouldn't even go to movies anymore but would spend the whole weekend wallowing in bed with the shades down and then reheating pasta), he
suspected that the minimum price of further conversation with her would
be an overpriced lunch of mesquite-grilled autumn vegetables and a bottle
of Sancerre for which he had no conceivable way of paying.

And so he stood and did nothing as the corner traffic light turned green
and Julia's cab drove out of sight. Rain was lashing the pavement in white,
infected-looking drops. Across the street, a long-legged woman in tight
jeans and excellent black boots had climbed out of the other cab.

That this woman was Chip's little sister, Denise—i.e., was the only attractive young woman on the planet whom he was neither permitted nor
inclined to feast his eyes on and imagine having sex with—seemed to him
just the latest unfairness in a long morning of unfairnesses.

Denise picked her way through the pools and rapids on the pavement
and joined Chip beneath the marquee.

"Listen," Chip said with a nervous smile, not looking at her, "I need to
ask you a big favor. I need you to hold the fort for me here while I find Eden
and get my script back. There's a major, quick set of corrections I have to
make."

As if he were a caddie or a servant, Denise handed him her umbrella and
brushed water and grit from the ankles of her jeans. Denise was the one
who'd instructed him to invite his parents to stop and have lunch in New
York today. She'd sounded like the World Bank dictating terms to a Latin
debtor state, because unfortunately Chip owed her some money. He owed
her whatever ten thousand and fifty-five hundred and four thousand and a
thousand dollars added up to.

"See," he explained, "Eden wants to read the script this afternoon some-time, and financially, obviously, it's critical that we—"

"You can't leave now," Denise said.

"It'll take me an hour," Chip said. "An hour and a half at most."

"Is Julia here?"

"No, she left. She said hello and left."

"You broke up?"

"I don't know. She's gotten herself medicated and I don't even trust—"

"Wait a minute. Wait a minute. Are you wanting to go to Eden's, or chasing Julia?"

Chip touched the rivet in his left ear. "Ninety per cent going to Eden's."

"Oh, Chip."

"No, but listen," he said, "she's using the word 'health' like it has some kind of absolute timeless meaning."

"This is Julia?"

"She takes pills for three months, the pills make her unbelievably obtuse, and the obtuseness then defines itself as mental health! It's like blindness defining itself as vision. 'Now that I'm blind, I can see there's nothing to see.' "

Denise sighed and let her shoulders droop. "What are you saying? You want to follow her and take away her medicine?"

"I'm saying the structure of the entire culture is flawed," Chip said. "I'm saying the bureaucracy has arrogated the right to define certain states of mind as 'diseased.' A lack of desire to spend money becomes a symptom of disease which requires expensive medication. Which medication then destroys the libido, in other words destroys the appetite for the one pleasure in life that's free, which means the person has to spend even *more* money on compensatory pleasures. The very definition of mental 'health' is the ability to participate in the consumer economy. When you buy into therapy, you're buying into buying. And I'm saying that I personally am losing the battle with a commercialized, medicalized, totalitarian modernity right this instant."

Denise closed one eye and opened the other very wide. "If I grant that these are interesting issues," she said, "will you stop talking about them and come upstairs with me?"

Chip shook his head. "There's a poached salmon in the fridge. A crème fraiche with sorrel."

"Has it occurred to you that Dad is sick?"

"An hour is all it's going to take. Hour and a half at most."

"I said has it occurred to you that Dad is sick?"

Chip had a vision of his father trembling and pleading in the doorway, and to block it out he tried to summon up an image of sex with Julia, with the azure-haired stranger, with Ruthie, with anyone, but all he could picture was a vengeful, Fury-like horde of disembodied breasts.

"The faster I find Eden and make those corrections," he said, "the sooner I'll be back. If you really want to help me."

An available cab was coming down the street. He made the mistake of looking at it, and Denise misunderstood him.

"I can't give you any more money," she said.

He recoiled as if she'd spat on him. "Jesus, Denise—"

"I'd like to but I can't."

"I wasn't asking you for money!"

"Because where does it end?"

He turned on his heel and walked into the downpour and marched toward University Place, smiling with rage. He was ankle deep in a boiling gray sidewalk-shaped lake. He was clutching Denise's umbrella in his fist without opening it, and still it seemed unfair to him, it seemed *not his fault*, that he was getting drenched.

(1999)

APARTMENT HOTEL

MR. and Mrs. Morrison lived in an apartment hotel in the East Thirties. They had moved there from an apartment hotel in the East Twenties that had been torn down to make an office building.

Although the dining-room opened at seven and closed at nine, they made it a rule to breakfast at eight. Their table was in a corner by the window and was distinguished from the other tables by a fern in an etched silver bowl. It was Mrs. Morrison's fern and Mrs. Morrison's bowl.

Sometimes she brought down a few fresh flowers and took the fern up to their sitting-room. She said she wanted to give it a breath of fresh air.

The sitting-room was full of personal touches. Even if Mrs. Morrison did live in a hotel she believed in trying to make it homelike.

The hotel management had provided the dark blue carpet and the dark blue draperies with tan fringe, but Mrs. Morrison had done wonders with them. The room was filled with useless little ornaments left over from the days when they had kept house.

Mrs. Morrison couldn't remember exactly when they had decided not to keep house. After the baby had died, the house in Twenty-second Street in Chelsea had seemed too big for them, and Mr. Morrison had suggested that they live in a hotel for the winter. He thought it might brighten her up a bit.

They had been living in hotels for thirty years now.

In the evenings they played two-handed rummy, or Mr. Morrison read aloud while Mrs. Morrison sewed. She had never been a slave to a book.

Sometimes the manager of the hotel would drop in to see if they were comfortable. They always were.

After Mr. Morrison left for his office in the mornings, Mrs. Morrison usually dropped in at Dennison's to work for a bit on the parchment shade she was making, or ran up to McCreery's to do a bit of shopping and perhaps to buy the new book of crocheted-work patterns. Sometimes in the afternoons a friend or two dropped in and Mrs. Morrison ordered hot water and toast and made tea in her own tea set.

At four, Mr. Morrison came home and they took a little walk before dinner. Mr. Morrison said he liked to work up an appetite.

ONE morning Mrs. Morrison finished her parchment shade. She could hardly believe it, as it was rather an elaborate shade. But she wrapped it in tissue paper and put her name on it and said she would call for it the next day. She didn't like to be seen carrying a parcel. She was like her mother that way. And as it was only half past eleven, she decided she would run up to Maillard's for lunch. She hadn't been to their new place.

As she settled herself in the bus and got her dime out, she planned what she would eat. She had just decided on a chicken patty with mushrooms and something a little sticky for dessert, when she noticed the young girl in the seat in front of her. She seemed very nervous. Every time the bus stopped, she squirmed about and tapped her fingers on the window sill, and several times, Mrs. Morrison thought, she was going to run out of the door.

At Thirty-fourth Street, a young man got on, and slid into the seat beside the girl. "Hello, Helpless," he said.

"Helpless is a kind name for it," she said.

"There's a shorter and uglier word, but I don't know it."

"Well, if you'll tell me where we went and what we did after we left George's, I'll believe you," she said.

"We went to Tony's. And we left you in the cab with George. You were talking perfectly all right. And pretty soon the cab-driver came in and said, 'Say, Mister, them two friends of yours is down the areaway.' "

"That's a dirty lie."

"You wouldn't move for quite a while. You said you were comfortable and wanted to talk."

"Well, I'm through. When I act like that it's time to quit. I mean it. What happened then?"

"Don't you remember saying you wanted to ride to Atlantic City in a hansom cab. You were a riot. And you kept wanting to dance, only George wouldn't get up because his shirt was bulging in front."

"Well, I'm through. I mean it. It seems to me I remember some other people. Didn't one man have a banjo?"

"You asked them over, and they were terrible. You thought you could sing, and finally the girl who was with this guy got sore and left."

"I asked them over? Well, I'm through."

They were silent for a minute.

"Where are you all going tonight?" she asked.

"Nick's."

"What's the matter with Tony's?"

"Oh, he's getting to be an awful crab. He put Roy out when he started to throw that cheese."

"Where's Nick's?"

"Six-forty-three West Eleventh Street. Say, look here, Foolish, you look terrible. How about just one whiskey sour."

"For medicinal purposes only. Just one."

"That's what I said. Just one. Come on. Pull yourself together."

They got off, and Mrs. Morrison rode on to Maillard's.

WHEN Mr. Morrison came home that evening, she had her hat on. Mr. Morrison noticed that it was her new hat. "I thought we might eat out for a change," she told him. "Walk down to the old part of town and find some little place there."

"Why, yes," said Mr. Morrison. "How about the Grosvenor?"

"Someone, I forget just who it was, was telling me of a little place in Eleventh Street. I think she said it was an Italian place."

"Good," said Mr. Morrison heartily. "I haven't had any spaghetti for a long time."

THE Eleventh Street house had a brownstone front, not unlike the house Mr. and Mrs. Morrison had lived in. There was no sign in front of it.

"Ring the bell, anyway," said Mrs. Morrison. "A great many places don't have signs. Tiffany's, for instance."

Mr. Morrison rang the bell.

A dark gentleman opened the door.

"What you want?" he asked.

"I beg your pardon," said Mr. Morrison. "But we heard that this place was a restaurant."

"You got a card?"

"Certainly," said Mr. Morrison. He handed the dark gentleman a card. It said "Harold Lamson Morrison" on it.

"You got the wrong place." The dark gentleman closed the door.

"Looks as though you had the wrong address, Mother," Mr. Morrison said. They turned back toward Fifth Avenue, and took the bus home.

It was just fifteen minutes before closing time when they entered the dining-room. The headwaiter showed them to their table. He knew they were late.

They studied the menu.

"I'll have the regular dinner, Harry," said Mrs. Morrison.

"Two regular dinners," Mr. Morrison told the waiter.

As Mrs. Morrison waited for her consommé vermicelli, she leaned over and picked a dead leaf from the fern in the etched silver bowl.

(1929)

MIDAIR

A SUNNY, windy day on the lower East Side of New York. The year is 1942. Sean, aged six, is being more or less pulled along the sidewalk by his father, who has shown up from nowhere to take him home from school. Sean tries to keep the pace, although he does not remember the last time he has seen this big, exuberant man, nor is he altogether sure that he trusts him. Mary, on the other side, is nine. Her legs are longer, and she seems happy, skipping every now and then, shouting into the wind, calling him Daddy. Sean cannot hear what they're saying except in fragments—the wind tears at the words. His hand, wrist, and part of his forearm are enclosed in his father's fist. The big man strides along, red-faced, chin jutting forward proudly, his whole carriage suggesting the eagerness and confidence of a soldier marching forward to receive some important, hard-won medal.

He is not a soldier, as Sean's mother has recently explained. He is not in the Army (although a war is going on) but in something called a rest home, where people go in order to rest. He does not seem tired, Sean thinks.

"It'll be a different story now, by God," his father says as they turn the corner onto Seventh Street. "A completely different story." Energy seems to radiate from the man like an electrical charge. His body carries a pale-blue corona, and when he speaks his white teeth give off white lightning. "What a day!" He lets go of the children's hands and makes a sweeping gesture. "An absolute pip of a day. Look at that blue sky! The clouds! Seventh Street! Look how vivid the colors are!"

Sean cannot look. He is preoccupied with the unnatural force of his father's enthusiasm. It is as if all that has been pointed out is too far away to be seen. The boy's awareness is focussed on the small bubble of space immediately surrounding himself, his father, and his sister. Within that area he sees clearly—as if his life depended on it—and there is no part of him left over to see anything else.

They reach the tenement building and climb the stoop. His father hesitates at the door.

"The key," he says.

"Mother has it," Mary says.

"You haven't got it?" He rolls his head in exasperation.

"I'm sorry." Mary is afraid she has failed him. "I'm sorry, Daddy."

Sean is uneasy with her use of the word "Daddy." It sounds strange, since they never use it. It is not part of their domestic vocabulary. On those extremely rare occasions when Sean, Mary, and their mother ever mention the man, the word they have always used is "Father."

Mrs. Rosenblum, second floor rear, emerges from the house.

"Good morning," his father says, smiling, catching the door. "In you go, children."

Mrs. Rosenblum has never seen this big man before but recognizes, from his expensive clothes and confident manner, that he is a gentleman, and the father of the children. A quick glance at Mary, smiling as he touches her head, confirms everything.

"Nice," Mrs. Rosenblum says. "Very nice."

Inside, Sean's father takes the steps two at a time. The children follow up to the top floor—the fourth—and find him standing at the door to the apartment, trying the knob.

"No key here, either, I suppose."

"It's the same one," Mary says.

He gives the door a hard push, as if testing. Then he steps back, looks around, and notices the iron ladder leading up to the hatch and the roof.

"Aha! More than one way to skin a cat." He strides over to the ladder and begins to climb. "Follow me, buckos. Up the mainmast!"

"Daddy, what are you doing?" Mary cries.

"We'll use the fire escape." He pushes up the hatch and sunlight pours down. "Come on. It's fun!"

Sean can hear the wind whistling up there as his father climbs through. Mary hesitates an instant and then mounts the ladder. As she approaches the top, Sean follows her. He ascends into the sunshine and the wind.

The big man moves rapidly across the tarred roof to the rear of the building and the twin hoops of the fire-escape railing. He shouts back at the children, but his words are lost. He beckons, turns, and grabs the railings. His feet go over the edge and he begins to descend. Then he stops—his head and shoulders visible—and shouts again. Mary moves forward, the big man sinks out of sight, and Sean follows.

The boy steps to the edge and looks over. His father is ten feet below, on the fire-escape landing, red face upturned.

"Come on!" The white teeth flash. "The window's open."

The wind whips Mary's skirt around her knees as she goes over. She has to stop and push the hair out of her eyes. When she reaches the landing below, Sean grabs the hoops. Five floors down, a sheet of newspaper flutters across the cement at the bottom of the airshaft. It seems no bigger than a page from a book. He climbs down. Pigeons rise from the airshaft and scatter. On the landing, he sees his father, already inside, lifting Mary through the kitchen window. He follows quickly on his own.

The kitchen, although entirely familiar in every detail, seems slightly odd in its totality. The abruptness of the entry—without the usual preparation of the other rooms—tinges the scene with unreality. Sean follows his father and sister through the kitchen, into the hall, and to the doorway of his mother's room. His father does not enter but simply stops and looks.

"Have you been here before?" Sean asks.

"Of course he has, silly," Mary says rapidly.

His father turns. "Don't you remember?"

"I don't think so," Sean says.

As they pass the main door to the apartment, toward the front of the hall, his father pauses to slip on the chain lock.

FOR more than an hour they have been rearranging the books on the living-room shelves, putting them in alphabetical order by author. Sean's father stops every now and then, with some favorite book, to do a dramatic reading. The readings become more and more dramatic. He leans down to the children to emphasize the dialogue, shouting in different voices, gesticulating with his free arm in the air, making faces. But then, abruptly, his mood changes.

"The windows are filthy," he says angrily, striding back and forth from one to another, peering at the glass. The books are forgotten now as he goes to the kitchen. Mary quickly pushes them over to the foot of the bookcase. Sean helps. While doing this, they look very quickly, almost furtively, into each other's eyes. It takes a fraction of a second, but Sean understands. He is aware that his father's unexplained abandonment of an activity in which he had appeared to be so deeply involved has frightened Mary. His own feelings are complex—he is gratified that she is scared, since in his opinion she should have been scared all along, while at the same time his own fear, because of hers, escalates a notch.

"What's going to happen?" Sean asks quietly.

"Nothing. It's O.K." She pretends not to be afraid.

"Get Mother." The sound of water running in the kitchen.

Mary considers this. "It's O.K. She'll come home from work the way she always does."

"That's a long time. That's too long."

The big man returns with a bucket and some rags. His face seems even more flushed. "We'll do it ourselves. Wait till you see the difference." He moves to the central window, and they are drawn in his wake. Sean recognizes a shift in the atmosphere: before, with the books, there was at least a pretense of the three of them doing something together—a game they might all enjoy—but now his father's attention has narrowed and intensified onto the question of the windows. He seems barely aware of the children.

He washes the panes with rapid, sweeping movements. Then he opens the lower frame, bends through, turns, and sits on the sill to do the outside. Sean can see his father's face, concentrated, frowning, eyes searching the glass for streaks.

Sean begins to move backward.

"No," Mary says quickly. "We have to stay."

The boy stops beside the rocking chair where his mother sits after dinner.

The big man reënters, and steps back to regard the results of his work. "Much better. Much, much better." He moves on to the next window. "Fresh water, Mary. Take the bucket."

Mary obeys, and goes back to the kitchen.

The big man stares down at the street. Sean stays by the rocking chair.

"You don't remember," the big man says. "Well, that's all right. Time is different for children. In any case, the past is behind us now. What counts is the future." He gives a short, barking laugh. "Another cliché rediscovered! But that's the way it is. You have to penetrate the clichés, you have to live them out to find out how true they are. What a joke!"

Mary brings the bucket of water to his side. Suddenly he moves closer to the window. He has seen something on the street.

"God damn." He moves back rapidly. He turns and runs down the hall to the kitchen. Sean and Mary can see him closing and locking the rear windows. "Bastards!" he shouts.

Mary moves sideways to glance through the window to the street.

"What is it?" Sean asks.

"An ambulance." Her voice is beginning to quaver. "It must be that ambulance."

Now he comes back into the living room and paces. Then he rushes to the newly washed window, opens it, and tears the gauzy curtains from the rod and throws them aside. Sean can see Mary flinch as the curtains are torn. The big man moves from one window to the next, opening them and tearing away the curtains. Wind rushes through the room. Torn curtains rise from the floor and swirl about.

He gathers the children and sits down on the couch, his arms around their shoulders. Sean feels crushed and tries to adjust his position, but his father only tightens his grip. The big man is breathing fast, staring into the hall, at the door.

"Daddy," Mary says. "It hurts."

A slight release of pressure, but Sean is still held so tightly to the man's side he can barely move.

"Oh, the bastards," his father says. "The tricky bastards."

The buzzer sounds. Then, after a moment, a knock on the door. The big man's grip tightens.

Another knock. The sound of a key. Sean watches the door open a few inches until the chain pulls it short. He sees the glint of an eye.

"Mr. Kennedy? This is Dr. Silverman. Would you open the door, please?"

"Alone, are you, Doctor?" An almost lighthearted tone.

A moment's pause. "No. I have Bob and James here with me." A calm voice, reassuring to Sean. "Please let us in."

"The goon squad," his father says.

"Bob in particular is very concerned. And so am I."

"Bob is a Judas."

"Mr. Kennedy. Be reasonable. We've been through this before, after all."

"No, no." As if correcting a slow student. "This is different. I'm through with you people. I'm through with all of that. I've come home, I'm here with my children, and I'm going to stay."

A pause. "Yes. I can see the children."

"We've been having a fine time. We've been washing the windows, Doctor." An almost inaudible chuckle.

"Mr. Kennedy, I implore you to open the door. We simply must come in. We must discuss your plans."

"I'm not going to open the door. And neither are you. What we have here, Doctor, is a Mexican standoff. Do you get my meaning?"

"I'm very sorry to hear you say that." Another pause—longer this time. "Bob would like a word with you."

"Mr. Kennedy? This is Bob." A younger voice.

"I'm not coming back, Bob. Don't try any crap with me. I know why you're here."

"I'm worried about you. You're flying. You know that."

"Got the little white jacket, eh, Bob? The one with the funny sleeves?"

"Look, if you don't come back they'll assign me to Mr. Farnsworth. You wouldn't do that to me. Please."

"Cut the crap, Bob."

"Listen. I'm with you. You know that. I mean, how many times have we talked about your—"

A tremendous crash as the door is kicked in, the wall splintering where the chain has come away. Sean is aware that things are happening very fast now, and yet he can see it all with remarkable clarity. Wood chips drift lazily through the air. Three men rush through the door—two in white uniforms, one in ordinary clothes. He knows they are running toward the couch as fast as they can—their faces frozen masks of strain—but time itself seems to have slowed down.

Still clamped to his father's side, Sean feels himself rise up into the air. He sees his father's other hand make a grab for Mary, who is trying to escape. He gets hold of her hair, but she twists away with a yell. Sean feels betrayed that she has gotten away. She was the one calling him Daddy. The wind roars as the big man rushes to the window and climbs out on the sill.

"Stop where you are!" he shouts back at the men.

Sean cannot see, but he senses that the men have stopped. He can hear Mary crying, hear the wind, and hear the sound of his father's heart racing under the rough tweed of his jacket. He stares down at the street, at the cracks in the sidewalk. With the very limited motion available to his arms, he finds his father's belt and hangs on with both fists.

"You bastards," his father shouts. "What you don't realize is I can do anything. Anything!"

Something akin to sleepiness comes over Sean. As time passes he realizes—a message from a distant outpost—that he has soiled himself. Finally, they are pulled back in, with great speed and strength, and fall to the floor. His father screams as the men cover him.

IN college, his father long dead, and all memory of his father's visit in 1942 completely buried, Sean looks for a wife. He is convinced that if he doesn't find someone before he graduates, he will have missed his chance for all time. The idea of living alone terrifies him, although he is not aware that it terrifies him. He lives as if he did not have a past, and so there is a great deal about himself of which he is not aware. He is entirely ignorant of his lack of awareness, and believes himself to be in full control of his existence. He zeroes in on a bright, rather guarded girl he meets in Humanities 301, and devotes himself to winning her hand. It is a long campaign, and the odds are against him—her family disapproves vehemently, for reasons that are never made clear, and she is more intelligent than Sean, and ambitious, in a way he is not, for power in some as yet unnamed career. She is older than he is. She is not afraid of living alone. Yet in the end his tenacity prevails. Graduate school provides no route for her ambition, she drifts for a bit, and finally capitulates over the telephone. Sean is exultant.

They are married by a judge in her parents' midtown brownstone. Sean is six feet two inches tall, weighs a hundred and thirty-three pounds, and appears, with his Irish, slightly acned face, to be all of seventeen. (He is actually twenty-two.) His wife is struck by the irony of the fact that more than half of the relatives watching the event are divorced. Sean is impressed by the activity outside the window during the ceremony. The New York Foundling Hospital is being torn down—the wrecker's ball exploding walls even as the absurdly short judge drones on. For both of them—in a moment of lucidity whose importance they are too young to recognize—the ceremony is anticlimactic, and faintly ridiculous.

Four years pass, and nothing happens. They both have a small monthly income from trust funds. She dabbles in an occasional project or temporary job but always retreats in mysterious frustration to the safety of their apartment. He writes a book, but it contains nothing, since he knows very little about people, or himself. He remains a boy; the marriage that was to launch him into maturity serves instead to extend his boyhood. Husband and wife, they remain children. They live together in good will, oddly sealed off from one another, and from the world. He dreams of people jumping out of windows, holding hands, in eerie accord. He has no idea what the dreams mean, or where they come from. She confesses that she has never believed in romantic love. They are both frightened of the outside, but they respond differently. She feels that what is out there is too dangerous to fool with. He feels that, however dangerous, it is only out there that strength can be found. In some vague, inchoate way, he knows he needs strength.

Privately, without telling him, she decides to have children. Philip is born. John is born. Sean is exultant.

A summer night in 1966. Sean drives down from Harlem, where he has gotten drunk in a jazz club. The bouncer, an old acquaintance, has sold him an ounce of marijuana. Sean carries it in a sealed envelope in his back pocket. He turns off the Henry Hudson Parkway at Ninety-sixth Street, slips along Riverside Drive for a couple of blocks, turns, and pulls up in front of Judy's house. It's a strange little building—five floors with a turret up the side, a dormer window on her top-floor apartment, bits of crenellation and decoration, like some miniature castle. A Rapunzel house.

He had met her on the sidelines during a soccer game. Kneeling on the grass, he had turned his head to follow the fullback's kick, and found himself looking instead at the slender, blue-jeaned thigh of the girl standing next to him. Perhaps it was the suddenness, the abrupt nearness of the splendid curve of her backside, the images sinking into him before he had time to protect himself. The lust he felt was so pure it seemed, for all its power, magically innocent, and he got to his feet and began talking to her. (She was eventually to disappear into medical school, but never, as it turned out, from his memory.)

He stares up at the dark window. Behind the window is a room, and in the room a bed, in which for a year he has been making love to Judy. She is gone now, away for a month, driving around France in a *deux-chevaux* Citroën leased by him as a gift. The room is dark and empty, and yet he has to go in. He does not question the urge. He simply gets out of the car and approaches the building. Once he is in motion, a kind of heat suffuses him. He experiences something like tunnel vision.

Inside, he scans the mailboxes. A few letters are visible behind the grille in hers. He opens the door with his key and runs up the stairs—turning at landings, climbing, turning, climbing, until he is there, at the top floor. It is midnight, and the building is silent. He slips the key into the lock, turns and pushes. The door will not open. He has forgotten the police lock, the iron bar she'd had installed before she left—with a separate locking mechanism. He doesn't have that key. He leans against the door for a moment, and the faint scent of the room inside reaches him. He is dizzy with the scent, and the door suddenly enrages him. The scent is inside, and he must get inside.

He pounds his shoulder against the glossy black wood in a steady rhythm, putting all his weight against it. The door shakes in its hinges, but he can feel the solidity of the iron bar in the center. There is not an iota of movement in the bar. He moves back in the hallway—halfway to the rear apartment—runs forward, raises his right leg, and kicks the central panel of the door. A terrific crash, but the door does not yield. He continues to run and kick, in a frenzy, until he starts falling down.

Out of breath, he sits on the stairs to the roof and looks at Judy's door. He cannot believe there is no way to get it open. The wood is cracked in several places. Finally, as his breathing slows, he gives up. The iron bar will never move.

Slowly, swirling like smoke, an idea emerges. He turns and looks up the stairs, into the darkness. After a moment he stands up, mounts the stairs, opens the hatch, and climbs out onto the roof. The air cools him—he is drenched with sweat. Purple sky. Stars. He crosses the flat part of the roof to the front of the building, where it suddenly drops off in a steep slope—a Rapunzel roof, tiled with overlapping slate. There is a masonry ridge, perhaps an inch high, at the bottom edge, fifteen feet down. He moves sideways until he comes to a place he estimates lies directly above the dormer window. He gets down on his belly and carefully slides his legs over onto the tiles, lowering more and more of himself onto the steep incline, testing to see if he can control his downward motion. Sufficient control seems possible, and, very slowly, he releases his grip on the roof and begins to slide. His face presses against the slate, and he can feel the sweat from his cheek on the slate. From somewhere off toward Amsterdam Avenue comes the sound of a siren.

He descends blindly and stops when his toes touch the ridge. Beyond the ridge, there is empty space and a clear drop to the sidewalk, but he is unafraid. He remains motionless for several moments, and his noisy brain falls still. He is no longer drunk. A profound calm prevails, a sense of peacefulness—as sweet, to him, as water to some traveller in the desert. Carefully, he slides down sideways until his entire body lies along the ridge. He raises his head and looks at the deserted street below—the pools of light under the street lamps, the tops of the parked cars, the square patterns of the cracks in the sidewalk—and there is a cleanness and orderliness to things. He becomes aware that there is a reality that lies behind the appearance of the world, a pure reality he has never sensed before, and the knowledge fills him with gratitude.

He moves his head farther out and looks for the dormer window. There it is. He had thought to hang on to the edge of the roof and swing himself down and into the window. In his mind, it had been a perfectly straightforward procedure. In his mind, he had known he could do anything—anything he was capable of imagining. But now, as he looks at the dormer window—too far away, full of tricky angles—he sees that the plan is impossible. He immediately discards the plan, as if he had been caught up in a story that ended abruptly. He no longer has any interest in getting into the apartment.

Moving slowly and carefully, as calm in his soul as the calmness in the great purple sky above him, he retreats. Using the friction of his arms and legs, of his damp palms and the sides of his shoes, he inches his way up the sloping roof. He reaches the top of the building.

Once inside, he closes the roof door behind him and descends rapidly. He passes the door to the apartment without a glance.

A$ his children are born, Sean begins to write a book about his past. At first he is ebullient, possessed by gaiety. He doesn't remember much—his childhood all jumbled, without chronology. There are only isolated scenes, places, sights and sounds, moods, in no apparent order. It seems a small thing to write down these floating memories, to play with them at a distance. It seems like fun.

His children, simply by coming into the world, have got him started. As the work gets difficult, the fact of his children sustains him in some roundabout fashion. His gaiety changes to a mood of taut attentiveness, as the past he had trivialized with his amnesia begins, with tantalizing slowness, to reveal itself. He knows hard work for the first time in his life, and he is grateful. Soon he finds himself in a kind of trance; after hours of writing he will look down at a page or two with a sense of awe, because the work is better than anything he could reasonably have expected of himself. He will live this way for four years. In his mind, his writing, his ability to write at all, is connected to his children.

He develops a habit of going into their room late at night. Blue light from the street lamp outside angles through the large windows to spill on the waxed wooden floor. Philip is three, sleeping on his side, his small hand holding a rubber frog. Sean crosses the room and looks at John, aged two. Behind delicate eyelids, his eyes move in a dream. Sean goes to a spot equidistant from both beds and sits down on the floor, his legs folded. He stares at the pale-blue bars of light on the floor and listens. He hears the children breathe. When they move, he hears them move. His mind clears. After half an hour he gets up, adjusts their blankets, and goes to bed.

A T a small dinner party with his wife, in Manhattan, he becomes aware that the host and hostess are tense and abstracted. The hostess apologizes and explains that she should have cancelled the dinner. There had been a tragedy that afternoon. The young couple living directly above, on the eighth floor, had left a window open, and their baby girl had somehow pulled herself up and fallen through to her death.

"You're white as a ghost," his wife says as they leave the table. "Sean, you're trembling!"

They forgo coffee, with apologies, and go home immediately. Sean drives fast, parks by a hydrant, and runs up the stoop into the house.

"It's O.K., it's O.K.," his wife says.

He nods to the sitter in the living room and keeps on going, up the stairs, to the children's room. They are asleep, safe in their beds.

"We have to get guardrails," he says, going to the windows, locking them. "Bars—those things—whatever they are."

"Yes. We will," his wife whispers. "O.K."

"All the windows. Front and back."

"Yes, yes. Don't wake them, now."

That night he must sleep in their room.

SEAN lies full length in the oversize bathtub, hot water to his chin. When he comes home from work (he writes in a small office a mile away), he almost always takes a bath. Philip and John push the door open and rush, stark naked, to the tub. They're about to be put to bed, but they've escaped. Sean doesn't move. Philip's head and shoulders are visible, while John, shorter, shows only his head. Their faces are solemn. Sean stares into their clear, intelligent eyes—so near—and waits, showing no expression, so as to draw the moment out. The sight of them is a profound refreshment.

"Do it, Daddy," Philip says.

"Do what?"

"The noise. When you wash your face."

Sean rises to a sitting position. He washes his face, and then rinses by bending forward and lifting cupped handfuls of water. He simultaneously blows and moans into the handfuls of water, making a satisfying noise. The boys smile. The drama of Daddy-in-the-bath fascinates them. They can't get enough of it.

Sean reaches out and lifts first one and then the other over the edge and into the tub. His hands encompass their small chests, and he can feel the life in them. The boys laugh and splash about, slippery as pink seals fresh from the womb. They hang on his neck and slide over his chest.

His wife comes in and pulls them up, into towels. They go off to bed. Later, in the kitchen, she says, "I wish you wouldn't do that."

"What?"

"In the bath like that."

He is nonplussed. "Good heavens. Why not?"

"It could scare them."

"But they love it!"

"It's icky."

"Icky," he repeats. He goes to the refrigerator for some ice. He can feel the anger starting, his face beginning to flush. He makes a drink and goes into the living room. The anger mounts as he hears the sounds of her working in the kitchen, making dinner. Abruptly, he puts down his drink, goes into the hall, down the stairs, and out the front door. He spends the evening in a bar frequented by writers and returns home drunk at three in the morning.

A few years later, Sean drives home from the office. He has worked late, missed dinner. He thinks about his boys, and begins to weep. He pulls off the expressway and parks in the darkness by the docks. It occurs to him that he is in bad trouble. The weeping has come out of nowhere, to overwhelm him, like some exotic physical reflex, and it could as well have happened on the street or in a restaurant. There is more pressure in him than he can control, or even gauge, his pretenses to the contrary notwithstanding. As he calms down, he allows himself to face the fact that his wife has begun to prepare for the end: a whisper of discreet activity—ice-skating with a male friend on weekends, veiled references to an unknown future, a certain coyness around the house. When he goes, he will have to leave the children. He starts the car, and the boys are in his mind; he feels the weight of their souls in his mind.

He unlocks the front door of the house, hangs his coat in the closet, and climbs the stairs. Silence. A fire burns in the fireplace in the empty living room. The kitchen and dining room are empty. He moves along the landing and starts up the second flight of stairs.

"Daddy." Philip is out of sight in his bedroom, but his voice is clear, his tone direct, as if they'd been talking together, as if they were in the middle of a conversation.

"I'm coming." Sean wonders why the house is so quiet. His wife must be up in the attic. John must be asleep.

"Why were you crying?" Philip asks.

Sean stops at the top of the stairs. His first thought is not how the boy knows but if the knowledge has scared him. He goes into the room, and there is Philip, wide awake, kneeling at the foot of his bed, an expectant look on his face.

"Hi." Sean can see the boy is not alarmed. Curious, focussed, but not scared.

"Why?" the boy asks. He is six years old.

"Grownups cry sometimes, you know. It's O.K."

The boy takes it in, still waiting.

"I'm not sure," Sean says. "It's complicated. Probably a lot of things. But it's O.K. I feel better now."

"That's good."

Sean senses the boy's relief. He sits down on the floor. "How did you know I was crying?" He has never felt as close to another human being as he does at this moment. His tone is deliberately casual.

The boy starts to answer, his intelligent face eager, animated. Sean watches the clearly marked stages: First, Philip draws a breath to begin speaking. He is confident. Second, he searches for language to frame what he knows, but, to his puzzlement, it isn't there. Third, he realizes he can't answer the question. He stares into the middle distance for several moments. Sean waits, but he has seen it all in the boy's face.

"I don't know," the boy says. "I just knew."

"I understand."

After a while the boy gives a sudden large yawn, and gets under the covers. Sean goes downstairs.

THE time arrives when he must tell the boys he is going away. Philip is eight, and John almost seven. They go up into the attic playroom. Sean masks the storm in his heart and explains that no one in the family is at fault. He has no choice—he must leave, and not live in the house anymore. As he says this, the boys glance quickly at each other—almost furtively— and Sean feels a special, sharp, mysterious pang.

TWELVE years later, Sean stands on line at Gate 6 in Boston's Logan Airport, waiting to check in for Eastern's 7:45 A.M. flight to Philadelphia. He is gray-haired, a bit thick around the middle, wears reading glasses low on his nose, and walks, as he moves closer to the desk, with a slight limp, from a cartilage operation on his right knee. He wears a dark suit and a trenchcoat, and carries a soft canvas overnight bag hanging from his shoulder.

"Morning." The attendant is a black woman with whom he has checked in every Monday morning for the last two years. "It's nowhere near full," she says. "I'll upgrade you now." Sean commutes weekly between the two cities, and the airline has provided him with a special card. When first class is not full, he gets a first-class seat at no extra charge. She hands him his boarding pass, and he nods as he moves away.

He sits down and waits for the boarding call. Businessmen surround him, two military officers, three stewardesses, a student carrying a book bag from the university in Boston where Sean teaches. He doesn't recognize the student but watches him abstractedly. Philip and John are that age now. Sean recalls that when his boys entered college, in Washington and Chicago, he found himself easing up on his own students in Boston, softening his style despite himself.

The flight is called. He surrenders his ticket and moves down the enclosed walkway to the open door of the plane. The stewardess recognizes him and takes his coat. He settles down in seat 2-A and accepts a cup of coffee. The ritual is familiar and reassuring. Sean is at ease.

It had not always been thus. When he'd begun commuting, Sean was tense in the air. It had been difficult for him to look out the window without a flash of panic. In his fear, he was abnormally sensitive to the other passengers—controlling his anger at loud conversations, conscious of any intrusion, however minute, into the space allotted to him. Expansive, relaxed people irritated him the most. He could not stand the way they threw their elbows about, or thoughtlessly stretched their legs, or clumsily bumped into his seat. He found himself hating the other passengers, cataloguing their faults like a miser counting money. But eventually, as he got used to flying, he began to recognize the oddness, the almost pathological oddness of his hatred, and it went away. Only on very rough flights did it recur.

Now he can gaze down through miles of empty space without fear. He wonders why, and concludes that both his former fear of heights and his present lack of fear are inexplicable. The stewardess brings breakfast, and his right knee cracks painfully as he adjusts his position.

The tenth summer of Sunday softball. The game Sean helped to organize had become a tradition in the town of Siasconset. Philip and John began as small boys and grew to young men playing the infield. Sean's second wife had taken pictures from the start, and the effect was that of time-lapse photography—a collapsed history in which the father grew older, the sons grew taller and stronger, and everyone else stayed more or less the same. Sean stood on the mound with a one-run lead, runner at first, and two outs. The batter was Gino, a power hitter. Sean threw an inside pitch and watched Gino's hips come around, watched the bat come around, and heard the snap of solid contact. The ball disappeared in speed toward third base. Sean turned to see John frozen in the air, impossibly high off the ground, feet together, toes pointed down, his legs and torso perfectly aligned in a smooth curve, a continuous brushstroke, his long arm pointing straight up at full extension, and there, nestled deep in the pocket of his glove, the white ball. Sean gave a shout of joy, dimly aware of pain in his knee, shouting all the way down as he fell, twisting, utterly happy, numb with pleasure.

The stewardess clears away his breakfast. Below, New York City slips past. He finds the old neighborhood, even the street, but he can't make out the house where his first wife still lives. They have retained good relations, and talk on the phone every month or so. His second, younger wife approves of the first, and vice versa. Sean is absurdly proud of this.

"Do you ever dream about me?" he had once asked her on the phone. "I mean, do I ever appear in your dreams?"

Slightly taken aback, she had laughed nervously. "No. What an odd question."

"I only ask because you crop up in mine. What is it—eleven years now, twelve? You still show up now and then."

The plane lands smoothly at the Philadelphia airport. Looping his bag over his shoulder, Sean is out the door, through the building, and into a cab.

"Downtown. The Drexler Building."

In his late forties, to his amazement, and through a process he never completely understood, the board of the Drexler Foundation had asked him to direct that part of their organization which gave money to the arts. It is work he enjoys.

He pays the driver and stares up at the Drexler Building—seventy stories of glass reflecting the clouds, the sky. Pushing through the big revolving door, he crosses the lobby, quickening his step as he sees the express elevator ready to leave. He jumps through just as the doors close behind him, pushes the button for the sixty-fifth floor, and turns.

For a split second he is disoriented. Philip, his older son, stands before him on the other side of the elevator, facing front. Sean's heart lurches, and then he sees that it is a young man of Philip's age, size, and general appearance, delivering a large envelope to Glidden & Glidden, on sixty-four. For a moment the two ideas overlap—the idea of Philip and the idea of the young man—and in that moment time seems to slow down. It is as if Sean had seen his son across a supernatural barrier—as if he, Sean, were a ghost haunting the elevator, able to see the real body of his son but unable to be seen by him. An almost unbearable sadness comes over him. As he emerges from this illusion, he knows full well that his son is hundreds of miles away at college, and yet he finds within himself a pressure of love for the young man so great it is all he can do to remain silent. The elevator ascends, and Sean regains control of himself. Now he can see the young man clearly—alert, a little edgy, clear blue eyes, a bit of acne.

"I hate elevators," the young man says, his eyes fixed on the lights above the door indicating the floors.

"I'm not crazy about them, but it beats walking."

The elevator approaches sixty-four, but then the lights go out, the emergency light comes on, and it stops between sixty-three and sixty-four. A slight bump downward. Sean grabs the rail involuntarily. Under the flat white light of the emergency bulb, the young man is pale, gaunt-looking.

"Oh my God," he says.

They fall a few feet more.

The young man presses himself into a corner. His eyes are wild.

Sean is utterly calm.

"Oh God oh God oh God." The young man's voice begins to rise.

"This has happened to me several times," Sean lies. "In Chicago. Once in

Baltimore. The elevators have brakes, non-electrical, separate from all the other systems, which automatically engage if the elevator exceeds a certain speed." This, he thinks, is the truth. "Do you understand what I'm saying?"

The young man's mouth is open, as if to scream. He looks in all directions, finally at Sean.

"It can't fall. It can't. Do you understand?"

"Yes." The young man swallows hard.

"We're perfectly safe."

Sean watches the young man as several minutes go by. He remains silent, remembering his own panic in airplanes, his own need for privacy on those occasions, guessing that the boy feels likewise. After another minute, however, he can see the fear rising again in the young man's face. Sean shrugs off his bag and crosses the space between them.

"Listen," he says quietly, "it's going to be O.K."

The young man is breathing fast. He stares at Sean without seeing him. Sean reaches out and takes the young man's head in his hands.

"I want you to listen to me, now. We are quite safe. Focus on me, now. I know we are safe, and if you focus on me *you* will know we are safe." The young man sees him now. He moves his head slightly in Sean's hands.

"Hypnotism," he whispers.

"No, for Christ's sake, it isn't hypnotism," Sean says. "We're going to stay like this until the lights come on. We're going to stay like this until the door opens, or they come get us, or whatever." Sean can feel the young man begin to calm down. He holds the boy's head gently and stares into his eyes. "Good. That's good."

After a while the lights come on, the elevator rises, and the doors open. The boy jumps out. "Come on, come on!" he cries.

Sean smiles. "This is sixty-four. I'm going to sixty-five."

The young man moves forward, but the door closes. The elevator goes up one floor, and Sean gets out.

That night, as he lies in bed waiting for sleep, Sean goes over the entire incident in his mind. He laughs aloud, remembering the young man's expression when he realized Sean was going to stay in the elevator.

Then he remembers the day in 1942 when his father showed up unexpectedly, took him home from school, washed the windows, and carried him out on the windowsill. He remembers looking down at the cracks in the sidewalk. Here, in the darkness, he can see the cracks in the sidewalk from more than forty years ago. He feels no fear—only a sense of astonishment.

(1984)

THE CATBIRD SEAT

M R. Martin bought the pack of Camels on Monday night in the most crowded cigar store on Broadway. It was theatre time and seven or eight men were buying cigarettes. The clerk didn't even glance at Mr. Martin, who put the pack in his overcoat pocket and went out. If any of the staff at F & S had seen him buy the cigarettes, they would have been astonished, for it was generally known that Mr. Martin did not smoke, and never had. No one saw him.

It was just a week to the day since Mr. Martin had decided to rub out Mrs. Ulgine Barrows. The term "rub out" pleased him because it suggested nothing more than the correction of an error—in this case an error of Mr. Fitweiler. Mr. Martin had spent each night of the past week working out his plan and examining it. As he walked home now he went over it again. For the hundredth time he resented the element of imprecision, the margin of guesswork that entered into the business. The project as he had worked it out was casual and bold, the risks were considerable. Something might go wrong anywhere along the line. And therein lay the cunning of his scheme. No one would ever see in it the cautious, painstaking hand of Erwin Martin, head of the filing department at F & S, of whom Mr. Fitweiler had once said, "Man is fallible but Martin isn't." No one would see his hand, that is, unless it were caught in the act.

Sitting in his apartment, drinking a glass of milk, Mr. Martin reviewed his case against Mrs. Ulgine Barrows, as he had every night for seven nights. He began at the beginning. Her quacking voice and braying laugh had first profaned the halls of F & S on March 7, 1941 (Mr. Martin had a head for dates). Old Roberts, the personnel chief, had introduced her as the newly appointed special adviser to the president of the firm, Mr. Fitweiler. The woman had appalled Mr. Martin instantly, but he hadn't shown it. He had given her his dry hand, a look of studious concentration, and a faint smile. "Well," she had said, looking at the papers on his desk, "are you lifting the oxcart out of the ditch?" As Mr. Martin recalled that moment, over his milk, he squirmed slightly. He must keep his mind on her crimes as a special adviser, not on her peccadillos as a personality. This he found difficult to do, in spite of entering an objection and sustaining it. The faults of the woman as a woman kept chattering on in his mind like an unruly witness. She had, for almost two years now, baited him. In the halls, in the elevator, even in his own office, into which she romped now and then like a circus horse, she was constantly shouting these silly questions at him. "Are you lifting the oxcart out of the ditch? Are you tearing up the pea patch? Are you hollering down the rain barrel? Are you scraping around the bottom of the pickle barrel? Are you sitting in the catbird seat?"

It was Joey Hart, one of Mr. Martin's two assistants, who had explained what the gibberish meant. "She must be a Dodger fan," he had said. "Red Barber announces the Dodger games over the radio and he uses those expressions—picked 'em up down South." Joey had gone on to explain one or two. "Tearing up the pea patch" meant going on a rampage; "sitting in the catbird seat" meant sitting pretty, like a batter with three balls and no strikes on him. Mr. Martin dismissed all this with an effort. It had been annoying, it had driven him near to distraction, but he was too solid a man to be moved to murder by anything so childish. It was fortunate, he reflected as he passed on to the important charges against Mrs. Barrows, that he had stood up under it so well. He had maintained always an outward appearance of polite tolerance. "Why, I even believe you like the woman," Miss Paird, his other assistant, had once said to him. He had simply smiled.

A gavel rapped in Mr. Martin's mind and the case proper was resumed. Mrs. Ulgine Barrows stood charged with willful, blatant, and persistent attempts to destroy the efficiency and system of F & S. It was competent, material, and relevant to review her advent and rise to power. Mr. Martin had got the story from Miss Paird, who seemed always able to find things out. According to her, Mrs. Barrows had met Mr. Fitweiler at a party, where she had rescued him from the embraces of a powerfully built drunken man who had mistaken the president of F & S for a famous retired Middle Western football coach. She had led him to a sofa and somehow worked upon him a monstrous magic. The aging gentleman had jumped to the conclusion there and then that this was a woman of singular attainments, equipped to bring out the best in him and in the firm. A week later he had introduced her into F & S as his special adviser. On that day confusion got its foot in the door. After Miss Tyson, Mr. Brundage, and Mr. Bartlett had been fired and Mr. Munson had taken his hat and stalked out, mailing in his resignation later, old Roberts had been emboldened to speak to Mr. Fitweiler. He mentioned that Mr. Munson's department had been "a little disrupted" and hadn't they perhaps better resume the old system there? Mr. Fitweiler had said certainly not. He had the greatest faith in Mrs. Barrows' ideas. "They require a little seasoning, a little seasoning, is all," he had added. Mr. Roberts had given it up. Mr. Martin reviewed in detail all the changes wrought by Mrs. Barrows. She had begun chipping at the cornices of the firm's edifice and now she was swinging at the foundation stones with a pickaxe.

Mr. Martin came now, in his summing up, to the afternoon of Monday, November 2, 1942—just one week ago. On that day, at 3 P.M., Mrs. Barrows had bounced into his office. "Boo!" she had yelled. "Are you scraping around the bottom of the pickle barrel?" Mr. Martin had looked at her from under his green eyeshade, saying nothing. She had begun to wander about the office, taking it in with her great, popping eyes. "Do you really need *all* these filing cabinets?" she had demanded suddenly. Mr. Martin's heart had jumped. "Each of these files," he had said, keeping his voice even, "plays an indispensable part in the system of F & S." She had brayed at him, "Well, don't tear up the pea patch!" and gone to the door. From there she had bawled, "But you sure have got a lot of fine scrap in here!" Mr. Martin could no longer doubt that the finger was on his beloved department. Her pickaxe was on the upswing, poised for the first blow. It had not come yet; he had received no blue memo from the enchanted Mr. Fitweiler bearing nonsensical instructions deriving from the obscene woman. But there was no doubt in Mr. Martin's mind that one would be forthcoming. He must act quickly. Already a precious week had gone by. Mr. Martin stood up in his living room, still holding his milk glass. "Gentlemen of the jury," he said to himself, "I demand the death penalty for this horrible person."

THE next day Mr. Martin followed his routine, as usual. He polished his glasses more often and once sharpened an already sharp pencil, but not even Miss Paird noticed. Only once did he catch sight of his victim; she swept past him in the hall with a patronizing "Hi!" At five-thirty he walked home, as usual, and had a glass of milk, as usual. He had never drunk anything stronger in his life—unless you could count ginger ale. The late Sam Schlosser, the S of F & S, had praised Mr. Martin at a staff meeting several years before for his temperate habits. "Our most efficient worker neither drinks nor smokes," he had said. "The results speak for themselves." Mr. Fitweiler had sat by, nodding approval.

Mr. Martin was still thinking about that red-letter day as he walked over to the Schrafft's on Fifth Avenue near Forty-sixth Street. He got there, as he always did, at eight o'clock. He finished his dinner and the financial page of the *Sun* at a quarter to nine, as he always did. It was his custom after dinner to take a walk. This time he walked down Fifth Avenue at a casual pace. His gloved hands felt moist and warm, his forehead cold. He transferred the Camels from his overcoat to a jacket pocket. He wondered, as he did so, if they did not represent an unnecessary note of strain. Mrs. Barrows smoked only Luckies. It was his idea to puff a few puffs on a Camel (after the rubbing-out), stub it out in the ashtray holding her lipstick-stained Luckies, and thus drag a small red herring across the trail. Perhaps it was not a good idea. It would take time. He might even choke, too loudly.

Mr. Martin had never seen the house on West Twelfth Street where Mrs. Barrows lived, but he had a clear enough picture of it. Fortunately, she had bragged to everybody about her ducky first-floor apartment in the perfectly darling three-story red-brick. There would be no doorman or other attendants; just the tenants of the second and third floors. As he walked along, Mr. Martin realized that he would get there before nine-thirty. He had considered walking north on Fifth Avenue from Schrafft's to a point from which it would take him until ten o'clock to reach the house. At that hour people were less likely to be coming in or going out. But the procedure would have made an awkward loop in the straight thread of his casualness, and he had abandoned it. It was impossible to figure when people would be entering or leaving the house, anyway. There was a great risk at any hour. If he ran into anybody, he would simply have to place the rubbing-out of Ulgine Barrows in the inactive file forever. The same thing would hold true if there were someone in her apartment. In that case he would just say that he had been passing by, recognized her charming house, and thought to drop in.

IT was eighteen minutes after nine when Mr. Martin turned into Twelfth Street. A man passed him, and a man and a woman, talking. There was no one within fifty paces when he came to the house, halfway down the block. He was up the steps and in the small vestibule in no time, pressing the bell under the card that said "Mrs. Ulgine Barrows." When the clicking in the lock started, he jumped forward against the door. He got inside fast, closing the door behind him. A bulb in a lantern hung from the hall ceiling on a chain seemed to give a monstrously bright light. There was nobody on the stair, which went up ahead of him along the left wall. A door opened down the hall in the wall on the right. He went toward it swiftly, on tiptoe.

"Well, for God's sake, look who's here!" bawled Mrs. Barrows, and her braying laugh rang out like the report of a shotgun. He rushed past her like a football tackle, bumping her. "Hey, quit shoving!" she said, closing the door behind them. They were in her living room, which seemed to Mr. Martin to be lighted by a hundred lamps. "What's after you?" she said. "You're as jumpy as a goat." He found he was unable to speak. His heart was wheezing in his throat. "I—yes," he finally brought out. She was jabbering and laughing as she started to help him off with his coat. "No, no," he said. "I'll put it here." He took it off and put it on a chair near the door. "Your hat and gloves, too," she said. "You're in a lady's house." He put his hat on top of the coat. Mrs. Barrows seemed larger than he had thought. He kept his gloves on. "I was passing by," he said. "I recognized—is there anyone here?" She laughed louder than ever. "No," she said, "we're all alone. You're as white as a sheet, you funny man. Whatever *has* come over you? I'll mix you a toddy." She started toward a door across the room. "Scotch-and-soda be all right? But say, you don't drink, do you?" She turned and gave him her amused look. Mr. Martin pulled himself together. "Scotch-and-soda will be all right," he heard himself say. He could hear her laughing in the kitchen.

Mr. Martin looked quickly around the living room for the weapon. He had counted on finding one there. There were andirons and a poker and something in a corner that looked like an Indian club. None of them would do. It couldn't be that way. He began to pace around. He came to a desk. On it lay a metal paper knife with an ornate handle. Would it be sharp enough? He reached for it and knocked over a small brass jar. Stamps spilled out of it and it fell to the floor with a clatter. "Hey," Mrs. Barrows yelled from the kitchen, "are you tearing up the pea patch?" Mr. Martin gave a strange laugh. Picking up the knife, he tried its point against his left wrist. It was blunt. It wouldn't do.

WHEN Mrs. Barrows reappeared, carrying two highballs, Mr. Martin, standing there with his gloves on, became acutely conscious of the fantasy he had wrought. Cigarettes in his pocket, a drink prepared for him—it was all too grossly improbable. It was more than that; it was impossible. Somewhere in the back of his mind a vague idea stirred, sprouted. "For heaven's sake, take off those gloves," said Mrs. Barrows. "I always wear them in the house," said Mr. Martin. The idea began to bloom, strange and wonderful. She put the glasses on a coffee table in front of a sofa and sat on the sofa. "Come over here, you odd little man," she said. Mr. Martin went over and sat beside her. It was difficult getting a cigarette out of the pack of Camels, but he managed it. She held a match for him, laughing. "Well," she said, handing him his drink, "this is perfectly marvellous. You with a drink and a cigarette."

Mr. Martin puffed, not too awkwardly, and took a gulp of the highball. "I drink and smoke all the time," he said. He clinked his glass against hers. "Here's nuts to that old windbag, Fitweiler," he said, and gulped again. The stuff tasted awful, but he made no grimace. "Really, Mr. Martin," she said, her voice and posture changing, "you are insulting our employer." Mrs. Barrows was now all special adviser to the president. "I am preparing a bomb," said Mr. Martin, "which will blow the old goat higher than hell." He had only had a little of the drink, which was not strong. It couldn't be that. "Do you take dope or something?" Mrs. Barrows asked coldly. "Heroin," said Mr. Martin. "I'll be coked to the gills when I bump that old buzzard off." "Mr. Martin!" she shouted, getting to her feet. "That will be all of that. You must go at once." Mr. Martin took another swallow of his drink. He tapped his cigarette out in the ashtray and put the pack of Camels on the coffee table. Then he got up. She stood glaring at him. He walked over and put on his hat and coat. "Not a word about this," he said, and laid an index finger against his lips. All Mrs. Barrows could bring out was "Really!" Mr. Martin put his hand on the doorknob. "I'm sitting in the catbird seat," he said. He stuck his tongue out at her and left. Nobody saw him go.

Mr. Martin got to his apartment, walking, well before eleven. No one saw him go in. He had two glasses of milk after brushing his teeth, and he felt elated. It wasn't tipsiness, because he hadn't been tipsy. Anyway, the walk had worn off all effects of the whiskey. He got in bed and read a magazine for a while. He was asleep before midnight.

MR. Martin got to the office at eight-thirty the next morning, as usual. At a quarter to nine, Ulgine Barrows, who had never before arrived at work before ten, swept into his office. "I'm reporting to Mr. Fitweiler now!" she shouted. "If he turns you over to the police, it's no more than you deserve!" Mr. Martin gave her a look of shocked surprise. "I beg your pardon?" he said. Mrs. Barrows snorted and bounced out of the room, leaving Miss Paird and Joey Hart staring after her. "What's the matter with that old devil now?" asked Miss Paird. "I have no idea," said Mr. Martin, resuming his work. The other two looked at him and then at each other. Miss Paird got up and went out. She walked slowly past the closed door of Mr. Fitweiler's office. Mrs. Barrows was yelling inside, but she was not braying. Miss Paird could not hear what the woman was saying. She went back to her desk.

Forty-five minutes later, Mrs. Barrows left the president's office and went into her own, shutting the door. It wasn't until half an hour later that Mr. Fitweiler sent for Mr. Martin. The head of the filing department, neat, quiet, attentive, stood in front of the old man's desk. Mr. Fitweiler was pale and nervous. He took his glasses off and twiddled them. He made a small, bruffing sound in his throat. "Martin," he said, "you have been with us more than twenty years." "Twenty-two, sir," said Mr. Martin. "In that time," pursued the president, "your work and your—uh—manner have been exemplary." "I trust so, sir," said Mr. Martin. "I have understood, Martin," said Mr. Fitweiler, "that you have never taken a drink or smoked." "That is correct, sir," said Mr. Martin. "Ah, yes." Mr. Fitweiler polished his glasses. "You may describe what you did after leaving the office yesterday, Martin," he said. Mr. Martin allowed less than a second for his bewildered pause. "Certainly, sir," he said. "I walked home. Then I went to Schrafft's for dinner. Afterward I walked home again. I went to bed early, sir, and read a magazine for a while. I was asleep before eleven." "Ah, yes," said Mr. Fitweiler again. He was silent for a moment, searching for the proper words to say to the head of the filing department. "Mrs. Barrows," he said finally, "Mrs. Barrows has worked hard, Martin, very hard. It grieves me to report that she has suffered a severe breakdown. It has taken the form of a persecution complex accompanied by distressing hallucinations." "I am very sorry, sir," said Mr. Martin. "Mrs. Barrows is under the delusion," continued Mr. Fitweiler, "that you visited her last evening and behaved yourself in an—uh—unseemly manner." He raised his hand to silence Mr. Martin's little pained outcry. "It is the nature of these psychological diseases," Mr. Fitweiler said, "to fix upon the least likely and most innocent party as the—uh—source of persecution. These matters are not for the lay mind to grasp, Martin. I've just had my psychiatrist, Dr. Fitch, on the phone. He would not, of course, commit himself, but he made enough generalizations to substantiate my suspicions. I suggested to Mrs. Barrows, when she had completed her—uh—story to me this morning, that she visit Dr. Fitch, for I suspected a condition at once. She flew, I regret to say, into a rage, and demanded—uh—requested that I call you on the carpet. You may not know, Martin, but Mrs. Barrows had planned a reorganization of your department—subject to my approval, of course, subject to my approval. This brought you, rather than anyone else, to her mind—but again that is a phenomenon for Dr. Fitch and not for us. So,

Martin, I am afraid Mrs. Barrows' usefulness here is at an end." "I am dreadfully sorry, sir," said Mr. Martin.

It was at this point that the door to the office blew open with the suddenness of a gas-main explosion and Mrs. Barrows catapulted through it. "Is the little rat denying it?" she screamed. "He can't get away with that!" Mr. Martin got up and moved discreetly to a point beside Mr. Fitweiler's chair. "You drank and smoked at my apartment," she bawled at Mr. Martin, "and you know it! You called Mr. Fitweiler an old windbag and said you were going to blow him up when you got coked to the gills on your heroin!" She stopped yelling to catch her breath and a new glint came into her popping eyes. "If you weren't such a drab, ordinary little man," she said, "I'd think you'd planned it all. Sticking your tongue out, saying you were sitting in the catbird seat, because you thought no one would believe me when I told it! My God, it's really too perfect!" She brayed loudly and hysterically, and the fury was on her again. She glared at Mr. Fitweiler. "Can't you see how he has tricked us, you old fool? Can't you see his little game?" But Mr. Fitweiler had been surreptitiously pressing all the buttons under the top of his desk and employees of F & S began pouring into the room. "Stockton," said Mr. Fitweiler, "you and Fishbein will take Mrs. Barrows to her home. Mrs. Powell, you will go with them." Stockton, who had played a little football in high school, blocked Mrs. Barrows as she made for Mr. Martin. It took him and Fishbein together to force her out of the door into the hall, crowded with stenographers and office boys. She was still screaming imprecations at Mr. Martin, tangled and contradictory imprecations. The hubbub finally died out down the corridor.

"I regret that this has happened," said Mr. Fitweiler. "I shall ask you to dismiss it from your mind, Martin." "Yes, sir," said Mr. Martin, anticipating his chief's "That will be all" by moving to the door. "I will dismiss it." He went out and shut the door, and his step was light and quick in the hall. When he entered his department he had slowed down to his customary gait, and he walked quietly across the room to the W20 file, wearing a look of studious concentration.

(1942)

SNOWING IN GREENWICH VILLAGE

T HE Maples had moved just the day before to West Thirteenth Street, and that evening they had Rebecca Cune over, because now they were so close. A tall, always slightly smiling girl with an absent manner, she allowed Richard Maple to slip off her coat and scarf even as she stood softly greeting Joan. Richard, moving with extra precision and grace because of the smoothness with which the business had been managed—though he and Joan had been married nearly two years, he was still so young-looking that people did not instinctively lay upon him hostly duties, and their reluctance worked in him a corresponding hesitancy, so that often it was his wife who poured the drinks while he sprawled on the sofa in the attitude of a favored and wholly delightful guest—entered the dark bedroom, entrusted the bed with Rebecca's clothes, and returned to the living room. How weightless her coat had seemed!

Rebecca, seated beneath the lamp, on the floor, one leg tucked under her, one arm up on the Hide-a-Bed that the previous tenants had not yet removed, was saying, "I had known her, you know, just for the day she taught me the job, but I said O.K. I was living in an awful place called a Hotel for Ladies. In the halls they had typewriters you put a quarter in."

Joan, straight-backed on a Hitchcock chair from her parents' home in Vermont, a damp handkerchief balled in her hand, turned to Richard and explained, "Before her apartment now, Becky lived with this girl and her boy friend."

"Yes, his name was Jacques," Rebecca said.

Richard asked, "You lived with them?" The arch composure of his tone was left over from the mood aroused in him by his successful and, in the dim bedroom, somewhat poignant—as if he were with great tact delivering a disappointing message—disposal of their guest's coat.

"Yes, and he insisted on having his name on the mailbox. He was terribly afraid of missing a letter. When my brother was in the Navy and came to see me and saw on the mailbox"—with three parallel movements of her fingers she set the names beneath in a column—

"Georgene Clyde
Rebecca Cune
Jacques Zimmerman,

he told me I had always been such a nice girl. Jacques wouldn't even move out so my brother would have a place to sleep. He had to sleep on the floor." She lowered her lids and looked in her purse for a cigarette.

"Isn't that wonderful?" Joan said, her smile broadening helplessly as she realized what an inane thing it had been to say. Her cold worried Richard. It had lasted seven days without improving. Her face was pale, mottled pink and yellow; this accentuated the Modiglianesque quality established by her long neck and oval blue eyes and her habit of sitting with her back straight, her head quizzically tilted, and her hands palms downward in her lap.

Rebecca, too, was pale, but in the consistent way of a drawing, perhaps (the weight of her lids and a certain virtuosity about the mouth suggested it) by da Vinci.

"Who would like some sherry?" Richard asked in a deep voice, from a standing position.

"We have some hard stuff if you'd rather," Joan said to Rebecca; from Richard's viewpoint the remark, like those advertisements that from varying angles read differently, contained the quite legible declaration that this time *he* would have to mix the Old-Fashioneds.

"The sherry sounds fine," Rebecca said. She enunciated all of her words distinctly, but in a faint, thin voice that disclaimed for them any consequence.

"I think too," Joan said.

"Good." Richard took from the mantel the five-dollar bottle of Tio Pepe that the second man on the Spanish-sherry account had given him. So that all could share in the drama of it, he uncorked the bottle in the living room. He posingly poured out three glasses, half full, passed them around, and leaned against the mantel (the Maples had never had a mantel before), swirling the liquid as the agency's wine expert had told him to do, thus liberating the esters and ethers, until his wife said, as she always did, it being the standard toast in her parents' home, "Cheers, dears!"

Rebecca continued the story of her first apartment. Jacques had never worked. Georgene never held a job more than three weeks. The three of them contributed to a kitty, to which all enjoyed equal access. Rebecca had a separate bedroom. Jacques and Georgene sometimes worked on comic strips; they pinned the bulk of their hopes on an adventure strip titled "Spade Malone Behind the Bamboo Curtain." One of their friends was a young Socialist who never washed and always had money because his father owned half of the West Side. During the day, when the two girls were off working, Jacques flirted with a Finnish girl upstairs, who kept dropping her mop onto the tiny balcony outside their window. "A real bombardier," Rebecca said. When Rebecca moved into a single apartment for herself and was all settled and happy, Georgene and Jacques offered to bring a mattress and sleep on her floor. Rebecca felt that the time had come for her to put her foot down. She said no. Later, Jacques married a girl other than Georgene.

"Cashews, anybody?" Richard suggested. He had bought a can at the corner delicatessen expressly for this visit, though if Rebecca had not been coming, he would have bought something else there on some other excuse, just for the pleasure of buying his first thing at the store where in the coming years he would purchase so much and become so well known.

"No, thank you," Rebecca said.

Richard was so far from expecting refusal that out of momentum he pressed them on her again, exclaiming, "Please! They're so good for you." She took two and bit one in half.

He offered the dish—a silver porringer given to the Maples as a wedding present and until yesterday, for lack of space, never unpacked—to his wife, who took a greedy handful. She looked so pale that he asked, "How do you feel?," not so much forgetting the presence of their guest as parading his concern—quite genuine, at that—before her.

"Fine," Joan said, edgily, and perhaps she did.

Though the Maples told some stories—how they had lived in a log cabin in a Y.M.C.A. camp for the first three months of their married life, how Bitsy Flaner, a friend of them all, was the only girl enrolled in Bentham Divinity School, how Richard's advertising work brought him into contact with Yogi Berra—they did not regard themselves (that is, each other) as raconteurs, and Rebecca's slight voice dominated the talk. She had a gift for odd things.

Her rich old cousin lived in a metal house, furnished with auditorium chairs. He was terribly afraid of fire. Right before the depression, he had built an enormous boat to take himself and some friends to Polynesia. All his friends lost their money in the crash. He did not. He made money. He made money out of everything. But he couldn't go on the trip alone, so the boat was still waiting in Oyster Bay—a huge thing, rising thirty feet out of the water. The cousin was a vegetarian. Rebecca had not eaten turkey for Thanksgiving until she was thirteen years old, because it was the family custom to go to the cousin's house on that holiday. The custom was dropped during the war, when the children's synthetic heels made black marks all over his asbestos floor. Rebecca's family had not spoken to the cousin since. "Yes, what got me," Rebecca said, "was the way each new wave of vegetables would come in as if it were a different course."

Richard poured the sherry around again and, because this made him the center of attention anyway, said, "Don't some vegetarians have turkeys molded out of crushed nuts for Thanksgiving?"

After a stretch of silence, Joan said, "I don't know." Her voice, unused for ten minutes, cracked on the last syllable. She cleared her throat, scraping Richard's heart.

"What would they stuff them with?" Rebecca asked, dropping an ash into the saucer beside her.

BEYOND and beneath the windows, there arose a clatter. Joan reached the windows first, Richard next, and lastly Rebecca, standing on tiptoe, elongating her neck. Six mounted police, standing in their stirrups, were galloping two abreast down Thirteenth Street. When the Maples' exclamations had subsided, Rebecca remarked, "They do it every night at this time. They seem awfully jolly, for policemen."

"Oh, and it's snowing!" Joan cried. She was pathetic about snow; she loved it so much, and in these last years had seen so little. "On our first night here! Our first *real* night." Forgetting herself, she put her arms around Richard, and Rebecca, where another guest might have turned away or smiled too widely, too encouragingly, retained without modification her sweet, absent look and studied, through the couple, the scene outdoors. The snow was not taking, on the wet street; only the hoods and tops of parked automobiles showed an accumulation.

"I think I'd best go," Rebecca said.

"Please don't," Joan said with an urgency Richard had not expected; clearly she was very tired. Probably the new home, the change in the weather, the good sherry, the currents of affection between herself and her husband that her sudden hug had renewed, and Rebecca's presence had become in her mind the inextricable elements of one enchanting moment.

"Yes, I think I'll go, because you're so snuffly and peakèd."

"Can't you just stay for one more cigarette? Dick, pass the sherry around."

"A teeny bit," Rebecca said, holding out her glass. "I guess I told you, Joan, about the boy I went out with who pretended to be a headwaiter."

Joan giggled expectantly. "No, honestly, you never did." She hooked her arm over the back of the chair and wound her hand through the slats, like a child assuring herself that her bedtime has been postponed. "What did he do? He imitated headwaiters?"

"Yes, he was the kind of guy who when we get out of a taxi and there's a grate giving out steam crouches down"—Rebecca lowered her head and lifted her arms—"and pretends he's the Devil."

The Maples laughed, less at the words themselves than at the way Rebecca had evoked the full situation by conveying, in her understated imitation, both her escort's flamboyant attitude and her own undemonstrative nature. They could see her standing by the taxi door, gazing with no expression as her escort bent lower and lower, seized by his own joke, his fingers writhing demoniacally as he felt horns sprout through his scalp, flames lick his ankles, and his feet shrivel into scarlet hoofs. Rebecca's gift, Richard realized, was not that of having odd things happen to her but that of representing, through the implicit contrast with her own sane calm, all things touching her as odd. This evening, too, might appear grotesque in her retelling: "Six policemen on horses galloped by, and she cried 'It's snowing!' and hugged him. He kept telling her how sick she was and filling us full of sherry."

"What else did he do?" Joan asked.

"At the first place we went to—it was a big night club on the roof of somewhere—on the way out he sat down and played the piano until a woman at a harp asked him to stop."

Richard asked, "Was the woman *playing* the harp?"

"Yes, she was strumming away." Rebecca made circular motions with her hands.

"Well, did he play the tune she was playing? Did he *accompany* her?" Petulance, Richard realized without understanding why, had entered his tone. Clarifying the incident had become strangely important, as if his confused picture of it were the product of deliberate deceit.

"No, he just sat down and played something else. I couldn't tell what it was. He didn't play very well."

"Is this *really* true?" Joan asked, egging her on.

"And then at the next place we went to, we had to wait at the bar for a table, and I looked around and he was walking among the tables asking people if everything was all right."

"Wasn't it awful?" said Joan.

"Yes, later he played the piano there, too. We were sort of the main attraction. Around midnight, he thought we ought to go out to Brooklyn to his sister's house. Here I was, exhausted. We got off the subway two stops too early, under the Manhattan Bridge. It was deserted, with nothing going by except black limousines. Miles above our heads"—she stared up, as though at a cloud, or the sun—"was the Manhattan Bridge and he kept saying it was the 'L.' We finally found some steps and two policemen who told us to go back to the subway."

"What does this amazing man do for a living?" asked Richard.

"He teaches school. He's quite bright." She stood up, stretching, and extended a long silvery-white arm. Richard got her coat and said he'd walk her home.

"It's only three-quarters of a block," Rebecca protested, in a voice free of any insistent inflection.

"You must walk her home, Dick," Joan said. "Pick up a pack of cigarettes." The idea of his walking in the snow seemed to please her, as if she were anticipating how he would bring back with him, in the snow on his shoulders and the coldness of his face, all the sensations of the walk she was not well enough to risk.

"You should stop smoking for a day or two," he told her.

Joan waved them goodbye from the head of the stairs.

THE snow, invisible except around street lights, exerted a fluttering, romantic pressure on their faces. "Coming down hard now," Richard said.

"Yes."

At the corner, where the snow gave the green light a watery blueness, her hesitancy in following him as he turned to walk with the light across Thirteenth Street led him to ask, "It is this side of the street you live on, isn't it?"

"Yes."

"I thought I remembered from the time we drove you back from the movies." The Maples had been living in the West Eighties then. "I remember I had an impression of big buildings."

"The church and the butchers' school," Rebecca said. "Every day about ten, when I'm going to work, the boys learning to be butchers come out for recess all bloody and laughing."

Richard looked up at the church; the steeple was fragmentarily silhouetted against the scattered lit windows of a tall improvement on Seventh Avenue. "Poor church," he said. "It's hard in the city for a steeple to be the tallest thing."

Rebecca said nothing—not even her habitual "Yes." He felt rebuked for being preachy. In his embarrassment, he directed her attention to the first next thing he saw—a poorly lettered sign above a great door. " 'Food Trades Vocational High School,' " he read aloud. "The people upstairs told us that our apartment was part of a duplex once, and the man in it was an Englishman who called himself a Purveyor of Elegant Produce. He kept a woman in there."

"Those big windows," Rebecca said, pointing up at an apartment house, "face mine across the street. I can look in and feel we are neighbors. Someone's always in there—I don't know what they do for a living."

After a few more steps, they halted, and Rebecca, in a voice that Richard imagined to be slightly louder than her ordinary one, said, "Do you want to come up and see where I live?"

"Sure." It seemed implausible to refuse.

They descended four concrete steps, opened a shabby orange door, entered an overheated half-basement lobby, and began to climb four flights of wooden stairs. Richard's suspicion on the street that he was trespassing beyond the public gardens of courtesy turned to certain guilt. Few experiences so savor of the illicit as mounting stairs behind a woman's fanny. Three years ago, Joan had lived in a fourth-floor walkup, in Cambridge. Richard never took her home, even when the whole business, down to the last intimacy, had become formula, without the fear that the landlord, justifiably furious, would leap from his door and devour him as they passed.

Opening her door, Rebecca said, "It's hot as hell in here," swearing for the first time in his hearing. She turned on a weak light. The room was small; slanting planes, the underside of the building's roof, intersecting the ceiling and walls, cut large prismatic volumes from Rebecca's living space. As he moved farther forward, toward Rebecca, who had not yet removed her coat, Richard perceived, on his right, an unexpected area, created where the steeply slanting roof extended itself to the floor. Here a double bed had been placed. Tightly bounded on three sides, the bed had the appearance not so much of a piece of furniture as of a permanently installed, blanketed platform. He quickly took his eyes from it and, unable to face Rebecca at once, stared at two kitchen chairs, a metal bridge lamp, around the rim of whose shade plump fish and helm wheels alternated, and a four-shelf bookcase—all of which, being slender and proximate to a tilting wall, had an air of threatened verticality.

"Yes, here's the stove on top of the refrigerator I told you about," Rebecca said. "Or did I?"

The refrigerator was several inches narrower than its burden, and the arrangement was T-shaped. He touched the stove's white side. "This room is quite sort of nice," he said.

"Here's the view," she said. He moved to stand beside her at the window, lifting aside the curtains and peering through tiny, flawed panes into the apartment across the street.

"That guy *does* have a huge window," Richard said.

She made a brief agreeing noise of "n"s.

Though all the lamps were on, the apartment across the street was empty. "Looks like a furniture store," he said. Rebecca had still not taken off her coat. "The snow's keeping up," he said.

"Yes. It is."

"Well"—this word too loud; he finished the sentence too softly—"thanks for letting me see it. I hope—have you read this?" He had noticed a copy of "Auntie Mame" lying on a hassock.

"I haven't had the time," she said.

"I haven't read it either. Just reviews. That's all I ever read."

This got him to the door. There, ridiculously, he turned. It was only at the door, he decided in retrospect, that her conduct was quite inexcusable: not only did she stand unnecessarily close but, by shifting the weight of her body to one leg and leaning her head sidewise, she lowered her height several inches, placing him in a dominating position exactly fitted to the broad, passive shadows she must have known were on her face.

"Well . . ." he said.

"Well." Her echo was immediate and possibly meaningless.

"Don't—don't let the b-butchers get you." The stammer, of course, ruined the joke, and her laugh, which had begun as soon as she had seen by his face that he would attempt something funny, was completed ahead of his utterance.

As he went down the stairs, she rested both hands on the banister and looked down toward the next landing. "Good night," she said.

"Night." He looked up; she had gone into her room. Oh, but they were close.

(1956)

I SEE YOU, BIANCA

MY friend Nicholas is about the only person I know who has no particular quarrel with the city as it is these days. He thinks New York is all right. It isn't that he is any better off than the rest of us. His neighborhood, like all our neighborhoods, is falling apart, with too many buildings half up and half down, and too many temporary sidewalks, and too many doomed houses with big Xs on their windows. The city has been like that for years now, uneasy and not very reasonable, but in all the shakiness Nicholas has managed to keep a fair balance. He was born here, in a house on 114th Street, within sight of the East River, and he trusts the city. He believes anyone with determination and patience can find a nice place to live and have the kind of life he wants here. His own apartment would look much as it does whether he lived in Rome or Brussels or Manchester. He has a floor through—two rooms made into one long room with big windows at each end, in a very modest brownstone, a little pre–Civil War house on East Twelfth Street near Fourth Avenue. His room is a spacious oblong of shadow and light—he made it like that, cavernous and hospitable—and it looks as though not two but ten or twenty rooms had contributed their best angles and their best corners and their best-kept secrets of depths and mood to it. Sometimes it seems to be the anteroom to many other rooms, and sometimes it seems to be the extension of many other rooms. It is like a telescope and at the same time it is like what you see through a telescope. What it is like, more than anything, is a private room hidden backstage in a very busy theatre where the season is in full swing. The ceiling, mysteriously, is covered in stamped tin. At night the patterned ceiling seems to move with the flickering shadows, and in the daytime an occasional shadow drifts slowly across the tin as though it was searching for a permanent refuge. But there is no permanence here—there is only the valiant illusion of a permanence that is hardly more substantial than the shadow that touches it. The house is to be torn down. Nicholas has his apartment by the month, no lease and no assurance that he will still be here a year or even three months from now. Sometimes the furnace breaks down in the dead of winter, and then there is a very cold spell for a few days until the furnace is repaired—the landlord is too sensible to buy a new furnace for a house that may vanish overnight. When anything gets out of order inside the apartment, Nicholas repairs it himself. (He thinks about the low rent he pays and not about the reason for the low rent.) When a wall or a ceiling has to be painted, he paints it. When the books begin to pile up on the floor, he puts up more shelves to join the shelves that now cover most of one long wall from the floor to the ceiling. He builds a cabinet to hide a bad spot in the end wall. The two old rooms, his one room, never had such attention as they are getting in their last days.

The house looks north and Nicholas has the second floor, with windows looking north onto Twelfth Street and south onto back yards and the backs and sides of other houses and buildings. The neighborhood is a kind of no man's land, bleak in the daytime and forbidding at night, very near to the Village but not part of the Village, and not a part, either, of the lower East Side. Twelfth Street at that point is very narrow and noisy. Elderly buildings that are not going to last much longer stand side by side with the enormous, blank façades of nearly new apartment houses, and there is a constant caravan of quarrelsome, cumbersome traffic moving toward the comparative freedom of Fourth Avenue. To his right Nicholas looks across the wide, stunted expanse of Fourth Avenue, where the traffic rolls steadily uptown. Like many exceedingly ugly parts of the city, Fourth Avenue is at its best in the rain, especially in the rain at night, when the whole scene, buildings, cars, and street, streams with such a black and garish intensity that it is beautiful, as long as one is safe from it—very safe, with both feet on the familiar floor of a familiar room filled with books, records, living plants, pictures and drawings, a tiny piano, chairs and tables and mirrors, and a long desk and a bed. All that is familiar is inside, and all the discontent is outside, and Nicholas can stand at his windows and look out on the noise and confusion with the cheerful interest of one who contemplates a puzzle he did not create and is not going to be called upon to solve. From the top of a tall filing cabinet near him, Bianca, his small white cat, also gazes at the street. It is afternoon now, and the sun is shining, and Bianca is there on the cabinet, looking out, only to be near Nicholas and to see what he sees. But she sees nothing.

What is that out there?

That is a view, Bianca.

And what is a view?

A view is where we are not. Where we are is never a view.

Bianca is interested only in where she is, and what she can see and hope to touch with her nose and paws. She looks down at the floor. She knows it well—the polished wood and the small rugs that are arranged here and there. She knows the floor—how safe it is, always there to catch her when she jumps down, and always very solid and familiar under her paws when she is getting ready to jump up. She likes to fly through the air, from a book-case on one side of the room to a table on the other side, flying across the room without even looking at the floor and without making a sound. But whether she looks at it or not, she knows the floor is always there, the dependable floor, all over the apartment. Even in the bathroom, under the old-fashioned bathtub, and even under the bed, and under the lowest shelf in the kitchen, Bianca finds the well-known floor that has been her ground—her playground and her proving ground—during all of her three years of life.

Nicholas has been standing and staring at rowdy Twelfth Street for a long time now, and Bianca, rising, stretching, and yawning on top of the filing cabinet, looks down at the floor and sees a patch of sunlight there. She jumps down and walks over to the patch of sun and sits in it. Very nice in the sun, and Bianca sinks slowly down until she is lying full length in the warmth. The hot strong light makes her fur whiter and denser. She is drowsy now. The sun that draws the color from her eyes, making them empty and bright, has also drawn all resistance from her bones, and she grows limp and flattens out into sleep. She is very flat there on the shining floor—flat and blurred—a thin cat with soft white fur and a blunt, patient Egyptian head. She sleeps peacefully on her side, with her front paws crossed and her back paws placed neatly one behind the other, and from time to time her tail twitches impatiently in her dream. But the dream is too frail to hold her, and she sinks through it and continues to sink until she lies motionless in the abyss of deepest sleep. There is glittering dust in the broad ray that shines on her, and now Bianca is dust-colored, paler and purer than white, and so weightless that she seems about to vanish, as though she were made of the radiance that pours down on her and must go when it goes.

Bianca is sleeping not far from Nicholas's bed, which is wide and low and stands sidewise against the wall. Behind the wall at that point is a long-lost fireplace, hidden away years before Nicholas took the apartment. But he has a second fireplace in the back part of the long room, and although it stopped working years ago, it was left open, and Nicholas has made a garden in it, a conservatory. The plants stand in tiers in the fireplace and on the floor close around it, and they flourish in the perpetual illumination of an electric bulb hidden in the chimney. Something is always in bloom. There are an ivy geranium, a rose geranium, and plain geraniums in pink and white. Then there are begonias, and feathery ferns, and a white violet, and several unnamed infant plants starting their lives in tiny pots. The jug for watering them all stands on the floor beside them, and it is kept full because Bianca likes to drink from it and occasionally to play with it, dipping in first one paw and then the other. She disturbs the water so that she can peer down into it and see the strange new depths she has created. She taps the leaves of the plants and then sits watching them. Perhaps she hopes they will hit back.

Also in this back half is Nicholas's kitchen, which is complete and well furnished, and separated from the rest of the room by a high counter. The kitchen gets the full light of one of the two windows that give him his back view. When he looks directly across, he sees the blank side wall of an old warehouse and, above, the sky. Looking straight down, he sees a neglected patch, a tiny wasteland that was once the garden of this house. It is a pathetic little spot of ground, hidden and forgotten and closed in and nearly sunless, but there is still enough strength in the earth to receive and nourish a stray ailanthus tree that sprouted there and grew unnoticed until it reached Nicholas's window. Nobody saw the little tree grow past the basement and the first floor because nobody lives down there, but once it touched the sill of Nicholas's room he welcomed it as though it was home at last after having delayed much too long on the way. He loved the tree and carried on about it as though he had been given the key to his inheritance, or a vision of it. He leaned out of the window and touched the leaves, and then he got out on the fire escape and hung over it, making sure it was healthy. He photographed it, and took a leaf, to make a drawing of it. And the little ailanthus, New York's hardship tree, changed at his touch from an overgrown weed to a giant fern of extraordinary importance. From the kitchen counter, Bianca watched, purring speculatively. Her paws were folded under her chest and her tail was curled around her. She was content. Watching Nicholas at the ailanthus was almost as good as watching him at the stove. When he climbed back into the room she continued to watch the few leaves that were high enough to appear, trembling, at the edge of the sill. Nicholas stood and looked at her, but she ignored him. As she stared toward the light her eyes grew paler, and as they grew paler they grew more definite. She looked very alert, but still she ignored him. He wanted to annoy her. He shouted at her. "Bianca," he shouted. "I see you!" Bianca narrowed her eyes. "I see you!" Nicholas yelled. "I see you, Bianca. I *see* you,

Bianca. I see you. I see you. I SEE you!" Then he was silent, and after a minute Bianca turned her head and looked at him, but only to show there was no contest—her will was stronger, why did he bother?—and then she looked away. She had won. She always did.

IN the summer it rains—sudden summer rain that hammers against the windowpanes and causes the ailanthus to stagger and shiver in gratitude for having enough water for once in its life. What a change in the weather, as the heavy breathless summer lifts to reveal a new world of freedom—free air, free movement, clean streets and clean roofs and easy sleep. Bianca stares at the rain as it streams down the glass of the window. One drop survives the battering and rolls, all in one piece, down the pane. Bianca jumps for it, and through the glass she catches it, flattening it with her paw so that she can no longer see it. Then she looks at her chilled paw and, finding it empty, she begins to wash it, chewing irritably at it. But one paw leads to another and she has four of them. She washes industriously. She takes very good care of her only coat. She is never idle, with her grooming to do, and her journeys to take, and then she attends on Nicholas. He is in and out of the apartment a good deal, and she often waits for him at the head of the stairs, so that he will see her first thing when he opens the door from the outside. When he is in the apartment she stays near him. If she happens to be on one of her journeys when he gets home, she appears at the window almost before he has taken off his coat. She goes out a good deal, up and down the fire escape and up and down the inside stairs that lead to the upper apartment and the roof. She wanders. Nicholas knows about it. He likes to think that she is free.

Bianca and the ailanthus provide Nicholas with the extra dimension all apartment dwellers long for. People who have no terraces and no gardens long to escape from their own four walls, but not to wander far. They only want to step outside for a minute. They stand outside their apartment houses on summer nights and during summer days. They stand around in groups or they sit together on the front steps of their buildings, taking the air and looking around at the street. Sometimes they carry a chair out, so that an old person can have a little outing. They lean out of their windows, with their elbows on the sills, and look into the faces of their neighbors at their windows on the other side of the street, all of them escaping from the rooms they live in and that they are glad to have but not to be closed up in. It should not be a problem, to have shelter without being shut away. The window sills are safety hatches into the open, and so are the fire escapes and the roofs and the front stoops. Bianca and the ailanthus make

Nicholas's life infinitely spacious. The ailanthus casts its new green light into his room, and Bianca draws a thread of his life all around the outside of the house and all around the inside, up and down the stairs. Where else does she go? Nobody knows. She has never been seen to stray from the walls of the house. Nicholas points out to his friends that it is possible to keep a cat in an apartment and still not make a prisoner of her. He says disaster comes only to those who attract it. He says Bianca is very smart, and that no harm will come to her.

She likes to sit on the window sills of the upper-floor tenants, but she never visits any of them unless they invite her in. She also likes to sit in the ruins of the garden Nicholas once kept on the roof. She watched him make the garden there. It was a real garden and grew well, until the top-floor tenant began to complain bitterly about his leaking ceiling. Even plants hardy enough to thrive in a thin bed of city dust and soot need watering. Nicholas still climbs to the roof, not to mourn his garden—it was an experiment, and he does not regret it—but to look about at the Gulliver world he lives in: the new buildings too tall for the streets they stand in and the older, smaller buildings out of proportion to everything except the past that will soon absorb them. From the street, or from any window, the city often seems like a place thrown up without regard for reason, and haunted by chaos. But from any rooftop the city comes into focus. The roof is in proportion to the building beneath it, and from any roof it can easily be seen that all the other roofs, and their walls, are in proportion to each other and to the city. The buildings are tightly packed together, without regard to size or height, and light and shadow strike across them so that the scene changes every minute. The struggle for space in Manhattan creates an oceanic uproar in the air above the streets, and every roof turns into a magic carpet just as soon as someone is standing on it.

Nicholas climbs to the roof by his fire escape, but when he leaves the roof to go back to his apartment he goes down through the house, down three flights to his own landing, or all the way down to the street floor. He likes the house and he likes to walk around in it. Bianca follows him. She likes to be taken for a walk. She likes to walk around the downstairs hall, where the door is that gives onto the street. It is an old hall, old and cramped, the natural entrance to the family place this house once was. To the left as you enter from the street there are two doors opening into what were once the sitting room and the dining room. The doors are always locked now—there are no tenants there. The hall is narrow, and it is cut in half by the stairs leading up to Nicholas's landing. Under the stairs, beside the door that leads down into the basement, there is a mysterious cubbyhole, big enough for galoshes, or wine bottles, or for a very small suitcase. Nobody knows what the cubbyhole was made for, but Bianca took it for one of her hiding places, and it was there Nicholas first looked for her when he realized he had not seen her all day—which is to say for about ten hours. He was certain she was in the cubbyhole, and that she wanted to be coaxed out. He called her from the landing, and then he went downstairs, calling her, and then he knelt down and peered into the dark little recess. Bianca was not there, and she was not on the roof, or under the bed, or down at the foot of the ailanthus trying to climb up, and she was not anywhere. Bianca was gone. She was nowhere to be found. She was nowhere.

There is no end to Bianca's story because nobody knows what happened to her. She has been gone for several months now. Nicholas has given up putting advertisements in the paper, and he took down all the little cards he put up in the cleaner's and in the grocery store and in the drugstore and the flower shop and the shoeshine parlor. He has stopped watching for her in the street. At first he walked through the street whispering her name, and then one night he found himself yelling for her. He was furious with her. He said to himself that if she turned up at that moment he would kill her. He would certainly not be glad to see her. All he wanted was, one way or another, to know whether she was alive or dead. But there was no word from Bianca, and no word from anyone with actual news of her, although the phone rang constantly with people who thought they had seen her, so that he spent a good many hours running around the neighborhood in answer to false reports. It was no good. She was gone. He reminded himself that he hadn't really wanted a cat. He had only taken Bianca because a friend of his, burdened with too many kittens, pleaded with him. He finds himself wondering what happened to Bianca, but he wonders less and less. Now, he tells himself, she has shrunk so that she is little more than an occasional irritation in his mind. He does not really miss her very much. After all, she brought nothing into the apartment with her except her silence. She was very quiet and not especially playful. She liked to roll and turn and paw the air in the moonlight, but otherwise she was almost sedate. But whatever she was, she is gone now, and Nicholas thinks that if he only knew for sure what happened to her he would have forgotten her completely by this time.

(1966)

YOU'RE UGLY, TOO

Y OU had to get out of them occasionally, those Illinois towns with the funny names: Paris, Oblong, Normal. Once, when the Dow Jones dipped two hundred points, a local paper boasted the banner headline "NORMAL MAN MARRIES OBLONG WOMAN." They knew what was important. They did! But you had to get out once in a while, even if it was just across the border to Terre Haute for a movie.

Outside of Paris, in the middle of a large field, was a scatter of brick buildings, a small liberal-arts college by the improbable name of Hilldale-Versailles. Zoë Hendricks had been teaching American history there for three years. She taught "The Revolution and Beyond" to freshmen and sophomores, and every third semester she had the senior seminar for majors, and although her student evaluations had been slipping in the last year and a half—*Professor Hendricks is often late for class and usually arrives with a cup of hot chocolate, which she offers the class sips of*—generally the department of nine men was pleased to have her. They felt she added some needed feminine touch to the corridors—that faint trace of Obsession and sweat, the light, fast clicking of heels. Plus they had had a sex-discrimination suit, and the dean had said, well, it was time.

The situation was not easy for her, they knew. Once, at the start of last semester, she had skipped into her lecture hall singing "Getting to Know You"—all of it. At the request of the dean, the chairman had called her into his office, but did not ask her for an explanation, not really. He asked her how she was and then smiled in an avuncular way. She said, "Fine," and he studied the way she said it, her front teeth catching on the inside of her lower lip. She was almost pretty, but her face showed the strain and ambition of always having been close but not quite. There was too much effort with the eyeliner, and her earrings, worn, no doubt, for the drama her features lacked, were a little frightening, jutting out the sides of her head like antennae.

"I'm going out of my mind," said Zoë to her younger sister, Evan, in Manhattan. *Professor Hendricks seems to know the entire soundtrack to "The King and I." Is this history?* Zoë phoned her every Tuesday.

"You always say that," said Evan, "but then you go on your trips and vacations and then you settle back into things and then you're quiet for a while and then you say you're fine, you're busy, and then after a while you say you're going crazy again, and you start all over." Evan was a part-time food designer for photo shoots. She cooked vegetables in green dye. She propped up beef stew with a bed of marbles and shopped for new kinds of silicone sprays and plastic ice cubes. She thought her life was O.K. She was living with her boyfriend of many years, who was independently wealthy and had an amusing little job in book publishing. They were five years out of college, and they lived in a luxury midtown high rise with a balcony and access to a pool. "It's not the same as having your own pool," Evan was always sighing, as if to let Zoë know that, as with Zoë, there were still things she, Evan, had to do without.

"Illinois. It makes me sarcastic to be here," said Zoë on the phone. She used to insist it was irony, something gently layered and sophisticated, something alien to the Midwest, but her students kept calling it sarcasm, something they felt qualified to recognize, and now she had to agree. It wasn't irony. "What is your perfume?" a student once asked her. "Room freshener," she said. She smiled, but he looked at her, unnerved.

Her students were by and large good Midwesterners, spacey with estrogen from large quantities of meat and eggs. They shared their parents' suburban values; their parents had given them things, things, things. They were complacent. They had been purchased. They were armed with a healthy vagueness about anything historical or geographic. They seemed actually to know very little about anything, but they were good-natured about it. "All those states in the East are so tiny and jagged and bunched up," complained one of her undergraduates the week she was lecturing on "The Turning Point of Independence: The Battle at Saratoga." "Professor Hendricks, you're from Delaware originally, right?" the student asked her.

"Maryland," corrected Zoë.

"Aw," he said, waving his hand dismissively. "New England."

Her articles—chapters toward a book called "Hearing the One About: Uses of Humor in the American Presidency"—were generally well received, though they came slowly for her. She liked her pieces to have something from every time of day in them—she didn't trust things written in the morning only—so she reread and rewrote painstakingly. No part of a day—its moods, its light—was allowed to dominate. She hung on to a piece for a year sometimes, revising at all hours, until the entirety of a day had registered there.

The job she'd had before the one at Hilldale-Versailles had been at a small college in New Geneva, Minnesota, Land of the Dying Shopping Mall. Everyone was so blond there that brunettes were often presumed to be from foreign countries. *Just because Professor Hendricks is from Spain doesn't give her the right to be so negative about our country.* There was a general emphasis on cheerfulness. In New Geneva you weren't supposed to be critical or complain. You weren't supposed to notice that the town had overextended and that its shopping malls were raggedy and going under. You were never to say you weren't "fine, thank you—and yourself?" You were supposed to be Heidi. You were supposed to lug goat milk up the hills and not think twice. Heidi did not complain. Heidi did not do things like stand in front of the new I.B.M. photocopier saying, "If this fucking Xerox machine breaks on me one more time, I'm going to slit my wrists."

But now in her second job, in her fourth year of teaching in the Midwest, Zoë was discovering something she never suspected she had: a crusty edge, brittle and pointed. Once she had pampered her students, singing them songs, letting them call her at home even, and ask personal questions, but now she was losing sympathy. They were beginning to seem different. They were beginning to seem demanding and spoiled.

"You act," said one of her senior-seminar students at a scheduled conference, "like your opinion is worth more than everyone else's in the class."

Zoë's eyes widened. "I *am* the teacher," she said. "I do get paid to act like that." She narrowed her gaze at the student, who was wearing a big leather bow in her hair like a cowgirl in a TV ranch show. "I mean, otherwise *everybody* in the class would have little offices and office hours." *Sometimes Professor Hendricks will take up the class's time just talking about movies she's seen.* She stared at the student some more, then added, "I bet you'd like that."

"Maybe I sound whiny to you," said the girl, "but I simply want my history major to mean something."

"Well, there's your problem," said Zoë, and, with a smile, she showed the student to the door. "I like your bow," she said.

Zoë lived for the mail, for the postman—that handsome blue jay—and when she got a real letter with a real full-price stamp from someplace else, she took it to bed with her and read it over and over. She also watched television until all hours and had her set in the bedroom—a bad sign. *Professor*

Hendricks has said critical things about Fawn Hall, the Catholic religion, and the whole state of Illinois. It is unbelievable. At Christmastime she gave twenty-dollar tips to the mailman and to Jerry, the only cabbie in town, whom she had gotten to know from all her rides to and from the Terre Haute airport, and who, since he realized such rides were an extravagance, often gave her cut rates.

"I'm flying in to visit you this weekend," announced Zoë.

"I was hoping you would," said Evan. "Charlie and I are having a party for Halloween. It'll be fun."

"I have a costume already. It's a bonehead. It's this thing that looks like a giant bone going through your head."

"Great," said Evan.

"It is, it's great."

"All I have is my moon mask from last year and the year before. I'll probably end up getting married in it."

"Are you and Charlie getting *married?*" Zoë felt slightly alarmed.

"Hmmmmmmmnnno, not immediately."

"Don't get married."

"Why?"

"Just not yet. You're too young."

"You're only saying that because you're five years older than I am and *you're* not married."

"*I'm* not married? Oh, my God," said Zoë, "I forgot to get married."

Zoë had been out with three men since she'd come to Hilldale-Versailles. One of them was a man in the municipal bureaucracy who had fixed a parking ticket she'd brought in to protest and then asked her out for coffee. At first, she thought he was amazing—at last, someone who did not want Heidi! But soon she came to realize that all men, deep down, wanted Heidi. Heidi with cleavage. Heidi with outfits. The parking-ticket bureaucrat soon became tired and intermittent. One cool fall day, in his snazzy, impractical convertible, when she asked him what was wrong he said, "You would not be ill served by new clothes, you know." She wore a lot of gray-green corduroy. She had been under the impression that it brought out her eyes, those shy stars. She flicked an ant from her sleeve.

"Did you have to brush that off in the car?" he said, driving. He glanced down at his own pectorals, giving first the left, then the right, a quick survey. He was wearing a tight shirt.

"Excuse me?"

He slowed down at an amber light and frowned. "Couldn't you have picked it up and thrown it outside?"

"The ant? It might have bitten me. I mean, what difference does it make?"

"It might have bitten you! Ha! How ridiculous! Now it's going to lay eggs in my car!"

The second guy was sweeter, lunkier, though not insensitive to certain paintings and songs, but too often, too, things he'd do or say would startle her. Once, in a restaurant, he stole the garnishes off her dinner plate and waited for her to notice. When she didn't, he finally thrust his fist across the table and said, "Look," and when he opened it, there was her parsley sprig and her orange slice crumpled to a wad. Another time, he described to her his recent trip to the Louvre. "And there I was in front of Delacroix's 'The Barque of Dante,' and everyone else had wandered off, so I had my own private audience with it, all those agonized shades splayed in every direction, and there's this motion in that painting that starts at the bottom, swirling and building up into the red fabric of Dante's hood, swirling out into the distance, where you see these orange flames—" He was breathless in the telling. She found this touching, and smiled in encouragement. "A painting like that," he said, shaking his head. "It just makes you shit."

"I have to ask you something," said Evan. "I know every woman complains about not meeting men, but really, on my shoots I meet a lot of men. And they're not all gay, either." She paused. "Not anymore."

"What are you asking?"

The third guy was a political-science professor named Murray Peterson, who liked to go out on double dates with colleagues whose wives he was attracted to. Usually, the wives would consent to flirt with him. Under the table sometimes there was footsie, and once there was even kneesie. Zoë and the husband would be left to their food, staring into their water glasses, chewing like goats. "Oh, Murray," said one wife, who had never finished her master's in physical therapy and wore great clothes. "You know, I know everything about you: your birthday, your license-plate number. I have everything memorized. But then that's the kind of mind I have. Once, at a dinner party, I amazed the host by getting up and saying goodbye to every single person there, first *and* last names."

"I knew a dog who could do that," said Zoë with her mouth full. Murray and the wife looked at her with vexed and rebuking expressions, but the husband seemed suddenly twinkling and amused. Zoë swallowed. "It was a Talking Lab, and after about ten minutes of listening to the dinner conversation this dog knew everyone's name. You could say, 'Take this knife to Murray Peterson,' and it would."

"Really," said the wife, frowning, and Murray Peterson never called again.

"Are you seeing anyone?" said Evan. "I'm asking for a particular reason. I'm not just being like Mom."

"I'm seeing my house. I'm tending to it when it wets, when it cries, when it throws up." Zoë had bought a mint-green ranch house near campus, though now she was thinking that maybe she shouldn't have. It was hard to live in a house. She kept wandering in and out of the rooms, wondering where she had put things. She went downstairs into the basement for no reason at all except that it amused her to own a basement. It also amused her to own a tree.

Her parents, in Maryland, had been very pleased that one of their children had at last been able to afford real estate, and when she closed on the house they sent her flowers with a congratulations card. Her mother had even U.P.S.'d a box of old decorating magazines saved over the years—photographs of beautiful rooms her mother used to moon over, since there never had been any money to redecorate. It was like getting her mother's pornography, that box, inheriting her drooled-upon fantasies, the endless wish and tease that had been her life. But to her mother it was a rite of passage that pleased her. "Maybe you will get some ideas from these," she had written. And when Zoë looked at the photographs, at the bold and beautiful living rooms, she was filled with longing. Ideas and ideas of longing.

Right now Zoë's house was rather empty. The previous owner had wallpapered around the furniture, leaving strange gaps and silhouettes on the walls, and Zoë hadn't done much about that yet. She had bought furniture, then taken it back, furnishing and unfurnishing, preparing and shedding, like a womb. She had bought several plain pine chests to use as love seats or boot boxes, but they came to look to her more and more like children's coffins, so she returned them. And she had recently bought an Oriental rug for the living room, with Chinese symbols on it she didn't understand. The salesgirl had kept saying she was sure they meant "Peace" and "Eternal Life," but when Zoë got the rug home she worried. What if they didn't mean "Peace" and "Eternal Life"? What if they meant, say, "Bruce Springsteen"? And the more she thought about it, the more she became convinced she had a rug that said "Bruce Springsteen," and so she returned that, too.

She had also bought a little baroque mirror for the front entryway, which, she had been told by Murray Peterson, would keep away evil spirits. The mirror, however, tended to frighten *her,* startling her with an image of a woman she never recognized. Sometimes she looked puffier and plainer than she remembered. Sometimes shifty and dark. Most times she just looked vague. "You look like someone I know," she had been told twice in the last year by strangers in restaurants in Terre Haute. In fact, sometimes she seemed not to have a look of her own, or any look whatsoever, and it began to amaze her that her students and colleagues were able to recognize her at all. How did they know? When she walked into a room, how did she look so that they knew it was she? Like this? Did she look like this? And so she returned the mirror.

"The reason I'm asking is that I know a man I think you should meet," said Evan. "He's fun. He's straight. He's single. That's all I'm going to say."

"I think I'm too old for fun," said Zoë. She had a dark bristly hair in her chin, and she could feel it now with her finger. Perhaps when you had been without the opposite sex for too long, you began to resemble them. In an act of desperate invention, you began to grow your own. "I just want to come, wear my bonehead, visit with Charlie's tropical fish, ask you about your food shoots."

She thought about all the papers on "Our Constitution: How It Affects Us" she was going to have to correct. She thought about how she was going in for ultrasound tests on Friday, because, according to her doctor and her doctor's assistant, she had a large, mysterious growth in her abdomen. Gallbladder, they kept saying. Or ovaries or colon. "You guys practice medicine?" asked Zoë, aloud, after they had left the room. Once, as a girl, she brought her dog to a vet, who had told her, "Well, either your dog has worms or cancer or else it was hit by a car."

She was looking forward to New York.

"Well, whatever. We'll just play it cool. I can't wait to see you, hon. Don't forget your bonehead," said Evan.

"A bonehead you don't forget," said Zoë.

"I suppose," said Evan.

The ultrasound Zoë was keeping a secret, even from Evan. "I feel like I'm dying," Zoë had hinted just once on the phone.

"You're not dying," said Evan, "you're just annoyed."

"ULTRASOUND," Zoë now said jokingly to the technician who put the cold jelly on her bare stomach. "Does that sound like a really great stereo system or what?"

She had not had anyone make this much fuss over her bare stomach since her boyfriend in graduate school, who had hovered over her whenever she felt ill, waved his arms, pressed his hands upon her navel, and drawled evangelically, "Heal! Heal for thy Baby Jesus' sake!" Zoë would laugh and they would make love, both secretly hoping she would get pregnant. Later they would worry together, and he would sink a cheek to her belly and ask whether she was late, was she late, was she sure, she might be late, and when after two years she had not gotten pregnant they took to quarrelling and drifted apart.

"O.K.," said the technician absently.

The monitor was in place, and Zoë's insides came on the screen in all their gray and ribbony hollowness. They were marbled in the finest gradations of black and white, like stone in an old church or a picture of the moon. "Do you suppose," she babbled at the technician, "that the rise in infertility among so many couples in this country is due to completely different species trying to reproduce?" The technician moved the scanner around and took more pictures. On one view in particular, on Zoë's right side, the technician became suddenly alert, the machine he was operating clicking away.

Zoë stared at the screen. "That must be the growth you found there," suggested Zoë.

"I can't tell you anything," said the technician rigidly. "Your doctor will get the radiologist's report this afternoon and will phone you then."

"I'll be out of town," said Zoë.

"I'm sorry," said the technician.

Driving home, Zoë looked in the rearview mirror and decided she looked—well, how would one describe it? A little wan. She thought of the joke about the guy who visits his doctor and the doctor says, "Well, I'm sorry to say, you've got six weeks to live."

"I want a second opinion," says the guy. *You act like your opinion is worth more than everyone else's in the class.*

"You want a second opinion? O.K.," says the doctor. "You're ugly, too." She liked that joke. She thought it was terribly, terribly funny.

She took a cab to the airport. Jerry the cabbie was happy to see her.

"Have fun in New York," he said, getting her bag out of the trunk. He liked her, or at least he always acted as if he did. She called him Jare.

"Thanks, Jare."

"You know, I'll tell you a secret: I've never been to New York. I'll tell you two secrets: I've never been on a plane." And he waved at her sadly as she pushed her way in through the terminal door. "Or an escalator!" he shouted.

The trick to flying safely, Zoë always said, was to never buy a discount ticket and to tell yourself you had nothing to live for anyway, so that when the plane crashed it was no big deal. Then, when it didn't crash, when you had succeeded in keeping it aloft with your own worthlessness, all you had to do was stagger off, locate your luggage, and, by the time a cab arrived, come up with a persuasive reason to go on living.

"YOU'RE here!" shrieked Evan over the doorbell, before she even opened the door. Then she opened it wide. Zoë set her bags on the hall floor and hugged Evan hard. When she was little, Evan had always been affectionate and devoted. Zoë had always taken care of her—advising, reassuring—until recently, when it seemed Evan had started advising and reassuring *her.* It startled Zoë. She suspected it had something to do with her being alone. It made people uncomfortable.

"How *are* you?"

"I threw up on the plane. Besides that, I'm O.K."

"Can I get you something? Here, let me take your suitcase. Sick on the plane. *Eeeyew.*"

"It was into one of those sickness bags," said Zoë, just in case Evan thought she'd lost it in the aisle. "I was very quiet."

The apartment was spacious and bright, with a view all the way downtown along the East Side. There was a balcony, and sliding glass doors. "I keep forgetting how nice this apartment is. Twenty-first floor, doorman . . ." Zoë could work her whole life and never have an apartment like this. So could Evan. It was Charlie's apartment. He and Evan lived in it like two kids in a dorm, beer cans and clothes strewn around. Evan put Zoë's bag away from the mess, over by the fish tanks. "I'm so glad you're here," she said. "Now what can I get you?"

Evan made them lunch—soup from a can and saltines.

"I don't know about Charlie," she said after they had finished. "I feel like we've gone all sexless and middle-aged already."

"Hmm," said Zoë. She leaned back into Evan's sofa and stared out the window at the dark tops of the buildings. It seemed a little unnatural to live up in the sky like this, like birds that out of some wrongheaded derring-do had nested too high. She nodded toward the lighted fish tanks and giggled. "I feel like a bird," she said, "with my own personal supply of fish."

Evan sighed. "He comes home and just sacks out on the sofa, watching fuzzy football. He's wearing the psychic cold cream and curlers, if you know what I mean."

Zoë sat up, readjusted the sofa cushions. "What's fuzzy football?"

"We haven't gotten cable yet. Everything comes in fuzzy. Charlie just watches it that way."

"Hmm, yeah, that's a little depressing," Zoë said. She looked at her hands. "Especially the part about not having cable."

"This is how he gets into bed at night." Evan stood up to demonstrate. "He whips all his clothes off, and when he gets to his underwear he lets it drop to one ankle. Then he kicks up his leg and flips the underwear in the air and catches it. I, of course, watch from the bed. There's nothing else. There's just that."

"Maybe you should just get it over with and get married."

"Really?"

"Yeah. I mean, you guys probably think living together like this is the best of both worlds, but—" Zoë tried to sound like an older sister; an older sister was supposed to be the parent you could never have, the hip, cool mom. "But I've always found that as soon as you think you've got the best of both worlds"—she thought now of herself, alone in her house, of the toad-faced cicadas that flew around like little men at night and landed on her screens, staring; of the size-14 shoes she placed at the doorstep, to scare off intruders; of the ridiculous, inflatable blowup doll someone had told her to keep propped up at the breakfast table—"it can suddenly twist and become the worst of both worlds."

"Really?" Evan was beaming. "Oh, Zoë. I have something to tell you. Charlie and I *are* getting married."

"Really." Zoë felt confused.

"I didn't know how to tell you."

"Yeah, I guess the part about fuzzy football misled me a little."

"I was hoping you'd be my maid of honor," said Evan, waiting. "Aren't you happy for me?"

"Yes," said Zoë, and she began to tell Evan a story about an award-winning violinist at Hilldale-Versailles—how the violinist had come home from a competition in Europe and taken up with a local man who made her go to all his summer softball games, made her cheer for him from the stands, with the wives, until she later killed herself. But when Zoë got halfway through, to the part about cheering at the softball games, she stopped.

"What?" said Evan. "So what happened?"

"Actually, nothing," said Zoë lightly. "She just really got into softball. You should have seen her."

Zoë decided to go to a late-afternoon movie, leaving Evan to chores she needed to do before the party—"I have to do them alone, really," she'd said, a little tense after the violinist story. Zoë thought about going to an art museum, but women alone in art museums had to look good. They always did. Chic and serious, moving languidly, with a great handbag. Instead, she walked down through Kips Bay, past an earring boutique called Stick It in Your Ear, past a hair salon called Dorian Gray. That was the funny thing about *beauty*, thought Zoë. Look it up in the yellow pages and you found a hundred entries, hostile with wit, cutesy with warning. But look up *truth*— Ha! There was nothing at all.

Zoë thought about Evan getting married. Would Evan turn into Peter Pumpkin Eater's wife? Mrs. Eater? At the wedding, would she make Zoë wear some flouncy lavender dress, identical with the other maids'? Zoë hated uniforms, had even in the first grade refused to join Elf Girls because she didn't want to wear the same dress as everyone else. Now she might have to. But maybe she could distinguish it. Hitch it up on one side with a clothespin. Wear surgical gauze at the waist. Clip to her bodice one of those pins that say in loud letters "SHIT HAPPENS."

At the movie—"Death by Number"—she bought strands of red licorice to tug and chew. She took a seat off to one side in the theatre. She felt strangely self-conscious sitting alone, and hoped for the place to darken fast. When it did, and the coming attractions came on, she reached inside her purse for her glasses. They were in a Baggie. Her Kleenex was also in a Baggie. So was her pen and her aspirin and her mints. Everything was in Baggies. This was what she'd become: *a woman alone at the movies with everything in a Baggie.*

AT the Halloween party, there were about two dozen people. There were people with ape heads and large hairy hands. There was someone dressed as a leprechaun. There was someone dressed as a frozen dinner. Some man had brought his two small daughters: a ballerina and a ballerina's sister, also dressed as a ballerina. There was a gaggle of sexy witches—women dressed entirely in black, beautifully made up and jewelled. "I hate those sexy witches. It's not in the spirit of Halloween," said Evan. Evan had abandoned the moon mask and dolled herself up as a hausfrau, in curlers and an apron, a decision she now regretted. Charlie, because he liked fish, because he owned fish and collected fish, had decided to go as a fish. He had fins, and eyes on the sides of his head. "Zoë! How are you! I'm sorry I wasn't here when you first arrived!" He spent the rest of his time chatting up the sexy witches.

"Isn't there something I can help you with here?" Zoë asked her sister. "You've been running yourself ragged." She rubbed her sister's arm, gently, as if she wished they were alone.

"Oh, God, not at all," said Evan, arranging stuffed mushrooms on a plate. The timer went off, and she pulled another sheetful out of the oven. "Actually, you know what you can do?"

"What?" Zoë put on her bonehead.

"Meet Earl. He's the guy I had in mind for you. When he gets here, just talk to him a little. He's nice. He's fun. He's going through a divorce."

"I'll try," Zoë groaned. "O.K.? I'll try." She looked at her watch.

When Earl arrived, he was dressed as a naked woman, steel wool glued strategically to a body stocking, and large rubber breasts protruding like hams.

"Zoë, this is Earl," said Evan.

"Good to meet you," said Earl, circling Evan to shake Zoë's hand. He stared at the top of Zoë's head. "Great bone."

Zoë nodded. "Great tits," she said. She looked past him, out the window at the city thrown glitteringly up against the sky; people were saying the usual things: how it looked like jewels, like bracelets and necklaces unstrung. You could see the clock of the Con Ed building, the orange-and-gold-capped Empire State, the Chrysler like a rocket ship dreamed up in a depression. Far west you could glimpse Astor Plaza, with its flying white roof like a nun's habit. "There's beer out on the balcony, Earl. Can I get you one?" Zoë asked.

"Sure, uh, I'll come along. Hey, Charlie, how's it going?"

Charlie grinned and whistled. People turned to look. "Hey, Earl," someone called from across the room. "Va-va-va-voom."

They squeezed their way past the other guests, past the apes and the sexy witches. The suction of the sliding door gave way in a whoosh, and Zoë and Earl stepped out onto the balcony, a bonehead and a naked woman, the night air roaring and smoky cool. Another couple were out there, too, murmuring privately. They were not wearing costumes. They smiled at Zoë and Earl. "Hi," said Zoë. She found the plastic-foam cooler, dug in and retrieved two beers.

"Thanks," said Earl. His rubber breasts folded inward, dimpled and dented, as he twisted open the bottle.

"Well," sighed Zoë anxiously. She had to learn not to be afraid of a man, the way, in your childhood, you learned not to be afraid of an earthworm or a bug. Often, when she spoke to men at parties, she rushed things in her mind. As the man politely blathered on, she would fall in love, marry, then find herself in a bitter custody battle with him for the kids and hoping for a reconciliation, so that despite all his betrayals she might no longer despise him, and, in the few minutes remaining, learn, perhaps, what his last name was and what he did for a living, though probably there was already too much history between them. She would nod, blush, turn away.

"Evan tells me you're a history professor. Where do you teach?"

"Just over the Indiana border into Illinois."

He looked a little shocked. "I guess Evan didn't tell me that part."

"She didn't?"

"No."

"Well, that's Evan for you. When we were kids we both had speech impediments."

"That can be tough," said Earl. One of his breasts was hidden behind his drinking arm, but the other shone low and pink, full as a strawberry moon.

"Yes, well, it wasn't a total loss. We used to go to what we called peach pearapy. For about ten years of my life, I had to map out every sentence in my mind, way ahead, before I said it. That was the only way I could get a coherent sentence out."

Earl drank from his beer. "How did you do that? I mean, how did you get through?"

"I told a lot of jokes. Jokes you know the lines to already. You can just say them. I love jokes. Jokes and songs."

Earl smiled. He had on lipstick, a deep shade of red, but it was wearing off from the beer. "What's your favorite joke?"

"Uh, my favorite joke is probably—O.K., all right. This guy goes into a doctor's office, and—"

"I think I know this one," interrupted Earl, eagerly. He wanted to tell it himself. "A guy goes into a doctor's office, and the doctor tells him he's got some good news and some bad news—that one, right?"

"I'm not sure," said Zoë. "This might be a different version."

"So the guy says, 'Give me the bad news first,' and the doctor says, 'O.K. You've got three weeks to live.' And the guy cries, 'Three weeks to live! Doctor, what is the good news?' And the doctor says, 'Did you see that secretary out front? I finally fucked her.' "

Zoë frowned.

"That's not the one you were thinking of?"

"No." There was accusation in her voice. "Mine was different."

"Oh," said Earl. He looked away and then back again. "What kind of history do you teach?"

"I teach American, mostly—eighteenth- and nineteenth-century." In graduate school, at bars the pickup line was always "So what's your century?"

"Occasionally, I teach a special theme course," she added. "Say, 'Humor and Personality in the White House.' That's what my book's on." She thought of something someone once told her about bowerbirds, how they build elaborate structures before mating.

"Your book's on *humor?*"

"Yeah, and, well, when I teach a theme course like that I do all the centuries." *So what's your century?*

"All three of them."

"Pardon?" The breeze glistened her eyes. Traffic revved beneath them. She felt high and puny, like someone lifted into Heaven by mistake and then spurned.

"Three. There's only three."

"Well, four, really." She was thinking of Jamestown, and of the Pilgrims coming here with buckles and witch hats to say their prayers.

"I'm a photographer," said Earl. His face was starting to gleam, his rouge smearing in a sunset beneath his eyes.

"Do you like that?"

"Well, actually, I'm starting to feel it's a little dangerous."

"Really?"

"Spending all your time in a dark room with that red light and all those chemicals. There's links with Parkinson's, you know."

"No, I didn't."

"I suppose I should wear rubber gloves, but I don't like to. Unless I'm touching it directly, I don't think of it as real."

"Hmm," said Zoë. Alarm buzzed mildly through her.

"Sometimes, when I have a cut or something, I feel the sting and think, *Shit*. I wash constantly and just hope. I don't like rubber over the skin like that."

"Really."

"I mean, the physical contact. That's what you want, or why bother?"

"I guess," said Zoë. She wished she could think of a joke, something slow and deliberate with the end in sight. She thought of gorillas, how when they had been kept too long alone in cages they would smack each other in the head instead of mating.

"Are you—in a relationship?" Earl suddenly blurted.

"Now? As we speak?"

"Well, I mean, I'm sure you have a relationship to your *work*." A smile, a little one, nestled in his mouth like an egg. She thought of zoos in parks, how when cities were under siege, during world wars, people ate the animals. "But I mean, with a *man*."

"No, I'm not in a relationship with a *man*." She rubbed her chin with her hand and could feel the one bristly hair there. "But my last relationship was with a very sweet man," she said. She made something up. "From Switzerland. He was a botanist—a weed expert. His name was Jerry. I called him Jare. He was so funny. You'd go to the movies with him and all he would notice was the plants. He would never pay attention to the plot. Once, in a jungle movie, he started rattling off all these Latin names, out loud. It was very exciting for him." She paused, caught her breath. "Eventually, he went back to Europe to, uh, study the edelweiss." She looked at Earl. "Are you involved in a relationship? With a *woman*?"

Earl shifted his weight and the creases in his body stocking changed, splintering outward like something broken. His pubic hair slid over to one hip, like a corsage on a saloon girl. "No," he said, clearing his throat. The steel wool in his underarms was inching down toward his biceps. "I've just gotten out of a marriage that was full of bad dialogue like 'You want more *space*? I'll give you more space!' *Clonk*. Your basic Three Stooges."

Zoë looked at him sympathetically. "I suppose it's hard for love to recover after that."

His eyes lit up. He wanted to talk about love. "But I keep thinking love should be like a tree. You look at trees and they've got bumps and scars from tumors, infestations, what have you, but they're still growing. Despite the bumps and bruises, they're—straight."

"Yeah, well," said Zoë, "where I'm from they're all married or gay. Did you see that movie 'Death by Number'?"

Earl looked at her, a little lost. She was getting away from him. "No," he said.

One of his breasts had slipped under his arm, tucked there like a baguette. She kept thinking of trees, of parks, of people in wartime eating the zebras. She felt a stabbing pain in her abdomen.

"Want some hors d'oeuvres?" Evan came pushing through the sliding door. She was smiling, though her curlers were coming out, hanging bedraggled at the ends of her hair like Christmas decorations, like food put out for the birds. She thrust forward a plate of stuffed mushrooms.

"Are you asking for donations or giving them away?" said Earl wittily. He liked Evan, and he put his arm around her.

"You know, I'll be right back," said Zoë.

"Oh," said Evan, looking concerned.

"Right back. I promise."

Zoë hurried inside, across the living room into the bedroom, to the adjoining bath. It was empty; most of the guests were using the half-bath near the kitchen. She flicked on the light and closed the door. The pain had stopped, and she didn't really have to go to the bathroom, but she stayed there anyway, resting. In the mirror above the sink, she looked haggard beneath her bonehead, violet-grays showing under the skin like a plucked and pocky bird's. She leaned closer, raising her chin a little to find the bristly hair. It was there, at the end of the jaw, sharp and dark as a wire. She opened the medicine cabinet, pawed through it until she found some tweezers. She lifted her head again and poked at her face with the metal tips, grasping and pinching and missing. Outside the door, she could hear two people talking low. They had come into the bedroom and were discussing something. They were sitting on the bed. One of them giggled in a false way. Zoë stabbed again at her chin, and it started to bleed a little. She pulled the skin tight along the jawbone, gripped the tweezers hard around what she hoped was the hair, and tugged. A tiny square of skin came away, but the hair remained, blood bright at the root of it. Zoë clenched her teeth. "Come on," she whispered. The couple outside in the bedroom were now telling stories, softly, and laughing. There was a bounce and squeak of mattress, and the sound of a chair being moved out of the way. Zoë aimed the tweezers carefully, pinched, then pulled gently, and this time the hair came, too, with a slight twinge of pain, and then a great flood of relief. "Yeah!" breathed Zoë. She grabbed some toilet paper and dabbed at her chin. It came away spotted with blood, and so she tore off some more and pressed hard until it stopped. Then she turned off the light, opened the door, and rejoined the party. "Excuse me," she said to the couple in the bedroom. They were the couple from the balcony, and they looked at her, a bit surprised. They had their arms around each other, and they were eating candy bars.

EARL was still out on the balcony, alone, and Zoë rejoined him there. "Hi," she said.

He turned around and smiled. He had straightened his costume out a bit, though all the secondary sex characteristics seemed slightly doomed, destined to shift and flip and zip around again any moment. "Are you O.K.?" he asked. He had opened another beer and was chugging.

"Oh, yeah. I just had to go to the bathroom." She paused. "Actually, I have been going to a lot of doctors recently."

"What's wrong?" asked Earl.

"Oh, probably nothing. But they're putting me through tests." She sighed. "I've had sonograms. I've had mammograms. Next week I'm going in for a candygram." He looked at her, concerned. "I've had too many gram words," she said.

"Here, I saved you these." He held out a napkin with two stuffed mushroom caps. They were cold and leaving oil marks on the napkin.

"Thanks," said Zoë, and pushed them both in her mouth. "Watch," she said with her mouth full. "With my luck it'll be a gallbladder operation."

Earl made a face. "So your sister's getting married," he said, changing the subject. "Tell me, really, what you think about love."

"Love?" Hadn't they done this already? "I don't know." She chewed thoughtfully and swallowed. "All right. I'll tell you what I think about love. Here is a love story. This friend of mine—"

"You've got something on your chin," said Earl, and he reached over to touch it.

"What?" said Zoë, stepping back. She turned her face away and grabbed at her chin. A piece of toilet paper peeled off it, like tape. "It's nothing," she said. "It's just—it's nothing."

Earl stared at her.

"At any rate," she continued, "this friend of mine was this award-winning violinist. She travelled all over Europe and won competitions; she made records, she gave concerts, she got famous. But she had no social life. So one day she threw herself at the feet of this conductor she had a terrible crush on. He picked her up, scolded her gently, and sent her back to her hotel room. After that, she came home from Europe. She went back to her old home town, stopped playing the violin, and took up with a local boy. This was in Illinois. He took her to some Big Ten bar every night to drink with his buddies from the team. He used to say things like 'Katrina here likes to play the violin' and then he'd pinch her cheek. When she once suggested that they go home, he said, 'What, you think you're too famous for a place like this? Well, let me tell you something. You may think you're famous, but you're not *famous* famous.' Two famouses. 'No one here's ever heard of you.' Then he went up and bought a round of drinks for everyone but her. She got her coat, went home, and shot a bullet through her head."

Earl was silent.

"That's the end of my love story," said Zoë.

"You're not at all like your sister," said Earl.

"Oh, really," said Zoë. The air had gotten colder, the wind singing minor and thick as a dirge.

"No." He didn't want to talk about love anymore. "You know, you should wear a lot of blue—blue and white—around your face. It would bring out your coloring." He reached an arm out to show her how the blue bracelet he was wearing might look against her skin, but she swatted it away.

"Tell me, Earl. Does the word 'fag' mean anything to you?"

He stepped back, away from her. He shook his head in disbelief. "You know, I just shouldn't try to go out with career women. You're all stricken. A guy can really tell what life has done to you. I do better with women who have part-time jobs."

"Oh, yes?" said Zoë. She had once read an article entitled "Professional Women and the Demographics of Grief." Or, no, it was a poem. *If there were a lake, the moonlight would dance across it in conniptions.* She remembered that line. But perhaps the title was "The Empty House: Aesthetics of Barrenness." Or maybe "Space Gypsies: Girls in Academe." She had forgotten.

Earl turned and leaned on the railing of the balcony. It was getting late. Inside, the party guests were beginning to leave. The sexy witches were already gone. "Live and learn," Earl murmured.

"Live and get dumb," replied Zoë. Beneath them on Lexington there were no cars, just the gold rush of an occasional cab. He leaned hard on his elbows, brooding.

"Look at those few people down there," he said. "They look like bugs. You know how bugs are kept under control? They're sprayed with bug hormones—female bug hormones. The male bugs get so crazy in the presence of this hormone they're screwing everything in sight—trees, rocks, everything but female bugs. Population control. That's what's happening in this country," he said drunkenly. "Hormones sprayed around, and now men are screwing rocks. Rocks!"

In the back, the Magic Marker line of his buttocks spread wide, a sketchy black on pink, like a funnies page. Zoë came up, slow, from behind, and gave him a shove. His arms slipped forward, off the railing, out over the street. Beer spilled out of his bottle, raining twenty stories down to the street.

"Hey, what are you doing!" he said, whipping around. He stood straight and readied, and moved away from the railing, sidestepping Zoë. "What the *hell* are you doing?"

"Just kidding," she said. "I was just kidding." But he gazed at her, appalled and frightened, his Magic Marker buttocks turned away now toward all of downtown, a naked pseudo woman with a blue bracelet at the wrist, trapped out on a balcony with—with *what?* "Really, I was just kidding!" Zoë shouted. The wind lifted the hair up off her head, skyward in spines behind the bone. If there were a lake, the moonlight would dance across it in conniptions. She smiled at him and wondered how she looked.

(1989)

SYMBOLS AND SIGNS

F OR the fourth time in as many years, they were confronted with the problem of what birthday present to take to a young man who was incurably deranged in his mind. Desires he had none. Man-made objects were to him either hives of evil, vibrant with a malignant activity that he alone could perceive, or gross comforts for which no use could be found in his abstract world. After eliminating a number of articles that might offend him or frighten him (anything in the gadget line, for instance, was taboo), his parents chose a dainty and innocent trifle—a basket with ten different fruit jellies in ten little jars.

At the time of his birth, they had already been married for a long time; a score of years had elapsed, and now they were quite old. Her drab gray hair was pinned up carelessly. She wore cheap black dresses. Unlike other women of her age (such as Mrs. Sol, their next-door neighbor, whose face was all pink and mauve with paint and whose hat was a cluster of brookside flowers), she presented a naked white countenance to the faultfinding light of spring. Her husband, who in the old country had been a fairly successful businessman, was now, in New York, wholly dependent on his brother Isaac, a real American of almost forty years' standing. They seldom saw Isaac and had nicknamed him the Prince.

That Friday, their son's birthday, everything went wrong. The subway train lost its life current between two stations and for a quarter of an hour they could hear nothing but the dutiful beating of their hearts and the rustling of newspapers. The bus they had to take next was late and kept them waiting a long time on a street corner, and when it did come, it was crammed with garrulous high-school children. It began to rain as they walked up the brown path leading to the sanitarium. There they waited again, and instead of their boy, shuffling into the room, as he usually did (his poor face sullen, confused, ill-shaven, and blotched with acne), a nurse they knew and did not care for appeared at last and brightly explained that he had again attempted to take his life. He was all right, she said, but a visit from his parents might disturb him. The place was so miserably under-staffed, and things got mislaid or mixed up so easily, that they decided not to leave their present in the office but to bring it to him next time they came.

Outside the building, she waited for her husband to open his umbrella and then took his arm. He kept clearing his throat, as he always did when he was upset. They reached the bus-stop shelter on the other side of the street and he closed his umbrella. A few feet away, under a swaying and dripping tree, a tiny unfledged bird was helplessly twitching in a puddle.

During the long ride to the subway station, she and her husband did not exchange a word, and every time she glanced at his old hands, clasped and twitching upon the handle of his umbrella, and saw their swollen veins and brown-spotted skin, she felt the mounting pressure of tears. As she looked around, trying to hook her mind onto something, it gave her a kind of soft shock, a mixture of compassion and wonder, to notice that one of the pas-sengers—a girl with dark hair and grubby red toenails—was weeping on the shoulder of an older woman. Whom did that woman resemble? She re-sembled Rebecca Borisovna, whose daughter had married one of the Soloveichiks—in Minsk, years ago.

The last time the boy had tried to do it, his method had been, in the doc-tor's words, a masterpiece of inventiveness; he would have succeeded had not an envious fellow-patient thought he was learning to fly and stopped him just in time. What he had really wanted to do was to tear a hole in his world and escape.

The system of his delusions had been the subject of an elaborate paper in a scientific monthly, which the doctor at the sanitarium had given to them to read. But long before that, she and her husband had puzzled it out for themselves. "Referential mania," the article had called it. In these very rare cases, the patient imagines that everything happening around him is a veiled reference to his personality and existence. He excludes real people from the conspiracy, because he considers himself to be so much more in-telligent than other men. Phenomenal nature shadows him wherever he goes. Clouds in the staring sky transmit to each other, by means of slow signs, incredibly detailed information regarding him. His inmost thoughts are discussed at nightfall, in manual alphabet, by darkly gesticulating trees.

Pebbles or stains or sun flecks form patterns representing, in some awful way, messages that he must intercept. Everything is a cipher and of everything he is the theme. All around him, there are spies. Some of them are detached observers, like glass surfaces and still pools; others, such as coats in store windows, are prejudiced witnesses, lynchers at heart; others, again (running water, storms), are hysterical to the point of insanity, have a distorted opinion of him, and grotesquely misinterpret his actions. He must be always on his guard and devote every minute and module of life to the decoding of the undulation of things. The very air he exhales is indexed and filed away. If only the interest he provokes were limited to his immediate surroundings, but, alas, it is not! With distance, the torrents of wild scandal increase in volume and volubility. The silhouettes of his blood corpuscles, magnified a million times, flit over vast plains; and still farther away, great mountains of unbearable solidity and height sum up, in terms of granite and groaning firs, the ultimate truth of his being.

WHEN they emerged from the thunder and foul air of the subway, the last dregs of the day were mixed with the street lights. She wanted to buy some fish for supper, so she handed him the basket of jelly jars, telling him to go home. Accordingly, he returned to their tenement house, walked up to the third landing, and then remembered he had given her his keys earlier in the day.

In silence he sat down on the steps and in silence rose when, some ten minutes later, she came trudging heavily up the stairs, smiling wanly and shaking her head in deprecation of her silliness. They entered their two-room flat and he at once went to the mirror. Straining the corners of his mouth apart by means of his thumbs, with a horrible, masklike grimace, he removed his new, hopelessly uncomfortable dental plate. He read his Russian-language newspaper while she laid the table. Still reading, he ate the pale victuals that needed no teeth. She knew his moods and was also silent.

When he had gone to bed, she remained in the living room with her pack of soiled playing cards and her old photograph albums. Across the narrow courtyard, where the rain tinkled in the dark against some ash cans, windows were blandly alight, and in one of them a black-trousered man, with his hands clasped under his head and his elbows raised, could be seen lying supine on an untidy bed. She pulled the blind down and examined the photographs. As a baby, he looked more surprised than most babies. A photograph of a German maid they had had in Leipzig and her fat-faced fiancé fell out of a fold of the album. She turned the pages of the book: Minsk, the Revolution, Leipzig, Berlin, Leipzig again, a slanting house front, badly out of focus. Here was the boy when he was four years old, in a park, shyly, with puckered forehead, looking away from an eager squirrel, as he would have from any other stranger. Here was Aunt Rosa, a fussy, angular, wild-eyed old lady, who had lived in a tremulous world of bad news, bankruptcies, train accidents, and cancerous growths until the Germans put her to death, together with all the people she had worried about. The boy, aged six—that was when he drew wonderful birds with human hands and feet, and suffered from insomnia like a grown-up man. His cousin, now a famous chess player. The boy again, aged about eight, already hard to understand, afraid of the wallpaper in the passage, afraid of a certain picture in a book, which merely showed an idyllic landscape with rocks on a hillside and an old cart wheel hanging from the one branch of a leafless tree. Here he was at ten— the year they left Europe. She remembered the shame, the pity, the humiliating difficulties of the journey, and the ugly, vicious, backward children he was with in the special school where he had been placed after they arrived in America. And then came a time in his life, coinciding with a long convalescence after pneumonia, when those little phobias of his, which his parents had stubbornly regarded as the eccentricities of a prodigiously gifted child, hardened, as it were, into a dense tangle of logically interacting illusions, making them totally inaccessible to normal minds.

All this, and much more, she had accepted, for, after all, living does mean accepting the loss of one joy after another, not even joys in her case, mere possibilities of improvement. She thought of the recurrent waves of pain that for some reason or other she and her husband had had to endure; of the invisible giants hurting her boy in some unimaginable fashion; of the incalculable amount of tenderness contained in the world; of the fate of this tenderness, which is either crushed or wasted, or transformed into madness; of neglected children humming to themselves in unswept corners; of beautiful weeds that cannot hide from the farmer.

IT was nearly midnight when, from the living room, she heard her husband moan, and presently he staggered in, wearing over his nightgown the old overcoat with the astrakhan collar that he much preferred to his nice blue bathrobe.

"I can't sleep!" he cried.

"Why can't you sleep?" she asked. "You were so tired."

"I can't sleep because I am dying," he said, and lay down on the couch.

"Is it your stomach? Do you want me to call Dr. Solov?"

"No doctors, no doctors," he moaned. "To the devil with doctors! We must get him out of there quick. Otherwise, we'll be responsible. . . .

Responsible!" He hurled himself into a sitting position, both feet on the floor, thumping his forehead with his clenched fist.

"All right," she said quietly. "We will bring him home tomorrow morning."

"I would like some tea," said her husband, and went out to the bathroom.

Bending with difficulty, she retrieved some playing cards and a photograph or two that had slipped to the floor—the knave of hearts, the nine of spades, the ace of spades, the maid Elsa and her bestial beau.

He returned in high spirits, saying in a loud voice, "I have it all figured out. We will give him the bedroom. Each of us will spend part of the night near him and the other part on this couch. We will have the doctor see him at least twice a week. It does not matter what the Prince says. He won't have much to say anyway, because it will come out cheaper."

The telephone rang. It was an unusual hour for it to ring. He stood in the middle of the room, groping with his foot for one slipper that had come off, and childishly, toothlessly, gaped at his wife. Since she knew more English than he, she always attended to the calls.

"Can I speak to Charlie?" a girl's dull little voice said to her now.

"What number do you want? . . . No. You have the wrong number."

She put the receiver down gently and her hand went to her heart. "It frightened me," she said.

He smiled a quick smile and immediately resumed his excited monologue. They would fetch him as soon as it was day. For his own protection, they would keep all the knives in a locked drawer. Even at his worst, he presented no danger to other people.

The telephone rang a second time. The same toneless, anxious young voice asked for Charlie.

"You have the incorrect number. I will tell you what you are doing. You are turning the letter 'o' instead of the zero." She hung up again.

They sat down to their unexpected, festive midnight tea. He sipped noisily; his face was flushed; every now and then he raised his glass with a circular motion, so as to make the sugar dissolve more thoroughly. The vein on the side of his bald head stood out conspicuously, and silvery bristles showed on his chin. The birthday present stood on the table. While she poured him another glass of tea, he put on his spectacles and reëxamined with pleasure the luminous yellow, green, and red little jars. His clumsy, moist lips spelled out their eloquent labels—apricot, grape, beach plum, quince. He had got to crab apple when the telephone rang again.

(1948)

POOR VISITOR

I T was my first day. I had come the night before, a gray-black and cold night before—as it was expected to be in the middle of January, though I didn't know that at the time—and I could not see anything clearly on the way in from the airport, even though there were lights everywhere. As we drove along, someone would single out to me a famous building, an important street, a park, a bridge that when built was thought to be a spectacle. In a daydream I used to have, all these places were points of happiness to me; all these places were lifeboats to my small drowning soul, for I would imagine myself entering and leaving them, and just that—entering and leaving over and over again—would see me through a bad feeling I did not have a name for. I only knew it felt a little like sadness. Now that I saw these places, they looked ordinary, dirty, worn down by so many people entering and leaving them in real life, and it occurred to me that I could not be the only person in the world for whom they were a fixture of fantasy. It was not my first bout with the disappointment of reality and it would not be my last. The undergarments that I wore were all new, bought for my journey, and as I sat in the car, twisting this way and that to get a good view of the sights before me, I was reminded of how uncomfortable the new can make you feel.

I got into an elevator, something I had never done before, and then I was in an apartment and seated at a table, eating food just taken from a refrigerator. In Antigua, where I came from, I had always lived in a house, and my house did not have a refrigerator in it. Everything I was experiencing—

the ride in the elevator, being in an apartment, eating day-old food that had been stored in a refrigerator—was such a good idea that I could imagine I would grow used to it and like it very much, but at first it was all so new that I had to smile with my mouth turned down at the corners. I slept soundly that night, but it wasn't because I was happy and comfortable—quite the opposite; it was because I didn't want to take in anything else.

That morning, the morning of my first day, the morning that followed my first night, was a sunny morning. It was not the sort of bright sun-yellow making everything curl at the edges, almost in fright, that I was used to, but a pale-yellow sun, as if the sun had grown weak from trying too hard to shine; but still it was sunny, and that was nice and made me miss my home less. And so, seeing the sun, I got up and put on a dress, a gay dress made out of madras cloth—the same sort of dress that I would wear if I were at home and setting out for a day in the country. It was all wrong. The sun was shining but the air was cold. It was the middle of January, after all. But I did not know that the sun could shine and the air remain cold; no one had ever told me. What a feeling that was! How can I explain? Something I had always known—the way I knew my skin was the color brown of a nut rubbed repeatedly with a soft cloth, or the way I knew my own name—something I took completely for granted, "the sun is shining, the air is warm," was not so. I was no longer in a tropical zone, and this re-alization now entered my life like a flow of water dividing formerly dry and solid ground, creating two banks, one of which was my past—so familiar and predictable that even my unhappiness then made me happy now just to think of it—the other my future, a gray blank, an overcast seascape on which rain was falling and no boats were in sight. I was no longer in a trop-ical zone and I felt cold inside and out, the first time such a sensation had come over me.

IN books I had read—from time to time, when the plot called for it—some-one would suffer from homesickness. A person would leave a not very nice situation and go somewhere else, somewhere a lot better, and then long to go back where it was not very nice. How impatient I would become with such a person, for I would feel that I was in a not very nice situation myself, and how I wanted to go somewhere else. But now I, too, felt that I wanted to be back where I came from. I understood it, I knew where I stood there. If I had had to draw a picture of my future then, it would have been a large gray patch surrounded by black, blacker, blackest.

What a surprise this was to me, that I longed to be back in the place that I came from, that I longed to sleep in a bed I had outgrown, that I longed to be with people whose smallest, most natural gesture would call up in me such a rage that I longed to see them all dead at my feet. Oh, I had imagined that with my one swift act—leaving home and coming to this new place—I could leave behind me, as if it were an old garment never to be worn again, my sad thoughts, my sad feelings, and my discontent with life in general as it presented itself to me. In the past, the thought of being in my present situation had been a comfort, but now I did not even have this to look forward to, and so I lay down on my bed and dreamt that I was eating a bowl of pink mullet and green figs cooked in coconut milk, and it had been cooked by my grandmother, which was why the taste of it pleased me so, for she was the person I liked best in all the world and those were the things I liked best to eat also.

The room in which I lay was a small room just off the kitchen—the maid's room. I was used to a small room, but this was a different sort of small room. The ceiling was very high and the walls went all the way up to the ceiling, enclosing the room like a box—a box in which cargo travelling a long way should be shipped. But I was not cargo. I was only an unhappy young woman living in a maid's room, and I was not even the maid. I was the young girl who watches over the children and goes to school at night. How nice everyone was to me, though, saying that I should regard them as my family and make myself at home. I believed them to be sincere, for I knew that such a thing would not be said to a member of their real family. After all, aren't family the people who become the millstone around your life's neck? On the last day I spent at home, my cousin—a girl I had known all my life, an unpleasant person even before her parents forced her to become a Seventh-Day Adventist—made a farewell present to me of her own Bible, and with it she made a little speech about God and goodness and blessings. Now it sat before me on a dresser, and I remembered how when we were children we would sit under my house and terrify and torment each other by reading out loud passages from the Book of Revelations, and I wondered if ever in my whole life a day would go by when these people I had left behind, my own family, would not appear before me in one way or another.

There was also a small radio on this dresser, and I had turned it on. At that moment, almost as if to sum up how I was feeling, a song came on some of the words of which were "Put yourself in my place, if only for a day; see if you can stand the awful emptiness inside." I sang these words to myself over and over, as if they were a lullaby, and I fell asleep again. This time I dreamt that I was holding in my hands one of my old cotton-flannel nightgowns, and it was printed with beautiful scenes of children playing with Christmas-tree decorations. The scenes printed on my nightgown were so real that I could actually hear the children laughing. I felt compelled to know where this nightgown came from, and I started to examine it furiously, looking for the label. I found it just where a label usually is, in the back, and it read "Made in Australia." I was awakened from this dream by the actual maid, a woman who had let me know right away, on meeting me, that she did not like me, and gave as her reason the way I talked. I thought it was because of something else, but I did not know what. As I opened my eyes, the word "Australia" stood between our faces, and I remembered then that Australia was settled as a prison for bad people, people so bad that they couldn't be put in a prison in their own country.

MY waking hours soon took on a routine. I walked four small girls to their school, and when they returned at midday I gave them a lunch of soup from a tin, and sandwiches. In the afternoon, I read to them and played with them. When they were away, I studied my books, and at night I went to school. I was unhappy. I looked at a map. The Atlantic Ocean stood between me and the place I came from, but would it have made a difference if it had been a teacup of water? I could not go back.

Outside, always it was cold, and everyone said that it was the coldest winter they had ever experienced; but the way they said it made me think they said this every time winter came around. And I couldn't blame them for not really remembering each year how unpleasant, how unfriendly winter weather could be. The trees with their bare, still limbs looked dead, and as if someone had just placed them there and planned to come back and get them later; all the windows of the houses were shut tight, the way windows are shut up when a house will be empty for a long time; when people walked on the streets they did it quickly, as if they were doing something behind someone's back, as if they didn't want to draw attention to themselves, as if being out in the cold too long would cause them to dissolve. How I longed to see someone lingering on a corner, trying to draw my attention to him, trying to engage me in conversation, someone complaining to himself in a voice I could overhear about a god whose love and mercy fell on the just and the unjust.

I wrote home to say how lovely everything was, and I used flourishing words and phrases, as if I were living life in a greeting card—the kind that has a satin ribbon on it, and quilted hearts and roses, and is expected to be so precious to the person receiving it that the manufacturer has placed a leaf of plastic on the front to protect it. Everyone I wrote to said how nice it was to hear from me, how nice it was to know that I was doing well, that I was very much missed, and that they couldn't wait until the day came when I returned.

ONE day the maid who said she did not like me because of the way I talked told me that she was sure I could not dance. She said that I spoke like a nun, I walked like one also, and that everything about me was so pious it made her feel at once sick to her stomach and sick with pity just to look at me. And so, perhaps giving way to the latter feeling, she said that we should dance, even though she was quite sure I didn't know how. There was a little portable record-player in my room, the kind that when closed up looked like a ladies' vanity case, and she put on a record she had bought earlier that day. It was a song that was very popular at the time—three girls, not older than I was, singing in harmony and in a very insincere and artificial way about love and so on. It was very beautiful all the same, and it was beautiful because it was so insincere and artificial. She enjoyed this song, singing at the top of her voice, and she was a wonderful dancer—it amazed me to see the way in which she moved. I could not join her and I told her why: the melodies of her song were so shallow, and the words, to me, were meaningless. From her face, I could see she had only one feeling about me: how sick to her stomach I made her. And so I said that I knew songs, too, and I burst into a calypso about a girl who ran away to Port-au-Spain, Trinidad, and had a good time, with no regrets.

THE household in which I lived was made up of a husband, a wife, and the four girl children. The husband and wife looked alike and their four children looked just like them. In photographs of themselves, which they placed all over the house, their six yellow-haired heads of various sizes were bunched as if they were a bouquet of flowers tied together by an unseen string. In the pictures, they smiled out at the world, giving the impression that they found everything in it unbearably wonderful. And it was not a farce, their smiles. From wherever they had gone, and they seemed to have been all over the world, they brought back some tiny memento, and they could each recite its history from its very beginning. Even when a little rain fell, they would admire the way it streaked through the blank air.

At dinner, when we sat down at the table—and did not have to say grace (such a relief; as if they believed in a God that did not have to be thanked every time you turned around)—they said such nice things to each other, and the children were so happy. They would spill their food, or not eat any

of it at all, or make up rhymes about it that would end with the words
"smelt bad." How they made me laugh, and I wondered what sort of parents I must have had, for even to think of such words in their presence I
would have been scolded severely, and I vowed that if I ever had children I
would make sure that the first words out of their mouths were bad ones.

IT was at dinner one night not long after I began to live with them that they
began to call me the Visitor. They said I seemed not to be a part of things, as
if I didn't live in their house with them, as if they weren't like a family to
me, as if I were just passing through, just saying one long Hallo!, and soon
would be saying a quick Goodbye! So long! It was very nice! For look at the
way I looked at them eating, Lewis said. Had I never seen anyone put a fork-
ful of French-cut green beans in his mouth before? This made Mariah
laugh, but almost everything Lewis said made Mariah happy, and so she
would laugh. When I didn't laugh also, Lewis said, Poor Visitor, poor
Visitor, over and over, a sympathetic tone to his voice, and then he told me
a story about an uncle he had who had gone to Canada and raised monkeys, and of how after a while the uncle loved monkeys so much and was so
used to being around them that he found actual human beings hard to
take. He had told me this story about his uncle before, and while he was
telling it to me this time I was remembering a dream I had had about them:
Lewis was chasing me around the house. I wasn't wearing any clothes. The
ground on which I was running was yellow, as if it had been paved with
cornmeal. Lewis was chasing me around and around the house, and
though he came close he could never catch up with me. Mariah stood at the
open windows saying, Catch her, Lewis, catch her. Eventually I fell down a
hole, at the bottom of which were some silver and blue snakes.
    When Lewis finished telling his story, I told them my dream. When I fin-
ished, they both fell silent. Then they looked at me and Mariah cleared her
throat, but it was obvious from the way she did it that her throat did not
need clearing at all. Their two yellow heads swam toward each other and,
in unison, bobbed up and down. Lewis made a clucking noise, then said,
Poor, poor Visitor. And Mariah said, Dr. Freud for Visitor. Then they
laughed in a soft, kind way. I had meant by telling them my dream that I
had taken them in, because only people who were very important to me
had ever shown up in my dreams, and I could see that they already understood that.

(1989)

IN GREENWICH,

THERE ARE MANY GRAVELLED WALKS

O N an afternoon in early August, Peter Birge, just returned from driving his mother to the Greenwich sanitarium she had to frequent at intervals, sat down heavily on a furbelowed sofa in the small apartment he and she had shared ever since his return from the Army a year ago. He was thinking that his usually competent solitude had become more than he could bear. He was a tall, well-built young man of about twenty-three, with a pleasant face whose even, standardized look was the effect of proper food, a good dentist, the best schools, and a brush haircut. The heat, which bored steadily into the room through a Venetian blind lowered over a half-open window, made his white T-shirt cling to his chest and arms, which were still brown from a week's sailing in July at a cousin's place on the Sound. The family of cousins, one cut according to the pattern of a two-car-and-country-club suburbia, had always looked with distaste on his precocious childhood with his mother in the Village and, the few times he had been farmed out to them during those early years, had received his healthy normality with ill-concealed surprise, as if they had clearly expected to have to fatten up what they undoubtedly referred to in private as "poor Anne's boy." He had only gone there at all, this time, when it became certain that the money saved up for a summer abroad, where his Army stint had not sent him, would have to be spent on one of his mother's trips to Greenwich, leaving barely enough, as it was, for his next, and final, year at the School of Journalism. Half out of disheartenment over his collapsed summer, half to provide himself with a credible "out" for

the too jovially pressing cousins at Rye, he had registered for some courses
at the Columbia summer session. Now these were almost over, too, leaving
a gap before the fall semester began. He had cut this morning's classes in
order to drive his mother up to the place in Connecticut.

He stepped to the window and looked through the blind at the convertible parked below, on West Tenth Street. He ought to call the garage for the
pickup man, or else, until he thought of someplace to go, he ought to hop
down and put up the top. Otherwise, baking there in the hot sun, the car
would be like a griddle when he went to use it, and the leather seats were
cracking badly anyway.

It had been cool when he and his mother started, just after dawn that
morning, and the air of the well-ordered countryside had had that almost
speaking freshness of early day. With her head bound in a silk scarf and her
chubby little chin tucked into the cardigan which he had buttoned on her
without forcing her arms into the sleeves, his mother, peering up at him
with the near-gaiety born of relief, had had the exhausted charm of a child
who has just been promised the thing for which it has nagged. Anyone
looking at the shingled hair, the feet in small brogues—anyone not close
enough to see how drawn and beakish her nose looked in the middle of her
little, round face, which never reddened much with drink but at the worst
times took on a sagging, quilted whiteness—might have thought the two of
them were a couple, any couple, just off for a day in the country. No one
would have thought that only a few hours before, some time after two, he
had been awakened, pounded straight up on his feet, by the sharp, familiar
cry and then the agonized susurrus of prattling that went on and on and
on, that was different from her everyday, artlessly confidential prattle only
in that now she could not stop, she could not stop, *she could not stop*, and
above the small, working mouth with its eliding, spinning voice, the glazed
button eyes opened wider and wider, as if she were trying to breathe
through them. Later, after the triple bromide, the warm bath, and the
crooning, practiced soothing he administered so well, she had hiccuped
into crying, then into stillness at last, and had fallen asleep on his breast.
Later still, she had awakened him, for he must have fallen asleep there in
the big chair with her, and with the weak, humiliated goodness which always followed these times she had even tried to help him with the preparations for the journey—preparations which, without a word between them,
they had set about at once. There'd been no doubt, of course, that she
would have to go. There never was.

He left the window and sat down again in the big chair, and smoked one
cigarette after another. Actually, for a drunkard—or an alcoholic, as people
preferred to say these days—his mother was the least troublesome of any.

He had thought of it while he packed the pairs of daintily kept shoes, the sweet-smelling blouses and froufrou underwear, the tiny, perfect dresses—of what a comfort it was that she had never grown raddled or blowzy. Years ago, she had perfected the routine within which she could feel safe for months at a time. It had gone on for longer than he could remember: from before the death of his father, a Swedish engineer, on the income of whose patents they had always been able to live fairly comfortably; probably even during her life with that other long-dead man, the painter whose model and mistress she had been in the years before she married his father. There would be the long, drugged sleep of the morning, then the unsteady hours when she manicured herself back into cleanliness and reality. Then, at about four or five in the afternoon, she and the dog (for there was always a dog) would make their short pilgrimage to the clubby, cozy little hangout where she would be a fixture until far into the morning, where she had been a fixture for the last twenty years.

Once, while he was at boarding school, she had made a supreme effort to get herself out of the routine—for his sake, no doubt—and he had returned at Easter to a new apartment, uptown, on Central Park West. All that this had resulted in was inordinate taxi fares and the repetitious nightmare evenings when she had gotten lost and he had found her, a small, untidy heap, in front of their old place. After a few months, they had moved back to the Village, to those few important blocks where she felt safe and known and loved. For they all knew her there, or got to know her—the aging painters, the newcomer poets, the omniscient news hacks, the military spinsters who bred dogs, the anomalous, sandalled young men. And they accepted her, this dainty hanger-on who neither painted nor wrote but hung their paintings on her walls, faithfully read their parti-colored magazines, and knew them all—their shibboleths, their feuds, the whole vocabulary of their disintegration, and, in a mild, occasional manner, their beds.

Even this, he could not remember not knowing. At ten, he had been an expert compounder of remedies for hangover, and of an evening, standing sleepily in his pajamas to be admired by the friends his mother sometimes brought home, he could have predicted accurately whether the party would end in a brawl or in a murmurous coupling in the dark.

It was curious, he supposed now, stubbing out a final cigarette, that he had never judged resentfully either his mother or her world. By the accepted standards, his mother had done her best; he had been well housed, well schooled, even better loved than some of the familied boys he had known. Wisely, too, she had kept out of his other life, so that he had never had to be embarrassed there except once, and this when he was grown, when she had visited his Army camp. Watching her at a post party for visitors, poised there, so chic, so distinctive, he had suddenly seen it begin: the fear, the scare, then the compulsive talking, which always started so innocently that only he would have noticed at first—that warm, excited, buttery flow of harmless little lies and pretensions which gathered its dreadful speed and content and ended then, after he had whipped her away, just as it had ended this morning.

On the way up this morning, he had been too clever to subject her to a restaurant, but at a drive-in place he was able to get her to take some coffee. How grateful they had both been for the coffee, she looking up at him, tremulous, her lips pecking at the cup, he blessing the coffee as it went down her! And afterward, as they flew onward, he could feel her straining like a homing pigeon toward their destination, toward the place where she felt safest of all, where she would gladly have stayed forever if she had just had enough money for it, if they would only let her stay. For there the pretty little woman and her dog—a poodle, this time—would be received like the honored guest that she was, so trusted and docile a guest, who asked only to hide there during the season of her discomfort, who was surely the least troublesome of them all.

HE had no complaints, then, he assured himself as he sat on the burning front seat of the convertible trying to think of somewhere to go. It was just that while others of his age still shared a communal wonder at what life might hold, he had long since been solitary in his knowledge of what life was.

Up in a sky as honestly blue as a flag, an airplane droned smartly toward Jersey. Out at Rye, the younger crowd at the club would be commandeering the hot blue day, the sand, and the water, as if these were all extensions of themselves. They would use the evening this way, too, disappearing from the veranda after a dance, exploring each other's rhythm-and-whiskey-whetted appetites in the backs of cars. They all thought themselves a pretty sophisticated bunch, the young men who had graduated not into a war but into its hung-over peace, the young girls attending junior colleges so modern that the deans had to spend all their time declaring that their girls were being trained for the family and the community. But when Peter looked close and saw how academic their sophistication was, how their undamaged eyes were still starry with expectancy, their lips still avidly open for what life would surely bring, then he became envious and awkward with them, like a guest at a party to whose members he carried bad news he had no right to know, no right to tell.

He turned on the ignition and let the humming motor prod him into a decision. He would drop in at Robert Vielum's, where he had dropped in quite often until recently, for the same reason that others stopped by at

Vielum's—because there was always likely to be somebody there. The door of Robert's old-fashioned apartment, on Claremont Avenue, almost always opened on a heartening jangle of conversation and music, which meant that others had gathered there, too, to help themselves over the pauses so endemic to university life—the life of the mind—and there were usually several members of Robert's large acquaintance among the subliterary, quasi-artistic, who had strayed in, ostensibly en route somewhere, and who lingered on hopefully on the chance that in each other's company they might find out what that somewhere was.

Robert was a perennial taker of courses—one of those non-matriculated students of indefinable age and income, some of whom pursued, with monkish zeal and no apparent regard for time, this or that freakishly peripheral research project of their own conception, and others of whom, like Robert, seemed to derive a Ponce de León sustenance from the young. Robert himself, a large man of between forty and fifty, whose small features were somewhat cramped together in a wide face, never seemed bothered by his own lack of direction, implying rather that this was really the catholic approach of the "whole man," alongside of which the serious pursuit of a degree was somehow foolish, possibly vulgar. Rumor connected him with a rich Boston family that had remittanced him at least as far as New York, but he never spoke about himself, although he was extraordinarily alert to gossip. Whatever income he had he supplemented by renting his extra room to a series of young men students. The one opulence among his dun-colored, perhaps consciously Spartan effects was a really fine record-player, which he kept going at all hours with selections from his massive collection. Occasionally he annotated the music, or the advance-copy novel that lay on his table, with foreign-language tags drawn from the wide, if obscure, latitudes of his travels, and it was his magic talent for assuming that his young friends, too, had known, had experienced, that, more than anything, kept them enthralled.

"*Fabelhaft!* Isn't it?" he would say of the Mozart. "Remember how they did it that last time at Salzburg!" and they would all sit there, included, belonging, headily remembering the Salzburg to which they had never been. Or he would pick up the novel and lay it down again. "*La plume de mon oncle,* I'm afraid. *La plume de mon oncle Gide. Eheu,* poor Gide!"—and they would each make note of the fact that one need not read that particular book, that even, possibly, it was no longer necessary to read Gide.

PETER parked the car and walked into the entrance of Robert's apartment house, smiling to himself, lightened by the prospect of company. After all,

he had been weaned on the salon talk of such circles; these self-fancying little bohemias at least made him feel at home. And Robert was cleverer than
most—it was amusing to watch him. For just as soon as his satellites
thought themselves secure on the promontory of some "trend" he had
pointed out to them, they would find that he had deserted them, had gone
on to another trend, another eminence, from which he beckoned, cocksure
and just faintly malicious. He harmed no one permanently. And if he concealed some skeleton of a weakness, some closeted Difference with the
Authorities, he kept it decently interred.

As Peter stood in the dark, soiled hallway and rang the bell of Robert's
apartment, he found himself as suddenly depressed again, unaccountably
reminded of his mother. There were so many of them, and they affected
you so, these charmers who, if they could not offer you the large strength,
could still atone for the lack with so many small decencies. It was ad-
mirable, surely, the way they managed this. And surely, after all, they
harmed no one.

Robert opened the door. "Why, hello— Why, hello, Peter!" He seemed
surprised, almost relieved. "Greetings!" he added, in a voice whose boom
was more in the manner than the substance. "Come in, Pietro, come in!"
He wore white linen shorts, a zebra-striped beach shirt, and huaraches, in
which he moved easily, leading the way down the dark hall of the apartment, past the two bedrooms, into the living room. All of the apartment
was on a court, but on the top floor, so it received a medium, dingy light
from above. The living room, long and pleasant, with an old white mantel,
a gas log, and many books, always came as a surprise after the rest of the
place, and at any time of day Robert kept a few lamps lit, which rouged the
room with an evening excitement.

As they entered, Robert reached over in passing and turned on the record-
player. Music filled the room, muted but insistent, as if he wanted it to patch
up some lull he had left behind. Two young men sat in front of the dead
gas log. Between them was a table littered with maps, an open atlas, travel
folders, glass beer steins. Vince, the current roomer, had his head on his
clenched fists. The other man, a stranger, indolently raised a dark, handsome head as they entered.

"Vince!" Robert spoke sharply. "You know Peter Birge. And this is Mario
Osti. Peter Birge."

The dark young man nodded and smiled, lounging in his chair. Vince
nodded. His red-rimmed eyes looked beyond Peter into some distance he
seemed to prefer.

"God, isn't it but hot!" Robert said. "I'll get you a beer." He bent over Mario
with an inquiring look, a caressing hand on the empty glass in front of him.

Mario stretched back on the chair, smiled upward at Robert, and shook his head sleepily. "Only makes me hotter." He yawned, spread his arms languorously, and let them fall. He had the animal self-possession of the very handsome; it was almost a shock to hear him speak.

Robert bustled off to the kitchen.

"Robert!" Vince called, in his light, pouting voice. "Get me a drink. Not a beer. A drink." He scratched at the blond stubble on his cheek with a nervous, pointed nail. On his round head and retroussé face, the stubble produced the illusion of a desiccated baby, until, looking closer, one imagined that he might never have been one, but might have been spawned at the age he was, to mummify perhaps but not to grow. He wore white shorts exactly like Robert's, and his blue-and-white striped shirt was a smaller version of Robert's brown-and-white, so that the two of them made an ensemble, like the twin outfits the children wore on the beach at Rye.

"You know I don't keep whiskey here." Robert held three steins deftly balanced, his heavy hips neatly avoiding the small tables which scattered the room. "You've had enough, wherever you got it." It was true, Peter remembered, that Robert was fonder of drinks with a flutter of ceremony about them—café brûlé perhaps, or, in the spring, a Maibowle, over which he could chant the triumphant details of his pursuit of the necessary woodruff. But actually one tippled here on the exhilarating effect of wearing one's newest façade, in the fit company of others similarly attired.

Peter picked up his stein. "You and Vince all set for Morocco, I gather."

"Morocco?" Robert took a long pull at his beer. "No. No, that's been changed. I forgot you hadn't been around. Mario's been brushing up my Italian. He and I are off for Rome the day after tomorrow."

The last record on the changer ended in an archaic battery of horns. In the silence while Robert slid on a new batch of records, Peter heard Vince's nail scrape, scrape along his cheek. Still leaning back, Mario shaped smoke with his lips. Large and facilely drawn, they looked, more than anything, accessible—to a stream of smoke, of food, to another mouth, to any plum that might drop.

"You going to study over there?" Peter said to him.

"Paint." Mario shaped and let drift another corolla of smoke.

"No," Robert said, clicking on the record arm. "I'm afraid Africa's démodé." A harpsichord began to play, its dwarf notes hollow and perfect. Robert raised his voice a shade above the music. "Full of fashion photographers. And little come-lately writers." He sucked in his cheeks and made a face. "Trying out their passions under the beeg, bad sun."

"Eheu, poor Africa?" said Peter.

Robert laughed. Vince stared at him out of wizened eyes. Not drink, so much, after all, Peter decided, looking professionally at the mottled cherub face before he realized that he was comparing it with another face, but lately left. He looked away.

"Weren't you going over, Peter?" Robert leaned against the machine.

"Not this year." Carefully Peter kept out of his voice the knell the words made in his mind. In Greenwich, there were many gravelled walks, un-shrubbed except for the nurses who dotted them, silent and attitudinized as trees. "Isn't that Landowska playing?"

"Hmm. Nice and cooling on a hot day. Or a fevered brow." Robert fiddled with the volume control. The music became louder, then lowered. "Vince wrote a poem about that once. About the Mozart, really, wasn't it, Vince? 'A lovely clock between ourselves and time.' " He enunciated daintily, pushing the words away from him with his tongue.

"Turn it off!" Vince stood up, his small fists clenched, hanging at his sides.

"No, let her finish." Robert turned deliberately and closed the lid of the machine, so that the faint hiss of the needle vanished from the frail, metro-nomic notes. He smiled. "What a time-obsessed crowd writers are. Now Mario doesn't have to bother with that dimension."

"Not unless I paint portraits," Mario said. His parted lips exposed his teeth, like some white, unexpected flint of intelligence.

"*Dolce far niente*," Robert said softly. He repeated the phrase dreamily, so that half-known Italian words—"*loggia*," the "Ponte Vecchio," the "Lungarno"—imprinted themselves one by one on Peter's mind, and he saw the two of them, Mario and Roberto now, already in the frayed-gold light of Florence, in the umber dusk of half-imagined towns.

A word, muffled, came out of Vince's throat. He lunged for the record-player. Robert seized his wrist and held it down on the lid. They were locked that way, staring at each other, when the doorbell rang.

"That must be Susan," Robert said. He released Vince and looked down, watching the blood return to his fingers, flexing his palm.

With a second choked sound, Vince flung out his fist in an awkward at-tempt at a punch. It grazed Robert's cheek, clawing downward. A thin line of red appeared on Robert's cheek. Fist to mouth, Vince stood a moment; then he rushed from the room. They heard the nearer bedroom door slam and the lock click. The bell rang again, a short, hesitant burr.

Robert clapped his hand to his cheek, shrugged, and left the room.

Mario got up out of his chair for the first time. "Aren't you going to ask who Susan is?"

"Should I?" Peter leaned away from the face bent confidentially near, curly with glee.

"His daughter," Mario whispered. "He said he was expecting his *daughter.* Can you imagine? *Robert!*"

Peter moved farther away from the mobile, pressing face and, standing at the window, studied gritty details of the courtyard. A vertical line of lighted windows, each with a glimpse of stair, marked the hallways on each of the five floors. Most of the other windows were dim and closed, or opened just a few inches above their white ledges, and the yard was quiet. People would be away or out in the sun, or in their brighter front rooms dressing for dinner, all of them avoiding this dark shaft that connected the backs of their lives. Or, here and there, was there someone sitting in the fading light, someone lying on a bed with his face pressed to a pillow? The window a few feet to the right, around the corner of the court, must be the window of the room into which Vince had gone. There was no light in it.

Robert returned, a Kleenex held against his cheek. With him was a pretty, ruffle-headed girl in a navy-blue dress with a red arrow at each shoulder. He switched on another lamp. For the next arrival, Peter thought, surely he will tug back a velvet curtain or break out with a heraldic flourish of drums, recorded by Red Seal. Or perhaps the musty wardrobe was opening at last and was this the skeleton—this girl who had just shaken hands with Mario, and now extended her hand toward Peter, tentatively, timidly, as if she did not habitually shake hands but today would observe every custom she could.

"How do you do?"

"How do you do?" Peter said. The hand he held for a moment was small and childish, the nails unpainted, but the rest of her was very correct for the eye of the beholder, like the young models one sees in magazines, sitting or standing against a column, always in three-quarter view, so that the picture, the ensemble, will not be marred by the human glance. Mario took from her a red dressing case that she held in her free hand, bent to pick up a pair of white gloves that she had dropped, and returned them with an avid interest which overbalanced, like a waiter's gallantry. She sat down, brushing at the gloves.

"The train was awfully dusty—and crowded." She smiled tightly at Robert, looked hastily and obliquely at each of the other two, and bent over the gloves, brushing earnestly, stopping as if someone had said something, and, when no one did, brushing again.

"Well, well, well," Robert said. His manners, always good, were never so to the point of clichés, which would be for him what nervous *gaffes* were for other people. He coughed, rubbed his cheek with the back of his hand, looked at the hand, and stuffed the Kleenex into the pocket of his shorts. "How was camp?"

Mario's eyebrows went up. The girl was twenty, surely, Peter thought.

"All right," she said. She gave Robert the stiff smile again and looked down into her lap. "I like helping children. They can use it." Her hands folded on top of the gloves, then inched under and hid beneath them.

"Susan's been counselling at a camp which broke up early because of a polio scare," Robert said as he sat down. "She's going to use Vince's room while I'm away, until college opens."

"Oh—" She looked up at Peter. "Then you aren't Vince?"

"No. I just dropped in. I'm Peter Birge."

She gave him a neat nod of acknowledgment. "I'm glad, because I certainly wouldn't want to inconvenience—"

"Did you get hold of your mother in Reno?" Robert asked quickly.

"Not yet. But she couldn't break up her residence term anyway. And Arthur must have closed up the house here. The phone was disconnected."

"Arthur's Susan's stepfather," Robert explained with a little laugh. "Number three, I think. Or is it *four*, Sue?"

Without moving, she seemed to retreat, so that again there was nothing left for the observer except the girl against the column, any one of a dozen with the short, anonymous nose, the capped hair, the foot arched in the trim shoe, and half an iris glossed with an expertly aimed photoflood. "Three," she said. Then one of the hidden hands stole out from under the gloves, and she began to munch evenly on a fingernail.

"Heavens, you haven't still got that *habit*!" Robert said.

"What a heavy papa you make, Roberto," Mario said.

She flushed, and put the hand back in her lap, tucking the fingers under. She looked from Peter to Mario and back again. "Then you're not Vince," she said. "I didn't think you were."

The darkness increased around the lamps. Behind Peter, the court had become brisk with lights, windows sliding up, and the sound of taps running.

"Guess Vince fell asleep. I'd better get him up and send him on his way." Robert shrugged, and rose.

"Oh, don't! I wouldn't want to be an inconvenience," the girl said, with a polite terror which suggested she might often have been one.

"On the contrary." Robert spread his palms, with a smile, and walked down the hall. They heard him knocking on a door, then his indistinct voice.

In the triangular silence, Mario stepped past Peter and slid the window up softly. He leaned out to listen, peering sidewise at the window to the right. As he was pulling himself back in, he looked down. His hands stiffened on the ledge. Very slowly he pulled himself all the way in and stood up. Behind him a tin ventilator clattered inward and fell to the floor. In the shadowy lamplight his too classic face was like marble which moved numbly. He swayed a little, as if with vertigo.

"I'd better get out of here!"

They heard his heavy breath as he dashed from the room. The slam of the outer door blended with Robert's battering, louder now, on the door down the hall.

"What's down there?" She was beside Peter, otherwise he could not have heard her. They took hands, like strangers met on a narrow footbridge or on one of those steep places where people cling together more for anchorage against their own impulse than for balance. Carefully they leaned out over the sill. Yes—it was down there, the shirt, zebra-striped, just decipherable on the merged shadow of the courtyard below.

Carefully, as if they were made of eggshell, as if by some guarded movement they could still rescue themselves from disaster, they drew back and straightened up. Robert, his face askew with the impossible question, was behind them.

AFTER this, there was the hubbub—the ambulance from St. Luke's, the prowl car, the two detectives from the precinct station house, and finally the "super," a vague man with the grub pallor and shamble of those who live in basements. He pawed over the keys on the thong around his wrist and, after several tries, opened the bedroom door. It was a quiet, unviolent room with a tossed bed and an open window, with a stagy significance acquired only momentarily in the minds of those who gathered in a group at its door.

MUCH later, after midnight, Peter and Susan sat in the bald glare of an all-night restaurant. With hysterical eagerness, Robert had gone on to the station house with the two detectives to register the salient facts, to help ferret out the relatives in Ohio, to arrange, in fact, anything that might still be arrangeable about Vince. Almost without noticing, he had acquiesced in Peter's proposal to look after Susan. Susan herself, after silently watching the gratuitous burbling of her father, as if it were a phenomenon she could neither believe nor leave, had followed Peter without comment. At his suggestion, they had stopped off at the restaurant on their way to her stepfather's house, for which she had a key.

"Thanks. I was starved." She leaned back and pushed at the short bang of hair on her forehead.

"Hadn't you eaten at all?"

"Just those pasty sandwiches they sell on the train. There wasn't any diner."

"Smoke?"

"I do, but I'm just too tired. I can get into a hotel all right, don't you think? If I can't get in at Arthur's?"

"I know the manager of a small one near us," Peter said. "But if you don't mind coming to my place, you can use my mother's room for tonight. Or for as long as you need, probably."

"What about your mother?"

"She's away. She'll be away for quite a while."

"Not in Reno, by any chance?" There was a roughness, almost a coarseness, in her tone, like that in the overdone camaraderie of the shy.

"No. My father died when I was eight. Why?"

"Oh, something in the way you spoke. And then you're so competent. Does she work?"

"No. My father left something. Does yours?"

She stood up and picked up her bedraggled gloves. "No," she said, and her voice was suddenly distant and delicate again. "She marries." She turned and walked out ahead of him.

He paid, rushed out of the restaurant, and caught up with her.

"Thought maybe you'd run out on me," he said.

She got in the car without answering.

They drove through the Park, toward the address in the East Seventies that she had given him. A weak smell of grass underlay the gas-blended air, but the Park seemed limp and worn, as if the strain of the day's effluvia had been too much for it. At the Seventy-second Street stop signal, the blank light of a street lamp invaded the car.

"Thought you might be feeling Mrs. Grundyish at my suggesting the apartment," Peter said.

"Mrs. Grundy wasn't around much when I grew up." The signal changed and they moved ahead.

They stopped in a street which had almost no lights along its smartly converted house fronts. This was one of the streets, still sequestered by money, whose houses came alive only under the accelerated, febrile glitter of winter and would dream through the gross summer days, their interiors deadened with muslin or stirred faintly with the subterranean clinkings of caretakers. No. 4 was dark.

"I would rather stay over at your place, if I have to," the girl said. Her voice was offhand and prim. "I hate hotels. We always stopped at them in between."

"Let's get out and see."

They stepped down into the areaway in front of the entrance, the car door banging hollowly behind them. She fumbled in her purse and took out a key, although it was already obvious that it would not be usable. In his childhood, he had often hung around in the areaways of old brownstones such as this had been. In the corners there had always been a soft, decaying smell, and the ironwork, bent and smeared, always hung loose and broken-toothed. The areaway of this house had been repaved with slippery flag; even in the humid night there was no smell. Black-tongued grillwork, with an oily shine and padlocked, secured the windows and the smooth door. Fastened on the grillwork in front of the door was the neat, square proclamation of a protection agency.

"You don't have a key for the padlocks, do you?"

"No." She stood on the curb, looking up at the house. "It was a nice room I had there. Nicest one I ever did have, really." She crossed to the car and got in.

He followed her over to the car and got in beside her. She had her head in her hands.

"Don't worry. We'll get in touch with somebody in the morning."

"I don't. I don't care about any of it, really." She sat up, her face averted. "My parents, or any of the people they tangle with." She wound the lever on the door slowly, then reversed it. "Robert, or my mother, or Arthur," she said, "although he was always pleasant enough. Even Vince—even if I'd known him."

"He was just a screwed-up kid. It could have been anybody's window."

"No." Suddenly she turned and faced him. "I should think it would be the best privilege there is, though. To care, I mean."

When he did not immediately reply, she gave him a little pat on the arm and sat back. "Excuse it, please. I guess I'm groggy." She turned around and put her head on the crook of her arm. Her words came faintly through it. "Wake me when we get there."

She was asleep by the time they reached his street. He parked the car as quietly as possible beneath his own windows. He himself had never felt more awake in his life. He could have sat there until morning with her sleep-secured beside him. He sat thinking of how different it would be at Rye, or anywhere, with her along, with someone along who was the same age. For they were the same age, whatever that was, whatever the age was of people like them. There was nothing he would be unable to tell her.

To the north, above the rooftops, the electric mauve of midtown blanked out any auguries in the sky, but he wasn't looking for anything like that. Tomorrow he would take her for a drive—whatever the weather. There were a lot of good roads around Greenwich.

(1950)

SOME NIGHTS WHEN NOTHING

HAPPENS ARE THE BEST

NIGHTS IN THIS PLACE

T HE boss of this saloon on Third Avenue often says he wishes there was such a thing as a speakeasy license because when all is said and done he'd rather have a speakeasy than an open saloon that everybody can come into the way they all are now. Not that he is exactly opposed to people coming in. They spend money, no denying that. But a speakeasy, you could control who comes in and it was more homelike and more often not crowded the way this saloon is now. Johnny, one of the hackmen outside, put the whole thing in a nutshell one night when they were talking about a certain hangout and Johnny said, "Nobody goes there anymore. It's too crowded."

The point is that some nights when there's hardly anybody in a gin mill and nothing happens, why, those are the best nights in one way of thinking. They're more interesting and not such a hullabaloo of juke-box music and everybody talking at once and all of it not amounting to any interest for the boss or any of the regulars, unless you'd count a lot of money coming in.

Like the other morning about half past two it was more like a speakeasy, only a few there and odd ones coming in that the boss knew well and didn't mind any of them, each one different than the other.

Jack Yee come in first. The boss was having a cup of tea. He's a regular old woman about having a cup of hot tea down at the far end of the bar every now and then. Jack Yee is a favorite of the boss. Jack is a Chinaman that weighs pradickly nothing at all but he'll live to be a hundred easy. He starts out from Pell Street or Doyers every night around midnight and comes up Third Avenue on a regular route selling little wooden statues they send over by the millions from China. He sells them to drunks in saloons and about three, four o'clock winds up his route selling them in a couple night clubs.

The boss asked Jack to have a cup of tea, because he's always glad to see Jack. He can't understand how anybody could be as thin as this Chinaman and still keep going up and down the avenue night after night. Coldest night, Jack got no overcoat, just a skinny raincoat tied around him and always smoking a cigarette that's stuck on his lower lip and bouncing when he talks. So Jack put down his bag of statues and had a cup of tea with the boss, and first thing you know what are they talking about but how tough it is talking Chinese for a language.

You must know the boss come from Dublin and naturally has no hint of talking Chinese, but like everything else he has ideas about it just the same. It's no sense trying to tell how Jack talks but what he says to the boss is that there's the same word means two things in Chinese. Depends on how you say it, this word, high and squeaky or low and groaning.

Jack says "*loo*" if you say it down low it means "mouth." Then he tells the boss if you say "*loo*" up high it means "trolley car."

"Oh my God!" says the boss to Jack while they have their cup of tea opposite each other on the bar. "Oh my God, Jack, the same word mean 'trolley car' and 'mouth'?"

Jack says yes, and then he makes it worse by saying another instance, you might say. He tells the boss when a Chinaman says "*pee-lo*," something like that, and says it low and moaning it means "a bird," and if he says the same thing high it means "come in!"

"Oh my God!" says the boss after another sip of tea. "The same word, Jack, mean 'come in' and 'bird'? And the same word mean 'mouth' and 'trolley car'? Then by God, Jack, if they're ever gonna make a start at getting anywhere they'll have to get that ironed out!"

With that, Jack is laughing because, like the boss says often, Chinamen are great people for laughing. They'd laugh if you shoot them. Fact is, he says that's what probally discourages the Japs, because the boss figures that Japs only grin but it has no meaning to it and Chinamen laugh from inside. They're great people, he says.

W HILE the boss and Jack Yee were finishing their tea, they gave up the Chinese language as a bad job entirely, and at that minute who came in finally but the sour-beer artist to get his Christmas money and this the middle of February. The sour-beer artist is quite a guy in his own way. In this neighborhood they got a tradition that at the couple of weeks before Christmas there has to be written on the mirror back of the bar "Merry Christmas and a Happy New Year." The sour-beer artist goes around and puts that on the mirror. He does it with sour beer saved in the place for the purpose. You write with sour beer on the glass and it makes shiny crystals in the writing. Anybody could do it, of course, if he has sour beer, but this artist writes it with curlicues and that's the tradition that it has to be written that way. They give him two bucks and a half for it, but he's a foresighted guy and he can see ahead he'll be drunk and wandering by Christmas and likely in trouble, so he leaves the two bucks and a half unpaid some places to collect it after Christmas, when he's broke and hungry. That's why he just come in the other night, to get the two and a half, and of course he was welcome. Turned out he got a little stretch on the island for fighting around New Year's and here he was, sober and hungry. So the boss gave him the dough and threw in some soup and a roast-beef sandwich, and out went the sour-beer artist, saying to the boss, "Thanks, Tim. I'll see you around Christmas time." And it is true for him that's about when he'll show up, no questions asked, in time to write the curlicues on the mirror. In some ways the sour-beer artist is a little unusual, but that's the kind comes in on the quiet nights nothing happens.

GIVING out the Christmas money to the sour-beer artist moved things back to Christmas for a few minutes in the place, and the boss got started into giving quite a speech on Christmas.

"I'm glad it's over, with office parties for Christmas starting unpleasantness," the boss says. "I mean I worry every Christmas about those office parties they have around here. Somebody always goes too far at them being chummy with the boss of their office, maybe one of the girls kissing him and then wondering for months afterward did she go too far. But Christmas is over and done with. The thing I remember about this one was something that I had a chance to sit back and have nothing to do with it. I was on a train going up to see a nephew of mine is in a seminary a little ways up in the state and it was Christmas Eve. Well, first of all, it's the bane of my life around here that if a drunk gets to be a nuisance, by God it is always another drunk only not so far gone that thinks he can handle him.

"A thousand times in here I've seen a man beginning to drive out other customers by noisiness, or butting in, or something like that—well, I'd just have my mind made up I'd do something about him, even throw him out cautious if necessary. And that minute, without fail, up would come another less drunk drunk and say, 'Lemme handle him! I can handle this cluck!' That's the horror of 'em all, because then you got two drunks instead of one.

"On the train, in come this guy with bundles and his overcoat half on half off, and the minute he got on I shrunk back in my seat. I ran into them like that so many times, I was thanking God I was not in it at all and it was in a train and not here in my place. He begun singing 'Silent Night' and so forth and next nudging the guy in the seat with him to sing it, and then got sore because the man wouldn't sing 'Silent Night' with him.

"Then the drunk started changing seats like they change places at the bar here when they get like that. And he was by then opening up bundles and trying to show presents to a decent, quiet girl in the train. And hollering 'Silent Night' all the while. It was bad. And do you know anything about trains? The conductor won't throw you off if he can help it. They got rules the conductor has to get a railroad cop. That's because guys sues that get thrown off trains.

"Now up came the second drunk, the kind there always is. 'Lemme handle him,' says the second drunk to the conductor, exactly word for word what the second drunk always says in the place here. 'No,' says the conductor, but that wouldn't do. The second one grabs the first one, and by then we're pulling into 125th Street. And of course there's no cop on hand when they wanted him, the cop probally having a Christmas Eve for himself somewhere away from the station. Off goes the first drunk, the second drunk on top of him, the bundles half in the car, and the first one's overcoat left behind and the train pulls out. I gave thanks to God for once there was two drunks and me no part of it, because I've had it so often, even with the 'Silent Night' part thrown in for Christmas."

IT was quite a speech about Christmas, nothing exciting but the boss was launched off on talking about it and it was one of those quiet nights nothing happens.

Still and all, Eddie Clancarty at the other end of the bar, drinking alone the way he mostly does, was trying to start an argument. He was hollering for a drink while the boss was talking about Christmas. People keep away from Eddie. He's quarrelsome. Came over here from the old country as a gossoon, and hardly made any friends because he'd take issue with everybody about everything. You can't say a word but what Eddie Clancarty would take you up on it.

"You bums, why don't you go into the Army?" Eddie hollered back at the other few in the place. "Whyn't you go into the Army?"

Without Clancarty hearing, one customer said to the boss, "Why don't you throw him out, he's always starting a fight?"

"Oh, leave him alone," says the boss. "He's going into the Army tomorrow." He went up and served Eddie a drink, then got away from him quick.

Well, it got to be near four o'clock, time to put the chairs on top of the tables and close up the place.

"We'll go over to Bickford's and have some scrambled eggs when I get the joint closed," said the boss to a couple of the customers with him, saying it low so Clancarty couldn't hear. The boss likes to wind up the night in Bickford's having some eggs and some more tea before he goes home, and reading who's dead in the *Tribune* and having a look at the entries in the *Mirror.*

"What're you heels talking about?" said nosy Clancarty. But nobody answered.

"Drink up, Eddie, we're closing!" said the boss. Eddie hollered some more but drank his drink.

In a minute or two they all had gone out on the sidewalk, some waiting in a little bunch while the boss locked the door. Clancarty was cursing at nothing at all, just in general, and started away by himself.

"Let him go," said the boss, though there was no need of it, with nobody stopping such a quarrelsome guy from going. The boss and the others started for Bickford's, and Clancarty was off the other way. The boss looked back at him going and said, "Now, isn't that a terrible thing? Sure I just bethought of it now! There he is, going into the Army tomorrow, and I can see plain as day what's the matter with him. The poor man has nobody at all to say good-bye to."

(1943)

J. D. SALINGER

SLIGHT REBELLION OFF MADISON

O N vacation from Pencey Preparatory School for Boys ("An Instructor for Every Ten Students"), Holden Morrisey Caulfield usually wore his chesterfield and a hat with a cutting edge at the "V" in the crown. While riding in Fifth Avenue buses, girls who knew Holden often thought they saw him walking past Saks' or Altman's or Lord & Taylor's, but it was usually somebody else.

This year, Holden's Christmas vacation from Pencey Prep broke at the same time as Sally Hayes' from the Mary A. Woodruff School for Girls ("Special Attention to Those Interested in Dramatics"). On vacation from Mary A. Woodruff, Sally usually went hatless and wore her new silverblu muskrat coat. While riding in Fifth Avenue buses, boys who knew Sally often thought they saw her walking past Saks' or Altman's or Lord & Taylor's. It was usually somebody else.

As soon as Holden got into New York, he took a cab home, dropped his Gladstone in the foyer, kissed his mother, lumped his hat and coat into a convenient chair, and dialled Sally's number.

"Hey!" he said into the mouthpiece. "Sally?"

"Yes. Who's that?"

"Holden Caulfield. How are ya?"

"Holden! I'm fine! How are you?"

"Swell," said Holden. "Listen. How are ya, anyway? I mean how's school?"

"Fine," said Sally. "I mean—you know."

"Swell," said Holden. "Well, listen. What are you doing tonight?"

Holden took her to the Wedgwood Room that night, and they both dressed, Sally wearing her new turquoise job. They danced a lot. Holden's style was long, slow side steps back and forth, as though he were dancing over an open manhole. They danced cheek to cheek, and when their faces got sticky from contact, neither of them minded. It was a long time between vacations.

They made a wonderful thing out of the taxi ride home. Twice, when the cab stopped short in traffic, Holden fell off the seat.

"I love you," he swore to Sally, removing his mouth from hers.

"Oh, darling, I love you, too," Sally said, and added, less passionately, "Promise me you'll let your hair grow out. Crew cuts are corny."

The next day was a Thursday and Holden took Sally to the matinée of "O Mistress Mine," which neither of them had seen. During the first intermission, they smoked in the lobby and vehemently agreed with each other that the Lunts were marvellous. George Harrison, of Andover, also was smoking in the lobby and he recognized Sally, as she hoped he would. They had been introduced once at a party and had never seen each other since. Now, in the lobby of the Empire, they greeted each other with the gusto of two who might frequently have taken baths together as small children. Sally asked George if he didn't think the show was marvellous. George gave himself a little room for his reply, bearing down on the foot of the woman behind him. He said that the play itself certainly was no masterpiece, but that the Lunts, of course, were absolute angels.

"Angels," Holden thought. "Angels. For Chrissake. *Angels.*"

After the matinée, Sally told Holden that she had a marvellous idea. "Let's go ice skating at Radio City tonight."

"All right," Holden said. "Sure."

"Do you mean it?" Sally said. "Don't just *say* it unless you mean it. I mean I don't *give* a darn, one way or the other."

"No," said Holden. "Let's go. It might be fun."

SALLY and Holden were both terrible ice skaters. Sally's ankles had a painful, unbecoming way of collapsing toward each other and Holden's weren't much better. That night there were at least a hundred people who had nothing better to do than watch the skaters.

"Let's get a table and have a drink," Holden suggested suddenly.

"That's the most marvellous idea I've heard all day," Sally said.

They removed their skates and sat down at a table in the warm inside lounge. Sally took off her red woollen mittens. Holden began to light matches. He let them burn down till he couldn't hold them, then he dropped what was left into an ashtray.

"Look," Sally said, "I have to know—are you or aren't you going to help me trim the tree Christmas Eve?"

"Sure," said Holden, without enthusiasm.

"I mean I have to know," Sally said.

Holden suddenly stopped lighting matches. He leaned forward over the table. "Sally, did you ever get fed up? I mean did you ever get scared that everything was gonna go lousy unless you did something?"

"Sure," Sally said.

"Do you like school?" Holden inquired.

"It's a terrific bore."

"Do you hate it, I mean?"

"Well, I don't hate it."

"Well, *I* hate it," said Holden. "Boy, do I hate it! But it isn't just that. It's everything. I hate living in New York. I hate Fifth Avenue buses and Madison Avenue buses and getting out at the center doors. I hate the Seventy-second Street movie, with those fake clouds on the ceiling, and being introduced to guys like George Harrison, and going down in elevators when you wanna go out, and guys fitting your pants all the time at Brooks." His voice got more excited. "Stuff like that. Know what I mean? You know something? You're the only reason I came home this vacation."

"You're sweet," said Sally, wishing he'd change the subject.

"Boy, I hate school! You oughta go to a boys' school sometime. All you do is study, and make believe you give a damn if the football team wins, and talk about girls and clothes and liquor, and—"

"Now, *listen,*" Sally interrupted. "Lots of boys get more out of school than that."

"I agree," said Holden. "But that's all *I* get out of it. See? That's what I mean. I don't get anything out of anything. I'm in bad shape. I'm in lousy shape. Look, Sally. How would you like to just beat it? Here's my idea. I'll borrow Fred Halsey's car and tomorrow morning we'll drive up to Massachusetts and Vermont and around there, see? It's beautiful. I mean it's wonderful up there, honest to God. We'll stay in these cabin camps and stuff like that till my money runs out. I have a hundred and twelve dollars with me. Then, when the money runs out, I'll get a job and we'll live some-where with a brook and stuff. Know what I mean? Honest to God, Sally, we'll have a swell time. Then, later on, we'll get married or something. Wuddaya say? C'mon! Wuddaya say? C'mon! Let's do it, huh?"

"You can't just *do* something like that," Sally said.

"Why not?" Holden asked shrilly. "Why the hell not?"

"Because you can't," Sally said. "You just can't, that's all. Supposing your money ran out and you didn't get a job—then what?"

"I'd get a job. Don't worry about that. You don't have to worry about that part of it. What's the matter? Don't you wanna go with me?"

"It isn't that," Sally said. "It's not that at all. Holden, we'll have lots of time to do those things—*all* those things. After you go to college and we get married and all. There'll be oodles of marvellous places to go to."

"No, there wouldn't be," Holden said. "It'd be entirely different."

Sally looked at him, he had contradicted her so quietly.

"It wouldn't be the same at all. We'd have to go downstairs in elevators with suitcases and stuff. We'd have to call up everyone and tell 'em goodbye and send 'em postcards. And I'd have to work at my father's and ride in Madison Avenue buses and read newspapers. We'd have to go to the Seventy-second Street all the time and see newsreels. Newsreels! There's always a dumb horse race and some dame breaking a bottle over a ship. You don't see what I mean at all."

"Maybe I don't. Maybe *you* don't, either," Sally said.

Holden stood up, with his skates swung over one shoulder. "You give me a royal pain," he announced quite dispassionately.

A little after midnight, Holden and a fat, unattractive boy named Carl Luce sat at the Wadsworth Bar, drinking Scotch-and-sodas and eating potato chips. Carl was at Pencey Prep, too, and led his class.

"Hey, Carl," Holden said, "you're one of these intellectual guys. Tell me something. Supposing you were fed up. Supposing you were going stark, staring mad. Supposing you wanted to quit school and everything and get the hell out of New York. What would you do?"

"Drink up," Carl said. "The hell with that."

"No, I'm serious," Holden pleaded.

"You've always got a bug," Carl said, and got up and left.

Holden went on drinking. He drank up nine dollars' worth of Scotch-and-sodas and at 2 A.M. made his way from the bar into the little anteroom, where there was a telephone. He dialled three numbers before he got the proper one.

"Hullo!" Holden shouted into the phone.

"Who is this?" inquired a cold voice.

"This is me, Holden Caulfield. Can I speak to Sally, please?"

"Sally's asleep. This is Mrs. Hayes. Why are you calling up at this hour, Holden?"

"Wanna talk Sally, Mis' Hayes. Very 'portant. Put her on."

"Sally's *asleep*, Holden. Call tomorrow. Good night."

"Wake 'er up. Wake 'er up, huh? Wake 'er up, Mis' Hayes."

"Holden," Sally said, from the other end of the wire. "This is me. What's the idea?"

"Sally? Sally, that you?"

"Yes. You're drunk."

"Sally, I'll come over Christmas Eve. Trim the tree for ya. Huh? Wuddaya say? Huh?"

"Yes. Go to bed now. Where are you? Who's with you?"

"I'll trim the tree for ya. Huh? Wuddaya say? Huh?"

"Yes. Go to bed now. Where are you? Who's with you?"

"I'll trim the tree for ya. Huh? O.K.?"

"Yes! Good night!"

"G'night. G'night, Sally baby. Sally sweetheart, darling."

Holden hung up and stood by the phone for nearly fifteen minutes. Then he put another nickel in the slot and dialled the same number again.

"*Hullo!*" he yelled into the mouthpiece. "Speak to Sally, please."

There was a sharp click as the phone was hung up, and Holden hung up, too. He stood swaying for a moment. Then he made his way into the men's room and filled one of the washbowls with cold water. He immersed his head to the ears, after which he walked, dripping, to the radiator and sat down on it. He sat there counting the squares in the tile floor while the water dripped down his face and the back of his neck, soaking his shirt collar and necktie. Twenty minutes later the barroom piano player came in to comb his wavy hair.

"Hiya, boy!" Holden greeted him from the radiator. "I'm on the hot seat. They pulled the switch on me. I'm getting fried."

The piano player smiled.

"Boy, you can play!" Holden said. "You really can play that piano. You oughta go on the radio. You know that? You're damn good, boy."

"You wanna towel, fella?" asked the piano player.

"Not me," said Holden.

"Why don't you go home, kid?"

Holden shook his head. "Not me," he said. "Not me."

The piano player shrugged and replaced the lady's comb in his inside pocket. When he left the room, Holden stood up from the radiator and blinked several times to let the tears out of his eyes. Then he went to the checkroom. He put on his chesterfield without buttoning it and jammed his hat on the back of his soaking-wet head.

His teeth chattering violently, Holden stood on the corner and waited for a Madison Avenue bus. It was a long wait.

(1946)

BROWNSTONE

THE camel, I had noticed, was passing, with great difficulty, through the eye of the needle. The Apollo flight, the four-minute mile, Venus in Scorpio, human records on land and at sea—these had been events of enormous importance. But the camel, practicing in near obscurity for almost two thousand years, was passing through. First the velvety nose, then the rest. Not many were aware. But if the lead camel and then perhaps the entire caravan could make it, the thread, the living thread of camels, would exist, could not be lost. No one could lose the thread. The prospects of the rich would be enhanced. "Ortega tells us that the business of philosophy," the professor was telling his class of indifferent freshmen, "is to crack open metaphors which are dead."

"I shouldn't have come," the Englishman said, waving his drink and breathing so heavily at me that I could feel my bangs shift. "I have a terrible cold."

"He would probably have married her," a voice across the room said, "with the exception that he died."

"Well, I am a personality that prefers not to be annoyed."

"We should all prepare ourselves for this eventuality."

A six-year-old was passing the hors d'oeuvres. The baby, not quite steady on his feet, was hurtling about the room.

"He's following me," the six-year-old said, in despair.
"Then lock yourself in the bathroom, dear," Inez replied.
"He always waits outside the door."
"He loves you, dear."
"Well, I don't like it."
"How I envy you," the minister's wife was saying to a courteous, bearded boy, "reading 'Magic Mountain' for the first time."

THE homosexual across the hall from me always takes Valium and walks his beagle. I borrow Valium from him from time to time, and when he takes a holiday the dog is left with me. On our floor of this brownstone, we are friends. Our landlord, Roger Somerset, was murdered last July. He was a kind and absentminded man, and on the night when he was stabbed there was a sort of requiem for him in the heating system. There is a lot of music in this building anyway. The newlyweds on the third floor play Bartók on their stereo. The couple on the second floor play clarinet quintets; their kids play rock. The girl on the fourth floor, who has been pining for two months, plays Judy Collins' "Maid of Constant Sorrow" all day long. We have a kind of orchestra in here. The ground floor is a shop. The owner of the shop speaks of our landlord's murder still. Shaking his head, he says that he suspects "foul play." We all agree with him. We changed our locks. But "foul play" seems a weird expression for the case.

IT is all weird. I am not always well. One block away (I often think of this), there was ten months ago an immense crash. Water mains broke. There were small rivers in the streets. In a great skyscraper that was being built, something had failed. The newspapers reported the next day that by some miracle only two people had been "slightly injured" by ten tons of falling steel. The steel fell from the eighteenth floor. The question that preoccupies me now is how, under the circumstances, slight injuries could occur. Perhaps the two people were grazed in passing by. Perhaps some fragments of the sidewalk ricocheted. I knew a deliverer of flowers who, at Sixty-ninth and Lexington, was hit by a flying suicide. Situations simply do not yield to the most likely structures of the mind. A "self-addressed envelope," if you are inclined to brood, raises deep questions of identity. Such an envelope, immutably itself, is always precisely where it belongs. "Self-pity" is just sadness, I think, in the pejorative. But "joking with nurses" fascinates me in the press. Whenever someone has been quite struck down, lost faculties, members of his family, he is said to have "joked with his nurses" quite a lot. What a mine of humor every nurse's life must be.

THE St. Bernard at the pound on Ninety-second Street was named Bonnie and would have cost five dollars. The attendant held her tightly on a leash of rope. "Hello, Bonnie," I said. Bonnie growled.

"I wouldn't talk to her if I was you," the attendant said.

I leaned forward to pat her ear. Bonnie snarled. "I wouldn't touch her if I was you," the attendant said. I held out my hand under Bonnie's jowls. She strained against the leash, and choked and coughed. "Now cut that out, Bonnie," the attendant said.

"Could I just take her for a walk around the block," I said, "before I decide?" "Are you out of your mind?" the attendant said. Aldo patted Bonnie, and we left.

I have a job, of course. I have had several jobs. I've had our paper's gossip column since last month. It is egalitarian. I look for people who are quite obscure, and report who is breaking up with whom and where they go and what they wear. The person who invented this new form for us is on antidepressants now. He lives in Illinois. He says there are people in southern Illinois who have not yet been covered by the press. I often write about families in Queens. Last week, I went to a dinner party on Park Avenue. After 1 A.M., something called the Alive or Dead Game was being played. Someone would mention an old character from Tammany or Hollywood. "Dead," "Dead," "Dead," everyone would guess. "No, no. Alive. I saw him walking down the street just yesterday," or "Yes. Dead. I read a little obituary notice about him last year." One of the little truths people can subtly enrage or reassure each other with is who—when you have looked away a month, a year—is still around.

Dear Tenant:

We have reason to believe that there are impostors posing as Con Ed repairmen and inspectors circulating in this area.

Do not permit any Con Ed man to enter your premises or the building, if possible.

The Precinct

MY cousin, who was born on February 29th, became a veterinarian. Some years ago, when he was twenty-eight (seven, by our childhood birthday count), he was drafted, and sent to Malaysia. He spent most of his military service there, assigned to the zoo. He operated on one tiger, which, in the course of abdominal surgery, began to wake up and wag its tail. The anesthetist grabbed the tail, and injected more sodium pentothal. That tiger survived. But two flamingos, sent by the city of Miami to Kuala Lumpur as a token of good will, could not bear the trip or the climate and, in spite of my cousin's efforts, died. There was also a cobra—the largest anyone in Kuala Lumpur could remember having seen. An old man had brought it, in an immense sack, from somewhere in the countryside. The zoo director called my cousin at once, around dinnertime, to say that an unprecedented cobra had arrived. Something quite drastic, however, seemed wrong with its neck. My cousin, whom I have always admired—for his leap-year birthday, for his pilot's license, for his presence of mind—said that he would certainly examine the cobra in the morning but that the best thing for it after its long journey must be a good night's rest. By morning, the cobra was dead.

My cousin is well. The problem is this. Hardly anyone about whom I deeply care at all resembles anyone else I have ever met, or heard of, or read about in the literature. I know an Israeli general who, in 1967, retook the Mitla Pass but who, since his mandatory retirement from military service at fifty-five, has been trying to repopulate the Ark. He asked me, over breakfast at the Drake, whether I knew any owners of oryxes. Most of the vegetarian species he has collected have already multiplied enough, since he has found and cared for them, to be permitted to run wild. The carnivorous animals, though, must still be kept behind barbed wire—to keep them from stalking the rarer vegetarians. I know a group that studies Proust one Sunday afternoon a month, and an analyst, with that Exeter laugh (embittered mooing noises, and mirthless heaving of the shoulder blades), who has the most remarkable terrorist connections in the Middle East.

THE New York Chinese cabdriver lingered at every corner and at every traffic light, to read his paper. I wondered what the news was. I looked over his shoulder. The illustrations and the type were clear enough: newspaper print, pornographic fiction. I leaned back in my seat. A taxi-driver who happened to be Oriental with a sadomasochistic cast of mind was not my business. I lit a cigarette, looked at my bracelet. I caught the driver's eyes a moment in the rearview mirror. He picked up his paper. "I don't think you ought to read," I said, "while you are driving." Traffic was slow. I saw his mirrored eyes again. He stopped his reading. When we reached my address, I did not tip him. Racism and prudishness, I thought, and reading over people's shoulders.

BUT there are moments in this place when everything becomes a show of force. He can read what he likes at home. Tipping is still my option. Another newspaper event, in our brownstone. It was a holiday. The superintendent normally hauls the garbage down and sends the paper up, by dumbwaiter, each morning. On holidays, the garbage stays upstairs, the paper on the sidewalk. At 8 A.M., I went downstairs. A ragged man was lying across the little space that separates the inner door, which locks, from the outer door, which doesn't. I am not a news addict. I could have stepped over the sleeping man, picked up my *Times*, and gone upstairs to read it. Instead, I knocked absurdly from inside the door, and said, "Wake up. You'll have to leave now." He got up, lifted the flattened cardboard he had been sleeping on, and walked away, mumbling and reeking. It would have been kinder, certainly, to let the driver read, the wino sleep. One simply cannot bear down so hard on all these choices.

WHAT is the point. That is what must be borne in mind. Sometimes the point is really who wants what. Sometimes the point is what is right or kind. Sometimes the point is a momentum, a fact, a quality, a voice, an intimation, a thing said or unsaid. Sometimes it's who's at fault, or what will happen if you do not move at once. The point changes and goes out. You cannot be forever watching for the point, or you lose the simplest thing: being a major character in your own life. But if you are, for any length of time, custodian of the point—in art, in court, in politics, in lives, in rooms—it turns out there are rear-guard actions everywhere. Now and then, a small foray is worthwhile. Just so that being constantly, complacently, thoroughly wrong does not become the safest position of them all. The point has never quite been entrusted to me.

THE conversation of "The Magic Mountain" and the unrequited love of six-year-olds occurred on Saturday, at brunch. "Bring someone new," Inez had said. "Not queer. Not married, maybe separated. John and I are breaking up." The invitation was not of a kind that I had heard before. Aldo, who lives with me between the times when he prefers to be alone, refused to come. He despises brunch. He detests Inez. I went, instead, with a lawyer who has been a distant, steady friend but who, ten years ago, when we first came to New York, had once put three condoms on the night table beside the phone. We both had strange ideas then about New York. Aldo is a gentle, orderly, soft-spoken man, slow to conclude. I try to be tidy when he is here, but I have often made his cigarettes, and once his manuscript, into the bed. Our paper's publisher is an intellectual from Baltimore. He has read Wittgenstein; he's always making unimpeachable remarks. Our music critic throws a tantrum every day, in print. Our book reviewer is looking for another job. He found that the packages in which all books are mailed could not, simply could not, be opened without doing considerable damage—through staples, tape, wire, fluttering gray stuff, recalcitrance—to the reviewer's hands. He felt it was a symptom of some kind—one of those cases where incompetence at every stage, across the board, acquired a certain independent force. Nothing to do with books, he thought, worked out at all. We also do the news. For horoscopes, there are the ladies' magazines. We just cannot compete.

MY late landlord was from Scarsdale. The Maid of Constant Sorrow is from Texas. Aldo is from St. Louis. Inez's versions vary about where she's from. I grew up in a New England mill town, where, in the early thirties, all the insured factories burned down. It has been difficult to get fire insurance in that region ever since. The owner of a hardware store, whose property adjoined an insured factory at the time, lost everything. Afterward, he walked all day along the railroad track, waiting for a train to run him down. Railroad service has never been very good up there. No trains came. His children own the town these days, for what it's worth. The two cobbled streets where black people always lived have been torn up and turned into a public park since a flood that occurred some years ago. Unprecedented rains came. Retailers had to destroy their sodden products, for fear of contamination. And the black section was torn up and seeded over in the town's rezoning project. No one knows where the blacks live now. But there are Negroes in the stores and schools, and on the football team. It is assumed that the park integrated the town. Those black families must be living somewhere. It is a mystery.

THE host, for some reason, was taking Instamatic pictures of his guests. It was not clear whether he was doing this in order to be able to show, at some future time, that there had been this gathering in his house. Or whether he thought of pictures in some voodoo sense. Or whether he found it difficult to talk. Or whether he was bored. Two underground celebrities—one of whom had become a sensation by never generating or exhibiting a flicker of interest in anything, the other of whom was known mainly for hanging around the first—were taking pictures, too. I was there with a movie star I've known for years. He had already been received in an enormous embrace by an Eastern European poet, whose hair was cut too short but who was neither as awkwardly spontaneous nor as drunk as he cared to seem. The party was in honor of the poet, who celebrated the occasion by insulting everyone and being fawned upon, by distinguished and undistinguished writers alike. "This group looks as though someone had torn up a few guest lists and floated the pieces on the air," somebody said.

PAUL: "Two diamonds."

INEZ: "Two hearts."

MARY: "Three clubs."

JOHN: "Four kings."

INEZ: "Darling, you know you can't just bid four kings."

JOHN: "I don't see why. I might have been bluffing."

INEZ: "No, darling. That's poker. This is bridge. And even in poker you can't just bid four kings."

JOHN: "No. Well, I guess we'd better deal another hand."

The friend of the underground sensation walked up to the actor and me and said hello. Then, in a verbal seizure of some sort, he began muttering obscenities. The actor said a few calming things that didn't work. He finally put his finger on the mutterer's lips. The mutterer bit that finger extremely hard, and walked away. The actor wrapped his finger in a paper napkin, and got himself another drink. We stayed till twelve.

I went to a women's college. We had distinguished faculty in everything, digs at Nuoro and Mycenae. We had a quality of obsession in our studies. For professors who had quarrelled with their wives at breakfast, those years of bright-eyed young women, never getting any older, must have been a trial. The head of the history department once sneezed into his best student's honors thesis. He slammed it shut. It was ultimately published. When I was there, a girl called Cindy Melchior was immensely fat. She wore silk trousers and gilt mules. One day, in the overheated classroom, she laid aside her knitting and lumbered to the window, which she opened. Then she lumbered back. "Do you think," the professor asked, "you are so graceful?" He somehow meant it kindly. Cindy wept. That year, Cindy's brother Melvin phoned me. "I would have called you sooner," he said, "but I had the most terrible eczema." All the service staff on campus in those days were black. Many of them were followers of Father Divine. They took new names in the church. I remember the year when a maid called Serious Heartbreak married a janitor called Universal Dictionary. At a meeting of the faculty last fall, the college president, who is new and male, spoke of raising money. A female professor of Greek was knitting—and working on Linear B, with an abacus before her. In our time, there was a vogue for madrigals. Some of us listened, constantly, to a single record. There was a phrase we could not decipher. A professor of symbolic logic, a French Canadian, had sounds that matched but a meaning that seemed unlikely: Sheep are no angels; come upstairs. A countertenor explained it, after a local concert: She'd for no angel's comfort stay. Not so likely, either.

THE Maid of Constant Sorrow said our landlord's murder marked a turning point in her analysis. "I don't feel guilty. I feel hated," she said. It is true, for a time, we all wanted to feel somehow a part—if only because violence offset the boredom of our lives. My grandfather said that some people have such extreme insomnia that they look at their watches every hour after midnight, to see how sorry they ought to be feeling for themselves. Aldo says he does not care what my grandfather said. My grandmother refused to concede that any member of the family died of natural causes. An uncle's cancer in middle age occurred because all the suitcases fell off the luggage rack onto him when he was in his teens, and so forth. Death was an acquired characteristic. My grandmother, too, used to put other people's ailments into the diminutive: strokelets were what her friends had. Aldo said he was bored to tearsies by my grandmother's diminutives.

WHEN I worked, for a time, in the infirmary of a branch of an upstate university, it was becoming more difficult with each passing semester, except in the most severe cases, to determine which students had mental or medical problems. At the clinic, young men with straggly beards and stained blue jeans wept alongside girls in jeans and frayed sweaters—all being fitted with contact lenses, over which they then wore granny glasses. There was no demand for prescription granny glasses at all. For the severely depressed, the paranoids, and the hallucinators, our young psychiatrists prescribed "mood elevators," pills that were neither uppers nor downers but which affected the bloodstream in such a way that within three to five weeks many sad outpatients became very cheerful, and several saints and historical figures became again Midwestern graduate students under tolerable stress. On one, not unusual, morning, the clinic had a call from an instructor in political science. "I am in the dean's office," he said. "My health is quite perfect. They want me to have a checkup."

"Oh?" said the doctor on duty. "Perhaps you could come in on Friday."

"The problem is," the voice on the phone said, "I have always thought myself, and been thought by others, a Negro. Now, through research, I have found that my family on both sides have always been white."

"Oh," the doctor on duty said. "Perhaps you could just take a cab and come over."

Within twenty minutes, the political-science instructor appeared at the clinic. He was black. The doctor said nothing, and began a physical examination. By the time his blood pressure was taken, the patient confided that his white ancestors were, in fact, royal. The mood elevators restored him. He and the doctor became close friends besides. A few months later, the instructor took a job with the government in Washington. Two weeks after that, he was calling the clinic again. "I have found new documentation," he said. "All eight of my great-grandparents were pure-blooded Germans—seven from Prussia, one from Alsace. I thought I should tell you, dear friend." The doctor suggested he come for the weekend. By Sunday afternoon, a higher dose of the pill had had its effect. The problem has not since recurred.

"ALL babies are natural swimmers," John said, lowering his two-year-old son gently over the side of the rowboat, and smiling. The child thrashed and sank. Aldo dived in and grabbed him. The baby came up coughing, not crying, and looked with pure fear at his father. John looked with dismay at his son. "He would have come up in a minute," John said to Aldo, who was dripping and rowing. "You have to give nature a chance."

"RESERVATIONS are still busy. Thank you for your patience," the voice of the airline kept saying. It was a recording. After it had said the same thing thirty-two times, I hung up. Scattered through the two cars of the Brewster–New York train last week were adults with what seemed to be a clandestine understanding of some sort. They did not look at each other. They stared out the windows, or read. "Um," sang a lady at our fourth stop on the way to Grand Central. She appeared to be reading the paper. She kept singing her

"Um," as one who is getting the pitch. A young man had already been whistling "Frère Jacques" for three stops. When the "Um" lady found her pitch and began to sing the national anthem, he looked at her with rage. The conductor passed through, punching tickets in his usual fashion, not in the aisle but directly over people's laps. Every single passenger was obliged to flick the tiny punched part of the ticket from his lap onto the floor. Conductors have this process as their own little show of force. The whistler and the singer were in a dead heat when we reached the city. The people with the clandestine understanding turned out to be inmates from an upstate asylum, now on leave with their families, who met them in New York.

I don't think much of writers in whom nothing is at risk. It is possible, though, to be too literal-minded about this question.
"$3000 for First Person Articles," for example:

> An article for this series must be a true, hitherto unpublished narrative of an unusual personal experience. It may be dramatic, inspirational, or humorous, but it must have, in the opinion of the editors, a quality of narrative and interest comparable to "How I Lost My Eye" (June '72) and "Attacked by a Killer Shark" (April '72). Contributions must be typewritten, preferably *double-spaced* . . .

I particularly like where the stress, the italics, goes.

IN Corfu, I once met a polo-playing Argentine Existential psychiatrist who had lived for months in a London commune. He said that on days when the ordinary neurotics in the commune were getting on each other's nerves the few psychopaths and schizophrenics in their midst retired to their rooms and went their version of berserk, alone. On days when the neurotics got along, the psychopaths calmed down, tried to make contact, cooked meals. It was, he said, as though the sun came out for them. I hope that's true. Although altogether too much of life is mood. I receive communications almost every day from an institution called the Center for Short-Lived Phenomena. They have reporting sources all over the world, and an extensive correspondence. Under the title "Type of Event: Biological," I have received postcards about the progress of the Dormouse Invasion of Formentera ("Apart from population density, the dormouse of Formentera had a peak of reproduction in 1970. All females checked were pregnant, and perhaps this fact could have been the source of the idea of an 'invasion' "), and the Northwest Atlantic Puffin Decline. I have followed the Tanzanian Army Worm Outbreak; the San Fernando Earthquake; the Green Pond Fish Kill ("80% of the numbers involved," the Center's post-card reports, "were mummichogs"); the Samar Spontaneous Soil Burn; the Hawaiian Monk Seal Disappearance; and, also, the Naini Tal Sudden Sky Brightening.

THOSE are accounts of things that do not last long, but if you become fa-mous for a single thing in this country, and just endure, it is certain you will recur enlarged. Of the eighteen men who were indicted for conspiracy to murder Schwerner, Goodman, and Chaney, seven were convicted by a Mississippi jury—a surprising thing. But then a year later, a man was wounded and a woman killed in a shootout while trying to bomb the house of some Mississippi Jews. It turned out that the informer, the man who had helped the bombers, and led the F.B.I. to them, was one of the convicted seven—the one, in fact, who was alleged to have killed two of the three boys who were found in that Mississippi dam. And what's more, and what's more, the convicted conspirator, alleged double killer, was paid thirty-six thousand dollars by the F.B.I. for bringing the bombers in. Yet the wave of anti-Semitic bombings in Mississippi stopped after the shootout. I don't know what it means. I am in this brownstone.

Last year, Aldo moved out and went to Los Angeles on a story. I called him to ask whether I could come. He said, "Are you going to stay this time?" I said I wasn't sure. I flew out quite early in the morning. On the plane, there was the most banal, unendurable pickup, lasting the whole flight. A young man and a young woman—he was Italian, I think; she was German—had just met, and settled on French as their only common lan-guage. They asked each other where they were from, and where they were going. They posed each other riddles. He took out a pencil and paper and sketched her portrait. She giggled. He asked her whether she had ever con-sidered a career as a model. She said she had considered it but she feared that all men in the field were after the same thing. He agreed. He began to tell slightly off-color stories. She laughed and reproached him. It was like that. I wondered whether these things were always, to captive eavesdrop-pers, so dreary.

WHEN I arrived at Aldo's door, he met me with a smile that seemed sur-prised, a little sheepish. We talked awhile. Sometimes he took, sometimes I held, my suitcase. I tried, I thought, a joke. I asked whether there was already a girl there. He said there was. He met me in an hour at the corner drugstore for a cup of coffee. We talked. We returned to the apartment. We had Scotch. That afternoon, quite late, I flew home. I called him from time to time. He had his telephone removed a few days later. Now, for a while, he's here again. He's doing a political essay. It begins, "Some things cannot be said too often, and some can." That's all he's got so far.

We had people in for drinks one night last week. The cork in the wine bottle broke. Somebody pounded it into the bottle with a chisel and a hammer. We went to a bar. I have never understood the feeling men seem to have for bars they frequent. A fine musician who was with us played Mozart, Chopin, and Beethoven on the piano. It seemed a great, impromptu occasion. Then he said, we thought, "I am now going to play some Yatz." From what he played, it turned out he meant jazz. He played it badly.

WE had driven in from another weekend in the country while it was still daylight. Lots of cars had their headlights on. We weren't sure whether it was for or against peace, or just for highway safety. Milly, a secretary in a brokerage office, was married in our ground-floor shop that evening. She cried hysterically. Her mother and several people from her home town and John, whose girl she had been before he married Inez, thought it was from sentiment or shyness, or some conventional reason. Milly explained it to Aldo later. She and her husband had really married two years before—the week they met, in fact—in a chapel in Las Vegas. They hadn't wanted to tell their parents, or anybody, until he finished law school. They had torn up their Las Vegas license. She had been crying out of some legal fear of being married twice, it turned out. Their best man, a Puerto Rican doctor, said his aunt had been mugged in a cemetery in San Juan by a man on horseback. She thought it was her husband, returned from the dead. She had required sedation. We laughed. My friend across the hall, who owns the beagle, looked very sad all evening. He said, abruptly, that he was cracking up, and no one would believe him. There were sirens in the street. Inez said she knew exactly what he meant: she was cracking up also. Her escort, an Italian jeweller, said, "I too. I too have it. The most terrible anguishes, anguishes all in the night."

Inez said she knew the most wonderful man for the problem. "He may strike you at first as a phony," she said, "but then, when you're with him, you find yourself naturally screaming. It's such a relief. And he teaches you how you can practice at home." Milly said she was not much of a screamer—had never, in fact, screamed in her life. "High time you did, then," Inez said. Our sportswriter said he had recently met a girl whose problem was stealing all the suède garments of house guests, and another, in her thirties, who cried all the time because she had not been accepted at Smith. We heard many more sirens in the streets. We all went home.

AT 4 A.M., the phone rang about fifty times. I did not answer it. Aldo suggested that we remove it. I took three Valium. The whole night was sirens, then silence. The phone rang again. It is still ringing. The paper goes to press tomorrow. It is possible that I know who killed our landlord. So many things point in one direction. But too strong a case, I find, is often lost. It incurs doubts, suspicions. Perhaps I do not know. Perhaps it doesn't matter. I think it does, though. When I wonder what it is that we are doing—in this brownstone, on this block, with this paper—the truth is probably that we are fighting for our lives.

(1973)

THE CAFETERIA

TRANSLATED, FROM THE YIDDISH, BY THE AUTHOR AND DOROTHEA STRAUS

E VEN though I have reached the point where a great part of my earn-
ings is given away in taxes, I still have the habit of eating in cafeterias
when I am by myself. I like to take a tray with a tin knife, fork, spoon, and
paper napkin and to choose at the counter the food I enjoy. Besides, I meet
there the *landsleit* from Poland, as well as all kinds of literary beginners
and readers who know Yiddish. The moment I sit down at a table, they
come over. "Hello, Aaron!" they greet me, and we talk about Yiddish literature, the Holocaust, the state of Israel, and often about acquaintances
who were eating rice pudding or stewed prunes the last time I was here
and are already in their graves. Since I seldom read a paper, I learn this
news only later. Each time, I am startled, but at my age one has to be ready
for such tidings. The food sticks in the throat; we look at one another in
confusion, and our eyes ask mutely, Whose turn is next? Soon we begin to
chew again. I am often reminded of a scene in a film about Africa. A lion
attacks a herd of zebras and kills one. The frightened zebras run for a while
and then they stop and start to graze again. Do they have a choice?

I cannot spend too long with these Yiddishists, because I am always busy.
I am writing a novel, a story, an article. I have to lecture today or tomorrow;
my datebook is crowded with all kinds of appointments for weeks and
months in advance. It can happen that an hour after I leave the cafeteria I
am on a train to Chicago or flying to California. But meanwhile we converse
in the mother language and I hear of intrigues and pettiness about which,
from a moral point of view, it would be better not to be informed. Everyone

tries in his own way with all his means to grab as many honors and as much love and prestige as he can. None of us learns from all these deaths. Old age does not cleanse us. We don't repent at the gate of Hell.

I have been moving around in this neighborhood for over thirty years—as long as I lived in Poland. I know each block, each house. There has been little building here on uptown Broadway in the last decades, and I have the illusion of having put down roots here. I have spoken in most of the synagogues. They know me in some of the stores and in the vegetarian restaurants. Women with whom I have had affairs live on the side streets. Even the pigeons know me; the moment I come out with a bag of feed, they begin to fly toward me from blocks away. It is an area that stretches from Ninety-sixth Street to Seventy-second Street and from Central Park to Riverside Drive. Almost every day on my walk after lunch, I pass the funeral parlor that waits for us and all our ambitions and illusions. Sometimes I imagine that the funeral parlor is also a kind of cafeteria where one gets a quick eulogy or *Kaddish* on the way to eternity.

The cafeteria people I meet are mostly men: old bachelors like myself, would-be writers, retired teachers, some with dubious doctorate titles, a rabbi without a congregation, a painter of Jewish themes, a few translators—all immigrants from Poland or Russia. I seldom know their names. One of them disappears and I think he is already in the next world; suddenly he reappears and he tells me that he has tried to settle in Tel Aviv or Los Angeles. Again he eats his rice pudding, sweetens his coffee with saccharin. He has a few more wrinkles, but he tells the same stories and makes the same gestures. It may happen that he takes a paper from his pocket and reads me a poem he has written.

IT was in the fifties that a woman appeared in the group who looked younger than the rest of us. She must have been in her early thirties; she was short, slim, with a girlish face, brown hair that she wore in a bun, a short nose, and dimples in her cheeks. Her eyes were hazel—actually, of an indefinite color. She dressed in a modest European way. She spoke Polish, Russian, and an idiomatic Yiddish. She always carried Yiddish newspapers and magazines. She had been in a prison camp in Russia and had spent some time in the camps in Germany before she obtained a visa for the United States. The men all hovered around her. They didn't let her pay the check. They gallantly brought her coffee and cheesecake. They listened to her talk and jokes. She had returned from the devastation still gay. She was introduced to me. Her name was Esther. I didn't know if she was unmarried, a widow, a divorcée. She told me she was working in a factory, where she sorted buttons. This fresh young woman did not fit into the group of elderly has-beens. It was also hard to understand why she couldn't find a better job than sorting buttons in New Jersey. But I didn't ask too many questions. She told me that she had read my writing while still in Poland, and later in the camps in Germany after the war. She said to me, "You are my writer."

The moment she uttered those words I imagined I was in love with her. We were sitting alone (the other man at our table had gone to make a telephone call), and I said, "For such words I must kiss you."

"Well, what are you waiting for?"

She gave me both a kiss and a bite.

I said, "You are a ball of fire."

"Yes, fire from Gehenna."

A few days later, she invited me to her home. She lived on a street between Broadway and Riverside Drive with her father, who had no legs and sat in a wheelchair. His legs had been frozen in Siberia. He had tried to run away from one of Stalin's slave camps in the winter of 1944. He looked like a strong man, had a head of thick white hair, a ruddy face, and eyes full of energy. He spoke in a swaggering fashion, with boyish boastfulness and a cheerful laugh. In an hour, he told me his story. He was born in White Russia but he had lived long years in Warsaw, Lodz, and Vilna. In the beginning of the thirties, he became a Communist and soon afterward a functionary in the Party. In 1939 he escaped to Russia with his daughter. His wife and the other children remained in Nazi-occupied Warsaw. In Russia, somebody denounced him as a Trotskyite and he was sent to mine gold in the north. The G.P.U. sent people there to die. Even the strongest could not survive the cold and hunger for more than a year. They were exiled without a sentence. They died together: Zionists, Bundists, members of the Polish Socialist Party, Ukrainian Nationalists, and just refugees, all caught because of the labor shortage. They often died of scurvy or beriberi. Boris Merkin, Esther's father, spoke about this as if it were a big joke. He called the Stalinists outcasts, bandits, sycophants. He assured me that had it not been for the United States Hitler would have overrun all of Russia. He told how prisoners tricked the guards to get an extra piece of bread or a double portion of watery soup, and what methods were used in picking lice.

Esther called out, "Father, enough!"

"What's the matter—am I lying?"

"One can have enough even of *kreplach*."

"Daughter, you did it yourself."

When Esther went to the kitchen to make tea, I learned from her father that she had had a husband in Russia—a Polish Jew who had volunteered in the Red Army and perished in the war. Here in New York she was courted by a refugee, a former smuggler in Germany who had opened a bookbinding factory and become rich. "Persuade her to marry him," Boris Merkin said to me. "It would be good for me, too."

"Maybe she doesn't love him."

"There is no such thing as love. Give me a cigarette. In the camp, people climbed on one another like worms."

I had invited Esther to supper, but she called to say she had the grippe and must remain in bed. Then in a few days' time a situation arose that made me leave for Israel. On the way back, I stopped over in London and Paris. I wanted to write to Esther, but I had lost her address. When I returned to New York, I tried to call her, but there was no telephone listing for Boris Merkin or Esther Merkin—father and daughter must have been boarders in somebody else's apartment. Weeks passed and she did not show up in the cafeteria. I asked the group about her; nobody knew where she was. "She has most probably married that bookbinder," I said to myself. One evening, I went to the cafeteria with the premonition that I would find Esther there. I saw a black wall and boarded windows—the cafeteria had burned. The old bachelors were no doubt meeting in another cafeteria, or an Automat. But where? To search is not in my nature. I had plenty of complications without Esther.

The summer passed; it was winter. Late one day, I walked by the cafeteria and again saw lights, a counter, guests. The owners had rebuilt. I entered, took a check, and saw Esther sitting alone at a table reading a Yiddish newspaper. She did not notice me, and I observed her for a while. She wore a man's fur fez and a jacket trimmed with a faded fur collar. She looked pale, as though recuperating from a sickness. Could that grippe have been the start of a serious illness? I went over to her table and asked, "What's new in buttons?"

She started and smiled. Then she called out, "Miracles do happen!"

"Where have you been?"

"Where did you disappear to?" she replied. "I thought you were still abroad."

"Where are our *cafeterianiks?*"

"They now go to the cafeteria on Fifty-seventh Street and Eighth Avenue. They only reopened this place yesterday."

"May I bring you a cup of coffee?"

"I drink too much coffee. All right."

I went to get her coffee and a large egg cookie. While I stood at the counter, I turned my head and looked at her. Esther had taken off her mannish fur hat and smoothed her hair. She folded the newspaper, which meant that she was ready to talk. She got up and tilted the other chair against the table as a sign that the seat was taken. When I sat down, Esther said, "You left without saying goodbye, and there I was about to knock at the pearly gates of Heaven."

"What happened?"

"Oh, the grippe became pneumonia. They gave me penicillin, and I am one of those who cannot take it. I got a rash all over my body. My father, too, is not well."

"What's the matter with your father?"

"High blood pressure. He had a kind of stroke and his mouth became all crooked."

"Oh, I'm sorry. Do you still work with buttons?"

"Yes, with buttons. At least I don't have to use my head, only my hands. I can think my own thoughts."

"What do you think about?"

"What not. The other workers are all Puerto Ricans. They rattle away in Spanish from morning to night."

"Who takes care of your father?"

"Who? Nobody. I come home in the evening to make supper. He has one desire—to marry me off for my own good and, perhaps, for his comfort, but I can't marry a man I don't love."

"What is love?"

"You ask me! You write novels about it. But you're a man—I assume you really don't know what it is. A woman is a piece of merchandise to you. To me a man who talks nonsense or smiles like an idiot is repulsive. I would rather die than live with him. And a man who goes from one woman to another is not for me. I don't want to share with anybody."

"I'm afraid a time is coming when everybody will."

"That is not for me."

"What kind of person was your husband?"

"How did you know I had a husband? My father, I suppose. The minute I leave the room, he prattles. My husband believed in things and was ready to die for them. He was not exactly my type but I respected him and loved him, too. He wanted to die and he died like a hero. What else can I say?"

"And the others?"

"There were no others. Men were after me. The way people behaved in the war—you will never know. They lost all shame. On the bunks near me one time, a mother lay with one man and her daughter with another. People were like beasts—worse than beasts. In the middle of it all, I dreamed about love. Now I have even stopped dreaming. The men who come here are terrible bores. Most of them are half mad, too. One of them tried to read me a forty-page poem. I almost fainted."

"I wouldn't read you anything I'd written."

"I've been told how you behave—no!"

"No is no. Drink your coffee."

"You don't even try to persuade me. Most men around here plague you and you can't get rid of them. In Russia people suffered, but I have never met as many maniacs there as in New York City. The building where I live is a madhouse. My neighbors are lunatics. They accuse each other of all kinds of things. They sing, cry, break dishes. One of them jumped out of the window and killed herself. She was having an affair with a boy twenty years younger. In Russia the problem was to escape the lice; here you're surrounded by insanity."

We drank coffee and shared the egg cookie. Esther put down her cup. "I can't believe that I'm sitting with you at this table. I read all your articles under all your pen names. You tell so much about yourself I have the feeling I've known you for years. Still, you are a riddle to me."

"Men and women can never understand one another."

"No—I cannot understand my own father. Sometimes he is a complete stranger to me. He won't live long."

"Is he so sick?"

"It's everything together. He's lost the will to live. Why live without legs, without friends, without a family? They have all perished. He sits and reads the newspapers all day long. He acts as though he were interested in what's going on in the world. His ideals are gone, but he still hopes for a just revolution. How can a revolution help him? I myself never put my hopes in any movement or party. How can we hope when everything ends in death?"

"Hope in itself is a proof that there is no death."

"Yes, I know you often write about this. For me, death is the only comfort. What do the dead do? They continue to drink coffee and eat egg cookies? They still read newspapers? A life after death would be nothing but a joke."

SOME of the *cafeterianiks* came back to the rebuilt cafeteria. New people appeared—all of them Europeans. They launched into long discussions in Yiddish, Polish, Russian, even Hebrew. Some of those who came from Hungary mixed German, Hungarian, Yiddish-German—then all of a sudden they began to speak plain Galician Yiddish. They asked to have their coffee in glasses, and held lumps of sugar between their teeth when they drank. Many of them were my readers. They introduced themselves and reproached me for all kinds of literary errors: I contradicted myself, went too far in descriptions of sex, described Jews in such a way that anti-Semites could use it for propaganda. They told me their experiences in the ghettos, in the Nazi concentration camps, in Russia. They pointed out one another. "Do you see that fellow—in Russia he immediately became a Stalinist. He denounced his own friends. Here in America he has switched to anti-Bolshevism." The one who was spoken about seemed to sense that he was being maligned, because the moment my informant left he took his cup of coffee and his rice pudding, sat down at my table, and said, "Don't believe a word of what you are told. They invent all kinds of lies. What could you do in a country where the rope was always around your neck? You had to adjust yourself if you wanted to live and not perish somewhere in Kazakhstan. To get a bowl of soup or a place to stay you had to sell your soul."

There was a table with a group of refugees who ignored me. They were not interested in literature and journalism but strictly in business. In Germany they had been smugglers. They seemed to be doing some shady business here, too; they whispered to one another and winked, counted their money, wrote long lists of numbers. Somebody pointed out one of them. "He had a store in Auschwitz."

"What do you mean, a store?"

"God help us. He kept his merchandise in the straw where he slept—a rotten potato, sometimes a piece of soap, a tin spoon, a little fat. Still, he did business. Later, in Germany, he became such a big smuggler they once took forty thousand dollars away from him."

Sometimes months passed between my visits to the cafeteria. A year or two had gone by (perhaps three or four; I lost count), and Esther did not show up. I asked about her a few times. Someone said that she was going to the cafeteria on Forty-second Street; another had heard that she was married. I learned that some of the *cafeterianiks* had died. They were beginning to settle down in the United States, had remarried, opened businesses, workshops, even had children again. Then came cancer or a heart attack. The result of the Hitler and Stalin years, it was said.

One day, I entered the cafeteria and saw Esther. She was sitting alone at a table. It was the same Esther. She was even wearing the same fur hat, but a strand of gray hair fell over her forehead. How strange—the fur hat, too, seemed to have grayed. The other *cafeterianiks* did not appear to be interested in her anymore, or they did not know her. Her face told of the time that had passed. There were shadows under her eyes. Her gaze was no longer so clear. Around her mouth was an expression that could be called bitterness, disenchantment. I greeted her. She smiled, but her smile immediately faded away. I asked, "What happened to you?"

"Oh, I'm still alive."

"May I sit down?"

"Please—certainly."

"May I bring you a cup of coffee?"

"No. Well, if you insist."

I noticed that she was smoking, and also that she was reading not the newspaper to which I contribute but a competition paper. She had gone over to the enemy. I brought her coffee and for myself stewed prunes—a remedy for constipation. I sat down. "Where were you all this time? I have asked for you."

"Really? Thank you."

"What happened?"

"Nothing good." She looked at me. I knew that she saw in me what I saw in her: the slow wilting of the flesh. She said, "You have no hair but you are white."

For a while we were silent. Then I said, "Your father—" and as I said it I knew that her father was not alive.

Esther said, "He has been dead for almost two years."

"Do you still sort buttons?"

"No, I became an operator in a dress shop."

"What happened to you personally, may I ask?"

"Oh nothing—absolutely nothing. You will not believe it, but I was sitting here thinking about you. I have fallen into some kind of trap. I don't know what to call it. I thought perhaps you could advise me. Do you still have the patience to listen to the troubles of little people like me? No, I didn't mean to insult you. I even doubted you would remember me. To make it short, I work but work is growing more difficult for me. I suffer from arthritis. I feel as if my bones would crack. I wake up in the morning and can't sit up. One doctor tells me that it's a disc in my back, others try to cure my nerves. One took X-rays and says that I have a tumor. He wanted me to go to the hospital for a few weeks, but I'm in no hurry for an operation. Suddenly a little lawyer showed up. He is a refugee himself and is connected with the German government. You know they're now giving reparation money. It's true that I escaped to Russia, but I'm a victim of the Nazis just the same. Besides, they don't know my biography so exactly. I could get a pension plus a few thousand dollars, but my dislocated disc is no good for the purpose because I got it later—after the camps. This lawyer says my only chance is to convince them that I am ruined psychically. It's the bitter truth, but how can you prove it? The German doctors, the neurologists, the psychiatrists require proof. Everything has to be according to the text-books—just so and no different. The lawyer wants me to play insane. Naturally, he gets twenty per cent of the reparation money—maybe more. Why he needs so much money I don't understand. He's already in his seventies, an old bachelor. He tried to make love to me and whatnot. He's half *meshuga* himself. But how can I play insane when actually I *am* insane? The whole thing revolts me and I'm afraid it will really drive me crazy. I hate swindle. But this shyster pursues me. I don't sleep. When the alarm rings in the morning, I wake up as shattered as I used to be in Russia when I had to walk to the forest and saw logs at four in the morning. Naturally, I take sleeping pills—if I didn't, I couldn't sleep at all. That is more or less the situation."

"Why don't you get married? You are still a good-looking woman."

"Well, the old question—there is nobody. It's too late. If you knew how I felt, you wouldn't ask such a question."

A few weeks passed. Snow had been falling. After the snow came rain, then frost. I stood at my window and looked out at Broadway. The passersby half walked, half slipped. Cars moved slowly. The sky above the roofs shone violet, without a moon, without stars, and even though it was eight o'clock in the evening the light and the emptiness reminded me of dawn. The stores were deserted. For a moment, I had the feeling I was in Warsaw. The telephone rang and I rushed to answer it as I did ten, twenty, thirty years ago—still expecting the good tidings that a telephone call was about to bring me. I said hello, but there was no answer and I was seized by the fear that some evil power was trying to keep back the good news at the last minute. Then I heard a stammering. A woman's voice muttered my name.

"Yes, it is I."

"Excuse me for disturbing you. My name is Esther. We met a few weeks ago in the cafeteria—"

"Esther!" I exclaimed.

"I don't know how I got the courage to phone you. I need to talk to you about something. Naturally, if you have the time and—please forgive my presumption."

"No presumption. Would you like to come to my apartment?"

"If I will not be interrupting. It's difficult to talk in the cafeteria. It's noisy and there are eavesdroppers. What I want to tell you is a secret I wouldn't trust to anyone else."

"Please, come up."

I gave Esther directions. Then I tried to make order in my apartment, but I soon realized this was impossible. Letters, manuscripts lay around on tables and chairs. In the corners books and magazines were piled high. I opened the closets and threw inside whatever was under my hand: jackets, pants, shirts, shoes, slippers. I picked up an envelope and saw to my amazement that it had never been opened. I tore it open and found a check. "What's the matter with me—have I lost my mind?" I said out loud. I tried to read the letter that came with the check, but I had misplaced my glasses; my fountain pen was gone, too. Well—and where were my keys? I heard a bell ring and I didn't know whether it was the door or the telephone. I opened the door and saw Esther. It must have been snowing again, because her hat and the shoulders of her coat were trimmed with white. I asked her in, and my neighbor, the divorcée, who spied on me openly with no shame—and, God knows, with no sense of purpose—opened her door and stared at my new guest.

Esther removed her boots and I took her coat and put it on the case of the Encyclopædia Britannica. I shoved a few manuscripts off the sofa so she could sit down. I said, "In my house there is sheer chaos."

"It doesn't matter."

I sat in an armchair strewn with socks and handkerchiefs. For a while we spoke about the weather, about the danger of being out in New York at night—even early in the evening. Then Esther said, "Do you remember the time I spoke to you about my lawyer—that I had to go to a psychiatrist because of the reparation money?"

"Yes, I remember."

"I didn't tell you everything. It was too wild. It still seems unbelievable, even to me. Don't interrupt me, I implore you. I'm not completely healthy— I may even say that I'm sick—but I know the difference between fact and illusion. I haven't slept for nights, and I kept wondering whether I should call you or not. I decided not to—but this evening it occurred to me that if I couldn't trust you with a thing like this then there is no one I could talk to. I read you and I know that you have a sense of the great mysteries—" Esther said all this stammering and with pauses. For a moment her eyes smiled, and then they became deeply sad and wavering.

I said, "You can tell me everything."

"I am afraid that you'll think me insane."

"I swear I will not."

Esther bit her lower lip. "I want you to know that I saw Hitler," she said.

Even though I was prepared for something unusual, my throat constricted. "When—where?"

"You see, you are frightened already. It happened three years ago—almost four. I saw him here on Broadway."

"On the street?"

"In the cafeteria."

I tried to swallow the lump in my throat. "Most probably someone resembling him," I said finally.

"I knew you would say that. But remember, you've promised to listen. You recall the fire in the cafeteria?"

"Yes, certainly."

"The fire has to do with it. Since you don't believe me anyhow, why draw it out? It happened this way. That night I didn't sleep. Usually when I can't sleep, I get up and make tea, or I try to read a book, but this time some power commanded me to get dressed and go out. I can't explain to you how I dared walk on Broadway at that late hour. It must have been two or three o'clock. I reached the cafeteria, thinking perhaps it stays open all night. I tried to look in, but the large window was covered by a curtain. There was a pale glow inside. I tried the revolving door and it turned. I went in and saw a scene I will not forget to the last day of my life. The tables were shoved together and around them sat men in white robes, like doctors or orderlies, all with swastikas on their sleeves. At the head sat Hitler. I beg you to hear me out—even a deranged person sometimes deserves to be listened to. They all spoke German. They didn't see me. They were busy with the Führer. It grew quiet and he started to talk. That abominable voice—I heard it many times on the radio. I didn't make out exactly what he said. I was too terrified to take it in. Suddenly one of his henchmen looked back at me and jumped up from his chair. How I came out alive I will never know. I ran with all my strength, and I was trembling all over. When I got home, I said to myself, 'Esther, you are not right in the head.' I still don't know how I lived through that night. The next morning, I didn't go straight to work but walked to the cafeteria to see if it was really there. Such an experience makes a person doubt his own senses. When I arrived, I found the place had burned down. When I saw this, I knew it had to do with what I had seen. Those who were there wanted all traces erased. These are the plain facts. I have no reason to fabricate such queer things."

We were both silent. Then I said, "You had a vision."

"What do you mean, a vision?"

"The past is not lost. An image from years ago remained present somewhere in the fourth dimension and it reached you just at that moment."

"As far as I know, Hitler never wore a long white robe."

"Perhaps he did."

"Why did the cafeteria burn down just that night?" Esther asked.

"It could be that the fire evoked the vision."

"There was no fire then. Somehow I foresaw that you would give me this kind of explanation. If this was a vision, my sitting here with you is also a vision."

"It couldn't have been anything else. Even if Hitler is living and is hiding out in the United States, he is not likely to meet his cronies at a cafeteria on Broadway. Besides, the cafeteria belongs to a Jew."

"I saw him as I am seeing you now."

"You had a glimpse back in time."

"Well, let it be so. But since then I have had no rest. I keep thinking about it. If I am destined to lose my mind, this will drive me to it."

The telephone rang and I jumped up with a start. It was a wrong number. I sat down again. "What about the psychiatrist your lawyer sent you to? Tell it to him and you'll get full compensation."

Esther looked at me sidewise and unfriendly. "I know what you mean. I haven't fallen that low yet."

I was afraid that Esther would continue to call me. I even planned to change my telephone number. But weeks and months passed and I never heard from her or saw her. I didn't go to the cafeteria. But I often thought about her. How can the brain produce such nightmares? What goes on in that little marrow behind the skull? And what guarantee do I have that the same sort of thing will not happen to me? And how do we know that the human species will not end like this? I have played with the idea that all of humanity suffers from schizophrenia. Along with the atom, the personality of *Homo sapiens* has been splitting. When it comes to technology, the brain still functions, but in everything else degeneration has begun. They are all insane: the Communists, the Fascists, the preachers of democracy, the writers, the painters, the clergy, the atheists. Soon technology, too, will disintegrate. Buildings will collapse, power plants will stop generating electricity. Generals will drop atomic bombs on their own populations. Mad revolutionaries will run in the streets, crying fantastic slogans. I have often thought that it would begin in New York. This metropolis has all the symptoms of a mind gone berserk.

But since insanity has not yet taken over altogether, one has to act as though there were still order—according to Vaihinger's principle of "as if." I continued with my scribbling. I delivered manuscripts to the publisher. I lectured. Four times a year, I sent checks to the federal government, the state. What was left after my expenses I put in the savings bank. A teller entered some numbers in my bankbook and this meant that I was provided for. Somebody printed a few lines in a magazine or newspaper, and this signified that my value as a writer had gone up. I saw with amazement that all my efforts turned into paper. My apartment was one big wastepaper basket. From day to day, all this paper was getting drier and more parched. I woke up at night fearful that it would ignite. There was not an hour when I did not hear the sirens of fire engines.

A year after I had last seen Esther, I was going to Toronto to read a paper about Yiddish in the second half of the nineteenth century. I put a few shirts in my valise as well as papers of all kinds, among them one that made me a citizen of the United States. I had enough paper money in my pocket to pay for a taxi to Grand Central. But the taxis seemed to be taken. Those that were not refused to stop. Didn't the drivers see me? Had I suddenly become one of those who see and are not seen? I decided to take the subway. On my way, I saw Esther. She was not alone but with someone I had known years ago, soon after I arrived in the United States. He was a frequenter of a cafeteria on East Broadway. He used to sit at a table, express opinions, criticize, grumble. He was a small man, with sunken cheeks the color of brick, and bulging eyes. He was angry at the new writers. He belittled the old ones. He rolled his own cigarettes and dropped ashes into the plates from which we ate. Almost two decades had passed since I had last seen him. Suddenly he appears with Esther. He was even holding her arm. I had never seen Esther look so well. She was wearing a new coat, a new hat. She smiled at me and nodded. I wanted to stop her, but my watch showed that it was late. I barely managed to catch the train. In my bedroom, the bed was already made. I undressed and went to sleep.

In the middle of the night, I awoke. My car was being switched, and I almost fell out of bed. I could not sleep anymore and I tried to remember the name of the little man I had seen with Esther. But I was unable to. The thing I did remember was that even thirty years ago he had been far from young. He had come to the United States in 1905 after the revolution in Russia. In Europe, he had a reputation as a speaker and public figure. How old must he be now? According to my calculations, he had to be in the late eighties—perhaps even ninety. Is it possible that Esther could be intimate with such an old man? But this evening he had not looked old. The longer I brooded about it in the darkness the stranger the encounter seemed to me. I even imagined that I had read somewhere in a newspaper that he had died. Do corpses walk around on Broadway? This would mean that Esther, too, was not living. I raised the window shade and sat up and looked out into the night—black, impenetrable, without a moon. A few stars ran along with the train for a while and then they disappeared. A lighted factory emerged; I saw machines but no operators. Then it was swallowed in the darkness and another group of stars began to follow the train. I felt confused and shaken. I was turning with the earth on its axis. I was circling with it around the sun and moving in the direction of a constellation whose name I had forgotten. Is there no death? Or is there no life?

I thought about what Esther had told me of seeing Hitler in the cafeteria. It had seemed utter nonsense, but now I began to reappraise the idea. If time and space are nothing more than forms of perception, as Kant argues, and quality, quantity, causality are only categories of thinking, why shouldn't Hitler confer with his Nazis in a cafeteria on Broadway? Esther didn't sound insane. She had seen a piece of reality that the heavenly censorship prohibits as a rule. She had caught a glimpse behind the curtain of the phenomena. I regretted that I had not asked for more details.

In Toronto, I had little time to ponder these matters, but when I returned to New York I went to the cafeteria for some private investigation. I met only one man I knew: a rabbi who had become an agnostic and given up his job. I asked him about Esther. He said, "The pretty little woman who used to come here?"

"Yes."

"I heard that she committed suicide."

"When—how?"

"I don't know. Perhaps we are not speaking about the same person."

No matter how many questions I asked and how much I described Esther, everything remained vague. Some young woman who used to come here had turned on the gas and made an end of herself—that was all the ex-rabbi could tell me.

I decided not to rest until I knew for certain what had happened to Esther and also to that half writer, half politician I remembered from East Broadway. But I grew busier from day to day. The cafeteria closed. The neighborhood changed. Years have passed and I have never seen Esther again. Yes, corpses do walk on Broadway. But why did Esther choose that particular corpse? She could have got a better bargain even in this world.

(1968)

PARTNERS

MISS TEAS WEDS FIANCÉ IN BRIDAL

THE marriage of Nancy Creamer Teas, daughter of Mr. and Mrs. Russell Ruckhyde Teas of Glen Frieburg, N.Y., and Point Pedro, Sri Lanka, to John Potomac Mining, son of Mr. Potomac B. Mining of Buffet Hills, Va., and the late Mrs. Mining, took place at the First Episcopal Church of the Port Authority of New York and New Jersey.

The bride attended the Bodice School, the Earl Grey Seminary, Fence Academy, Railroad Country Day School, and the Credit School, and made her début at the Alexander Hamilton's Birthday Cotillion at Lazard Frères. She is a student in the premedical program at M.I.T. and will spend her junior year at Cartier & Cie. in Paris.

The bridegroom recently graduated from Harvard College. He spent his junior year at the Pentagon, a military concern in Washington, D.C. He will join his father on the board of directors of the Municipal Choate Assistance Corporation. His previous marriage ended in divorce.

CABINET, DELOS NUPTIALS SET

Ellen Frances Cabinet, a self-help student at Manifest Destiny Junior College, plans to be married in August to Wengdell Delos, a sculptor, of Tampa, Fla. The engagement was announced by the parents of the future bride, Mr. and Mrs. Crowe Cabinet of New York. Mr. Cabinet is a consultant to the New York Stock Exchange.

Mr. Delos's previous marriage ended in an undisclosed settlement. His sculpture is on exhibition at the New York Stock Exchange. He received a B.F.A. degree from the Wen-El-Del Company, a real-estate-development concern with headquarters in Tampa.

MISS BURDETTE WED TO MAN

Pews Chapel aboard the Concorde was the setting for the marriage of Bethpage Burdette to Jean-Claude LaGuardia Case, an account executive for the Junior Assemblies. Maspeth Burdette was maid of honor for her sister, who was also attended by Massapequa Burdette, Mrs. William O. Dose, and Mrs. Hodepohl Inks.

The parents of the bride, Dr. and Mrs. Morris Plains Burdette of New York, are partners in Conspicuous Conception, an art gallery and maternity-wear cartel.

The ceremony was performed by the Rev. Erasmus Tritt, a graduate of Skidmore Finishing and Divinity School and president of Our Lady of the Lake Commuter Airlines. The Rev. Tritt was attended by the flight crew. The previous marriages he has performed all ended in divorce.

DAISY LAUDERDALE FEATURED AS BRIDE

Daisy Ciba Lauderdale of Boston was married at the Presbyterian Church and Trust to Gens Cosnotti, a professor of agribusiness at the Massachusetts State Legislature. There was a reception at the First Court of Appeals Club.

The bride, an alumna of the Royal Doulton School and Loot University, is the daughter of Mr. and Mrs. Cyrus Harvester Lauderdale. Her father is retired from the family consortium. She is also a descendant of Bergdorf Goodman of the Massachusetts Bay Colony. Her previous marriage ended in pharmaceuticals.

Professor Cosnotti's previous marriage ended in a subsequent marriage. His father, the late Artaud Cosnotti, was a partner in the Vietnam War. The bridegroom is also related somehow to Mrs. Bethlehem de Steel of Newport, R.I., and Vichy, Costa Rica; Brenda Frazier, who was a senior partner with Delta, Kappa & Epsilon and later general manager of marketing for the U.S. Department of State; I. G. Farben, the former King of England; and Otto von Bismarck, vice-president of the Frigidaire Division of General Motors, now a division of The Hotchkiss School.

AFFIANCEMENT FOR MISS CONVAIR

Archbishop and Mrs. Marquis Convair of Citibank, N.Y., have made known the engagement of their daughter, Bulova East Hampton Convair, to the Joint Chiefs of Staff of Arlington County, Va. Miss Convair is a holding company in the Bahamas.

All four grandparents of the bride-to-be were shepherds and shepherdesses.

(1980)

THE EVOLUTION OF KNOWLEDGE

T HERE is something wrong with the floors of our apartment in New York. Not even our superintendent can do anything about it, for the cause of the trouble lies beyond his reach; it may, in fact, be traced back to the incongruities of Progress and to the decay of Western Civilization. Also to my two children, especially my son Vieri, who is seven. Every bounce of Vieri's ball on the floor evokes the spirit of Mr. Feinstein and sets into motion a long line of actions and reactions, which end in Mr. Feinstein's pounding on the radiator pipe or on his ceiling right under our feet. The spirit of Mr. Feinstein grows bigger, bigger, bigger, until *everything* is Mr. Feinstein. Vieri, in fact, is the real Sorcerer's Apprentice with that ball—tum ti, tum ti, tatata, tum ti, tum ti . . .

But there was a time when Mr. Feinstein didn't allow his spirit to reach us through his ceiling. He kept his fuming downstairs. That is why I think the story should be told; it is a highly philosophical story, because it proves that knowledge is not static but instead is constantly in the process of evolution.

Three years ago, when Mr. Feinstein pounded on the radiator, we did not care. Then, one day, I met him in the elevator. Though we had never happened to meet before, each of us knew instinctively who the other was, so, man to man, we had one of those bitter exchanges of words, just off the limits of politeness, that are usually accompanied by acceleration of the heartbeat and heavy breathing. Alas, in our case the exchange was also marked by an uncontrollable relapse into our foreign accents. Though this last hampered the free flow of profanity, it was how I learned that Mr.

Feinstein came from Saxony, and how he, who has lived in my country, understood that I came from Tuscany. But what we chiefly managed to convey to each other was that "Man must sleep" (his theory) and "Children must jump" (mine). The next time we met, we realized that we were both haters of hate more than of each other, so we tried to solve the problem by means of diplomatic negotiation. "We exiles," I said, "are always in a state of repressed emotion." He nodded and then explained, with many apologies, that the floor squeaked terribly even when I walked on it barefoot, and I explained, with my own apologies, that I had intended for some time to buy carpets for all the rooms, "but you know . . ." And he said, "Don't I know! You must not misunderstand me, please. It's not your fault. The floors haven't been repaired for the last two years, because of the war. So, you see, it's definitely one of those things that cannot be helped."

I thanked him for the acquittal, and he had an even more encouraging observation for me. Children's noise was also just one of those things that could not be helped, he said. I said, "You're much too kind, and, to tell you the truth, my children should learn how to behave." "Oh, no," he said, and I knew that he was growing political in his thoughts, because his face became quite sombre. "We have all suffered too much because of this idea of restraint," he said. "I, who was brought up in the strictest discipline, am now all in favor of the American system. Children here may do just as they please. They grow healthier, freer."

I nodded gratefully and, feeling that I must now repay him for his understanding, began to search my mind for something very bad to say against my children, something that would even make them appear to be unworthy of this blessed American freedom. But before I could formulate a reply, he made a demand. "All I ask you to do," he said, "is to have the children wear slippers on Saturdays and Sundays until at least ten in the morning, for that's the only time in the week that I can rest a little."

"This is indeed very little to ask," I said, "and I assure you that it will be done."

When I entered my apartment and found my family gathered in plenary session in the kitchen, I announced that I had just had a pleasant talk with the man downstairs. To my wife, I said, by way of comment, "A very civilized, kind person, really," and to the children, by way of injunction, "All he wants from you is that on Saturdays and Sundays, until after ten in the morning, you walk with your slippers on and don't play ball. Can you imagine anything easier than that?" They immediately saw the adventure in a program of this kind; the idea of connecting their slippers with a given period of time seemed full of mystery and charm. Vieri told me that he would watch the clock and the very instant the hand touched the first tiny portion of the figure 10, he would throw his slippers against the ceiling. And Bimba, who is only five, immediately went to her room and came back to the kitchen, where we were sitting, with her slippers and Vieri's, to rehearse the Feast of Liberation.

"No, no!" I shouted, and my wife shouted, "No, no!" But since the slippers were already flying in all directions and landing in the sink, on the gas rings, behind the icebox, and on the breakfast table, I saw that the situation was desperate, and I commanded silence. Then I made an announcement.

"First of all," I said, "when he says ten o'clock, he doesn't mean that at ten sharp we have to start making a lot of noise. Ten o'clock means some time in the middle of the morning. We don't want to impose on his kindness."

"Impose?" Vieri asked. "What does that mean?"

"Now, look," I said. "The idea is this: We don't want to be unkind to this man." And I went on to explain that on Saturday and Sunday mornings we would go to the park if the weather was fine or play quiet games at home if it rained.

IN back of our apartment building, above the parkway and the Hudson, there is a wild cliff covered with rocks and trees. This is where all the children of the apartment house play, and in summer or on mild winter days many of the grownups sit there in deck chairs and hate the children while enjoying the view of the boats on the river. My wife sometimes goes to the cliff with the children in the afternoon, and it was there, a few days after our family session, that she first met Mrs. Feinstein. From her, she learned that Mr. Feinstein had been a writer in Germany and that he was now again trying to write, in a new language. He had a quiet office downtown where he worked five days a week, but the shattering experiences of the past in Germany and the difficulty of mastering English had so discouraged him that after a day of writing he could hardly sleep at night, which was why he had to have his rest on Saturdays and Sundays. Mrs. Feinstein also expressed the hope that we would see more of each other and become friends. "You see," said my wife to me later, after recounting all this, "it's really a matter of honor for us to make up for our past sins and show that we are able to bring up our children to be civilized human beings."

"Yes, indeed," I said, "especially as the Feinsteins have asked little enough of us. We won't even try to become real friends with them until after we've given them reason to respect us."

Thus began our ordeal.

The first Saturday morning, both children put on their slippers and climbed on the table in their bedroom to reach for the picture books on the top shelf. I was in my room looking at the paper when I heard the most frightful noise. I rushed into the children's room and saw that all the big books and a box filled with wooden blocks, plus three or four wooden cows, had fallen on the floor. The children were blaming each other for the disaster, and they at once began a battle of shoes, books, and marbles. Needless to say, the reaction from downstairs was none too kind, and we learned later that even though we had gone out for the entire afternoon, Mr. Feinstein had found it impossible to repair the damage done to his sleep that day.

I was lucky enough not to see Mr. Feinstein for a whole week after the incident, but one day my wife met his wife when they were both waiting their turns at the washing machine in the basement. My wife renewed our pledge to keep to the ten-o'clock limit on weekends. This happened on a Friday, so very early the next morning, before the children could wake up, I went into their room and put their slippers in a place where they would be sure to see them. Next to the slippers, I put colored pencils, toys, and other accepted items of pre-breakfast entertainment. Everything went splendidly that one day—so splendidly, in fact, that we often recalled the occasion later and said among ourselves, "Why can't we have another December 17th?" But the fact is that we just didn't; in our family, at least, history does not repeat itself.

A couple of months later, rumors began to reach us from reliable sources, as they say in the papers, to the effect that Mr. Feinstein always spoke of us as "the parents of the two noisy children." Not a friendly word about us. This struck my wife and me painfully, and what disturbed us even more was to learn from one of our neighbors that Mr. Feinstein had received bad news from his family in Europe and was quite depressed.

My wife and I then held a secret meeting to plan a new strategy. It was a Monday morning and we had just got the children off to school.

"I am more worried about ourselves than about Mr. Feinstein," said my wife. "What will become of us in the future when, instead of trying to teach the children not to make noise, we will want to teach them not to wage aggressive wars on their neighbors?"

"The future is not yet," I said, "so don't worry."

The next morning, I stopped in at my children's school and consulted the school psychologist, whom I had come to know and like. He said, "Very simple, my friend. If you want to impress upon your children the notion that Mr. Feinstein is asleep, you must first believe it yourself. It's like the psychology of selling—you can never sell a thing in which you yourself have no faith. And furthermore," he said, "your methods are dictatorial. You can't ask children for exceptional behavior on Saturdays without any previous training. Try to approach Saturday by degrees. Accumulate a capital of habit, act artificially by minor doses, until Saturday comes to them naturally, without a shock."

I thanked him very much for his advice and began that same day to think in terms of Saturday. Mr. Feinstein was away in his office downtown, but I was beginning to prepare a nice silence for him upstairs. It was a wonderful feeling. I almost saw myself as a young bride preparing the first meal for her husband, hours before he comes back from the office. I walked cautiously, even typed cautiously (for I work at home), and when the children returned from school, I said to them, "Let's all work together for a better Saturday."

"Hurrah!" they shouted. "Let's work right away! May we use our shovels?"

"Children!" I whispered in my new velveted, tired voice. "Please, my dear, good, gentle children! Come, let's sit peacefully together and have silent fun!" And while saying this, I caressed their heads and closed my eyes to suggest peace.

I have come to the point at which my critics (among them my wife) accuse me of having brought violence into my advocacy of peace. They may be right; perhaps I am too passionate a character anyway. Well, it was Thursday afternoon and the children were playing in their room while I was writing in the living room. Needless to say, Mr. Feinstein was not at home. Suddenly I heard the sound of hammering. I emerged from the nineteenth century in Rome, in which my work had submerged me, to ask my wife with anguish, "What time is it?" Saturday morning was in my subconscious, so much so that I began to plead with my son to stop hammering. My wife took his side against me; she said he had every right to play with his tool kit. I tried everything, even literature. I said, "If Thursday is here, can Saturday be far behind? Think of that poor man downstairs, who will be asleep in less than two days from now!" Neither Vieri nor my wife was impressed.

That night, I committed my greatest mistake. I went downstairs and asked Mr. Feinstein to help me, and although he said again that those two mornings on the weekend were all he cared for, I insisted so earnestly that he made two more demands: a 1-to-3 P.M. silence on Sundays and a nightly silence after nine. It was a little too much, I felt, but after all I'd asked for it. In fairness to Mr. Feinstein, I must say that he did what he could to help me, pounding his disapproval on the radiator pipe each time we played the victrola or I typed after nine. Since his approval was not shown by any applause but was simply left to our guess, our hopeful guessing, plus those occasional ghostlike rappings on the radiator, seemed to summon up Mr. Feinstein's spirit. The whole family began to flee from it. We withdrew to the kitchen and lived there like fugitives; we talked to our guests in whispers and always told them not to walk too confidently, lest the spirit wake up.

One evening, while we were having guests—Mr. Feinstein was, of course, present in spirit—my wife observed that our lot had not improved much with exile; in Italy the tyrant had been constantly awake over us, here he was asleep under our feet. The joke was such a success that one of our guests, laughing convulsively, drummed on the floor with his heels, and at once—bang, bang—the spirit replied. Before long, the phrase "Mr. Feinstein is asleep" was no longer a phrase; it was a dogma. It was, in fact, the Law. I vaguely recall that this was the period when I could no longer work on my historical research, and while my actions were all devoted to the defense of Mr. Feinstein's sleep, my thoughts centered on hating him. Finally, a friend gave me a key to his apartment, so that I could go there to work in peace. But the fact was that I went there only to be able to hate Mr. Feinstein without interruptions. In the meantime, the children went on making a lot of noise, and they even began taking liberties with Mr. Feinstein such as I would never have dared. One day, my son met him in the elevator. It was the eve of the long Easter holidays, the thought of which was already filling me with dread. Mr. Feinstein said to Vieri, "You are lucky to have such a long vacation." "Yes, I am," answered Vieri with a smile, "but you're not."

At this point, I went to see the school psychologist again. He suggested that I now try the progressive method; namely, teach while playing, in the manner of the modern school. I thanked him for the idea, and the same day I began to make many jokes to the children about Mr. Feinstein, the monster downstairs. I taught them to call him Sleepyhead, and whenever his name was mentioned, we made snoring noises. Then the expression was coined: "As lazy as Mr. Feinstein." This worked pretty well until Mr. Feinstein fell sick and actually had to stay in bed all the time. Vieri had taken up bouncing his ball again, so, to save the day, I at once established a Feinstein Prize for silence.

Unfortunately, one Sunday afternoon not long after, while I was walking through the park with my children, we met a group of friends who were on their way to pay us a visit with their own children, six in all. As it was a beautiful day, we decided to stay outdoors and not go back to our apartment until teatime. When we started on our way home, I noticed that each of my friends' children was armed with a ball and that one of them had iron cleats on his shoes, and I began to warn them of the "monster" that lived under our feet. My children helped me, volunteering the usual epithets and noises, and suddenly, whom did we see passing us but Mr. Feinstein, his face pale and stern. He must have been returning from a

Sunday walk in the park and certainly had come up behind us and heard everything. He stared at me and said in a dignified tone that stabbed my heart, "Good afternoon."

I did not sleep that night. One always hates to be caught by an enemy in the act of abusing him behind his back, but what made things worse in my case was that I liked Mr. Feinstein as a person and would have given anything to be forgiven by him. "Horrible!" I thought. "Instead of understanding the delicacy of our motives, he will understand only the indelicacy of our remarks." So, after hours of nightmare, I decided that the only thing to do was face the situation squarely and go to him. But, alas, before I did so bad fortune willed it that I meet him right in front of my door. He wasn't coming to see me, that I knew, but I said, "Mr. Feinstein, I would like to talk to you. Won't you come in?" He hesitated, entered, and sat down without saying a word. Despite my confusion, I immediately noticed that in person he occupied a much smaller portion of the air than did his spirit. I had been unjust. And he looked much kinder than his spirit, too.

"I don't know why you want to see me," he began. "Are you looking for inspiration for more vulgar stunts to teach your children? As a matter of fact," he continued, moving his chair back noisily and preparing to leave, "I don't know what made me accept your offer to come in in the first place."

I was almost speechless, but instinctively said what I now always said to my guests: "Please be careful, we have—" And my finger was pointed toward the floor. He understood, for his face reddened and he said with rage, "Never mind! I'm up here now, not downstairs!" I blushed and sank back on my chair, then stuttered, "Now, Mr. Feinstein, you, who are a philosopher—"

He interrupted me. "I don't see what that has to do with the fact that you teach your children to insult a man who has done you no harm. If that's the way Italian children are brought up, I can almost believe that Italy needs a Mussolini!"

"Please!" I said. "There is no reason why you should insult me! Listen to me, now. I myself never used bad words against you."

"But you laughed when your children used them. You even encouraged them. I heard what you said in the park. So you can hear me 'snore like a pig,' can you?"

"I? We? No, indeed, I never said so."

"You *did* say so. I heard you!"

"I was only joking."

"Only joking! Respect for your neighbor is a joke to you. I knew it all the time, but for a while I thought that you were merely a little casual, like most Italians. But now I know. Respect for others means nothing to you, and you even take pleasure in persecuting others with your jokes. You are a Fascist!"

"Sir!" I cried. "That you should insult me in my own home! I can prove to you that I have fought Fascism, that I have written dozens of articles denouncing all forms of persecution."

"You may have done so, but my experience with you is just the opposite. You have constantly disregarded my very modest demands, and on top of this you make me out a clown to amuse your children. That, sir, is more than I—"

"Please, please!" I said. "All my friends can be witnesses to the fact that your demands for quiet are the only thing I've taken seriously for the last two years. It is, in fact, *I* who may reproach *you* for making me a nervous wreck. Unintentionally, I admit, but still—"

"I?" said he, growing terribly pale. "I? I have made *you* a nervous wreck? All *my* friends are my witnesses, sir, that all I ever asked of you was a few hours of silence a week. Is *that* what makes you a wreck? You and your children have made *me* a wreck! How on earth can you have the nerve to claim that my asking you for those few hours of silence that I never got has made you a wreck! That is indeed Fascist!"

"Sir," I said, "please listen! I admit you never got your rest, and I'm sorry, but you don't know how many sleepless nights I've spent trying to prepare the rest you never got. And let me tell you also that this all came about because I tried to be kind to you. First, I tried to offer you two hours and a quarter of quiet, then three hours, and soon quiet for you became the ruling principle of our existence. Your sleep, Mr. Feinstein, ruled my life! And how could I persuade the children to obey these rules without pretending that I was taking their part against you? If you are to enjoy the sleep of the just, you must allow me to insult you unjustly. If the children know that you are a good man, they will want you to be so good as to cope with their noise, while if they think that you are a monster, they will respect you to avoid trouble."

"But that *is* Fascism! That is horrible! Couldn't you have told them that I was very sick?"

"I did once, when you were, but it didn't help. Besides, though I'm not superstitious, I hate to talk lightly about sickness. To mention it may tempt the Fates."

He looked at me, bit his lip, then said, "Why didn't you just call me a fool?"

"Who was I to do that?" I said. "And you, sir, why did you always ask with such kindness, and look so pale? That made me act the way I did."

He frowned, looked at me again, and then we both started laughing and my wife came in with a bottle of wine and some wineglasses. The children, too, came running in, and started jumping so hard that this time it was for the protection of the house itself that we had to stop them. "I guess," said Mr. Feinstein now, "this all goes back to the incongruities of Progress."

"Also," I said, "to the decay of Western Civilization."

"Perhaps, too, though only a little, to these darling children here," he said.

"Yes," I said, "or to me, who am silly enough to live in town. Let's drink now and be friends."

So our friendship was sealed, and upon leaving Mr. Feinstein said, "Frankly, I prefer your noise to all that unfair propaganda against me. It's bad enough that the grownups should scare each other with lies. Let's spare these babies if we can."

"This time," I said, "I am *sure* I can keep my promise."

But, alas, this time, too, it was a mistake to make a promise. For now every time I think of my good friend Mr. Feinstein, even late at night, I hope the children will play ball, jump, or do something awful, just to let him know that he has friends upstairs, real friends, and that his name is not being taken in vain. Yet he's so nervous now, so jittery, so sad (and, needless to say, his spirit still sometimes manifests itself by the usual rappings), that I still am afraid to let the children act like children. The result is that I never quite know whether to give rest to his body or to his soul.

(1947)

THE WAY WE LIVE NOW

A T first he was just losing weight, he felt only a little ill, Max said to Ellen, and he didn't call for an appointment with his doctor, according to Greg, because he was managing to keep on working at more or less the same rhythm, but he did stop smoking, Tanya pointed out, which suggests he was frightened, but also that he wanted, even more than he knew, to be healthy, or healthier, or maybe just to gain back a few pounds, said Orson, for he told her, Tanya went on, that he expected to be climbing the walls (isn't that what people say?) and found, to his surprise, that he didn't miss cigarettes at all and revelled in the sensation of his lungs' being ache-free for the first time in years. But did he have a good doctor, Stephen wanted to know, since it would have been crazy not to go for a checkup after the pressure was off and he was back from the conference in Helsinki, even if by then he was feeling better. And he said, to Frank, that he would go, even though he was indeed frightened, as he admitted to Jan, but who wouldn't be frightened now, though, odd as that might seem, he hadn't been worrying until recently, he avowed to Quentin, it was only in the last six months that he had the metallic taste of panic in his mouth, because becoming seriously ill was something that happened to other people, a normal delusion, he observed to Paolo, if one was thirty-eight and had never had a serious illness; he wasn't, as Jan confirmed, a hypochondriac. Of course, it was hard not to worry, everyone was worried, but it wouldn't do to panic, because, as Max pointed out to Quentin, there wasn't anything one could do except wait and hope, wait and start being careful, be careful, and hope. And even if one did prove to be ill, one shouldn't give up, they had new treatments that promised an arrest of the disease's inexorable course, research was progressing. It seemed that everyone was in touch with everyone else several times a week, checking in, I've never spent so many hours at a time on the phone, Stephen said to Kate, and when I'm exhausted after the two or three calls made to me, giving me the latest, instead of switching off the phone to give myself a respite I tap out the number of another friend or acquaintance, to pass on the news. I'm not sure I can afford to think so much about it, Ellen said, and I suspect my own motives, there's something morbid I'm getting used to, getting excited by, this must be like what people felt in London during the Blitz. As far as I know, I'm not at risk, but you never know, said Aileen. This thing is totally unprecedented, said Frank. But don't you think he ought to see a doctor, Stephen insisted. Listen, said Orson, you can't force people to take care of themselves, and what makes you think the worst, he could be just run-down, people still do get ordinary illnesses, awful ones, why are you assuming it has to be *that*. But all I want to be sure, said Stephen, is that he understands the options, because most people don't, that's why they won't see a doctor or have the test, they think there's nothing one can do. But is there anything one can do, he said to Tanya (according to Greg), I mean what do I gain if I go to the doctor; if I'm really ill, he's reported to have said, I'll find out soon enough.

AND when he was in the hospital, his spirits seemed to lighten, according to Donny. He seemed more cheerful than he had been in the last months, Ursula said, and the bad news seemed to come almost as a relief, according to Ira, as a truly unexpected blow, according to Quentin, but you'd hardly expect him to have said the same thing to all his friends, because his relation to Ira was so different from his relation to Quentin (this according to Quentin, who was proud of their friendship), and perhaps he thought Quentin wouldn't be undone by seeing him weep, but Ira insisted that couldn't be the reason he behaved so differently with each, and that maybe he was feeling less shocked, mobilizing his strength to fight for his life, at the moment he saw Ira but overcome by feelings of hopelessness when Quentin arrived with flowers, because anyway the flowers threw him into a bad mood, as Quentin told Kate, since the hospital room was choked with flowers, you couldn't have crammed another flower into that room, but surely you're exaggerating, Kate said, smiling, everybody likes flowers. Well, who wouldn't exaggerate at a time like this, Quentin said sharply. Don't you think *this* is an exaggeration. Of course I do, said Kate gently, I was only teasing, I mean I didn't mean to tease. I know that, Quentin said, with tears in his eyes, and Kate hugged him and said well, when I go this evening I guess I won't bring flowers, what does he want, and Quentin said, according to Max, what he likes best is chocolate. Is there anything else, asked Kate, I mean like chocolate but not chocolate. Licorice, said Quentin, blowing his nose. And besides that. Aren't *you* exaggerating now, Quentin said, smiling. Right, said Kate, so if I want to bring him a whole raft of stuff, besides chocolate and licorice, what else. Jelly beans, Quentin said.

HE didn't want to be alone, according to Paolo, and lots of people came in the first week, and the Jamaican nurse said there were other patients on the floor who would be glad to have the surplus flowers, and people weren't afraid to visit, it wasn't like the old days, as Kate pointed out to Aileen, they're not even segregated in the hospital anymore, as Hilda observed, there's nothing on the door of his room warning visitors of the possibility of contagion, as there was a few years ago; in fact, he's in a double room and, as he told Orson, the old guy on the far side of the curtain (who's clearly on the way out, said Stephen) doesn't even have the disease, so, as Kate went on, you really should go and see him, he'd be happy to see you, he likes having people visit, you aren't not going because you're afraid, are you. Of course not, Aileen said, but I don't know what to say, I think I'll feel awkward, which he's bound to notice, and that will make him feel worse, so I won't be doing him any good, will I. But he won't notice anything, Kate said, patting Aileen's hand, it's not like that, it's not the way you imagine, he's not judging people or wondering about their motives, he's just happy to see his friends. But I never was really a friend of his, Aileen said, you're a friend, he's always liked you, you told me he talks about Nora with you, I know he likes me, he's even attracted to me, but he respects you. But, according to Wesley, the reason Aileen was so stingy with her visits was that she could never have him to herself, there were always others there already and by the time they left still others had arrived, she'd been in love with him for years, and I can understand, said Donny, that Aileen should feel bitter that if there could have been a woman friend he did more than occasionally bed, a woman he really loved, and my God, Victor said, who had known him in those years, he was crazy about Nora, what a heartrending couple they were, two surly angels, then it couldn't have been she.

AND when some of the friends, the ones who came every day, waylaid the doctor in the corridor, Stephen was the one who asked the most informed questions, who'd been keeping up not just with the stories that appeared several times a week in the *Times* (which Greg confessed to have stopped reading, unable to stand it anymore) but with articles in the medical journals published here and in England and France, and who knew socially one of the principal doctors in Paris who was doing some much-publicized research on the disease, but his doctor said little more than that the pneumonia was not life-threatening, the fever was subsiding, of course he was still weak but he was responding well to the antibiotics, that he'd have to complete his stay in the hospital, which entailed a minimum of twenty-one days on the I.V., before she could start him on the new drug, for she was optimistic about the possibility of getting him into the protocol; and when Victor said that if he had so much trouble eating (he'd say to everyone, when they coaxed him to eat some of the hospital meals, that food didn't taste right, that he had a funny metallic taste in his mouth) it couldn't be good that friends were bringing him all that chocolate, the doctor just smiled and said that in these cases the patient's morale was also an important factor, and if chocolate made him feel better she saw no harm in it, which worried Stephen, as Stephen said later to Donny, because they wanted to believe in the promises and taboos of today's high-tech medicine but here this reassuringly curt and silver-haired specialist in the disease, someone quoted frequently in the papers, was talking like some oldfangled country G.P. who tells the family that tea with honey or chicken soup may do as much for the patient as penicillin, which might mean, as Max said, that they were just going through the motions of treating him, that they were not sure about what to do, or rather, as Xavier interjected, that they didn't know what the hell they were doing, that the truth, the real truth, as Hilda said, upping the ante, was that they didn't, the doctors, really have any hope.

OH, no, said Lewis, I can't stand it, wait a minute, I can't believe it, are you sure, I mean are they sure, have they done all the tests, it's getting so when the phone rings I'm scared to answer because I think it will be someone telling me someone else is ill; but did Lewis really not know until yesterday, Robert said testily, I find that hard to believe, everybody is talking about it, it seems impossible that someone wouldn't have called Lewis; and perhaps Lewis did know, was for some reason pretending not to know already, because, Jan recalled, didn't Lewis say something months ago to Greg, and not only to Greg, about his not looking well, losing weight, and being worried about him and wishing he'd see a doctor, so it couldn't come as a total surprise. Well, everybody is worried about everybody now, said Betsy, that seems to be the way we live, the way we live now. And, after all, they were once very close, doesn't Lewis still have the keys to his apartment, you know the way you let someone keep the keys after you've broken up, only a little because you hope the person might just saunter in, drunk or high, late some evening, but mainly because it's wise to have a few sets of keys strewn around town, if you live alone, at the top of a former commercial building that, pretentious as it is, will never acquire a doorman or even a resident superintendent, someone whom you can call on for the keys late one night if you find you've lost yours or have locked yourself out. Who else has keys, Tanya inquired, I was thinking somebody might drop by tomorrow before coming to the hospital and bring some treasures, because the other day, Ira said, he was complaining about how dreary the hospital room was, and how it was like being locked up in a motel room, which got everybody started telling funny stories about motel rooms they'd known, and at Ursula's story, about the Luxury Budget Inn in Schenectady, there was an uproar of laughter around his bed, while he watched them in silence, eyes bright with fever, all the while, as Victor recalled, gobbling that damned chocolate. But, according to Jan, whom Lewis's keys enabled to tour the swank of his bachelor lair with an eye to bringing over some art consola-tion to brighten up the hospital room, the Byzantine icon wasn't on the wall over his bed, and that was a puzzle until Orson remembered that he'd recounted without seeming upset (this disputed by Greg) that the boy he'd recently gotten rid of had stolen it, along with four of the *maki-e* lacquer boxes, as if these were objects as easy to sell on the street as a TV or a stereo. But he's always been very generous, Kate said quietly, and though he loves beautiful things isn't really attached to them, to things, as Orson said, which is unusual in a collector, as Frank commented, and when Kate shud-dered and tears sprang to her eyes and Orson inquired anxiously if he, Orson, had said something wrong, she pointed out that they'd begun talk-ing about him in a retrospective mode, summing up what he was like, what made them fond of him, as if he were finished, completed, already a part of the past.

PERHAPS he was getting tired of having so many visitors, said Robert, who was, as Ellen couldn't help mentioning, someone who had come only twice and was probably looking for a reason not to be in regular atten-dance, but there could be no doubt, according to Ursula, that his spirits had dipped, not that there was any discouraging news from the doctors, and he seemed now to prefer being alone a few hours of the day; and he told Donny that he'd begun keeping a diary for the first time in his life, because he wanted to record the course of his mental reactions to this astonishing turn of events, to do something parallel to what the doctors were doing, who came every morning and conferred at his bedside about his body, and that perhaps it wasn't so important what he wrote in it, which amounted, as he said wryly to Quentin, to little more than the usual banalities about terror and amazement that this was happening to him, to him also, plus the usual remorseful assessments of his past life, his pardonable superficialities, capped by resolves to live better, more deeply, more in touch with his work and his friends, and not to care so passionately about what people thought of him, interspersed with admonitions to himself that in this situation his will to live counted more than anything else and that if he really wanted to live, and trusted life, and liked himself well enough (down, ol' debbil Thanatos!), he *would* live, he would be an exception; but perhaps all this, as Quentin ruminated, talking on the phone to Kate, wasn't the point, the point was that by the very keeping of the diary he was accumulating something to reread one day, slyly staking out his claim to a future time, in which the diary would be an object, a relic, in which he might not actually reread it, because he would want to have put this ordeal behind him, but the diary would be there in the drawer of his stupendous Majorelle desk, and he could already, he did actually say to Quentin one late sunny afternoon, propped up in the hospital bed, with the stain of chocolate framing one corner of a heartbreaking smile, see himself in the penthouse, the October sun streaming through those clear windows instead of this streaked one, and the diary, the pathetic diary, safe inside the drawer.

IT doesn't matter about the treatment's side effects, Stephen said (when talking to Max), I don't know why you're so worried about that, every strong treatment has some dangerous side effects, it's inevitable, you mean otherwise the treatment wouldn't be effective, Hilda interjected, and anyway, Stephen went on doggedly, just because there *are* side effects it doesn't mean he has to get them, or all of them, each one, or even some of them. That's just a list of all the possible things that could go wrong, because the doctors have to cover themselves, so they make up a worst-case scenario, but isn't what's happening to him, and to so many other people, Tanya interrupted, a worst-case scenario, a catastrophe no one could have imagined, it's too cruel, and isn't everything a side effect, quipped Ira, even *we* are all side effects, but we're not bad side effects, Frank said, he likes having his friends around, and we're helping each other, too; because his illness sticks us all in the same glue, mused Xavier, and, whatever the jealousies and grievances from the past that have made us wary and cranky with each other, when something like this happens (the sky is falling, the sky is falling!) you understand what's really important. I agree, Chicken Little, he is reported to have said. But don't you think, Quentin observed to Max, that being as close to him as we are, making time to drop by the hospital every day, is a way of our trying to define ourselves more firmly and irrevocably as the well, those who aren't ill, who aren't going to fall ill, as if what's happened to him couldn't happen to us, when in fact the chances are that before long one of us will end up where he is, which is probably what he felt when he was one of the cohort visiting Zack in the spring (you never knew Zack, did you?), and, according to Clarice, Zack's widow, he didn't come very often, he said he hated hospitals, and didn't feel he was doing Zack any good, that Zack would see on his face how uncomfortable he was. Oh, he was one of those, Aileen said. A coward. Like me.

AND after he was sent home from the hospital, and Quentin had volunteered to move in and was cooking meals and taking telephone messages and keeping the mother in Mississippi informed, well, mainly keeping her from flying to New York and heaping her grief on her son and confusing the household routine with her oppressive ministrations, he was able to work an hour or two in his study, on days he didn't insist on going out, for a meal or a movie, which tired him. He seemed optimistic, Kate thought, his appetite was good, and what he said, Orson reported, was that he agreed when Stephen advised him that the main thing was to keep in shape, he was a fighter, right, he wouldn't be who he was if he weren't, and was he ready for the big fight, Stephen asked rhetorically (as Max told it to Donny), and he said you bet, and Stephen added it could be a lot worse, you could have gotten the disease two years ago, but now so many scientists are working on it, the American team and the French team, everyone bucking for that Nobel Prize a few years down the road, that all you have to do is stay healthy for another year or two and then there will be good treatment, real treatment. Yes, he said, Stephen said, my timing is good. And Betsy, who had been climbing on and rolling off macrobiotic diets for a decade, came up with a Japanese specialist she wanted him to see but thank God, Donny reported, he'd had the sense to refuse, but he did agree to see Victor's visualization therapist, although what could one possibly visualize, said Hilda, when the point of visualizing disease was to see it as an entity with contours, borders, here rather than there, something limited, something you were the host of, in the sense that you could disinvite the disease, while this was so total; or would be, Max said. But the main thing, said Greg, was to see that he didn't go the macrobiotic route, which might be harmless for plump Betsy but could only be devastating for him, lean as he'd always been, with all the cigarettes and other appetite-suppressing chemicals he'd been welcoming into his body for years; and now was hardly the time, as Stephen pointed out, to be worried about cleaning up his act, and eliminating the chemical additives and other pollutants that we're all blithely or not so blithely feasting on, blithely since we're healthy, healthy as we can be; so far, Ira said. Meat and potatoes is what I'd be happy to see him eating, Ursula said wistfully. And spaghetti and clam sauce, Greg added. And thick cholesterol-rich omelettes with smoked mozzarella, suggested Yvonne, who had flown from London for the weekend to see him. Chocolate cake, said Frank. Maybe not chocolate cake, Ursula said, he's already eating so much chocolate.

AND when, not right away but still only three weeks later, he was accepted into the protocol for the new drug, which took considerable behind-the-scenes lobbying with the doctors, he talked less about being ill, according to Donny, which seemed like a good sign, Kate felt, a sign that he was not feeling like a victim, feeling not that he *had* a disease but, rather, was living *with* a disease (that was the right cliché, wasn't it?), a more hospitable arrangement, said Jan, a kind of cohabitation which implied that it was something temporary, that it could be terminated, but terminated how, said Hilda, and when you say hospitable, Jan, I hear hospital. And it was encouraging, Stephen insisted, that from the start, at least from the time he was finally persuaded to make the telephone call to his doctor, he was willing to say the name of the disease, pronounce it often and easily, as if it were just another word, like boy or gallery or cigarette or money or deal, as in no big deal, Paolo interjected, because, as Stephen continued, to utter the name is a sign of health, a sign that one has accepted being who one is, mortal, vulnerable, not exempt, not an exception after all, it's a sign that one is willing, truly willing, to fight for one's life. And we must say the name, too, and often, Tanya added, we mustn't lag behind him in honesty, or let him feel that, the effort of honesty having been made, it's something done with and he can go on to other things. One is so much better prepared to help him, Wesley replied. In a way he's fortunate, said Yvonne, who had taken care of a problem at the New York store and was flying back to London this evening, sure, fortunate, said Wesley, no one is shunning him, Yvonne went on, no one's afraid to hug him or kiss him lightly on the mouth, in London we are, as usual, a few years behind you, people I know, people who would seem to be not even remotely at risk, are just terrified, but I'm impressed by how cool and rational you all are; you find us cool, asked

Quentin. But I have to say, he's reported to have said, I'm terrified, I find it very hard to read (and you know how he loves to read, said Greg; yes, reading is his television, said Paolo) or to think, but I don't feel hysterical. I feel quite hysterical, Lewis said to Yvonne. But you're able to *do* something for him, that's wonderful, how I wish I could stay longer, Yvonne answered, it's rather beautiful, I can't help thinking, this utopia of friendship you've assembled around him (this pathetic utopia, said Kate), so that the disease, Yvonne concluded, is not, anymore, out there. Yes, don't you think we're more at home here, with him, with the disease, said Tanya, because the imagined disease is so much worse than the reality of him, whom we all love, each in our fashion, having it. I know for me his getting it has quite demystified the disease, said Jan, I don't feel afraid, spooked, as I did before he became ill, when it was only news about remote acquaintances, whom I never saw again after they became ill. But you know you're not going to come down with the disease, Quentin said, to which Ellen replied, on her behalf, that's not the point, and possibly untrue, my gynecologist says that everyone is at risk, everyone who has a sexual life, because sexuality is a chain that links each of us to many others, unknown others, and now the great chain of being has become a chain of death as well. It's not the same for you, Quentin insisted, it's not the same for you as it is for me or Lewis or Frank or Paolo or Max, I'm more and more frightened, and I have every reason to be. I don't think about whether I'm at risk or not, said Hilda, I know that I was afraid to know someone with the disease, afraid of what I'd see, what I'd feel, and after the first day I came to the hospital I felt so relieved. I'll never feel that way, that fear, again; he doesn't seem different from me. He's not, Quentin said.

ACCORDING to Lewis, he talked more often about those who visited more often, which is natural, said Betsy, I think he's even keeping a tally. And among those who came or checked in by phone every day, the inner circle as it were, those who were getting more points, there was still a further competition, which was what was getting on Betsy's nerves, she confessed to Jan; there's always that vulgar jockeying for position around the bedside of the gravely ill, and though we all feel suffused with virtue at our loyalty to him (speak for yourself, said Jan), to the extent that we're carving time out of every day, or almost every day, though some of us are dropping out, as Xavier pointed out, aren't we getting at least as much out of this as he is. Are we, said Jan. We're rivals for a sign from him of special pleasure over a visit, each stretching for the brass ring of his favor, wanting to feel the most wanted, the true nearest and dearest, which is inevitable with

someone who doesn't have a spouse and children or an official in-house
lover, hierarchies that no one would dare contest, Betsy went on, so we are
the family he's founded, without meaning to, without official titles and
ranks (we, we, snarled Quentin); and is it so clear, though some of us, Lewis
and Quentin and Tanya and Paolo, among others, are ex-lovers and all of
us more or less than friends, which one of us he prefers, Victor said (now
it's us, raged Quentin), because sometimes I think he looks forward more to
seeing Aileen, who has visited only three times, twice at the hospital and
once since he's been home, than he does you or me; but, according to
Tanya, after being very disappointed that Aileen hadn't come, now he was
angry, while, according to Xavier, he was not really hurt but touchingly
passive, accepting Aileen's absence as something he somehow deserved.
But he's happy to have people around, said Lewis; he says when he doesn't
have company he gets very sleepy, he sleeps (according to Quentin), and
then perks up when someone arrives, it's important that he not feel ever
alone. But, said Victor, there's one person he hasn't heard from, whom he'd
probably like to hear from more than most of us; but she didn't just vanish,
even right after she broke away from him, and he knows exactly where she
lives now, said Kate, he told me he put in a call to her last Christmas Eve,
and she said it's nice to hear from you and Merry Christmas, and he was
shattered, according to Orson, and furious and disdainful, according to
Ellen (what do you expect of her, said Wesley, she was burned out), but Kate
wondered if maybe he hadn't phoned Nora in the middle of a sleepless
night, what's the time difference, and Quentin said no, I don't think so, I
think he wouldn't want her to know.

AND when he was feeling even better and had regained the pounds he'd
shed right away in the hospital, though the refrigerator started to fill up
with organic wheat germ and grapefruit and skimmed milk (he's worried
about his cholesterol count, Stephen lamented), and told Quentin he could
manage by himself now, and did, he started asking everyone who visited
how he looked, and everyone said he looked great, so much better than a
few weeks ago, which didn't jibe with what anyone had told him at that
time; but then it was getting harder and harder to know how he looked, to
answer such a question honestly when among themselves they wanted to
be honest, both for honesty's sake and (as Donny thought) to prepare for the
worst, because he'd been looking like *this* for so long, at least it seemed so
long, that it was as if he'd always been like this, how did he look before, but
it was only a few months, and those words, pale and wan-looking and fragile, hadn't they always applied? And one Thursday Ellen, meeting Lewis at

the door of the building, said, as they rode up together in the elevator, how is he *really?* But you see how he is, Lewis said tartly, he's fine, he's perfectly healthy, and Ellen understood that of course Lewis didn't think he was perfectly healthy but that he wasn't worse, and that was true, but wasn't it, well, almost heartless to talk like that. Seems inoffensive to me, Quentin said, but I know what you mean, I remember once talking to Frank, somebody, after all, who has volunteered to do five hours a week of office work at the Crisis Center (I know, said Ellen), and Frank was going on about this guy, diagnosed almost a year ago, and so much further along, who'd been complaining to Frank on the phone about the indifference of some doctor, and had gotten quite abusive about the doctor, and Frank was saying there was no reason to be so upset, the implication being that *he,* Frank, wouldn't behave so irrationally, and I said, barely able to control my scorn, but Frank, Frank, he has every reason to be upset, he's dying, and Frank said, said according to Quentin, oh, I don't like to think about it that way.

AND it was while he was still home, recuperating, getting his weekly treatment, still not able to do much work, he complained, but, according to Quentin, up and about most of the time and turning up at the office several days a week, that bad news came about two remote acquaintances, one in Houston and one in Paris, news that was intercepted by Quentin on the ground that it could only depress him, but Stephen contended that it was wrong to lie to him, it was so important for him to live in the truth; that had been one of his first victories, that he was candid, that he was even willing to crack jokes about the disease, but Ellen said it wasn't good to give him this end-of-the-world feeling, too many people were getting ill, it was becoming such a common destiny that maybe some of the will to fight for his life would be drained out of him if it seemed to be as natural as, well, death. Oh, Hilda said, who didn't know personally either the one in Houston or the one in Paris, but knew *of* the one in Paris, a pianist who specialized in twentieth-century Czech and Polish music, I have his records, he's such a valuable person, and, when Kate glared at her, continued defensively, I know every life is equally sacred, but that *is* a thought, another thought, I mean, all these valuable people who aren't going to have their normal fourscore as it is now, these people aren't going to be replaced, and it's such a loss to the culture. But this isn't going to go on forever, Wesley said, it can't, they're bound to come up with something (they, they, muttered Stephen), but did you ever think, Greg said, that if some people don't die, I mean even if they can keep them alive (they, they, muttered Kate), they continue to be carriers, and that means, if you have a conscience, that you

can never make love, make love fully, as you'd been wont—wantonly, Ira
said—to do. But it's better than dying, said Frank. And in all his talk about
the future, when he allowed himself to be hopeful, according to Quentin,
he never mentioned the prospect that even if he didn't die, if he were so fortunate as to be among the first generation of the disease's survivors, never
mentioned, Kate confirmed, that whatever happened it was over, the way
he had lived until now, but, according to Ira, he did think about it, the end
of bravado, the end of folly, the end of trusting life, the end of taking life for
granted, and of treating life as something that, samurai-like, he thought
himself ready to throw away lightly, impudently; and Kate recalled, sighing, a brief exchange she'd insisted on having as long as two years ago,
huddling on a banquette covered with steel-gray industrial carpet on an
upper level of The Prophet and toking up for their next foray onto the dance
floor: she'd said hesitantly, for it felt foolish asking a prince of debauchery
to, well, take it easy, and she wasn't keen on playing big sister, a role, as
Hilda confirmed, he inspired in many women, are you being careful, honey,
you know what I mean. And he replied, Kate went on, no, I'm not, listen, I
can't, I just can't, sex is too important to me, always has been (he started
talking like that, according to Victor, after Nora left him), and if I get it, well,
I get it. But he wouldn't talk like that now, would he, said Greg; he must feel
awfully foolish now, said Betsy, like someone who went on smoking, saying
I can't give up cigarettes, but when the bad X-ray is taken even the most be-
sotted nicotine addict can stop on a dime. But sex isn't like cigarettes, is it,
said Frank, and, besides, what good does it do to remember that he was
reckless, said Lewis angrily, the appalling thing is that you just have to be
unlucky once, and wouldn't he feel even worse if he'd stopped three years
ago and had come down with it anyway, since one of the most terrifying
features of the disease is that you don't know when you contracted it, it
could have been ten years ago, because surely this disease has existed for
years and years, long before it was recognized; that is, named. Who knows
how long (I think a lot about that, said Max) and who knows (I know what
you're going to say, Stephen interrupted) how many are going to get it.

I'M feeling fine, he's reported to have said whenever someone asked him
how he was, which was almost always the first question anyone asked. Or:
I'm feeling better, how are you? But he said other things, too. I'm playing
leapfrog with myself, he is reported to have said, according to Victor. And:
There must be a way to get something positive out of this situation, he's reported to have said to Kate. How American of him, said Paolo. Well, said
Betsy, you know the old American adage: When you've got a lemon, make

lemonade. The one thing I'm sure I couldn't take, Jan said he said to her, is becoming disfigured, but Stephen hastened to point out the disease doesn't take that form very often anymore, its profile is mutating, and, in conversation with Ellen, wheeled up words like blood-brain barrier; I never thought there was a barrier *there*, said Jan. But he mustn't know about Max, Ellen said, that would really depress him, please don't tell him, he'll have to know, Quentin said grimly, and he'll be furious not to have been told. But there's time for that, when they take Max off the respirator, said Ellen; but isn't it incredible, Frank said, Max was fine, not feeling ill at all, and then to wake up with a fever of a hundred and five, unable to breathe, but that's the way it often starts, with absolutely no warning, Stephen said, the disease has so many forms. And when, after another week had gone by, he asked Quentin where Max was, he didn't question Quentin's account of a spree in the Bahamas, but then the number of people who visited regularly was thinning out, partly because the old feuds that had been put aside through the first hospitalization and the return home had resurfaced, and the flickering enmity between Lewis and Frank exploded, even though Kate did her best to mediate between them, and also because he himself had done something to loosen the bonds of love that united the friends around him, by seeming to take them all for granted, as if it were perfectly normal for so many people to carve out so much time and attention for him, visit him every few days, talk about him incessantly on the phone with each other; but, according to Paolo, it wasn't that he was less grateful, it was just something he was getting used to, the visits. It had become, with time, a more ordinary kind of situation, a kind of ongoing party, first at the hospital and now since he was home, barely on his feet again, it being clear, said Robert, that I'm on the B list; but Kate said, that's absurd, there's no list; and Victor said, but there is, only it's not he, it's Quentin who's drawing it up. He wants to see us, we're helping him, we have to do it the way he wants, he fell down yesterday on the way to the bathroom, he mustn't be told about Max (but he already knew, according to Donny), it's getting worse.

WHEN I was home, he is reported to have said, I was afraid to sleep, as I was dropping off each night it felt like just that, as if I were falling down a black hole, to sleep felt like giving in to death, I slept every night with the light on; but here, in the hospital, I'm less afraid. And to Quentin he said, one morning, the fear rips through me, it tears me open; and, to Ira, it presses me together, squeezes me toward myself. Fear gives everything its hue, its high. I feel so, I don't know how to say it, exalted, he said to Quentin. Calamity is an amazing high, too. Sometimes I feel *so* well, so powerful, it's as if I could jump out of my skin. Am I going crazy, or what? Is it all this attention and coddling I'm getting from everybody, like a child's dream of being loved? Is it the drugs? I know it sounds crazy but sometimes I think this is a *fantastic* experience, he said shyly; but there was also the bad taste in the mouth, the pressure in the head and at the back of the neck, the red, bleeding gums, the painful, if pink-lobed, breathing, and his ivory pallor, color of white chocolate. Among those who wept when told over the phone that he was back in the hospital were Kate and Stephen (who'd been called by Quentin), and Ellen, Victor, Aileen, and Lewis (who were called by Kate), and Xavier and Ursula (who were called by Stephen). Among those who didn't weep were Hilda, who said that she'd just learned that her seventy-five-year-old aunt was dying of the disease, which she'd contracted from a transfusion given during her successful double bypass of five years ago, and Frank and Donny and Betsy, but this didn't mean, according to Tanya, that they weren't moved and appalled, and Quentin thought they might not be coming soon to the hospital but would send presents; the room, he was in a private room this time, was filling up with flowers, and plants, and books, and tapes. The high tide of barely suppressed acrimony of the last weeks at home subsided into the routines of hospital visiting, though more than a few resented Quentin's having charge of the visiting book (but it was Quentin who had the idea, Lewis pointed out); now, to insure a steady stream of visitors, preferably no more than two at a time (this, the rule in all hospitals, wasn't enforced here, at least on his floor; whether out of kindness or inefficiency, no one could decide), Quentin had to be called first, to get one's time slot, there was no more casual dropping by. And his mother could no longer be prevented from taking a plane and installing herself in a hotel near the hospital; but he seemed to mind her daily presence less than expected, Quentin said; said Ellen it's we who mind, do you suppose she'll stay long. It was easier to be generous with each other visiting him here in the hospital, as Donny pointed out, than at home, where one minded never being alone with him; coming here, in our twos and twos, there's no doubt about what our role is, how we should be, collective, funny, distracting, undemanding, light, it's important to be light, for in all this dread there is gaiety, too, as the poet said, said Kate. (His eyes, his glittering eyes, said Lewis.) His eyes looked dull, extinguished, Wesley said to Xavier, but Betsy said his face, not just his eyes, looked soulful, warm; whatever is there, said Kate, I've never been so aware of his eyes; and Stephen said, I'm afraid of what my eyes show, the way I watch him, with too much intensity, or a phony kind of casualness, said Victor. And, unlike at home, he was clean-shaven each morning, at whatever hour they visited him; his curly hair was always combed; but he complained that the nurses had changed since he was here the last time, and that he didn't like the change, he wanted everyone to be the same. The room was furnished now with some of his personal effects (odd word for one's things, said Ellen), and Tanya brought drawings and a letter from her nine-year-old dyslexic son, who was writing now, since she'd purchased a computer; and Donny brought champagne and some helium balloons, which were anchored to the foot of his bed; tell me about something that's going on, he said, waking up from a nap to find Donny and Kate at the side of his bed, beaming at him; tell me a story, he said wistfully, said Donny, who couldn't think of anything to say; *you're* the story, Kate said. And Xavier brought an eighteenth-century Guatemalan wooden statue of St. Sebastian with upcast eyes and open mouth, and when Tanya said what's that, a tribute to eros past, Xavier said where I come from Sebastian is venerated as a protector against pestilence. Pestilence symbolized by arrows? Symbolized by arrows. All people remember is the body of a beautiful youth bound to a tree, pierced by arrows (of which he always seems oblivious, Tanya interjected), people forget that the story continues, Xavier continued, that when the Christian women came to bury the martyr they found him still alive and nursed him back to health. And he said, according to Stephen, I didn't know St. Sebastian didn't die. It's undeniable, isn't it, said Kate on the phone to Stephen, the fascination of the dying. It makes me ashamed. We're learn-ing how to die, said Hilda, I'm not ready to learn, said Aileen; and Lewis, who was coming straight from the other hospital, the hospital where Max was still being kept in I.C.U., met Tanya getting out of the elevator on the tenth floor, and as they walked together down the shiny corridor past the open doors, averting their eyes from the other patients sunk in their beds, with tubes in their noses, irradiated by the bluish light from the television sets, the thing I can't bear to think about, Tanya said to Lewis, is someone dying with the TV on.

HE has that strange, unnerving detachment now, said Ellen, that's what upsets me, even though it makes it easier to be with him. Sometimes he was querulous. I can't stand them coming in here taking my blood every morn-ing, what are they doing with all that blood, he is reported to have said; but where was his anger, Jan wondered. Mostly he was lovely to be with, always saying how are *you*, how are you feeling. He's so sweet now, said Aileen. He's so nice, said Tanya. (Nice, nice, groaned Paolo.) At first he was very ill, but he was rallying, according to Stephen's best information, there was no fear of his not recovering this time, and the doctor spoke of his being dis-charged from the hospital in another ten days if all went well, and the mother was persuaded to fly back to Mississippi, and Quentin was readying the penthouse for his return. And he was still writing his diary, not showing it to anyone, though Tanya, first to arrive one late-winter morning, and finding him dozing, peeked, and was horrified, according to Greg, not by anything she read but by a progressive change in his handwriting: in the recent pages, it was becoming spidery, less legible, and some lines of script wandered and tilted about the page. I was thinking, Ursula said to Quentin, that the difference between a story and a painting or photograph is that in a story you can write, He's still alive. But in a painting or a photo you can't show "still." You can just show him being alive. He's still alive, Stephen said.

[1986]

DO THE WINDOWS OPEN?

FOR several years I was afraid to ride the South Fork Bus. Then one day I rode it. The day itself was over, since I couldn't get my courage up for the afternoon bus to New York, but I did make it to the 7 P.M. For one year I had driven myself back and forth from East Hampton to New York. It had taken me ten years to manage this feat. Then, all of a sudden, after almost mastering it, I could never do it again.

Even when I drove the better but longer way onto the Northern State Parkway and across the Triborough Bridge and down the crater-filled F.D.R. Drive to get to my apartment in SoHo, the trip became so horrible that I couldn't keep doing it. Once I crossed that bridge at night in a thunderstorm with cars speeding past me on the left and right. But the part of the Grand Central Parkway near LaGuardia started to cause the no-breathing attacks after a few trips. Nothing like the more serious attacks of paralysis of the lungs that used to overcome me on the worse route—the Long Island Expressway and the deadly approach to the Midtown Tunnel, with trucks passing on the right and three lanes of headlights coming toward me on the left.

On one of my last trips a single truck caused one of these attacks. I thought I could drive among trucks! And anyway, how many trucks could there be at night? There could be a whole highway full of trucks at night on the Long Island Expressway, and one of these trucks in front of me had an open cargo, if it could be called a cargo—a load of dust. Dust was its cargo, probably asbestos dust was what it was filled with, and this asbestos dust was not packed up in barrels and tied down but simply heaped onto the back and covered with a thin gray sheet. The sheet was not even tied down, so it flapped around and the dust was blowing into the air, and there was no way to see through these gusts of asbestos dust.

I'll pass the truck, I thought—because I had learned how to pass, with "Così Fan Tutte" playing, but I quickly discovered that I hadn't learned to pass on a curve with no visibility, no matter what opera of Mozart's was on and no matter how loud. I was trying to pass the asbestos truck on the left, I had my signal on, only a few seconds had gone by while I was waiting for a part of the road that was not curved. But whenever one came up, the dust would start to blow, and it would be a case of trying to pass into dust through dust to nowhere, just like actual death as we imagine it. As I waited these few seconds with Karl Böhm conducting Alfredo Kraus, cars began to squeeze in and pass on the right. Couldn't they tell that I was going to pass at the proper moment?

My last trip took place on a rainy night. Although I had listened to the weather reports all day and they had warned only of occasional light rain, heavy rain overtook the road at the safe, wide, empty part east of Manorville. Before I could get into the right lane, a gigantic white-and-blue vehicle roared past, going sixty or seventy, splashing highway water so that I was completely blinded for several seconds. This vehicle was the South Fork Bus. I thought, "It would be better to be on the South Fork Bus than to be passed on the right by it in a rainstorm."

I prepared myself for that first trip on the bus by seeing someone else off. The passenger I chose to see off was my husband. "It's not so bad," I said. Nothing is so bad if it isn't summer. The people, the things they have with them and on them; namely, their faces, their bodies, their hair styles—none of this is so bad in cold weather. But even as I said that it wasn't so bad I noticed that the seats were too close together, and I couldn't help wondering what it would be like to be aboard when the vehicle filled up with humans and departed from pleasant, tree-lined Main Street. When it got *onto the road. Onto the road,* with fifty other humans and their paraphernalia. *Onto the Expressway.* The thought filled me with horror.

My husband did not mind his time on the bus. He said things like "I work, I read, I sleep. It's great—I'm not driving."

I would never be able to work, read, or sleep. I was still working on a series of photographs of flowers in decline, and there wouldn't be any flowers on the bus. My other project was to photograph the reproductive surgeon Dr. Arnold Loquesto with his dog, and they wouldn't be on the bus, either. Reading in vehicles caused nausea, and sleeping on a bus on a highway was out of the question. "Are there seat belts?" I asked my husband.

"No. Why? You mean you're afraid to ride the South Fork Bus?"

"Not afraid. Do the windows open?"

"No. Windows on these new things don't open anymore. Why—you need the windows to open?"

"It would be better if they could be opened."

"But who wants to open the windows on the Long Island Expressway?" he said.

AS the departure time approached for my first trip on the bus, I thought that this must be the way people feel when waiting to board a plane. They're always telling us that cars are more dangerous than planes. Why not be afraid of both? I'll take half a Xanax to enable me to get aboard, I decided. A kindly periodontist had prescribed some for a root-extraction session, and I had eleven pills left. People I knew in Southampton and East Hampton were always trying to get my Xanax away from me. One of these people was an anxious flower arranger. Once, in a discussion of highway driving, he mentioned that he couldn't drive on the Expressway at all. He told me this with a look of fear in his large, blue, flower-arranging eyes. These driving conversations had made him my favorite person to talk to in Southampton and East Hampton. "The traffic will be over by six, but then it will be dark," he said. "Aren't you afraid to drive in the dark?"

"It's not the dark. It's the headlights," I said.

"Yes! The headlights make me crazy. Forget it. I can't even do it in the daylight. My last time I broke into a sweat, the panic started, and when I got to the city I ran to St. Patrick's to say a prayer."

I had confided in a religious, panic-stricken flower arranger. Which was more scary, his religious fervor or his discussion of floral arrangements for funerals? Both gave me shivers.

I felt brave as I waited out in the cold night for the South Fork Bus. Very few people waited with me. This bus is so big, I thought—it must be safer than a car. "We're the biggest thing on the road," a confident middle-aged male passenger said to everyone in a spirit of camaraderie as the bus came down the street. But I was not the comrade of any of the passengers on the South Fork Bus, I thought as I watched them board on that first dark winter night.

I determined that the safest seat would be on the right and in the middle. In a crash the front of the bus would fold up, crunching together the driver and the first few rows. The left side would go right into those three lanes of oncoming headlights that I had studied during my own driving experiences. The back would smash together if the bus was hit from behind. The middle could jackknife, but I'd heard that this kind of accident was rare.

The back seats were near the bathroom, and an important rule in travelling and in dining out is to avoid sitting near plumbing. Yet, even with this rule seeming to make perfect sense, certain passengers on the South Fork Bus chose the bathroom corner as their most desired place to sit. After watching a series of almost normal-looking individuals head for various sections of the middle and front, I saw that a tall man, all in black leather, was heading right for the seat across from the dreaded bathroom door. He was between fifty and sixty, and almost bald—he had some hair, but it was very short and gray. Probably he was a member of some sadomasochist-black-leather Hampton set, the first of his kind I'd ever seen. The minute he got to the back I heard a loud cough. Not a normal cough. A loud, choking, grunting, screaming kind of cough. Maybe his choosing the back seat was simply a matter of wanting to cough alone, to save his fellow-passengers the experience of hearing this cough at closer range, and to preserve whatever dignity a black-leather sado man could have. Before everyone was seated he coughed again. Other people were getting afraid, not just me. I figured I had gotten to the normal amount of fear with that half a Xanax in my brain. I saw that some had not even noticed the cough and were getting themselves ready for the trip with their newspapers and shopping bags and parcels.

People were making themselves comfortable—they didn't think that this was going to be their last day on earth. One woman had a special neck pillow, another had a lap robe. Others had beverages—coffee, tea, and juice. Although the South Fork Bus was known for giving out free Perrier, these passengers could not wait. They had magazines and books, and about half of them had headphones. The other half were going to take naps. Naps were planned for the Long Island Expressway! I saw people adjusting their seats backward into other people's knee space. Certain passengers were polite and consulted the people behind them, others did whatever they pleased. Supposedly in warmer weather, when I was in Nova Scotia or Maine, fights broke out about this and other things.

The first step I had to take to get ready was to tie myself into my seat with the belt from my reversible alpaca coat. I will have to remember to take this alpaca seat belt off the armrests when I arrive in Manhattan, I thought, because it would be impossible to get another. The one thing of value that I had learned from seeing a Viennese psychiatrist in his newly restored Art Deco building on Central Park West was information on how to obtain this coat. As I went up in the splendid elevator I couldn't help staring at the coat on a woman who looked exactly my age—at the time, thirty-nine. She was

kind enough to volunteer the name of a store in England, and several over-
seas phone calls enabled me to have the same coat. Having read that the
wrong kind of seat belt can be more dangerous than none at all, I knew
that this was the wrong kind, the kind that causes ruptured spleens and
herniated other organs. Still I kept to my plan and tied one end of the belt to
the outer armrest and the other end to the center armrest.

Next I would get some Mozart into my earphones—I would add Mozart
to my brain, along with the Xanax. This winning combination had helped
me through oral surgery, where they have a new device—a pellet gun to
shoot bullets of Novocain into the roof of the mouth. It had helped me not
to faint as I heard those bullets shoot in, and felt them, too.

I had decided that this trip would not require a Mozart opera. A piano
sonata would be enough—a trio, a string quartet, or a divertimento might
work. Before I could get my earphones on, the extremely weird hostess appeared. She said her name was Cindy, and began giving the rules of the
South Fork Bus. She must have graduated from the est program or some
kind of mind-training course, because she was so overly agreeable and
pleasant that there had to be a reason for it. "She's an est graduate," I remembered my haircutter, Francine, saying of a certain hair-streaker when
I asked "Why is she so cheerful?" "You mean it's that fake cheer?" I asked.
"More or less," she said. "At first we couldn't stand it, but then we got used
to it." Unlike Francine, I couldn't get used to things.

How had Cindy come to the point in life where she could stand to ride
back and forth on the Long Island Expressway, I wondered, and I thought it
was something she might wonder, too. Maybe, before her trips, she smoked
several ounces of marijuana to keep from wondering. Because even the est
in her background wouldn't have been enough to allow her to act this way.

Then there was the driver—a red-haired, middle-aged woman who looked
as if she had just spent the day in front of a TV, smoking packs of Camels in
preparation for her long drive on the South Fork Bus, where smoking was not
allowed, "and that includes the restroom." I was thankful for that rule, and I
thought I had so many things to be thankful for that if I survived the trip I
might run to St. Patrick's, too.

Just into the andante grazioso—I was tied in tightly—I saw that Cindy
had made her way up the aisle and was being argued with by a spoiled-
looking sixty-year-old man in a heavy, gray, hand-knitted sweater. The passenger wanted to be allowed to use his eastbound ticket to ride westbound.
This was strictly forbidden, but the passenger had a reason why it shouldn't
be forbidden in his case. Cindy had twisted herself into a physical position
of sympathy and understanding, bending over the passenger with her head
tilted and her body turned so that the next passenger was only an inch or

two from her hip joint. "It's really something that we're not allowed to do in any case, but I do understand why you think your case is different, and you know what, I *am* going to do it, but if this were ever known I would lose my job—not that this should be anything for you to concern yourself with." Perhaps the marijuana dose had kicked in to the point where she'd lost all concept of time and didn't know how long this conversation was going on.

As I watched the other passengers calmly paying their fares, it occurred to me that most of the men on the left side of the bus looked like antique dealers. The proportion seemed greater than the proportion viewed in other activities around the town. The junk-bond traders from Southampton had not yet boarded. When they did board, they would be angry that the good seats had been taken by this kind of passenger. But at least then it would be time to get that Perrier. The hostess had promised this.

PASSENGERS at Southampton turned out to have more materialistic and less intellectual paraphernalia than passengers from East Hampton. One woman with platinum-blond hair had five big shopping bags from the Saks Fifth Avenue Southampton branch, and she was in an angry mood. She'd been drinking. I could smell the alcohol particles in the air. She was one of those fifty-five-year-old women who always wear black or red, or both together. A red cashmere turtleneck sweater—everything else, including the coat she took off when she sat down, was black—and all those pieces of jewelry I couldn't identify except for the Rolex watch and the Cartier watch. She had one of each, plus several other kinds of gold bracelets. She was sitting right across the aisle, so I could study her jewelry the whole trip if I needed to.

At last, it was time for the refreshments. But not only wasn't it Perrier, it was some cheap club soda in a plastic bottle and served in plastic cups. All along I had thought that it was going to be individual green glass bottles for everyone. The hostess was asking people if they wanted little bags of peanuts and even asked some, "Would you like two?" Several were saying yes. One antique dealer had to ask if he could have two. Just the kind of thing I was afraid of but could not imagine—soon the entire bus had the odor of chewed peanuts. How long would the peanut odor last with the poor ventilation system was something I couldn't get off my mind. Why hadn't these people heard that peanuts are contaminated by the carcinogenic mold aflatoxin?

I noticed that other men had just as poor peanut-eating styles as my husband. Maybe my husband was not so bad. Maybe men are like this, as my exercise teacher, the dancer Katherine Glass, used to say. One man emptied the bag of peanuts into his hand, then threw them all at once into his mouth. Another one held the opened packet to his mouth with his head back and tapped the packet to get the peanuts out.

The time had come to complain about the temperature. It was about one hundred degrees in the bus. People were tearing off their cashmere scarves and sweaters. "We're trying to control the heat," Cindy said. "I know it's awful." Soon there was no heat. The platinum-blond, jewelry-laden passenger was getting angrier as she put her black coat back on. I saw that she was eating peanuts, even though she needed to lose ten pounds—her wrists were fattened up under her gold watches. One of the antique dealers didn't mind the wildly fluctuating temperature conditions, but he was complaining that his overhead light didn't aim right on his newspaper.

Somewhere around Manorville, Cindy made an announcement. "As you may have noticed we are having a lot of trouble temperature-wise," she said. "We can't control the heat, but we want you all to know that we're trying." Unfortunately, I had taken my earphones off to hear this announcement. Now I had the word "temperature-wise" stamped into my brain, and I also realized that the coughing man was still coughing at timed intervals. It was not a real cough, I suddenly knew, but a sign of Tourette's syndrome, where the afflicted person involuntarily shouts obscenities and has no recollection of having done so. This man had mastered the cough as a disguise, or he had not yet reached the obscenity stage. Perhaps it began with a cough—I couldn't recall, although this was my husband's favorite disease to read about.

Still, this was a better way to ride than driving myself, I thought, even though it was one hundred degrees for half the trip and thirty for the other half. I decided I would become a regular rider of the South Fork Bus throughout the winter. No one even noticed when I untied myself from my seat.

THEN there was the trip back. Nobody had told me what it was like to board the South Fork Bus at Fortieth Street and Third Avenue. I had only my husband's version of the facts, which was "It's right near my office—a perfect short walk." But, then, the opinion of a man who works in midtown, an architect who would choose to spend his life in the ugliest part of midtown—what is the opinion of this man worth? There are so many ugly office buildings in midtown now, and his is the ugliest. When you see this building you can think only one thing. "WHY?" is the thing. "Why? Why? Why?" But when you read architects' explanations of why this or that is in their plans, they have answers. Not that anyone would ask an architect why, just as no one would put an architect in jail for crimes of architecture; there is already such a prison-space shortage.

On a particularly deformed strip of the low Sixties around Second Avenue there is a building that's constructed of a material which cannot be identified. It's a color between that of a dead salmon and a dead rat. How can this be possible when these colors are so far apart? It's possible because they've been mixed together the way dog food was mixed together before there were any health regulations about its contents. Ground-up parts of old dead anything still go into dog food, apparently, things Ralph Nader says are in hot dogs—lips, ears, hooves. There are even worse ones, which Ralph Nader doesn't always list.

Why can't buildings be built according to the specifications of Prince Charles, I thought when first I saw the sight of East Fortieth Street. Why can't Prince Charles be in charge? East Fortieth Street was filled with gigantic, new gray-and-black buildings—if the sky was blue on any day, there would be no way to see it.

A commandant from the bus company was lining up the prisoners in some kind of cavernous space on East Fortieth Street—it wasn't clear what the space was, but some architect must have described it as something. It was a kind of mall space without any stores, thus combining the worst parts of city life and suburb life. The commandant was drinking coffee out of a plastic-foam cup. He had a look that identified his origins as Montauk and Poland. Yet he was in charge here, with an evil smile that could have meant the buses were not headed for any Hampton. His smile hinted that he knew about all kinds of things that were going to go wrong on the trip.

As I looked around I saw that I was trapped, waiting on East Fortieth Street in a cavernous nowhere surrounded by midtown. I was gripped by horror at the thought of what it would be like to stroll aimlessly through this part of Manhattan. Always have a purpose and walk rapidly between appointments, to work, and on errands. In this way you cannot be overwhelmed, overtaken, enveloped by the mammoth emptiness of square gray spaces and buildings. Your tiny remnant of a soul, crushed into a minute fragment of itself by travelling the streets of New York—your soul can't be obliterated if you keep walking. Walk briskly, ride, escape if it's over fifty degrees, wear dark glasses if the sun is out, stay near Central Park on the Upper East Side, never go to a business district on weekends, never even be in New York on a weekend. Even a Friday is not safe—don't let yourself try to imagine what it would feel like to be on Park Avenue and Forty-sixth Street on a Sunday in the summer. You would be the only one there— maybe a lost tourist or a derelict in some state of delirium tremens would be someone to share the empty corner with. Your view would include the

Scaffold Building, a building designed to incorporate the look of metal scaffolding into its façade.

By talking to the commandant as if I had normal, casual thoughts on my mind—I was getting to like him—I found out that the bus was on the way down from the Seventy-third Street stop: the better, Upper East Side, first stop. I knew that the passengers who had boarded there would have that smug first-stop look on their privileged Upper East Side faces. But when the bus pulled up I saw that some of them had chosen those dangerous first-row seats. How stupid people could be, even if they lived on the Upper East Side. It was then I decided that in the future I'd go uptown to Seventy-third Street, all the way from SoHo, in order to board the bus with this smug group.

On the trips from Long Island, I discovered that any kind of person could get on the bus at any stop. One ride from East Hampton started out so well that I wasn't prepared for what I soon saw. It was still cold out, and something like a real winter day from the past. It was almost dusk and I could see out the window that the sky looked as if it might snow, but I knew that in the new greenhouse weather this was not a realistic hope. As I waited for the bus to start, I was thinking about what the pharmacist in "The Stranger" says to Orson Welles, the Nazi Franz Kindler: "Looks like it's coming up for snow." My view of the sky and my happy memory of that film were both suddenly obstructed by a six-feet-six creature who looked exactly like Frankenstein, except for his face, which was kinder and sweeter than the monster's face. He did have that protruding frontal bone in his forehead, but his forehead was small and low. He had to fold up his long arms and legs in order to get into the tiny space provided by the bus company for its passengers, the way you have to fold a marionette to get it into its little box. I felt sorry for the man as I noticed his long wristbones sticking out of his jacket sleeves, which were several inches too short. His pants legs were much too short, also. He sat down in the seat across from mine. He wore a reddish-brown box-plaid suit and a lopsided Frankenstein-style toupee, the exact same color brown as his suit. The toupee was tilted too far forward, and, underneath, his own normal-colored hair was visible—darker brown with gray. I'd seen this kind of toupee mistake on other men, including something I thought I saw on Dennis Hopper. The box-plaid colors of his suit were turquoise blue and orange. He wore an orange shirt to match one color and white socks with turquoise blue stripes around the tops to match the other. Before long he took out a bag with his lunch or dinner. The meal appeared to be a liverwurst sandwich, and after eating this sandwich he ate two bananas. Then he took out a bag of Pepperidge Farm cookies. When I checked to see which kind of Pepperidge Farm cookie such a man would choose, I was surprised to see that it was Chessmen. In my whole life of acquaintance with this brand of cookie I'd never seen anyone buy or eat Chessmen. The Frankenstein man ate about half a bag of Chessmen and then began to read the *Times Book Review*. He was a big man, he had to eat a lot, I tried to tell myself. Still, there could never be a reason to eat liverwurst, or animals in any form.

I found out that bad things happened at East Seventy-third Street, too. Once, a woman with a German accent was complaining, in a voice between crying and screaming, about the "air conditions," and the journey had not yet even begun. The woman was about forty-eight but still had long, straight black hair and bangs, as if it were the nineteen-sixties and she were twenty. "What is that terrible odor?" she was asking the driver in her hysterical voice. Other passengers joined the debate.

"It's food," one said. "People are eating lunch."

"It's something else, in addition to that—it's some kind of fumes!" she said.

People quickly skipped over what it was to how they could avoid this trip on the South Fork Bus. Two elderly gentlemen in suède jackets with fringes said that you could avoid Penn Station by taking a taxi over the Fifty-ninth Street Bridge to Hunter's Point, the place the Long Island Railroad started from—some barren, deadly yard in Queens where gangland shootouts and drug transactions probably took place.

Down in the dirty, gray Forties, the first-stop people seemed to be on the verge of awareness of the seriousness of the air problem, but before a rebellion could start, the bus stopped and the doors opened to let in the angry midtown line. Before things could settle down I heard sounds of a scuffle a few rows behind me. I heard punching sounds—maybe two men had started to punch each other. I didn't want to see. The reason for the fight turned out to be that one passenger didn't want a new passenger to sit next to him and said so. The new passenger, a dark-skinned man, took this to be a racial insult. The seated man explained that he needed two seats for himself because he was tall.

After the altercation was over I heard some swearing and heavy breathing, but I couldn't tell which was coming from which passenger. A lightskinned, sixty-year-old African-Spanish-American woman tried to keep the insulted man calm by turning back toward his seat and reciting outdated anti-racist slogans. After a while she turned around, and she and her own seatmate began chatting about other things.

The sun was beating into the bus on all sides—even though it was January, the temperature outside was about seventy degrees. By then we were near the exits of the hot, truck-packed Thirties, but this did not deter her from happily telling her seatmate that she had ordered up some Chinese food for lunch before the trip, and that her husband was a judge. I thought that ordering up Chinese food on a warm afternoon before a long bus ride was wrong. Then I imagined the sixty-five-year-old judge, probably a corrupt Housing Court judge, in his black robes downtown in his chambers with all the other corrupt judges. The judge's wife and her seatmate were becoming the best of friends, even though the seatmate was a rich-looking white woman, about five feet nine, wearing black toreador pants, ballet slippers, and eight or ten bracelets. As her bracelets clinked together she confessed that she had been a cruise-ship attendant—it sounded like a confession—and she had married an airline executive and they had a little boy, who'd been born when they lived in Senegal. When asked about the maternity treatment in Senegalese hospitals, she said, "It was fine. They have you hang from a tree by your wrists." I began to feel ill when I heard this, even though I knew that the use of gravity had to be better than the American method of lying on a table. It was the picture of the former cruise-ship attendant in labor, hanging from a tree—this picture plus the combination of the heat, the fumes, the Chinese lunch of the woman married to the judge presiding downtown in Housing Court. The Mozart in my earphones could not help me transcend this.

Every now and then the former cruise-ship attendant would laugh with inappropriate abandon. I decided that she must be drunk. In order to distract myself, I made a plan to ask Dr. Loquesto about the technique of childbirth she'd described, but on second thought I realized that it might enrage him. I'd once heard him yell at someone who asked his opinion of the birthing chair, "Great, the doctor has to sit on the floor in a raincoat!" Everything seemed worse when I remembered this.

IT was another muggy January day at the midtown location that same winter when I realized I could never again ride the South Fork Bus. It was Thursday afternoon and I was aiming for the bus that left East Seventy-third Street at one o'clock. Because of some kind of demonstration, there was the thick, slow, miserable kind of traffic on the way up Park Avenue. The taxi-driver suggested we go to the midtown stop. I said O.K., although I had a fear of midtown, and then we agreed that the only thing demonstrations ever accomplished was traffic.

I asked the midtown commandant where to get some coffee, even though I wanted tea, and he pointed me to a kind of hellhole combination stationery-and-coffee shop. In the hellhole I saw midtown individuals of every wretched sort, and stuffed animals of the poorest quality made, yet in the back, behind every other kind of thing a midtown person would want—for example, a cheap kind of foldup umbrella, a lavender rabbit, and the most dreaded candies and magazines known to man—there was a little Indian man whose job was dispensing coffee and tea. I was surprised to see a selection of herbal teas on a shelf behind him. I ordered a peppermint tea and a black coffee. I thought, I'll try the tea; if it doesn't help me feel any better, I'll try the coffee; if it makes me feel worse, I'll switch back to the tea.

Behind my small suitcase in the line for the South Fork Bus, fifteen more people had arrived during the ten minutes I was gone. These passengers were sick to see a long line on a January afternoon. A former débutante who I knew would be getting off at Southampton was behind me. She said that once it was so crowded she had to ask to sit next to someone. "I asked if I could sit there and the person said, 'No,' " she said.

"What reason did the person give?" I asked.

"No reason," she said. "Just 'no.' It took me a long time to get over that incident."

"I'd never get over it," I said. "I haven't had to ask and people haven't had to ask me yet," I said, picturing the three-hundred-pound man I saw once. No one asked to sit next to him, and after a while you had to feel sorry for him, since his great girth was obviously the reason. But as he settled into the trip and discovered that he knew the couple in front of him and began to tell them about his new life in Water Mill, you had to hate him. Because in his new life, although he was around fifty-five, his new wife and he had a one-year-old son named Jake, Josh, or Zack, and his wife and son watched the sun rise each day before she went for her three-mile run on the beach. A very typical description, I thought, as I heard him say his house was right on the beach and then ask the couple where their house was. They said their house was right on the highway. Now, that was a surprise. He didn't know what to say to that. This was as embarrassing to hear as hearing a couple say that their son was a pornography star or a follower of the Reverend Moon. There was nothing to say in reply. The couple didn't seem to mind that their house was on the highway. They took it lightly; it was their same house they'd had all these years. Maybe the highway was not so busy twenty years ago. Still, that was no excuse, and the couple and the three-hundred-pound man all knew it.

That trip, starting with the demonstration and the débutante, clinched it. I got on the bus, sipping my tea and coffee alternately, and found that neither one was helping. The seventh seat on the right was taken by what looked like a purple sweatshirt with a tough-looking woman inside. It was going to have to be the eighth, closer to the center accordion divider of the bus. This was the new, extra-large bus, which appeared to be two pieces of a bus joined together by a flimsy vinyl connector. In a crash, the back section would fly off and smash into everything—cars, trucks, trees. The front, at least, would still be steered by the driver, this time an angry-looking, red-faced thug who would probably have a seizure because of his poor physical condition, which I judged to be high blood pressure and arteriosclerosis.

The débutante sat in the front with a friend who had gotten on uptown. Very quickly, I saw that someone was going to ask to sit next to me, because the new passengers, to their dismay, were having to sit with other passengers all over the bus. First they'd walk through the front section and through the accordion to the back, thinking that certainly there would be empty seats in the back. Then they'd come dejectedly back to the front and survey the choices. In front of me, in the seventh seat, a woman—the purple sweatshirt—with horribly bleached hair was asked by a man if the seat was occupied. I couldn't tell what she said, but he left and went to the back. I was studying what had gone wrong with the hair-dyeing process when a man came by and asked me if the seat next to me was occupied. I had to tell the truth, because if you lied to a decent specimen, a worse one would be coming by next. I should be flattered that this man has chosen me, I thought, because this man was perfect as men go. He was (1) clean—clean as a man can be. His hair was clean, his bluejeans were clean, his boots were clean, his cotton socks were clean, his skin was clean and, as an added bonus, it was perfect skin, too. (2) He was only about forty. (3) He was wearing a wedding ring. (4) He had a book. He wasn't going to bother me.

Across the aisle from the purple sweatshirt, a most elegant man had sat down next to an elderly lady. The elegant man wore a perfect, lightweight gray flannel pin-striped suit, a blue striped shirt, and a blue striped tie. I wondered how the elegant man had just the right weight suit for this warm winter's day. He was an investment banker, I was sure, because these guys have all the right clothes no matter what else is wrong with them. One thing wrong with this man was his face. His face was too small, his features were too small for a man's face, but what could he do? He was a man. He couldn't get out of it. He wore black shoes—a mark against him—but at least they didn't have gold hardware. His hair was too long for his profession, and it was thin on top, but he didn't let this bother him, and he bravely combed it back the way he'd always combed it. He had a suntan on his small-featured face, but not too much of a suntan, and his hands were tan and smooth-looking, as if he'd never done anything with them but handle financial papers and cut a twig in his garden. This man was going to get off at Southampton. I imagined him in prep school. I imagined his whole privileged life of about forty-nine years and how he might have managed to keep his hands like that. Servants hammered and sawed things for him in Southampton, and superintendents and porters helped with things at home on Park Avenue.

Before we had even taken off I saw that the elegant man was talking in a cordial way to the purple sweatshirt. What could he have to say to her? He was not looking directly at her when I heard him say, "I keep mine out on the East End." I realized that he was smiling warmly at her dog, her dog that was the reason no one sat with her—her dog sat in the window seat, although dogs were not allowed on the South Fork Bus. He spoke directly to the dog, and, to my astonishment, he called the dog "pooch." "Hi, pooch," I believe he said. I couldn't tell what kind of dog it was. It looked a bit like the elegant man himself, with little tiny features on its little tiny face, but its face was a squashed, flat, light-brown fur thing, and his was not. The dog had big ears surrounding its tiny, bashed-in fur face, and the man's ears were normal-sized.

I saw that my seatmate was listening to his Walkman, a newer and more expensive model than mine, and that he was reading his book. There was no way to see what he was reading, but I saw that his hands were not only clean, they were beautiful. The more I stared at his hands, the more grateful I felt to have him sitting there. His long legs in those tight, but not too tight, clean, naturally faded bluejeans were not only good legs, they were great legs, but his hands were perfect hands, and suddenly I had the urge to grab one and kiss it.

Once we were out of the tunnel, I noticed that across the aisle the elegant man and the purple sweatshirt were exchanging newspapers—he had the *Wall Street Journal,* and the sweatshirt had the *Times.* They were friends now, just because of this dog. They were smiling at each other with each exchange of sections, and there were seven sections altogether. If they were in a Mozart opera, they might get up and dance a minuet. How could he like her so much just because she had this dog? It didn't seem possible, because he was so elegant and she was such a slob. He'd smile his courtly smile and she'd smile glowingly back even though she couldn't have been interested in him, since he was some kind of neuter man.

By the time we reached Manorville, I saw that the elegant man had stopped reading. He was becoming fidgety. When he saw that the bus was stopping at Manorville he got more fidgety. He mentioned to his seatmate, the elderly lady, that this was really too much, to have to stop at

Manorville—the trip was taking four hours instead of two, the traffic was terrible, and now all these new stops.

Soon after Manorville he started to bite his nails. But he didn't manage to bite them. He would start, and then think better of it. Just a small nibble starting at the index finger and going across all the way. Then he began to run his hands through his hair. He'd run his hands through, and then he'd stop, and start to bite those nails again, but he never got into it. The hair, next the nails, and then he began with his ears. Rubbing his finger around the rim of his ear madly and almost poking it into the center of the ear. Then he'd look out the window and squirm around in his seat and start with his nails again. At one point he started to take a huge chomp out of all four fingers at once but reconsidered and stopped.

This elegant man is going to go crazy on this bus, I realized, and I had those few Xanax with me. This is what they were for, but I couldn't offer; he'd have to ask, and he would never ask. I became afraid of what would happen if he continued this way to Southampton. But he did continue. Look out the window, I tried to direct him by mental telepathy, which I didn't believe in. Look out at the beautiful country view, look at the landscape. See the sky, see the fields, see the trees, calm down, you are almost at your destination. But he would not calm down. The hair-running, the brink of nail-biting, the ear-rubbing; and then he added nose-rubbing to it—a quick flick across each side of that tiny Pekinese nose was added to the routine. There was nothing left for him to do but put his face into his palms and rub his eyebrows and forehead upward in a final act of desperation— and then he did this, too.

I'm not going to watch anymore, I decided, even though the best view was out his window. I tried looking out the window next to my seatmate and saw to my alarm that the clean, beautiful-hand man was writing inside the cover of his book. I had no trouble seeing that he was keeping a diary, a moment-by-moment diary of his trip on the South Fork Bus. "3:04. This f——— bus!" it said. I looked at another section and saw that he was also writing about some failed relationship. I hoped it was not with a man. It appeared to be about his innermost feelings, feelings that I thought men did not wish to express, but here he was expressing them in a diary. When I saw a sentence that began, "So many feelings," I decided not to read on.

If I closed my eyes and concentrated on my sonata, either one of these two passengers could go berserk and I wouldn't see in time to escape. Neither one was calming down. The sweatshirt and her dog were asleep. The diarist put away the book and started taking deep breaths. I decided to speak. "We're not even at Southampton," I said to him, "and it's four o'clock."

"It's always late," he said, as if he might start to cry. "I hate this bus. At least . . . the train . . . I can walk around."

"Do the windows open?" I asked.

"No, but you can go to the end of the car and get some air," he said.

Finally, at Southampton, the elegant man suddenly turned calm and polite; he was helping the elderly lady on with her coat. People knew him. They were all getting off together, shaking their heads in disgust.

"Where are you getting off?" I asked the diarist.

"East Hampton," he said. "I can walk home. I live on Further Lane."

I could see that he was used to having people gasp when he said the name of his street, because this clean, half-crazed man lived on the most beautiful and expensive lane in East Hampton. The elegant, more crazed man must have lived on the most beautiful lane in Southampton—Pond Lane, or one of those Neck Lane roads.

Even though it had started to rain by the time we got to East Hampton, I knew that these two men would change their clothes and go out running. I couldn't run, but I could walk so fast it would be just as good for the heart.

On my walk I'd try to think of a new means of transportation. I'd heard that people hired retired policemen to drive them back and forth. It was only four times the price of the bus. I knew a young man who had gone to police school but flunked out because of his mistakes in choosing his uniform. The police hat he'd purchased was too large and kept falling over his eyes, and his shoes were too small to chase petty criminals in. Maybe his rates would be lower.

I could get a part-time job to pay the flunked-out police trainee his cutrate price. I had no skills for the real world and didn't know anyone gainfully employed except for the flower arranger and a macrobiotic chef. I could ask them if they needed any help. I could work arranging flowers by day and cooking brown rice at night. If only I'd shared those Xanax with the flower arranger, but drugs had become so hard to get. Dr. Loquesto had once given me a prescription for one Demerol for a medical test. The flower arranger had told me that his dog knocked over a bottle containing his last few pills and then tried to lick them up. The flower arranger had to scramble around the floor trying to salvage the licked pills for himself.

I'd always listened attentively to his floral techniques. "First, I mossed up the table, then I strewed calla lilies in wet Oasis—you know, the green foam Oasis?—then I draped ivy. . . ." People preferred live flower arrangements to photographs of flowers in decline. I had to accept this. While we worked on arrangements, we could talk about flowers and pills and herbal remedies. The medium-strength Xanax was a pale-peach color, the same shade as the Apricot Beauty tulip we both admired. The mild strength was white, like a

White Emperor tulip. An even higher strength was light purple, my hair-cutter, Francine, had told me. "They're for extreme cases," she explained. I pictured a lilac and a freesia. Valerian root could induce calm and sleep. Echinacea drops had antibiotic properties and came from the coneflower.

I'd have to hear the word "moss" turned into a verb. Dr. Loquesto didn't mind hearing the word "laser" conjugated as a verb. I minded, but in my new job I wouldn't even have the authority to say " 'Moss' is not a verb." Still, if I could learn to moss up tables and strew calla lilies in wet Oasis, maybe I could earn enough to hire the flunked-out trainee with the big hat to drive me back and forth. That was my plan.

(1992)

THE MENTOCRATS

O F my graduating class in grade school, only three of us passed the entrance tests for Townsend Harris High School, the special city prep for bright boys. Karl Denling and I passed with 89's, Benny Frankel with a gaudy 97. As freshmen, we continued to live in the same neighborhood and travelled together on the Third Avenue trolley. Benny and Karl would compare their homework and I would copy mine from one or the other.

In the course of our freshman year Benny achieved a lordly and careless preëminence. I had an inkling of the extent to which that carelessness was cultivated, because in spite of the boast that he never opened a book outside of class the homework was produced without fail each morning. But I wasn't fool enough to contradict him, not while I had the benefit of his labors. Benny Frankel in turn pretended to believe me when I said I could do the quarter-mile in fifty seconds flat. For a time we had a marvellous working relationship. If only because Benny was the one boy I knew who had read both the "Count of Monte Cristo" and the d'Artagnan series, he would have been a pleasant companion. It was regrettable that his tastes shifted from Dumas to Balzac so soon.

Benny was scrawny and terribly small. He even had tortoise-shell glasses. It must have been because he looked so much like a grind that he insisted on maintaining he never did a lick of homework. He really did spend much less time at it than Karl, and strictly speaking, he told the truth when he said he never studied at home. He had to do his work at the library, because more often than not the gas was turned off in the base- ment room on Seventy-seventh Street where he lived with his mother, and they had to light the place with a candle. Even when they had gas the place was pretty dismal. Benny's mother had a pushcart stand on Second Avenue and got home so late at night there seemed to be no point in mak- ing the beds. And everything from the walls to the worn oilcloth on the table was damp. If I sat too long on a chair my pants would stick to me moistly.

Mrs. Frankel sold fruits in season. She didn't hawk her wares, because her voice was ineffectual; she just stood in front of the cart and waited for buyers to come. In the wintertime she smashed up all the available crates and tried to keep a fire going in an ashcan. When the crates gave out she would peel off a sweater or two and wrap them around her ankles. Her wind-chapped red face made her look cold even during the warm months. All year round she was bundled into the same sweaters and shawls. Neither her clothes nor her face ever changed, and whenever we came by she asked Benny the same question: "Will you come help me clean up tonight?" And Benny would say, "You know damn well I'll come."

Once I bought a box of peaches from her, and she asked, "Benny a smart boy in school?"

"Oh yes. Very."

"I know." She gave me my change. "Don't tell him I asked. I know he's smart."

Another time I passed the stand with Benny and bought an apple for three cents. Benny took the money out of her hand and gave it back to me.

"You're a friend of mine," he said.

I didn't want to take the apple for nothing and returned the three cents to Mrs. Frankel. He took the pennies out of her hand and threw them quickly into the gutter.

"He's my friend, I tell you," Benny said. "What do you take his money for?"

"I'm sorry. Don't holler on me like that."

I couldn't say anything, and we left her. At the corner I turned back and saw Mrs. Frankel searching for the pennies in the gutter.

We walked up Seventy-ninth Street without knowing where we wanted to go.

"What do you hang around that track team for?" Benny said. "What's the sense in it? You run back and forth, and where are you? In fifteen years you'll die of athlete's heart."

"I don't strain myself."

"That's not the idea. How can you stand being in the company of those pinheads day after day? It's a wonder those morons manage to stay eligible."

THIS eventually led to a rift. I was crazy about running and stayed with it, and finally Benny gave me up in disgust. When I stopped copying his homework my grades fell off badly. For this and other reasons I regretted the loss of his friendship, but I had my pride. After a while we began pretending not to notice each other in the streetcar. And in time I could follow Benny's progress only through Karl Denling, who maintained civil relations with everyone.

It was Karl who told me about the stunt Benny pulled at the dual meet between the math teams of Stuyvesant and Harris. A dual meet of that sort is held between teams of five contestants, who are given a set of algebra problems to be solved within a stipulated time limit. It occurred to Benny that if he could somehow distract the attention of the Stuyvesant team his own side would have a great advantage. So he released a laboratory white mouse during the contest and it scampered up and down until the Stuyvesant boys went for it. The Harris team, who had been told what was going to happen, remained at work and won the meet.

Benny didn't always need trickery to put over his triumphs. There was nothing phony about the way he copped the freshman medals in Algebra, English, and History. Pride or no pride, on the day of the awards I went over to his locker to see those medals and feel them. Karl was with him.

"I'm glad you came," Benny said. "I got something to say to you."

"You suppose they're real gold?" I said.

"What's the difference what they are?" he said mildly. "Keep up with your track and one of these days you'll win a silver cup that'll be worth ten times as much as these."

I didn't quite know how to take him. "Is that what you wanted to talk to me about?"

"No, this is something important. Let's go where they can't overhear us."

The three of us went to a stone bench on the campus.

"It's a dizzy scheme, if you ask me," Karl said.

"So stay out of it if you think so. I'm not so sure I want you in on it anyway," Benny said.

"Well, go ahead, tell him."

"It's this. Did you ever read 'The Thirteen,' by Honoré de Balzac?"

"No," I said.

"You want to," Benny said. "It's some book. All about thirteen guys who swore they'd stick together all their lives and help each other in every way possible. By the time they got through they were the most powerful organization in France. Just thirteen smart guys. I got the idea of getting up an outfit like that right here in New York, young guys like us. There's no end of things we could do if we worked it right."

"Who'd be the thirteen guys?" I said.

"We wouldn't have to make it thirteen at first. We could start with the three of us as a base. I got the whole thing figured. I'm not letting you in on it just because you're friends of mine. I think we're the three smartest guys in the class. That's the one requirement we'll have for membership—a man will have to be extra smart. And we'll call ourselves the Mentocrats."

"Mentocrats?"

"Yeah. Mental aristocrats. Get it? Mentocrats. Thirteen of the smartest guys in the country working together. Pooling their brains. That's power."

"If anybody crossed us up, then what?" I said.

"Just this." Benny drew a finger across his throat. "But nobody will. There will be a probationary period of a year for every new member, and then the Oath. Nobody will want to violate *that* Oath, not the way I got it framed. I tell you this is foolproof. I'll let you see the Oath tonight. Can you meet me in front of the Seventy-ninth Street library at nine?"

"Nine? My mother won't let me out that late," Karl said.

"You know, I don't think I want you," Benny said. "If you had any will power you'd make it. Brains aren't all that's needed in a Mentocrat. It takes guts. No, I don't think you *would* do."

"Well, I can't get out that late. But even if you don't let me in, you can depend on me keeping it a secret."

"I know I can," said Benny slowly. "You know what's good for you."

OFFHAND I couldn't see Benny's plan either, but I declared myself in. I spent a good part of the afternoon thinking up amendments to the Oath I hadn't seen, and at nine I met Benny in front of the library. He carried a large package.

"Let's go where we can talk," he said.

"Down the docks?"

"No good. You know Dolan's Express office next to my house?"

"Yes."

"They leave the skylight on their back room open at nights. We could climb down and talk away all night without being interrupted. And they got a typewriter in there. I want to type out some copies of this Oath so it looks like something."

"How can you climb down a skylight?"

He tapped his package. "Rope."

We went up to Benny's roof and he showed me the open skylight. The climb looked easy enough. No slipup in any of Benny's plans.

"Karl's yellow," he said.

"He stinks."

We climbed through the skylight, using our rope. Dolan's office was a small room in back of the garage. All it had was a desk and cabinet and a couple of chairs and the typewriter which Benny had mentioned. You had to hand it to Benny. He had even thought of bringing a candle. He sat in the swivel chair and put his feet on the desk and laughed. I laughed, too.

"This is the life," Benny said.

We looked in the drawers and they were full of all kinds of stuff—typing paper, pencils, envelopes.

"Let's see the Oath."

Benny tightened up. "Listen, boy," he said. "What do you say we take some of this? The typewriter, I mean, and all the paper. We'll need it to make the organization look like something."

"No."

"Yes."

"All right," I said. "Dolan's got plenty of dough."

Benny went out into the garage and found a gunnysack. We slipped all the paper and envelopes and the typewriter and a box of pencils into the sack and tied up its mouth with the end of our rope. For a moment we stared at each other in excitement.

"Heave-ho," Benny said. "Yo-ho-ho and a Dough-Dough-Dolan."

Then somebody began pounding on the garage door. We looked out, and a flashlight was playing all over the shiny cars.

"Somebody saw us," I said. "Somebody saw you when you went out for the gunnysack."

"You go first. You can climb faster."

I began shinnying up the rope. It was thin and nearly cut into my palms. The full gunnysack swung round and round under me. Nearing the roof, I gashed my hand on the aluminum setting of the skylight. I pulled my legs after me through the opening and turned back to give Benny a hand. But by then a policeman had him around the neck and Benny just had time to yell, "Beat it, beat it, run!"

I jumped two feet across to Benny's roof and ran down the stairs and out the back yard and over the fence and through a basement to Seventy-sixth Street and up Seventy-sixth, with my hand bleeding and my eyes not seeing. I looked back to find out if anyone followed, but my eyes were blurred and I just ran on, brushing past newsstands and people. Finally I stepped into a doorway and stayed there a full two hours before going home.

BENNY didn't come to school the next day. I expected the police to pick me up after class, but they didn't come either. In the afternoon I went past the market, and Mrs. Frankel's stand was empty. For three days she stayed away.

On the fourth day she resumed her place, but I still had had no word of Benny. I stood that for several more days, and then I went to Mrs. Frankel's stand and asked for a dime's worth of oranges. Mrs. Frankel looked the same. All her sweaters were still dark-green with age and her face was red and wind-chapped—a little swollen, perhaps.

"You don't have to buy the oranges. You the other boy?"

"Yes, Ma'am."

"It is all right. What's the use you should get in trouble too? Benny wouldn't say nothing about you."

"Where is he?"

"They take him to orphan home," Mrs. Frankel said. "Don't worry. Benny wouldn't say nothing about you. Even they hit him, he wouldn't say nothing. But if maybe they should hit him too much, he would tell. Anyhow, they couldn't take you away. You got a papa."

"When is he coming back?"

"I don't know. Go away now if you don't want oranges."

"Yes, I want the oranges." She gave them to me in a bag and I paid her.

The same day I got a letter from Benny in which he also said I shouldn't worry, because he never would tell on me. He asked me not to answer, because they read all incoming mail. He said he would write again and send me the Oath of the Mentocrats, but he never did.

I don't know what ever became of Benny Frankel. All this happened ten years ago and still I haven't heard. I know he can't be doing so well in a money way, because a short while back I was travelling uptown on the Second Avenue bus and saw his mother standing beside her curb stand. Karl Denling hasn't heard of him, either. I ran into Karl on Times Square recently. Said he was an accountant now and doing pretty well.

(1939)

THE TREATMENT

WAS going to be late. A fat woman in a vertically quilted brown parka—
she looked like a walking onion—had kept everyone waiting in heavy
snow at Ninety-sixth and Broadway while she argued with the crosstown-
bus driver. She was trying to get him to take a transfer from the day before. She
insisted, loudly, that a downtown driver had just issued the transfer to her.

"It couldn't be, lady," the driver said. His Caribbean accent, his delicate
features, the touch of gray at his temples made him seem like an aristocrat
with favors to dispense, especially in the presence of the bulging woman
and the freezing masses outside.

"I'm telling you not five minutes ago," the woman said.

"And I'm telling you that he couldn't have any transfers from yesterday,"
the driver said. "They are destroyed each day."

Holding aloft the slip of blue paper, the woman turned around and
shouted at the rest of us, bunched up against the snow and wind blasting
off the Hudson, "Five minutes ago! Five minutes!"

During the silent glaring that followed, another crosstown bus stopped
across the street, and among the passengers who got off were a bunch of
Coventry School seniors, dressed only in sports jackets and slacks and running shoes. In two hours some of them would jostle their way into my
Advanced Placement English class, and I would give them broadly farcical
interpretations of the first half of "Billy Budd" until one of the quicker ones
began to suspect that I was putting them on.

"Hey, Mr. Singer," one boy called.

"Yo, Lenny, where ya headed?" another shouted, probably taking the weather as permission for impertinence.

If I'd wanted to answer the question, I would have said, "I'm going to see my psychoanalyst, Dr. Ernesto Morales." And if I'd wanted to amplify a bit I'd have added, "He's a Cuban, and a devout Catholic, apparently. There's a crucifix in the waiting room and another one on the wall behind his chair. I got his name from the school psychologist." And if I were histrionic, like the fat woman, I would have gone on, yelling my plaint for all to hear: "You see, boys, I am in real trouble. My mother died when I was six, my father and I are barely on speaking terms, and my girlfriend left me two months ago. When I told her I was thinking about ending it all, she said she thought that was an unlikely course of action for someone who at the age of twenty-eight was afraid to venture outside his own Zip Code. And I'm not going to be head of the Upper School next year after all. I told the headmaster he was kidding himself about his reasons for wanting to expand the scholarship program. He thought they were altruistic, and I thought they had more to do with wanting a league championship in football."

But no. It would never do even to allude to my problems to the boys. First of all, I wasn't so crazy that I didn't know how boring my plight would be to most people. The banality of evil is far outstripped by the banality of anxiety neurosis. Second, the kids weren't my friends, and, third, even though they weren't my friends, they were all I had left. Anyway, I wouldn't be seeing Dr. Morales much longer. He was a madman for whom conservative Freudianism was merely a flag of convenience, and I was just trying to keep him at a distance as I planned my escape—into what, I had no idea. The school psychologist must have been crazy herself.

"How long are we going to allow ourselves to be treated like this?" the fat woman demanded of the wind.

"Come on," I said. "Here." I was third in line, and I reached around the person in front of me and handed the fat woman a token.

The woman snatched it from my hand. "It's not the money," she said angrily. "It's the way we are treated. But obviously you don't care about that. So all right, all right." She put the token and the transfer into her purse and took out another transfer. She turned around, the fabric of her casing sighing against the metal panels of the bus's entryway, and handed the second transfer to the driver.

"Can you beat it?" the driver said to me as I paid my fare.

TEN minutes after my session should have started, I pushed the buzzer outside the door of the brownstone in which Dr. Morales's office occupied the rear of the top floor, and he buzzed me in. In the stuffy, overheated waiting room, the noise machine, which looked like a Starship Enterprise gizmo, was hissing away. The machine could sound like anything—wind in a cane field outside Havana, a wave receding on a beach, a tiger's warning—but today it was just static. I looked out the window, which was flanked by two big flower-pots out of which *Cacti freudii derelicti* thornily protruded. In the backyard of the house across the way, snow was building up on the back of the huge sow.

"Yes, I know the story of this pig," Dr. Morales had said a few weeks ear-lier. "This was David Letterman's house, and he had this statue installed in the yard. And when he moved he did not take the pig."

"It's strange," I said.

"I agree," Dr. Morales said, "but what is even stranger to me is that you have not mentioned it before now. You have been coming three times a week for how long—two months now?"

"Four," I said. "But who's counting?"

"We shall get back to your anger in a moment," he said. "But right now perhaps you could talk a little about why you did not bring up such an odd thing for such a long time."

This was as far as I got in my recollection of the pig conversation, which had quickly and typically put us at swords' points, when Dr. Morales opened the door to his inner office. He was beaming, as usual, and was bent at the waist the customary ten degrees, in what I took to be sarcastic defer-ence. This upper-body inclination made him seem even shorter than he was. He had on a white shirt and the vest and trousers of a three-piece suit, and his shoulders ballooned out like a miniature stevedore's. Light bounced off his shiny bald head, and behind his straight, heavy, broomlike black beard and narrow mustache, he was smiling the gleefully diabolical smile he always smiled. "Good morning, Mr. Singer," he said in his insinuating way—his voice, as always, even more flamboyantly Spanished in reality than it was in my memory. "Please come in."

"There was this fat woman on the bus," I started out after I lay down on the couch. I told him the rest. "She was probably on her way to *her* analyst," I said at the end. "Life in the city. How can someone let herself get so fat?"

"What do *you* think?" Dr. Morales said.

"Well, I suppose with some people it's just their metabolism or glands or something."

"So you are apologizing for her and for yourself."

"Myself?"

"With this 'Well, I suppose.' This is a habit, as I have pointed out before. You guess, you suppose, you think maybe. You castrate yourself before it happens what you so fear—that if you display your balls someone else will cut them off. Preëmptive self-castration."

"Opinions are testicles?"

"Yes. And so are feelings. You are amused, but this is the case. And people do not let themselves get fat, by the way. Again we have this passivity. They make themselves fat."

"Well, so why do they do it?"

"You must tell me what you think."

"It *could* be physical. They might—"

Dr. Morales dropped some papers on the floor. As he picked them up, he said, "Now we are like—what do you call them?—a champster on a wheel."

"Hamster. But sometimes it must be physiological."

"When it is, it is boring. As boring as this conversation. Unfortunate, maybe even tragic, but boring. The majority are fat because they want to be fat. They feel entitled to have more room and more attention than other people. They talk too loudly and they take up two seats on the bus. They cheave themselves around, and everyone else has to make room for them. And excuses, as you are doing. If you go to the mountain for a hike with them they get out of breath going up the hill and you have to wait for them. They want attention, and they are saying they should not have to take responsibility for what they do."

Dr. Morales paused. "You are smiling again, I can tell."

"It seems to me so outrageous as to be funny," I said.

"But were you not angry at this woman?"

"Of course. I told you."

"Then why do you laugh at me when I am denouncing her?"

The office was silent except for the ticking of the wind-driven snow against the windows.

"Maybe it's because it would never enter my mind to go on a mountain hike with a fat person."

"Again the 'maybe.' You disavow your anger, and you do not have the courage of your own contempt. She is a clown, I am a clown, the entire world is a circus, correct? But even then it is only *maybe* that the whole world is a circus and everyone except you is a clown. I must tell you honestly that I do not know how to proceed right now."

"I did not disavow my anger," I said.

"Ah, but you did, you did," Dr. Morales said. "You presented it as if it were a play and you were a character but in the audience at the same time. You had even a title for it, as I recall. The Life of the City."

"Life in the City," I said.

"Now, really, Mr. Singer, I must protest. You are correcting me and resisting the treatment at every drop of the hat. You do not want intercourse but frottage."

"All right. I was angry at the fat woman on the bus."

"Oh, thank the good Lord Jesus Christ. Why?"

"Because she stole a token from me."

"No."

"She made me late for the session."

"At last the penis goes inside the vagina. But not quite yet with the ejaculation."

"What did I miss? Oh, I get it. Me. I made myself late."

"And at whom are you angry?"

"Myself?"

"Why?"

"Because I was late? By the way, is there a makeup test if I fail?"

"You know, Mr. Singer, you are a gigantic pain in the ass. *Now, again, why were you angry at yourself?"*

"I already said: because I was naughty."

"AND SO AT LAST WE HAVE FINALLY MADE THE BABY," Dr. Morales declaimed.

"But I already said that."

"No, you will have to pardon me, Mr. Singer, but you said first that you were angry at yourself because you were late. The second time, you said it was because you were naughty. Now, do not sigh this way, please. You are an English teacher. You know that the choice of words always matters."

"So I was naughty, like a little boy."

"Exactly." Dr. Morales shuffled his papers.

"When I'm late, I'm always testing you or trying to provoke you."

"Yes, especially if you could express a little less like a quadratic equation, with a little more feeling. You are a little boy who takes down his pants and shows his penis and testicles and anus, all the dirty parts, to see if your mommy will love you anyway, even though you are naughty. You are angry at yourself because you are in reality an adult who has allowed his unconscious to be seen. You also use your lateness to get me off the tracks of your more serious problems and to get extra attention for yourself."

"Like being a fat person."

"Oho! We have engendered twins today. Yes, the fat lady makes passengers wait. You make me wait. You are amused again."

"All your patients probably do the same kind of thing."

"This is guesswork, and in any case, much as you might like to, you cannot throw your arm on my shoulders and talk to me as a colleague about my other patients."

"The guy after me is often late."

"Perhaps he does not have a regular appointment time. You are hunting with blinders on and without a license."

"Sometimes when I leave I see him running down the street."

Dr. Morales yawned loudly. The wind moaned around the windows, as if nature itself wanted his special attention. The radiator behind his chair clanked and spluttered, the noise machine in the waiting room hissed, and the air seemed closer and hotter than ever. At length he said, "Are you not tired, are you not tired, Mr. Singer, from lifting these sandbags and throwing them up against the treatment here? You are only hurting yourself, you know. And the more construction you perform up on this bunker, the more clearly you can be seen."

"Then what's the problem? If it's all grist for the mill, it doesn't matter what I talk about, right?"

Another yawn, this one downright theatrical.

"I guess that to you, people who are fat or late for the ordinary little neurotic reasons must be just as boring as those whose pituitaries have run amok or who get detained by a police roadblock. It must be excruciating for you."

"Nor do I need your sympathy, Mr. Singer. And I do not recall saying that your neurosis was little. You have now succeeded in filling up fifteen of the forty minutes available with dramaturgical exercises, procedural pettiness, philosophical speculation, an attempt to join the New York Psychoanalytic Institute and form a partnership with me, and condescension to the tedium of my practice. Not one mention of the headmaster who has reneged on his promise, not one mention of the woman who left you, not one mention of the joy of teaching, not one mention of the sadness you must feel about your estrangement from your father, not one mention of what you are doing in your sex life these days. I suspect that your being late is in fact not a plea for attention but a reluctance to tell me that you have been masturbating."

"I'm sorry. I guess I was just struck by how boring many aspects of your work must be, and I said what was on my mind, as you are always haranguing me to do."

A long silence ensued.

"You are so kind to think of my working conditions," Dr. Morales said. "Perhaps you would like to vary my routine for me by going outside and taking a walk in the snow in the Park?"

"Well, you have been yawning and rearranging your papers back there."

"I must congratulate you. You have graduated from being my partner to being my analyst. Shall we go?"

"You're serious?"

"There are no jokes, Mr. Singer."

THE sun was up high enough behind the clouds to give the air the bright, false-spring light that always marks an hour or two of daytime snow-storms, before afternoon arrives and the gloom lowers. The wind was coming from behind us, at the same speed we were walking, and the snow had retired from fine urgency to flaky slowness, its movement more horizontal than vertical, so that as Dr. Morales and I walked to the end of the block we seemed to be moving without moving. He had on a coat and hat so bulbous and red and shiny—it must have been some sort of weird new synthetic fabric—that he looked like a postmodern mountain climber or an explorer or astronaut. He didn't appear to notice the glances he got from nearly everyone we passed but charged ahead as if he had just caught sight of some lunar objective. I tried to keep up.

We entered the Park at Ninetieth Street and went down a little hill. Paths that had been shovelled were already re-covered by snow, and the banks stood three or four feet high on either side. We walked in silence for a few minutes, following a course that took us—appropriately, it occurred to me—in a large circle. At the halfway point, Dr. Morales asked, "What are you thinking about?," and I said, "Not much." When we got back to where we had started, I stopped and scooped up some snow, made it into a snow-ball, and threw it at a tree about fifty feet off. It nicked the trunk.

"What a beautiful day, yes?" said Dr. Morales, beaming at the winter-scape as if he had created it himself. "It makes you feel like a kid, no?"

"Yes," I said. "But you couldn't have had much weather like this in Cuba."

"You are still at point counterpoint, eh, Mr. Singer?"

"Just an observation," I said, moving off down the path. "Sometimes a cigar is a cigar."

"Yes, but not, I believe, when you light it and then try to ram it up some-one's ass." He hadn't resumed walking, and when I turned to face him he looked, now, less exploratory than extraterrestrially Bolshevik, with the snow—which was intensifying again—swirling about him. He stood per-fectly upright in his carapace, a few feet away, gazing at me austerely, as if I had failed to hold my share of the line against the Fascists outside Leningrad. Off to the side, some schoolboys on an outing tossed a Frisbee back and forth. Dr. Morales picked up some snow, compacted it vigorously, and, encumbered as he was, fired it at the tree I'd aimed at. Bull's-eye.

"I don't think this treatment is getting me anywhere," I said.

"You must give it time, Mr. Singer."

"I want to stop."

"Please do not do that, Mr. Singer."

"I thought this whole process was supposed to be more sympathetic, kinder."

"That is what you want? Someone to be kind to you?"

"Yes," I said, and, with that, tears welled into my eyes. "Yes, that's what I want."

"I'm afraid this is not my function. What I shall try to do, if you will permit me, is to help you learn how to obtain from others what it is that you want."

The tears were now starting from my eyes, as if expelled by some great interior pressure, and even as I wept I smiled in childlike delight to feel such sudden lightness across my shoulders, such relief in not being able to govern myself. Dr. Morales walked along the path toward me. Despite what he had said, I expected that he might put his arm around my shoulders or explain that it was for my own good that he remained so aloof and exigent— some little gesture of concern. But even in the face of my weeping he didn't let go an inch, and what I got, after a Frisbee player ran between us, his coat flapping and his orange scarf trailing behind him like a pennant, was "I am sorry but our time is up. I must return to my office."

We walked out of the Park once again in silence, and Dr. Morales once again struck a lively pace. I hastened along in order not to lag behind like a child, which is very much what I felt like as I tried to wipe the snot and tears from my face with the back of a snow-crusted glove. At Fifth Avenue, Dr. Morales gave me a single formal nod of the head and hurried off toward his office. I got on the westbound crosstown bus, and there was the fat woman, occupying two of the seats reserved for the elderly and handicapped.

HE must work out. His striding through the snow, his dead shot with the snowball, his billowing shoulders have led me to imagine him at a gym, lifting weights and then putting in half an hour on a Nordic. Next to a priest. It's some kind of special, exclusively Catholic gym that I imagine, serving only the various brands of maniacal, too-bright-a-gleam-in-the-eye types that that religion appears to breed. The spirit of the place is martial. The fanatics go there and harden their bodies into worthy vessels of the all-consuming vocations they follow. So we have mafiosi grunting and sweating alongside philosophy professors, and young, sharklike politicians holding the ankles of supermarket managers as they do situps with barbells. Scattered throughout the cavernous facility, whose only ungrotty feature is a south-facing stained-glass window, are those who have gone the whole hog and become priests. And there is also a sprinkling of zealots who have somehow landed in the

"helping professions"—tyrannical nurse supervisors, militant social workers, and one or two lunatic analysts like Dr. Morales. Commitment and determination burn like fire in the air around them.

This vision comes to me on my way to a session with Dr. Morales as I
walk through the little hollow where we stood in the snow, me crying, Dr.
Morales not relenting. It's spring now—one of the few genuine springs I
can remember in New York. After the snow on the back of David Letterman's pig melted, there were soft, cool days and chilly nights, with weeks'
worth of trees fuzzing up with foliage, and none of the usual foretastes of
the heat of summer, and no six-day block of rain and rawness.

I still feel as though in that blizzard I lost a battle in the war I wage tri-
weekly with Dr. Morales, but it evidently instilled in me a love of combat, for
I have gone on seeing him, holding in reserve the ultimate weapon: quit-
ting. Soon after the al-fresco session, in fact, I took to leaving every morning at exactly the same time and walking across the Park, to make sure I
wouldn't be late, feeling a shade less desperate but not wanting to acknowledge it officially, for fear it wouldn't last, muttering all the way, rehearsing the devastating termination remarks that have yet to be delivered.
As the weather has turned, I've been making the trip more and more
quickly, and I think, now, how this morning's conversation might go if Dr.
Morales were to indulge me and himself in a ceasefire:

ME: Have you noticed that I'm not late anymore? This morning I was actually ten minutes *early.*

DR. MORALES: Yes, I have noticed. And why do you suppose this is?

ME: I think it's just that I'm getting into better shape and doing the walk
faster and haven't adjusted for the difference yet.

DR. MORALES: I see. Do you take any other exercise?

ME: No.

DR. MORALES: Then I doubt that this walk alone is putting you in better condition.

ME: Well, you ought to know.

DR. MORALES: And what does this mean?

ME: I just remember when we went to the Park in the snow that day. You
seemed to be in very good shape yourself, the way you strode around and
threw that snowball. Walter Johnson. And you look as though you lift
weights or something.

DR. MORALES: The Big Train, yes?

ME: Yes.

DR. MORALES: You are amazed I know this?

ME: Yes.

DR. MORALES: Yet you know that baseball is if anything more popular in Cuba than it is here?

ME: Yes, I guess so.

DR. MORALES: No guesses, Mr. Singer. And you also sound surprised that I am in shape. You remark on this as though it defied credibility, like a snake with tits.

ME: I'm surprised you would have the time—that's all.

DR. MORALES: Well, as you know, it is not my custom to discuss details of my personal life, but since you are so interested, I will tell you that you happen to be right—I do go to the gymnasium.

ME: Every day?

DR. MORALES: No, this would be impossible with the routine I follow. At my age the body must rest between these kinds of workouts. So, then, what do I do? I go every other day. I fool the body by letting it rest. That is essentially what you do—get the body ready for strenuous work and then fool it on a regular basis. Sometimes, when the body is ready the next day, I fool it even more completely by taking another day off.

I can't help laughing as I picture my invented Dr. Morales resolutely shunning the gym every other day, pulling the wool over his body's eyes. That image reminds me of his hirsute face and his stiff smile as he told me the time was up, the son of a bitch, and my own smile fades.

ME: Have you noticed that I'm not late anymore? This morning I was ten minutes *early!*

DR. MORALES: Yes, I did notice. You must know that this would be very disruptive when the buzzer rings in the middle of someone else's session, and I wonder if you are not becoming jealous of the time I spend with other patients.

(1990)

ARRANGEMENT IN BLACK

AND WHITE

T HE woman with the pink velvet poppies wreathed round the assisted gold of her hair traversed the crowded room at an interesting gait combining a skip with a sidle, and clutched the lean arm of her host.

"Now I got you!" she said. "Now you can't get away!"

"Why, hello," said her host. "Well. How are you?"

"Oh, I'm finely," she said. "Just simply finely. Listen. I want you to do me the most terrible favor. Will you? Will you please? Pretty please?"

"What is it?" said her host.

"Listen," she said. "I want to meet Walter Williams. Honestly, I'm just simply crazy about that man. Oh, when he sings! When he sings those spirituals! Well, I said to Burton, 'It's a good thing for you Walter Williams is colored,' I said, 'or you'd have lots of reason to be jealous.' I'd really love to meet him. I'd like to tell him I've heard him sing. Will you be an angel and introduce me to him?"

"Why, certainly," said her host. "I thought you'd met him. The party's for him. Where is he, anyway?"

"He's over there by the bookcase," she said. "Let's wait till those people get through talking to him. Well, I think you're simply marvellous, giving this perfectly marvellous party for him, and having him meet all these white people, and all. Isn't he terribly grateful?"

"I hope not," said her host.

"I think it's really terribly nice," she said. "I do. I don't see why on earth it isn't perfectly all right to meet colored people. I haven't any feeling at all about it—not one single bit. Burton—oh, he's just the other way. Well, you know, he comes from Virginia, and you know how they are."

"Did he come tonight?" said her host.

"No, he couldn't," she said. "I'm a regular grass widow tonight. I told him when I left, 'There's no telling what I'll do,' I said. He was just so tired out, he couldn't move. Isn't it a shame?"

"Ah," said her host.

"Wait till I tell him I met Walter Williams!" she said. "He'll just about die. Oh, we have more arguments about colored people. I talk to him like I don't know what, I get so excited. 'Oh, don't be so silly,' I say. But I must say for Burton, he's heaps broader-minded than lots of these Southerners. He's really awfully fond of colored people. Well, he says himself, he wouldn't have white servants. And you know, he had this old colored nurse, this regular old nigger mammy, and he just simply loves her. Why, every time he goes home, he goes out in the kitchen to see her. He does, really, to this day. All he says is, he says he hasn't got a word to say against colored people as long as they keep their place. He's always doing things for them—giving them clothes and I don't know what all. The only thing he says, he says he wouldn't sit down at the table with one for a million dollars. 'Oh,' I say to him, 'you make me sick, talking like that.' I'm just terrible to him. Aren't I terrible?"

"Oh, no, no, no," said her host. "No, no."

"I am," she said. "I know I am. Poor Burton! Now, me, I don't feel that way at all. I haven't the slightest feeling about colored people. Why, I'm just crazy about some of them. They're just like children—just as easy-going, and always singing and laughing and everything. Aren't they the happiest things you ever saw in your life? Honestly, it makes me laugh just to hear them. Oh, I like them. I really do. Well, now, listen, I have this colored laundress, I've had her for years, and I'm devoted to her. She's a real character. And I want to tell you, I think of her as my friend. That's the way I think of her. As I say to Burton, 'Well, for Heaven's sakes, we're all human beings!' Aren't we?"

"Yes," said her host. "Yes, indeed."

"Now this Walter Williams," she said. "I think a man like that's a real artist. I do. I think he deserves an awful lot of credit. Goodness, I'm so crazy about music or anything, I don't care what color he is. I honestly think if a person's an artist, nobody ought to have any feeling at all about meeting them. That's absolutely what I say to Burton. Don't you think I'm right?"

"Yes," said her host. "Oh, yes."

"That's the way I feel," she said. "I just can't understand people being narrow-minded. Why, I absolutely think it's a privilege to meet a man like

Walter Williams. Now, I do. I haven't any feeling at all. Well, my goodness, the good Lord made him, just the same as He did any of us. Didn't He?"

"Surely," said her host. "Yes, indeed."

"That's what I say," she said. "Oh, I get so furious when people are narrow-minded about colored people. It's just all I can do not to say something. Of course, I do admit when you get a bad colored man, they're simply terrible. But as I say to Burton, there are some bad white people, too, in this world. Aren't there?"

"I guess there are," said her host.

"Why, I'd really be glad to have a man like Walter Williams come to my house and sing for us, some time," she said. "Of course, I couldn't ask him on account of Burton, but I wouldn't have any feeling about it at all. Oh, can't he sing! Isn't it marvellous, the way they all have music in them? It just seems to be right *in* them. Come on, let's us go on over and talk to him. Listen, what shall I do when I'm introduced? Ought I to shake hands? Or what?"

"Why, do whatever you want," said her host.

"I guess maybe I'd better," she said. "I wouldn't for the world have him think I had any feeling. I think I'd better shake hands, just the way I would with anybody else. That's just exactly what I'll do."

They reached the tall young Negro, standing by the bookcase. The host performed introductions; the Negro bowed.

"How do you do?" he said. "Isn't it a nice party?"

The woman with the pink velvet poppies extended her hand at the length of her arm and held it so, in fine determination, for all the world to see, until the Negro took it, shook it, and gave it back to her.

"Oh, how do you do, Mr. Williams," she said. "Well, how do you do. I've just been saying, I've enjoyed your singing so awfully much. I've been to your concerts, and we have you on the phonograph and everything. Oh, I just enjoy it!"

She spoke with great distinctness, moving her lips meticulously, as if in parlance with the deaf.

"I'm so glad," he said.

"I'm just simply crazy about that 'Water Boy' thing you sing," she said. "Honestly, I can't get it out of my head. I have my husband nearly crazy, the way I go around humming it all the time. Oh, he looks just as black as the ace of—er. Well, tell me, where on earth do you ever get all those songs of yours? How do you ever get hold of them?"

"Why," he said, "there are so many different—"

"I should think you'd love singing them," she said. "It must be more fun. All those darling old spirituals—oh, I just love them! Well, what are you doing, now? Are you still keeping up your singing? Why don't you have another concert, some time?"

"I'm having one the sixteenth of this month," he said.

"Well, I'll be there," she said. "I'll be there, if I possibly can. You can count on me. Goodness, here comes a whole raft of people to talk to you. You're just a regular guest of honor! Oh, who's that girl in white? I've seen her some place."

"That's Katherine Burke," said her host.

"Good Heavens," she said, "is that Katherine Burke? Why, she looks entirely different off the stage. I thought she was much better-looking. I had no idea she was so terribly dark. Why, she looks almost like—Oh, I think she's a wonderful actress! Don't you think she's a wonderful actress, Mr. Williams? Oh, I think she's marvellous. Don't you?"

"Yes, I do," he said.

"Oh, I do, too," she said. "Just wonderful. Well, goodness, we must give some one else a chance to talk to the guest of honor. Now, don't forget, Mr. Williams, I'm going to be at that concert if I possibly can. I'll be there applauding like everything. And if I can't come, I'm going to tell everybody I know to go, anyway. Don't you forget!"

"I won't," he said. "Thank you so much."

The host took her arm and piloted her firmly into the next room.

"Oh, my dear," she said. "I nearly died! Honestly, I give you my word, I nearly passed away. Did you hear that terrible break I made? I was just going to say Katherine Burke looked almost like a nigger. I just caught myself in time. Oh, do you think he noticed?"

"I don't believe so," said her host.

"Well, thank goodness," she said, "because I wouldn't have embarrassed him for anything. Why, he's awfully nice. Just as nice as he can be. Nice manners, and everything. You know, so many colored people, you give them an inch, and they walk all over you. But he doesn't try any of that. Well, he's got more sense, I suppose. He's really nice. Don't you think so?"

"Yes," said her host.

"I liked him," she said. "I haven't any feeling at all because he's a colored man. I felt just as natural as I would with anybody. Talked to him just as naturally, and everything. But honestly, I could hardly keep a straight face. I kept thinking of Burton. Oh, wait till I tell Burton I called him 'Mister'!"

(1927)

CARLYLE TRIES POLYGAMY

F OR a while anyway an Africamerican man named Carlyle Bedlow
lived in one large, sunny room in a brownstone on lower Edgecombe
Avenue in Harlem, U.S.A. Like many men he had a polygamous nature,
which did not make him promiscuous. And neither had he married. But
over the years he usually seemed to have two or three steady lady friends.

Often they overlapped, and sometimes they repeated. First he would have
one woman, for example Glora Glamus. Then he would meet another one,
like Senegale Miller. Then he would shuttle back and forth between the two.
On the way he might meet a third. Then he would shuttle around among
the three, travelling from the Bronx to Manhattan to Brooklyn. Then the
first woman would get tired of his intermittency and break it off. Then he
would meet another woman shuttling back and forth between the second
two. Occasionally he would disappear to his room in Harlem, where he
lived alone and never let anyone visit except his brother and his widowed
mother, who rarely came because she did not like climbing the three flights
of steps to his room.

Carlyle Bedlow kept his room neat and clean. Since he never entertained
any women there, he had a firm narrow bed, which he made up into a
couch each morning. His clothes he kept in a large closet and three black
footlockers. A high-grade Navajo rug (handmade by the Etcitty sisters) covered the polished-wood floor. In the corner near the window sat an EzeeGuy
chair, where by sunlight or lamp he would relax and read science-fiction
novels, a pile of which he stacked beside the chair.

Sometimes he would look up from his reading and think about the two more or less steady lady friends he had kept for the past ten years. Actually Glora had occupied a place in his heart for about thirty years. In the beginning he loved her madly but could not win her because she loved Carlyle's mentor in the hustling life, the society baker and contract killer C. C. (Cooley) Johnson. Eventually, when she realized that Cooley Johnson would never love anybody, she and Carlyle began a relationship that produced a daughter, Carlotta, now twelve years old. Carlyle and Glora had broken it off fifty times, but had made up fifty-one times. Besides, they both adored Carlotta. So did Carlyle's mother, though she did not like professional barmaid Glora, considering her barky and brassy and boastful.

The second lady friend in Carlyle's life had a child for him as well, an eight-year-old daughter named Mali. He had met Mali's mama, Senegale Miller, at a jump-up given by the Rastafarian *bredda* who supplied high-quality cannabis that Carlyle sold to his high-society clientele, affluent former Woodstockians who had returned to the lap of luxury but secretly still smoked the blessed herb and did not want the world to know it.

Senegale Miller possessed luxuriant glistening black dreadlocks reaching to the small of her back which had never known scissors or comb. Raised in the cockpit country of Arawaka and descended from Maroons (who fought their way out of slavery in the seventeen-thirties), she had not worn shoes until coming to America. She stood six feet tall in her smooth cocoa-buttered chocolate-colored skin and had the grace of a seal in water. Carlyle's mother did not like Senegale either, mostly because she could not understand her thick accent, but, as she did with Carlotta, she showered Mali with gifts.

Carlotta and Mali got along very well, better than most big and little sisters. Sometimes Carlyle borrowed his brother's RoadStar sedan and without telling their mothers took the two girls anywhere they wanted to go, the beach or zoo or circus or rodeo or amusement park. He walked behind them, an unobtrusive shepherd, enjoying the sight of them whispering, cavorting, holding hands.

RECENTLY their mothers had become jealous of each other. They had known of each other for the past three years, when Senegale had tracked him down to Glora's house in the Bronx, demanding money for Mali's school uniforms. Before that, he had kept them separated in different parts of the city, Senegale in Brooklyn and Glora in the Bronx. Once they learned about each other, they did not stop talking and asking about each other.

In the Bronx, Glora might inquire, "When you getting your monkey woman to cut off that bush of hair and get a regular look, baby?"

In Brooklyn, Senegale would comment, "Is only a foolfool woulda make him babymudda to work into said wicked atmosphere, man no see it."

In the Bronx, Glora might wonder, "Why you don't go to court for custody of that cute little Mali, then report that bitch to immigration?"

In Brooklyn, Senegale would ponder, "Why you must keep on with the old woman when you kyan find rest and fulfillment in I-arm of this daughter of King Solomon?"

At times the verbal struggle they waged in his ears became so intense that Carlyle would retreat to his sunny Harlem room and rest in his EzeeGuy until his ears repaired themselves. He would not see either woman for a week. His brother, who knew something of his dilemma, told him that the blessed Koran gave a man permission to maintain four women, which did not help. Carlyle could barely manage two.

"Then you must cut one loose, my brother. Keep the relationship with your offspring, but call it off with one of the mothers." His brother had decided to wait till the Provider sent him a woman, abstaining from sex for several years, though Carlyle suspected he had a woman stashed somewhere. "You must choose!"

But Carlyle loved both women, Glora for her mocha beauty and her fast mouth, Senegale for her chocolate beauty and her independent spirit, and could not choose between them. Reclining in his EzeeGuy, he would puff a spliff and try to envision life without one or the other of them. He had always loved Glora; Senegale had stomped into his life with her goofy belief in the divinity of Ethiopia just when he had started to get sour, making him aware of some motivating force in the world besides money. Until Senegale came along he had not known how much he loved Glora, because falling in love with Senegale reminded him that he had love inside himself to give. So suddenly he also found himself in love with Glora again.

Carlyle could not decide between them. But something had to change. Then one day he encountered Brother Ben selling juice and astrology books at the corner of 125th Street and Frederick Douglass, and the brother launched into his tired polygamy rap, which goes:

Vietnam + Homosexuality + Prison + Heroin + AIDS + Crack had so reduced the male Africamerican population as to make polygamy the only way for Africamerican culture to sustain itself. Each man had to accept his responsibility. Each woman had to realize that only by accepting the other women in her man's life could she get a man to call her own. Then of course once a man had gathered his women together he might organize them to make dried-flower arrangements or some such product—

"But Brother Ben," Carlyle interrupted. "You have a nuclear family under your own roof, a wife you've loved for years and two beautiful daughters like mine. And besides, no other woman would have you!"

Brother Ben blinked, but continued his rap undeterred as Carlyle ambled away. But Brother Ben had made one usable point: perhaps Carlyle should bring together his two warring lady friends for a sitdown. Give them the opportunity to say bad things to each other face to face without making Carlyle's brain the battleground. Perhaps they could work out what he could not. At least they might blow off some bad gas.

CARLYLE arranged to have both meet him on a Tuesday evening at one of Harlem's few surviving gems, the Golden Grouse Bar & Restaurant. He liked breakfast better than dinner at the Grouse but did not expect anybody to eat very much. However, red-clad Glora tipped in first and quickly ordered an immense fried-chicken dinner with scalloped potatoes and tossed salad and peach cobbler and the Grouse's special punch. Before her food had arrived, Senegale appeared in olive drab, her dreadlocks wrapped (out and back like a praying mantis) in the Nationalist colors. She carried various tubs of her own I-tall delicacies because she did not trust the cook at the Grouse to keep the bacon grease out of the peanut oil.

The two women sat silently glaring across the table at each other and consumed all that the waitress and Senegale had carried to the table, near the end of the thirty-minute meal Senegale sampling the peach cobbler and Glora quenching her thirst with the homemade ginger beer. Together they covered their belches and tittered.

Then they both put fire under his sorry brown butt! Thought the sight of this simple country cow pie would do what? But make I tell all the world that I-woman never fear no old higgler till yet, no see it! Sure don't see what jive hustle he think he pulling with this tired B.S. but this sister came a long way to tell ev'rybody that this just won't hardly go down! Because I-love that I-woman keeping for said man spring from the most high mountain of New Zion! Besides this brother have deluded himself into thinking that because I love him that mean I need him when he be too dim to see I got my own house on Barnes Avenue in the Bronx all bought and paid for with mops and tips, and also got by far the best of his never-do-nothing buttocks in his daughter Carlotta. Which I-sister kyan strenuously affirm and illustrate as him give I-woman nothing of value but sweet likkle Mali, and she quite valu-able. They glowered at him.

So now what, *bumbasukka?*

"I just wanted to see if we all couldn't maybe find a way to get along," Carlyle said simply. "I can't help myself but I love you both. And I been mainly true to you two for the past ten years." He heard and despised the quiet desperation in his voice. "I mean, the kids don't seem to defend each other."

The women agreed. Dem two pickney hitch up like sea and sand, no see it. Looking so cute and fly in they little matching outfits, hooking it up on the phone when this fool think he sneaking them out on the sly to take them someplace like my child don't come tell her mama ev'rything that be goin' on, turkey! All the while dem aburn up phone wire, no see it, talkin' bout my sister dis and my sister dat, Carlotta why and Carlotta what for. And many times Carlotta have said, "Mama, why can't Mali spend the night?"

Well they could certainly agree to arrange that. Senegale expressed her gratitude that Mali would spend time on safer Bronx streets than those in the part of Brooklyn in which she presently resided where posses marauded in broad daylight and as soon as she found suitable accommodations, perhaps with members of her extended family in New Jersey, she would willingly offer similar hospitality to Carlotta. Strangely enough, Glora's aforementioned two-family semidetached featured a smaller second-floor space, which she had recently listed with Sister Edward's Realty, seeking tenants, five hundred dollars a month for two-bedrooms-kitchen-living-room-bath, use of washer-dryer, easy walking distance to the I.R.T.—but Senegale knew the way because she had already visited there at least once. They shook on it, bracelets and bangles jangling.

On the first of the following month, two jaunty I-dren driving a yellow van, puffing spliffs and blasting St. Donald Drummond and the Skatalites on their trunk-size cassette player, delivered Senegale and Mali Miller, along with two mahogany beds, a sofa and an overstuffed chair, a dish cabinet, a kitchen table and chairs, large cartons of clothes, books, utensils, dishes and pots, a cast-iron Dutchie, tools, raffia, leather hides for belts and sandals, and one calico puss cat named Kiki, to *chez* Glora Glamus, Bronx, N.Y. Soon the house filled with incessant female activity. Carlotta and Mali and their girlfriends (neighborhood pre-teens quickly forming a crew) seemed to make no distinction between upstairs and downstairs, roaming freely throughout every room under the roof, as likely to sleep in one as in the other of their two bedrooms, eating wherever hunger and opportunity struck them, though both avoided Glora's rhubarb pie as well as Senegale's steamed okra. And the two women began to take the step-aerobics class and do weights at the local NUBODi exercise salon on White Plains Road, working off their stress and excess energy with the rest of the sisters. Around the corner on Paulding Avenue, Carlyle's mother loved living near to both of her two darlings, though she still barely tolerated their mothers.

AFTER completing his hustling chores, Carlyle Bedlow spends more time in his one large room in the brownstone on lower Edgecombe Avenue, Harlem, U.S.A. Since he no longer travels to Brooklyn except on business to the Promenade or Park Slope, and can visit his two daughters at one address, he gets to see them both more often than in the days before polygamy, a definite improvement in his life. But now that his two lady friends live within whispering distance of each other Carlyle finds his sexual style stunted. Whenever he hopes to bed down with one woman, he knows the other woman knows his exact whereabouts and keeps expecting one or the other or the kids to burst through the door. Occasionally he gets over. But more often than not cool winds sweep his loins. The women load him with lists of things to do and buy. He completes his errands for them, then returns to the solitude and quiet of his room. His brother visits, assuring him that Carlyle has done the honest, manly thing, brought out everything into the open, creating a healthier environment for his children, that with each woman knowing where she fits into the Grand Scheme, they will all live happily ever after. For a while anyway.

(1997)

CHILDREN ARE BORED ON SUNDAY

T HROUGH the wide doorway between two of the painting galleries, Emma saw Alfred Eisenburg standing before "The Three Miracles of Zenobius," his lean, equine face ashen and sorrowing, his gaunt frame looking undernourished, and dressed in a way that showed he was poorer this year than he had been last. Emma herself had been hunting for the Botticelli all afternoon, sidetracked first by a Mantegna she had forgotten, and then by a follower of Hieronymus Bosch, and distracted, in an English room as she was passing through, by the hot invective of two ladies who were lodged (so they bitterly reminded one another) in an outrageous and expensive mare's-nest at a hotel on Madison. Emma liked Alfred, and once, at a party in some other year, she had flirted with him slightly for seven or eight minutes. It had been spring, and even into that modern apartment, wherever it had been, while the cunning guests, on their guard and highly civilized, learnedly disputed on aesthetic and political subjects, the feeling of spring had boldly invaded, adding its nameless, sentimental sensations to all the others of the buffeted heart; one did not know and never had, even in the devouring raptures of adolescence, whether this was a feeling of tension or of solution—whether one flew or drowned.

In another year, she would have been pleased to run into Alfred here in the Metropolitan on a cold Sunday, when the galleries were thronged with out-of-towners and with people who dutifully did something self-educating on the day of rest. But this year she was hiding from just such people as Alfred Eisenburg, and she turned quickly to go back the way she had come, past the Constables and Raeburns. As she turned, she came face to face with Salvador Dali, whose sudden countenance, with its unlikely mustache and its histrionic eyes, familiar from the photographs in public places, momentarily stopped her dead, for she did not immediately recognize him and, still surprised by seeing Eisenburg, took him also to be someone she knew. She shuddered and then realized that he was merely famous, and she penetrated the heart of a guided tour and proceeded safely through the rooms until she came to the balcony that overlooks the medieval armor, and there she paused, watching two youths of high-school age examine the joints of an equestrian's shell.

She paused because she could not decide what to look at now that she had been denied the Botticelli. She wondered, rather crossly, why Alfred Eisenburg was looking at it and why, indeed, he was here at all. She feared that her afternoon, begun in such a burst of courage, would not be what it might have been; for this second's glimpse of him—who had no bearing on her life—might very well divert her from the pictures, not only because she was reminded of her ignorance of painting by the presence of someone who was (she assumed) versed in it but because her eyesight was now bound to be impaired by memory and conjecture, by the irrelevant mind-portraits of innumerable people who belonged to Eisenburg's milieu. And almost at once, as she had predicted, the air separating her from the school-boys below was populated with the images of composers, of painters, of writers who pronounced judgments, in their individual argot, on Hindemith, Ernst, Sartre, on Beethoven, Rubens, Baudelaire, on Stalin and Freud and Kierkegaard, on Toynbee, Frazer, Thoreau, Franco, Salazar, Roosevelt, Maimonides, Racine, Wallace, Picasso, Henry Luce, Monsignor Sheen, the Atomic Energy Commission, and the movie industry. And she saw herself moving, shaky with apprehensions and Martinis, and with the belligerence of a child who feels himself laughed at, through the apartments of Alfred Eisenburg's friends, where the shelves were filled with everyone from Aristophanes to Ring Lardner, where the walls were hung with reproductions of Seurat, Titian, Vermeer, and Klee, and where the record cabinets began with Palestrina and ended with Copland.

These cocktail parties were a *modus vivendi* in themselves for which a new philosophy, a new ethic, and a new etiquette had had to be devised. They were neither work nor play, and yet they were not at all beside the point but were, on the contrary, quite indispensable to the spiritual life of the artists who went to them. It was possible for Emma to see these occasions objectively, after these many months of abstention from them, but it was still not possible to understand them, for they were so special a case, and so unlike any parties she had known at home. The gossip was different, for one thing, because it was stylized, creative (integrating the whole of the garrotted, absent friend), and all its details were precise and all its conceits were Jamesian, and all its practitioners sorrowfully saw themselves in the role of Pontius Pilate, that hero of the untoward circumstance. (It has to be done, though we don't want to do it; 'tis a pity she's a whore, when no one writes more intelligent verse than she.) There was, too, the matter of the drinks, which were much worse than those served by anyone else, and much more plentiful. They dispensed with the fripperies of olives in Martinis and cherries in Manhattans (God forbid! They had no sweet teeth), and half the time there was no ice, and when there was, it was as likely as not to be suspect shavings got from a bed for shad at the corner fish store. Other species, so one heard, went off to dinner after cocktail parties certainly no later than half past eight, but no one ever left a party given by an Olympian until ten, at the earliest, and then groups went out together, stalling and squabbling at the door, angrily unable to come to a decision about where to eat, although they seldom ate once they got there but, with the greatest formality imaginable, ordered several rounds of cocktails, as if they had not had a drink in a month of Sundays. But the most surprising thing of all about these parties was that every now and again, in the middle of the urgent, general conversation, this cream of the enlightened was horribly curdled, and an argument would end, quite literally, in a bloody nose or a black eye. Emma was always astounded when this happened and continued to think that these outbursts did not arise out of hatred or jealousy but out of some quite unaccountable quirk, almost a reflex, almost something physical. She never quite believed her eyes—that is, was never altogether convinced that they were really beating one another up. It seemed, rather, that this was only a deliberate and perfectly honest demonstration of what might have happened often if they had not so diligently dedicated themselves to their intellects. Although she had seen them do it, she did not and could not believe that city people clipped each other's jaws, for, to Emma, urban equalled urbane, and ichor ran in these Augustans' veins.

A S she looked down now from her balcony at the atrocious iron clothes below, it occurred to her that Alfred Eisenburg had been just such a first-generation metropolitan boy as these two who half knelt in lithe and eager attitudes to study the glittering splints of a knight's skirt. It was a kind of childhood she could not imagine and from the thought of which she turned away in secret, shameful pity. She had been really stunned when she first came to New York to find that almost no one she met had gluttonously read Dickens, as she had, beginning at the age of ten, and because she was only twenty when she arrived in the city and unacquainted with the varieties of cultural experience, she had acquired the idea, which she was never able to shake entirely loose, that these New York natives had been deprived of this and many other innocent pleasures because they had lived in apartments and not in two- or three-story houses. (In the early years in New York, she had known someone who had not heard a cat purr until he was twenty-five and went to a houseparty on Fire Island.) They had played hide-and-seek dodging behind ash cans instead of lilac bushes and in and out of the entries of apartment houses instead of up alleys densely lined with hollyhocks. But who was she to patronize and pity them? Her own childhood, rich as it seemed to her on reflection, had not equipped her to read, or to see, or to listen, as theirs had done; she envied them and despised them at the same time, and at the same time she feared and admired them. As their attitude implicitly accused her, before she beat her retreat, she never looked for meanings, she never saw the literary-historical symbolism of the cocktail party but went on, despite all testimony to the contrary, believing it to be an occasion for getting drunk. She never listened, their manner delicately explained, and when she talked she was always lamentably off key; often and often she had been stared at and had been told, "It's not the same thing at all."

Emma shuddered, scrutinizing this nature of hers, which they all had scorned, as if it were some harmless but sickening reptile. Noticing how cold the marble railing was under her hands, she felt that her self-blame was surely justified; she came to the Metropolitan Museum not to attend to the masterpieces but to remember cocktail parties where she had drunk too much and had seen Alfred Eisenburg, and to watch schoolboys, and to make experience out of the accidental contact of the palms of her hands with a cold bit of marble. What was there to do? One thing, anyhow, was clear and that was that today's excursion into the world had been premature; her solitude must continue for a while and perhaps it would never end. If the sight of someone so peripheral, so uninvolving as Alfred Eisenburg could scare her so badly, what would a cocktail party do? She almost fainted at the thought of it, she almost fell headlong, and the boys, abandoning the coat of mail, dizzied her by their progress toward an emblazoned tabard.

In so many words, she wasn't fit to be seen. Although she was no longer mutilated, she was still unkempt; her pretensions needed brushing; her ambiguities needed to be cleaned; her evasions would have to be completely overhauled before she could face again the terrifying learning of someone like Alfred Eisenburg, a learning whose components cohered into a central personality that was called "intellectual." She imagined that even the boys down there had opinions on everything political and artistic and metaphysical and scientific, and because she remained, in spite of all her opportunities, as green as grass, she was certain they had got their head start because they had grown up in apartments, where there was nothing else to do but educate themselves. This being an intellectual was not the same thing as dilettantism; it was a calling in itself. Emma, for example, did not even know whether Eisenburg was a painter, a writer, a composer, a sculptor, or something entirely different. When, seeing him with the composers, she had thought he was one of them; when, the next time she met him, at a studio party, she decided he must be a painter; and when, on subsequent occasions, everything had pointed toward his being a writer, she had relied altogether on circumstantial evidence and not on anything he had said or done. There was no reason to suppose that he had not looked upon her as the same sort of variable and it made their anonymity to one another complete. Without the testimony of an impartial third person, neither she nor Eisenburg would ever know the other's actual trade. But his specialty did not matter, for his larger designation was that of "the intellectual," just as the man who confines his talents to the nose and throat is still a doctor. It was, in the light of this, all the more extraordinary that they had had that lightning-paced flirtation at a party.

Extraordinary, because Emma could not look upon herself as an intellectual. Her private antonym of this noun was "rube," and to her regret—the regret that had caused her finally to disappear from Alfred's group—she was not even a bona-fide rube. In her store clothes, so to speak, she was often taken for an intellectual, for she had, poor girl, gone to college and had never been quite the same since. She would not dare, for instance, go up to Eisenburg now and say that what she most liked in the Botticelli were the human and compassionate eyes of the centurions' horses, which reminded her of the eyes of her own Great-Uncle Graham, whom she had adored as a child. Nor would she admit that she was delighted with a Crivelli Madonna because the peaches in the background looked exactly like marzipan, or that Goya's little red boy inspired in her only the pressing desire to go out immediately in search of a plump cat to stroke. While she knew that feelings like these were not really punishable, she had not perfected the art of tossing them off; she was no flirt. She was a bounty jumper in the war between Great-Uncle Graham's farm and New York City, and liable to court-martial on one side and death on the other. Neither staunchly primitive nor confidently *au courant*, she rarely knew where she was at. And this was her Achilles' heel: her identity was always mistaken, and she was thought to be an intellectual who, however, had not made the grade. It was no use now to cry that she was not, that she was a simon-pure rube; not a soul would believe her. She knew, deeply and with horror, that she was thought merely stupid.

It was possible to be highly successful as a rube among the Olympians, and she had seen it done. Someone calling himself Nahum Mothersill had done it brilliantly, but she often wondered whether his name had not helped him, and, in fact, she had sometimes wondered whether that had been his real name. If she had been called, let us say, Hyacinth Derryberry, she believed she might have been able, as Mothersill had been, to ask who Ezra Pound was. (This struck her suddenly as a very important point; it was endearing, really, not to know who Pound was, but it was only embarrassing to know who he was but not to have read the "Cantos.") How different it would have been if education had not meddled with her rustic nature! Her education had never dissuaded her from her convictions, but certainly it had ruined the looks of her mind—painted the poor thing up until it looked like a mean, hypocritical, promiscuous malcontent, a craven and apologetic fancy woman. Thus she continued secretly to believe (but *never* to confess) that the apple Eve had eaten tasted exactly like those she had eaten when she was a child visiting on her Great-Uncle Graham's farm, and that Newton's observation was no news in spite of all the hue and cry. Half the apples she had eaten had fallen out of the tree, whose branches she had shaken for this very purpose, and the Apple Experience included both the descent of the fruit and the consumption of it, and Eve and Newton and Emma understood one another perfectly in this particular of reality.

EMMA started. The Metropolitan boys, who, however bright they were, would be boys, now caused some steely article of dress to clank, and she instantly quit the balcony, as if this unseemly noise would attract the crowd's attention and bring everyone, including Eisenburg, to see what had happened. She scuttered like a quarry through the sightseers until she found an empty seat in front of Rembrandt's famous frump, "The Noble Slav"—it was this kind of thing, this fundamental apathy to most of Rembrandt, that made life in New York such hell for Emma—and there, upon the plum velours, she realized with surprise that Alfred Eisenburg's had been the last familiar face she had seen before she had closed the door of her tomb.

In September, it had been her custom to spend several hours of each day walking in a straight line, stopping only for traffic lights and outlaw taxicabs, in the hope that she would be tired enough to sleep at night. At five o'clock—and gradually it became more often four o'clock and then half past three—she would go into a bar, where, while she drank, she seemed to be reading the information offered by the *Sun* on "Where to Dine." Actually she had ceased to dine long since; every few days, with effort, she inserted thin wafers of food into her repelled mouth, flushing the frightful stuff down with enormous drafts of magical, purifying, fulfilling applejack diluted with tepid water from the tap. One weighty day, under a sky that grimly withheld the rain, as if to punish the whole city, she had started out from Ninetieth Street and had kept going down Madison and was thinking, as she passed the chancery of St. Patrick's, that it must be nearly time and that she needed only to turn east on Fiftieth Street to the New Weston, where the bar was cool, and dark to an almost absurd degree. And then she was hailed. She turned quickly, looking in all directions until she saw Eisenburg approaching, removing a gray pellet of gum from his mouth as he came. They were both remarkably shy and, at the time, she had thought they were so because this was the first time they had met since their brief and blameless flirtation. (How curious it was that she could scrape off the accretions of the months that had followed and could remember how she had felt on that spring night—as trembling, as expectant, as altogether young as if they had sat together underneath a blooming apple tree.) But now, knowing that her own embarrassment had come from something else, she thought that perhaps his had, too, and she connected his awkwardness on that September day with a report she had had, embedded in a bulletin on everyone, from her sole communicant, since her retreat, with the Olympian world. This informant had run into Alfred at a party and had said that he was having a very bad time of it with a divorce, with poverty, with a tempest that had carried off his job, and, at last, with a psychoanalyst, whose fees he could not possibly afford. Perhaps the nightmare had been well under way when they had met beside the chancery. Without alcohol and without the company of other people, they had had to be shy or their suffering would have shown in all its humiliating dishabille. Would it be true still if they should inescapably meet this afternoon in an Early Flemish room?

SUDDENLY, on this common level, in this state of social displacement, Emma wished to hunt for Alfred and urgently tell him that she hoped it had not been as bad for him as it had been for her. But naturally she was not so naïve, and she got up and went purposefully to look at two Holbeins. They pleased her, as Holbeins always did. The damage, though, was done, and she did not really see the pictures; Eisenburg's hypothetical suffering and her own real suffering blurred the clean lines and muddied the lucid colors. Between herself and the canvases swam the months of spreading, cancerous distrust, of anger that made her seasick, of grief that shook her like an influenza chill, of the physical afflictions by which the poor victimized spirit sought vainly to wreck the arrogantly healthy flesh.

Even that one glance at his face, seen from a distance through the lowing crowd, told her, now that she had repeated it to her mind's eye, that his cheeks were drawn and his skin was gray (no soap and water can ever clean away the grimy look of the sick at heart) and his stance was tired. She wanted them to go together to some hopelessly disreputable bar and to console one another in the most maudlin fashion over a lengthy succession of powerful drinks of whiskey, to compare their illnesses, to marry their invalid souls for these few hours of painful communion, and to babble with rapture that they were at last, for a little while, no longer alone. Only thus, as sick people, could they marry. In any other terms, it would be a mésalliance, doomed to divorce from the start, for rubes and intellectuals must stick to their own class. If only it could take place—this honeymoon of the cripples, this nuptial consummation of the abandoned—while drinking the delicious amber whiskey in a joint with a juke box, a stout barkeep, and a handful of tottering derelicts; if it could take place, would it be possible to prevent him from marring it all by talking of secondary matters? That is, of art and neurosis, art and politics, art and science, art and religion? Could he lay off the fashions of the day and leave his learning in his private entrepôt? Could he, that is, see the apple fall and not run madly to break the news to Newton and ask him what on earth it was all about? Could he, for her sake (for the sake of this pathetic rube all but weeping for her own pathos in the Metropolitan Museum), forget the whole dispute and, believing his eyes for a change, admit that the earth was flat?

It was useless for her now to try to see the paintings. She went, full of intentions, to the Van Eyck diptych and looked for a long time at the souls in Hell, kept there by the implacable, impartial, and genderless angel who stood upon its closing mouth. She looked, in renewed astonishment, at Jo Davidson's pink, wrinkled, embalmed head of Jules Bache, which sat, a trinket on a fluted pedestal, before a Flemish tapestry. But she was really conscious of nothing but her desire to leave the museum in the company of Alfred Eisenburg, her cousin-german in the territory of despair.

So she had to give up, two hours before the closing time, although she had meant to stay until the end, and she made her way to the central stairs, which she descended slowly, in disappointment, enviously observing the people who were going up, carrying collapsible canvas stools on which they would sit, losing themselves in their contemplation of the pictures. Salvador Dali passed her, going quickly down. At the telephone booths, she hesitated, so sharply lonely that she almost looked for her address book, and she did take out a nickel, but she put it back and pressed forlornly forward against the incoming tide. Suddenly, at the storm doors, she heard a whistle and she turned sharply, knowing that it would be Eisenburg, as, of course, it was, and he wore an incongruous smile upon his long, El Greco face. He took her hand and gravely asked her where she had been all this year and how she happened to be here, of all places, of all days. Emma replied distractedly, looking at his seedy clothes, his shaggy hair, the green cast of his white skin, his deep black eyes, in which all the feelings were dishevelled, tattered, and held together only by the merest faith that change *had* to come. His hand was warm and her own seemed to cling to it and all their mutual necessity seemed centered here in their clasped hands. And there was no doubt about it; he had heard of her collapse and he saw in her face that she had heard of his. Their recognition of each other was instantaneous and absolute, for they cunningly saw that they were children and that, if they wished, they were free for the rest of this winter Sunday to play together, quite naked, quite innocent. "What a day it is! What a place!" said Alfred Eisenburg. "Can I buy you a drink, Emma? Have you time?"

She did not accept at once; she guardedly inquired where they could go from here, for it was an unlikely neighborhood for the sort of place she wanted. But they were *en rapport*, and he, wanting to avoid the grownups as much as she, said they would go across to Lexington. He needed a drink after an afternoon like this—didn't she? Oh, Lord, yes, she did, and she did not question what he meant by "an afternoon like this" but said that she would be delighted to go, even though they would have to walk on eggs all the way from the Museum to the place where the bottle was, the peace pipe on Lexington. Actually, there was nothing to fear; even if they had heard catcalls, or if someone had hooted at them, "Intellectual loves Rube!," they would have been impervious, for the heart carved in the bark of the apple tree would contain the names Emma and Alfred, and there were no perquisites to such a conjugation. To her own heart, which was shaped exactly like a valentine, there came a winglike palpitation, a delicate exigency, and all the fragrance of all the flowery springtime love affairs that ever were seemed waiting for them in the whiskey bottle. To mingle their pain, their handshake had promised them, was to produce a separate entity, like a child that could shift for itself, and they scrambled hastily toward this profound and pastoral experience.

(1948)

JAMES STEVENSON

NOTES FROM A BOTTLE

(A BOTTLE CONTAINING THE FOLLOWING NOTES WAS DISCOVERED ON A
MOUNTAINSIDE ON ASCENSION ISLAND, IN THE SOUTH ATLANTIC.)

MARCH 23rd. 7 A.M.: Looked out the window of my apartment, saw that the water was up to the second story all along Eighty-sixth Street. Yesterday, the movie marquees toward Lexington were still visible at twilight, but this morning they are gone. There were, of course, no lights last night—there has been no electricity in the city for three days. (No telephones, no water, no heat, no television. Heat and telephone service had been gone for several days before that, owing to the fuel strike and the phone strike. Some portable radios still work, but they receive only the grainy sound of static.) A light snow is falling.

4 P.M.: It is almost dark again, and the water is approaching the fourth floor. No planes or helicopters were seen today; the airports were probably the first to flood, and any planes that managed to get aloft would have run out of fuel by now. It looks like another night of parties and celebrations. Across the street, candles and flashlight beams move about in the windows, and in our building loud, cheerful voices can be heard echoing in the fire stairs. There is a lot of shrieking and laughter. The children, as usual, are riding bicycles up and down the halls, as adults—bundled up in all manner of clothing, and carrying drinks and candles—roam the building, going from one party to another. The Williamses, who were supposed to go on a cruise, have been dancing around in their vacation clothes—Audrey in a fur coat and bathing suit, Harold in a mask and flippers. A lot of things have been thrown out of windows; Ed Shea on 7 was tossing an orange back and forth to somebody in the building across the street; one group was

skimming L.P. records, throwing them like Frisbees. There has been a good deal of horseplay. Carson on 8 would lean out his window and drop a paper bag full of flour on any head that was sticking out below. The biggest party last night was in the MacNeills' on 4—Alice played the piano, and everyone sang and danced until around three. (Today, a group of volunteers is moving the piano up to the Webers' on 6, just in case, and the Webers intend to have everybody in.) Phil Lewis amused everybody last night, saying that an ark was on its way and that it was going to take two people from the upper East Side. Martin, the doorman, has been drunk for a couple of days; he opened the Wenkers' apartment on 10—they're in Spain—and he has been holding court up there, dispensing the Wenkers' liquor with a free hand. There is still no explanation for the flood, beyond rumors shouted from one building to another. A lot of activity on Eighty-sixth Street during the day. For a while, everyone was throwing piles of flaming newspapers out their windows and watching them float away, burning, and there was considerable boat traffic—outboards, rowboats, a Circle Line boat with a crowd aboard, a small tug, a speedboat full of howling drunks towing a water skier in a black wet-suit. An hour ago, the Mayor went by, smiling grimly, in a large Chris-Craft cruiser with the city flag on the stern, the deck jammed with officials. Presumably, the water has reached Gracie Mansion by now, although the mansion is on high ground.

MARCH 24th. 3 P.M.: The water is now just below my windows on the ninth floor. There is nothing to do but watch. The water is filthy—there had been the six-week garbage strike, and all the city's garbage is awash—and the seagulls are everywhere, feasting. A number of people came up to stay in my apartment during the night, but they have left now and gone to a higher floor. They all arrived with apologies and genial remarks, but when they left they did so without fanfare—simply disappeared, one or two at a time, when I wasn't looking. I'd hear the door click shut, and I'd know they'd gone upstairs. There has been constant speculation on the cause of the flood—an atomic test in the Arctic is a popular explanation—but no one has any information at all, and no one really expects any. Those of us who have lived here for any length of time have become hardened: one simply waits. Langford, the lawyer, who recently moved to New York and lives on 8, was furious at first. "Why haven't we been informed?" he kept demanding. "I have contacts in Washington. . . ." But when I saw him a few minutes ago—he was standing in the hall, eating a once-frozen TV dinner—he was brooding, and when others spoke to him he didn't reply.

5 P.M.: The strangest thing is the silence of the city. No car noises, honking, sirens. Bodies float by, tangled in wreckage—furniture, lumber, trash. Suddenly a boat's horn, but then it is silent again—extraordinary silence. The loudest sound, except when the gulls come near, is the slap of water just below the windowsill, or the scrape of something bumping the window air-conditioner.

MARCH 25th: We are on the roof now. I have no idea what time it is, but it is daylight. The lower buildings have been submerged, the tall office buildings stand like tombstones above the heaving waves. There are white-caps toward Central Park. An ocean liner stood by the Pan Am Building for a while, then moved out to sea. Our rooftop is packed with people; many huddle against the chimneys, trying to keep away from the bitter wind. Alice MacNeill—her piano was abandoned on 8—tried to get everyone to sing "Nearer My God to Thee," but there was little response. No one wants to accept the situation as final, and yet everyone is keeping to himself. Langford, I notice, has moved toward the tallest TV antenna and has stationed himself near its base. He dreams, I suppose, that when the water covers the roof and the skylights and the chimneys, he will shinny up the pole and cling to the top. In his mind, probably, the water will rise until it reaches his ankles, and then stop. That is his hope. Then the water will recede, go down, down, down—and he will be saved. The water is swirling around the skylights now. The wind shifts. The waves are coming straight in from the Atlantic.

(1969)

MAN IN THE MIDDLE

OF THE OCEAN

A RNOLD Darcy was a civil engineer who worked for the city as a building-plans examiner. He handled skyscrapers, one of three men in the department who O.K.'d blueprints on construction twelve stories and higher, and it was a fairly important position, but, like everybody else on a fixed salary these days, Darcy was trapped by inflation. He lived at the end of the subway line, way out in Jackson Heights, in one of those modern, close, cluttered-up, three-room apartments. A Phi Beta Kappa, he was married and had one child. Darcy didn't particularly get along with his wife. They were married a good number of years now, ten or so.

He'd come home from work; he'd change his shirt and carefully hang up his suit, saving his good clothes so that he'd look neat in the morning; he'd go into the kitchen and greet his wife. "Darling," he would say. "Dear. Sweetheart. How are you, lover? Did you have a vexing day? Did the washing machine break down?" He'd kiss her. It was an artificial, painful performance, slightly ridiculous under the circumstances, but Darcy went through this rigamarole, he faithfully made the effort every night, because the pediatrician advised it for the sake of their son, to create a solid family atmosphere. Gary, a city child, was afflicted with a mysterious collection of allergies, and the doctors said the allergies were no doubt due to a basic sense of insecurity induced by the strained situation in the home. When Darcy came home from the Municipal Building, Gary would generally be in the living room, all by himself in there, looking at the television while he had his dinner. Darcy had to eat in the kitchen, at the kitchen table.

That was the way it was in that apartment in Jackson Heights. Darcy never blamed Natalie, his wife. He understood. He knew how the countless petty household cares and frictions could wear away on a person over the years. After all, to illustrate with a specific instance, Natalie worked hard all day, fighting with the butcher, watching the budget, running to the doctors with Gary and his rashes, and then when she'd come home and see Darcy, say, calmly playing Mozart's Symphony No. 40 in G Minor on the phonograph attachment—well, naturally she'd lose control and let go with a mean, caustic remark. It was human and probably didn't mean as much as it seemed.

One evening as Darcy was sitting at the kitchen table eating his dinner in an unhappy peace, the phone rang. His wife promptly flung a dish towel on the sink, and muttered something under her breath.

"What?" Darcy said.

"Nothing," Natalie said. "I wasn't talking to you. I was talking to myself. Your sister called. I told her you weren't home."

"Rita called?" Darcy said, a little stupidly, not wanting trouble.

"Don't sit there like a lummox—talk to her," Natalie said. "Answer the phone, it's ringing!"

Darcy winced. Rita and his mother were an old running argument in that house, the familiar, distressing, in-law problem. Natalie always claimed he spent too much time with his mother and sister, that he had no right to give them money every week when he had enough trouble supporting his own family, that his mother smothered Gary with excessive affection and had a bad influence on the child, and so on—all the rest of it. But when Darcy picked up the phone, it wasn't Rita at all. It was Arthur Colie. Colie and a man named Charles Angus were the two other examiners with whom Darcy worked down at the department. Colie was calling now to say something very urgent had turned up and they had to see him right away. Colie told him where to meet them, at an address over in Manhattan.

Darcy put the phone back on the rest. He couldn't imagine what Angus and Colie wanted with him or what could have turned up that was so terribly urgent, but on the other hand he knew he couldn't afford to keep them waiting. Charlie Angus was a power downtown. He had all kinds of political pull and had a hundred different subtle ways of making your life miserable for you if you tried to antagonize him.

"Flies to his mother the minute she calls him," Natalie said. She still had it in her head, of course, that it had been Rita on the phone.

"I am not flying to my mother the minute she calls me," Darcy said quietly, with dignity, but he couldn't do a thing with Natalie. She was boiling. He patiently explained it had been Colie on the phone, not Rita or his mother—just Arthur Colie and Charles Angus. They wanted to see him, something had turned up, business, and he made it clear why it was only expedient to keep in the good graces of a man like Angus, but it was hopeless. Natalie wouldn't even listen to him.

Darcy understood. He knew it was a fixation with his wife, a subconscious resentment directed against his mother and sister because Natalie herself had never had any family life of her own, having lost her mother and father when she was still a child. Darcy sympathized. He made allowances. Psychologically everything was clear to him. But nevertheless it wasn't very satisfactory.

He put on the shirt he had just taken off. He put on his good suit, and he left to see what Angus and Colie wanted.

DARCY had a vague, peculiar feeling something was wrong as soon as he reached the address Colie had given him over the phone. It was an exclusive-looking apartment hotel in the East Sixties, just off Fifth Avenue. Darcy stepped from the elevator into a fantastically lavish apartment—a triplex with one whole wall in the living room nothing but a big plate-glass window overlooking Central Park. It was the first time in his life he had even been in a triplex, although, of course, he had examined the plans of many of them in the course of his duties at the department.

At first, Darcy couldn't make head or tail of the whole business. He was so baffled he probably looked comical. There was a full-fledged party going on. He spotted Angus and Colie, but it wasn't easy getting to them in the crowd. Everybody was laughing and drinking and making noise, everybody was terribly friendly, everybody obviously was trying to get you in a good humor, and there were girls there—party girls, no question about it, the kind you read about in the papers. They were all made up and very young. Darcy kept blinking his eyes in wonder, like a fool, but he made a few guarded inquiries and soon discovered that the host, a man too busy to be present even at his own party, was Adolph Eckworth, a well-known public figure. Instantly everything became revealed to Darcy. Adolph Eckworth was the 990 Corporation, a construction group interested in putting up a forty-story hotel. Down at the office, Darcy, Colie, and Angus were right in the middle of examining the 990 Corporation plans. This whole party, Darcy saw now, was nothing but a clever, unscrupulous attempt to bring improper influence to bear upon them.

He went into action at once. Surreptitiously he caught Colie's eye, signalled to Angus, and drew them over to the bathroom. Darcy wanted to warn them.

"Do you know who's running this party?" he said as soon as he had locked the bathroom door. "Do you realize whose place we're in? Do you know why they invited us?"

He stopped. He stared at them. They were both grinning from ear to ear. They grinned at him as though they had just pulled the most delicious surprise in the world. It dawned on Darcy. How naïve could you get? Angus and Colie, of course, knew all about the deal, whatever it was. They were already part of it. They wanted him to come in with them—that was why they had called him.

"This is no candy-box proposition," Angus began. "These fellers ain't coming around Christmastime with no lousy three-dollar box of cigars, believe me. . . ."

Darcy got his breath back. "I don't want anything to do with it," he said, and turned at once to unlock the bathroom door. The general public impression about what goes on in city government to the contrary, Darcy had never before in his Civil Service experience come face to face with a clearcut, out-and-out graft situation. He was shocked. He was also scared. The only thing he could think of was to get out of that fancy place as fast as he could. Angus and Colie, no longer grinning, were pulling at his shoulder, trying to make him listen, but he was so determined or panicked that there was no holding him.

"Include me out!" he said. He got the door unlocked and broke away.

You heard about graft, you read about it—the costly gifts, expense accounts, trips on yachts to Florida, party girls—but when you came upon it in person, the effect was altogether different. There was an impact, hard and unnerving and ugly, like witnessing a bad automobile accident or being on the scene while a holdup was taking place. Darcy was still very much excited and upset when he got home, and as he crossed the threshold, he was suddenly filled with a deep sense of misgiving. He started to worry. In his bones, he knew he hadn't heard the last of the matter from Arthur Colie and Charlie Angus. Darcy knew those boys weren't finished with him, not by a long shot.

Natalie was in the kitchen. "No courage whatsoever," she said, still firmly convinced he had gone to his mother's. "A grown-up man scared to death of his own mother. Nincompoop."

"What?" Darcy said, groggy and sinking, this disheartening, unfair insult coming now on top of everything. "What did you call me?"

"Nincompoop," Natalie said. "Nincompoop, with all the college degrees. Has the nervous disposition of a fly." She walked out of the kitchen and went into the living room, to get ready for bed. The Darcys slept in the living room, on a couch that opened up. Gary had the bedroom.

THE factor of safety that the city insisted on was extremely conservative, in some cases perhaps as much as three to one. Roughly, where any competent engineering authority would have been satisfied with, say, a steel support two inches deep, the city required five or six inches—a brutal expense, a brutal waste of precious rental space, all the room being taken up by the structural steel.

"Morally," Colie argued the next morning, when he and Angus went to work on Darcy, "morally we're not even doing anything wrong." After all, they weren't robbing anybody, were they? Nobody was getting hurt. Two inches or six inches, the 990 building wasn't going to fall down and kill a million people, no matter what.

It was a beautifully worked-out proposition, Colie said, perfectly safe. Who was going to start digging into a mountain of blueprints? How could anyone ever find out? By shaving the safety factor in just the steel-frame requirements alone, the examiners could easily—and so unobtrusively—save the builders hundreds of thousands. And the 990 Corporation, a hard-hitting, realistic bunch of go-getters, were ready to pay off handsomely for any favorable consideration. Colie wanted to weep. Without Darcy, he and Angus couldn't do a thing; their hands were tied.

"Have a heart," Colie said. "Show *me* a little consideration." Colie had personal difficulties which were common knowledge around the office. He was bitterly infatuated with his wife, who was a big headache. She was supposed to be some kind of beauty, but she had expensive tastes and didn't care how much money she spent, and so Colie was always in the clutches of the loan sharks. It was one of those unfortunate marital relationships—he had to pay through the nose for every single, solitary thing Mrs. Colie ever gave him or no sale. She had the upper hand. "Do you realize I owe in four figures?" Colie said. "Thousands, not hundreds. Thousands!"

"Don't be a goddam freak—take!" Angus said, breaking in impatiently. He was baffled, honestly unable to figure out a man like Darcy. "What the hell is it anyway?" Angus said. "You got a grudge against money?" He was an uncomplicated person, very direct and practical, without sensitivity. He was the one, with all his contacts, who had brought in the deal in the first place.

"Why not, for Christ sake?" he said. "The dentist calls up, suddenly your kid needs braces, his teeth are crooked—is it a tragedy? Six, seven hundred bucks they charge nowadays for braces—does it ruin you? No! It's a drop in the bucket, you don't even feel the damn six hundred. See, you'll become a wonderful father, a wonderful, generous husband. They'll look up to you with respect—you'll send your wife on cruises! Darcy, you got an idea the kind of dough this outfit is willing to hand out? There's eight thousand dollars in this for you, eight G—is this a sum of money you habitually sneeze at?"

Darcy shuddered, the size of the bribe only making him more frightened than ever. It turned out that Angus had bragged. He had told the Eckworth people he could deliver, that he had the deal all set and sealed, and it would put him in an acute embarrassing personal position if trouble developed now. He had given his word. "Make me out a monkey," Angus said, "and so help me, Darcy, you'll regret it!"

Angus and Colie made threats. They argued and begged. They hammered away at Darcy all day long, catching him in the office, in the halls, in the men's washroom, but nothing helped. Darcy wouldn't budge. He didn't give his reasons. He wouldn't even discuss the subject. It just wasn't in him to take a bribe or do anything off color, that was all. It was unthinkable.

"Stubborn like an ox," Angus said. "Who could ever foresee a cockeyed contingency like this? Goddam ethical kiyoodle!"

Around four o'clock in the afternoon, a forceful woman, no longer young but with a remarkably well-preserved figure for her age, suddenly came barging into the office where Darcy, Colie, and Angus worked. She was Mrs. Colie, and she was very angry, all tight and swollen up. She marched straight up to her husband and threw a set of keys on the drafting table before him.

"Eileen, what is this?" Colie said.

"The keys," she said. "The house keys. What do you think it is—a horse and carriage? I sent the laundry out. You'll get your gray suit back from the cleaners on Thursday." She was going to Lake Placid with friends and she was leaving immediately. It seemed a mink stole had just been repossessed.

"Dearest, don't make a scene," Colie begged. The door was wide open and everybody in the place could hear her. "Not in here, dearest. Not in front of the whole office—"

Colie reached out to restrain her, but she promptly knocked his hands down, backing away from him. "Don't you touch me! Keep your hands off!" she screamed. "You're always pulling and grabbing. That's why I have to go to Lake Placid. I need a rest. You're oversexed!"

"Eileen!" Colie said in horror, choking and shutting his eyes.

"It's love, love, love—morning, noon, and night," Mrs. Colie said. "Promises! You promise the moon, you buy me mink stoles, but when it comes down to business—baloney. I don't know when I'm coming back!"

She turned, walked out, and slammed the door. Colie knew it was useless to follow her. Absent-mindedly he picked up the keys and put them in his pocket.

"A man lives in a tiny overcrowded apartment," he said, his voice thin and anguished. "A man lives way out in Jackson Heights. He hasn't got a decent suit of clothes to his name. You offer him a gilt-edged proposition on a platter, and he don't want it!"

AFTER that, there was no holding Colie back. He became altogether intemperate and didn't seem to care what kind of language he used with Darcy. There was a bar-and-grill in the heart of the City Hall district, and after working hours Colie and Angus got Darcy squeezed in one of the alcoves there and battered away at him like a pair of maniacs. They kept it up for two solid hours, until Darcy was sick, literally sick, at his stomach.

He didn't get home until long past seven o'clock. No one would talk to him. Gary, of course, was in the living room, his attention taken up with the television, and as for Natalie, she kept busy at the range and wouldn't even look at her husband. He felt low. He could hardly swallow the food. It was as though the world was caving in on him. The atmosphere in the kitchen was oppressive. Natalie was in a terrible temper. He was befuddled by the whole Eckworth situation. And in the next room Gary was sitting at the bridge table like one of those potbellied Asiatic idols, fierce and implacable, with his compulsory television programs, with his mysterious allergies, with his everlasting, infernal basic sense of insecurity.

As soon as Darcy had had his dinner, Natalie let go. It was odd—it was somehow touching, and it didn't make much sense—but no matter how mad she might be at him, she waited until he finished eating before she started up. She wanted him to have a good meal inside of him, at least, before she began squabbling and getting him aggravated.

"Under no conditions," she said, straight out of the blue, "are we going to have dinner at your mother's this or any other weekend." Darcy looked up, groping helplessly for the cause of this outbreak, but it soon came out that it had no cause; Natalie was jumping to conclusions, as usual. Nobody had said anything about having dinner at his mother's. Rita had called up again, but it wasn't the phone call that had set Natalie off this time. It was the two hours he had spent at the Old Commercial. Natalie had put two and two together, and claimed she knew perfectly well where he had been and why. He had gone to his mother's again. Natalie claimed she had it all worked out, she understood everything now. Gary had a birthday coming up early next month and the possessive old woman, Natalie said, was only scheming and putting on the pressure to have a party, a dinner. That was what the whole hullabaloo was about—the phone calls, the visits.

"Oh, Natalie, for goodness' sake," Darcy said, squirming in torment. He started wearily, hopelessly, to tell her about Angus and Colie wanting him to accept a bribe, that he had been at the Old Commercial with them all the time.

"Don't tell me it was business," Natalie broke in. "Don't try to cover up. You're only lying."

"I'm lying?" Darcy said.

"Look at him, how self-righteous he is—butter wouldn't melt in his mouth," Natalie said. "That's the trouble with people like you, you rationalize. You justify every selfish, rotten thing you do. I always say you're the worst kind of a person there is—a good person. You're hypocrites. Get out of the kitchen, I have to clean up!"

Darcy went into the living room. His head was spinning. Suddenly the good cowboys started galloping after the bad cowboys, and Gary, who kept a bicycle horn at his side for just such occasions, promptly began honking away in a crazy fit, rooting his heroes along. Darcy begged him to stop, but Gary had no pity and honked all through the chase.

THE next morning Darcy sat down at the breakfast table dizzy with lack of sleep, no appetite in him.

"Drink your orange juice," Natalie said. She was in a rush. Gary was dawdling in the bedroom and she had to get him out for school.

"I don't want it," Darcy said.

"Drink it," Natalie said. "I went to the trouble of squeezing it for you, don't let it go to waste."

"Natalie," Darcy began, "this morning I just don't happen to feel like—"

"Drink it up!" she said, blazing out at him. "Drink it or I'll throw it in your face!"

DARCY went to work. In the ten or eleven years of their marriage, he said to himself, he and Natalie had had their moments of distress, but they had never descended to such a sordid level. He had known for some time that his marriage was deteriorating, and for all he knew now, it was ruined for good, but he was so eaten away by the Eckworth business that he couldn't even stop and take the time to worry about Natalie and his marriage. When he walked into his office, Angus and Colie were standing there waiting for him.

Darcy held fast. As the day wore on, however, scrambling around and trying to fight back, he was less and less able to think clearly, and somehow his mind seemed to get hung up on the mechanics of bribetaking. To be perfectly honest, perhaps by this time he would have been willing to go in on the deal, except that he was overwhelmed by the maze of complications that would follow. "I wouldn't even know how to go about it," he said, protesting. What did they do, pay you by check or in cash? Even if it was in cash, you had to deposit the money eventually, and wouldn't the bankbooks, the bank entries, give you away? And what about the income tax? How did a person declare a bribe?

Angus slapped the drafting board hard. "O.K.," he said. "It's over. You agreed."

"I agreed?" Darcy said. "When? All I said, I said did they pay you by check or in cash—"

"Cash, cash," Angus said. "What that screwball finds to worry about! Income taxes! Didn't you ever hear of safe-deposit vaults? You buy a box for four dollars and you got no troubles. Now what's there left to kick about? So that's what I said—it's over. Thank God! What a time he give me! Boy!"

Angus now acted as though everything was settled. He turned away from Darcy, went to the drafting tables, and started getting together the blueprints of the 990 Corporation building.

Colie was bewildered. He couldn't understand what was going on, he said.

"The subject's closed," Angus said, cold and businesslike. As far as Colie could see, nothing had been arrived at, just words.

"Go away, don't bother me," Angus said. "He agreed—he can't back out."

"Ridiculous!" Darcy said when Colie turned to him. "Silliest thing I ever heard of. He misconstrued what I said. I was just asking academically."

"Angus, what's the good?" Colie pleaded. "He's a fanatic. You know him—a will of iron. He'll only go to the Commissioner or the D.A.—wherever they go to give information. He'll talk!"

"No, he won't," Angus said. "What do you think—those parties are going to stand by idle? They won't sit in jail. If he squeals, they will come and get him. They will kill him!" Tight-lipped and unyielding, he picked up the bundle of blueprints and walked out of the office, taking the rest of the day off. A few seconds after he left, Rita, Darcy's sister, walked in. "It's disgusting," she said. "I have to get docked an hour just to see my brother—I can't reach you on the phone." What she had come to see him about was Gary's birthday. There was some justification for Natalie's suspicions, after all. On account of the occasion, Darcy's mother wanted to see the child this evening. This was, of course, strictly against Natalie's objections—the old excessive affection argument—but Rita went on shrilly, "Momma has a right, too. She's his grandmother. She's got a present to give him, a sweater she knitted all by herself."

"Rita, please!" Darcy said, but his sister refused to let him say a word.

"Natalie doesn't have to know. You can meet Momma outside in the park. Bring Gary downstairs to the park after dinner, after Captain Video— it's still light. For God's sake, Arnold, she worked on the sweater three whole weeks!"

Darcy was dazed. His head was reeling and there was something wrong with his eyes—he couldn't seem to focus very well. He nodded and said he'd meet his mother in the park—anything to get rid of Rita—and finally she left.

"What did I do?" Colie said, moaning to himself. He had been through a terrible time the last day or two and couldn't stand the thought now of having anybody's life on his conscience. "Oh, what did I go and get myself all involved for? All for a mink stole and a few lousy pieces of jewelry—I should have my head examined!"

ALL through the little visit with his mother in the neighborhood park, Darcy's mind raced in circles. He saw how diabolically effective Angus's tactics were. He, Darcy, would be presented with what amounted to a *fait accompli*. He faced the very real threat of murder or of serious bodily injury at the least if he tried to do anything about it. And in the meantime he had to intervene constantly and stop his mother. She was knocking Natalie.

"Momma, please!" Darcy said. "Gary's listening. It's not right."

"What am I saying? I'm only remarking," the old woman said, and innocently went on chattering to the boy.

In time, the visit was over. Gary took the present and thanked his grandmother, and Darcy was at last able to lead him back to the apartment. It was Natalie's turn tonight to go to the movies—she and Darcy went separately, an arrangement necessitated by financial stringencies but nevertheless without doubt one cause accounting for the poor success of their marriage—and Darcy hoped with all his heart that when he returned, his wife would be gone. But when he and Gary entered the apartment, there she was, right in the foyer, still fixing her hat at the mirror.

She kept talking to Gary, asking him did he have a nice time in the park? Did he go on the swing? Did he play with Donald?

"No, I didn't play with Donald," Gary said.

"You didn't?" Natalie said. "Why? Why didn't you play with Donald?"

Darcy wanted to groan aloud. Here it came. He just didn't have the energy in him for another flare-up with Natalie, and didn't know what he would do if she let out at him now, but luck was with him; Gary remembered his television programs, in the nick of time, and went darting off into the living room.

"What happened in the park?" Natalie said, confronting her husband.

"Nothing," Darcy said. "Absolutely nothing."

"Then why didn't he play with Donald?" she said. "Did they have a fight? Answer me."

"Natalie!" Darcy said. Something had got into him. It was an involuntary outburst. He found himself holding her by the shoulders, almost shaking her. She looked at him in wonder.

"Let go of my dress," she said, "you're getting it all wrinkled."

"What happened to you, Natalie? How did it happen?" He gripped her shoulders tighter. He couldn't stop himself. He had had more than he could stand, but maybe it was all really because he saw her now—for once—not in an apron and house dress but wearing a nice blue linen dress, with white gloves and a little white piqué hat. She looked pretty, fresh and youthful, and it made him ache to see her like this. "How the dickens does a person change so completely?" he cried.

He reminded her how it had been ten and eleven years ago—how they took ferryboat rides all over New York Bay, how they spent whole afternoons just walking together in the Botanical Gardens, how they went to Lewisohn Stadium and Carnegie Hall and discussed Toscanini by the hour. He even reminded her of the time she had bought him a book of Japanese poems in translation.

"What are you talking about?" she said, flushing. "What book of Japanese poems?"

"Yes, Japanese poems—you remember, 'The Jade Garden,' " he went on passionately, still, however, holding his voice down—that hushed, agonized, damnable technique the Darcys had developed over the years so that they could have their quarrels and not disturb Gary and his inner equilibrium. "When I was in the hospital," Darcy said. "When I had my tonsils out."

"A remainder," she said, twisting and turning, trying to escape, to get away from his eyes. "Forty-seven cents—I bought it in a drugstore. What are you bringing that up for now, after all these years—"

She stopped. She became suddenly transformed, the guilt and unhappiness in her turning all at once into a blind, senseless rage. "What is that?" she said, pointing. "How did *that* get there? Did *she* give it to him?"

It was the sweater, lying on a chair in the foyer. Darcy had forgotten. Distracted as he was, he had forgotten all about the sweater!

"Is that why you took Gary to the park—to meet your mother? Is that why he couldn't play with Donald?"

"Yes!" Darcy said. "Yes! I *took* him to meet my mother."

"Didn't I expressly forbid it? Didn't I tell you a million times I never wanted that woman near him again?"

"She's his grandmother," Darcy said. "She has a right. I don't care what you told me!"

Natalie then became altogether uncontrolled and did something so painful, so dismaying, so unspeakable, that a shiver went through Darcy. She spat in his face.

"Natalie," he said, "Natalie, don't you ever do that again."

"I'll do it whenever I feel like!" she said, and spat in his face again.

Darcy struck her—not hard, a glancing blow, more a light slap really than a blow. He immediately regained control over himself and turned away, now ignoring her completely.

She was still hysterical. "You'll do everything I tell you, do you hear me? After I go, you'll open the couch and fix the bed. You'll give Gary his bath. You'll put him to sleep. You'll mop the floor. And you'll stay away from your mother. Nincompoop," she said. "Coward!"

SHE left. The place was very quiet now except, of course, for the gunplay and Western voices in the living room. "Got the petition ready, Lester?" "Comin' along slow, Dude. Folks ain't a-signin'. . . ."

Darcy wasn't in the least worked up and bedevilled any longer. It was surprising how clearheaded you could become, once you made your mind up on a definite course of action, regardless of the possible consequences. It was a relief. Darcy was tired of being helpless and uncertain all the time, flopping around like a man drowning in the middle of the ocean. Darcy was tired of meanness.

He calmly supervised Gary's play when the child finished with the television and turned to his electric trains. Later, he got the boy ready for bed, taking out his pajamas, giving him his bath, watching him brush his teeth. When Gary fell asleep, Darcy opened the couch in the living room and arranged the bedding, although he wouldn't be sleeping there tonight. He packed his briefcase—they had one good suitcase and he preferred to let Natalie have it. And now as he waited for the time to pass, he sat in Gary's bedroom and looked at the face of his son, sweet and dear in sleep.

In Darcy's apartment house, they had the self-service elevator and the stairs. You could always tell when somebody downstairs in the lobby took the elevator—you heard a certain click. Around eleven o'clock, the click came, and Darcy knew his wife was on the way up. He could leave now. Gary would only be alone in the apartment a few seconds. Darcy picked up the briefcase and went out into the hall and part way down the first flight of stairs. In another moment or two, the elevator door swung open. In the murky lighting from the landing, he watched his wife as she walked across the tiled hall to the door of their apartment, never once realizing that he was standing there looking at her all the time. She opened the door and went in, and Darcy walked swiftly on down the stairs.

ANGUS was a bachelor and had a swanky bachelor's apartment in a residential hotel on the West Side. Darcy took the subway and went straight down there, late as it was. He walked in and said without preliminary that he was having no part of the 990 business. He wouldn't be bulldozed and he wanted the blueprints—nobody was presenting *him* with a *fait accompli*. Darcy spoke with grim determination, but Angus, who naturally had no way of knowing what had transpired that evening at the Jackson Heights apartment, never dreamed he was dealing with a radically changed man and made the mistake of treating him lightly.

"Jack Dalton of the U.S. Marines," Angus said. The blueprints were staying right where they were, Angus said. Everything was going to proceed exactly according to schedule, and there wasn't a damn thing Darcy could do about it, so what was he raising an unnecessary holler for? Angus said talk, talk, but in the last analysis Darcy knew good and well he would cave in and back down when the going got rough.

"You think so?" Darcy said.

"Sure," Angus said. "What the hell are you going around trying to create an impression for? You're a nonentity."

Darcy socked him on the nose, for the second time that night resorting to physical violence. Angus's eyes streamed profusely. He brought his hand up to his nose and then looked into his palm but his nose wasn't bleeding. "Boy!" he said, gulping.

Darcy banged out of the place. He didn't need the blueprints. The way he felt now, he didn't care about *fait accomplis* or reprisals or anything, and when he reached the sidewalk downstairs, he was still so charged with nervous tension that he did a nonsensical, almost deranged thing, one of those oddity items you always read in the papers: He attacked a car. It was parked in front of the building where Angus lived, a big black convertible—that fat, hateful symbol of graft, that smug reward for corruption, along with Angus's swanky bachelor apartment, along with the two-hundred-and-fifty-dollar custom-tailored suits he always wore. Darcy methodically went to work on the tires, letting the air out.

A short, stout, middle-aged man Darcy had never seen before in his life came trotting out of the apartment building, dancing on the tips of his toes and holding up his hands in consternation. "Here, here, young man!" he exclaimed. "What *is* this? Stop! Please leave my car alone!"

"What?" Darcy said, glaring. The stranger took fright immediately and went scurrying back into the building. For a moment, Darcy thought of running after him to explain, to apologize, but then he realized that he'd get in trouble if he hung around there any longer, that he might be arrested.

What did I need all this excitement for, he asked himself. What have I done? What good is it? He felt deflated, the reaction setting in now, and as he walked along the dead deserted streets, his mind grew filled with dismal second thoughts. He was married to Natalie, he had a child to support. How *can* I leave them, he wondered. And what was I trying to prove up there in the hotel, socking Angus on the nose? When you come right down to it, nobody stands up to professional hoodlums. In his heart, Darcy was beginning to suspect the ignominious truth: that in all likelihood he *would* cave in; that he would probably go right back to Natalie; that in the end you never succeeded in changing anything. And what did I want from the car, he wondered dejectedly—a car owned, no doubt, by a thoroughly re-spectable man who has worked hard and honorably to obtain it? The car surely was the most idiotic thing of all.

DARCY rode to the St. George Hotel in Brooklyn—a local train all the way, making every station stop at that time of night—and got a room in the old wing. In the morning, he got up and shaved and showered, but he didn't go to work.

For the next four days, he didn't do much of anything. He kept pretty close to the hotel, wandering around in the lobby, looking at the people there at the bars or downstairs in the swimming pool. It was a weird, unreal kind of existence and soon Darcy had the feeling the hotel personnel were beginning to stare at him. Maybe Darcy imagined the stares, but in any case on the morning of the fifth day he checked out of the hotel, and went down to the department.

As he walked in, Angus took one look at him and immediately let out a strange, mystifying howl. "See?" he yelled, not at Darcy but at Colie. "See, you dumb little pest? There he is! I told you—I didn't make the deal! Nobody murdered him! Nobody abducted him! Do you believe me now?"

"Leave me alone," Colie said. "I'm exhausted. I'm a mental wreck."

"Conscience, conscience!" Angus said bitterly.

Darcy watched and listened in wonder, but actually it wasn't so mystifying, and in a few moments he had it all straightened out. What had happened was that when the office called up to inquire where he was, Natalie, understandably enough, was too ashamed to tell the truth—that her husband had left her following a domestic quarrel. She had been evasive. She had said she had no idea where he was or why he had gone away or what had happened to him.

Colie had feared the worst. He had thought Angus had made the deal secretly, and that the thugs had already gotten ahold of Darcy. And so, night and day, every minute of the time Darcy had spent at the St. George, Colie had been on Angus's neck, driving him crazy.

"You wait," Angus said, talking to Darcy now. "You'll get yours yet." Angus was sick and tired of everything. The 990 deal was dead. He had brought the blueprints back to the office and called all bets off, explaining that he was in no position to undertake ambitious ventures. "I'll take care of you," he said to Darcy, and walked out of the office, still muttering angrily.

Colie and Darcy worked side by side all day, and then when it was time to go home, Colie stood up and insisted on shaking hands. "Personally, I think you made the wrong decision," he said sadly. Apparently Mrs. Colie was still away at Lake Placid. "But if that's the way you felt about it, then that's the way it had to be. Because people have to go according to their makeup. What's the use? We're none of us strong enough to fight against our nature. I know."

He turned and left. Darcy waited a few moments and then walked to the elevators in the hall.

The thousands and thousands of Civil Service employees poured out of the big, dirty municipal buildings and streamed off to the various subway entrances. Soon, in the whole City Hall district there were only scattered groups of people here and there on the streets. Darcy idled about, drifting aimlessly. After some time, he walked into the Old Commercial and managed to kill an hour or two there. Around eight o'clock, he got up from the table and did what he knew all along he would do. He went into the phone booth and called up Natalie.

She didn't burst out at him or cry when she heard his voice at the other end of the wire. She kept controlled. They were both stiff and self-conscious.

"I'm coming home," Darcy said.

"Oh?" Natalie said.

Darcy faltered. "I don't quite know how to take that as an answer. What do you mean, 'Oh'?"

"Nothing—'Oh' . . ."

"Do you want me to come home?"

"Where are you?"

"Where am I? What difference does it make where I am? I'm in a public phone booth, downtown. Do you want me to come home?"

"Do what you like. Whatever will make you happy."

Again Darcy halted. "I don't quite know how to take that as an—"

"Do you love me?" Natalie interrupted.

"What?" Darcy said.

"Do you love me?"

"Yes," Darcy said.

She kept silent. Darcy didn't know what to say, and for a moment or two they just stayed there holding the phone at each end, nothing happening. Finally Natalie spoke. "Then all right," she said, slowly, quietly, and hung up.

Gary was asleep in the bedroom when Darcy came home. The house was quiet. It looked tidy and neat and pleasant. Natalie didn't speak. She wasn't mad—just neutral. Darcy didn't say anything, either. Natalie brought him his dinner—lamb chops, green peas, and a glass of milk. When she had finished putting the food on the table, she quickly left the kitchen.

Darcy could tell the lamb chops were specially prepared; they were pan-broiled and looked appetizing. He started to cut into one of them, but just then he saw the note. It hadn't been there a moment before. Natalie must have slipped it onto the table as she walked out of the kitchen. He put his knife and fork down and took the note.

This is what it said:

Dear Arnold,

You have always said how wonderful it was to have a nice home and a wife and a son such as you have. At least, I know, you are really a devoted family man. But I must admit that I do not really know you as well as I thought, because of what you did. I realize it was done in a moment of great anger, despair, and frustration. But you must never do this again, at least without consulting me first. We must discuss things. There must be no concealed problems that cause needless inner conflicts.

Arnold, I think you are really very nice. I am very unhappy away from you and I know that now. You are good-natured, intelligent, and you like to do favors for other people. Of course, you have a few faults. You are quite stubborn and you have admitted this yourself. Another fault is the fact that you are too impulsive and emotional. Every expression on my face, every word and gesture of mine seems to affect you to a degree never intended by me.

I propose not to say anything further to you about the awful thing you did. Let it all be forgotten. Gary was very ill when you left and I was all alone. I have no parents, sisters, or brothers. That is why you should never have done what you did! Between Gary and you, I was frantic. Then, I couldn't tell anyone about this! The whole time, I never slept and ate practically nothing. I lost eleven pounds in four days.

Gary is much better. At first, he will be a little shy with you; but I believe he will forget eventually. Act normally with him, as though nothing untoward took place.

> Love,
> *Your Natalie*

He finished the note and started to read it all over again, but suddenly he stopped. He couldn't go on. He folded the paper carefully and then covered it with his hand. Now the refrigerator motor hit, the current automatically switching on the way it does in electric refrigerators. Darcy started counting silently, one, two, three, four, five, continuing until the current should go off again. In the stillness of the kitchen, the motor throbbed and throbbed, like a beating heart, and Darcy counted fiercely, concentrating his whole mind on this pointless, peculiar little task.

(1953)

MESPOULETS OF THE SPLENDIDE

WHEN I say '*Le chien est utile*,' there is one proposition. When I say '*Je crois que le chien est utile*,' there are two. When I say, '*Je crois que le chien est utile quand il garde la maison*,' how many propositions are there?"

"Three."

"Very good."

Mespoulets, the waiter whose bus boy I was, nodded gravely in approval. At that moment Monsieur Victor, the maître d'hôtel, walked through our section of tables, and the other waiters nearby stopped talking to each other, straightened a tablecloth here, moved a chair there, arranged their side towels smoothly over their arms, tugged at their jackets, and pulled their bow ties. Only Mespoulets was indifferent. He walked slowly toward the pantry, past Monsieur Victor, holding my arm. I walked with him and he continued the instruction.

" '*L'abeille fait du miel*.' The verb '*fait*' in this sentence in itself is insufficient. It does not say what the bee does, therefore we round out the idea by adding the words '*du miel*.' These words are called '*un complément*.' The sentence '*L'abeille fait du miel*' contains then what?"

"It contains one verb, one subject, and one complement."

"Very good, excellent. Now run down and get the Camembert, the *salade escarole*, the hard water crackers, and the demitasse for Mr. Frank Munsey on Table Eighty-six."

.   .   .

THE day was one of the rare ones when Mespoulets and I had a guest at our tables. Our station was on the low rear balcony of the main dining room of a hotel I shall call the Splendide, a vast and luxurious structure which, I regret to say, gave up its unequal struggle with economics not long after the boom days and has since been converted into an office building.

Before coming to America I had worked a short while in a hotel in the Tyrol that belonged to my uncle. German was my native language and I knew enough English to get along in New York City, but my French was extremely bad. The French language in all its aspects was a passion with Mespoulets, and he had plenty of time to teach it to me. Our tables—Nos. 81, 82, and 86—were in a noisy, drafty corner of the balcony. They stood facing the stairs from the dining room and were between two doors. One door led to the pantry and was hung on whining hinges. On wet days it sounded like an angry cat and it was continually kicked by the boots of waiters rushing in and out with trays in their hands. The other door led to a linen closet.

The waiters and bus boys squeezed by our tables, carrying trays. The ones with trays full of food carried them high over their heads; the ones with dirty dishes carried them low, extended in front. They frequently bumped into each other and there would be a crash of silver, glasses, and china, and cream trickling over the edges of the trays in thin streams. When this happened, Monsieur Victor would race to our section, followed by his captains, to direct the cleaning up of the mess and pacify the guests. It was a common sight to see people standing in our section, napkins in hand, complaining and brushing themselves off and waving their arms angrily in the air.

Monsieur Victor used our tables as a kind of penal colony to which he sent guests who were notorious cranks, people who had forgotten to tip him over a long period of time and needed a reminder, undesirables who looked out of place in better sections of the dining room, and guests who were known to linger for hours over an order of hors-d'œuvres and a glass of milk while well-paying guests had to stand at the door waiting for a table.

Mespoulets was the ideal man for Monsieur Victor's purposes. He complemented Monsieur Victor's plan of punishment. He was probably the worst waiter in the world and I had become his bus boy after I fell down the stairs into the main part of the dining room with twelve pheasants *à la Souvaroff.* When I was sent to him to take up my duties as his assistant, he introduced himself by saying, "My name is easy to remember. Just think of 'my chickens'—'*mes poulets*'—Mespoulets."

He was a kind man and I suppose that is one reason he was never fired for his magnificent incompetence. In a hotel conducted in the European tradition, as the Splendide was, an employee's personal virtues were justly weighed against his professional shortcomings, and men who might have been better at their jobs were kept on because they were good fathers or because they played an interesting game of chess. Mespoulets, besides being kind, was a talented penman. It was he who wrote the menus for private parties, he who, with beautiful flourishes, made out the cards for banquets.

Rarely did any guest who was seated at one of our tables leave the hotel with a desire to come back again. If there was any broken glass around the dining room, it was always in our spinach. The occupants of Tables Nos. 81, 82, and 86 shifted in their chairs, stared at the pantry door, looked around and made signs of distress at other waiters and captains while they waited for their food. When the food finally came, it was cold and was often not what had been ordered. While Mespoulets explained what the unordered food was, telling in detail how it was made and what the ingredients were, and offered hollow excuses, he dribbled mayonnaise, soup, or mint sauce over the guests, upset the coffee, and sometimes even managed to break a plate or two. I helped him as best I could.

At the end of a meal, Mespoulets usually presented the guest with somebody else's check, or it turned out that he had neglected to adjust the difference in price between what the guest had ordered and what he had got. By then the guest just held out his hand and cried, "Never mind, never mind, give it to me, just give it to me! I'll pay just to get out of here! Give it to me, for God's sake!" Then the guest would pay and go. He would stop on the way out at the maître d'hôtel's desk and show Monsieur Victor and his captains the spots on his clothes, bang on the desk, and swear he would never come back again. Monsieur Victor and his captains would listen, make faces of compassion, say "Oh!" and "Ah!," and look darkly toward us across the room and promise that we would be fired the same day. But the next day we would still be there.

IN the hours between meals, while the other waiters were occupied filling salt and pepper shakers, oil and vinegar bottles, and mustard pots, and counting the dirty linen and dusting the chairs, Mespoulets would walk to a table near the entrance, right next to Monsieur Victor's own desk, overlooking the lounge of the hotel. There he adjusted a special reading lamp which he had demanded and obtained from the management, spread a piece of billiard cloth over the table, and arranged on top of this a large blotter and a small one, an inkstand, and half a dozen penholders. Then he

drew up a chair and seated himself. He had a large assortment of fine copper pen points of various sizes, and he sharpened them on a piece of sand-
paper. He would select the pen point and the holder he wanted and begin to
make circles in the air. Then, drawing toward him a gilt-edged place card or
a crested one, on which menus were written, he would go to work. When
he had finished, he arranged the cards all over the table to let them dry, and
sat there at ease, only a step or two from Monsieur Victor's desk, in a sector
invaded by other waiters only when they were to be called down or to be
discharged, waiters who came with nervous hands and frightened eyes to
face Monsieur Victor. Mespoulet's special talent set him apart, and he was
further distinguished by the fact that he was permitted to wear glasses, a
privilege denied all other waiters no matter how nearsighted or astigmatic.
He was permitted to wear glasses, of course, because he was a penman.

It was said of Mespoulets variously that he was the father, the uncle, or
the brother of Monsieur Victor. It was also said of him that he had once
been the director of a lycée in Paris. The truth was that he had never known
Monsieur Victor on the other side, and I do not think there was any secret
between them, only an understanding, a subtle sympathy of some kind. I
got to know Mespoulets intimately. I learned that at one time he had been a
tutor to a family in which there was a very beautiful daughter and that this
was something he did not like to talk about. He loved animals almost as
dearly as he loved the French language. He had taken it upon himself to
watch over the fish which were in an aquarium in the outer lobby of the
hotel, he fed the pigeons in the courtyard, and he extended his interest to
the birds and beasts and crustaceans that came alive to the kitchen. He
begged the cooks to deal quickly, as painlessly as could be, with lobsters and
terrapins. If a guest brought a dog to our section, Mespoulets was mostly
under the table with the dog. It got well fed and it left with a bone between
its teeth, trailing happily after its master, who usually was fuming.

AT mealtime, while we waited for the few guests who came our way,
Mespoulets sat out in the linen closet on a small box where he could keep an
eye on our tables through the partly open door. He leaned comfortably
against a pile of tablecloths and napkins. At his side was an ancient
"Grammaire Française," and while his hands were folded in his lap, the
palms up, the thumbs cruising over them in small, silent circles, he made
me repeat exercises, simple, compact, and easy to remember. He knew
them all by heart and soon I did, too. He made me go over and over them
until my pronunciation was right. All of them were about animals. There
were: "The Sage Salmon," "The Cat and the Old Woman," "The Society of

Beavers," "The Bear in the Swiss Mountains," "The Intelligence of the Partridge," "The Lion of Florence," and "The Bird in a Cage."

We started with "The Sage Salmon" in January that year and were at the end of "The Bear in the Swiss Mountains" when the summer garden opened in May. At that season business fell off for dinner, and all during the summer we were busy only at luncheon. Mespoulets had time to go home in the afternoons and he suggested that I continue studying there.

He lived in the house of a relative on West Twenty-fourth Street. On the sidewalk in front of the house next door stood a large wooden horse, painted red, the sign of a saddlemaker. Across the street was a place where horses were auctioned off, and up the block was an Italian poultry market with a picture of a chicken painted on its front. Hens and roosters crowded the market every morning.

Mespoulets occupied a room and bath on the second floor rear. The room was papered green and over an old couch hung a print of van Gogh's "Bridge at Arles," which was not a common picture then. There were book-shelves, a desk covered with papers, and over the desk a large bird cage hanging from the ceiling.

In this cage, shaded with a piece of the hotel's billiard cloth, lived a miserable old canary. It was bald-headed, its eyes were like peppercorns, its feet were no longer able to cling to the roost, and it sat in the sand, in a corner, looking like a withered chrysanthemum that had been thrown away. On summer afternoons, near the bird, we studied "The Intelligence of the Partridge" and "The Lion of Florence."

Late in August, on a chilly day that seemed like fall, Mespoulets and I began "The Bird in the Cage." The lesson was:

L'OISEAU EN CAGE

Voilà sur ma fenêtre un oiseau qui vient visiter le mien. Il a peur, il s'en va, et le pauvre prisonnier s'attriste, s'agite comme pour s'échapper. Je ferais comme lui, si j'étais à sa place, et cependant je le retiens. Vais-je lui ouvrir? Il irait voler, chanter, faire son nid; il serait heureux; mais je ne l'aurais plus, et je l'aime, et je veux l'avoir. Je le garde. Pauvre petit, tu seras toujours prisonnier; je jouis de toi aux dépens de ta liberté, je te plains, et je te garde. Voilà comme le plaisir l'emporte sur la justice.

Mespoulets looked up at the bird and said to me, "Find some adjective to use with 'fenêtre,' 'oiseau,' 'peur,' 'nid,' 'liberté,' 'plaisir,' and 'justice,' " and while I searched for them in our dictionary, he went to a shelf and took from it a cigar box. There was one cigar in it. He took this out, wiped off the box with his handkerchief, and then went to a drawer and got a large penknife, which he opened. He felt the blade. Then he went to the cage, took the bird out, laid it on the closed cigar box, and quickly cut off its head. A little pond of transparent, oily blood appeared on the cigar box. One claw opened slowly and the bird and its head lay still.

Mespoulets washed his hands, rolled the box, the bird, and knife into a newspaper, put it under his arm, and took his hat from a stand. We went out and walked up Eighth Avenue. At Thirty-fourth Street he stopped at a trash can and put his bundle into it. "I don't think he wanted to live any more," he said.

(1940)

OVER BY THE RIVER

T HE sun rose somewhere in the middle of Queens, the exact moment
of its appearance shrouded in uncertainty because of a cloud bank.
The lights on the bridges went off, and so did the red light in the lantern of
the lighthouse at the north end of Welfare Island. Seagulls settled on the
water. A newspaper truck went from building to building dropping off
heavy bundles of, for the most part, bad news, which little boys carried inside on their shoulders. Doormen smoking a pipe and dressed for a walk in
the country came to work after a long subway ride and disappeared into
the service entrances. When they reappeared, by way of the front elevator,
they had put on with their uniforms a false amiability and were prepared
for eight solid hours to make conversation about the weather. With the
morning sun on them, the apartment buildings far to the west, on
Lexington Avenue, looked like an orange mesa. The pigeons made bub-
bling noises in their throats as they strutted on windowsills high above the
street.

All night long, there had been plenty of time. Now suddenly there
wasn't, and this touched off a chain explosion of alarm clocks, though in
some instances the point was driven home without a sound: Time is interior to animals as well as exterior. A bare arm with a wristwatch on it
emerged from under the covers and turned until the dial was toward the
light from the windows.

"What time is it?"

"Ten after."

"It's always ten after," Iris Carrington said despairingly, and turned over in bed and shut her eyes against the light. Also against the clamor of her desk calendar: *Tuesday 11, L. 3:30 Dr. de Santillo . . . 5:30–7:30? . . . Wednesday 1:45, Mrs. McIntosh speaks on the changing status of women. 3:30 Dr. F . . . Friday 11C. Get Albertha . . . Saturday, call Mrs. Stokes. Ordering pads. L ballet 10:30. 2 Laurie to Sasha's. Remaining books due at library. Explore dentists. Supper at 5. Call Margot . . .*

Several minutes passed.

"Oh my God, I don't think I can make it," George Carrington said, and put his feet over the side of the bed, and found he could make it, after all. He could bend over and pick up his bathrobe from the floor, and put it on, and find his slippers, and close the window, and turn on the radiator valve. Each act was easier than the one before. He went back to the bed and drew the covers closer around his wife's shoulders.

Yawning, stretching, any number of people got up and started the business of the day. Turning on the shower. Dressing. Putting their hair up in plastic curlers. Squeezing toothpaste out of tubes that were all but empty. Squeezing orange juice. Separating strips of bacon.

The park keepers unlocked the big iron gates that closed the river walk off between Eighty-third and Eighty-fourth Streets. A taxi coming from Doctors Hospital was snagged by a doorman's whistle. The wind picked up the dry filth under the wheels of parked cars and blew it now this way, now that. A child got into an orange minibus and started on the long, devious ride to nursery school and social adjustment.

"Have you been a good girl?" George inquired lovingly, through the closed door of the unused extra maid's room, where the dog slept on a square of carpet. Puppy had not been a good girl. There was a puddle of urine—not on the open newspaper he had left for her, just in case, but two feet away from it, on the black-and-white plastic-tile floor. Her tail quivering with apology, she watched while he mopped the puddle up and disposed of the wet newspaper in the garbage can in the back hall. Then she followed him through the apartment to the foyer, and into the elevator when it came.

There were signs all along the river walk:

NO DOGS

NO BICYCLES

NO THIS

NO THAT

He ignored them with a clear conscience. If he curbed the dog beforehand, there was no reason not to turn her loose and let her run—except that sometimes she stopped and arched her back a second time. When shouting and waving his hands didn't discourage her from moving her bowels, he took some newspaper from a trash container and cleaned up after her.

At the flagpole, he stood looking out across the river. The lights went off all the way up the airplane beacon, producing an effect of silence—as if somebody had started to say something and then decided not to. The tidal current was flowing south. He raised his head and sniffed, hoping for a breath of the sea, and smelled gasoline fumes instead.

Coming back, the dog stopped to sniff at trash baskets, at cement copings, and had to be restrained from greeting the only other person on the river walk—a grey-haired man who jogged there every morning in a gym suit and was afraid of dogs. He smiled pleasantly at George, and watched Puppy out of the corner of his eyes, so as to be ready when she leapt at his throat.

A tanker, freshly painted, all yellow and white, and flying the flag of George had no idea what country until he read the lettering on the stern, overtook him, close in to shore—so close he could see the captain talking to a sailor in the wheelhouse. To be sailing down the East River on a ship that was headed for open water . . . He waved to them and they waved back, but they didn't call out to him *Come on, if you want to,* and it was too far to jump. It came to him with the seriousness of a discovery that there was no place in the world he would not like to see. Concealed in this statement was another that he had admitted to himself for the first time only recently. There were places he would never see, experiences of the first importance that he would never have. He might die without ever having heard a nightingale.

When they stepped out of the elevator, the dog hurried off to the kitchen to see if there was something in her dish she didn't know about, and George settled down in the living room with the *Times* on his lap and waited for a glass of orange juice to appear at his place at the dining-room table. The rushing sound inside the walls, as of an underground river, was Iris running her bath. The orange juice was in no hurry to get to the dining-room table. Iris had been on the phone daily with the employment agency and for the moment this was the best they could offer: twenty-seven years old, pale, with dirty blond hair, unmarried, overattached to her mother, and given to burning herself on the antiquated gas stove. She lived on tea and cigarettes. Breakfast was all the cooking she was entrusted with; Iris did the rest. Morning after morning his boiled egg was hard enough to take on a picnic. A blind man could not have made a greater hash of half a grapefruit. The coffee was indescribable. After six weeks there was a film of grease over everything in the kitchen. Round, jolly, neat, professionally trained, a marvellous cook, the mother was everything that is desirable in a servant except that, alas, she worked for somebody else. She drifted in and out of the apartment at odd hours, deluding Iris with the hope that some of her accomplishments would, if one were only patient, rub off on her daughter.

"Read," a voice said, bringing him all the way back from Outer Mongolia.

"Tonight, Cindy."

"Read! Read!"

He put the paper down and picked her up and when she had settled comfortably in his lap he began: " 'Emily was a guinea pig who loved to travel. Generally she stayed home and looked after her brother Arthur. But every so often she grew tired of cooking and mending and washing and ironing; the day would seem too dark, and the house too small, and she would have a great longing to set out into the distance. . . .' "

Looking down at the top of her head as he was reading, he felt an impulse to put his nose down and smell her hair. Born in a hurry she was. Born in one hell of a hurry, half an hour after her mother got to the hospital.

LAURIE Carrington said, "What is the difference, what is the difference between a barber and a woman with several children?" Nobody answered, so she asked the question again.

"I give up," Iris said.

"Do you know, Daddy?"

"I give up too, we all give up."

"A barber . . . has razors to shave. And the woman has shavers to raise."

He looked at her over the top of his half-glasses, wondering what ancestor was responsible for that reddish-blond hair.

"That's a terribly funny one, Laurie," he said. "That's the best one yet," and his eyes reverted to the editorial page. A nagging voice inside his head informed him that a good father would be conversing intelligently with his children at the breakfast table. But about what? No intelligent subject of conversation occurred to him, perhaps because it was Iris's idea in the first place, not his.

He said, "Cindy, would you like a bacon sandwich?"

She thought, long enough for him to become immersed in the *Times* again, and then she said, "I would like a piece of bacon and a piece of toast. But not a bacon sandwich."

He dropped a slice of bread in the toaster and said, "Py-rozz-quozz-gill"—a magic word, from one of the Oz books. With a grinding noise the bread disappeared.

"Stupid Cindy," Laurie remarked, tossing her head. But Cindy wasn't fooled. Laurie used to be the baby and now she wasn't anymore. She was the oldest. And what she would have liked to be was the oldest *and* the baby. About lots of things she was very piggy. But she couldn't whistle. Try though she might, *whhih, whhih, whhih,* she couldn't. And Cindy could.

The toast emerged from the toaster and Iris said, "Not at the breakfast table, Cindy." The morning was difficult for her, clouded with amnesia, with the absence of energy, with the reluctance of her body to take on any action whatever. Straight lines curved unpleasantly, hard surfaces presented the look of softness. She saw George and the children and the dog lying at her feet under the table the way one sees rocks and trees and cottages at the seashore through the early-morning fog; just barely recognizable they were.

"WHY is a church steeple—"

"My gloves," he said, standing in the front hall, with his coat on.

"They're in the drawer in the lowboy," Iris said.

"Why is a church steeple—"

"Not those," he said.

"Why is a—"

"Laurie, Daddy is talking. Look in the pocket of your chesterfield."

"I did."

"Yes, dear, why is a church steeple."

"Why is a church steeple like a maiden aunt?"

"I give up."

"Do you know, Daddy?"

"No. I've looked in every single one of my coats. They must be in my raincoat, because I can't find that either."

"Look in your closet."

"I did look there." But he went into the bedroom and looked again anyway. Then he looked all through the front-hall closet, including the mess on the top shelf.

Iris passed through the hall with her arms full of clothes for the washing machine. "Did you find your raincoat?" she asked.

"I must have left it somewhere," he said. "But where?"

He went back to the bedroom and looked in the engagement calendar on her desk, to see where they had been, and it appeared that they hadn't been anywhere.

"Where did we go when we had Albertha to babysit?"

"I don't remember."

"We had her two nights."

"Did we? I thought we only went out one night last week."

She began to make the bed. Beds—for it was not one large bed, as it appeared to be in the daytime, but twin beds placed against each other with a king-sized cotton spread covering them both. When they were first married they slept in a three-quarter bed from his bachelor apartment. In time this became a double bed, hard as a rock because of the horsehair mattress. Then it also proved to be too small. For he developed twitches. While he was falling asleep his body beside her would suddenly flail out, shaking the bed and waking her completely. Six or seven times this would happen. After which he would descend at last into a deep sleep and she would be left with insomnia. So now there were twin beds, and even then her bed registered the seismic disturbances in his, though nothing like so much.

"We went to that benefit. With Francis," she said.

"Oh . . . I think I did wear my raincoat that night. No, I wore the coat with the velvet collar."

"The cleaner's?"

"No."

"I don't see how you could have left your raincoat somewhere," she said. "I never see you in just a suit. Other men, yes, but never you."

He went into the hall and pulled open a drawer of the lowboy and took out a pair of grey gloves and drew them on. They had been his father's and they were good gloves but too small for him. His fingers had burst open the seams at the end of the fingers. Iris had mended them, but they would not stay sewed, and so he went to Brooks and bought a new pair—the pair he couldn't find.

"The Howards' dinner party?" he said.

"That was the week before. Don't worry about it," Iris said. "Cindy, what have you been doing?"—meaning hair full of snarls, teeth unbrushed, at twenty-five minutes past eight.

"It makes me feel queer not knowing where I've been," George said, and went out into the foyer and pressed the elevator button. From that moment, he was some other man. Their pictures were under his nose all day but he had stopped seeing them. He did not even remember that he had a family, until five o'clock, when he pushed his chair back from his desk, reached for his hat and coat, and came home, cheerfully unrepentant. She forgave him now because she did not want to deal with any failure, including his, until she had had her second cup of coffee. The coffee sat on the living-room mantelpiece, growing cold, while she brushed and braided Cindy's hair.

"Stand still! I'm not hurting you."

"You are too."

The arm would not go into the sweater, the leggings proved to be on backwards, one mitten was missing. And Laurie wild because she was going to be late for school.

The girls let the front door bang in spite of all that had been said on the subject, and in a moment the elevator doors opened to receive them. The quiet then was unbelievable. With the *Times* spread out on the coffee table in the living room, and holes in the Woman's Page where she had cut out recipes, she waited for her soul, which left her during the night, to return and take its place in her body. When this happened she got up suddenly and went into the bedroom and started telephoning: Bloomingdale's, Saks, the Maid-to-Order service, the children's school, the electrician, the pediatrician, the upholsterer—half the population of New York City.

OVER the side of the bed Cindy went, eyes open, wide awake. In her woolly pyjamas with feet in them. Even though it was dark outside—the middle of the night—it was only half dark in the bedroom. There was a blue night-light in the wall plug by the doll's house, and a green night-light in the bathroom, beside the washbasin, and the door to the bathroom was partly open. The door to the hall was wide open and the hall light was on, but high up where it wasn't much comfort, and she had to pass the closed door of Laurie's room and the closed door to the front hall. Behind both these doors the dark was very dark, unfriendly, ready to spring out and grab her, and she would much rather have been back in her bed except it was not safe there either, so she was going for help.

When she got to the door at the end of the hall, she stood still, afraid to knock and afraid not to knock. Afraid to look behind her. Hoping the door would open by itself and it did. Her father—huge, in his pyjamas, with his hair sticking up and his face puffy with sleep. "Bad dream?" he asked.

Behind him the room was all dark except for a little light from the hall. She could see the big windows—just barely—and the great big bed, and her mother asleep under a mound of covers. And if she ran past him and got into the bed she would be safe, but it was not allowed. Only when she was sick. She turned and went back down the hall, without speaking but knowing that he would pick up his bathrobe and follow her and she didn't have to be brave anymore.

"What's Teddy doing on the floor?" he said, and pulled the covers up around her chin, and put his warm hand on her cheek. So nice to have him do this—to have him there, sitting on the edge of her bed.

"Can you tell me what you were dreaming about?"

"Tiger."

"Yes? Well that's too bad. Were you very frightened?"

"Yes."

"Was it a big tiger?"

"Yes."

"You know it was only a dream? It wasn't a real tiger. There aren't any tigers in New York City."

"In the zoo there are."

"Oh yes, but they're in cages and can't get out. Was this tiger out?"

"Yes."

"Then it couldn't have been a real tiger. Turn over and let me rub your back."

"If you rub my back I'll go to sleep."

"Good idea."

"If I go to sleep I'll dream about the tiger."

"I see. What do you want me to do?"

"Get in bed with me."

What with Teddy and Raggedy Ann and Baby Dear, and books to look at in the morning, and the big pillow and the little pillow, things were a bit crowded. He put his hand over his eyes to shut out the hall light and said, "Go to sleep," but she didn't, even though she was beginning to feel drowsy. She was afraid he was going to leave her—if not right this minute then pretty soon. He would sit up in bed and say *Are you all right now?* and she would have to say *Yes*, because that was what he wanted her to say. Sometimes she said no and they stayed a little longer, but they always went away in the end.

After a while, her eyes closed. After still another while, she felt the bed heave under her as he sat up. He got out of bed slowly and carefully and fixed the covers and put the little red chair by the bed so she wouldn't fall out. She tried to say *Don't go*, but nothing happened. The floorboards creaked under the carpeting as he crossed the room. In the doorway he turned and looked at her, one last look, and she opened her eyes wide so he would know she wasn't asleep, and he waved her a kiss, and that was the last of him, but it wasn't the last of her. Pretty soon, even though there wasn't a sound, she knew something was in the room. Hiding. It was either hiding behind the curtains or it was hiding in the toy closet or it was hiding behind the doll's house or it was behind the bathroom door or it was under the bed. But wherever it was it was being absolutely still, waiting for her to close her eyes and go to sleep. So she kept them open, even though her eyelids got heavier and heavier. She made them stay open. And when they closed she opened them again right afterward. She kept opening them as long as she could, and once she cried out *Laurie!* very loud, but in her mind only. There was no sound in the room.

The thing that was hiding didn't make any sound either, which made her think maybe it wasn't a tiger after all, because tigers have a terrible roar that they roar, but it couldn't have been anything else, for it had stripes and a tail and terrible teeth and eyes that were looking at her through the back of the little red chair. And her heart was pounding and the tiger knew this, and the only friend she had in the world was Teddy, and Teddy couldn't move, and neither could Raggy, and neither could she. But the tiger could move. He could do anything he wanted to except roar his terrible roar, because then the bedroom door would fly open and they would come running.

She looked at the tiger through the back of the little red chair, and the tiger looked at her, and finally it thrashed its tail once or twice and then went and put its head in the air-conditioner.

That isn't possible. . . . But it was. More and more of his body disappeared into the air-conditioner, and finally there was only his tail, and then only the tip of his tail, and when that was gone so was she.

THE young policeman who stood all night on the corner of East End Avenue and Gracie Square, eight stories below, was at the phone box, having a conversation with the sergeant on the desk. This did not prevent him from keeping his eyes on an emaciated junkie who stood peering through the window of the drugstore, past the ice-cream bin, the revolving display of paperbacks, the plastic toys, hair sprays, hand creams, cleansing lotions, etc., at the prescription counter. The door had a grating over it but the plate-glass window did not. One good kick would do it. It would also bring the policeman running.

The policeman would have been happy to turn the junkie in, but he didn't have anything on him. Vagrancy? But suppose he had a home? And suppose it brought the Civil Liberties Union running? The policeman turned his back for a minute and when he looked again the junkie was gone, vanished, nowhere.

Though it was between three and four in the morning, people were walking their dogs in Carl Schurz Park. Amazing. Dreamlike. And the sign on the farther shore of the river that changed back and forth continually was enough to unhinge the mind: PEARLWICK HAMPERS became BATHROOM HAMPERS, which in turn became PEARLWICK HAMPERS, and sometimes for a fraction of a second BATHWICK HAMPERS.

In the metal trash containers scattered here and there along the winding paths of the park were pieces of waxed paper that had been around food but nothing you could actually eat. The junkie didn't go into the playground because the gates were locked and it had a high iron fence around it. He could have managed this easily by climbing a tree and dropping to the cement on the other side. Small boys did it all the time. And maybe in there he would have found something—a half-eaten Milky Way or Mounds bar that a nursemaid had taken from a child with a finicky appetite—but then he would have been locked in instead of out, and he knew all there was to know about that: Sing Sing, Rikers Island, Auburn, Dannemora. His name is James Jackson, and he is a figure out of a nightmare—unless you happen to know what happened to him, the steady rain of blows about his unprotected head ever since he was born, in which case it is human life that seems like a nightmare. The dog walkers, supposing—correctly—that he had a switchblade in his pocket and a certain amount of experience in using it, chose a path that detoured around him. The wind was out of the southeast and smelled of the sea, fifteen miles away on the other side of Long Beach and Far Rockaway. The Hell Gate section of the Triborough Bridge was a necklace of sickly-green incandescent pearls. When the policeman left his post and took a turn through the south end of the park, the junkie was sitting innocently on a bench on the river walk. He was keeping the river company.

And when the policeman got back to his post a woman in a long red coat was going through the trash basket directly across the street from him. She was harmless. He saw her night after night. And in a minute she would cross over and tell him about the doctor at Bellevue who said she probably dreamed that somebody picked the lock of her door while she was out buying coffee and stole her mother's gold thimble.

The threads that bound the woman in the long red coat to a particular address, to the family she had been born into, her husband's grave in the Brooklyn cemetery, and the children who never wrote except to ask for money, had broken, and she was now free to wander along the street, scavenging from trash containers. She did not mind if people saw her, or feel that what she was doing was in any way exceptional. When she found something useful or valuable, she stuffed it in her dirty canvas bag, the richer by a pair of sandals with a broken strap or a perfectly clean copy of "Sartor Resartus." What in the beginning was only an uncertainty, an uneasiness, a sense of the falsity of appearances, a suspicion that the completely friendly world she lived in was in fact secretly mocking and hostile, had proved to be true. Or rather, had become true—for it wasn't always. And meanwhile, in her mind, she was perpetually composing a statement, for her own use and understanding, that would cover this situation.

Three colored lights passed overhead, very high up and in a cluster, blinking. There were also lights strung through the park at intervals, and on East End Avenue, where taxicabs cruised up and down with their roof-lights on. Nobody wanted them. As if they had never in their life shot through a red light, the taxis stopped at Eighty-third Street, and again at Eighty-fourth, and went on when the light turned green. East End Avenue was as quiet as the grave. So were the side streets.

With the first hint of morning, this beautiful quiet came to an end. Stopping and starting, making a noise like an electric toaster, a Department of Sanitation truck made its way down Eighty-fourth Street, murdering sleep. Crash. Tinkle. More grinding. Bump. Thump. Voices. A brief silence and then the whole thing started up again farther down the street. This was followed by other noises—a parked car being warmed up, a maniac in a sports car with no muffler. And then suddenly it was the policeman's turn to be gone. A squad car drove by, with the car radio playing an old Bing Crosby song, and picked him up.

Biding his time, the junkie managed to slip past the service entrance of one of the apartment buildings on East End Avenue without being seen. Around in back he saw an open window on the ground floor with no bars over it. On the other hand he didn't know who or what he would find when he climbed through it, and he shouldn't have waited till morning. He stood flattened against a brick wall while a handyman took in the empty garbage cans. The sound of retreating footsteps died away. The door to the service entrance was wide open. In a matter of seconds James Jackson was in and out again, wheeling a new ten-speed Peugeot. He straddled the bicycle as if he and not the overweight insurance broker in 7E had paid good money for it, and rode off down the street.

"'CLOUDY with rain or showers . . .' Cindy, did you know you dreamt about a tiger last night?"

"Cindy dreamt about a tiger?" Iris said.

"Yes. What happened after I left?"

"Nothing."

"Congratulations. I dreamt the air-conditioner in our room broke and we couldn't get anybody to come and fix it."

"Is it broken?" Iris asked.

"I don't know. We'll have to wait till next summer to find out."

"GOOD morning, Laurie. Good morning, Cindy," Jimmy the daytime elevator man said cheerfully. No answer. But no rudeness intended either. They did not know they were in the elevator.

The red-haired doorman at No. 7 Gracie Square stretched out his arms and pretended he was going to capture Cindy. This happened morning after morning, and she put up with it patiently.

"Taxi!" people wailed. *"Taxi!"* But there were no taxis. Or if one came along there was somebody in it. The doorman of No. 10 stood in the middle of East End Avenue and blew his whistle at nothing. On a balcony five stories above the street, a man lying on his back with his hips in the air was being put through his morning exercises by a Swedish masseur. The tired middle-aged legs went up and down like pistons. Like pistons, the elevators rose and fell in all the buildings overlooking the park, bringing the maids and laundresses up, taking men with briefcases down. The stationery store and the cleaners were now open. So was the luncheonette.

The two little girls stopped, took each other by the hand, and looked carefully both ways before they crossed the car tunnel at No. 10. On the river walk Laurie saw an acquaintance and ran on ahead. Poor Cindy! At her back was the park—very agreeable to play in when she went there with her mother or the kindergarten class, but also frequented by rough boys with water pistols and full of bushes it could be hiding in—and on her right was the deep pit alongside No. 10; it could be down there, below the sidewalk and waiting to spring out when she came along. She did not look to see if it was there but kept well over to the other side, next to the outer railing and the river. A tug with four empty barges was nosing its way upstream. The Simpsons' cook waved to Cindy from their kitchen window, which looked out on the river walk, and Cindy waved back.

In the days when George used to take Laurie to kindergarten because she was too small to walk to school by herself, he had noticed her—a big woman with blond braids in a crown around her head. And one day he said, "Shall we wave to her and see what happens?" Sometimes her back was turned to the window and she didn't know that Cindy and Laurie were there. They did not ever think of her except when they saw her, and if they had met her face to face she would have had to do all the talking.

Laurie was waiting at the Eighty-third Street gate. "Come on," she said.

"Stupid-head," Cindy said.

They went into the school building together, ignoring the big girls in camel's-hair coats who held the door open for them. But it wasn't like Jimmy the elevator man; they knew the big girls were there.

Sitting on the floor of her cubby, with her gym sneakers under her bottom and her cheek against her green plaid coat, Cindy felt safe. But Miss Nichols kept trying to get her to come out. The sandbox, the blocks, the crayons—Cindy said no to them all, and sucked her thumb. So Miss Nichols sat down on a little chair and took Cindy on her lap.

"If there was a (   )?" Cindy asked finally.

In a soft coaxing voice Miss Nichols said, "If there was a what?"

Cindy wouldn't say what.

THE fire engines raced down Eighty-sixth Street, sirens shrieking and horns blowing, swung south through a red light, and came to a stop by the alarm box on the corner of East End Avenue and Gracie Square. The firemen jumped down and stood talking in the middle of the street. The hoses remained neatly folded and the ladders horizontal. It was the second false alarm that night from this same box. A county fair wouldn't have made more commotion under their windows but it had happened too often and George and Iris Carrington went on sleeping peacefully, flat on their backs, like stone figures on a medieval tomb.

IN the trash basket on the corner by the park gates there was a copy of the *Daily News* which said, in big letters, "TIGER ESCAPES," but that was a different tiger; that tiger escaped from a circus in Jamestown, R.I.

"WHAT *is* it?" Iris asked, in the flower shop. "Why are you pulling at my skirt?"

The flower-shop woman (pink-blond hair, Viennese accent) offered Cindy a green carnation, and she refused to take it. "You don't like flowers?" the woman asked, coyly, and the tiger kept on looking at Cindy from behind some big, wide rubbery green leaves. "She's shy," the flower-shop woman said.

"Not usually," Iris said. "I don't know what's got into her today."

She gave the woman some money, and the woman gave her some money and some flowers, and then she and Cindy went outside, but Cindy was afraid to look behind her. If the tiger was following them, it was better not to know. For half a block she had a tingling sensation in the center of her back, between her shoulder blades. But then, looking across the street, she saw that the tiger was not back there in the flower shop. It must have left when they did, and now it was looking at her from the round hole in a cement mixer.

The lights changed from red to green, and Iris took her hand and started to cross over.

"I want to go that way," Cindy said, holding back, until the light changed again. Since she was never allowed on the street alone, she was not really afraid of meeting the tiger all by herself. But what if some day it should walk into the elevator when Jimmy wasn't looking, and get off at their floor, and hide behind Laurie's bicycle and the scooters. And what if the front door opened and somebody came out and pressed the elevator button and the tiger got inside when they weren't looking. And what if—

"Oh, please don't hold back, Cindy! I'm late as anything!"

So, dangerous as it was, she allowed herself to be hurried along home.

Tap, tap, tap . . .

In the night this was, just after Iris and George had got to sleep.

"Oh, no!" Iris moaned.

But it was. When he opened the door, there she stood.

Tap, tap . . .

That same night, two hours later. Sound asleep but able to walk and talk, he put on his bathrobe and followed her down the hall. Stretched out beside her, he tried to go on sleeping but he couldn't. He said, "What were you dreaming about this time?"

"Sea-things."

"What kind of seethings?"

"Sea-things under the sea."

"Things that wiggled?"

"Yes."

"Something was after you?"

"Yes."

"Too bad. Go to sleep."

Tap, tap . . .

This time as he heaved himself up, Iris said to him, "*You* lie still."

She got up and opened the door to the hall and said, "Cindy, we're tired and we need our sleep. I want you to go back to your bed and stay there."

Then they both lay awake, listening to the silence at the other end of the hall.

"I came out of the building," Iris said, "and I had three letters that Jimmy had given me, and it was raining hard, and the wind whipped them right out of my hand."

He took a sip of his drink and then said, "Did you get them?"

"I got two of them. One was from the Richards children, thanking me for the toys I sent when Lonnie was in the hospital. And one was a note from Mrs. Mills. I never did find the third. It was a small envelope, and the handwriting was Society."

"A birthday party for Cindy."

"No. It was addressed to Mr. and Mrs. George Carrington. Cocktail party, probably."

He glanced at the windows. It was already dark. Then, the eternal optimist (also remembering the time he found the button that flew off her coat and rolled under a parked car on Eighty-fifth Street): "Which way did it blow? I'll look for it tomorrow."

"Oh, there's no use. You can see by the others. They were reduced to pulp by the rain, in just that minute. And anyway, I did look, this afternoon."

In the morning, he took the Seventy-ninth Street crosstown bus instead of the Eighty-sixth, so that he could look for the invitation that blew away. No luck. The invitation had already passed through a furnace in the Department of Sanitation building on Ninetieth Street and now, in the form of ashes, was floating down the East River on a garbage scow, on its way out to sea.

The sender, rebuffed in this first tentative effort to get to know the Carringtons better, did not try again. She had met them at a dinner party, and liked them both. She was old enough to be Iris's mother, and it puzzled her that a young woman who seemed to be well-bred and was quite lovely-looking and adored "Middlemarch" should turn out to have no manners, but she didn't brood about it. New York is full of pleasant young couples, and if one chooses to ignore your invitation the chances are another won't.

"DID you hear Laurie in the night?" Iris said.

"No. Did Laurie have a nightmare?"

"Yes. I thought you were awake."

"I don't think so."

He got up out of bed and went into the children's room and turned on the radiators so they wouldn't catch cold. Laurie was sitting up in bed reading.

"Mommy says you had a bad dream last night."

"There were three dreams," she said, in an overdistinct voice, as if she were a grown woman at a committee meeting. "The first dream was about Miss Stevenson. I dreamed she wasn't nice to me. She was like the wicked witch."

"Miss Stevenson loves you."

"And the second dream was about snakes. They were all over the floor. It was like a rug made up of snakes, and very icky, and there was a giant, and Cathy and I were against him, and he was trying to shut me in the room where the snakes were, and one of the snakes bit me, but he wasn't the kind of snake that kills you, he was just a mean snake, and so it didn't hurt. And the third dream was a happy dream. I was with Cathy and we were skating together and pulling our mommies by strings."

WITH his safety razor ready to begin a downward sweep, George Carrington studied the lathered face in the mirror of the medicine cabinet. He shook his head. There was a fatal flaw in his character: Nobody was ever as real to him as he was to himself. If people knew how little he cared whether they lived or died, they wouldn't want to have anything to do with him.

THE dog moved back and forth between the two ends of the apartment, on good terms with everybody. She was in the dining room at mealtimes, and in the kitchen when Iris was getting dinner (when quite often something tasty fell off the edge of the kitchen table), and she was there again just after dinner, in case the plates were put on the floor for her to lick before they went into the dishwasher. In the late afternoon, for an hour before it was time for her can of beef-and-beef-by-products, she sat with her front paws crossed, facing the kitchen clock, a reminding statue. After she had been fed, she went to the living room and lay down before the unlit log fire in the fireplace and slept until bedtime. In the morning, she followed Iris back and forth through room after room, until Iris was dressed and ready to take her out. "Must you nag me so?" Iris cried, but the dog was not in-timidated. There was something they were in agreement about, though only one of them could have put it in words: It is a crime against Nature to keep a hunting dog in the city. George sometimes gave her a slap on her haunches when she picked up food in the gutter or lunged at another dog. And if she jerked on her leash he jerked back, harder. But with Iris she could do anything—she could even stand under the canopy and refuse to go anywhere because it was raining.

Walking by the river, below Eightieth Street, it wasn't necessary to keep her on a leash, and while Iris went on ahead Puppy sniffed at the godfor-saken grass and weeds that grew between the cement walk and the East River Drive. Then she overtook Iris, at full speed, overshot the mark, and came charging back, showing her teeth in a grin. Three or four times she did this, as a rule—with Iris applauding and congratulating her and cheering her on. It may be a crime against Nature to keep a hunting dog in the city, but this one was happy anyway.

AFTER a series of dreams in which people started out as one person and ended up another and he found that there was no provision for getting from where he was to where he wanted to go and it grew later and later and even after the boat had left he still went on packing his clothes and what he thought was his topcoat turned out to belong to a friend he had not seen for seventeen years and naked strangers came and went, he woke and thought he heard a soft tapping on the bedroom door. But when he got up and opened it there was no one there.

"Was that Cindy?" Iris asked as he got back into bed.

"No. I thought I heard her, but I must have imagined it."

"I thought I heard her too," Iris said, and turned over.

At breakfast he said, "Did you have any bad dreams last night?" but Cindy was making a lake in the middle of her oatmeal and didn't answer.

"I thought I heard you tapping on our door," he said. "You didn't dream about a wolf, or a tiger, or a big black dog?"

"I don't remember," she said.

"YOU'LL never guess what I just saw from the bedroom window," Iris said.

He put down his book.

"A police wagon drove down Eighty-fourth Street and stopped, and two policemen with guns got out and went into a building and didn't come out. And after a long while two more policemen came and *they* went into the building, and pretty soon they all came out with a big man with black hair, handcuffed. Right there on Eighty-fourth Street, two doors from the corner."

"Nice neighborhood we live in," he said.

"DADDY, Daddy, Daddy, Daddy!" came into his dreams without waking him, and what did wake him was the heaving of the other bed as Iris got up and hurried toward the bedroom door.

"It was Cindy," she said when she came back.

"Dream?" he asked.

"Yes."

"I heard her but went on dreaming myself."

"She doesn't usually cry out like that."

"Laurie used to."

Why all these dreams, he wondered, and drifted gently back to sleep, as if he already knew the answer. She turned and turned, and finally, after three-quarters of an hour, got up and filled the hot-water bottle. What for days had been merely a half-formed thought in the back of her mind was now suddenly, in the middle of the night, making her rigid with anxiety. She needed to talk, and couldn't bring herself to wake him. What she wanted to say was they were making a mistake in bringing the children up in New York City. Or even in America. There was too much that there was no way to protect them from, and the only sensible thing would be to pull up stakes now, before Laurie reached adolescence. They could sublet the apartment until the lease ran out, and take a house somewhere in the South of France, near Aix perhaps, and the children could go to a French school, and they could all go skiing in Switzerland in the winter, and Cindy could have her own horse, and they both would acquire a good French accent, and be allowed to grow up slowly, in the ordinary way, and not be jaded by one premature experience after another, before they were old enough to understand any of it.

With the warmth at her back, and the comforting feeling that she had found the hole in the net, gradually she fell asleep too.

But when she brought the matter up two days later he looked at her blankly. He did not oppose her idea but neither did he accept it, and so her hands were tied.

A S usual, the fathers' part in the Christmas program had to be rehearsed beforehand. In the small practice room on the sixth floor of the school, their masculinity—their grey flannel or dark-blue pin-striped suits, their size 9, 10, 11, 11½, and 12 shoes, their gold cufflinks, the odor that emanated from their bodies and from their freshly shaved cheeks, their simple assurance, based on, among other things, the *Social Register* and the size of their income—was incongruous. They were handed sheets of music as they came in, and the room was crammed with folding chairs, all facing the ancient grand piano. With the two tall windows at their backs they were missing the snow, which was a pity. It went up, down, diagonally, and in centrifugal motion—all at once. The fact that no two of the star-shaped crystals were the same was a miracle, of course, but it was a miracle that everybody has long since grown accustomed to. The light outside the windows was cold and grey.

"Since there aren't very many of you," the music teacher said, "you'll have to make up for it by singing enthusiastically." She was young, in her late twenties, and had difficulty keeping discipline in the classroom; the girls took advantage of her good nature, and never stopped talking and gave her their complete attention. She sat down at the piano now and played the opening bars of "O come, O come, Emmanuel/And ransom captive I-i-i-zrah-el . . ."

Somebody in the second row exclaimed, "Oh God!" under his breath. The music was set too high for men's voices.

"The girls will sing the first stanza, you fathers the second—"

The door opened and two more fathers came in.

"—and all will sing the third."

With help from the piano (which they would not have downstairs in the school auditorium) they achieved an approximation of the tune, and the emphasis sometimes fell in the right place. They did their best, but the nineteenth-century words and the ninth-century plainsong did not go well together. Also, one of the fathers had a good strong clear voice, which only made the others more self-conscious and apologetic. They would have been happier without him.

The music teacher made a flip remark. They all laughed and began again. Their number was added to continually as the door opened and let in the sounds from the hall. Soon there were no more vacant chairs; the latecomers had to stand. The snow was now noticeably heavier, and the singing had more volume. Though they were at some pains to convey, by their remarks to one another and their easy laughter, that this was not an occasion to be taken seriously, nevertheless the fact that they were here was proof of the contrary: they all had offices where they should have been and salaries they were not at this moment doing anything to earn. Twenty-seven men with, at first glance, a look of sameness about them, a round, composite, youngish, unrevealing, New York face. Under closer inspection, this broke down. Not all the eyes were blue, nor were the fathers all in their middle and late thirties. The thin-faced man at the end of the second row could not have been a broker or a lawyer or in advertising. The man next to him had survived incarceration in a Nazi prison camp. There was one Negro. Here and there a head that was not thickly covered with hair. Their speaking voices varied, but not so much as they conceivably might have—no Texas drawl, for instance. And all the fingernails were clean, all the shoes were shined, all the linen was fresh.

Each time they went over the hymn it was better. They clearly needed more rehearsing, but the music teacher glanced nervously at the clock and said, "And now 'In Dulci Jubilo.' "

Those who had forgotten their Latin, or never had any, eavesdropped on those who knew how the words should be pronounced. The tune was powerful and swept everything before it, and in a flush of pleasure they finished together, on the beat, loudly, making the room echo. They had forgotten about the telephone messages piling up on their desks beside the unopened mail. They were enjoying themselves. They could have gone on singing for another hour. Instead, they had to get up and file out of the room and crowd into the elevators.

In spite of new costumes, new scenery, different music, and—naturally—a different cast, the Christmas play was always the same. Mary and Joseph proceeded to Bethlehem, where the inns were full, and found shelter in the merest suggestion of a stable. An immature angel announced to very unlikely shepherds the appearance of the Star. Wise Men came and knelt before the plastic Babe in Mary's arms. And then the finale: the Threes singing and dancing with heavenly joy.

"How did it sound?" George asked, in the crowd on the stairs.

"Fine," Iris said.

"Really? It didn't seem to me—maybe because we were under the balcony—it didn't seem as if we were making any sound at all."

"No, it was plenty loud enough. What was so nice was the two kinds of voices."

"High and low, you mean?"

"The fathers sounded like bears. Adorable."

IN theory, since it was the middle of the night, it was dark, but not the total suffocating darkness of a cloudy night in the country. The city, as usual, gave off light—enough so that you could see the island in the middle of the river, and the three bridges, and the outlines of the little houses on East End Avenue and the big apartment buildings on Eighty-sixth Street, and the trees and shrubs and lampposts and comfort station in the park. Also a woman standing by the railing of the river walk.

There was no wind. The river was flowing north and the air smelled of snow, which melted the moment it touched any solid object, and became the shine on iron balustrades and on the bark of trees.

The woman had been standing there a long time, looking out over the water, when she began awkwardly to pull herself up and over the curved iron spikes that were designed, by their size and shape, to prevent people from throwing themselves into the river. In this instance they were not enough. But it took some doing. There was a long tear in the woman's coat and she was gasping for breath as she let herself go backward into space.

· · ·

THE sun enters Aquarius January 20th and remains until February 18th. *"An extremely good friend can today put into motion some operation that will be most helpful to your best interest, or else introduce you to some influential person. Go out socially in the evening on a grand scale. Be charming."*

THE cocktail party was in a penthouse. The elevator opened directly into the foyer of the apartment. And the woman he was talking to—or rather, who was talking to him—was dressed all in shades of brown.

"I tried to get you last summer," she said, "but your wife said you were busy that day."

"Yes," he said.

"I'll try you again."

"Please do," somebody said for him, using his mouth and tongue and vocal cords—because it was the last thing in the world he wanted, to drive halfway across Long Island to a lunch party. "We hardly ever go anywhere," he himself said, but too late, after the damage had been done.

His mind wandered for an instant as he took in—not the room, for he was facing the wrong way, but a small corner of it. And in that instant he lost the thread of the story she was telling him. She had taken her shoe off in a movie theatre and put her purse down beside it, and the next thing he knew they refused to do anything, even after she had explained what happened and that she must get in. Who "they" were, get in where, he patiently waited to find out, while politely sharing her indignation.

"But imagine!" she exclaimed. "They said, 'How valuable was the ring?' "

He shook his head, commiserating with her.

"I suppose if it hadn't been worth a certain amount," she went on, "they wouldn't have done a thing about it."

The police, surely, he thought. Having thought at first it was the manager of the movie theatre she was talking about.

"And while they were jimmying the door open, people were walking by, and nobody showed the slightest concern. Or interest."

So it wasn't the police. But who was it, then? He never found out, because they were joined by another woman, who smiled at him in such a way as to suggest that they knew each other. But though he searched his mind and her face—the plucked eyebrows, the reserved expression in the middle-aged eyes—and considered her tweed suit and her diamond pin and her square figure, he could not imagine who she was. Suppose somebody—suppose Iris came up and he had to introduce her?

The purse was recovered, with the valuable ring still in it, and he found himself talking about something that had occupied his thoughts lately. And in his effort to say what he meant, he failed to notice what happened to the first woman. Suddenly she was not there. Somebody must have carried her off, right in front of his unseeing eyes.

". . . but it isn't really distinguishable from what goes on in dreams," he said to the woman who seemed to know him and to assume that he knew her. "People you have known for twenty or thirty years, you suddenly discover you didn't really know how they felt about you, and in fact you don't know how anybody feels about anything—only what they *say* they feel. And suppose that isn't true at all? You decide that it is better to act as if it is true. And so does everybody else. But it is a kind of myth you are living in, wide awake, with your eyes open, in broad daylight."

He realized that the conversation had become not only personal but intimate. But it was too late to back out now.

To his surprise she seemed to understand, to have felt what he had felt. "And one chooses," she said, "between this myth and that."

"Exactly! If you live in the city and are bringing up children, you decide that this thing is not safe—and so you don't let them do it—and that thing *is* safe. When, actually, neither one is safe and everything is equally dangerous. But for the sake of convenience—"

"And also so that you won't go out of your mind," she said.

"And so you won't go out of your mind," he agreed. "Well," he said after a moment, "that makes two of us who are thinking about it."

"In one way or another, people live by myths," she said.

He racked his brain for something further to say on this or any other subject.

Glancing around at the windows, which went from floor to ceiling, the woman in the tweed suit said, "These vistas you have here."

He then looked and saw black night, with lighted buildings far below and many blocks away. "From our living room," he said, "you can see all the way to the North Pole."

"We live close to the ground," she said.

But where? Cambridge? Princeton? Philadelphia?

"In the human scale," he said. "Like London and Paris. Once, on a beautiful spring day, four of us—we'd been having lunch with a visiting Englishman who was interested in architecture—went searching for the sky. Up one street and down the next."

She smiled.

"We had to look for it, the sky is so far away in New York."

They stood nursing their drinks, and a woman came up to them who seemed to know her intimately, and the two women started talking and he turned away.

ON her way into the school building, Laurie joined the flood from the school bus, and cried, "Hi, Janet . . . Hi, Connie . . . Hi, Elizabeth . . ." and seemed to be enveloped by her schoolmates, until suddenly, each girl having turned to some other girl, Laurie is left standing alone, her expression unchanged, still welcoming, but nobody having responded. If you collect reasons, this is the reason she behaved so badly at lunch, was impertinent to her mother, and hit her little sister.

HE woke with a mild pain in his stomach. It was high up, like an ulcer pain, and he lay there worrying about it. When he heard the sound of shattered glass, his half-awake, oversensible mind supplied both the explanation and the details: two men, putting a large framed picture into the trunk compartment of a parked car, had dropped it, breaking the glass. Too bad . . . And with that thought he drifted gently off to sleep.

In the morning he looked out of the bedroom window and saw three squad cars in front of the drugstore. The window of the drugstore had a big star-shaped hole in it, and several policemen were standing around looking at the broken glass on the sidewalk.

THE sneeze was perfectly audible through two closed doors. He turned to Iris with a look of inquiry.

"Who sneezed? Was that you, Laurie?" she called.

"That was Cindy," Laurie said.

In principle, Iris would have liked to bring them up in a Spartan fashion, but both children caught cold easily and their colds were prolonged, and recurring, and overlapping, and endless. Whether they should or shouldn't be kept home from school took on the unsolvability of a moral dilemma—which George's worrying disposition did nothing to alleviate. The sound of a child coughing deep in the chest in the middle of the night would make him leap up out of a sound sleep.

She blamed herself when the children came down with a cold, and she blamed them. Possibly, also, the school was to blame, since the children played on the roof, twelve stories above the street, and up there the winds were often much rawer, and teachers cannot, of course, spend all their time going around buttoning up the coats of little girls who have got too hot from running.

She went and stood in the doorway of Cindy's room. "No sneezing," she said.

Sneeze, sneeze, sneeze.

"Cindy, if you are catching another cold, I'm going to shoot myself," Iris said, and gave her two baby-aspirin tablets to chew, and some Vitamin C drops, and put an extra blanket on her bed, and didn't open the window, and in the morning Cindy's nose was running.

"Shall I keep her home from school?" Iris asked, at the breakfast table.

Instead of answering, George got up and looked at the weather thermometer outside the west window of their bedroom. "Twenty-seven," he said, when he came back. But he still didn't answer her question. He was afraid to answer it, lest it be the wrong answer, and she blame him. Actually, there was no answer that was the right answer: They had tried sending Cindy to school and they had tried not sending her. This time, Iris kept her home from school—not because she thought it was going to make any difference but so the pediatrician, Dr. de Santillo, wouldn't blame her. Not that he ever said anything. And Cindy got to play with Laurie's things all morning. She played with Laurie's paper dolls until she was tired, and left them all over the floor, and then she colored in Laurie's coloring book, and Puppy chewed up one of the crayons but not one of Laurie's favorites—not the pink or the blue—and then Cindy rearranged the furniture in Laurie's doll house so it was much nicer, and then she lined up all Laurie's dolls in a row on her bed and played school. And when it was time for Laurie to come home from school she went out to the kitchen and played with the egg-beater. Laurie came in, letting the front door slam behind her, and dropped her mittens in the hall and her coat on the living-room rug and her knitted cap on top of her coat, and started for her room, and it sounded as if she had hurt herself. Iris came running. What a noise Laurie made. And stamping her foot, Cindy noted disapprovingly. And tears.

"Stop screaming and tell me what's the matter!" Iris said.

"Cindy, I hate you!" Laurie said. "I hate you, I hate you!"

Horrible old Laurie . . .

But in the morning when they first woke up it was different. She heard Laurie in the bathroom, and then she heard Laurie go back to her room. Lying in bed, Cindy couldn't suck her thumb because she couldn't breathe through her nose, so she got up and went into Laurie's room (entirely forgetting that her mother had said that in the morning she was to stay out of

Laurie's room because she had a cold) and got in Laurie's bed and said, "Read, read." Laurie read her the story of "The Tinder Box," which has three dogs in it—a dog with eyes as big as saucers, and a dog with eyes as big as millwheels, and a third dog with eyes as big as the Round Tower of Copenhagen.

Tap, tap, tap on the bedroom door brought him entirely awake. "What's Laurie been reading to her?" he asked, turning over in bed. That meant it was Iris's turn to get up. While she was pulling herself together, they heard tap, tap, tap again. The bed heaved.

"What's Laurie been reading to you?" she asked as she and Cindy went off down the hall together. When she came back into the bedroom, the light was on and he was standing in front of his dresser, with the top drawer open, searching for Gelusil tablets.

"Trouble?" she said.

STANDING in the doorway of Cindy's room, in her blue dressing gown, with her hairbrush in her hand, Iris said, "Who sneezed? Was that you, Cindy?"

"That was Laurie," Cindy said.

So after that Laurie got to stay home from school too.

"I saw Phyllis Simpson in Gristede's supermarket," Iris said. "Their cook committed suicide."

"How?"

"She threw herself in the river."

"No!"

"They think she must have done it sometime during the night, but they don't know exactly when. They just came down to breakfast and she wasn't there. They're still upset about it."

"When did it happen?"

"About a month ago. Her body was found way down the river."

"What a pity. She was a nice woman."

"You remember her?"

"Certainly. She always waved to the children when I used to walk them to school. She waved to me too, sometimes. From the kitchen window. What made her do such a thing?"

"They have no idea."

"She was a big woman," he said. "It must have been hard for her to pull herself up over that railing. It's quite high. No note or anything?"

"No."

"Terrible."

ON St. Valentine's Day, the young woman who lived on tea and cigarettes and was given to burning herself on the gas stove eloped to California with her mother, and now there was no one in the kitchen. From time to time, the employment agency went through the formality of sending someone for Iris to interview—though actually it was the other way round. And either the apartment was too large or they didn't care to work for a family with children or they were not accustomed to doing the cooking as well as the other housework. Sometimes they didn't give any reason at all.

A young woman from Haiti, who didn't speak English, was willing to give the job a try. It turned out that she had never seen a carpet sweeper before, and she asked for her money at the end of the day.

WALKING the dog at seven-fifteen on a winter morning, he suddenly stopped and said to himself, "Oh God, somebody's been murdered!" On the high stone stoop of one of the little houses on East End Avenue facing the park. Somebody in a long red coat. By the curve of the hip he could tell it was a woman, and with his heart racing he considered what he ought to do. From where he stood on the sidewalk he couldn't see the upper part of her body. One foot—the bare heel and the strap of her shoe—was sticking out from under the hem of the coat. If she'd been murdered, wouldn't she be sprawled out in an awkward position instead of curled up and lying on her side as though she was in bed asleep? He looked up at the house. Had they locked her out? After a scene? Or she could have come home in the middle of the night and discovered that she'd forgotten to take her key. But in that case she'd have spent the night in a hotel or with a friend. Or called an all-night locksmith.

He went up three steps without managing to see any more than he had already. The parapet offered some shelter from the wind, but even so, how could she sleep on the cold stone, with nothing over her?

"Can I help you?"

His voice sounded strange and hollow. There was no answer. The red coat did not stir. Then he saw the canvas bag crammed with the fruit of her night's scavenging, and backed down the steps.

· · ·

NOW it was his turn. The sore throat was gone in the morning, but it came back during the day, and when he sat down to dinner he pulled the extension out at his end and moved his mat, silver, and glass farther away from the rest of them.

"If you aren't sneezing, I don't think you need to be in Isolation Corner," Iris said, but he stayed there anyway. His colds were prolonged and made worse by his efforts to treat them; made worse still by his trying occasionally to disregard them, as he saw other people doing. In the end he went through box after box of Kleenex, his nose white with Noxzema, his eyelids inflamed, like a man in a subway poster advertising a cold remedy that, as it turned out, did not work for him. And finally he took to his bed, with a transistor radio for amusement and company. In his childhood, being sick resulted in agreeable pampering, and now that he was grown he preferred to be both parties to this pleasure. No one could make him as comfortable as he could make himself, and Iris had all but given up trying.

ON a rainy Sunday afternoon in March, with every door in the school building locked and the corridors braced for the shock of Monday morning, the ancient piano demonstrated for the benefit of the empty practice room that it is one thing to fumble through the vocal line, guided by the chords that accompany it, and something else again to be genuinely musical, to know what the composer intended—the resolution of what cannot be left uncertain, the amorous flirtation of the treble and the bass, notes taking to the air like a flock of startled birds.

THE faint clicking sounds given off by the telephone in the pantry meant that Iris was dialling on the extension in the master bedroom. And at last there was somebody in the Carringtons' kitchen again—a black woman in her fifties. They were low on milk, and totally out of oatmeal, canned dog food, and coffee, but the memo pad that was magnetically attached to the side of the Frigidaire was blank. Writing down things they were out of was not something she considered part of her job. When an emergency arose, she put on her coat and went to the store, just as if she were still in North Carolina.

The sheet of paper that was attached to the clipboard hanging from a nail on the side of the kitchen cupboard had the menus for lunch and dinner all written out, but they were for yesterday's lunch and dinner. And though it was only nine-thirty, Bessie already felt a mounting indignation at being kept in ignorance about what most deeply concerned her. It was an old-fashioned apartment, with big rooms and high ceilings, and the kitchen was a considerable distance from the master bedroom; nevertheless, it was just barely possible for the two women to live there. Nature had designed them for mutual tormenting, the one with an exaggerated sense of time, always hurrying to meet a deadline that did not exist anywhere but in her own fancy, and calling upon the angels or whoever is in charge of amazing grace to take notice that she had put the food on the hot tray in the dining room at precisely one minute before the moment she had been told to have dinner ready; the other with not only a hatred of planning meals but also a childish reluctance to come to the table. When the minute hand of the electric clock in the kitchen arrived at seven or seven-fifteen or whatever, Bessie went into the dining room and announced in an inaudible voice that dinner was ready. Two rooms away, George heard her by extrasensory perception and leapt to his feet, and Iris, holding out her glass to him, said, "Am I not going to have a second vermouth?"

To his amazement, on Bessie's day off, having cooked dinner and put it on the hot plate, Iris drifted away to the front of the apartment and read a magazine, fixed her hair, God knows what, until he discovered the food sitting there and begged her to come to the table.

"THEY said they lived in Boys Town, and I thought Jimmy let them in because he's Irish and Catholic," Iris said. "There was nothing on the list I wanted, so I subscribed to *Vogue,* to help them out. When I spoke to Jimmy about it, he said he had no idea they were selling subscriptions, and he never lets solicitors get by him—not even nuns and priests. Much as he might want to. So I don't suppose it will come."

"It might," George said. "Maybe they were honest."

"He thought they were workmen because they asked for the eleventh floor. The tenants on the eleventh floor have moved out and Jimmy says the people who are moving in have a five years' lease and are spending fifty thousand dollars on the place, which they don't even *own.* But anyway, what they did was walk through the apartment and then down one floor and start ringing doorbells. The super took them down in the back elevator without asking what they were doing there, and off they went. They tried the same thing at No. 7 and the doorman threw them out."

WALKING the dog before breakfast, if he went by the river walk he saw in the Simpsons' window a black-haired woman who did not wave to him or even look up when he passed. That particular section of the river walk was haunted by an act of despair that nobody had been given a chance to understand. Nothing that he could think of—cancer, thwarted love, melancholia—seemed to fit. He had only spoken to her once, when he and Iris went to a dinner party at the Simpsons' and she smiled at him as she was helping the maid clear the table between courses. If she didn't look up when he passed under her window it was as though he had been overtaken by a cloud shadow—until he forgot all about it, a few seconds later. But he could have stopped just once, and he hadn't. When the window was open he could have called out to her, even if it was only "Good morning," or "Isn't it a beautiful day?"

He could have said, *Don't do it.* . . .

Sometimes he came back by the little house on East End Avenue where he had seen the woman in the red coat. He invariably glanced up, half expecting her to be lying there on the stoop. If she wasn't there, where was she?

In the psychiatric ward of Bellevue Hospital was the answer. But not for long. She and the doctor got it straightened out about her mother's gold thimble, and he gave her a prescription and told her where to go in the building to have it filled, and hoped for the best—which, after all, is all that anybody has to hope for.

THE weather thermometer blew away one stormy night and after a week or two George brought home a new one. It was round and encased in white plastic, and not meant to be screwed to the window frame but to be kept inside. It registered the temperature outside by means of a wire with what looked like a small bullet attached to the end of it. The directions said to drill a hole through the window frame, but George backed away from all that and, instead, hung the wire across the sill and closed the window on it. What the new thermometer said bore no relation to the actual temperature, and drilling the hole had a high priority on the list of things he meant to do.

There was also a racial barometer in the apartment that registered *Fair* or *Stormy*, according to whether Bessie had spent several days running in the apartment or had just come back from a weekend in her room in Harlem.

The laundress, so enormously fat that she had to maneuver her body around, as if she were the captain of an ocean liner, was a Muslim and hated all white people and most black people as well. She was never satisfied with the lunch Bessie cooked for her, and Bessie objected to having to get lunch for her, and the problem was solved temporarily by having her eat in the luncheonette across the street.

She quit. The new laundress was half the size of the old one, and sang alto in her church choir, and was good-tempered, and fussy about what she had for lunch. Bessie sometimes considered her a friend and sometimes an object of derision, because she believed in spirits.

So did Bessie, but not to the same extent or in the same way. Bessie's mother had appeared to her and her sister and brother, shortly after her death. They were quarrelling together, and her mother's head and shoulders appeared up near the ceiling, and she said they were to love one another. And sometimes when Bessie was walking along the street she felt a coolness and knew that a spirit was beside her. But the laundress said, "All right, go ahead, then, if you want to," to the empty air and, since there wasn't room for both of them, let the spirit precede her through the pantry. She even knew who the spirit was.

IT was now spring on the river, and the river walk was a Chinese scroll which could be unrolled, by people who like to do things in the usual way, from right to left—starting at Gracie Square and walking north. Depicted were:

A hockey game between Loyola and St. Francis de Sales

Five boys shooting baskets on the basketball court

A seagull

An old man sitting on a bench doing columns of figures

A child drawing a track for his toy trains on the pavement with a piece of chalk

A paper drinking cup floating on the troubled surface of the water

A child in pink rompers pushing his own stroller

A woman sitting on a bench alone, with her face lifted to the sun

A Puerto Rican boy with a transistor radio

Two middle-aged women speaking German

A bored and fretful baby, too hot in his perambulator, with nothing to look at or play with, while his nurse reads

The tugboat Chicago pulling a long string of empty barges upstream

A little girl feeding her mother an apple

A helicopter

A kindergarten class, in two sections

Clouds in a blue sky

A flowering cherry tree

Seven freight cars moving imperceptibly, against the tidal current, in the wake of the Herbert E. Smith

A man with a pipe in his mouth and a can of Prince Albert smoking tobacco on the bench beside him

A man sorting his possessions into two canvas bags, one of which contains a concertina

Six very small children playing in the sandpile, under the watchful eyes of their mothers or nursemaids

An oil tanker

A red-haired priest reading a pocket-size New Testament

A man scattering bread crumbs for the pigeons

The Coast Guard cutter CG 40435 turning around just north of the lighthouse and heading back towards Hell Gate Bridge

A sweeper with his bag and a ferruled stick

A little boy pointing a red plastic pistol at his father's head

A pleasure yacht

An airplane

A man and a woman speaking French

A child on a tricycle

A boy on roller skates

A reception under a striped tent on the lawn of the mayor's house

The fireboat station

The Franklin Delano Roosevelt Drive, a cinder path, a warehouse, seagulls, and so on

Who said *Happiness is the light shining on the water. The water is cold and dark and deep. . . .*

"IT'S perfectly insane," George said when he met Iris coming from Gristede's with a big brown paper bag heavy as lead under each arm and relieved her of them. "Don't we still have that cart?"

"Nobody in the building uses them."

"But couldn't you?"

"No," Iris said.

"ALL children," Cindy said wisely, leaning against him, with her head in the hollow of his neck, "all children think their mommy and daddy are the nicest."

"And what about you? Are you satisfied?"

She gave him a hug and a kiss and said, "I think you and Mommy are the nicest mommy and daddy in the whole world."

"And I think you are the nicest Cindy," he said, his eyes moist with tears.

They sat and rocked each other gently.

. . .

AFTER Bessie had taken the breakfast dishes out of the dishwasher, she went into the front, dragging the vacuum cleaner, to do the children's rooms. She stood sometimes for five or ten minutes, looking down at East End Avenue—at the drugstore, the luncheonette, the rival cleaning establishments (side by side and, according to rumor, both owned by the same person), the hairstyling salon, and the branch office of the Chase Manhattan Bank. Together they made a canvas backdrop for a procession of people Bessie had never seen before, or would not recognize if she had, and so she couldn't say to herself, "There goes old Mrs. Maltby," but she looked anyway, she took it all in. The sight of other human beings nourished her mind. She read them as people read books. Pieces of toys, pieces of puzzles that she found on the floor she put on one shelf or another of the toy closet in Cindy's room, gradually introducing a disorder that Iris dealt with periodically, taking a whole day out of her life. But nobody told Bessie she was supposed to find the box the piece came out of, and it is questionable whether she could have anyway. The thickness of the lenses in her eyeglasses suggested that her eyesight was poorer than she let on.

She was an exile, far from home, among people who were not like the white people she knew and understood. She was here because down home she was getting forty dollars a week and she had her old age to think of. She and Iris alternated between irritation at one another and sudden acts of kindness. It was the situation that was at fault. Given halfway decent circumstances, men can work cheerfully and happily for other men, in offices, stores, and even factories. And so can women. But if Iris opened the cupboard or the icebox to see what they did or didn't contain, Bessie popped out of her room and said, "Did you want something?" And Iris withdrew, angry because she had been driven out of her own kitchen. In her mind, Bessie always thought of the Carringtons as "my people," but until she had taught them to think of themselves as her people her profound capacity for devotion would go unused; would not even be suspected.

You can say that life is a fountain if you want to, but what it more nearly resembles is a jack-in-the-box.

HALF awake, he heard the soft whimpering that meant Iris was having a nightmare, and he shook her. "I dreamt you were having a heart attack," she said.

"Should you be dreaming that?" he said. But the dream was still too real to be joked about. They were in a public place. And he couldn't be moved.

He didn't die, and she consulted with doctors. Though the dream did not progress, she could not extricate herself from it but went on and on, feeling the appropriate emotions but in a circular way. Till finally the sounds she made in her sleep brought about her deliverance.

THE conversation at the other end of the hall continued steadily—not loud but enough to keep them from sleeping, and he had already spoken to the children once. So he got up and went down the hall. Laurie and Cindy were both in their bathroom, and Cindy was sitting on the toilet. "I have a stomach ache," she said.

He started to say, "You need to do bizz," and then remembered that the time before she had been sitting on the toilet doing just that.

"And I feel dizzy," Laurie said.

"I heard it," Iris said as he got back into bed.

"That's why she was so pale yesterday."

And half an hour later, when he got up again, Iris did too. To his surprise. Looking as if she had lost her last friend. So he took her in his arms.

"I hate everything," she said.

ON the top shelf of his clothes closet he keeps all sorts of things—the overflow of phonograph records, and the photograph albums, which are too large for the bookcases in the living room. The snapshots show nothing but joy. Year after year of it.

ON the stage of the school auditorium, girls from Class Eight, in pastel-colored costumes and holding arches of crêpe-paper flowers, made a tunnel from the front of the stage to the rear right-hand corner. The pianist took her hands from the keys, and the headmistress, in sensible navy blue, with her hair cut short like a man's, announced, "Class B becomes Class One."

Twenty very little girls in white dresses marched up on the stage two by two, holding hands.

George and Iris Carrington turned to each other and smiled, for Cindy was among them, looking proud and happy as she hurried through the tunnel of flowers and out of sight.

"Class One becomes Class Two." Another wave of little girls left their place in the audience and went up on the stage and disappeared into the wings.

"Class Two becomes Class Three."

Laurie Carrington, her red hair shining from the hairbrush, rose from her seat with the others and started up on the stage.

"It's too much!" George said, under his breath.

Class Three became Class Four, Class Four became Class Five, Class Five became Class Six, and George Carrington took a handkerchief out of his right hip pocket and wiped his eyes. It was their eagerness that undid him. Their absolute trust in the Arrangements. Class Six became Class Seven, Class Seven became Class Eight. The generations of man, growing up, growing old, dying in order to make room for more.

"Class Eight becomes Class Nine, and is now in the Upper School," the headmistress said, triumphantly. The two girls at the front ducked and went under the arches, taking their crêpe-paper flowers with them. And then the next two, and the next, and finally the audience was left applauding an empty stage.

"COME here and sit on my lap," he said, by no means sure Laurie would think it worth the trouble. But she came. Folding her onto his lap, he was aware of the length of her legs, and the difference of her body; the babyness had departed forever, and when he was affectionate with her it was always as if the moment were slightly out of focus; he felt a restraint. He worried lest it be too close to making love to her. The difference was not great, and he was not sure whether it existed at all.

"Would you like to hear a riddle?" she asked.

"All right."

"Who was the fastest runner in history?"

"I don't know," he said, smiling at her. "Who was?"

"Adam. He was the first in the human race. . . . Teeheeheeheehee, wasn't that a good one?"

WAKING in the night, Cindy heard her mother and father laughing behind the closed door of their room. It was a sound she liked to hear, and she turned over and went right back to sleep.

"WHAT was that?"

He raised his head from the pillow and listened.

"Somebody crying 'Help!' " Iris said.

He got up and went to the window. There was no one in the street except a taxi-driver brushing out the back seat of his hack. Again he heard it. Somebody being robbed. Or raped. Or murdered.

"Help . . ." Faintly this time. And not from the direction of the park. The taxi-driver did not look up at the sound, which must be coming from inside a building somewhere. With his face to the window, George waited for the sound to come again and it didn't. Nothing but silence. If he called the police, what could he say? He got back into bed and lay there, sick with horror, his knees shaking. In the morning maybe the *Daily News* would have what happened.

But he forgot to buy a *News* on his way to work, and days passed, and he no longer was sure what night it was that they heard the voice crying "Help!" and felt that he ought to go through weeks of the *News* until he found out what happened. If it was in the *News*. And if something happened.

(1974)

BASTER

T HE recipe came in the mail:

> Mix semen of three men.
> Stir vigorously.
> Fill turkey baster.
> Recline.
> Insert nozzle.
> Squeeze.
>
> Ingredients:
> 1 pinch Stu Wadsworth
> 1 pinch Jim Freeson
> 1 pinch Wally Mars

There was no return address but Tomasina knew who had sent it: Diane, her best friend and, recently, fertility specialist. Ever since Tomasina's latest catastrophic breakup, Diane had been promoting what they referred to as Plan B. Plan A they'd been working on for some time. It involved love and a wedding. They'd been working on Plan A for a good eight years. But in the final analysis—and this was Diane's whole point—Plan A had proved much too idealistic. So now they were giving Plan B a look.

Plan B was more devious and inspired, less romantic, more solitary, sadder, but braver, too. It stipulated borrowing a man with decent teeth, body, and brains, free of the major diseases, who was willing to heat himself up with private fantasies (they didn't have to include Tomasina) in order to bring off the tiny sputter that was indispensable to the grand achievement of having a baby. Like twin Schwarzkopfs, the two friends noted how the field of battle had changed of late: the reduction in their artillery (they'd both just turned forty); the increasing guerrilla tactics of the enemy (men didn't even come out into the open anymore); and the complete dissolution of the code of honor. The last man who'd got Tomasina pregnant—not the boutique investment banker, the one before him, the Alexander Technique instructor—hadn't even gone through the motions of proposing marriage. His idea of honor had been to split the cost of the abortion. There was no sense denying it: the finest soldiers had quit the field, joining the peace of marriage. What was left was a ragtag gang of adulterers and losers, hit-and-run types, village-burners. Tomasina had to give up the idea of meeting someone she could spend her life with. Instead, she had to give birth to someone who would spend life with her.

But it wasn't until she received the recipe that Tomasina realized she was desperate enough to go ahead. She knew it before she'd even stopped laughing. She knew it when she found herself thinking, Stu Wadsworth I could maybe see. But Wally Mars?

TOMASINA—I repeat, like a ticking clock—was forty. She had pretty much everything she wanted in life. She had a great job as an assistant producer of the "CBS Evening News with Dan Rather." She had a terrific, adult-sized apartment on Hudson Street. She had good looks, mostly intact. Her breasts weren't untouched by time, but they were holding their own. And she had new teeth. She had a set of gleaming new bonded teeth. They'd whistled at first, before she got used to them, but now they were fine. She had biceps. She had an I.R.A. kicked up to a hundred and seventy-five thousand dollars. But she didn't have a baby. Not having a husband she could take. Not having a husband was, in some respects, preferable. But she wanted a baby.

"After thirty-five," the magazine said, "a woman begins to have trouble conceiving." Tomasina couldn't believe it. Just when she got her head on straight, her body started falling apart. Nature didn't give a damn about her maturity level. Nature wanted her to marry her college boyfriend. In fact, from a purely reproductive standpoint, nature would have preferred that she marry her *high-school* boyfriend. While Tomasina had been going on about her life, she hadn't noticed it: the eggs pitching themselves into oblivion, month by month. She saw it all now. While she canvassed for RIPIRG in college, her uterine walls had been thinning. While she got her journalism degree, her ovaries had cut estrogen production. And while she slept with as many men as she wanted, her fallopian tubes had begun to narrow, to clog. *During her twenties.* That extended period of American childhood. The time when, educated and employed, she could finally have some fun. Tomasina once had five orgasms with a cabdriver named Ignacio Veranes while parked on Gansevoort Street. He had a bent, European-style penis and smelled like flan. Tomasina was twenty-five at the time. She wouldn't do it again, but she was glad she'd done it then. So as not to have regrets. But in eliminating some regrets you create others. She'd only been in her twenties. She'd been playing around was all. But the twenties become the thirties, and a few failed relationships put you at thirty-five, when one day you pick up *Mirabella* and read, "After thirty-five, a woman's fertility begins to decrease. With each year, the proportion of miscarriages and birth defects rises."

It had risen for five years now. Tomasina was forty years one month and fourteen days old. And panicked, and sometimes not panicked. Sometimes perfectly calm and accepting about the whole thing.

She thought about them, the little children she never had. They were lined at the windows of a ghostly school bus, faces pressed against the glass, huge-eyed, moist-lashed. They looked out, calling, "We understand. It wasn't the right time. We understand. We *do.*"

The bus shuddered away, and she saw the driver. He raised one bony hand to the gearshift, turning to Tomasina as his face split open in a smile.

The magazine also said that miscarriages happened all the time, without a woman's even noticing. Tiny blastulas scraped against the womb's walls and, finding no purchase, hurtled downward through the plumbing, human and otherwise. Maybe they stayed alive in the toilet bowl for a few seconds, like goldfish. She didn't know. But with three abortions, one official miscarriage, and who knows how many unofficial ones, Tomasina's school bus was full. When she awoke at night, she saw it slowly pulling away from the curb, and she heard the noise of the children packed in their seats, that cry of children indistinguishable between laughter and scream.

EVERYONE knows that men objectify women. But none of our sizing up of breasts and legs can compare with the cold-blooded calculation of a woman in the market for semen. Tomasina was a little taken aback by it herself, and yet she couldn't help it: once she made her decision, she began to see men as walking spermatozoa. At parties, over glasses of Barolo (soon to be giving it up, she drank like a fish), Tomasina examined the specimens who came out of the kitchen, or loitered in the hallways, or held forth from the armchairs. And sometimes, her eyes misting, she felt that she could discern the quality of each man's genetic material. Some semen auras glowed with charity; others were torn with enticing holes of savagery; still others flickered and dimmed with substandard voltage. Tomasina could ascertain health by a guy's smell or complexion. Once, to amuse Diane, she'd ordered every male party guest to stick out his tongue. The men had obliged, asking no questions. Men always oblige. Men *like* being objectified. They thought that their tongues were being inspected for nimbleness, toward the prospect of oral abilities. "Open up and say ah," Tomasina kept commanding, all night long. And the tongues unfurled for display. Some had yellow spots or irritated taste buds, others were blue as spoiled beef. Some performed lewd acrobatics, flicking up and down or curling upward to reveal spikes depending from their undersides like the antennae of deep-sea fish. And then there were two or three that looked perfect, opalescent as oysters and enticingly plump. These were the tongues of the married men, who'd already donated their semen—in abundance—to the lucky women taxing the sofa cushions across the room. The wives and mothers who were nursing other complaints by now, of insufficient sleep and stalled careers—complaints that to Tomasina were desperate wishes.

AT this point, I should introduce myself. I'm Wally Mars. I'm an old friend of Tomasina's. Actually, I'm an old boyfriend. We went out for three months and seven days in the spring of 1985. At the time, most of Tomasina's friends were surprised that she was dating me. They said what she did when she saw my name on the ingredient list. They said, "Wally Mars?" I was considered too short (I'm only five feet four), and not athletic enough. Tomasina loved me, though. She was crazy about me for a while. Some dark hook in our brains, which no one could see, linked us up. She used to sit across the table, tapping it and saying, "What else?" She liked to hear me talk.

    She still did. Every few weeks she called to invite me to lunch. And I always went. At the time all this happened, we made a date for a Friday. When I got to the restaurant, Tomasina was already there. I stood behind the hostess station for a moment, looking at her from a distance and getting ready. She was lounging back in her chair, sucking the life out of the first of the three cigarettes she allowed herself at lunch. Above her head, on a ledge, an enormous flower arrangement exploded into bloom. Have you noticed? Flowers have gone multicultural, too. Not a single rose, tulip, or daffodil lifted its head from the vase. Instead, jungle flora erupted: Amazonian orchids, Sumatran flytraps. The jaws of one flytrap trembled, stimulated by Tomasina's perfume. Her hair was thrown back over her bare shoulders.

She wasn't wearing a top—no, she was. It was flesh-colored and skintight. Tomasina doesn't exactly dress corporate, unless you could call a brothel a kind of corporation. What she has to display was on display. (It was on display every morning for Dan Rather, who had a variety of nicknames for Tomasina, all relating to Tabasco sauce.) Somehow, though, Tomasina got away with her chorus-girl outfits. She toned them down with her maternal attributes: her homemade lasagna, her hugs and kisses, her cold remedies.

At the table, I received both a hug and kiss. "Hi, hon!" she said, and pressed herself against me. Her face was all lit up. Her left ear, inches from my cheek, was a flaming pink. I could feel its heat. She pulled away and we looked at each other.

"So," I said. "Big news."

"I'm going to do it, Wally. I'm going to have a baby."

We sat down. Tomasina took a drag on her cigarette, then funnelled her lips to the side, expelling smoke.

"I just figured, Fuck it," she said. "I'm forty. I'm an adult. I can do this." I wasn't used to her new teeth. Every time she opened her mouth it was like a flashbulb going off. They looked good, though, her new teeth. "I don't care what people think. People either get it or they don't. I'm not going to raise it all by myself. My sister's going to help. And Diane. You can babysit, too, Wally, if you want."

"Me?"

"You can be an uncle." She reached across the table and squeezed my hand. I squeezed back.

"I hear you've got a list of candidates on a recipe," I said.

"What?"

"Diane told me she sent you a recipe."

"Oh, that." She inhaled. Her cheeks hollowed out.

"And I was on it or something?"

"Old boyfriends." Tomasina exhaled upward. "All my old boyfriends."

Just then the waiter arrived to take our drink order.

Tomasina was still gazing up at her spreading smoke. "Martini up very dry two olives," she said. Then she looked at the waiter. She kept looking. "It's Friday," she explained. She ran her hand through her hair, flipping it back. The waiter smiled.

"I'll have a Martini, too," I said.

The waiter turned and looked at me. His eyebrows rose and then he turned back to Tomasina. He smiled again and went off.

As soon as he was gone, Tomasina leaned across the table to whisper in my ear. I leaned, too. Our faces touched. And then she said, "What about him?"

"Who?"

"Him."

She indicated with her head. Across the restaurant, the waiter's tensed buns retreated, dipping and weaving.

"He's a *waiter.*"

"I'm not going to marry him, Wally. I just want his sperm."

"Maybe he'll bring some out as a side dish."

Tomasina sat back, stubbing out her cigarette. She pondered me from a distance, then reached for cigarette No. 2. "Are you going to get all hostile again?"

"I'm not being hostile."

"Yes, you are. You were hostile when I told you about this and you're acting hostile now."

"I just don't know why you want to pick the waiter."

She shrugged. "He's cute."

"You can do better."

"Where?"

"I don't know. A lot of places." I picked up my soup spoon. I saw my face in it, tiny and distorted. "Go to a sperm bank. Get a Nobel Prize winner."

"I don't just want smart. Brains aren't everything." Tomasina squinted, sucking in smoke, then looked off dreamily. "I want the whole package."

I didn't say anything for a minute. I picked up my menu. I read the words "Fricassée de Lapereau" nine times. What was bothering me was this: the state of nature. It was becoming clear to me—clearer than ever—what my status was in the state of nature: it was low. It was somewhere around hyena. This wasn't the case, as far as I knew, back in civilization. I'm a catch, pragmatically speaking. I make a lot of money, for one thing. *My* I.R.A. is pumped up to two hundred and fifty-four thousand dollars. But money doesn't count, apparently, in the selection of semen. The waiter's tight buns counted for more.

"You're against the idea, aren't you?" Tomasina said.

"I'm not *against* it. I just think, if you're going to have a baby, it's best if you do it with somebody else. Who you're in love with." I looked up at her. "And who loves you."

"That'd be great. But it's not happening."

"How do you know?" I said. "You might fall in love with somebody tomorrow. You might fall in love with somebody six months from now." I looked away, scratching my cheek. "Maybe you've already met the love of your life and don't even know it." Then I looked back into her eyes. "And then you realize it. And it's too late. There you are. With some stranger's baby."

Tomasina was shaking her head. "I'm forty, Wally. I don't have much time."

"I'm forty, too," I said. "What about me?"

She looked at me closely, as though detecting something in my tone, then dismissed it with a wave. "You're a man. You've got time."

AFTER lunch, I walked the streets. The restaurant's glass door launched me into the gathering Friday evening. It was four-thirty and already getting dark in the caverns of Manhattan. From a striped chimney buried in the asphalt, steam shot up into the air. A few tourists were standing around it, making low Swedish sounds, amazed by our volcanic streets. I stopped to watch the steam, too. I was thinking about exhaust, anyway, smoke and exhaust. That school bus of Tomasina's? Looking out one window was my kid's face. *Our* kid's. We'd been going out three months when Tomasina got pregnant. She went home to New Jersey to discuss it with her parents and returned three days later, having had an abortion. We broke up shortly after that. So I sometimes thought of him, or her, my only actual, snuffed-out offspring. I thought about him right then. What would the kid have looked like? Like me, with buggy eyes and potato nose? Or like Tomasina? Like her, I decided. With any luck, the kid would look like her.

FOR the next few weeks I didn't hear anything more. I tried to put the whole subject out of my mind. But the city wouldn't let me. Instead, the city began filling with babies. I saw them in elevators and lobbies and out on the sidewalk. I saw them straitjacketed into car seats, drooling and ranting. I saw babies in the park, on leashes. I saw them on the subway, gazing at me with sweet, gummy eyes over the shoulders of Dominican nannies. New York was no place to be having babies. So why was everybody having them? Every fifth person on the street toted a pouch containing a bonneted larva. They looked like they needed to go back inside the womb.

Mostly you saw them with their mothers. I always wondered who the fathers were. What did they look like? How big were they? Why did they have a kid and I didn't? One night I saw a whole Mexican family camping out in a subway car. Two small children tugged at the mother's sweatpants while the most recent arrival, a caterpillar wrapped in a leaf, suckled at the wineskin of her breast. And across from them, holding the bedding and the diaper bag, the progenitor sat with open legs. No more than thirty, small, squat, paint-spattered, with the broad flat face of an Aztec. An ancient face, a face of stone, passed down through the centuries into those overalls, this hurtling train, this moment.

The invitation came five days later. It sat quietly in my mailbox amid bills and catalogues. I noticed Tomasina's return address and ripped the envelope open.

On the front of the invitation a champagne bottle foamed out the words:

nant!

preg

ting

get

I'm

Inside, cheerful green type announced, "On Saturday, April 13, Come Celebrate Life!"

The date, I learned afterward, had been figured precisely. Tomasina had used a basal thermometer to determine her times of ovulation. Every morning before getting out of bed, she took her resting temperature and plotted the results on a graph. She also inspected her underpants on a daily basis. A clear, albumeny discharge meant that her egg had dropped. She had a calendar on the refrigerator, studded with red stars. She was leaving nothing to chance.

I thought of cancelling. I toyed with fictitious business trips and tropical diseases. I didn't want to go. I didn't want there to be parties like this. I asked myself if I was jealous or just conservative and decided both. And then, of course, in the end, I did go. I went to keep from sitting at home thinking about it.

TOMASINA had lived in the same apartment for eleven years. But when I got there that night it looked completely different. The familiar speckled pink carpeting, like a runner of olive loaf, led up from the lobby, past the same dying plant on the landing, to the yellow door that used to open to my key. The same mezuzah, forgotten by the previous tenants, was still tacked over the threshold. According to the brass marker, 2-A, this was still the same high-priced one-bedroom I'd spent ninety-eight consecutive nights in almost ten years ago. But when I knocked and then pushed open the door I didn't recognize it. The only light came from candles scattered around the living room. While my eyes adjusted, I groped my way along the wall to the closet—it was right where it used to be—and hung up my coat. There was a candle burning on a nearby chest, and, taking a closer look, I began to get some idea of the direction Tomasina and Diane had gone with the party decorations. Though inhumanly large, the candle was nevertheless an exact replica of the male member in proud erection, the detailing almost hyperrealistic, right down to the tributaries of veins and the sandbar of the scrotum. The phallus's fiery tip illuminated two other objects on the table: a clay facsimile of an ancient Canaanite fertility goddess of the type sold at feminist bookstores and New Age emporiums, her womb domed, her breasts bursting; and a package of Love incense, bearing the silhouette of an entwined couple.

I stood there as my pupils dilated. Slowly the room bodied forth. There were a lot of people, maybe as many as seventy-five. It looked like a Halloween party. Women who all year secretly wanted to dress sexy *had* dressed sexy. They wore low-cut bunny tops or witchy gowns with slits up the side. Quite a few were stroking the candles provocatively or fooling around with the hot wax. But they weren't young. Nobody was young. The men looked the way men have generally looked for the past twenty years: uncomfortable yet agreeable. They looked like me.

Champagne bottles were going off, just like on the invitation. After every pop a woman would shout, "Ooops, I'm pregnant!" and everyone would laugh. Then I did recognize something: the music. It was Jackson Browne. One of the things I used to find endearing about Tomasina was her anti-quated and sentimental record collection. She still had it. I could remember dancing to this very album with her. Late one night, we just took off our clothes and started dancing all alone. It was one of those spontaneous living-room dances you have at the beginning of a relationship. On a hemp rug we twirled each other around, naked and graceless in secret, and it never happened again. I stood there, remembering, until someone came up from behind.

"Hey, Wally."

I squinted. It was Diane.

"Just tell me," I said, "that we don't have to watch."

"Relax. It's totally PG. Tomasina's going to do it later. After everybody's gone."

"I can't stay long," I said, looking around the room.

"You should see the baster we got. Four ninety-five, on sale at Macy's basement."

"I'm meeting someone later for a drink."

"We got the donor cup there, too. We couldn't find anything with a lid. So we ended up getting this plastic toddler's cup. Roland already filled it up."

Something was in my throat. I swallowed.

"Roland?"

"He came early. We gave him a choice between a *Hustler* and a *Penthouse.*"

"I'll be careful what I drink from the refrigerator."

"It isn't in the refrigerator. It's under the sink in the bathroom. I was worried somebody *would* drink it."

"Don't you have to freeze it?"

"We're using it in an hour. It keeps."

I nodded, for some reason. I was beginning to be able to see clearly now. I could see all the family photographs on the mantel. Tomasina and her dad. Tomasina and her mom. The whole Genovese clan up in an oak tree. And then I said, "Call me old-fashioned but . . ." and trailed off.

"Relax, Wally. Have some champagne. It's a party."

The bar had a bartender. I waved off the champagne and asked for a glass of Scotch, straight. While I waited, I scanned the room for Tomasina. Out loud, though pretty quietly, I said, with bracing sarcasm, "Roland." That was just the kind of name it would have to be. Someone out of a medieval epic. "The Sperm of Roland." I was getting whatever enjoyment I could out of this when suddenly I heard a deep voice somewhere above me say, "Were you talking to me?" I looked up, not into the sun, exactly, but into its anthropomorphic representation. He was both blond *and* orange, and large, and the candle behind him on the bookshelf lit up his mane like a halo.

"Have we met? I'm Roland DeMarchelier."

"I'm Wally Mars," I said. "I thought that might be you. Diane pointed you out to me."

"Everybody's pointing me out. I feel like some kind of prize hog," he said, smiling. "My wife just informed me that we're leaving. I managed to negotiate for one more drink."

"You're married?"

"Seven years."

"And she doesn't mind?"

"Well, she *didn't*. Right now I'm not so sure."

What can I say about his face? It was open. It was a face used to being looked at, looked into, without flinching. His skin was a healthy apricot color. His eyebrows, also apricot, were shaggy like an old poet's. They saved his face from being too boyish. It was this face Tomasina had looked at. She'd looked at it and said, "You're hired."

"My wife and I have two kids. We had trouble getting pregnant the first time, though. So we know how it can be. The anxiety and the timing and everything."

"Your wife must be a very open-minded woman," I said. Roland narrowed his eyes, making a sincerity check—he wasn't stupid, obviously (Tomasina had probably unearthed his S.A.T. scores). Then he gave me the benefit of the doubt. "She says she's flattered. I know I am."

"I used to go out with Tomasina," I said. "We used to live together."
"Really?"
"We're just friends now."
"It's good when that happens."
"She wasn't thinking about babies back when we went out," I said.
"That's how it goes. You think you have all the time in the world. Then boom. You find you don't."
"Things might have been different," I said. Roland looked at me again, not sure how to take my comment, and then looked across the room. He smiled at someone and held up his drink. Then he was back to me. "That didn't work. My wife wants to go." He set down his glass and turned to leave. "Nice to meet you, Wally."

"Keep on plugging," I said, but he didn't hear me, or pretended not to.
I'd already finished my drink, so I got a refill. Then I went in search of Tomasina. I shouldered my way across the room and squeezed down the hall. I stood up straight, showing off my suit. A few women looked at me, then away. Tomasina's bedroom door was closed, but I still felt entitled to open it.

She was standing by the window, smoking and looking out. She didn't hear me come in, and I didn't say anything. I just stood there, looking at her. What kind of dress should a girl wear to her Insemination Party? Answer: The one Tomasina had on. This wasn't skimpy, technically. It began at her neck and ended at her ankles. Between those two points, however, an assortment of peepholes had been ingeniously razored into the fabric, revealing a patch of thigh here, a glazed hipbone there; up above, the white sideswell of a breast. It made you think of secret orifices and dark canals. I counted the shining patches of skin. I had two hearts, one up, one down, both pumping.

And then I said, "I just saw Secretariat."
She swung around. She smiled, though not quite convincingly. "Isn't he gorgeous?"
"I still think you should have gone with Isaac Asimov." She came over and we kissed cheeks. I kissed hers, anyway. Tomasina kissed mostly air. She kissed my semen aura.
"Diane says I should forget the baster and just sleep with him."
"He's married."
"They all are." She paused. "You know what I mean."
I made no sign that I did. "What are you doing in here?" I asked.
She took two rapid-fire puffs on her cigarette, as though to fortify herself. Then she answered, "Freaking out."
"What's the matter?"
She covered her face with her hand. "This is depressing, Wally. This isn't

how I wanted to have a baby. I thought this party would make it fun, but it's just depressing." She dropped her hand and looked into my eyes. "Do you think I'm crazy? You do, don't you?"

Her eyebrows went up, pleading. Did I tell you about Tomasina's freckle? She has this freckle on her lower lip like a piece of chocolate. Everybody's always trying to wipe it off.

"I don't think you're crazy, Tom," I said.

"You don't?"

"No."

"Because I trust you, Wally. You're mean, so I trust you."

"What do you mean I'm mean?"

"Not bad mean. Good mean. I'm not crazy?"

"You want to have a baby. It's natural."

Suddenly Tomasina leaned forward and rested her head on my chest. She had to lean down to do it. She closed her eyes and let out a long sigh. I put my hand on her back. My fingers found a peephole and I stroked her bare skin. In a warm, thoroughly grateful voice, she said, "You get it, Wally. You totally get it."

She stood up and smiled. She looked down at her dress, adjusting it so that her navel showed, and then took my arm.

"Come on," she said. "Let's go back to the party."

I didn't expect what happened next. When we came out, everybody cheered. Tomasina held onto my arm and we started waving to the crowd like a couple of royals. For a minute I forgot about the purpose of the party. I just stood arm in arm with Tomasina, and accepted the applause. When the cheers died down, I noticed that Jackson Browne was still playing. I leaned over and whispered to Tomasina, "Remember dancing to this song?"

"Did we dance to this?"

"You don't remember?"

"I've had this album forever. I've probably danced to it a thousand times." She broke off. She let go of my arm.

My glass was empty again.

"Can I ask you something, Tomasina?"

"What?"

"Do you ever think about you and me?"

"Wally, don't." She turned away and looked at the floor. After a moment, in a reedy, nervous voice, she said, "I was really screwed up back then. I don't think I could have stayed with anybody."

I nodded. I swallowed. I told myself not to say the next thing. I looked over at the fireplace, as though it interested me, and then I said it: "Do you ever think about our kid?"

The only sign that she'd heard me was a twitch next to her left eye. She took a deep breath, let it out. "That was a long time ago."

"I know. It's just that when I see you going to all this trouble I think it could be different sometimes."

"I don't think so, Wally." She picked a piece of lint off the shoulder of my jacket, frowning. Then she tossed it away. "God! Sometimes I wish I was Benazir Bhutto or somebody."

"You want to be Prime Minister of Pakistan?"

"I want a nice, simple, arranged marriage. Then after my husband and I sleep together he can go off and play polo."

"You'd like that?"

"Of course not. That would be horrible." A tress fell into her eyes and she backhanded it into place. She looked around the room. Then she straightened up and said, "I should mingle."

I held up my glass. "Be fruitful and multiply," I said. And Tomasina squeezed my arm and was gone.

I stayed where I was, drinking from my empty glass to have something to do. I looked around the room for any women I hadn't met. There weren't any. Over at the bar, I switched to champagne. I had the bartender fill my glass three times. Her name was Julie and she was majoring in art history at Columbia University. While I was standing there, Diane stepped into the middle of the room and clinked her glass. Other people followed and the room got quiet.

"First of all," Diane began, "Before we kick everyone out of here, I'd like to make a toast to tonight's oh-so-generous donor, Roland. We conducted a nationwide search and, let me tell you, the auditions were gruelling." Everybody laughed. Somebody shouted, "Roland left."

"He left? Well, we'll toast his semen. We've still got that." More laughter, a few drunken cheers. Some people, men and women both now, were picking up the candles and waving them around.

"And, finally," Diane went on, "finally, I'd like to toast our soon-to-be-expecting—knock on wood—mother. Her courage in seizing the means of production is an inspiration to us all." They were pulling Tomasina out onto the floor now. People were hooting. Tomasina's hair was falling down. She was flushed and smiling. I tapped Julie on the arm, extending my glass. Everyone was looking at Tomasina when I turned and slipped into the bathroom.

After shutting the door, I did something I don't usually do. I stood and looked at myself in the mirror. I stopped doing that, for any prolonged period, at least twenty years ago. Staring into mirrors was best at around thirteen. But that night I did it again. In Tomasina's bathroom, where we'd once showered and flossed together, in that cheerful, brightly tiled grotto, I presented myself to myself. You know what I was thinking? I was thinking about nature. I was thinking about hyenas again. The hyena, I remembered, is a fierce predator. Hyenas even attack lions on occasion. They aren't much to look at, hyenas, but they do O.K. for themselves. And so I lifted my glass. I lifted my glass and toasted myself: "Be fruitful and multiply."

The cup was right where Diane had said it would be. Roland had placed it, with priestly care, on top of a bag of cotton balls. The toddler cup sat enthroned on a little cloud. I opened it and inspected his offering. It barely covered the bottom of the cup, a yellowish scum. It looked like rubber cement. It's terrible, when you think about it. It's terrible that women need this stuff. It's so *paltry*. It must make them crazy, having everything they need to create life but this one meagre leaven. I rinsed Roland's out under the faucet. Then I checked to see that the door was locked. I didn't want anybody to burst in on me.

THAT was ten months ago. Shortly after, Tomasina got pregnant. She swelled to immense proportions. I was away on business when she gave birth in the care of a midwife at St. Vincent's. But I was back in time to receive the announcement:

> Tomasina Genovese proudly announces
> the birth of her son,
> Joseph Mario Genovese,
> on January 15, 1996.
> 5 lbs. 3 oz.

The small size alone was enough to clinch it. Nevertheless, bringing a Tiffany spoon to the little heir the other day, I settled the question as I looked down into his crib. The potato nose. The buggy eyes. I'd waited ten years to see that face at the school-bus window. Now that I did, I could only wave goodbye.

(1996)

THE SECOND TREE FROM THE CORNER

E VER have any bizarre thoughts?" asked the doctor.
Mr. Trexler failed to catch the word. "What kind?" he said.

"Bizarre," repeated the doctor, his voice steady. He watched his patient for any slight change of expression, any wince. It seemed to Trexler that the doctor was not only watching him closely but was creeping slowly toward him, like a lizard toward a bug. Trexler shoved his chair back an inch and gathered himself for a reply. He was about to say "Yes" when he realized that if he said yes the next question would be unanswerable. Bizarre thoughts, bizarre thoughts? Ever have any bizarre thoughts? What kind of thoughts *except* bizarre had he had since the age of two?

Trexler felt the time passing, the necessity for an answer. These psychiatrists were busy men, overloaded, not to be kept waiting. The next patient was probably already perched out there in the waiting room, lonely, worried, shifting around on the sofa, his mind stuffed with bizarre thoughts and amorphous fears. Poor bastard, thought Trexler. Out there all alone in that misshapen antechamber, staring at the filing cabinet and wondering whether to tell the doctor about that day on the Madison Avenue bus.

Let's see, bizarre thoughts. Trexler dodged back along the dreadful corridor of the years to see what he could find. He felt the doctor's eyes upon him and knew that time was running out. Don't be so conscientious, he said to himself. If a bizarre thought is indicated here, just reach into the bag and pick anything at all. A man as well supplied with bizarre thoughts as you are should have no difficulty producing one for the record. Trexler darted into the bag, hung for a moment before one of his thoughts, as a hummingbird pauses in the delphinium. No, he said, not that one. He darted to another (the one about the rhesus monkey), paused, considered. No, he said, not that.

Trexler knew he must hurry. He had already used up pretty nearly four seconds since the question had been put. But it was an impossible situation—just one more lousy, impossible situation such as he was always getting himself into. When, he asked himself, are you going to quit maneuvering yourself into a pocket? He made one more effort. This time he stopped at the asylum, only the bars were lucite—fluted, retractable. Not here, he said. Not this one.

He looked straight at the doctor. "No," he said quietly. "I never have any bizarre thoughts."

The doctor sucked in on his pipe, blew a plume of smoke toward the rows of medical books. Trexler's gaze followed the smoke. He managed to make out one of the titles, "The Genito-Urinary System." A bright wave of fear swept cleanly over him, and he winced under the first pain of kidney stones. He remembered when he was a child, the first time he ever entered a doctor's office, sneaking a look at the titles of the books—and the flush of fear, the shirt wet under the arms, the book on t.b., the sudden knowledge that he was in the advanced stages of consumption, the quick vision of the hemorrhage. Trexler sighed wearily. Forty years, he thought, and I still get thrown by the title of a medical book. Forty years and I still can't stay on life's little bucky horse. No wonder I'm sitting here in this dreary joint at the end of this woebegone afternoon, lying about my bizarre thoughts to a doctor who looks, come to think of it, rather tired.

The session dragged on. After about twenty minutes, the doctor rose and knocked his pipe out. Trexler got up, knocked the ashes out of his brain, and waited. The doctor smiled warmly and stuck out his hand. "There's nothing the matter with you—you're just scared. Want to know how I know you're scared?"

"How?" asked Trexler.

"Look at the chair you've been sitting in! See how it has moved back away from my desk? You kept inching away from me while I asked you questions. That means you're scared."

"Does it?" said Trexler, faking a grin. "Yeah, I suppose it does."

They finished shaking hands. Trexler turned and walked out uncertainly along the passage, then into the waiting room and out past the next patient, a ruddy pin-striped man who was seated on the sofa twirling his hat nervously and staring straight ahead at the files. Poor, frightened guy, thought Trexler, he's probably read in the *Times* that one American male out of every two is going to die of heart disease by twelve o'clock next

Thursday. It says that in the paper almost every morning. And he's also probably thinking about that day on the Madison Avenue bus.

A week later, Trexler was back in the patient's chair. And for several weeks thereafter he continued to visit the doctor, always toward the end of the afternoon, when the vapors hung thick above the pool of the mind and darkened the whole region of the East Seventies. He felt no better as time went on, and he found it impossible to work. He discovered that the visits were becoming routine and that although the routine was one to which he certainly did not look forward, at least he could accept it with cool resignation, as once, years ago, he had accepted a long spell with a dentist who had settled down to a steady fooling with a couple of dead teeth. The visits, moreover, were now assuming a pattern recognizable to the patient.

Each session would begin with a résumé of symptoms—the dizziness in the streets, the constricting pain in the back of the neck, the apprehensions, the tightness of the scalp, the inability to concentrate, the despondency and the melancholy times, the feeling of pressure and tension, the anger at not being able to work, the anxiety over work not done, the gas on the stomach. Dullest set of neurotic symptoms in the world, Trexler would think, as he obediently trudged back over them for the doctor's benefit. And then, having listened attentively to the recital, the doctor would spring his question: "Have you ever found anything that gives you relief?" And Trexler would answer, "Yes. A drink." And the doctor would nod his head knowingly.

As he became familiar with the pattern Trexler found that he increasingly tended to identify himself with the doctor, transferring himself into the doctor's seat—probably (he thought) some rather slick form of escapism. At any rate, it was nothing new for Trexler to identify himself with other people. Whenever he got into a cab, he instantly became the driver, saw everything from the hackman's angle (and the reaching over with the right hand, the nudging of the flag, the pushing it down, all the way down along the side of the meter), saw everything—traffic, fare, everything—through the eyes of Anthony Rocco, or Isidore Freedman, or Matthew Scott. In a barbershop, Trexler was the barber, his fingers curled around the comb, his hand on the tonic. Perfectly natural, then, that Trexler should soon be occupying the doctor's chair, asking the questions, waiting for the answers. He got quite interested in the doctor, in this way. He liked him, and he found him a not too difficult patient.

It was on the fifth visit, about halfway through, that the doctor turned to Trexler and said, suddenly, "What do you want?" He gave the word "want" special emphasis.

"I d'know," replied Trexler uneasily. "I guess nobody knows the answer to that one."

"Sure they do," replied the doctor.

"Do *you* know what *you* want?" asked Trexler narrowly.

"Certainly," said the doctor. Trexler noticed that at this point the doctor's chair slid slightly backward, away from him. Trexler stifled a small, internal smile. Scared as a rabbit, he said to himself. Look at him scoot!

"What *do* you want?" continued Trexler, pressing his advantage, pressing it hard.

The doctor glided back another inch away from his inquisitor. "I want a wing on the small house I own in Westport. I want more money, and more leisure to do the things I want to do."

Trexler was just about to say, "And what are those things you want to do, Doctor?" when he caught himself. Better not go too far, he mused. Better not lose possession of the ball. And besides, he thought, what the hell goes on here, anyway—me paying fifteen bucks a throw for these séances and then doing the work myself, asking the questions, weighing the answers. So he wants a new wing! There's a fine piece of theatrical gauze for you! A new wing.

Trexler settled down again and resumed the role of patient for the rest of the visit. It ended on a kindly, friendly note. The doctor reassured him that his fears were the cause of his sickness, and that his fears were unsubstantial. They shook hands, smiling.

Trexler walked dizzily through the empty waiting room and the doctor followed along to let him out. It was late; the secretary had shut up shop and gone home. Another day over the dam. "Goodbye," said Trexler. He stepped into the street, turned west toward Madison, and thought of the doctor all alone there, after hours, in that desolate hole—a man who worked longer hours than his secretary. Poor, scared, overworked bastard, thought Trexler. And that new wing!

It was an evening of clearing weather, the Park showing green and desirable in the distance, the last daylight applying a high lacquer to the brick and brownstone walls and giving the street scene a luminous and intoxicating splendor. Trexler meditated, as he walked, on what he wanted. "What do you want?" he heard again. Trexler knew what he wanted, and what, in general, all men wanted; and he was glad, in a way, that it was both inexpressible and unattainable, and that it wasn't a wing. He was satisfied to remember that it was deep, formless, enduring, and impossible of fulfillment, and that it made men sick, and that when you sauntered along Third Avenue and looked through the doorways into the dim saloons, you could sometimes pick out from the unregenerate ranks the ones who had not forgotten, gazing steadily into the bottoms of the glasses on the long chance that they could get another little peek at it. Trexler found himself renewed by the remembrance that what he wanted was at once great and microscopic, and that although it borrowed from the nature of large deeds and of youthful love and of old songs and early intimations, it was not any one of these things, and that it had not been isolated or pinned down, and that a man who attempted to define it in the privacy of a doctor's office would fall flat on his face.

Trexler felt invigorated. Suddenly his sickness seemed health, his dizziness stability. A small tree, rising between him and the light, stood there saturated with the evening, each gilt-edged leaf perfectly drunk with excellence and delicacy. Trexler's spine registered an ever so slight tremor as it picked up this natural disturbance in the lovely scene. "I want the second tree from the corner, just as it stands," he said, answering an imaginary question from an imaginary physician. And he felt a slow pride in realizing that what he wanted none could bestow, and that what he had none could take away. He felt content to be sick, unembarrassed at being afraid; and in the jungle of his fear he glimpsed (as he had so often glimpsed them before) the flashy tail feathers of the bird courage.

Then he thought once again of the doctor, and of his being left there all alone, tired, frightened. (The poor, scared guy, thought Trexler.) Trexler began humming "Moonshine Lullaby," his spirit reacting instantly to the hypodermic of Merman's healthy voice. He crossed Madison, boarded a downtown bus, and rode all the way to Fifty-second Street before he had a thought that could rightly have been called bizarre.

(1947)

REMBRANDT'S HAT

R UBIN, in careless white cloth hat or visorless soft round cap, however one described it, wandered with unexpressed or inexpressive thoughts up the stairs from his studio in the basement of a New York art school where he made his sculpture, to a workshop on the second floor, where he taught it. Arkin, the art historian, a hypertensive, impulsive bachelor of thirty-four—a man often swept by strong feeling, he thought—about a dozen years younger than the sculptor, observed him through his open office door, wearing his cap among a crowd of art students and teachers he wandered amid along the hall during a change of classes. In his white hat he stands out and apart, the art historian thought. It illumines a lonely inexpressiveness arrived at after years of experience. Though it was not entirely apt, he imagined a lean white animal—hind, stag, goat?—staring steadfastly, but despondently, through trees of a dense wood. Their gazes momentarily interlocked and parted. Rubin hurried to his workshop class.

Arkin was friendly with Rubin though they were not really friends. Not his fault, he felt; the sculptor was a very private person. When they talked he listened looking away, as though guarding his impressions. Attentive, apparently, he seemed to be thinking of something else—his sad life, no doubt, if saddened eyes, a faded green mistakable for gray, necessarily denote sad life. Once in a while he uttered an opinion—usually a flat statement about the nature of life, or art, never much about himself; and he said absolutely nothing about his work. "Are you working, Rubin?" Arkin was reduced to. "Of course I'm working." "What are you doing, if I may ask?" "I have a thing going."

There Arkin let it lie.

Once, in the faculty cafeteria, listening to the art historian discourse at long length on the work of Jackson Pollock, the sculptor's anger had momentarily flared.

"The world of art ain't necessarily in your eyes."

"I have to believe that what I see is there," Arkin had politely but stiffly responded.

"Have you ever painted?" asked Rubin.

"Painting is my life," retorted Arkin.

Rubin, with dignity, reverted to silence. That evening, leaving the building, they tipped hats to each other over small smiles.

In recent years, after his wife left him and costume and headdress became a mode among students, Rubin had taken to wearing various odd hats from time to time, and this white one was the newest, resembling Nehru's Congress Party cap, but rounded, a cross between a cantor's hat and a bloated yarmulke; or it was perhaps like a French judge's in Rouault, or a working doctor's in a Daumier print. Rubin wore it like a crown. Maybe it kept his head warm under the cold skylight of his large studio.

When the sculptor afterward again passed along the crowded hall on his way down to his studio that day, Arkin, who had been reading a fascinating article on Giacometti, put it down and went quickly into the hall. He was in an ebullient mood he could not explain to himself and told Rubin he very much admired his hat.

"I'll tell you why I like it so much. It looks like Rembrandt's hat that he wears in one of the middle-aged self-portraits, the really profound ones, I think the one in the Rijksmuseum in Amsterdam. May it bring you the best of luck."

Rubin, who had for a moment looked as though he were struggling to say something extraordinary, fixed Arkin in a strong stare and hurried downstairs. That ended the incident, though not the art historian's pleasure in his observation.

Arkin later remembered that when he had come to the art school via an assistant curator's job in a museum in St. Louis seven years ago, Rubin had been working in wood; he now welded triangular pieces of scrap iron to construct his sculptures. Working at one time with a hatchet, later a modified small meat cleaver, he had reshaped driftwood pieces out of which he had created some arresting forms. Dr. Levis, the director of the school, had talked the sculptor into giving an exhibition of his altered driftwood objects in one of the downtown galleries near where Levis lived. Arkin, in his first term at the school, had gone on the subway to see the show one brisk winter's day. This man is an original, he thought; maybe his work will be, too. Rubin had refused a gallery *vernissage* and on the opening day the place was nearly deserted. The sculptor, as though escaping his hacked forms, had retreated into a storage room at the rear of the gallery and stayed there, looking at pictures. Arkin, after reflecting whether he ought to, sought him out to say hello, but seeing Rubin seated on a crate with his back to him, examining a folio of somebody's prints without once turning to see who had come into the room, he silently shut the door and departed. Although in time two notices of the show appeared, one dreadful, the other mildly favorable, the sculptor seemed unhappy about exhibiting his work and hadn't for years. Nor had there been any sales. Recently, when Arkin had casually suggested it might be a good idea to show what he was doing with his welded-iron triangles, Rubin, after a wildly inexpressive moment, had answered, "Don't bother playing around with that idea."

The day after the art historian's remarks in the hall to Rubin about his white cap, it disappeared from sight—gone totally; for a while he wore on his head nothing but his heavy reddish hair. And a week or two later, though he could momentarily not believe it, it seemed to Arkin that the sculptor was actively avoiding him. He guessed the man was no longer using the staircase to the right of his office but was coming up from the basement on the other side of the building, where his corner workshop room was anyway, so he wouldn't have to pass Arkin's open door. When he was certain of this, Arkin felt at first uneasy, then experienced intermittent moments of strong anger.

Have I offended him in some way? the art historian asked himself. If so, what did I say that's so offensive? All I did was remark on the hat in one of Rembrandt's self-portraits and say it looked like the cap he was wearing that day. How can that be so offensive?

He then thought: No offense where none's intended. All I had was good will to him. He's shy and might have been embarrassed in some way— maybe my exuberant voice in the presence of students. If that's so, it's no fault of mine. And if that's not it, I don't know what's the matter other than his nature. Maybe he hasn't been feeling well, or it's some momentary *mishigas*—nowadays there are more ways of insult without meaning to than ever before—so why raise up a sweat over it? I'll wait it out.

But as weeks, then a couple of months went by and Rubin continued to shun the art historian—he saw the sculptor only at faculty meetings when Rubin attended them; and once in a while glimpsed him going up or down the left staircase; or sitting in the Fine Arts secretary's office poring over long inventory lists of supplies for sculpture—Arkin thought, Maybe the man is having a nervous breakdown. He did not believe it. One day they met by chance in the men's room and Rubin strode out without a word. Arkin, incensed, felt for the sculptor surges of hatred. He didn't like people who didn't like him. Here I make a sociable, innocent remark to the son of a bitch—at worst it might be called innocuous—and to him it's an insult. I know the type, I'll give him tit for tat. Two can play.

But when he had calmed down and was reasonable, Arkin continued to wonder and worry over what might have gone wrong. I've always thought I was good in human relationships. He had a worrisome nature and wore a thought ragged if in it lurked a fear the fault was his own. Arkin searched the past. He had always liked the sculptor even though Rubin offered only his fingertip in friendship; yet Arkin had been friendly—courteous, interested in his work, and respectful of his dignity, almost visibly weighted with unspoken thoughts. Had it, he often wondered, something to do with his mentioning—suggesting—not long ago, the possibility of a new exhibition of his sculpture, to which Rubin had reacted as though his life were threatened?

It was then he recalled that he had never told Rubin how he had responded to his hacked driftwood show—never once commented on it, although he had signed the guestbook and the sculptor surely knew he had been there. Arkin hadn't liked the show, yet had wanted to seek Rubin out to name one or two interesting pieces. But when he had located him in the storage room, intently involved with a folio of prints, lost in hangdog introspection so deeply he had been unwilling, or unable, to greet whoever was standing at his back—hiding, really—Arkin had said to himself, better let it be. He had ducked out of the gallery without saying a word. Nor had he mentioned the driftwood exhibition thereafter. Was this kindness cruel? In some cases unsaid things were worse than things said. Something Rubin might think about if he hadn't.

Still it's not very likely he's avoiding me so long after the fact for that alone, Arkin reflected. If he was disappointed, or irritated, or both, by my not mentioning his driftwood show, he would then and there have stopped talking to me if he was going to stop talking. But he didn't. He seemed as friendly as ever, according to his measure, and he isn't a dissembler. And when I afterward suggested the possibility of a new show he obviously wasn't eager to have—which touched him to torment on the spot—he wasn't at all impatient with me but only started staying out of my sight after the business of his white cap, whatever that meant to him. Maybe it wasn't my mention of the cap itself that's annoyed him. Maybe it's a cumulative thing—three minuses for me? Arkin felt it was probably cumulative; still, it seemed that the cap remark had mysteriously wounded Rubin most, because nothing that had happened before had threatened their relationship, such as it was, and it was then at least amicable, pleasant. Having thought it through to this point, Arkin had to admit to himself he did not know why Rubin acted as strangely as he was now acting.

Off and on the art historian considered going down to the basement to the sculptor's studio and there apologizing to him if he had said something inept, which he certainly hadn't meant to do. He would ask Rubin if he'd mind telling him what it was that bothered him; if it was something *else* he had inadvertently said or done, he would apologize for that and clear things up. It would be mutually beneficial. One early spring day he made up his mind to visit Rubin after his seminar that afternoon, but one of his students, a bearded printmaker, had found out it was Arkin's thirty-fifth birthday and presented him with a white ten-gallon Stetson that the student's father, a travelling salesman, had brought back from Waco, Texas.

"Wear it in good health, Mr. Arkin," said the student. "Now you're one of the good guys."

Arkin was wearing the hat going up the stairs to his office, accompanied by the student who had given it to him, when they encountered the sculptor, who grimaced, then glowered in disgust. Arkin was upset, though he felt at once the force of this uncalled-for reaction indicated that, indeed, the hat remark had been taken by Rubin as an insult. After the bearded student left Arkin, he placed the Stetson on his worktable, it had seemed to him, before going to the men's room; and when he returned the cowboy hat was gone. The art historian frantically searched for it in his office and even hurried to his seminar room to see whether it could possibly have landed up there, someone having snatched it as a joke. It was not in the seminar room. Smoldering in resentment, Arkin thought of rushing down and confronting Rubin nose to nose in his studio, but could not bear the thought. What if he hadn't taken it?

Now both of them evaded the other; but after a period of rarely meeting, they began, ironically, Arkin thought, to encounter one another everywhere—even in the streets of various neighborhoods, especially near galleries on Madison or Fifty-seventh or in SoHo, or on entering or leaving movie houses, and on occasion about to go into stores near the art school; each then hastily crossed the street to skirt the other, twice ending up standing close by on the sidewalk. In the art school both refused to serve together on committees. One, if he entered the lavatory and saw the other, stepped outside and remained a distance away till he had left. Each hurried to be first into the basement cafeteria at lunchtime, because when one followed the other in and observed him standing on line at the counter or already eating at a table, alone or in the company of colleagues, invariably he left and had his meal elsewhere. Once, when they came in together they hurriedly departed together. After often losing out to Rubin, who could get to the cafeteria easily from his studio, Arkin began to eat sandwiches in his office. Each had become a greater burden to the other, Arkin felt, than he would have been if only one were doing the shunning. Each was in the other's mind to a degree and extent that bored him. When they met unexpectedly in the building after turning a corner or opening a door, or had come face to face on the stairs, one glanced at the other's head to see what, if anything, adorned it; they then hurried by, or away in opposite directions. Arkin as a rule wore no hat unless he had a cold, then he usually wore a black woollen knit hat all day; and Rubin lately affected a railroad engineer's cap. The art historian felt a growth of repugnance for the other. He hated Rubin for hating him and beheld hatred in Rubin's eyes.

"It's your doing," he heard himself mutter to himself to the other. "You brought me to this, it's on your head."

After hatred came coldness. Each froze the other out of his life; or froze him in.

One early morning, neither looking where he was going as he rushed into the building to his first class, they bumped into each other in front of the arched art-school entrance. Angered, insulted, both started shouting. Rubin, his face flushed, called Arkin murderer, and the art historian retaliated by calling the sculptor thief. Rubin smiled in scorn, Arkin in pity; they then fled.

Afterward in imagination Arkin saw them choking one another. He felt faint and had to cancel his class. His weakness became nausea, so he went home and lay in bed, nursing a severe occipital headache. For a week he slept badly, felt tremors in his sleep; he ate next to nothing. "What has this bastard done to me?" he cried aloud. Later he asked, "What have I done to myseif?" I'm in this against the will, he thought. It had occurred to him that he found it easier to judge paintings than to judge people. A woman had said this to him once, but he had denied it indignantly. Arkin answered neither question and fought off remorse. Then it went through him again that he ought to apologize, if only because if Rubin couldn't he could. Yet he feared an apology would cripple his craw.

HALF a year later, on his thirty-sixth birthday, Arkin, thinking of his lost cowboy hat and having heard from the Fine Arts secretary that Rubin was home sitting shivah for his recently deceased mother, was drawn to the sculptor's studio—a jungle of stone and iron figures—to search for the hat. He found a discarded welder's helmet but nothing he could call a cowboy hat. Arkin spent hours in the large skylighted studio, minutely inspecting the sculptor's work in welded triangular iron pieces, set amid broken stone statuary he had been collecting for years—decorative garden figures placed charmingly among iron flowers seeking daylight. Flowers were what Rubin was mostly into now, on long stalks with small corollas, on short stalks with petalled blooms. Some of the flowers were mosaics of triangles fixing white stones and broken pieces of thick colored glass in jewelled forms. Rubin had in the last several years come from abstract driftwood sculptures to figurative objects—the flowers, and some uncompleted, possibly abandoned, busts of men and women colleagues, including one that vaguely resembled Rubin in a cowboy hat. He had also done a lovely sculpture of a dwarf tree. In the far corner of the studio was a place for his welding torch and gas tanks as well as arc-welding apparatus, crowded by open heavy wooden boxes of iron triangles of assorted size and thickness. The art historian slowly studied each sculpture and after a while thought he understood why talk of a new exhibition had threatened Rubin. There was perhaps one fine piece, the dwarf tree, in the whole iron jungle. Was this what he was afraid he might confess if he fully expressed himself?

Several days later, while preparing a lecture on Rembrandt's self-portraits, Arkin, examining the slides, observed that the portrait of the painter he had remembered as the one he had seen in the Rijksmuseum in Amsterdam was probably hanging in Kenwood House in London. And neither hat the painter wore in either gallery, though both were white, was that much like Rubin's cap. This observation startled the art historian. The Amsterdam portrait was of Rembrandt in a white turban he had wound around his head; the London portrait was him in a studio cap or beret worn slightly cocked. Rubin's white thing looked more like an assistant cook's cap in Sam's Diner than it did like either of Rembrandt's hats in the large oils, or in the other self-portraits Arkin showed himself on slides. What those had in common was the unillusioned honesty of his gaze. In his self-created mirror the painter beheld distance, objectivity, painted to stare out of his right eye; but the left looked out of bedrock, beyond quality. Yet the expression of each of the portraits seemed magisterially sad; or was this what life was if, when Rembrandt painted, he did not paint the sadness?

After studying the pictures projected on the small screen in his dark office, Arkin felt he had, in truth, made a referential error, confusing the hats. Even so, what had Rubin, who no doubt was acquainted with the self-portraits, or may have had a recent look at them—at *what* had he taken offense? Whether I was right or wrong, so what if his white cap made me think of Rembrandt's hat and I told him so? That's not throwing rocks at his head, so what bothered him? Arkin felt he ought to be able to figure it out. Therefore suppose Rubin was Arkin and Arkin Rubin—suppose it was me in his hat: "Here I am an aging sculptor with only one show, which I never had confidence in and nobody saw. And, standing close by, making critical pronouncements one way or another, is this art historian Arkin, a big-nosed, gawky, overcurious gent, friendly but no friend of mine because he doesn't know how to be. That's not his talent. An interest in art we have in common but not much more. Anyway, Arkin, maybe not because it means anything in particular—who says he knows what he means?—mentions Rembrandt's hat on my head and wishes me good luck in my work. So say he meant well—it's still more than I can take. In plain words it irritates me. The mention of Rembrandt, considering the quality of my work and what I am feeling generally about life, is a fat burden on my soul because it makes me ask myself once more—but once too often—why am I going on this way if this is the kind of sculptor I am going to be for the whole rest of my life? And since Arkin makes me think the same unhappy things no matter what he says to me—or even what he doesn't say, as for instance about my driftwood show—who wants to hear more? From then on I avoid the guy—like forever."

Afterward, after staring at himself in the mirror in the men's room, Arkin wandered on every floor of the building and then wandered down to Rubin's studio. He knocked on the door. No one answered. After a moment he tested the knob; it gave, he thrust his head into the room and called Rubin's name. Night lay on the skylight. The studio was lit with many dusty bulbs but Rubin was not present. The forest of iron sculptures was. Arkin went among the iron flowers and broken stone garden pieces to see if he had been wrong in his judgment. After a while he felt he hadn't been.

He was staring at the dwarf tree when the door opened and Rubin, wearing his railroad engineer's cap, in astonishment entered.

"It's a beautiful sculpture," Arkin got out, "the best in the room, I'd say."

Rubin stared at him in flushed anger, his face lean; he had grown long reddish sideburns. His eyes were for once green rather than gray. His mouth worked nervously, but he said nothing.

"Excuse me, Rubin, I came in to tell you I got those hats I mentioned to you some time ago mixed up."

"Damn right you did."

"Also for letting things get out of hand for a while."

"Damn right."

Rubin, though he tried not to, then began to cry. He wept silently, his shoulders shaking, tears seeping through his coarse fingers on his face. Arkin had taken off.

They stopped avoiding each other and spoke pleasantly when they met, which wasn't often. One day, Arkin, when he went into the men's room, saw Rubin regarding himself in the mirror in his white cap, the one that seemed to resemble Rembrandt's hat. He wore it like a crown of failure and hope.

(1973)

SHOT: A NEW YORK STORY

$\int$ HE, Zona, went along the avenues of the East Side of Manhattan, turned up the brownstone side streets of the Seventies and the Nineties on the way to the houses of her group. Once there, she would iron shirts, untangle the vacuum, and at times would be called to put on her black uniform and pass the smoked salmon curling on squares of pumpernickel at cocktail parties. Occasionally, one of the group might see Zona racing up Madison Avenue in the late evening, passing swiftly by the windows where the dresses and scarves and jewelry stood or lay immobile in the anxious night glitter of the high-priced. Zona would, of course, be making her way home, although not one of her people was certain just where that home might be. Somewhere in the grainy, indivisible out-there: area code 718, and what did that signify—the Bronx, Queens? She was tall, very thin; in her black coat, her thick black hair topping her black face, she seemed to be flying with the migratory certainty of some wide-winged black bird.

Her rushing movements were also noticeable about the house. She flew with the dust cloth—swish, swish, swish over the tabletops and a swipe at the windowsills; a splash here and there in the sink; a dash to recover the coat of a not quite sober cocktail guest. Yet, for all this interesting quickness of hand and foot, she was imperturbable, courteous, not given to chatter. And she was impressive; yes, impressive—that was said about Zona. A bit of the nunnery about her, black virgin from some sandy Christian village on the Ivory Coast. So you might say, in a stretch.

A decorator; a partner in an old-print shop; a flute player, female; and a retired classics professor, who liked to sit reading in a wheelchair. To him, Zona would say: Up, up, move, move, and he might spring to his feet or he might not. Such was Zona's group. She had been passed along to them by some forgotten homesteader, perhaps the now dead photographer from *Life*, who took her picture and used it in a spread on Somalia. These random dwellers did not see much of each other, but each had passed through the sponge of Manhattan, where even a more or less reclusive person like the professor had a bulky address book filled with friends, relatives, window-washers, foot doctors, whatever—a tattered memorial with so many weird scratches and revisions it might have been in Sanskrit.

It was at the decorator's apartment that the messenger first stopped. Tony's was a place on the first floor of a brownstone in the Seventies—a more or less rent-controlled arrangement, since the owner, an old lady, did not want to sell and did not want to fix anything: a standoff. Except for leaks and such matters, Tony was content to do up his own place in his own manner. And a neat number it was, if always in transition, since he bought at auction, tarted the stuff up with a bit of fabric, and sold to his clients, when he had clients. Freelance, that's what he was. A roving knight available for hire. But, even if his sofa had disappeared, Tony had his rosy walls in a six-coat glaze, and a handsome Englishy telescope that stood in a corner, a tôle chandelier done in a leaf design of faded greens and reds, and lots of things here and there. But not too many.

It was near the end of a nice autumn day when his doorbell rang. Lovely September air, and gather it while ye may, for tomorrow in New York a smoky heat could move across the two rivers and hang heavy as leather on your eyebrows. Tony, at the sound of the bell, looked through the peephole and saw before him a young black face, not very black, almost yellow. His mind rushed to accommodate the vision, and, talking to himself, even doing a little dance, he went through his inner dialogue. Ring the bell, open the door. You-have-got-to-be-kidding. This is New York, fella. . . . And so on. Nevertheless, curiosity had its power, and when a finger from the great city touched the bell once more, Tony called out in as surly and as confident a tone as he could summon, What's up?

There was a pause, and the young caller answered in a fading voice. He said: *From Zona.*

Whoa. Come again. Not in a million years could anyone make up the name of Zona and present it on Tony's doorstep under a rare blue-pink sky. Tony looked again through the opening. From Zona was wearing a tangerine-colored jacket, he noticed. Not bad. The latchkey lay near at hand, and with it in his pocket Tony stepped out on the stoop, closing the door behind him, and there they were, the two of them.

The young man shifted uneasily and it fell to Tony to proceed like a busy interpreter at court. From Zona, are you? And there was a nod. Zona? Now here's a coincidence. I had a few friends in the other night. Not many— about six, nothing special. But I could have used a little class in the presentation, you know how it is, and that made me think of Zona right away, but no answer from her. Tony took in the handsome, young, light-skinned face, with its black, black eyes and black, black oily curls. So what is your errand?

Zona passed away. That was the message from the slim youth, about fifteen in Tony's arithmetic.

Zona passed away. You mean dead?

Passed away, the young man repeated, leaving Tony to meet the challenge of whatever was in order—information, emotion? I call that downright horrible news, he said. Such a wonderful person, a gem of a person, Zona. You sure have my sympathy, for what it's worth.

And then, as they stood on the steps, Tony now braced on the iron railing, a car alarm went off. A loud, oppressive, rhythmical whine, urging, Help, help! When at last it came to an abrupt, electronic end, Tony said: Be my witness. There's not a soul on that side of the street, not a soul when it went off and not a soul there now.

It's like the wind sets them off, the boy offered.

Very good, Tony said. Very good. They remind me of a screaming brat, spoiled, nothing wrong, just wanting attention. Something like that. Rotten, screeching Dodge or Plymouth or whatever it is.

The young man gave a hesitant smile before settling back into silence.

Well, business is business, and Tony gathered himself together and asked with true sweetness: What can I do for you, sir?

We're not able to make arrangements for Zona. The young man shifted and brought his doleful countenance up to meet Tony's eyes, with their flashing curiosity blinking bright in the pleasant sun.

Tony held fast to the railing. I want very much to do something for Zona, he said. And he found himself adding, like a parson, Zona who did so much for us.

The afternoon was retreating; schoolboys and schoolgirls, women with groceries, nurses with prams. Family life and double-parked maintenance trucks of electricians, pipe fitters, floor sanders taking off for the boroughs. Such sad news you have brought to my door, Tony said. And unfortunately I cannot meet the news as I would like. Consolation, all that. I don't have any cash around just now. . . . Maybe I could write you a check somehow or send something later.

Checks are hard to handle, the caller said, to which Tony replied with emphasis: *You are telling me.*

In truth, Tony didn't have any money. As he often expressed it: I don't have any money to speak of, and have you ever thought what a silly phrase that "to speak of" is? Tony didn't have any money. What he had were debts, piling up as they always did, month after month after month. Nothing ever seemed to place him ahead. Ahead? Not even in balance. When he got paid for a job or sold something, by the time the payment came through he owed most of it.

He borrowed from his friends, had borrowed from his sister until that source dried up in a ferocious finale. When reproached or reminded of a default, Tony was something grand to see and to hear. He attacked the lender and carried on with tremendous effrontery, often weeping in his rage. I don't need you to tell me that I owe you money. Don't you think I know that? Do I have to sit here and tell you that damned money is on my mind day and night? And then, in a change of pace, he would crumble, or appear to do so. Listen. I've been having a really rough time. Just now. This wonderful United States economy is in a god-awful mess. Right down there in the mud, as I see it. Or haven't you had reason to notice? You have no idea what borrowing is like, Tony would go on in an aggrieved tone. I hope you never have to go through it yourself, believe me. Borrowing from friends is the worst of it. Sheer hell on earth. Better Con Ed and the phone company after you every day, better than a friend out there waiting . . . With the utilities and all that, there are thousands in the same shitty hole. Those companies don't know you, wouldn't know you on the street, thank God. But with pals, it's torture on the rack.

Take it easy, Tony. Calm down. Everything will work out—and such was the end of that bit of troublesome arrears. Settled.

Autumn leaves lay in damp clumps along the curbs. Some of them still struggling to be yellow and red as they fell from faraway trees and were somehow carried into the treeless streets. Thinking of autumn leaves brought Tony's mind to the first vodka of the evening. It was time to step back through the door with its polished brass knocker in the shape of a lion's head. Time for his little bar alcove and zinc sink encased in pine, his American Back Porch period; time to get ice from the Sub-Zero, High-Tech period. It was time to relax, watch the evening news and, after that, "Hard Copy" or "A Current Affair." But the lovers didn't know *the wife was waiting!* That sort of problem.

Poor Zona, he said. I'd give the old eyeteeth to help you out. I really would, believe me. I know what you folks are going through, but things are a little tight with me at this point in time. That is, right now.

Tony was from Memphis. It had long been understood by him and his world in New York that he had a special sort of down-home, churchgoing way with black people. Perhaps he did, with his loquacity, curiosity, good humor—when he wasn't in a rage. There were, indeed, some occasions when he was more "Southern" than others.

The financial aspect of the transaction on the stoop in the East Seventies seemed to have blown away to rest elsewhere, like the leaves. This resolution, if you could call it that, left Tony free to ask: What's your name, fella?

My name is Carlos.

Carlos, is it? A bit out of the way to my ear. But then I don't know just where Zona got her name, either. And you might ask how I come to be Tony, like an Italian. Never laid eyes on one till I was your age.

That went by without interference, and Tony prepared for a retreat. Zona was a fine person, a special individual. Kind of a lady in her bearing. Of the old school, as they say. And how old was she? No time for that now. Time for the zinc-sink folly. He directed Carlos to another of Zona's group when he saw the young man looking at what appeared to be a list.

Check out Joseph, he said. But don't turn up before seven. He works. As a goodbye offering for Carlos, Tony went into his act, accent and all. Joseph's a good ole boy. And, just between us, he's got pigs at the trough, chickens scootin' round the yard, hay in the barn, and preserves in the cellar. Definitely not hungry, if you get my drift.

Carlos bowed his head and made his way down the stoop. Now, Tony wondered, just what was I going on about? Carlos, not even Southern, for God's sake. But, Southern or not, he called out to the disappearing tangerine back, God bless!

Inside, double-locked, vodka in hand, he rang up Joseph and gave a synopsis and foretold the boy's visit.

What did Zona die of? Joseph wanted to know.

Don't ask me. Just passed away.

AT seven-fifteen the elevator man called Joseph's apartment and said that a young man named Zona wanted to be brought up, and Joseph said, Bring him up. It was an awful moment at the door, with the young man saying, Zona passed away.

Yes, I know. Tony rang me. It's very sad news indeed. I've known Zona for fifteen years. A long time for New York, I guess.

Joseph worked in a distinguished print shop on Madison Avenue, a shop owned by a distinguished dealer, a Jewish refugee from Germany. Joseph himself was a second-generation Jewish refugee from Germany. He had been brought up in America by his parents, who left Germany in the mid-nineteen-thirties, went first to England and then to New York. They left with some of their family money, and in New York the father became a successful accountant and the mother trained with Karen Horney and went into practice as a therapist. The parents died and did not leave Joseph penniless, even if what had seemed a lot in the nineteen-seventies didn't seem much at all now.

He had studied history and French at the University of Michigan in Ann Arbor, a happy place for him, which confirmed his parents' notion that young persons of foreign birth should experience the country outside New York. Several years after graduation, he married a Michigan girl and they came to the city, where he learned the old-print business from the Master. It was not long before the Michigan girl found life too old-print—too German and all that. For Joseph the marriage seemed mysteriously to dissolve, but his bride used the word "disintegrate" with unflattering fervor. She took some of Joseph's inheritance and left Joseph with his natural sentimentality and diffidence increased. She left him also in some way frightened, even though cheerfulness was his outward aspect and went handily with his stocky, plumpish figure.

Joseph was wearing a black suit, a shirt of blue stripes, and a black tie. Business wear, except that he was in his socks. The therapeutic walk of twenty blocks up Madison Avenue had taken its toll on his feet, as he explained to Carlos. He invited the young man into a study off the living room, where there was a large desk. Here Joseph planned to talk to Carlos and to write out a check in honor of Zona. Of course it was a difficult meeting, since Joseph lacked Tony's chattering, dominating intimacy with every cat and dog and beggar (Sorry, man, out of change) on the street.

Please be at ease. Uh, Carlos, isn't it? Be at ease, Joseph said. And he sent the young man to sink into an old leather chair. Here in this dark cubicle, with the desk taking up most of the space and books on the floor, Joseph switched on the lights dug into the ceiling. Under the not entirely friendly illumination, the face of Carlos was a warm, light brown, the color of certain packing envelopes. With his eyes a swim of black and his oily black curls, Carlos looked like a figure in a crowded painting of some vivid historical scene, a face peering over the gleaming shoulders of white bodies, a face whose presence would need to be interpreted by scholars. Joseph found himself lost in this for a moment or two but could not name the painting, if any, that he was trying to recall.

No, no, he said. This is going too fast. No hurry, no hurry. He led Carlos into the kitchen and brought forth a bottle of Pellegrino. They took their glasses and Joseph had the idea of showing Carlos around the flat. In a mournful voice, he said: Carlos, this was Zona's place.

The apartment was on the overstuffed side, like Joseph himself. It had been *done* by Tony, and that was the cause of their meeting. Tony's contributions were window drapery that rolled up in a scalloped pattern, a sofa in something that looked like tapestry and ended in a band of fringe around the bottom—those and the recessed ceiling lights. For the rest, there was a mahogany dining table, with six heavy high-backed chairs spread around the three rooms. The bedroom had a suite done in an ivory color with a lot of gilt on its various components, a dated bunch of pieces coldly reigning amidst the glossy white walls.

While the apartment was being renovated, Joseph had announced that he didn't intend to buy any large pieces, because he had his mother's things in storage. Tony rolled his eyes and said: A catastrophe lies ahead. And, not long after, he came face to face with the accumulation of objects as heavy and strong, and spread around as helplessly, as old, dull-eyed mammoths. Tony blew a smoke ring at Joseph and exclaimed: I wouldn't believe it. It's wonderful. Park Avenue Early Jewish!

He wanted everything sent off to Tepper's auction house. Estate sale, Joseph. Estate sale. Joseph was taken with a fit of sentimental stubbornness, and most of the loot remained. Sometimes, when friends came around, he would smile, wave his arm about, and say, Here you have it. Early Jewish. Of course, he had his prints, his library, his silver, some old clocks. And he had Zona, whom he seldom saw, but whose presence in his life was treasured. Her hours, once a week, with a single gentleman out of the house, unlike the freelance Tony, were whatever suited her. Sometimes Joseph was at home in the late afternoon and they collided. Rapid, graceful, and courteous, she filled him with the most pleasurable emotions. The wastebaskets were emptied, the sheets on the ivory-and-gilt bed changed, a few shirts, not his best, ironed. There was that, but even more it was the years, the alliance, the black bird herself.

He directed Carlos back to the room with the desk and, hesitating, uncertain of his ground, he said: Tell me what happened to Zona. That is, if you don't mind.

Zona was shot, Carlos said, lowering his gaze to the wrinkled kilim on the floor.

Joseph drank from the water glass. Then he put it down and pressed his plump hands together. Shot. What a miserable ending for Zona. Such a— what shall I say about her? In truth, Joseph did not have words to describe Zona. He often felt: I love Zona. But that did not appear to be an appropriate expression somehow. For love, although fearful of the details, he asked: Who shot Zona?

Carlos said: Mister Joseph, they haven't got him yet. The one who did it.

You mean on the street? Just like that?

It was with the driver. Her livery driver.

Livery driver?

The driver with the car who drove her around to her places, brought her into town in the morning and met her at their corner and drove her home. For a long time, it's been. Some years, the arrangement. Martin was his name.

Joseph said: Martin shot Zona?

Carlos looked at him with a curious, long glance, a look of impatience, as if he could not believe Joseph did not comprehend what he knew so well himself. Carefully, he said: Martin didn't shoot Zona. She always sat in front with him. They were both shot.

Joseph, near to a sob, said: You must mean a robbery or something like that.

That's what it was. A fare that came in on the car radio. Got in the back seat and that was it.

There it was. It was time for Joseph to ask, What can I do for Zona? Carlos said they were having trouble with the arrangements, and when Joseph got his pen to write a check, Carlos said, Checks are hard. We don't have any banks especially. Any that know us. So, in the end, Joseph found two hundred dollars and Carlos rose to leave. I'll take it to her sister.

Whose sister?

Zona's sister. My mother. And in the gloom he was escorted to the elevator and went down to the street, where now rain splashed and wind blew.

Joseph phoned Tony and said, Shot. And Tony said, Shot? Wouldn't you just know it?

Joseph said, There's a sister.

Whose sister?

Zona's sister. That's who we're talking about, right? The sister is the mother of Carlos. It's horrible to think of Zona gone like that. From the back seat.

Tony said, What back seat? But Joseph declined. Nothing, Tony, nothing. Just shot.

Tony said: History of this goddam city—at least a footnote to the history of these fucking times. The whole place is a firing range, up and down and across.

Joseph said: Zona's not a footnote to me. I loved Zona.

Didn't we all? came back over the wire.

THE next morning, Carlos arrived at a town house on East Ninety-first Street, the house of Cynthia, the flute player. The door was ajar and noise could be heard inside—voices, a phonograph, a telephone ringing and answered. Carlos pushed the bell button and waited next to a stone urn of faltering geraniums. After a time, a young girl, about his age, called out for Granny, and after a minute or two here came Cynthia in a smock. This time the opening line was: I'm Carlos. From Zona.

How nice. Come in, come in. You are welcome here.

There were boots and umbrellas in the hallway, coats hanging on pegs, newspapers stacked for recycling—quite a busy entrance, you'd have to say.

Carlos was led into the front parlor, where there was a piano, along with bookcases, two-seater sofas, and a big, lumpy armchair by the window, to which he was directed. Cynthia drew a chair very near to him, and her greenish, amiable eyes gazed into his liquid black ones and at last she said: I missed Zona this week. You know—Carlos, is it?—that I consider it very brave of Zona to set foot into my jungle. An army couldn't handle it. You can see that, I'm sure. But Zona found things to do, and I am much in her debt.

Carlos looked aside. Zona passed away, he said.

Cynthia sat up straight as a rod in her chair and looked up at the ceiling for a long time. At last she said: I wasn't prepared for this. Passed on from this life, Zona. Just like that.

Zona passed away, he repeated, and Cynthia seemed lost in contemplation, meditation of some kind. Oh, oh, passed away. I'm sorry. I'm sorry. I hope it was an easy death. An easy passage after a hard, honorable life.

Carlos said: No, Ma'am. It wasn't easy. Zona was shot.

Cynthia drew her chair nearer, brought her golden-gray head so close that Carlos tilted his black curls back a bit. Then Cynthia placed her long fingers on his hand and drew his other brown hand over her own so that they were in a clasp like that practiced in progressive churches. Shot, you say. More than the heart can bear.

Cynthia grew up in Baltimore, went to the Curtis Institute, in Philadelphia, had a three-week summer session in Paris with Rampal, and in her younger years had played for a time in the Baltimore Symphony Orchestra. Then she came with her husband and daughter to New York and bought the house on Ninety-first Street. Thirty-nine thousand it cost then, she would say. Only that. The money had come from the closing of her grandfather's Baltimore business, a handsome store where well-to-do women could buy dresses, coats and satin lingerie, cologne and face powder. Three floors in a fine downtown brick building, clerks long in service, and seamstresses with pins in their mouths while making alterations. Ours was a *select* business, she would say with an ironical lilt and the special tone of

Unitarian modesty. It was very well known and much respected in the community. To be that, you had to be somewhat cool to ordinary people. You didn't want them to look at things and then go pale at the price. But the doors were welcoming to one and all on the Day After the Fourth of July Sale. A yearly excitement it was, people in line at seven in the morning.

Releasing the hand of Carlos, Cynthia said: Tell me what you and your family have been going through. She passed him a damp cookie and a cat entered the room and settled on his lap. Carlos ate the cookie and stroked the cat. Looking hard at Cynthia, he said in a tone of apology: You see, I never met any of the people Zona worked for before this happened. I don't know just what they might want to hear.

I want to hear what you can bear to tell, Cynthia said.

In a breathless rush, Carlos told about the livery car that had taken Zona back and forth to her work, about the passenger who got in from the radio call and hadn't been caught yet. And he added that his mother, Zona's sister, would have come round to the people but she was home crying herself crazy.

I will attend Zona's funeral, Cynthia said. I want to be there. For me, it would be an honor. And it occurs to me that if you wish I might play a little music. Something suitable, of course.

Carlos raised his hand to interrupt. It was time to complete his errand: We haven't been able to make the arrangements for Zona.

Cynthia said at this point: Funeral arrangements cost much more than they need to. I read a book about that—although I didn't need to be informed about the ways of such institutions.

Carlos, a diver at the tip of the board, fixed his glance on Cynthia's bright head of white hair, with the brown streaks turning golden. He said: She's been there a week while we couldn't make the arrangements. They put them in the ground, like in a field, they say.

Been where?

With the city down where they keep them. If you can't make the arrangements to transfer, they put them—

Oh, Cynthia said. You mean Potter's Field?

Carlos said: That sounds like it.

The granddaughter who had opened the door came into the room and introductions were made. As she was going out, she said to Carlos: You're cute.

This young person is in a state of bereavement, Cynthia called to the girl. And she added: Neither of my grandchildren is musical. They can't sing "Adeste Fideles" in tune. A deprivation.

Pigeons rested on the sills of the long, handsome, smeary windows still divided into the original panes and now interrupted only by a rusty air-conditioner. I can't take it all in, Cynthia said. I would like to know what Zona's family needs.

What we want, Ma'am, he said, what we want is a coffin on a train, and a few of us family will go down and have her buried in Opelika.

Opelika? Where is that?

Alabama. Zona's town.

Opelika, Alabama. What a pretty name.

The ground down there's paid for, Carlos explained.

Cynthia drew a pencil from the pocket of her smock, found a pad, and began to write on it. I have probably waited too long to sell this house, she said. The prices are falling fast—the darkness deepening, as the hymn goes.

Cynthia and her chamber-music group occasionally held concerts in this house, and at one of those Joseph had brought Tony along. Tony, when the invitation came, said: I might have guessed you'd go for that, Joseph. German.

During the wine and cheese, inferior quality indeed, Tony approached Cynthia and in an excited mode informed her: You are sitting on a million bucks here—if not exactly in mint condition. He noted the panelling, the high ceilings, and the matching fireplaces of decorated marble on the first floor. Assets you have here. A million for sure, at the bottom.

Tony was floating like a sturdy little boat on the waters of the house market. A million for the property and another mil *at least* to do it up. They're terrorists, these buyers. They like to gut the place, break down walls, even move the staircase so they can put a powder room under it. Space, dear lady, that's the ticket. Space is what you have to sell.

Of course, Cynthia stayed on. The house, the space, was all she had to leave her daughter, the way things looked. She rented rooms to students, gave lessons, while lamenting that the lesson-takers were mostly girls and few strong enough for the instrument. In these rooms now she was contemplating life and death with Carlos. It was calculated that a thousand dollars was needed to rescue Zona. And there was the problem with cashing checks, and just two days before they would, down there at the city, before they would—

Please, please, Carlos. Don't speak of it. More than the heart can bear.

Cynthia's finances were more than a little murky. Her husband, when they moved to New York, had worked for a publishing group that put out *Family Days*. Perhaps he got a bit overloaded on that, and he squared the circle, so to speak, and shifted to *Liberty*, when that magazine was around. He also shifted to an ignorant girl in the mail room. Cynthia was left to provide for her daughter, who quit Barnard College in her freshman year, took up with a boy from Columbia, and went up to New Hampshire with him to pursue carpentry and to produce two daughters. Cynthia had bits of trust funds from the old Baltimore emporium, from a childless uncle, and from her father, who declined the clothing business and went into a small local bank, not very successfully. He raised his nice, musical daughter, who ended up on the flute.

At last, toward noon, with the temperamental city sun shining one minute and disappearing the next, as if turning a corner, Cynthia found a sweater and put her arm through the arm of Carlos, and the odd tandem made its way down Lexington Avenue to the Chemical Bank. Inside the bank, the odd tandem became an alarming couple; Carlos like a thief avoiding eye contact with the teller, a young Indian woman in a sari, and Cynthia, in an old gentlewoman's untidy fluster, withdrawing a thousand dollars in fifties and twenties.

They stood outside in humbling confusion until the money in two envelopes was passed into the hands of Carlos. Off in a gallop to the subway and to do the paperwork down there where they were impatiently holding the body of Zona. Alert the River Jordan Twenty-Four-Hour Funeral Service. And at last meet the train rolling down to Washington, D.C.; there a crunching change of cars, a wait, before wheeling through state after state, through West Virginia, passing the memory of the prehistoric Mound Builders and the rusting scaffolds of the anthracite-coal counties. On to the point of the Chattanooga Campaign, down to the grass and myrtle of the cemetery lying in the Alabama autumn. Journey's end.

Adios, Carlos. Au revoir, Zona. Rest in peace in Opelika.

Cynthia recounted the dire circumstances to Joseph, who said, I loved Zona. A great hole in my life, this is. It's like planting a field of seeds and none of them coming up. In a manner of speaking.

Cynthia said: Nothing for Planned Parenthood this year. But no matter, no matter.

Tony, informed, said: They love funerals.

(1993)

A FATHER-TO-BE

THE strangest notions had a way of forcing themselves into Rogin's mind. Just thirty-one and passable-looking, with short black hair, small eyes, but a high, open forehead, he was a research chemist, and his mind was generally serious and dependable. But on a snowy Sunday evening while this stocky man, buttoned to the chin in a Burberry coat and walking in his preposterous gait—feet turned outward—was going toward the subway, he fell into a peculiar state.

He was on his way to have supper with his fiancée. She had phoned him a short while ago and said, "You'd better pick up a few things on the way."

"What do we need?"

"Some roast beef, for one thing. I bought a quarter of a pound coming home from my aunt's."

"Why a quarter of a pound, Joan?" said Rogin, deeply annoyed. "That's just about enough for one good sandwich."

"So you have to stop at a delicatessen. I had no more money."

He was about to ask, "What happened to the thirty dollars I gave you on Wednesday?," but he knew that would not be right.

"I had to give Phyllis money for the cleaning woman," said Joan.

Phyllis, Joan's cousin, was a young divorcée, extremely wealthy. The two women shared an apartment.

"Roast beef," he said, "and what else?"

"Some shampoo, sweetheart. We've used up all the shampoo. And hurry, darling, I've missed you all day."

"And I've missed you," said Rogin, but to tell the truth he had been worrying most of the time. He had a younger brother whom he was putting through college. And his mother, whose annuity wasn't quite enough in these days of inflation and high taxes, needed money, too. Joan had debts he was helping her to pay, for she wasn't working. She was looking for something suitable to do. Beautiful, well-educated, aristocratic in her attitude, she couldn't clerk in a dime store; she couldn't model clothes (Rogin thought this made girls vain and stiff, and he didn't want her to); she couldn't be a waitress or a cashier. What could she be? Well, something would turn up, and meantime Rogin hesitated to complain. He paid her bills—the dentist, the department store, the osteopath, the doctor, the psychiatrist. At Christmas, Rogin almost went mad. Joan bought him a velvet smoking jacket with frog fasteners, a beautiful pipe, and a pouch. She bought Phyllis a garnet brooch, an Italian silk umbrella, and a gold cigarette holder. For other friends, she bought Dutch pewter and Swedish glassware. Before she was through, she had spent five hundred dollars of Rogin's money. He loved her too much to show his suffering. He believed she had a far better nature than his. She didn't worry about money. She had a marvelous character, always cheerful, and she really didn't need a psychiatrist at all. She went to one because Phyllis did and it made her curious. She tried too much to keep up with her cousin, whose father had made millions in the rug business.

While the woman in the drugstore was wrapping the shampoo bottle, a clear idea suddenly arose in Rogin's thoughts: Money surrounds you in life as the earth does in death. Superimposition is the universal law. Who is free? No one is free. Who has no burdens? Everyone is under pressure. The very rocks, the waters of the earth, beasts, men, children—everyone has some weight to carry. This idea was extremely clear to him at first. Soon it became rather vague, but it had a great effect nevertheless, as if someone had given him a valuable gift. (Not like the velvet smoking jacket he couldn't bring himself to wear, or the pipe it choked him to smoke.) The notion that all were under pressure and affliction, instead of saddening him, had the opposite influence. It put him in a wonderful mood. It was extraordinary how happy he became and, in addition, clear-sighted. His eyes all at once were opened to what was around him. He saw with delight how the druggist and the woman who wrapped the shampoo bottle were smiling and flirting, how the lines of worry in her face went over into lines of cheer, and the druggist's receding gums did not hinder his kidding and friendliness. And in the delicatessen, also, it was amazing how much Rogin noted and what happiness it gave him simply to be there.

. . .

DELICATESSENS on Sunday night, when all other stores are shut, will overcharge you ferociously, and Rogin would normally have been on guard, but he was not tonight, or scarcely so. Smells of pickle, sausage, mustard, and smoked fish overjoyed him. He pitied the people who would buy the chicken salad and chopped herring; they could do it only because their sight was too dim to see what they were getting—the fat flakes of pepper on the chicken, the soppy herring, mostly vinegar-soaked stale bread. Who would buy them? Late risers, people living alone, waking up in the darkness of the afternoon, finding their refrigerators empty, or people whose gaze was turned inward. The roast beef looked not bad, and Rogin ordered a pound.

While the storekeeper was slicing the meat, he yelled at a Puerto Rican kid who was reaching for a bag of chocolate cookies, "Hey, you want to pull me down the whole display on yourself? You, *chico*, wait a half a minute." This storekeeper, though he looked like one of Pancho Villa's bandits, the kind that smeared their enemies with syrup and staked them down on anthills, a man with toadlike eyes and stout hands made to clasp pistols hung around his belly, was not so bad. He was a New York man, thought Rogin—who was from Albany himself—a New York man toughened by every abuse of the city, trained to suspect everyone. But in his own realm, on the board behind the counter, there was justice. Even clemency.

The Puerto Rican kid wore a complete cowboy outfit—a green hat with white braid, guns, chaps, spurs, boots, and gauntlets—but he couldn't speak any English. Rogin unhooked the cellophane bag of hard circular cookies and gave it to him. The boy tore the cellophane with his teeth and began to chew one of those dry chocolate discs. Rogin recognized his state—the energetic dream of childhood. Once, he, too, had found these dry biscuits delicious. It would have bored him now to eat one.

What else would Joan like? Rogin thought fondly. Some strawberries? "Give me some frozen strawberries. And heavy cream. And some rolls, cream cheese, and some of those rubber-looking gherkins."

"What rubber?"

"Those, deep green, with eyes. Some ice cream might be in order, too."

He tried to think of a compliment, a good comparison, an endearment, for Joan when she'd open the door. What about her complexion? There was really nothing to compare her sweet, small, daring, shapely, timid, defiant, loving face to. How difficult she was, and how beautiful!

AS Rogin went down into the stony, odorous, metallic, captive air of the subway, he was diverted by an unusual confession made by a man to his friend. These were two very tall men, shapeless in their winter clothes, as if their coats concealed suits of chain mail.

"So, how long have you known me?" said one.

"Twelve years."

"Well, I have an admission to make," he said. "I've decided that I might as well. For years I've been a heavy drinker. You didn't know. Practically an alcoholic."

But his friend was not surprised, and he answered immediately, "Yes, I did know."

"You knew? Impossible! How could you?"

Why, thought Rogin, as if it could be a secret! Look at that long, austere, alcohol-washed face, that drink-ruined nose, the skin by his ears like turkey wattles, and those whiskey-saddened eyes.

"Well, I did know, though."

"You couldn't have. I can't believe it." He was upset, and his friend didn't seem to want to soothe him. "But it's all right now," he said. "I've been going to a doctor and taking pills, a new revolutionary Danish discovery. It's a miracle. I'm beginning to believe they can cure you of anything and everything. You can't beat the Danes in science. They do everything. They turned a man into a woman."

"That isn't how they stop you from drinking, is it?"

"No. I hope not. This is only like aspirin. It's super-aspirin. They call it the aspirin of the future. But if you use it, you have to stop drinking."

Rogin's illuminated mind asked of itself while the human tides of the subway swayed back and forth, and cars linked and transparent like fish bladders raced under the streets: How come he thought nobody would know what everybody couldn't help knowing? And, as a chemist, he asked himself what kind of compound this new Danish drug might be, and started thinking about various inventions of his own, synthetic albumen, a cigarette that lit itself, a cheaper motor fuel. Ye gods, but he needed money! As never before. What was to be done? His mother was growing more and more difficult. On Friday night, she had neglected to cut up his meat for him, and he was hurt. She had sat at the table motionless, with her long-suffering face, severe, and let him cut his own meat, a thing she almost never did. She had always spoiled him and made his brother envy him. But what she expected now! Oh, Lord, how he had to pay, and it had never even occurred to him formerly that these things might have a price.

Seated, one of the passengers, Rogin recovered his calm, happy, even clairvoyant state of mind. To think of money was to think as the world wanted you to think; then you'd never be your own master. When people said they wouldn't do something for love or money, they meant that love and money were opposite passions and one the enemy of the other. He went on to reflect how little people knew about this, how they slept through life, how small a light the light of consciousness was. Rogin's clean, snub-nosed face shone while his heart was torn with joy at these deeper thoughts of our ignorance. You might take this drunkard as an example, who for long years thought his closest friends never suspected he drank. Rogin looked up and down the aisle for this remarkable knightly symbol, but he was gone.

However, there was no lack of things to see. There was a small girl with a new white muff; into the muff a doll's head was sewn, and the child was happy and affectionately vain of it, while her old man, stout and grim, with a huge scowling nose, kept picking her up and resettling her in the seat, as if he were trying to change her into something else. Then another child, led by her mother, boarded the car, and this other child carried the very same doll-faced muff, and this greatly annoyed both parents. The woman, who looked like a difficult, contentious woman, took her daughter away. It seemed to Rogin that each child was in love with its own muff and didn't even see the other, but it was one of his foibles to think he understood the hearts of little children.

A foreign family next engaged his attention. They looked like Central Americans to him. On one side the mother, quite old, dark-faced, white-haired, and worn out; on the other a son with the whitened, porous hands of a dishwasher. But what was the dwarf who sat between them—a son or a daughter? The hair was long and wavy and the cheeks smooth, but the shirt and tie were masculine. The overcoat was feminine, but the shoes—the shoes were a puzzle. A pair of brown oxfords with an outer seam like a man's, but Baby Louis heels like a woman's—a plain toe like a man's, but a strap across the instep like a woman's. No stockings. That didn't help much. The dwarf's fingers were beringed, but without a wedding band. There were small grim dents in the cheeks. The eyes were puffy and concealed, but Rogin did not doubt that they could reveal strange things if they chose and that this was a creature of remarkable understanding. He had for many years owned De la Mare's "Memoirs of a Midget." Now he took a resolve; he would read it. As soon as he had decided, he was free from his consuming curiosity as to the dwarf's sex and was able to look at the person who sat beside him.

THOUGHTS very often grow fertile in the subway, because of the motion, the great company, the subtlety of the rider's state as he rattles under streets and rivers, under the foundations of great buildings, and Rogin's mind had already been strangely stimulated. Clasping the bag of groceries from which there rose odors of bread and pickle spice, he was following a train of reflections, first about the chemistry of sex determination, the

X and Y chromosomes, hereditary linkages, the uterus, afterward about his brother as a tax exemption. He recalled two dreams of the night before. In one, an undertaker had offered to cut his hair, and he had refused. In another, he had been carrying a woman on his head. Sad dreams, both! Very sad! Which was the woman—Joan or Mother? And the undertaker—his lawyer? He gave a deep sigh, and by force of habit began to put together his synthetic albumen that was to revolutionize the entire egg industry.

Meanwhile, he had not interrupted his examination of the passengers and had fallen into a study of the man next to him. This was a man whom he had never in his life seen before but with whom he now suddenly felt linked through all existence. He was middle-aged, sturdy, with clear skin and blue eyes. His hands were clean, well-formed, but Rogin did not approve of them. The coat he wore was a fairly expensive blue check such as Rogin would never have chosen for himself. He would not have worn blue suède shoes, either, or such a faultless hat, a cumbersome felt animal of a hat encircled by a high, fat ribbon. There are all kinds of dandies, not all of them are of the flaunting kind; some are dandies of respectability, and Rogin's fellow-passenger was one of these. His straight-nosed profile was handsome, yet he had betrayed his gift, for he was flat-looking. But in his flat way he seemed to warn people that he wanted no difficulties with them, he wanted nothing to do with them. Wearing such blue suède shoes, he could not afford to have people treading on his feet, and he seemed to draw about himself a circle of privilege, notifying all others to mind their own business and let him read his paper. He was holding a *Tribune,* and perhaps it would be overstatement to say that he was reading. He was holding it.

His clear skin and blue eyes, his straight and purely Roman nose—even the way he sat—all strongly suggested one person to Rogin: Joan. He tried to escape the comparison, but it couldn't be helped. This man not only looked like Joan's father, whom Rogin detested; he looked like Joan herself. Forty years hence, a son of hers, provided she had one, might be like this. A son of hers? Of such a son, he himself, Rogin, would be the father. Lacking in dominant traits as compared with Joan, his heritage would not appear. Probably the children would resemble her. Yes, think forty years ahead, and a man like this, who sat by him knee to knee in the hurtling car among their fellow-creatures, unconscious participants in a sort of great carnival of transit—such a man would carry forward what had been Rogin.

This was why he felt bound to him through all existence. What were forty years reckoned against eternity! Forty years were gone, and he was gazing at his own son. Here he was. Rogin was frightened and moved. "My son! My son!" he said to himself, and the pity of it almost made him burst into tears. The holy and frightful work of the masters of life and death brought this about. We were their instruments. We worked toward ends we thought were our own. But no! The whole thing was so unjust. To suffer, to labor, to toil and force your way through the spikes of life, to crawl through its darkest caverns, to push through the worst, to struggle under the weight of economy, to make money—only to become the father of a fourth-rate man of the world like this, so flat-looking, with his ordinary, clean, rosy, un-interesting, self-satisfied, fundamentally bourgeois face. What a curse to have a dull son! A son like this, who could never understand his father. They had absolutely nothing, but nothing, in common, he and this neat, chubby, blue-eyed man. He was so pleased, thought Rogin, with all he owned and all he did and all he was that he could hardly unfasten his lip. Look at that lip, sticking up at the tip like a little thorn or egg tooth. He wouldn't give anyone the time of day. Would this perhaps be general forty years from now? Would personalities be chillier as the world aged and grew colder? The inhumanity of the next generation incensed Rogin. Father and son had no sign to make to each other. Terrible! Inhuman! What a vision of existence it gave him. Man's personal aims were nothing, illusion. The life force occupied each of us in turn in its progress toward its own fulfillment, trampling on our individual humanity, using us for its own ends like mere dinosaurs or bees, exploiting love heartlessly, making us engage in the so-cial process, labor, struggle for money, and submit to the law of pressure, the universal law of layers, superimposition!

What the blazes am I getting into? Rogin thought. To be the father of a throwback to *her* father. The image of this white-haired, gross, peevish old man with his ugly selfish blue eyes revolted Rogin. This was how his grand-son would look. Joan, with whom Rogin was now more and more dis-pleased, could not help that. For her, it was inevitable. But did it have to be inevitable for him? Well, then, Rogin, you fool, don't be a damned instru-ment. Get out of the way!

But it was too late for this, because he had already experienced the sen-sation of sitting next to his own son, his son and Joan's. He kept staring at him, waiting for him to say something, but the presumptive son remained coldly silent though he must have been aware of Rogin's scrutiny. They even got out at the same stop—Sheridan Square. When they stepped to the platform, the man, without even looking at Rogin, went away in a different direction in his detestable blue-checked coat, with his rosy, nasty face.

THE whole thing upset Rogin very badly. When he approached Joan's door and heard Phyllis's little dog Henri barking even before he could knock, his face was very tense. "I won't be used," he declared to himself. "I have my own right to exist." Joan had better watch out. She had a light way of by-passing grave questions he had given earnest thought to. She always assumed no really disturbing thing would happen. He could not afford the luxury of such a carefree, debonair attitude himself, because he had to work hard and earn money so that disturbing things would *not* happen. Well, at the moment this situation could not be helped, and he really did not mind the money if he could feel that she was not necessarily the mother of such a son as his subway son or entirely the daughter of that awful, obscene father of hers. After all, Rogin was not himself so much like either of his parents, and quite different from his brother.

Joan came to the door, wearing one of Phyllis's expensive housecoats. It suited her very well. At first sight of her happy face, Rogin was brushed by the shadow of resemblance; the touch of it was extremely light, almost figmentary, but it made his flesh tremble.

She began to kiss him, saying, "Oh, my baby. You're covered with snow. Why didn't you wear your hat? It's all over its little head"—her favorite third-person endearment.

"Well, let me put down this bag of stuff. Let me take off my coat," grumbled Rogin, and escaped from her embrace. Why couldn't she wait making up to him? "It's so hot in here. My face is burning. Why do you keep the place at this temperature? And that damned dog keeps barking. If you didn't keep it cooped up, it wouldn't be so spoiled and noisy. Why doesn't anybody ever walk him?"

"Oh, it's not really so hot here! You've just come in from the cold. Don't you think this housecoat fits me better than Phyllis? Especially across the hips. She thinks so, too. She may sell it to me."

"I hope not," Rogin almost exclaimed.

She brought a towel to dry the melting snow from his short, black hair. The flurry of rubbing excited Henri intolerably, and Joan locked him up in the bedroom, where he jumped persistently against the door with a rhythmic sound of claws on the wood.

Joan said, "Did you bring the shampoo?"

"Here it is."

"Then I'll wash your hair before dinner. Come."

"I don't want it washed."

"Oh, come on," she said, laughing.

Her lack of consciousness of guilt amazed him. He did not see how it could be. And the carpeted, furnished, lamplit, curtained room seemed to stand against his vision. So that he felt accusing and angry, his spirit sore and bitter, but it did not seem fitting to say why. Indeed, he began to worry lest the reason for it all slip away from him.

They took off his coat and his shirt in the bathroom, and she filled the sink. Rogin was full of his troubled emotions; now that his chest was bare he could feel them even more distinctly inside, and he said to himself, "I'll have a thing or two to tell her pretty soon. I'm not letting them get away with it. 'Do you think,' he was going to tell her, 'that I alone was made to carry the burden of the whole world on me? Do you think I was born just to be taken advantage of and sacrificed? Do you think I'm just a natural resource, like a coal mine, or oil well, or fishery, or the like? Remember, that I'm a man is no reason why I should be loaded down. I have a soul in me no bigger or stronger than yours. Take away the externals, like the muscles, deeper voice, and so forth, and what remains? A pair of spirits, practically alike. So why shouldn't there also be equality? I can't always be the strong one.' "

"Sit here," said Joan, bringing up a kitchen stool to the sink. "Your hair's gotten all matted."

He sat with his breast against the cool enamel, his chin on the edge of the basin, the green, hot, radiant water reflecting the glass and the tile, and the sweet, cool, fragrant juice of the shampoo poured on his head. She began to wash him.

"You have the healthiest-looking scalp," she said. "It's all pink."

He answered, "Well, it should be white. There must be something wrong with me."

"But there's absolutely nothing wrong with you," she said, and pressed against him from behind, surrounding him, pouring the water gently over him until it seemed to him that the water came from within him, it was the warm fluid of his own secret loving spirit overflowing into the sink, green and foaming, and the words he had rehearsed he forgot, and his anger at his son-to-be disappeared altogether, and he sighed, and said to her from the water-filled hollow of the sink, "You always have such wonderful ideas, Joan. You know? You have a kind of instinct, a regular gift."

(1955)

FAREWELL, MY LOVELY APPETIZER

Add Smorgasbits to your ought-to-know department, the newest of the three Betty Lee products. What in the world! Just small mouth-size pieces of herring and of pinkish tones. We crossed our heart and promised not to tell the secret of their tinting.

—*Clementine Paddleford's food column*
in the Herald Tribune.

The "Hush-Hush" Blouse. We're very hush-hush about his name, but the celebrated shirtmaker who did it for us is famous on two continents for blouses with details like those deep yoke folds, the wonderful shoulder pads, the shirtband bow!

—*Russeks adv. in the Times.*

I CAME down the sixth-floor corridor of the Arbogast Building, past the World Wide Noodle Corporation, Zwinger & Rumsey, Accountants, and the Ace Secretarial Service, Mimeographing Our Specialty. The legend on the ground-glass panel next door said, "Atlas Detective Agency, Noonan & Driscoll," but Snapper Driscoll had retired two years before with a .38 slug between the shoulders, donated by a snowbird in Tacoma, and I owned what good will the firm had. I let myself into the crummy anteroom we kept to impress clients, growled good morning at Birdie Claflin.

"Well, you certainly look like something the cat dragged in," she said. She had a quick tongue. She also had eyes like dusty lapis lazuli, taffy hair, and a figure that did things to me. I kicked open the bottom drawer of her desk, let two inches of rye trickle down my craw, kissed Birdie square on her lush, red mouth, and set fire to a cigarette.

"I could go for you, sugar," I said slowly. Her face was veiled, watchful. I stared at her ears, liking the way they were joined to her head. There was something complete about them; you knew they were there for keeps. When you're a private eye, you want things to stay put.

"Any customers?"

"A woman by the name of Sigrid Bjornsterne said she'd be back. A looker."

"Swede?"

"She'd like you to think so."

I nodded toward the inner office to indicate that I was going in there, and went in there. I lay down on the davenport, took off my shoes, and bought myself a shot from the bottle I kept underneath. Four minutes later, an ash blonde with eyes the color of unset opals, in a Nettie Rosenstein basic black dress and a baum-marten stole, burst in. Her bosom was heaving and it looked even better that way. With a gasp she circled the desk, hunting for some place to hide, and then, spotting the wardrobe where I keep a change of bourbon, ran into it. I got up and wandered out into the anteroom. Birdie was deep in a crossword puzzle.

"See anyone come in here?"

"Nope." There was a thoughtful line between her brows. "Say, what's a five-letter word meaning 'trouble'?"

"Swede," I told her, and went back inside. I waited the length of time it would take a small, not very bright boy to recite "Ozymandias," and, inching carefully along the wall, took a quick gander out the window. A thin galoot with stooping shoulders was being very busy reading a paper outside the Gristede store two blocks away. He hadn't been there an hour ago, but then, of course, neither had I. He wore a size-seven dove-colored hat from Browning King, a tan Wilson Brothers shirt with pale-blue stripes, a J. Press foulard with a mixed-red-and-white figure, dark blue Interwoven socks, and an unshined pair of ox-blood London Character shoes. I let a cigarette burn down between my fingers until it made a small red mark, and then I opened the wardrobe.

"Hi," the blonde said lazily. "You Mike Noonan?" I made a noise that could have been "Yes," and waited. She yawned. I thought things over, decided to play it safe. I yawned. She yawned back, then, settling into a corner of the wardrobe, went to sleep. I let another cigarette burn down until it made a second red mark beside the first one, and then I woke her up. She sank into a chair, crossing a pair of gams that tightened my throat as I peered under the desk at them.

"Mr. Noonan," she said, "you—you've got to help me."

"My few friends call me Mike," I said pleasantly.

"Mike." She rolled the syllable on her tongue. "I don't believe I've ever heard that name before. Irish?"

"Enough to know the difference between a gossoon and a bassoon."

"What is the difference?" she asked. I dummied up; I figured I wasn't giving anything away for free. Her eyes narrowed. I shifted my two hundred pounds slightly, lazily set fire to a finger, and watched it burn down. I could see she was admiring the interplay of muscles in my shoulders. There wasn't any extra fat on Mike Noonan, but I wasn't telling her that. I was playing it safe until I knew where we stood.

When she spoke again, it came with a rush. "Mr. Noonan, he thinks I'm trying to poison him. But I swear the herring was pink—I took it out of the jar myself. If I could only find out how they tinted it. I offered them money, but they wouldn't tell."

"Suppose you take it from the beginning," I suggested.

She drew a deep breath. "You've heard of the golden spintria of Hadrian?" I shook my head. "It's a tremendously valuable coin believed to have been given by the Emperor Hadrian to one of his proconsuls, Caius Vitellius. It disappeared about 150 A.D., and eventually passed into the possession of Hucbald the Fat. After the sack of Adrianople by the Turks, it was loaned by a man named Shapiro to the court physician, or hakim, of Abdul Mahmoud. Then it dropped out of sight for nearly five hundred years, until last August, when a dealer in second-hand books named Lloyd Thursday sold it to my husband."

"And now it's gone again," I finished.

"No," she said. "At least, it was lying on the dresser when I left, an hour ago." I leaned back, pretending to fumble a carbon out of the desk, and studied her legs again. This was going to be a lot more intricate than I had thought. Her voice got huskier. "Last night I brought home a jar of Smorgasbits for Walter's dinner. You know them?"

"Small mouth-size pieces of herring and of pinkish tones, aren't they?"

Her eyes darkened, lightened, got darker again. "How did you know?"

"I haven't been a private op nine years for nothing, sister. Go on."

"I—I knew right away something was wrong when Walter screamed and upset his plate. I tried to tell him the herring was supposed to be pink, but he carried on like a madman. He's been suspicious of me since—well, ever since I made him take out that life insurance."

"What was the face amount of the policy?"

"A hundred thousand. But it carried a triple-indemnity clause in case he died by sea food. Mr. Noonan—Mike"—her tone caressed me—"I've got to win back his confidence. You could find out how they tinted that herring."

"What's in it for me?"

"Anything you want." The words were a whisper. I leaned over, poked open her handbag, counted off five grand.

"This'll hold me for a while," I said. "If I need any more, I'll beat my spoon on the high chair." She got up. "Oh, while I think of it, how does this golden spintria of yours tie in with the herring?"

"It doesn't," she said calmly. "I just threw it in for glamour." She trailed past me in a cloud of scent that retailed at ninety rugs the ounce. I caught her wrist, pulled her up to me.

"I go for girls named Sigrid with opal eyes," I said.

"Where'd you learn my name?"

"I haven't been a private snoop twelve years for nothing, sister."

"It was nine last time."

"It seemed like twelve till *you* came along." I held the clinch until a faint wisp of smoke curled out of her ears, pushed her through the door. Then I slipped a pint of rye into my stomach and a heater into my kick and went looking for a bookdealer named Lloyd Thursday. I knew he had no connection with the herring caper, but in my business you don't overlook anything.

THE thin galoot outside Gristede's had taken a powder when I got there; that meant we were no longer playing girls' rules. I hired a hack to Wanamaker's, cut over to Third, walked up toward Fourteenth. At Twelfth a mink-faced jasper made up as a street cleaner tailed me for a block, drifted into a dairy restaurant. At Thirteenth somebody dropped a sour tomato out of a third-story window, missing me by inches. I doubled back to Wanamaker's, hopped a bus up Fifth to Madison Square, and switched to a cab down Fourth, where the second-hand bookshops elbow each other like dirty urchins.

A flabby hombre in a Joe Carbondale rope-knit sweater, whose jowl could have used a shave, quit giggling over the Heptameron long enough to tell me he was Lloyd Thursday. His shoe-button eyes became opaque when I asked to see any first editions or incunabula relative to the *Clupea harengus*, or common herring.

"You got the wrong pitch, copper," he snarled. "That stuff is hotter than Pee Wee Russell's clarinet."

"Maybe a sawbuck'll smarten you up," I said. I folded one to the size of a postage stamp, scratched my chin with it. "There's five yards around for anyone who knows why those Smorgasbits of Sigrid Bjornsterne's happened to be pink." His eyes got crafty.

"I might talk for a grand."

"Start dealing." He motioned toward the back. I took a step forward. A second later a Roman candle exploded inside my head and I went away from there. When I came to, I was on the floor with a lump on my sconce the size of a lapwing's egg and big Terry Tremaine of Homicide was bending over me.

"Someone sapped me," I said thickly. "His name was—"

"Webster," grunted Terry. He held up a dog-eared copy of Merriam's Unabridged. "You tripped on a loose board and this fell off a shelf on your think tank."

"Yeah?" I said skeptically. "Then where's Thursday?" He pointed to the fat man lying across a pile of erotica. "He passed out cold when he saw you cave." I covered up, let Terry figure it any way he wanted. I wasn't telling him what cards I held. I was playing it safe until I knew all the angles.

In a seedy pharmacy off Astor Place, a stale Armenian, whose name might have been Vulgarian but wasn't, dressed my head and started asking questions. I put my knee in his groin and he lost interest. Jerking my head toward the coffee urn, I spent a nickel and the next forty minutes doing some heavy thinking. Then I holed up in a phone booth and dialed a clerk I knew called Little Farvel, in a delicatessen store on Amsterdam Avenue. It took a while to get the dope I wanted because the connection was bad and Little Farvel had been dead two years, but we Noonans don't let go easily.

BY the time I worked back to the Arbogast Building, via the Weehawken ferry and the George Washington Bridge to cover my tracks, all the pieces were in place. Or so I thought up to the point she came out of the wardrobe holding me between the sights of her ice-blue automatic.

"Reach for the stratosphere, gumshoe." Sigrid Bjornsterne's voice was colder than Horace Greeley and Little Farvel put together, but her clothes were plenty calorific. She wore a forest-green suit of Hockanum woollens, a Knox Wayfarer, and baby crocodile pumps. It was her blouse, though, that made tiny red hairs stand up on my knuckles. Its deep yoke folds, shoulder pads, and shirt-band bow could only have been designed by some master craftsman, some Cézanne of the shears.

"Well, Nosy Parker," she sneered, "so you found out how they tinted the herring."

"Sure—grenadine," I said easily. "You knew it all along. And you planned to add a few grains of oxylbutane-cheriphosphate, which turns the same shade of pink in solution, to your husband's portion, knowing it wouldn't show in the post-mortem. Then you'd collect the three hundred g's and join Harry Pestalozzi in Nogales till the heat died down. But you didn't count on me."

"You?" Mockery nicked her full-throated laugh. "What are you going to do about it?"

"This." I snaked the rug out from under her and she went down in a swirl of silken ankles. The bullet whined by me into the ceiling as I vaulted over the desk, pinioned her against the wardrobe.

"Mike." Suddenly all the hatred had drained away and her body yielded to mine. "Don't turn me in. You cared for me—once."

"It's no good, Sigrid. You'd only double-time me again."

"Try me."

"O.K. The shirtmaker who designed your blouse—what's his name?" A shudder of fear went over her; she averted her head. "He's famous on two continents. Come on, Sigrid, they're your dice."

"I won't tell you. I can't. It's a secret between this—this department store and me."

"They wouldn't be loyal to *you*. They'd sell you out fast enough."

"Oh, Mike, you mustn't. You don't know what you're asking."

"For the last time."

"Oh, sweetheart, don't you see?" Her eyes were tragic pools, a cenotaph to lost illusions. "I've got so little. Don't take that away from me. I—I'd never be able to hold up my head in Russeks again."

"Well, if that's the way you want to play it . . ." There was silence in the room, broken only by Sigrid's choked sob. Then, with a strangely empty feeling, I uncradled the phone and dialed Spring 7-3100.

For an hour after they took her away, I sat alone in the taupe-colored dusk, watching lights come on and a woman in the hotel opposite adjusting a garter. Then I treated my tonsils to five fingers of firewater, jammed on my hat, and made for the anteroom. Birdie was still scowling over her crossword puzzle. She looked up crookedly at me.

"Need me any more tonight?"

"No." I dropped a grand or two in her lap. "Here, buy yourself some stardust."

"Thanks, I've got my quota." For the first time I caught a shadow of pain behind her eyes. "Mike, would—would you tell me something?"

"As long as it isn't clean," I flipped to conceal my bitterness.

"What's an eight-letter word meaning 'sentimental'?"

"Flatfoot, darling," I said, and went out into the rain.

(1944)

David Remnick is the editor of *The New Yorker.* He began his career as a sportswriter for *The Washington Post* and won the Pulitzer Prize in 1994 for *Lenin's Tomb.* He is also the author of *Resurrection, The Devil Problem and Other True Stories,* a collection of essays, and *King of the World.* He lives in New York City with his wife and three children.

ABOUT THE TYPE

This book was set in Photina, a typeface designed by José Mendoza in 1971. It is an elegant design with high legibility, and its close character fit has made it a popular choice for use in distinguished magazines and art gallery publications.

T